KU-696-115

V

FRENCH

Vol. 5-6, *frontis.*

THE

Masterpiece Library of Short Stories

The Thousand Best Complete Tales of all Times and all Countries

Selected by

AN INTERNATIONAL BOARD
OF EMINENT CRITICS

Sir William Robertson Nicoll, LL.D.

Sir Arthur Quiller-Couch
Clement Shorter
George Saintsbury, LL.D.
Richard le Gallienne
Brander Matthews, Litt.D.

Sir Frederick Wedmore
Sir Edmund Gosse, C.B., LL.D.
W. P. Trent, LL.D.
Carl Van Doren
Thomas Seccombe

Edited by

Sir J. A. Hammerton

V. FRENCH

LONDON
THE EDUCATIONAL BOOK COMPANY LIMITED

Special Edition in 10 double-volumes issued by Allied Newspapers, Ltd., in association with The Educational Book Co. Ltd.

Editorial Board

Editorial Note

A SHORT story may be a mere anecdote of three hundred words or a work of ten or fifteen thousand. In content it may be anything from a glimpse of character, an incident, to a highly finished picture of life. But it should be a complete work of imagination, its effect achieved with a minimum of personages and events.

TO select the best thousand examples was a task that could be achieved only on arbitrary lines. As to length, three thousand words was the ideal average, but this excluded some of the finest stories, so exceptions had to be allowed. National characteristics also had consideration. Another test was the value of a story as illustrating the development of the art.

PROBLEMS of arrangement were not entirely solved by classification according to the country of each writer's origin. This puts Richard Steele into the Irish volume and separates those ideal literary partners Agnes and Egerton Castle. But it is the best possible arrangement for the work, and the index makes reference easy. The inclusion of a series of stories of the War became possible when the War itself ruled out all modern German work.

A WORD as to the method of selection. The General Editor prepared a trial list of titles which were submitted to all the members of the Editorial Board, who rejected and added according to their individual tastes and knowledge. These individual lists were then collated and the final list evolved. The thousand stories selected are therefore representative of the combined opinion of the whole group of editors. A very few modifications of the final list were made necessary by difficulties of copyright and considerations of Anglo-Saxon taste in certain translations from foreign literatures.

MOST of the foreign stories have been specially translated, and all copyrights, in both stories and translations, the use of which authors and publishers have courteously permitted, are duly credited at the end of each volume.

J. A. H.

Contents of Volume V

THE FRENCH STORY-TELLERS

From Jules Claretie to Paul Hervieu

DURING the period covered by this volume, the French mind was overshadowed by the disasters of the war with Germany and the loss of Alsace-Lorraine. All the most living branches of French art and thought were moulded by the influence of the terrible year. The leading men of the younger generation made a complete break with the ideas of the Second Empire. The romantic movement in prose, poetry, drama, and painting was severely condemned, as being the source of the atmosphere of theatrical splendour in which Napoleon III and his school of adventurers had flourished to the detriment of the nation.

In bitter revulsion from all their dreams and illusions, the French resolved to know the worst about themselves and about everybody else. Their national feeling of depression coincided with a universal sentiment of melancholy, engendered by the researches of Darwin and Lyell, the philosophy of Herbert Spencer and Taine, and the critical studies in religious history made by Renan and Strauss.

France became the mistress of the age of disillusion. Her poets and novelists of the new school had little faith in either God or man, and under various forms started a realistic movement in art which, however, eventually proved to be creative rather than destructive. The Frenchmen did not intend to depict the plain, simple, commonplace truth. They were too much embittered for that. It was the flayed and bleeding truth that they wanted—something with violence, anger, and heartache in it. They were in a militant mood, and cultivated bitterness of soul as a tonic medicine for their race.

JULES CLARETIE

In their hands, both the novel and the short story became, for the time, as acrid as the tales of Dean Swift. In fact, Swift was one of their favourite authors. Yet there remained men of a quieter frame of mind, such as Jules Claretie (1840–1914), who continued to regard literature as a pleasant recreation, seeking rather gracefully to distract and amuse his readers than to agitate and exhaust their perturbed minds. Claretie was especially interested in theatrical life, and became the director of the Comédie Française. His best short stories, such as "Boum-Boum," often touch on the light romance of the stage. His more serious study of crime, "Catissou," is admirably framed in a sketch of wandering showmen, while his ironic episode of "The Last Stage" is a telling miniature drama. Claretie's serious thoughts were expressed in works on contemporary history. He used his art to keep his countrymen cheerful in misfortune.

ÉMILE POUVILLON

Émile Pouvillon (1840–1906) was a writer of a more sombre cast of mind. He lived in the country and wrote about country life, with a sober severity recalling that of Thomas Hardy in his early period. He loved the fields, woods, and open air, but he did not regard the country folk in the romantic light which George Sand had made fashionable. Yet he was far from being so ferocious a realist as was Zola, and as his quiet, subtle tale of "Duck Shooting" shows, there was a remarkable degree of fine tender feeling strongly working beneath his reserved nature.

CATULLE MENDÈS

Catulle Mendès (1841–1909), on the other hand, had no reserve and little fineness of feeling. He was a French Jew, brilliant, exuberant, and versatile. His enemies called him "the ape of all the masters," and there was sufficient truth in this unkindly criticism to make it cut deeply. Mendès represented some of the worst sides of the Parisian life of his time: he was as decadent as the fashionable Greeklings of the age of Nero. Nevertheless, there was a really remarkable amount of skill in his facile art. He originated nothing, but absorbed everything, and when he liked he could tell a simple tale like " The Mirror " with the perfect simplicity of the art that knows how to conceal itself.

FRANÇOIS COPPÉE

Simplicity was also the master quality in the work of François Coppée (1842–1908). But it was not a matter of art with Coppée, it was an expression of character. He had the classic temper in mind and style, and his best work in verse and prose is likely to survive that of several of his contemporaries who still enjoy more renown than he did.

Coppée was profoundly affected by the defeat of his country, and, like the writers of the realistic school, he thought that the national misfortune was largely due to the prevailing mood created by the leaders of the romantic movement. Therefore he went back to a classic reticence of language, but chose his heroes and heroines from the lower French middle classes, who had been a target for ridicule by his predecessors. In " A Miracle " he gently satirises the free-thinking plutocracy of his country. In " The Substitute " he pleads for charity for the criminal class manufactured in the slums of every great city. In his story of " The Gold Coin " his feeling for the broken waifs of modern civilisation again finds dramatic expression.

Although Coppée was full of pity for the unfortunate and ever seeking to find sources of consolation in religion, his eyes were as keen as those of any realist, and, like the fine artist he was, he liked to study, as in " An Accident," the hardest cases of life. His art, however, is more clearly shown in the next sketch, " Died at Sea." This is built on half-a-dozen words concerning a Breton superstition : yet the effect obtained is as memorable as anything in the volume. The tale seems to be a loosely written anecdote, prolonged for pages when it might have been put into a short paragraph. But this is not so : Coppée was as careful as Poe in using every device of the short story with effectiveness.

TINSEAU—PAUL ARÈNE

In Léon de Tinseau (b. 1844) we indeed touch one of the lighter French disciples of Poe, who had been introduced to French readers by Baudelaire. Tinseau strives purely for effect in his amusing story of " The Black Pearl." The idea of it is as far-fetched as possible, but so humorous and original that it is well worth selecting as an example of pure brilliance. Probably Tinseau's friend, Paul Arène (1843–1896), would not be pleased if he had lived to see that his tale of " Uncle Sambuq's Fortune " had been chosen as his masterpiece in short-story writing. For Arène was the chief disciple of Zola, and at times took himself very seriously as a realist. But, as a matter of fact, he was naturally a jovial creature, and his pleasant little farce fairly represents the quality of his easy and trained talent.

ANATOLE FRANCE

Of Anatole France (1844–1924), who by the chance of chronology followed Arène, there is not space enough fully to speak. For Anatole France was one of the greatest writers his country had produced, and after the death of Tolstoy his fame overshadowed that of all other living princes of literature. The son of a bookseller in Paris, Anatole France, whose proper name was Jacques Anatole Thibault, was a striking example of a man of talent who made himself a man of genius. He began by executing graceful variations on the themes of men who seemed superior to him.

The only peculiar gift he displayed was that of a studious bookworm, devoted to literary criticism. At first he might fairly have been called, with Mendès, " the ape of all the masters." The field of his reproductive art extended from Greek literature to contemporary French poetry and novel-writing.

Great, however, as was his scholarship, he carried it with lightness and grace, and developed a mixture of wit and humour that soon made his novels very readable. Then suddenly he changed. A love affair altered his character, and with a fierce fire burning at his heart he became the prophet of revolution and anarchy. Scarcely anything in modern civilisation escaped the biting flame of his tortured mind.

Once he had been the perfect Mandarin of letters, understudying Renan in the art of cold aristocratic irony. " The Procurator of Judea " ranks as his masterpiece in Renanism. It contains the essence of the Breton historian's studies in the origins of Christianity, and is conceived with a deliberate disdainful disregard for all easy means of making its effect. The writer parades his scholarship, and wilfully delays to approach his real subject-matter, yet when he says in the last line what he intended to say, the preceding mass of confused details draws together into the finest perspective effect in the art of literature.

Anatole France has another tale of similar kind constructed around Gallio, but it is too long to be called a short story, and is not so absolutely perfect in form as " The Procurator of Judea." He has often been compared with Voltaire, but he had more depth and passion and a higher sense of beauty than the older French sceptic. The modern master of disillusion and despair keenly feels what he and all men like him have lost when they gave up the faith of their childhood. Anatole France understood the value of the rarest and finest Christian virtues, and when he was not laughing at himself or railing at the wickedness of man, he brooded upon the Sermon on the Mount and wished that he could believe in it. Thus it came that the greatest of modern infidels, while satirising in "Putois" the currents of mind that make for credulity, produced in "The Juggler of Notre Dame" one of the most exquisite Christian legends published in western Europe since the Reformation.

The stories entitled "In the Reign of Terror" and "Springtime in the Year Two" are two of those studies in the drama of the great revolution, from which Anatole France approached the general problem of the overthrow of modern civilisation.

He pictured the great revolution in the light of his personal experiences during the communard insurrection in Paris. At first he had been dismayed by the outbreak of mob violence in his own days, and in middle life he seemed to be as cynical a conservative as was Renan. It is the sufferings of French noblewomen that interest him in the two stories mentioned, and there is an echo of Renan's "l'Abbesse de Jouarre" in both of them. But in "A Gift of Death," one of the shortest of all short tales, there is expressed, or rather indicated, an intensity of true feeling, showing that Anatole France was moving towards that outburst of emotion which at last made him, in spite of some grave defects of character, the master-mind of Europe in the days before the Great War.

OCTAVE MIRBEAU

In the house of art there are many mansions, and though Octave Mirbeau, Jacques Normand, Jean Richepin, and Richard O'Monroy fall variously below Anatole France in general achievement, their best stories all possess qualities of distinction. Octave Mirbeau (1848–1917) was a novelist and dramatist of the realistic school, but his larger works, though popular at the time, lacked fresh and intrinsic power. In an effort to equal Zola, Mirbeau merely strained himself, and afterwards lapsed into the position of a capable literary confectioner. His original, fine, true talent, however, is displayed in his earlier short pieces, such as the sympathetic tale of a village dog "Turc."

JACQUES NORMAND

Jacques Normand (1848–1931) was never pretentious. His light entertaining way of writing long delighted the taste of the French public, that wanted a good short story served up with their daily news. Normand was regarded as the literary omelette maker to the Paris Press, and, for a long time, no regard was paid to the brilliant rapid art underlying his inexhaustible facility in verse and prose. His little railway comedy, "The P.L.M. Express," is characteristic of his agreeable talent.

JEAN RICHEPIN

Utterly unlike Normand was Jean Richepin (1849–1926) when he first won recognition by shock effect. To Richepin, the literary and artistic professionalism of the Latin quarter was boredom. He satirises it in "Bonjour, Monsieur," which is an attack upon the fashion for quintessence of style started by Mallarmé. Richepin went gypsying along country lanes with vagabonds, and in his first works specialised in the crudest popular language. He mellowed, however, under success, and became one of the sanest forces in modern French literature, and his tale of happy child-life, "Totor's Drum," shows him in a kindly fatherly mood.

RICHARD O'MONROY

Richard O'Monroy (1849–1916), whose longer works are already almost forgotten, was more decent in language than Richepin but more cynical in character. He saw life from the wings of the stage, and, like his friend Claretie, watched with pitiful amusement the struggles and intrigues of actresses and ballet-dancers. Madame Manchaballe, the heroine of "The Fugue" and "The Violin," is a biting sketch of a certain theatrical type that Dickens might have drawn.

GUY DE MAUPASSANT

The amused cynicism of all the group of writers to which O'Monroy belonged was but a passing whim of mind compared with the tremendous ferocity of soul of Guy de Maupassant (1850–1893). A young Norman nobleman, laboriously trained in literary craft by his friend Flaubert, Maupassant was the incarnation of the spirit of France under defeat. He was born with madness working in him, and, like his brother, he died mad, his last hallucination being that war with Germany had again broken out and that he was marching, radiant and happy at last, to death in battle. From the opening to the end of his period of sane work, Maupassant attacked his countrymen, often with a bitter injustice that only his mental malady and sombre patriotism could excuse.

His originality, force, and versatility are quite or almost incomparable. Only Mr. Rudyard Kipling can rank beside him, and he is more various than the English writer. His " Necklace " has nothing in it but its workmanship, but that makes it classic. " The Necklace " is the source of a thousand later stories. " Ulrich the Guide " is a study of terror based on Maupassant's own Alpine experiences. " The Prisoners " is one of his rare comedies of the Franco-German war, while his striking study of " A Coward " is a memorable essay in psychology, which has often been imitated.

In " The Little Soldier " Maupassant is in a rare mood of pity, and finely, reticently suggests the tragedy of a loyal friendship between men broken by a woman's love. " The Bit of String," one of the famous studies of Norman life, is a thing that Swift might have written. " Among the Peasants " is an attack upon the Norman, who occupies in France somewhat the same position that the Scotsman occupies in England. It is doubtful if " The House with the Green Shutters " would have been written if Maupassant had never turned his fierce, mad eyes upon the Norman peasant and village shopkeeper. No assault by Carlyle or Ruskin upon their countrymen approached in penetrating power the quiet fury with which Maupassant moved among his Normans.

" The Two Fishermen " discloses Maupassant in a gentler mood, for he is telling of Frenchmen who died for their country. " Moonlight " is one of his high masterpieces—poetic, natural, simple, and unforgettable. " The Dowry " is a pretty study in irony, and though it is unlike Maupassant to combine irony with prettiness, he does it perfectly. There is prettiness again in " The Colonel's Story," but with a large moral underneath it connected with the revival of the warlike cult of Joan of Arc. The satiric note is resumed in " How he won the Legion of Honour," a story remarkable for the influence it had upon Anatole France when he turned upon the politicians of his country.

" The Accursed Bread " is a masterpiece of bitterness, and " Old Judas," the last of our Maupassant collection, is a thing of horror saved only by its reticent art from exceeding the bounds of literature. As Maupassant's agony of mind increased, he rose in his work to the height of Greek tragedy, but also wandered into the uttermost depths of horror. Yet, savagely as he lashed his own people, he loved them, and though he seemed to do nothing in his life but insist upon their faults, he was one of the regenerators of France.

JUDITH GAUTIER—PIERRE LOTI

After him came a new school of writers, who thought that the work of destructive criticism was complete and that it was time to clarify, strengthen, and assuage the spirit of their race. There first arose an exotic group that sought for solace in strange, picturesque, far-off scenes. Judith Gautier (1850–1917), daughter of the famous French poet, turned to the Orient, and in such exquisite pieces of orientalism as "Zin-Gou" took refuge in a new palace of art. Pierre Loti (Louis M. J. Viaud) (1850–1923), a brilliant, melancholy naval officer, wandered about the South Sea Islands and Japan in search of the spirit of romance that had been killed, so he thought, in Europe, by factory owners, men of science, and realistic novelists. Yet, he is best in intimate, humble, homely things, such as the wall of roses in "The Wall Opposite" and the sparrow in "An Old Convict's Sorrow."

PAUL BOURGET

Paul Bourget (b. 1852), from whose work we have selected "The Portrait of the Doge" and "The Brother of Mr. Viple," became one of the leaders of the constructive school. He began as a disciple to Taine and Renan in scepticism, and displayed a striking power of analysing neurotic conditions of feeling. He was neurotic himself, but by an effort of will, inspired by patriotism, he pulled himself together, and rallying to the conservative class, that largely officered the French army and navy, was transformed into a fervent nationalist.

"The Portrait of the Doge" gives the quintessence of Bourget's art in his earlier period. The plot is rather commonplace and sentimental; but that does not matter. Bourget shows no gift for narration. He is a social philosopher, using the novel and the short story, because these forms of literature were more popular than the essay. The special field of study in which, with Henry James, he is a master, is the strangely mingled society of all the pleasure-seeking wealthy classes of the new world and the old, gathering about the grand hotels and cosmopolitan centres of France, England, and Italy.

In the present story, he brings together the bustling plutocracy of the United States, the impoverished Venetian nobility, and the idle French aristocracy. The strings by which he makes the characters move around the sale of an Italian masterpiece are of no importance. Hundreds of writers could do this part of the tale better than Bourget. The great merit of his story is that in it, with a few clear strokes, he portrays the spirit of a remarkable crisis in social history, when America was exporting heiresses and importing costly works of art. First of all writers, Bourget perceived this movement and divined some of its importance. That is why "The Portrait of the Doge" is a very remarkable short story.

"The Brother of Mr. Viple" illustrates another side of Bourget's genius. From it there suddenly flames out the embittered feelings of patriotism that led him at last into the nationalist camp. The story is far better composed than the previous one. Bourget is no longer setting coldly down his ideas about foreigners and new amalgams of cosmopolitanism: he is writing about his own feelings, and the result is a fiery masterpiece.

RENÉ BAZIN

The younger writer, René Bazin (1853–1932), three of whose stories we give, was struck by the depopulation of the French countryside. In a novel of resounding fame he attracted and alarmed the French public, and continued in a series of delicate and true stories of country life, written with classic simplicity, to revive the French spirit and charm it back to the fertile soil from which all its strength was drawn. "The Raspberry Harvest" is remarkable for its plot. "The Saviours of the White Wine" is a quiet study of national character, while the story of "The Fourth Beggar" is a vivid and exquisite allegory.

JULES LEMAÎTRE

Jules Lemaître (1853–1914) was a convert to nationalism, like Bourget and Bazin. At first he shared with Anatole France the sinister glory of leading the sceptic school of literature. Inspired, like Anatole France, directly by Renan, he dabbled in picturesque mysticism, and without believing in what he wrote, related finely coloured legends of the Middle Ages, such as "The Sculptor." With equal artistic zest he played with classic paganism as in "The Siren," and with orientalism in "The Khan's Wives." But "The Funeral of Firdousi" is, in spite of its Baghdad scenery, a telling satirical picture of French literary life, Firdousi being Victor Hugo. During this period, Lemaître was also an amused student of life in the Latin quarter, as is shown in his entertaining story of "Garnoteau's Three Manners." The man was, however, at heart a creature of tenderness, and his pathetic story of "The White Marriage" has an incomparable quality of sweetness. Lemaître ends by contemning his own fine literary genius, and it is as an anti-republican politician, and a fierce opponent of all political tricksters, that we see him spending almost his last energies.

MALIN TO HERVIEU

In the string of writers that follow, each with a single story, the back-wash of the two main movements in French life trickles into the mould of the short story. Henri Malin (b. 1852), Léon Hennique (b. 1852), Pontsevrez (1854–1910), Alphonse Allais (1855–1905), George de Lys (b. 1855), and Jean Reibrach (1855–1927) have their peculiar quality in the art that had become especially French. Each in his field could write as well as Paul Hervieu (1857–1915). Yet Hervieu, by the sombre fire of his mind, that burns as clearly in the three tales that we give as in his famous dramas, has a weight of imagination that is more impressive. Hervieu joined neither of the main parties in French literature, he remained a realist of the Maupassant school, yet there was more hopefulness in his view than in that of the broken and despairing Norman. A certain harshness and rigour in his art were the marks of his work of the best period, but in all his criticisms of French society there was a constructive intention.

E. W.

JULES CLARETIE
1840–1914

BOUM-BOUM

THE child was lying stretched out on his little white bed, his wide-open eyes gazing straight before him, with that strange fixed expression of the sick who already perceive what the living cannot see.

The mother, at the foot of the bed wringing her hands to keep from weeping, marked, in an agony of grief, the progress of the malady on the poor pinched face of the little one. The father, a sturdy labourer, forced back from his red eyes the tears that burned his eyelids.

The day broke clear and sweet, a beautiful morning in June, and lighted up the narrow room in the Rue des Abbesses, where little François, the child of Jacques Legrand and of Madeleine Legrand, his wife, was dying.

He was seven years old. Fair and rosy, and so strong; lively as a cricket had been this little one, not three weeks before. But he had caught a fever, and one evening they brought him home from school with his head heavy and his hands very hot. From that time he had been there on his bed; saying, over and over again in his delirium, when he saw the little shoes, so carefully blacked, which his mother had placed in a corner:

" You can throw them away now, little François's shoes! Little François will not wear them! Little François will not go to school any more—never, never! "

Then the father cried, moaned: " Hush, hush, little one! " and the mother, very pale, hid her golden head in his pillow, so that little François might not hear her crying.

That night the child had not been delirious; but for two days the doctor had been anxious about a strange depression that resembled a giving way to death, as if at seven years the little one had no longer any desire to live. He was worn and silent and sad, moving his thin face from side to side on the pillow, the smile gone from his pinched lips, and his haggard eyes searching, seeing no one knew what, over there, very far off.

" Heaven, perhaps! " thought Madeleine, trembling.

When they tried to get him to take some tea, some syrup, a little bouillon, he refused. He refused everything.

" Do you want anything, François? "

" No, I don't want anything."

" He must be got out of it," the doctor had said—" this terrible stupor! You are his father and mother; you know your own child. Try to find something that will put new life into the little body, that will call back to earth the spirit that is already hovering among the clouds! "

And he went away.

" Try! "

Yes, without doubt, they knew him well, their François! They knew how he loved to take a walk in the country on Sunday afternoon, and to come back to Paris on his father's shoulders laden with hawthorn flowers, or to see Punch and Judy on the Champs Elysées with the little rich children. Jacques Legrand had bought toys for François—a kaleidoscope, gilded soldiers; he took them out and set them up on the child's bed, he made them dance before the wandering eyes, and, near to tears himself, tried to make the little one laugh.

" See, here is a big fight going on—bang! Boom! And this is the general. We saw a general one time, in the Bois de Boulogne, do you remember? If you are a good boy and drink your tea I will buy you a real general with a cloth coat and gold epaulets. Would you like that—tell me—a general? "

" No," replied the child, in the hard voice caused by the fever.

" Would you like a pistol, some new marbles—a bow and arrows? "

" No," repeated the little voice, short and almost cruel.

And to everything they said, to all the dolls and balloons they promised, the little voice—while the parents looked at each other in despair—answered: " No, no, no! "

" But isn't there something you want, baby-child? " asked his mother. " Why, you used to want a lot of things. Tell me—tell your own mama," and she put her cheek down in his pillow and whispered it in his ear, softly, like a secret. Then the child, with a strange look, sat upright in his bed, and stretching an eager little hand toward some invisible object, answered, all of a sudden, his voice at the same time pleading and commanding:

" I want *Boum-Boum*! "

Boum-Boum!

Poor Madeleine cast a terrified look at her husband. What was the little one saying? Could it be the delirium again—the dreadful delirium—that had come back?

Boum-Boum!

She did not understand it, and she was afraid of the strange words that the child kept repeating, as if, not having dared to formulate his dream before, he now clung to it with an invincible obstinacy.

"Yes, Boum-Boum! Boum-Boum! Boum-Boum! I want Boum-Boum!"

The mother seized her husband's hand frantically, saying, in a low voice, like a madwoman:

"What can it mean, Jacques? He is gone! He is gone!"

But there was a smile on the toil-hardened features of the father—a smile almost happy, and yet dazed, like that of the condemned man who hears of the possibility of freedom.

Boum-Boum! He remembered well the morning of Easter Monday, when he had taken François to the circus. He could still hear the child's shrieks of delight when the clown, the beautiful clown, covered with gold spangles and with a great resplendent butterfly on the breast of his black domino, came dancing on to the stage, went about on all-fours with a little rider on his back, stood, straight and stiff, on his head waving his feet in the air, or caught big felt caps on his head, one after the other, till they formed a pyramid, and, at each round, at each new trick, like a gay refrain, with a droll smile lighting up his face, he gave the same cry, repeated the same word, accompanied each time by a bang from the orchestra: *Boum-Boum!*

Boum-Boum! And each time he said it the whole circus rang with applause and the little one gave his delighted laugh. Boum-Boum! It was this Boum-Boum, it was the clown of the circus, it was this favourite of all that part of the city, that little François wanted to see, that he wanted to have, and that he could not have and could not see because he was lying there so ill on his little white bed.

That evening Jacques Legrand brought the boy a jointed clown, all covered with spangles, which he had bought in a shop. It was very dear—the price of four of his days of toil! But he would have given twenty, thirty—he would have given the price of a whole year—to bring a smile to the pale lips of his darling.

The child looked at the toy a moment as it lay glittering on the white sheets; then, sadly:

"That isn't Boum-Boum! I want to see Boum-Boum!"

Ah, if Jacques could have wrapped him up in the bedclothes and carried him to the circus, and showed him the clown dancing beneath the bright lights, and said to him, "Look!" But he did better, Jacques, he went to the circus and asked the address of the clown, and timidly, his knees shaking with emotion, he mounted one by one the stairs that led to the artist's apartment at Montmartre. It was a bold thing for him to do, Jacques. But, after all, comedians were very willing to sing, to give recitations, at the houses of the great. Perhaps the clown—oh, for anything he liked—would consent to come and bid François good-morning. Never mind; how was he received there, Jacques Legrand, at Boum-Boum's house?

It was no longer Boum-Boum! It was M. Morens, and the beautiful room, with its books and pictures and objects of art, gave just the right setting to a charming man, who took Jacques into a little study, like a physician's.

Jacques looked at him, not recognising the clown, and turned and twisted his felt cap in his hands. The other waited. Then the father excused his coming. It was unusual, what he had come to ask—he would never have done it—pardon, excuse—but, after all, it was for the little one. "Such a darling, *monsieur*! And so intelligent! Always the first in his class, except in arithmetic, which he couldn't understand. A dreamer, the little one—yes, a dreamer; and the proof—listen—the proof."

Jacques hesitated and stammered; then, recovering his courage, he finished in a breath:

"The proof is that he wants to see you, that he thinks of nothing but you, and that you are there, before him, like a star that he wants to have, and that he looks at!"

When the father had finished he was very pale, with great drops of perspiration on his forehead. He did not dare look at the clown, who was standing with his eyes fixed on the labourer. And what would the great Boum-Boum say? Would he dismiss him, would he take him for a madman, would he show him the door?

"Where do you live?" asked Boum-Boum.

"Oh, very near! Rue des Abbesses!"

"Come!" said the other. "He wants to see Boum-Boum, your little boy. Very well, he shall see Boum-Boum!"

When the door opened for the clown Jacques Legrand cried joyously to his son: "François, you're in luck, rascal! Here he is—here's Boum-Boum!"

A smile of joy came over the child's face. He raised himself on his mother's arm and turned his head toward the two men who were entering. For a moment he tried to think who the gentleman was at his father's side in the long coat, who was smiling at him, but whom he did not know; and when they told him, "It's Boum-Boum!" he let himself fall back slowly, sadly, with his forehead against the pillow. There he lay, his eyes fixed, his beautiful big blue eyes that looked beyond the walls of the little chamber and sought for the spangles and the butterfly of Boum-Boum as a lover seeks for his idol.

"No," said the child, in a voice that was no longer harsh, but so sad—"no, it's not Boum-Boum."

The clown, standing near the little bed, looked down at the sick baby gravely, tenderly; then, saying, with a glance at the anxious father, at the heart-broken mother, " He is right; it isn't Boum-Boum! " he went out.

" I shall never see Boum-Boum any more! I shall never see Boum-Boum any more! " repeated the child, and already the little voice talked to the angels. Perhaps Boum-Boum was off there—off there where little François was soon going.

And suddenly—it was not so much as a half-hour since the clown disappeared—the door was thrown open just as before, and there, in his black spangled tights, a little yellow tuft on his head, a golden butterfly on his breast and another on his back, and a great smile spreading from ear to ear on his beautiful powdered face, was Boum-Boum, the real Boum-Boum, the Boum-Boum of the circus, the people's Boum-Boum, little François's Boum-Boum, Boum-Boum!

And on his little white bed, the joy of life in his eyes, laughing, crying, happy, saved, the child clapped his little thin hands, cried bravo, and said, with the gaiety of a seven-year-old, which flashes out all of a sudden like a lighted match:

" It's Boum-Boum! It's Boum-Boum this time! Here's Boum-Boum! Hurrah for Boum-Boum! How d' y' do, Boum-Boum? "

When the doctor came back that day he found, seated by little François's pillow, a clown with whitened face, who made the child laugh again, and who said, stirring a lump of sugar into a cup of medicine:

" You know, if you don't drink this, little François, like a good boy, Boum-Boum won't come back any more."

And the child obeyed.

" Isn't that good? "

" Very good! Thank you, Boum-Boum! "

" Doctor," said the clown to the physician, " you mustn't be jealous, but I certainly think that my tricks have done him as much good as your medicines! "

The father and mother wept, but this time it was with joy.

And until little François was out of bed a carriage from Montmartre stopped every day at the labourer's door on the Rue des Abbesses and a man got out, enveloped in a great coat, with the collar turned up, and underneath, dressed for the circus, with the spangles and the great gold butterfly.

" How much do I owe you, *monsieur*? " said Jacques Legrand, at the end, to *monsieur* the clown when the child sat up for the first time; " because I must owe you something! "

The clown held out to the parents the two large hands of a gentle Hercules:

" A hearty hand-shake," he said.

Then, pressing two big kisses on the baby's cheeks where the roses were coming back, he added, laughing:

" And permission to have on my visiting-cards, ' Boum-Boum, medical acrobat and physician-in-ordinary to little François! ' "

CATISSOU

JULES CLARETIE

THE corporal sat astride a cane-bottomed chair in front of the gendarme quarters at Pierrebuffière and smoked his pipe; slowly the smoke curled upwards in regular lines, forming circles which gradually expanded, quivered, and finally vanished in the warm air of this July evening.

Martial Tharaud had seen many similar circles of smoke act in just the same way aLove the cannon's mouth.

He was now taking life easily in his little garden, the head of a family, with a corporal's stripes on his sleeve, and wished for nothing better—not even to become sergeant, because then he would probably have to go to Eymoutiers, Saint-Léonard, or Limoges. He was fond of his little corner at Pierrebuffière, fond of those roses which he had grafted himself, and fond of that creeping plant which ran along the white walls of the house and hung in wreaths around the tin tricolour flag suspended over the door.

As the corporal smoked he watched some boys who, at a short distance from him, were playing upon a hillock at the game of *pique-romme,* in which they threw long pointed pieces of iron into the ground, as though throwing at a target. Occasionally he cried warningly to them: " Take care, there, youngsters; mind you don't run them into your feet! "

Then he turned round and looked over his shoulder through the open window at a pretty, dark-complexioned woman, still young, who was bustling about the kitchen where the pots and pans shone like silver; he smiled at her and said as he puffed away: " They *are* having a game, the little rascals! "

Then the woman, with bare arms—nice white arms, half covered with flour—came to the window-sill, put her jolly, energetic-looking face (red with the heat of the stove) out of the window, and looked towards the boys, who were excitedly throwing their pieces of iron at the mark.

" Go along! there's no danger! Besides, it makes them skilful and brave! "

" And gives them an appetite for your *clafoutis,* Catissou! "

The *clafoutis*—a Limousin dish as solid as the thick cabbage soup of the country districts—was already baking in the oven, with its black cherries stuck in the flour like bricks in mortar.

" Is the *clafoutis* cooking all right? " asked the corporal.

And Catissou shrugged her shoulders as if to say: " Are you foolish? Is your housekeeper in the habit of neglecting her pastry? "

II

" A good woman," said Martial Tharaud to us a moment afterwards as we passed him with a nod.

He was in the humour for a gossip.

" Yes, yes " (he became loquacious when speaking of Catissou), " she's a good woman; and a sturdy woman, too. To see her make the kettle boil and wash the children—we have three, all boys; see them over there?—nobody would believe she had been on show at the fairs! And yet it's true enough! Oh, it's quite a story! I'll tell you all about it.

" It is about ten years ago—I had just left the chasseurs and entered the gendarmerie at Limoges, and that suited me, because I belong to that part. The adjutant told us one morning that there was a splendid capture to be made. A worthy old man named Coussac, a foreman builder, had been murdered in his own house at Montmailler, and there was no clue to the identity of the assassin. That was in September. We had to search the highways and byways; and the adjutant, M. Boudet (he's captain now), told the sergeant, the corporals, and the men to redouble their vigilance and keep their eyes open; and if we met any suspicious-looking persons under the chestnut trees or along the high roads we were to seize them without hesitation and haul them up before the authorities.

" Information had been sent all over the district, and also to Châteauneuf, Ambazac, everywhere, even to Bellac. In a word, the whole department was on the alert.

" Now, it's all very fine to tell you to arrest all suspicious-looking individuals, but you must not always judge by appearances. There are many worthy people who have very evil-looking faces. Why, I knew a man whose looks would have brought him to the guillotine or the galleys; yet he was a man who might have taken a prize for upright conduct! It's true enough! He gave away all he had to the poor—a perfect saint, my word on it! And there are others who look like saints, but who ought to have the handcuffs put on at once.

" Still, we were told to arrest them; and so we did. We ran in some of those natives of Lorraine who come to Sauviat and Saint-Yrieix to buy china-ware, you know; we took up hawkers, old men, yellow-looking beggars—as yellow as their bags; and we even ran in some silly people who were roaming about without any knowledge of the place. But not one of them was capable of giving that fillip to old Coussac. So the time went on, and we could not lay hands on the Montmailler murderer.

" And it wasn't an easy thing at all to find out who had killed the old foreman builder. We had scarcely any clue, and we did not know how to set to work.

" Well! one day I was at the gendarme quarters, about to curry-comb my horse, when a handsome young woman, with eyes like sloes and lips as red as cherries, came up to me and said: ' Well! have you any news of the murderer after all this time? I am the daughter of Léonard Coussac! '

" It made me start when I heard that, I tell you! She spoke so energetically, and her eyes flashed so angrily, that I felt as though I ought to be ashamed of myself for not having taken a grip of the collar of that scoundrel who had killed the young woman's father. Then I tried to clear myself by explaining that it was not exactly our fault, that we had very little information about the murderer, and so on; but she looked at me straight in the eyes, in such a manner that I felt I was making a mess of it.

" ' Now, look here, miss,' I said suddenly, stopping in the midst of my excuses. ' I would willingly risk an arm or a leg, if necessary, to catch that scoundrel! ' And I meant it, too. And it wasn't exactly what you call—er—professional duty which made me say it. It was those confounded black eyes which seemed all on fire. ' But, you see, we want a clue! '

" ' A clue? ' Then she shrugged her shoulders. ' What about the hand? ' she asked. ' Isn't that a clue? '

" ' The hand? What hand? '

" Then Catherine Coussac—her name was Catherine, *Catissou* in our country dialect—told me the story of the crime, a story which, I confess, made my blood run cold.

III

" It was one September evening when poor old Coussac was killed, and it was as warm as a summer day. In his house he had the money which Mr. Sabourdy, the contractor he worked for, had left with him before starting for Guéret. He had about ten thousand francs besides that, for he had to pay the men and meet two bills which would be due in two or three days. It was Saturday. After he had paid the men, the foreman builder returned home, pleased, and with a good appetite. He ate his cabbage soup and some dumplings, and after the meal his mother went upstairs to rest on the bed, as she was rather tired, while old Coussac and his daughter Catissou remained in the downstairs room, sitting near the chest where the money was. He was reading the *Almanach Limousin* which had just come out, and she was knitting a woollen stocking.

" You must understand that Coussac's rooms were at the back of the house, overlooking the garden. The one on the ground floor, in which Coussac and his daughter were then sitting, had a window about five feet from the ground, with inside shutters which were usually closed in the evening; but that evening the window had been left slightly open, because the old man felt rather warm. He was reading by the light of a shaded lamp, and Catissou heard him turn over the pages of the *Almanach* at regular intervals. She has often told me that, as she was working away mechanically, the tick-tick of the clock, and the rustle of the paper as the leaves were regularly turned over, made her feel drowsy.

" Suddenly she lifted her head from her work with a yawn to see if it wasn't time to go to bed, and she saw—she thought at first that she was mistaken or dreaming—she saw between the shutters a hand, a big hand, a thick, wide hand with something terrifying about it, something which Catissou noticed at once—the four fingers were almost as thick as the thumb, and were all the same size, and all as long as one another, just as if they had been cut off at a certain point. But they had not been cut off, for they had nails; only they all finished in a line. This frightful hand with the spatulated fingers—that's what Dr. Boutsilloux called them—glided along the shutters like a great spider, and it was evidently trying to push back the shutters without making a noise; it remained there almost motionless as Catissou looked up, as though the man to whom it belonged guessed that she was looking at it.

" For a moment Catherine thought that her eyes had been affected by the light of the lamp, causing her to see black and red spots as you do when you look at the sun. She opened them wide, and saw the hand gliding over the woodwork nearer and nearer. Catissou could no longer doubt the reality of what she saw, and tried to cry out; but she seemed choked, as if the hand were strangling her, and she could not utter a sound.

" She jumped up, stretched her arm out towards Coussac, and shook him by the sleeve, pointing to the terrible hand at the window. But, at the very moment when old Coussac turned and perceived the hand, the shutter was pushed violently back and the window opened very quickly, which caused the door of the room to open, admitting a draught of air which blew out the lamp and left Catherine and her father in the dark.

" Then there was the noise of a heavy body jumping into the

room, and Coussac endeavoured to find a knife in the drawer of the table on which he was reading—a knife to defend himself, and, above all, Catissou and Mr. Sabourdy's money; but, before he could open the drawer, he was seized by the throat, and felt something cold enter his body under the neck near the heart. Catissou could see nothing, but she guessed what was taking place, and she uttered a scream. Bang! A blow from a fist like a hammer on her head, and she fell senseless. The man must have had cat's eyes; he could see everything, and took good aim. If Catissou was not killed by the knife, it was because it had broken off short; still, the fist was enough for the man's purpose in her case.

"How long the poor girl remained insensible, she could not say; but when she came to herself she was still in the lower room, and her grandmother in her night-dress, with a face as white as a sheet, was trying to restore poor old Léonard, who was dying.

"Of course you can guess that the chest had been broken open, and the thousand-franc notes stolen.

"What an awful night that was! It will be many a long day before it is forgotten in the Montmailler suburb. The neighbours were called up, the garden was searched, a guard put round the houses, and the houses searched from top to bottom. They found the imprints of iron-tipped boots in the flower-beds; instructions were given that these marks should not be touched, and the size was carefully measured. Every place round about was searched, but to no purpose. And, in the meantime, Coussac was dying, and his mother, half crazy with grief and rage, was saying what she would do if she only got hold of the assassin.

"As for Catherine, who was half mad too, the sight of that terrible hand, with the four fingers of the same length, gliding, gliding over the oaken shutter like a field-spider or a crab-fish, was continually before her eyes.

"You can guess that everything that could be done was done to find the wretch who had sent the worthy man to 'Louyat,' that's what they call the cemetery at Limoges; the parson told me that the name comes from 'Alleluia.' Yes, everything possible was done, but I say again there was no clue! Of course, there was the hand, as Catissou told me at the barracks; but nobody knew a man with a hand like that in the whole of that part of the country—he would soon have been noticed. They questioned the men who worked with old Coussac, one after another. No, they did not know any one with such a fist; and you could not suspect any of them. They were all decent fellows; they liked to wet their whistles a bit, but that isn't a crime. Besides, none of them knew that Mr. Sabourdy had left other money than the wages with Coussac. Who, then, could the rascal be who had such a hand as Catissou had seen?

"One day a journeyman butcher came and told us that he well remembered one day having a quarrel with a big, evil-looking fellow, who had pulled out a knife; and the butcher had noticed, as he had pulled out this Nontron knife from his pocket, that this fellow had a very peculiar hand, a big, hairy hand with all the fingers of the same size! Now, the knife that had killed Léonard Coussac was a Nontron knife. But the butcher knew nothing about this man, and nobody else had seen the fellow at Limoges, so we could only believe that the butcher was humbugging us. And still the hunt went on, but it was no good; and I was in a rare state about it, I was, for I had said to Catissou, looking her full in the face: 'Come, Miss Catissou, answer me plainly; what would you give to the one who brought your father's murderer to you with a rope round his neck?' and she had not answered in words, but had become quite pale, and you should have seen her eyes, her beautiful black eyes! They were full of tears, and they promised—something!

"Still, even that could not help me to find the wretch.

"At last, seeing that not one of the 12th, from the colonel to the last gendarme, could put his hand upon the fellow, Catherine said: 'Very well; if *you* can't find him, *I* will!'

"She left her situation as dressmaker, and asked the police authorities for permission to take part in the fairs. That surprised us all; but it surprised me especially, when in every place where there was any entertainment on, we saw a large canvas poster with a portrait of Catherine Coussac, dressed in pink tights, with a red velvet jacket, short skirt, and copper fish-scales; and above this picture were the words, in big letters, *Woman Torpedo Fish.*

"What a name! It was quite strange enough for Catherine to mix up with mountebanks at all—although they are as good as other people, ay, and even better than a good many other people we meet. Still, it was surprising enough for her to become a strolling player or such like; but *Woman Torpedo Fish,* that beat all! Of course you know that the torpedo is a fish which gives you an electric shock if you touch it—a fish which seems to have an electric machine in its body. Well, by some electrical arrangement, when you touched Catherine Coussac's hand you received an electric shock.

"It was not necessary for me to *touch* her to be electrified; I only had to *look* at her. Look at her now; she is twenty-eight and a little stouter, but she's still pretty. Well, ten years ago, when she used to wear that lace cap on her black hair—that lace cap which the silly women have thrown aside for hats like the ladies wear—well, very few people who passed her went on their way without looking back at her! Such a figure she had; and such a complexion! There were some handsome girls in Limoges, but

Catherine was the handsomest, though I say it as shouldn't.

" Didn't she draw the people to the booth! She didn't want a big band like the Corvi Circus, nor a lot of gag like the troupe which plays the *Tour de Nesle*. Not a bit of it; she just showed herself; people said, ' I say, that's a pretty girl! ' and they went in.

IV

" One day, at Magnac Laval—it was Shrove Tuesday—I went in with the other people to see the *Woman Torpedo Fish*. There she was on a little stage, and old Mrs. Coussac, Léonard's mother, sat below, squatting like a witch, and frowning at every one who came in, as though she would like to throw a spell upon them. Since the murder of her son she had become sullen, and she scarcely said anything but ' So they won't take him to the guillotine, the rascal who killed my son! '

" I stepped forward. Catherine recognised me; and, as I stopped in front of her, and thought how well the costume suited her, she smiled, and said to me in a significant tone: ' Oh, it is you; but it isn't *your* hand I am looking for.' And her black eyes blazed again, with a look of madness almost.

" Then I understood what the brave girl was doing. Then I knew why she was going all over the country, disguised as a mountebank. The recollection of that frightful hand was always present, and she held out her own white little hand—as soft as satin, but as strong as a vice—to every one, hoping in this way to recognise the hand with the fingers all of the same size.

" That was her own idea! That was the only clue, but it would be sufficient for her, she thought. It was not an easy task to find that fellow—almost as bad as looking for a needle in a haystack. And yet there is always a chance that a murderer will come and prowl round the scene of his crime. Blood seems to attract like a magnet, that's what *I* think. Of course, the man had fled from Limoges after the crime and might still be far away, but he would come back and have a look at Montmailler at some time or other; so the *Woman Torpedo Fish* had the chances in her favour that she would see him again and recognise that hand—that hand which seemed to haunt her to such an extent that she has told me that she often dreamt it was round her neck, strangling her.

" In this way Catherine went about from place to place with old Mrs. Coussac. The electric woman's van went wherever it could, drawn by an old horse which had served in the gendarmerie. From fair to fair they dragged along, the mother and the daughter, and they must have covered miles enough to make a journey round the world. They saw Auvergne, Bordeaux, Angoulême, Tours, and right on to Orléans—and a good many other places, too, in the south. But it was in the department of Haute-Vienne that they felt most confident of success. They said to each other: 'That is where he did it, and that is where he will be taken!' A superstitious idea, perhaps, but you can't help such things.

"Women soon get at the bottom of things, I tell you. They are as artful as can be.

"Well, one day—I remember it as if it was yesterday, it was the 22nd of May and a Tuesday also—the booths were making no end of a row upon the Place Royale—Place de la République. There were roundabouts, waxworks, athletic sports, performing monkey, Pezon's menagerie, everything you could think of, including, of course, the *Woman Torpedo Fish*.

"Catherine, fresh as a daisy, walked about on the platform outside, pointing to the picture of herself and crying out: 'Walk up, walk up, ladies and gentlemen! Just about to begin!' while poor old Widow Coussac, looking a hundred years old, as yellow as a guinea, as thin as a rake, and coughing in a way that made your heart ache, glared around at the people.

"'Walk up, walk up, walk up!'

"I walked up like the other people, except that, as I went in, I said, 'Good-morning, miss,' to Catissou.

"'Good-morning, gendarme,' she answered.

"She knew my name perfectly well, but she only gave me my title. It seemed to me that it was as good as saying: 'Although you are a gendarme, you don't know how to nab people who murder poor old men, do you?' and, besides, she had a right to call me 'gendarme,' because I was in uniform.

"Well, there I was inside. There were about twenty persons in the booth, men and women; and while Catissou smiled at them, old Mrs. Coussac, squatting in a corner, glared at them as usual.

"I can see it all now, just as if I was there. Catissou, standing on the stage with a red curtain for the background, with spangles in her hair, a rose in her breast, and, as a contrast to all this red, a pair of plump, white arms, and pretty shoulders, and a head—well, a head pretty enough to turn the heads of all the men who saw her. The sun shone through the canvas upon Catissou, making the imitation fish-scales, which she had sewn upon her garments, shine like diamonds.

"There she was, explaining to the audience what sort of a thing this electric fish is, where it lives, how the Arabs call it 'Thunder,' and what a shock it gives you, as if you had been struck by lightning; and how—but there, it's all done with now, and very likely Catissou herself has forgotten it, although she has said it so many times. But she had it at her fingers' ends at that time, and said it right off as pat as a lawyer; and the audience sat with their mouths wide open taking it all in, and devouring Catissou with their eyes, which proves that they had good taste.

"After that, she held out her hand as usual, and said to them: 'Walk up and shake hands and feel the electric shock! Don't be afraid; it won't hurt you!' All hands were held out to touch Catissou's dainty little hand; some laughed at the sensation, others shook their hands and looked rather angry.

"I sat there, looking on and feeling just a little jealous at all those people mauling Catherine's pretty hand, when all at once I saw her go as pale as death, and spring upon one of the hands like a dog at a piece of meat.

"Right in front of her stood a tall, herculean fellow, with curly red hair showing under a fur cap. He wore a starched blue blouse over a countryman's jacket, and had wide, square shoulders, a protruding lower jaw—I was looking at him sideways—and temples that hid his eyes from any one looking at him from my position. No beard, only a few hairs visible on his white, dull face. An evil-looking face it was. Catissou was looking him straight in the face and holding his hand—it seemed enormous in her small, woman's hand—in a frenzied grasp, as if her life depended upon it.

"A shiver passed through me, and I said to myself: 'That's the man!'

"Yes, she held him; held him with all her might. And she said to the great fellow, who had suddenly turned as pale as she had:

"'Who killed Léonard Coussac?'

"He started back and tried to free his hand from the grasp of the *Woman Torpedo Fish*. Ah! Catissou didn't require any electrical arrangement to give *that* man a shock! He drew back his hand without being able to get it out of Catherine's grasp. 'Let me go, will you!' he said, trying to push her away. 'Are you mad?' He turned his head this way and that way, his eyes, wild with rage and fear, looking for a way of escape.

"'Wretch!' cried Catissou, sinking her fingers in his flesh as she tried to tighten her grasp, 'it was *you* who did it—you! *you!* YOU!'

"She shook him as a dog does a rat, and he was so stupefied he did not know what to do. But he soon recovered himself. He got his hand free from Catherine's fingers and dealt her a blow with it on the shoulder, which made her sink on her knees; then he turned towards the door like a wild boar.

"The audience was scared and made a rush for the door. The man made a bound, pushing the people before him, when I, by a quick movement, placed myself in front of him. He was a head taller than I was, and an evil look appeared on his face as I lifted my arm and seized him by the blouse.

"'I arrest you in the name of the law!'

"His reply was a blow, which would have sent me rolling, perhaps, if I had not been rendered strong by the presence of Catherine. As it was, I took very little notice of it and held him tight, struggling with him and dragging him about. I wouldn't loose him, you would have had to cut my hand off first. And all the time he was trying to stun me or break my skull by hitting me about the head. All at once—whizz—a knife sank into my flesh just below the neck, in the very same place as old Coussac had been struck. I have the scar now. Seems to have been the usual place for the rascal to strike!

"He reckoned on killing me, but the collar of my uniform stopped the blow a bit, and the blade of the knife—a Nontron knife, with a yellow handle—cut the collar clean through and gave me a nick in the flesh, that's all.

"I gripped the wrist of the hand that held the knife and held it above my head. If it came down again, it would be all up with me—*me*, a gendarme! So the knife was in the air over my head like the sword of Damo—what do you call him, Damocles?—yes, Damocles; and round the handle of the knife were the four fingers, all the same size, which had enabled Catherine Coussac to recognise the murderer of her father.

"I suppose the struggle did last some little time, but it seemed much longer to me. The blood was running from my wound, and I felt I was losing strength. I must leave go of the arm, and the knife would——. I made an effort; then, just in the nick of time, the good-for-nothing rascal gave a yell—such a yell it was! He gave a jump and started backwards as if to free himself from something, and he stepped backwards so quickly that he fell over something on to the ground, dragging me with him. He had fallen over old Mrs. Coussac, who had actually bitten him in the leg as the best way to make him leave go of me.

"We struggled about on the floor, but not for long. Catherine was up and helped me by getting the knife away from him, and I fastened my right hand on his throat and nearly strangled him. Then up came Sergeant Bugead and a comrade, attracted by the noise, and we soon had the handcuffs on the fellow, and they took him off through the crowd, who, now that he was unable to do anything, became very brave and wanted to lynch him.

"It was about time that help came, for I was done up. I felt myself going, and I fainted from loss of blood—fainted! Wasn't it silly for a gendarme to faint?

"And as I went off I had a feeling that I was being supported by a pair of white arms, and above me, I fancied I could see, not the Nontron knife, but Catherine's eyes, looking tenderly at me.

V

"Well, that's how a good marriage was brought about. My wound got well, of course, or you wouldn't see me here; but it got well twice as quick because Catherine looked after it. And when I got about again, she said plainly: 'Look here now! You suit me and I suit you. I swear I'll be a good wife to you!' Catherine's marriage was the last pleasure old Mrs. Coussac enjoyed, poor old woman! No! I make a mistake; her last piece of happiness was hearing that sentence had been passed on the murderer of Léonard Coussac.

"He turned out to be a bricklayer's labourer who had applied to Mr. Sabourdy for work, and had overheard about the money being entrusted to old Coussac. His greed had been excited, and he had committed the murder. He had done it quite alone; no accomplice. After the murder he had gone to Paris, then come back to Guéret, and then to Limoges, all the money gone and on the look-out for work. And he evidently wasn't particular what sort of work, either! He hardly took the trouble to defend himself at the trial. He seemed to say: 'You've got me. So much the worse for me!' He was condemned to death. He tried to cheat the executioner by knocking his head against the wall of his cell. But he didn't succeed, and the executioner had him after all.

"At the trial the judge complimented me. I don't say that for the sake of boasting, but because it's true. But I had no need of his compliments, nor of anything else. I had got Catissou, and that was enough for me. However, on the wedding-day, my captain's wedding gift was a corporal's stripes; and I tell you I was pleased at that. And since then—well, if you want to see a happy man, look at me!

"Catissou has had ever so many offers from theatrical managers to go on show—even from Australia. The newspapers had been full of her, and that made the managers eager to get her. But Catissou only laughed at it. She's got something else to do now. She has to wash the children, pipeclay my epaulettes, look after the poultry, and superintend the house—and she does superintend the house, too, and the corporal as well!

"No, no! Catissou is not an artiste. But if there should ever be a crime committed in these parts, and they can't find the man who did it, I wouldn't mind backing Catissou against all the detectives they like to employ!"

VI

The corporal knocked out the ashes of his pipe on his left thumbnail and was about to fill up again, when Catherine Tharaud came to the door, making a pretty picture, surrounded by the creeping plant, with the rays of the setting sun falling upon her.

"Come along, Martial," she said, with a pleasant smile, "the *clafoutis* is ready, and the soup, too. Call the little ones."

Martial Tharaud arose, put his hands up to his mouth, and called out to the boys, who were still enjoying their game:

"Hallo, there! Come along, you little rascals! Soup is ready!"

The boys ran up to him, and, as they all went inside, he took off his military cap and gaily saluted us.

THE LAST STAGE

Jules Claretie

A VERY dear friend told me this story. We had been talking of the strange things that happen in life—things a thousand times more wonderful and more romantic than the inventions of novelists—and he mentioned that this little drama had been played in his presence and that the actors had been known to him.

"You and I must go to Mézières together," he added, "and there I will introduce you to one of the heroes of the story. Ah! by no means yet have all the stories been told; the most astonishing ones still wait to be published. Who knows, too, how many secrets each one of us carries away at death—secrets buried within the conscience, and stifled for ever under the graveyard stone?"

Could my friend, Eugène Decary, be aware how closely these words applied to himself? And that his story of Jean Chevaucheux was the last he was to tell me? Fine spirit! Brave heart which beat in vain for all that was beautiful and good on earth! Thy rare soul has taken flight, thy warm heart is silent now!

This was the story as Eugène told it to me.

My father, he said, lived at Rethel, in the main road of the town. How well I remember the house with its slate roof and projecting beams—a hospitable house if ever there was one. The poor travellers knew it was good to call there. If they came with empty wallets, they left with those wallets filled.

One evening when we were seated by the fireside, my father smoking his pipe and gazing at the red-hot cinders on the hearth, my mother ironing the family linen, and I reading, we suddenly heard a loud noise outside, and then a lad with a frightened face came bursting into the house.

"Why, what is the matter?" said my father.

"A soldier has fallen down at your door—he's tired to death," answered the lad.

My father always had an affection for soldiers. He sprang up at once, rushed to the door, and before I could overtake him, was back in the house carrying a young soldier—as though the burden was a sack of corn. My mother quickly wheeled a big arm-chair up to the fire, and my father having placed the young man in it, said, looking at him tenderly:

"Is it possible that you are tramping the roads in the state you are in?"

Pitiful indeed was the condition of the young soldier. So pale and thin, his hair sticking to his forehead with perspiration, the veins on his temples swollen to the thickness of your little finger, his face begrimed with the dust of the high road. Although it was October, and the nights were beginning to be cold, great beads of sweat were on the poor fellow's brow as if we were in the heat of summer. He must have been walking a long way, for his shoes were worn out, and we could see that the leather had been cut to pieces by sharp stones. The upper leather of the left shoe was torn right away from the sole, and the foot was bleeding.

He lay in the chair without moving, his head thrown back, his eyes half open, his face deathly white.

My mother had some soup on the fire in no time, besides bringing out a flagon of wine.

"Tut!" said my father, "his feet are the chief thing."

With that he was on his knees before the poor fellow, cutting and tearing away all that remained of the shoes. Horribly swollen and blistered were the young soldier's feet, reminding me of the feet of the martyrs in the pictures that some of the Spanish artists have painted. My father, with a handkerchief dipped in vinegar, washed and dressed the wounds.

"Get some lint," he said to me.

My mother handed me some linen from the press and I tore it up.

By this time the soldier had begun to come round. He looked at us—at my father, at my mother, at me, and at two or three neighbours who had dropped in—glancing at us one after the other. Evidently he was trying to understand what had happened to him. No longer was he facing the high road with its sharp stones, or the vast uninhabited woods. He was in a comfortable room, where the beams of polished oak shone from the ceiling. A table covered with a snowy white cloth was before him; and on the table was a brown earthen tureen full of steaming cabbage soup, which gave out a most appetising odour.

Presently, raising himself and resting on the arms of the chair, he said to my father, in broken accents:

"But,—monsieur,—you—you—do not know who I am!"

"Well, we must make each other's acquaintance at table, then," my father replied with a smile.

Our dinner had already taken place, but my father, to keep the soldier company, sat down to the table facing him and examined the regimental buttons of his greatcoat. My mother having filled his plate and my father his glass, the young soldier ate and drank with tremendous appetite.

"Ah!" said my father suddenly, and pointing at the same time to a little tin box which was fastened by a cord to the soldier's neck, "you have served your time, then, for I see you've got your discharge there. But what the devil are you doing, then, eh? Trying to kill yourself on the high road? I have it—no money to pay for a seat on the *diligence*, eh?"

"I've got my discharge money," said the soldier, "and my mother would have sent me the fare and more if I had wanted it. But—well, I couldn't ride, that's all."

"I quite understand," said my father, calling for another bottle of wine, though he really hadn't the least idea what the soldier meant.

When he had finished at the table the soldier tried to walk; but he staggered on his feet and fell back in the chair with a moan. I noticed the tears coming to his eyes; and seeing that he was young, thin, and wiry, and had a face that, despite weariness, showed considerable energy, I was sure he was not the man to weep at trifles. These tears in his eyes puzzled me.

"I cannot walk before to-morrow!" said the soldier in a tone of vexation and disappointment.

"Walk!" cried my mother in alarm.

"To think of resuming your tramp!" exclaimed my father.

The soldier shook his head.

"You don't understand," he said. "I must go on! I have vowed to do it."

My father looked at the young man intently, with a glance of silent, earnest questioning.

"Let me tell you all about it," said the soldier, "for I think you have saved my life, and I owe it to you to tell you who I am.

"I come from Mézières, where my father is a wood-cutter. He is an honest man, and not unlike you in the face, monsieur. My name is Jean Chevaucheux. Seven years ago I was drawn for the conscription, and I was wildly in love with Marguerite Servan—a girl, oh, so good and so pretty. I had already asked for her hand, and her father had not said 'No.' But then at the same time there was Pierre Puvioux, who had also asked to marry her. Pierre Puvioux is about my own age, and he is a good fellow, so open-hearted; of course I ought to have hated him as a rival, but he remained my friend. Judge if this was not so.

"Daddy Servan had given me his hand and had said: 'I am willing to have you for my son-in-law, but you must get Marguerite's consent.' But when the question was put to Marguerite she said that while she was quite willing to have me for her husband, she felt just the same towards Pierre. She loved us both equally, and could not choose between the two. At the same time she certainly could not marry both of us.

"I must confess that for a little while I was in great fear. For it was said in Mézières that Puvioux had a rich aunt who was going to buy him a substitute; and then if he stayed behind he would surely marry Marguerite. As I knew that being poor I should have to go, I felt as if I heard the sound of their wedding bells deafening my ears and breaking my heart.

"There is no one to compare with Marguerite Servan. If I lose her now after waiting seven years, on my word of honour, I think I must blow my brains out. But fortunately Pierre Puvioux's aunt did not buy him off; as it happened she died, leaving nothing but debts behind her. He hadn't a sou any more than I had, and the two of us were obliged to shoulder arms and wait for the order to march.

"One evening Daddy Servan, taking each of us by the arm, led us to a cabaret. Then, while we disposed of a bottle of Moselle, he said:

"'My boys, I love you both with all my heart, for both of you are worthy Ardennais, and the one is as good as the other. One of you shall be my son-in-law—that's a bargain; for Marguerite will wait the seven years. She has no preference either for you, Puvioux, or for you, Chevaucheux; but she loves both of you equally, and which of you is chosen by Fate to be her husband will be a happy man. Now, then, this is the condition which will decide who is to marry my daughter. Both of you will go away on the same day and it is quite likely you will come back on the same day. Very well, the one who on his return is the first to shake hands with Daddy Servan and to say to him, "Hullo! here I am; I've served my time!" that one, I swear, shall marry Marguerite.'

"I was amazed and could hardly believe my ears. I glanced at Pierre and he looked at me, and though we were both in great distress it was all we could do to keep from laughing.

"But Daddy Servan was not in fun at all. He had thought out this plan for getting over the difficulty and he meant to stick to it. When I saw he was thoroughly in earnest I gave the old man my hand and swore I would act fairly, that I would use neither trickery nor violence, and that if Pierre Puvioux got back first to Mézières I would agree to his marrying Marguerite. Then Pierre rose and took a similar oath that he would deal fairly by me. After that we shook hands, and Daddy Servan said:

"'Now it rests with you two. All you have got to do is to see that no bullet catches you, and to come back safe and sound.'

" He filled up our glasses again, and we took a farewell drink.

" Before I left the town, after our marching orders had come, I determined to see Marguerite for the last time. But no sooner was I beneath her window—it was just getting dusk—than I saw some one else drawing near. It was Pierre Puvioux. He seemed annoyed at finding me there, and I wasn't exactly pleased to see him. For a minute we stood facing one another, our eyes on the ground, like a pair of fools. Then, by my faith, a wave of courage swept suddenly over me, and I said to Puvioux: ' Let us enter the house together.'

" ' Why, certainly,' he agreed.

" We said our good-byes to Marguerite. Though she listened to us in silence, there were tears on her long brown eyelashes. All of a sudden Pierre left off speaking and burst into sobs, and I followed suit. So there we were, all three, crying and shaking hands and saying nothing.

" Next day the *diligence* carried us off from Mézières, and when it started rattling over the stones I could have thrown myself from the roof in the hope of being crushed under its wheels; it was worse when a man from Lorraine, who was sitting next to me, began singing in a dreary voice one of the songs of his country; for his words seemed to say to me, ' It's all over with you, my poor Jean: you will never see her again! '

" Life is full of strange accidents," Jean Chevaucheux went on. " Pierre and I left our native town at the same hour and were put into the same regiment. This vexed me at first. I would rather he had been farther off, for you can easily understand that my feelings were not altogether friendly towards him. But soon came the thought, if Pierre is near me I shall at least be able to talk to him of Marguerite, and there will be some comfort in that. And then I said to myself, ' After all what are seven years? Seven years won't kill me! '

" Pierre Puvioux and I became close friends in the regiment, for he was a good sort, with a heart of gold. Sharing the same quarters we often talked of the country, of Daddy Servan, of Marguerite—just to pass the time, you understand. We often wrote to Mézières, each one telling the other what he had said in his letter. Of course it was a struggle, but we carried it out loyally. Then when letters came in reply from Marguerite or Daddy Servan they were addressed to both of us, wished us both equally good luck, and brought us both an equal supply of hope. So, of course, you may be sure both of us went on hoping.

" Then, one day, our Colonel made me a corporal. I was proud and sorry at the same time, for, you see, Pierre and I were now no longer equals. The stripes on my arm gave me authority over him, and that is a distinct superiority in the eyes of the people of the Ardennes. But, you know, I am not bad-natured, and I wasn't stuck up. On the contrary my rank chiefly distressed me; for my stripes prevented me talking in the old way with Pierre. It seemed to me, thinking it over, that there was only one way of getting rid of what embarrassed us. I missed roll-call one day on purpose, and for that my rank was taken away from me. But think of my bad luck! I only gave up my stripes in order that Puvioux might have them! It was enough to make one gnaw one's finger-tips off! However, it gave Pierre the chance of proving his friendship, and he did it without making any fuss; so that at the end of a week he was deprived of his rank. After that our tunics were safe enough from alteration, and we were doomed to remain privates.

" 'A good job,' said Puvioux.

" 'Lucky for us,' I replied.

" The seven years came to an end—there is no need for me to tell you what happened day by day. Our discharge and the return route papers, all duly signed, were handed to us.

" 'Now,' I said to Puvioux, 'at last our time is up, and we can set off home.'

" 'Yes,' he answered, 'they are waiting for us there.'

" 'You know,' I said, 'that the contest won't be finally settled before we are both of us back at Mézières, and the one who has lost has declared the struggle to have been fairly carried out.'

" 'That's right,' Puvioux replied.

" We embraced, and then—the other morning—we started off for Mézières, with good shoes on our feet and stout sticks in our hands. Did I tell you we had been on garrison duty at Angers? It's a fine stretch of road from there, if you like! My faith! Since I started I seem to have walked round the world!

" We set off together, not saying much, but thinking a good deal and walking even more. It was fearfully hot, horribly dusty, and the air as heavy as lead. Half-way through one of our stages I threw myself down by the side of the road, exhausted, my legs too stiff to carry me any farther.

" 'Are you stopping to rest?' asked Puvioux.

" 'Yes,' I replied.

" 'Good-bye, then,' he said, going on.

" 'Good-bye till our next meeting,' I called after him.

" I watched him stride away, walking as firmly as though he had only just commenced the journey. When a bend of the road took him out of sight and I could see him no more, I felt utterly alone and forsaken, and a horrible sense of despair overwhelmed me. I fought against it, and rose up to continue the march. Short as the rest was, it had done me good and put new courage in me. I pressed on, on, on, and did so well that after a time I caught up with Puvioux and passed him.

"But at the end of the day, though well in front of my rival, I was quite done up. I stopped at an inn, intending to get a little sleep—only a little. I actually slept through the whole night and only awoke at daybreak. Of course I was enraged.

"'Has anybody seen a soldier go by on foot?' I called out. 'A soldier? why, yes, monsieur, last night very late. He asked for a drink of water.'

"Ah! so Puvioux had passed me in his turn! I hurried off, but at three o'clock in the afternoon I had not overtaken him, nor yet at six o'clock. I rested for a while in the evening while I took some food, and then on again I went. I felt sure Puvioux could not be much ahead of me now. It was late at night when I stopped—for there is a limit to a man's strength—and at the wayside public-house where I had knocked and found admission, I came upon Puvioux, pale as death, sitting in an arm-chair. He started at seeing me, and was not unnaturally annoyed. We said very little to each other: what was there indeed for us to talk about? Besides, we were so horribly tired.

"It was a question which of us would be up first next morning, and I was the one: and that next morning was this morning. I have been walking all day, with very short rests, for, you know, we are near to Mézières. I know my map of France now! The last stage—oh, my God! if I should arrive too late!"

Jean Chevaucheux became silent at the thought.

"And what of Pierre Puvioux?" said my father. "Has he overtaken you again?"

"No!" exclaimed Chevaucheux; "and if only I could go on now I should be saved."

"Go on! In the state you are now in! Impossible."

"Yes. My feet are so swollen—cut badly. But, to-morrow——?"

"By to-morrow you will have rested and will be able to walk."

"Do you mean that?" the soldier asked with pleading eyes.

"I can promise it."

"Oh! but you are kind to me."

"That's all right," said my father.

He advised the soldier to go to bed at once, for his bed was ready, and it was then ten o'clock.

The poor fellow desired nothing better. He shook hands warmly with all of us before going up to the room which had been prepared for him.

My father was up before daybreak next morning, anxious to see what the weather was like. While he stood looking up at the sky from an open window, he heard a heavy step in the street below, and made out in the dim uncertain light a soldier making his way painfully in the direction of Mézières.

"On the march already?" said my father. The soldier halted.

"Are you off, then?" continued my father.

The soldier looked up, trying to make out who it was who called to him.

"Is that Jean Chevaucheux?" asked my father.

"No," came the answer; "it is Pierre Puvioux."

And, as though spurred on by the name Jean Chevaucheux, he went off with quickened speed and was soon out of my father's sight.

"Hullo!" said my father, "poor Chevaucheux will have to stir his stumps if he means to overtake that brave young fellow! And with that he went at once to the room where Jean had gone to bed. The young soldier, already up, was examining his feet by the light of a candle.

"Victory!" he cried on seeing my father. "I am strong and well again, and out of pain. To the road!"

"Yes, and quickly, too," said my father, "for Puvioux has passed through Rethel."

"Pierre Puvioux?"

"Yes, I have just spoken to him. He went under my window, and is pressing on like a madman."

"*Bon Dieu!*" cried Chevaucheux as if he were stunned. He repeated this exclamation while fastening his knapsack. But when the knapsack was on his shoulders he said, "Well, instead of being discouraged at what you have told me, it has put new heart into me."

My mother had risen too by this time, and was downstairs filling a wallet with provisions for Chevaucheux. But he wouldn't take it, insisting that he was not hungry, and all he would accept was a flask of brandy. But he put on a pair of my father's stout walking boots, and went off full of confidence, blessing my mother, and leaning on my father's arm for the first few steps.

It was daylight now, and for half an hour my father bore Jean Chevaucheux company. The young soldier walked uprightly, in spite of his damaged feet, which must have pained him horribly; but he was very silent, and seemed to be wrapped in thought.

"Well, it is time to say good-bye now," said my father. "Good luck to you, and God be with you."

"Monsieur Decary," said Jean Chevaucheux at this, "will you allow me to embrace you?"

They were in each other's arms in a moment. Chevaucheux wept, and there was moisture in my father's eyes.

"But this won't do," said my father, the first to recover himself. "We are losing time. *En route! en route!*"

So they parted, and Jean marched off on the road to Mézières.

We had no news of Jean Chevaucheux for three or four years, but we often talked about the night when the young soldier came wounded and worn out to our house. What had become of him? And what was the end of that romantic love-story which had so strange a beginning?

One day my father had business to do in Mézières, and took me with him. When we reached the town he made for the first barber's shop in order to get shaved; but at the door of the shop sat a sturdy infant enjoying the sunshine and blocking the way with plump, outstretched legs.

"Won't you let me pass?" said my father amiably.

"No, I won't let 'oo pass," the child answered.

Just then a man in his shirt-sleeves appeared in the shop—evidently the father, for he picked up the young gentleman and held him in his arms, saying:

"What are you up to, Pierre? Do you want to drive away our customers?"

I recognised the voice at once, and so did my father.

We looked at the barber. He looked at us. Then suddenly all three of us burst into a simultaneous exclamation. The barber was Jean Chevaucheux. With flushed and beaming face he instantly held out his hand.

"Ah! is it really you? And to think that I have never written to you—ungrateful wretch that I am! And you never heard? Yes, it was I who won the bride! I arrived first—first, you know!"

He rushed to the back of the shop, and called out:

"Marguerite! Marguerite! come quickly!" He seemed almost out of his senses with joy.

A pretty woman with fair complexion and blue eyes appeared. Her demeanour was gentle and pensive, almost a little sad.

"You see this—this gentleman," Jean cried excitedly. "It was he who saved me at Rethel—the night before I reached your father's. Monsieur Decary—whom I have told you about so often."

"Ah!" Marguerite exclaimed, with a beautiful smile. Looking at us with her large, calm eyes, she bowed and thanked us gently. Then, as her husband still went on recalling the past, she turned to him with a glance that was beseeching, and perhaps a little reproachful.

But Jean never noticed it.

"Ah!" he cried, "and it is to you, monsieur, I owe my happiness! Look at my son, my little Pierre—it was by my wife's wish that he was called Pierre—isn't he a fine fellow? My shop, which is doing a first-rate business; my wife, whom I worship; and my little Pierre—I owe them all to you!"

ÉMILE POUVILLON
1840–1906

DUCK SHOOTING

" AND when is the wedding? " I asked my friend, Vidian Sorède.

We had not seen each other for years, and he was telling me of his approaching marriage, while the carriage, which had come to fetch me on the arrival of the night train, took us, all booted and rigged out from head to foot, to the meeting-place at Saint Nazaire, where the famous wild-duck shooting, praised on every occasion by my friend, was about to take place.

" My marriage? " replied Vidian; " it was settled to take place just before Lent, the contract drawn up, the wedding presents ordered at Toulouse. And now everything is put off to Easter, or to Trinity Sunday, perhaps. A whim of my future sister-in-law! I do not know what has come over her. Very bright, very charming and friendly with me when she came from the convent school. Then all of a sudden a complete change; a face of woe. She is upset at any talk about the marriage. Swears she will die of grief if she is separated from her sister."

" Jealous of you? "

" No doubt. Unless it is some religious mania working in her. She has her own ideas about marriage. Men horrify her, and she is scarcely fifteen. She wants a good whipping."

" A spoilt child! Unless . . . You do not think . . . It cannot be that . . ."

An explanation had struck me, but the matter was so delicate I hesitated to speak of it. Useless to trouble this simple-hearted Vidian, and put him perhaps on a false trail.

Besides, our chat was over: we had arrived. Beneath the pale radiance of the stars, the house of the Rudelles, the future parents by marriage of my friend Sorède, loomed before us, big and lonely, between the lake, the mountain, and the sea. The approach of the duck shooting filled it that night with a joyful tumult. In a very large dining-room, used for long country meals and yearly feasts, the lady of the house and her two daughters were looking after the guests, while our host, a patriarch in marsh boots, a sailor's oilskin over his shoulder, went from one to the other shaking hands and exchanging forecasts of the weather.

A little on one side, in the bay of a window, Vidian was talking gaily to his sweetheart, Estelle, a lovely girl, a flower of twenty years, with a splendid figure. Thérèse, the younger girl, watched them from afar, with evil glances showing beneath her eyelashes, sudden flashes that lighted up for the moment her long pale form, pale with almost the greenish tinge of growing youth. Jealous certainly. But of whom? of Vidian, or of Estelle?

Our host, however, signed to us to depart. Not a moment to lose if we wished to surprise the velvet ducks, and surround them in their nocturnal haunts.

Outside the day was breaking. Behind us, westward, above the black mass of the houses of Saint Nazaire, the Canigou shot aloft, a white phantom alongside the pale-blue chaos of the Albères. Opposite, between a terrace of vineyards and the thin line of an isthmus of sand that separated it from the sea, the widespread sheet of a lake twinkled behind a curtain of wandering haze.

Boats were waiting for us a few steps from the house: a score of black-bottomed wherries, with prows rising in a crosier shape, like the ships of the ancient Greeks. Primitive also, in keeping with his boat, was the silent chewer of quids, a pensioned sailor, who helped us with our boxes of cartridges and our spare oars.

At the order of Rudelle, supreme head and organiser of the shoot, the flotilla got under way and set out to conquer the lake. Upright in the bows, we scanned the sky-line in search of the famous velvet ducks. Nothing yet. Not a sign of life on the vast plain just beginning to be wrinkled by the early morning breeze. Then, as the wind grew in strength, the mists lifted. On our left, then, close to the shore, a movement was seen.

Sometimes bright, sometimes obscure, according as they turned their backs or bellies to the light, flocks of sea-birds arose, oscillating between the land and the lake. Ducks! In long, in slow movements, like a swarm of anxious ghosts on the banks of Styx, they floated, frightened, hesitating between the noises of the land and the line of boats that cut off their retreat from the side of the lake. But soon, as under orders, the different individuals fell into their places and the wild whirl was organised. Two flocks with their leaders and their rear-guard drew off in a spiral climb, and when they were out of reach of our guns, passed slowly over our heads and disappeared like travelling clouds towards the high seas.

"Good-bye to the common ducks, and welcome to the velvet ducks! Can you see them over there?" said Vidian to me. "The dance is about to begin. Attention!"

The boats now were deploying in a semicircle towards the shore. At the same time some black points were stirring on the water: the heavy wings arose, fell back again, and restless heads appeared between two dives. The velvet-backs were there. A gunshot made them resolved to flee. But instead of the skilful and well-ordered retreat of the ordinary ducks, this was the wild chance scurry of a stampede. In twos and threes the birds rose up and tried to pass over the wall of boats. Taken between two fires and half massacred, they stopped in full flight and fell back in heaps on the water. And after them came others—a fusillade of fifteen minutes' sheer slaughter.

Vidian never stopped firing and recharging. He thought no more about his marriage, Vidian. Love was far away, and the smile of his dark-haired lady-love and the hostile glance of the little sister were forgotten. He was given over entirely to the passion of the hunter, the joy of murder. And the faces of the other shooters, in view on the neighbouring boats, had all the same expression of triumphant brutality. The elemental feelings of the race, the privateers and the fierce mountain fighters of old, came fully out in the cries and the gestures of these civilised men, plunged for the moment back into the barbarity of their ancestors. The spectacle of the victims, the dead bodies heaped up in the bottom of our boat, aggravated the repugnance, the nausea with which this festival of blood and death filled me. And the carnage, finishing here, began again farther off. The flotilla, dispersed for the moment in search of the wounded and the dead, reformed and dashed in pursuit of the unhappy creatures escaped from the slaughter. My gorge rose. I pretended I was tired by my long journey and sickened by the motion of the boat dancing on the waves. I landed.

Stretched out on the warm sands of the dune, I watched the flotilla lessen in size as it went far away over the lake. I heard the sound of the firing move away and thin out. Then, suddenly, all around me the sweetness of silence and the boon of solitude were felt. Some chickens were pecking on the threshold of the fisherman's hut, a hut of reeds that evoked the stillness of the desert, the melancholy of some African shore. At my feet some bees were plundering the first frail flowers of spring, and through a break in the dunes the surf of the sea reached me with a vision of a sail, of a fringe of foam twinkling suddenly on the crest of a wave. Abruptly, with a bewildered beat of wings, the velvet-backs alighted two steps from the shore. Ignorant of danger, forgetful of the others, of the unhappy creatures who fell over there under the guns, they will soon begin to play, to pitch over, to dig in the mud in search of food. . . . The arrival of Vidian and his boat interrupted my reflections. Vidian was exalted—three double shots, and I don't know how many single ones, a score and a half of coots, and as many velvet-backs—a triumph!

My want of interest extinguished his enthusiasm. Our return

was a dull affair. As though the last shot fired in the air by the hunters had wounded the sun, daylight faded very quickly. On high, towards the sunset, the snows of the Canigou took on mournful tints and livid, ghastly colours. The lake grew pale. The agonies of dying birds, palpitating in the hollow of the waves, trails of feathers floated here and there, funereal flotsam. In silence we let ourselves sway to the rhythm of the slow melody—an old song in Catalanian—that the old rower sang to the knocking of his oars against the rowlocks.

Madame Rudelle and her daughters were waiting for us at the landing-stage, cries of joy welcomed the hunters, and Vidian was hailed as the king of the battue. But Thérèse was upset at the sight of the blood remaining on the hand of the hero.

"You are wounded!" she exclaimed, in an outburst that revealed the secret of her heart, of her little sorrowful heart that did not know its own feelings.

"Little silly!" laughed Estelle. "Don't you see it is only the blood of the birds!"

The boats were beached, the kill was counted and taken into the house. As soon as they entered the hunters sat down and gathered round the table. It was the bestiality of eating after the brutality of carnage, and jokes, hunting stories, boasts of wonderful kills, suggested by the day's shooting and deep draughts of wine.

I watched Thérèse, silent before an empty plate. Sulking over the dinner as she had over the shooting, the sad child spied on Vidian and Estelle who were sitting opposite her, and, isolated amid the laughing and chatter, pursuing their loving conversation.

At dessert, one of the guests proposed the health of the lovers. Glasses were raised in their honour, but Thérèse's glass slipped from her fingers and broke as it fell on the table. The act had been beyond her strength! She had fainted. They carried her away, pale as a corpse. Estelle and Vidian accompanied the bearers as far as the bedroom. The meal ended, the guests departed, before the sick girl appeared again.

"Good news!" said Vidian to me a little later, as we in turn left Saint Nazaire. Thérèse has recovered, and I shall be married in a month. She knew well what she was doing, the little sly thing. Thanks to her attack of nerves, she has got what she was asking for. Her parents have given up trying to tame her, and are sending her back to the convent. Let her stay there and leave us alone, especially as she now wants to become a nun.

We climbed up the hill above the village. Below, the lake slept under the moon. The straw huts of the fishermen by the shore, the farmsteads in the vineyards, with their hedges of cypress and thuyas, slumbered, wrapped in the stillness of night. But my nerves, still vibrating from the double drama of the day, were bent on evoking in my mind, across the peace and silence of the present hour, the images of murder and sorrow that had shaken them since the morning. I thought of the velvet-backs, I thought of Thérèse. I had before me now the scared flight, with necks stretched out to the sea, of the poor innocent birds reeling under the gun-fire, now the pale figure of the little passionate child, struck down in a moment by the storms of this world, and who escaped, with beating wings, towards heaven.

CATULLE MENDÈS
1841–1909

THE MIRROR

I

In that kingdom there was not a single looking-glass. All the mirrors you hang on the walls, all the hand-mirrors, all those that are worn on the *chatelaine* had been broken into a thousand pieces by order of the queen. If the smallest bit of looking-glass was found, no matter whose house it was, the queen always put the occupants of that house to death with horrible tortures. The reason for this curious proceeding can be explained. The queen was so appallingly ugly that the most hideous monsters would have appeared handsome beside her; and not only was she quite aware of her ugliness and determined to avoid all risk of seeing a reflection of herself when she went about the town, but there was some comfort in the knowledge that at least others were not able to see their beauty. What profit was it to have the most beautiful eyes in the world, a mouth as glorious as roses, and to put flowers in your hair if you were not allowed to see your head-dress, or your mouth, or your eyes? You could not even hope to see your reflection in the streams and lakes, for all rivers and ponds in that country were hidden under cunningly-joined stone slabs. The wells whence water was drawn were so deep that you could not see their surface, and instead of buckets flat troughs were used that made reflection impossible. The consequent distress surpasses all description—especially among coquettes, who were no more rare there than in other countries.

II

But a maiden named Jacinthe, living in the suburbs of that town, was not quite so unhappy as the rest; for she had a lover who took the place of a mirror to some extent by always telling her how beautiful she was. Jacinthe blushed, but not because she was afraid, when this lover asked her to marry him; and when she smiled it was not in a spirit of pleasantry at the thought of saying "No." The trouble was that the wicked queen came to hear the news of the engagement; for the queen's one joy was to spoil the happiness of others. Besides, she hated Jacinthe above all the rest, because Jacinthe was the most beautiful maiden in all the realm.

III

A few days before the wedding, when Jacinthe happened to be walking in the orchard, an old woman came towards her, begging. Suddenly the old woman fell back with a cry of horror, as though she had nearly trodden on a toad.

"Heavens! what's this I see?" she exclaimed.

"What's the matter, my good woman, what is it you see? Tell me," asked Jacinthe.

"The ugliest thing in the whole world."

"Well, I'm sure that isn't me," Jacinthe said with a smile.

"Alas! poor child, but it is you. I am very old, but in all my life never have I met any one so hideous as you are."

"You mean to tell me that I am ugly—I?"

"A thousand times uglier than words can tell."

. . . . .

The old woman, who must have been some wicked fairy and a friend of the wicked queen, had vanished with a cruel and mocking laugh. Jacinthe, weeping bitterly, had dropped on a seat under the apple-trees.

IV

It seemed impossible to distract Jacinthe's mind from her trouble. "I am ugly! I am ugly!" she kept saying, over and over again. It was in vain that her lover swore by every oath he could think of that the opposite was true. To his earnest request that the wedding-day should be fixed, Jacinthe would reply:

"What? I become your wife! That must never be. I love you far too dearly to give you so hideous a thing as I am for a wife."

What could be done? The only way to prove the old woman a liar, and to convince Jacinthe of the truth, was to let her see herself in a looking-glass. But there was no looking-glass in the whole kingdom, and out of terror of the queen no workman durst make one.

"I must go to the court," Jacinthe's lover said at last. "However savage the queen may be, the sight of my tears and Jacinthe's beauty are bound to move her."

V

"Well, what is the matter?" said the wicked queen. "Who are these people, and what do they want with me?"

"Your majesty, the most miserable lover in all the world is before you."

"That's a good reason certainly for worrying me."

"Have pity on us, your majesty."

"But what concern have I with your lovers' quarrels?"

"If you would but allow a mirror——"

"How dare you allude to a mirror," said the queen rising up, trembling with rage and gnashing her teeth.

"Pardon me, I beseech you, your majesty, and do not be angry, but deign to listen to me. This maiden whom you see before you suffers under a most extraordinary delusion. She thinks that she is ugly——"

"So she is," the queen interrupted, with an ill-tempered laugh. "She is quite right. I don't think I ever saw a more hideous object."

Jacinthe felt that she could die of grief at these words. It was impossible for her to doubt any longer her appearance, since in the queen's eyes, no less than in the eyes of the beggar woman, she was ugly. Slowly her gaze fell, and with a face as pale as death she sank in a faint on the steps of the throne. But her lover, on hearing the queen's cruel words, was not by any means prepared to give up all as lost. He called out loudly that either the queen was mad or she had some special reason for her monstrous lie.

There was no time to say more, for the guards quickly seized him and held him fast. Then the queen gave a sign, and the executioner, who was always near the throne in case he might be wanted at any minute, stepped forward.

"Do your duty," said the queen, pointing to the man who had insulted her.

Calmly did the executioner raise his mighty sword; suddenly two utterly discordant cries were heard. Jacinthe, not recalling where she was, and slowly opening her eyes, had caught sight of herself in the bright naked steel, and had shouted for joy at seeing her own fascinatingly beautiful face.

The other cry came from the queen. It was a cry of pain, a death-rattle. For the ugly and wicked queen, seeing her own face also in this unexpected mirror, had died of shame and anger at the sight.

FRANÇOIS COPPÉE
1842–1908

A MIRACLE

On that morning, which was the morning before Christmas, two important events happened simultaneously—the sun rose, and so did M. Jean-Baptiste Godefroy.

Unquestionably the sun, illuminating suddenly the whole of Paris with its morning rays, is an old friend, regarded with affection by everybody. It is particularly welcome after a fortnight of misty atmosphere and grey skies, when the wind has cleared the air and allowed the sun's rays to reach the earth again. Besides all this the sun is a person of importance. Formerly, he was regarded as a god, and was called Osiris, Apollo, and I don't know what else. But do not imagine that because the sun is so important he is of greater influence than M. Jean-Baptiste Godefroy, millionaire banker, director of the *Comptoir Général de Crédit,* administrator of several big companies, deputy and member of the General Council of the Eure, officer of the Legion of Honour, etc. etc. And whatever opinion the sun may have about himself, he certainly has not a higher opinion than M. Jean-Baptiste Godefroy has of *him*self. So we are authorised to state, and we consider ourselves justified in stating, that on the morning in question, at about a quarter to eight, the sun and M. Jean-Baptiste Godefroy rose.

Certainly the manner of rising of these two great powers mentioned was not the same. The good old sun began by doing a great many pretty actions. As the sleet had, during the night, covered the bare branches of the trees in the boulevard Malesherbes, where the *hôtel* Godefroy is situated, with a powdered coating, the sun, a true magician, amused himself by transforming the branches into great bouquets of red coral. At the same time he scattered his rays impartially on those poor passers-by whom necessity sent out, so early in the morning, to gain their daily bread. He even had a smile for the poor clerk, in thin overcoat, hurrying to his office, as well as for the little dressmaker, shivering under her insufficient clothing; for the workman carrying half a loaf under his arm, for the car-conductor as he punched the tickets, and for the dealer in roast chestnuts, who was roasting his first panful. In short, the sun gave pleasure to everybody in the world.

M. Jean-Baptiste Godefroy, on the contrary, rose in quite a different frame of mind. On the previous evening he had dined with the Minister for Agriculture. The dinner, from the removal of the *potage* to the salad, bristled with truffles, and the banker's stomach, aged forty-seven years, experienced the burning and biting of pyrosis. So the manner in which M. Jean-Baptiste Godefroy rang for his valet-de-chambre was so expressive that, as he got some warm water for his master's shaving, Charles said to the kitchen-maid:

"There he goes! The monkey is barbarously ill-tempered again this morning. My poor Gertrude, we're in for a bad day."

Then, walking on tiptoe, with eyes modestly cast down, he entered the chamber of his master, opened the curtains, lit the fire, and made all the necessary preparations for the toilet, with the discreet demeanour and respectful gestures of a sacristan placing the sacred vessels on the altar for the priest.

"What sort of weather this morning?" demanded M. Godefroy curtly, as he buttoned his undervest of grey swandown upon a stomach that was already a little too prominent.

"Very cold, sir," replied Charles meekly. "At six o'clock the thermometer marked seven degrees above zero. But, as you will see, sir, the sky is quite clear, and I think we are going to have a fine morning."

In stropping his razor, M. Godefroy approached the window, drew aside one of the hangings, looked on the boulevard, which was bathed in brightness, and made a slight grimace which bore some resemblance to a smile.

It is all very well to be perfectly stiff and correct, and to know that it is bad taste to show feeling of any kind in the presence of domestics, but the appearance of the roguish sun in the middle of December sends such a glow of warmth to the heart that it is impossible to disguise the fact. So M. Godefroy deigned, as before observed, to smile. If some one had whispered to the opulent banker that his smile had anything in common with that of the printer's boy, who was enjoying himself by making a slide on the pavement, M. Godefroy would have been highly incensed. But it really was so all the same; and during the space of one minute this man who was so occupied by business matters, this leading light in the financial and political worlds, indulged in the childish pastime of watching the passers-by, and following with his eyes the files of conveyances as they gaily rolled in the sunshine.

But pray do not be alarmed. Such a weakness could not last long. People of no account, and those who have nothing to do, may be able to let their time slip by in doing nothing. It is very well for women, children, poets, and riff-raff. M. Godefroy had other fish to fry; and the work of the day promised to be exceptionally heavy. From half-past eight to ten o'clock he had a meeting at his office with a certain number of gentlemen, all of whom bore a striking resemblance to M. Godefroy. Like him, they were very nervous; they had risen with the sun, they were all *blasés,* and they all had the same object in view—to make money.

After an early luncheon (taken at the close of the meeting), M. Godefroy had to jump into his carriage and fly to the Bourse to exchange a few words with other gentlemen who had also risen at dawn, but who had not the least spark of imagination among them. (The conversations were always on the same subject—money.)

From there, without losing an instant, M. Godefroy had to rush off to preside over another meeting of acquaintances, equally with himself without compassion or tenderness. At this meeting, held round a baize-covered table, strewn with heaps of papers and well provided with ink-wells, the talk would again turn on money, and various methods of making it.

After the aforesaid meeting he, in his capacity of deputy, had to appear before several commissions (always held in rooms where there were baize-covered tables and ink-wells and heaps of papers). There he would find men as devoid of sentiment as he was, all utterly incapable of neglecting any occasion of making money, but who, nevertheless, had the extreme goodness to sacrifice several hours of the afternoon to the glory of France.

When he had shaved himself carefully, sparing the narrow strip of pepper-and-salt beard round his chin, as that gave him the air of a trustworthy family man in the eyes of the electors in Auverge and of fools in general, M. Godefroy put on a morning suit of perfect cut and finish, showing that the old beau nearing fifty had not ceased trying to please. Then he descended to his cabinet, where he received the file of men who were entirely occupied by one thought—that of augmenting their capital. These gentlemen discussed several projected enterprises, all of them of considerable importance, notably that of a new railroad to be laid across a remote desert. Another scheme was for the founding of monster works in the environs of Paris, another of a mine to be worked in one of the South American republics. It goes without saying that no one asked if the railway would have passengers or goods to carry, or if the proposed works should manufacture cotton night-caps or distil whisky; whether the mine was to produce gold or inferior copper: certainly not. The talk of M. Godefroy's morning callers turned exclusively upon the profits which it would be possible to realise during the week which should follow the issue of the shares. They discussed particularly the values of the shares, which they knew would be destined before long to be worth less than the paper on which they were printed in fine style.

These conversations, bristling with figures, lasted till ten o'clock precisely, and then the director of the *Comptoir Général de Crédit,* who, by the way, was an honest man—at least, as honest as is to be found in business—courteously conducted his last visitor to the head of the stairway. The visitor named was an old villain, as rich as Crœsus, who, by a not uncommon chance, enjoyed the general esteem of the public; whereas, had justice been done to him, he would have been lodging at the expense of the State in one of those large establishments provided by a thoughtful government for smaller delinquents; and there he would have pursued a useful and healthy calling for a lengthy period, the exact length having been fixed by the judges of the supreme court. But M. Godefroy showed him out relentlessly, notwithstanding his importance—it was absolutely necessary to be at the Bourse at 11 o'clock—and went into the dining-room.

It was a luxuriously furnished room. The furniture and plate would have served to endow a cathedral. Nevertheless, notwithstanding that M. Godefroy took a gulp of bicarbonate of soda, his indigestion refused to subside, and consequently he could only take the scanty breakfast of a dyspeptic. In the midst of such luxury, and under the eye of a well-paid butler, M. Godefroy could only eat a couple of boiled eggs and nibble a little mutton chop. The man of money trifled with dessert—took only a crumb of Roquefort—not more than two cents' worth. Then the door opened and an overdressed but charming little child—young Raoul, four years old—the son of the great financier, entered the room, accompanied by his German nursery governess.

This event occurred every day at the same hour—a quarter to eleven, precisely, while the carriage which was to take the banker to the Bourse stood ready for the man who had only a quarter of an hour to give to paternal sentiment. It was not that he did not love his son. He did love him—nay, he adored him, in his own particular way. But then, you know, business *is* business.

At the age of forty-two, when already worldly-wise and *blasé,* he had fancied himself in love with the daughter of one of his club friends—Marquis de Neufontaine, an old rascal—a nobleman, but one whose card-playing was more than open to suspicion, and who certainly would have been expelled from the club but for the influence of M. Godefroy. The nobleman was only too happy to become the father-in-law of a man who would pay his debts, and without any scruples he handed over his daughter—a simple and ingenuous child of seventeen, who was taken from a convent to be married—to the worldly banker. The girl, doubtless, was sweet and pretty, but she had no dowry except numerous aristocratic prejudices and romantic illusions, and her father thought he was fortunate in getting rid of her on such favourable terms.

M. Godefroy, the son of a miserly old lawyer of Andelys, had always remained a man of the people, and intensely vulgar. In spite of his improved circumstances, he had not improved. His entire lack of tact and refinement was painful to his young wife, whose tenderest feelings he ruthlessly and thoughtlessly trampled upon. Things were looking unpromising, when, happily for her, Madame Godefroy died in giving birth to her firstborn. When he spoke of his deceased wife, the banker waxed poetical, although had she lived they would have been divorced in six months. His son he loved dearly for several reasons—first, because the child was an only son; secondly, because he was a scion of two such houses as Godefroy and Neufontaine; finally, because the man of money had naturally great respect for the heir to many millions.

So the youngster had golden rattles and other similar toys, and was brought up like a young Dauphin. But his father, overwhelmed with business worries, could never give the child more than fifteen minutes per day of his precious time—and, as on the day mentioned, it was always during " cheese "—and for the rest of the day the father abandoned the child to the care of the servants.

" Good-morning, Raoul."

" Good-morning, papa."

And the company director, having put his serviette away, sat young Raoul on his left knee, took the child's head between his big paws, and in stroking and kissing it actually forgot all his money matters and even his note of the afternoon, which was of great importance to him, as by it he could gain quite an important amount of patronage.

" Papa," said little Raoul suddenly, " will Father Christmas put anything in my shoe to-night? "

The father answered with " Yes, if you are a good child." This was very striking from a man who was a pronounced freethinker, who always applauded every anti-clerical attack in the Chamber with a vigorous " Hear, hear." He made a mental note that he must buy some toys for his child that very afternoon.

Then he turned to the nursery governess with:

" Are you quite satisfied with Raoul, Mademoiselle Bertha? "

Mademoiselle Bertha became as red as a peony at being addressed, as if the question were scarcely *comme il faut,* and replied by a little imbecile snigger, which seemed fully to satisfy M. Godefroy's curiosity about his son's conduct.

" It's fine to-day," said the financier, " but cold. If you take Raoul to Monceau Park, mademoiselle, please be careful to wrap him up well."

Mademoiselle, by a second fit of idiotic smiling, having set at rest M. Godefroy's doubts and fears on that essential point, he kissed his child, left the room hastily, and in the hall was enveloped in his fur coat by Charles, who also closed the carriage door. Then the faithful fellow went off to the café which he frequented in the Rue de Miromesnil, where he had promised to meet the coachman of the baroness who lived opposite, and play a game of billiards, thirty up—and spot-barred, of course.

Thanks to the brown bay—for which a thousand francs over and above its value was paid by M. Godefroy as a result of a sumptuous snail supper given to that gentleman's coachman by the horse-dealer—thanks to the expensive brown bay which certainly went well, the financier was able to get through his many engagements satisfactorily. He appeared punctually at the Bourse, sat at several committee tables, and at a quarter to five, by voting with the ministry, he helped to reassure France and Europe that the rumours of a ministerial crisis had been totally unfounded. He voted with the ministry because he had succeeded in obtaining the favours which he demanded as the price of his vote.

After he had thus nobly fulfilled his duty to himself and his country, M. Godefroy remembered what he had said to his child on the subject of Father Christmas, and gave his coachman the address of a dealer in toys. There he bought, and had put in his carriage, a fantastic rocking-horse mounted on castors—a whip in each ear; a box of leaden soldiers—all as exactly alike as those grenadiers of the Russian regiment of the time of Paul I, who all had black hair and snub noses; and a score of other toys, all equally striking and costly. Then, as he returned home, softly reposing in his well-swung carriage, the rich banker, who, after all, was a father, began to think with pride of his little boy and to form plans for his future.

When the child grew up he should have an education worthy of a prince, and he would be one, too, for there was no longer any aristocracy except that of money, and his boy would have a capital of about 30,000,000 francs.

If his father, the son of a pettifogging provincial lawyer, who had formerly dined in the Latin Quarter when in Paris, and had remarked every evening when putting on a white tie that he looked as fine as if he were going to a wedding—if his father had been able to accumulate an enormous fortune, and to become thereby a power in the republic; if he had been able to marry a young lady, one of whose ancestors had fallen at Marignan, what an important personage little Raoul might become.

M. Godefroy built all sorts of air-castles for his boy, forgetting that Christmas is the birthday of a very poor little Child, who was born in a stable, where the parents only found lodging through charity.

In the midst of the banker's dreams the coachman cried: "Door, please," and drove into the yard. As he went up the steps M. Godefroy was thinking that he had barely time to dress for dinner; but on entering the vestibule he found all the domestics crowded in front of him in a state of alarm and confusion. In a corner, crouching on a seat, was the German nursery-governess, crying. When she saw the banker she buried her face in her hands and wept still more copiously than before. M. Godefroy felt that some misfortune had happened.

"What's the meaning of all this? What's amiss? What has happened?"

Charles, the *valet de chambre,* a sneaking rascal of the worst type, looked at his master with eyes full of pity and stammered: "Mr. Raoul——"

"My boy?"

"Lost, sir. The stupid German did it. Since four o'clock this afternoon he has not been seen."

The father staggered back like one who had been hit by a ball. The German threw herself at his feet, screaming: "Mercy, mercy!" and the domestics all spoke at the same time.

"Bertha didn't go to *parc Monceau.* She lost the child over there on the fortifications. We have sought him all over, sir. We went to the office for you, sir, and then to the Chamber, but you had just left. Just imagine, the German had a rendezvous with her lover every day, beyond the ramparts, near the gate of Asnières. What a shame! It is a place full of low gipsies and strolling players. Perhaps the child has been stolen. Yes, sir, we informed the police at once. How could we imagine such a thing? A hypocrite, that German! She had a rendezvous, doubtless, with a countryman—a Prussian spy, sure enough!"

His son lost! M. Godefroy seemed to have a torrent of blood rushing through his head. He sprang at Mademoiselle, seized her by the arms and shook her furiously.

"Where did you lose him, you miserable girl? Tell me the truth before I shake you to pieces. Do you hear? Do you hear?"

But the unfortunate girl could only cry and beg for mercy.

The banker tried to be calm. No, it was impossible. Nobody would dare to steal *his* boy. Somebody would find him and bring him back. Of that there could be no doubt. He could scatter money about right and left, and could have the entire police force at his orders. And he would set to work at once, for not an instant should be lost.

"Charles, don't let the horse be taken out. You others, see that this girl doesn't escape. I'm going to the Prefecture."

And M. Godefroy, with his heart thumping against his sides as if it would break them, his hair wild with fright, darted into his carriage, which at once rolled off as fast as the horse could take it. What irony! The carriage was full of glittering playthings, which sparkled every time a gaslight shone on them. For the next day was the birthday of the Divine Infant at whose cradle wise men and simple shepherds alike adored.

" My poor little Raoul! Poor darling! Where is my boy? " repeated the father as in his anguish he dug his nails into the cushions of the carriage. At that moment all his titles and decorations, his honours, his millions, were valueless to him. He had one single idea burning in his brain. " My poor child! Where is my child? "

At last he reached the Prefecture of Police. But no one was there—the office had been deserted for some time.

" I am M. Godefroy, deputy from L'Eure—— My little boy is lost in Paris; a child of four years. I must see the Prefect."

He slipped a louis into the hand of the *concierge*.

The good old soul, a veteran with a grey moustache, less for the sake of the money than out of compassion for the poor father, led him to the Prefect's private apartments. M. Godefroy was finally ushered into the room of the man in whom were centred all his hopes. He was in evening dress, and wore a monocle; his manner was frigid and rather pretentious. The distressed father, whose knees trembled through emotion, sank into an armchair, and, bursting into tears, told of the loss of his boy—told the story stammeringly and with many breaks, for his voice was choked by sobs.

The Prefect, who was also father of a family, was inwardly moved at the sight of his visitor's grief, but he repressed his emotion and assumed a cold and self-important air.

" You say, sir, that your child has been missing since four o'clock."

" Yes."

" Just when night was falling, confound it. He isn't at all precocious, speaks very little, doesn't know where he lives, and can't even pronounce his own name? "

" Unfortunately that is so."

" Not far from Asnières gate? A suspected quarter. But cheer up. We have a very intelligent *Commissaire de Police* there. I'll telephone to him."

. . . .

The distressed father was left alone for five minutes. How his temples throbbed and his heart beat!

Then, suddenly, the Prefect reappeared, smiling with satisfaction. " Found! "

Whereupon M. Godefroy rushed to the Prefect, whose hand he pressed till that functionary winced with the pain.

"I must acknowledge that we were exceedingly fortunate. The little chap is blond, isn't he? Rather pale? In blue velvet? Black felt hat, with a white feather in it?"

"Yes, yes; that's he. That's my little Raoul."

"Well, he's at the house of a poor fellow down in that quarter who had just been at the police office to make his declaration to the Commissaire. Here's his address, which I took down: '*Pierron, rue des Cailloux, Levallois-Perret.*' With good horses you may reach your boy in less than an hour. Certainly, you won't find him in an aristocratic quarter; his surroundings won't be of the highest. The man who found him is only a small dealer in vegetables."

But that was of no importance to M. Godefroy, who, having expressed his gratitude to the Prefect, leaped down the stairs four at a time, and sprang into his carriage. At that moment he realised how devotedly he loved his child. As he drove away he no longer thought of little Raoul's princely education and magnificent inheritance. He was decided never again to hand over the child entirely to the hands of servants, and he also made up his mind to devote less time to monetary matters and the glory of France and attend more to his own. The thought also occurred to him that France wouldn't be likely to suffer from the neglect. He had hitherto been ashamed to recognise the existence of an old-maid sister of his father, but he decided to send for her to his house. She would certainly shock his lackeys by her primitive manners and ideas. But what of that? She would take care of his boy, which to him was of much more importance than the good opinion of his servants. The financier, who was always in a hurry, never felt so eager to arrive punctually at a committee meeting as he was to reach the lost little one. For the first time in his life he was longing through pure affection to take the child in his arms.

The carriage rolled rapidly along in the clear, crisp night air down boulevard Malesherbes; and, having crossed the ramparts and passed the large houses, plunged into the quiet solitude of suburban streets. When the carriage stopped M. Godefroy saw a wretched hovel, on which was the number he was seeking; it was the house where Pierron lived. The door of the house opened immediately, and a big, rough-looking fellow with red moustache appeared. One of his sleeves was empty. Seeing the gentleman in the carriage, Pierron said cheerily: "So you are the little one's father. Don't be afraid. The little darling is quite safe," and, stepping aside in order to allow M. Godefroy to pass, he placed his finger on his lips with: "Hush! The little one is asleep!"

Yes, it was a real hovel. By the dim light of a little oil lamp

M. Godefroy could just distinguish a dresser from which a drawer was missing, some broken chairs, a round table on which stood a beer-mug which was half empty, three glasses, some cold meat on a plate, and on the bare plaster of the wall two gaudy pictures—a bird's-eye view of the Exposition of 1889, with the Eiffel Tower in bright blue, and the portrait of General Boulanger when a handsome young lieutenant. This last evidence of weakness of the tenant of the house may well be excused, since it was shared by nearly everybody in France. The man took the lamp and went on tiptoe to the corner of the room where, on a clean bed, two little fellows were fast asleep. In the little one, around whom the other had thrown a protecting arm, M. Godefroy recognised his son.

" The youngsters were tired to death, and so sleepy," said Pierron, trying to soften his rough voice. " I had no idea when you would come, so gave them some supper and put them to bed, and then I went to make a declaration at the police office. Zidore generally sleeps up in the garret, but I thought they would be better here, and that I should be better able to watch them."

M. Godefroy, however, scarcely heard the explanation. Strangely moved, he looked at the two sleeping infants on an iron bedstead and covered with an old blanket which had once been used either in barracks or hospital. Little Raoul, who was still in his velvet suit, looked so frail and delicate compared with his companion that the banker almost envied the latter his brown complexion.

" Is he your boy? " he asked Pierron.

" No," answered he. " I am a bachelor, and don't suppose I shall ever marry, because of my accident. You see, a dray passed over my arm—that was all. Two years ago a neighbour of mine died, when that child was only five years old. The poor mother really died of starvation. She wove wreaths for the cemeteries, but could make nothing worth mentioning at that trade—not enough to live. However, she worked for the child for five years, and then the neighbours had to buy wreaths for her. So I took care of the youngster. Oh, it was nothing much, and I was soon repaid. He is seven years old, and is a sharp little fellow, so he helps me a great deal. On Sundays and Thursdays, and the other days after school, he helps me push my hand-cart. Zidore is a smart little chap. It was he who found your boy."

" What! " exclaimed M. Godefroy; " that child! "

" Oh, he's quite a little man, I assure you. When he left school he found your child, who was walking on ahead, crying like a fountain. He spoke to him and comforted him like an old grandfather. The difficulty is, that one can't easily understand what your little one says—English words are mixed up with German and French. So we couldn't get much out of him, nor could we learn his address. Zidore brought him to me—I wasn't far away; and then all the old women in the place came round chattering and croaking like so many frogs, and all full of advice.

" 'Take him to the police,' said some.

" But Zidore protested.

" 'That would scare him,' said he, for like all Parisians, he has no particular liking for the police—and besides, your little one didn't wish to leave him. So I came back here with the child as soon as I could. They had supper, and then off to bed. Don't they look sweet? "

When he was in his carriage, M. Godefroy had decided to reward the finder of his child handsomely—to give him a handful of that gold so easily gained. Since entering the house he had seen a side of human nature with which he was formerly unacquainted—the brave charity of the poor in their misery. The courage of the poor girl who had worked herself to death weaving wreaths to keep her child; the generosity of the poor cripple in adopting the orphan, and above all, the intelligent goodness of the little street Arab in protecting the child who was still smaller than himself—all this touched M. Godefroy deeply and set him reflecting. For the thought had occurred to him that there were other cripples who needed to be looked after as well as Pierron, and other orphans as well as Zidore. He also debated whether it would not be better to employ his time looking after them, and whether money might not be put to a better use than merely gaining money. Such was his reverie as he stood looking at the two sleeping children. Finally, he turned round to study the features of the greengrocer, and was charmed by the loyal expression in the face of the man, and his clear, truthful eyes.

" My friend," said M. Godefroy, " you and your adopted son have rendered me an immense service. I shall soon prove to you that I am not ungrateful. But, for to-day—I see that you are not in comfortable circumstances, and I should like to leave a small proof of my thankfulness."

But the hand of the cripple arrested that of the banker, which was diving into his coat-pocket where he kept bank-notes.

" No, sir; no! Anybody else would have done just as we have done. I will not accept any recompense; but pray don't take offence. Certainly, I am not rolling in wealth, but please excuse my pride—that of an old soldier; I have the Tonquin medal—and I don't wish to eat food which I haven't earned."

" As you like," said the financier; " but an old soldier like you is capable of something better. You are too good to push a hand-cart. I will make some arrangement for you, never fear."

The cripple responded by a quiet smile, and said coldly: " Well, sir, if you really wish to do something for me——"

" You'll let me care for Zidore, won't you? " cried M. Godefroy, eagerly.

" That I will, with the greatest of pleasure," responded Pierron, joyfully. " I have often thought about the child's future. He is a sharp little fellow. His teachers are delighted with him."

Then Pierron suddenly stopped, and an expression came over his face which M. Godefroy at once interpreted as one of distrust. The thought evidently was: " Oh, when he has once left us he'll forget us entirely."

" You can safely pick the child up in your arms and take him to the carriage. He'll be better at home than here, of course. Oh, you needn't be afraid of disturbing him. He is fast asleep, and you can just pick him up. He must have his shoes on first, though."

Following Pierron's glance, M. Godefroy perceived on the hearth, where a scanty coke fire was dying out, two pairs of children's shoes—the elegant ones of Raoul, and the rough ones of Zidore. Each pair contained a little toy and a package of bonbons.

" Don't think about that," said Pierron in an abashed tone. " Zidore put the shoes there. You know children still believe in Christmas and the child Jesus, whatever scholars may say about fables; so, as I came back from the *commissaire,* as I didn't know whether your boy would have to stay here to-night, I got those things for them both."

At which the eyes of M. Godefroy, the freethinker, the hardened capitalist, and *blasé* man of the world, filled with tears.

He rushed out of the house, but returned in a minute with his arms full of the superb mechanical horse, the box of leaden soldiers, and the rest of the costly playthings bought by him in the afternoon, and which had not even been taken out of the carriage.

" My friend, my dear friend," said he to the greengrocer, " see, these are the presents which Christmas has brought to my little Raoul. I want him to find them here, when he awakens, and to share them with Zidore, who will henceforth be his playmate and friend. You'll trust me now, won't you? I'll take care both of Zidore and of you, and then I shall ever remain in your debt, for not only have you found my boy, but you have also reminded me, who am rich and lived only for myself, that there are other poor who need to be looked after. I swear by these two sleeping children, I won't forget them any longer."

Such is the miracle which happened on the 24th of December of last year, ladies and gentlemen, at Paris, in the full flow of modern egotism. It doesn't sound likely—that I own; and I am compelled to attribute this miraculous event to the influence of the Divine Child who came down to earth nearly nineteen centuries ago to command men to love one another.

THE SUBSTITUTE

FRANÇOIS COPPÉE

HE was scarcely ten years old when he was first arrested as a vagabond.

He spoke thus to the judge:

" I am called Jean François Leturc, and for six months I was with the man who sings and plays upon a cord of catgut between the lanterns at the Place de la Bastille. I sang the refrain with him, and after that I called, ' Here's all the new songs, ten centimes, two sous! ' He was always drunk, and used to beat me. That is why the police picked me up the other night. Before that I was with the man who sells brushes. My mother was a laundress, her name was Adèle. At one time she lived on the ground-floor at Montmartre. She was a hard-working woman and was fond of me. She made money because she had for customers waiters in the cafés, and they use a good deal of linen. On Sundays she used to put me to bed early so that she could go to the ball. On week-days she sent me to the Christian Brothers, where I learned to read. Well, the sergent-de-ville whose beat was in our street used always to stop before our windows to talk with her—a good-looking chap, with a medal from the Crimea. They were married, and after that everything went wrong. He didn't take to me, and turned mother against me. Every one had a blow for me, and so, to get out of the house, I spent whole days in the Place Clichy, where I knew the mountebanks. My father-in-law lost his place, and my mother her work. She used to go out washing to take care of him; this gave her a cough—the steam. . . . She is dead at Lamboisière. She was a good woman. Since that I have lived with the seller of brushes and the catgut scraper. Are you going to send me to prison? "

He said this openly, cynically, like a man. He was a little ragged street-arab, as tall as a boot, his forehead hidden under a queer mop of yellow hair.

Nobody claimed him, and they sent him to the Reform School.

Not very intelligent, idle, clumsy with his hands, the only trade he could learn there was not a good one—that of reseating straw chairs. However, he was obedient, naturally quiet and silent, and he did not seem to be profoundly corrupted by that school of vice.

But when, in his seventeenth year, he was thrown out again on the streets of Paris, he unhappily found there his prison comrades, all great scamps, exercising their dirty professions: teaching dogs to catch rats in the sewers, and blacking shoes on ball nights in the passage of the Opéra—amateur wrestlers, who permitted themselves to be thrown by the Hercules of the booths—or fishing at noon-time from rafts; all of these occupations he followed to some extent, and some months after he came out of the house of correction he was arrested again for a petty theft—a pair of old shoes prigged from a shop-window. Result: a year in the prison of Sainte Pélagie, where he served as valet to the political prisoners.

He lived in much surprise among this group of prisoners, all very young, negligent in dress, who talked in loud voices, and carried their heads in a very solemn fashion. They used to meet in the cell of one of the oldest of them, a fellow of some thirty years, already a long time in prison and quite a fixture at Sainte Pélagie—a large cell, the walls covered with coloured caricatures, and from the window of which one could see all Paris—its roofs, its spires, and its domes—and far away the distant line of hills, blue and indistinct upon the sky. There were upon the walls some shelves filled with volumes and all the old paraphernalia of a fencing-room: broken masks, rusty foils, breast-plates, and gloves that were losing their tow. It was there that the "politicians" used to dine together, adding to the everlasting "soup and beef," fruit, cheese, and pints of wine which Jean François went out and got by the can—a tumultuous repast interrupted by violent disputes, and where, during the dessert, the "Carmagnole" and "Ca Ira" were sung in full chorus. They assumed, however, an air of great dignity on those days when a new-comer was brought in among them, at first entertaining him gravely as a citizen, but on the morrow using him with affectionate familiarity and calling him by his nickname. Great words were used there: Corporation, Responsibility, and phrases quite unintelligible to Jean François—such as this, for example, which he once heard imperiously put forth by a frightful little hunchback who blotted some writing-paper every night:

"It is done. This is the composition of the Cabinet: Raymond, the Bureau of Public Instruction; Martial, the Interior; and for Foreign Affairs, myself."

His time done, he wandered again around Paris, watched afar by the police, after the fashion of cockchafers, made by cruel children to fly at the end of a string. He became one of those fugitive and timid beings whom the law, with a sort of coquetry, arrests and releases by turn—something like those platonic fishers who, in order that they may not exhaust their fish-pond, throw immediately back into the water the fish which has just come out of the net. Without a suspicion on his part that so much honour had been done to so sorry a subject, he had a special bundle of memoranda in the mysterious portfolios of the Rue de Jérusalem. His name was written in round hand on the grey paper of the cover, and the notes and reports, carefully classified, gave him his successive appellations. " Name, Leturc," " the prisoner Leturc," and, at last, " the criminal Leturc."

He was two years out of prison, dining where he could, sleeping in night lodging-houses and sometimes in lime-kilns, and taking part with his fellows in interminable games of pitch-penny on the boulevards near the barriers. He wore a greasy cap on the back of his head, carpet slippers, and a short white blouse. When he had five sous he had his hair curled. He danced at Constant's at Montparnasse; bought for two sous to sell for four at the door of Bobino, the jack of hearts or the ace of clubs serving as a countermark; sometimes opened the door of a carriage; led horses to the horse-market. From the lottery of all miserable employments he drew a goodly number.

Who can say if the atmosphere of honour which one breathes as a soldier, if military discipline might not have saved him?

Taken, in a cast of the net, with some young loafers who robbed drunkards sleeping on the streets, he denied very earnestly having taken part in their expeditions. Perhaps he told the truth, but his antecedents were accepted in lieu of proof, and he was sent for three years to Poissy. There he made coarse playthings for children, was tattooed on the chest, learned thieves' slang and the penal code. A new liberation, and a new plunge into the sink of Paris; but very short this time, for at the end of six months at the most he was again compromised in a night robbery, aggravated by climbing and breaking—a serious affair, in which he played an obscure rôle, half dupe and half fence. On the whole his complicity was evident, and he was sent for five years at hard labour. His grief in this adventure was above all in being separated from an old dog which he had found on a dung-heap, and cured of the mange. The beast loved him.

Toulon, the ball and chain, the work in the harbour, the blows from a stick, wooden shoes on bare feet, soup of black beans dating from Trafalgar, no tobacco money, and the terrible sleep in a camp swarming with convicts; that was what he experienced for five broiling summers and five winters raw with the Mediterranean wind. He came out from there stunned, was sent under surveillance to Vernon, where he worked some time on the river.

Then, an incorrigible vagabond, he broke his exile and came again to Paris. He had his savings, fifty-six francs, that is to say, time enough for reflection. During his absence his former wretched companions had dispersed. He was well hidden, and slept in a loft at an old woman's, to whom he represented himself as a sailor, tired of the sea, who had lost his papers in a recent shipwreck, and who wanted to try his hand at something else. His tanned face and his calloused hands, together with some sea phrases which he dropped from time to time, made his tale seem probable enough.

One day when he risked a saunter in the streets, and when chance had led him as far as Montmartre, where he was born, an unexpected memory stopped him before the door of the Christian Brothers, where he had learned to read. As it was very warm the door was open, and by a single glance the passing outcast was able to recognise the peaceful schoolroom. Nothing was changed: neither the bright light shining in at the great windows, nor the crucifix over the desk, nor the rows of benches with the tables furnished with inkstands and pencils, nor the table of weights and measures, nor the map where pins stuck in still indicated the operations of some ancient war. Heedlessly and without thinking, Jean François read on the blackboard the words of the Evangelist which had been set there as a copy:

"Joy shall be in heaven over one sinner that repenteth, more than over ninety and nine just persons, which need no repentance."

It was undoubtedly the hour for recreation, for the Brother Professor had left his chair, and, sitting on the edge of a table, was telling a story to the boys who surrounded him with eager and attentive eyes. What a bright and innocent face he had, that beardless young man, in his long black gown, and white necktie, and great ugly shoes, and his badly cut brown hair streaming out behind! All the simple figures of the children of the people who were watching him seemed scarcely less childlike than his; above all when, delighted with some of his own simple clerical pleasantries, he broke out in an open and frank peal of laughter which showed his white and regular teeth, a peal so contagious that all the scholars laughed loudly in their turn. It was such a sweet, simple group in the bright sunlight, which lighted their dear eyes and their blond curls.

Jean François looked at them for some time in silence, and for the first time in that savage nature, all instinct and appetite, there awoke a mysterious, a tender emotion. His heart, that seared and hardened heart, unmoved when the convict's cudgel or the heavy whip of the watchman fell on his shoulders, beat oppressively. In that sight he saw again his infancy; and closing his eyes sadly, the prey to torturing regret, he walked quickly away.

Then the words written on the blackboard came back to his mind.

"If it wasn't too late after all!" he murmured; "if I could again, like others, eat honestly my brown bread, and sleep my fill without nightmare! The spy must be sharp who recognises me. My beard, which I shaved off down there, has grown out thick and strong. One can burrow somewhere in the great ant-hill, and work can be found. Whoever is not worked to death in the hell of the galleys comes out agile and robust, and I learned there to climb ropes with loads upon my back. Building is going on everywhere here, and the masons need helpers. Three francs a day! I never earned so much. Let me be forgotten, and that is all I ask."

He followed his courageous resolution; he was faithful to it, and after three months he was another man. The master for whom he worked called him his best workman. After a long day upon the scaffolding, in the hot sun and the dust, constantly bending and raising his back to take the hod from the man at his feet and pass it to the man over his head, he went for his soup to the cook-shop, tired out, his legs aching, his hands burning, his eyelids stuck with plaster, but content with himself, and carrying his well-earned money in a knot in his handkerchief. He went out now without fear, since he could not be recognised in his white mask, and since he had noticed that the suspicious glances of the policeman were seldom turned on the tired workman. He was quiet and sober. He slept the sound sleep of fatigue. He was free!

At last—oh, supreme recompense!—he had a friend!

This was a fellow-workman like himself, named Savinien, a little peasant with red lips who had come to Paris with his stick over his shoulder and a bundle on the end of it, fleeing from the wine-shops and going to mass every Sunday. Jean François loved him for his piety, for his candour, for his honesty, for all that he himself had lost, and so long ago. It was a passion, profound and unrestrained, which transformed him by fatherly cares and attentions. Savinien, himself of a weak and egotistical nature, let things take their course, satisfied only in finding a companion who shared his horror of the wine-shop. The two friends lived together in a fairly comfortable lodging, but their resources were very limited. They were obliged to take into their room a third companion, an old Auvergnat, gloomy and rapacious, who found it possible out of his meagre salary to save something with which to buy a place in his own country. Jean François and Savinien were always together. On holidays they together took long walks in the environs of Paris, and dined under an arbour in one of those small country inns where there are a great many mushrooms in the sauces and innocent rebusses on the napkins. There Jean François learned from his friend all that lore of which they who are born in the city are ignorant; learned the names of the trees, the flowers, and the plants; the various seasons for harvesting; he heard eagerly the thousand details of a laborious country life—the autumn sowing, the winter tasks, the splendid celebrations of harvest and vintage days, the sound of the mills at the waterside, and the flails striking the ground, the tired horses led to water, and the hunting in the morning mist; and, above all, the long evenings around the fire of vine-shoots, that were shortened by some marvellous stories. He discovered in himself a source of imagination before unknown, and found a singular delight in the recital of events so placid, so calm, so monotonous.

One thing troubled him, however: it was the fear lest Savinien might learn something of his past. Sometimes there escaped from him some low word of thieves' slang, a vulgar gesture—vestiges of his former horrible existence—and he felt the pain one feels when old wounds reopen; the more because he fancied that he sometimes saw in Savinien the awakening of an unhealthy curiosity. When the young man, already tempted by the pleasures which Paris offers to the poorest, asked him about the mysteries of the great city, Jean François feigned ignorance and turned the subject; but he felt a vague inquietude for the future of his friend.

His uneasiness was not without foundation. Savinien could not long remain the simple rustic that he was on his arrival in Paris. If the gross and noisy pleasures of the wine-shop always repelled him, he was profoundly troubled by other temptations, full of danger for the inexperience of his twenty years. When spring came he began to go off alone, and at first he wandered about the brilliant entrance of some dancing-hall, watching the young girls who went in with their arms around each other's waists, talking in low tones. Then, one evening, when lilacs perfumed the air and the call to quadrilles was most captivating, he crossed the threshold, and from that time Jean François observed a change, little by little, in his manners and his visage. He became more frivolous, more extravagant. He often borrowed from his friend his scanty savings, and he forgot to repay. Jean François, feeling that he was abandoned, jealous and forgiving at the same time, suffered and was silent. He felt that he had no right to reproach him, but with the foresight of affection he indulged in cruel and inevitable presentiments.

One evening, as he was mounting the stairs to his room, absorbed in his thoughts, he heard, as he was about to enter, the sound of angry voices, and he recognised that of the old Auvergnat who lodged with Savinien and himself. An old habit of suspicion made him stop at the landing-place and listen to learn the cause of the trouble.

"Yes," said the Auvergnat, angrily, "I am sure that some one has opened my trunk and stolen from it the three louis that I had hidden in a little box; and he who has done this thing must be one of the two companions who sleep here, if it were not the servant Maria. It concerns you as much as it does me, since you are the master of the house, and I will drag you to the courts if you do not let me at once break open the valises of the two masons. My poor gold! It was here yesterday in its place, and I will tell you just what it was, so that if we find it again nobody can accuse me of having lied. Ah, I know them, my three beautiful gold-pieces, and I can see them as plainly as I see you! One piece was more worn than the others; it was of greenish gold, with a portrait of the great emperor. The other was a great old fellow with a queue and epaulettes; and the third, which had on it a Philippe with whiskers, I had marked with my teeth. They don't trick me. Do you know that I only wanted two more like that to pay for my vineyard? Come, search these fellows' things with me, or I will call the police! Hurry up!"

"All right," said the voice of the landlord; "we will go and search with Maria. So much the worse for you if we find nothing, and the masons get angry. You have forced me to it."

Jean François' soul was full of fright. He remembered the embarrassed circumstances and the small loans of Savinien, and how sober he had seemed for some days. And yet he could not believe that he was a thief. He heard the Auvergnat panting in his eager search, and he pressed his closed fists against his breast as if to still the furious beating of his heart.

"Here they are!" suddenly shouted the victorious miser. "Here they are, my louis, my dear treasure; and in the Sunday vest of that little hypocrite of Limousin! Look, landlord, they are just as I told you. Here is the Napoleon, the man with a queue, and the Philippe that I have bitten. See the dents! Ah, the little beggar with the sanctified air. I should have much sooner suspected the other. Ah, the wretch! Well, he must go to the convict prison."

At this moment Jean François heard the well-known step of Savinien coming slowly up the stairs.

He is going to his destruction, thought he. Three stories. I have time!

And, pushing open the door, he entered the room, pale as death, where he saw the landlord and the servant stupefied in a corner, while the Auvergnat, on his knees, in the disordered heap of clothes, was kissing the pieces of gold.

"Enough of this," he said, in a thick voice; "I took the money and put it in my comrade's trunk. But that was too bad. I am a thief, but not a Judas. Call the police; I will not try to escape, only I must say a word to Savinien in private. Here he is."

In fact, the little Limousin had just arrived, and seeing his crime discovered, believing himself lost, he stood there, his eyes fixed, his arms hanging.

Jean François seized him forcibly by the neck, as if to embrace him; he put his mouth close to Savinien's ear, and said to him in a low, supplicating voice:

"Keep quiet."

Then turning towards the others:

" Leave me alone with him. I tell you I won't go away. Lock us in if you wish, but leave us alone."

With a commanding gesture he showed them the door.

They went out.

Savinien, broken by grief, was sitting on the bed, and lowered his eyes without understanding anything.

" Listen," said Jean François, who came and took him by the hands. " I understand! You have stolen three gold-pieces to buy some trifle for a girl. That costs six months in prison. But one only comes out from there to go back again, and you will become a pillar of police courts and tribunals. I understand it. I have been seven years at the Reform School, a year at Sainte Pélagie, three years at Poissy, five years at Toulon. Now, don't be afraid. Everything is arranged. I have taken it on my shoulders."

" It is dreadful," said Savinien; but hope was springing up again in his cowardly heart.

" When the elder brother is under the flag, the younger one does not go," replied Jean François. " I am your substitute, that's all. You care for me a little, do you not? I am paid. Don't be childish —don't refuse. They would have taken me again one of these days, for I am a runaway from exile. And then, do you see, that life will be less hard for me than for you. I know it all, and I shall not complain if I have not done you this service for nothing, and if you swear to me that you will never do it again. Savinien, I have loved you well, and your friendship has made me happy. It is through it that, since I have known you, I have been honest and pure, as I might always have been, perhaps, if I had had, like you, a father to put a tool in my hands, a mother to teach me my prayers. It was my sole regret that I was useless to you, and that I deceived you concerning myself. To-day I have unmasked in saving you. It is all right. Do not cry, and embrace me, for already I hear heavy boots on the stairs. They are coming with the *posse,* and we must not seem to know each other so well before those chaps."

He pressed Savinien quickly to his breast, then pushed him from him, when the door was thrown wide open.

It was the landlord and the Auvergnat, who brought the police.

Jean François sprang forward to the landing-place, held out his hands for the handcuffs, and said, laughing, " Forward, bad lot! "

To-day he is at Cayenne, condemned for life as an incorrigible.

THE GOLD COIN

FRANÇOIS COPPÉE

WHEN Lucien de Hem saw his last note for a hundred francs drawn up by the rake of the banker, he rose from the roulette table where he had just lost the remains of his little fortune, which he had gathered together for this supreme battle: he felt giddy and thought he was going to fall.

His head dazed, his knees giving way, he threw himself on the big leather seat that ran all round the gaming-room. For some minutes he looked vaguely at the clandestine den, in which he had wrecked the best years of his youth, gazed at the worn faces of the gamblers, harshly lighted by three great reflectors, listened to the light friction of the gold on the cloth, thought what he should do now that he was completely ruined, remembered he had at home in a chest of drawers the army pistols with which his father, General de Hem, when but a captain, had fought bravely at the attack on Zaatcha: then, broken with fatigue, he fell into a profound sleep.

When he awoke, his mouth felt sticky, he saw by a look of the clock that he had barely slept half an hour, and he felt a strong desire to get a breath of fresh air. The hands marked a quarter to midnight. While rising and stretching his arms, Lucien remembered it was Christmas Eve, and by an ironic turn of his memory he saw himself again as a little child, putting his shoes in the fireplace before he went to bed.

At this moment, old Dronski, a pillar of the gaming-hell, the traditional Pole, wearing a threadbare coat, adorned with braid and grease stains, came up to Lucien and mumbled some words in his grey, dirty beard.

"Lend me just five francs, sir. Look! for two days I have not left the club, and for two days the 'seventeen' has not come up. Laugh at me if you like, but you can cut off my hand if all at once, at the stroke of midnight, the number does not turn up."

Lucien de Hem shrugged his shoulders. He hadn't even in his pockets enough to pay this tax which the frequenters of the place call the "hundred sous of the Pole." He went into the outer room, put on his hat and coat and went down the stairs with the agility of a man in a fever.

During the four hours that Lucien had been shut up in the gaming-house, the snow had fallen thickly, and the street—one of the central streets of Paris, narrow, and edged by high houses—was quite white. In the cleansed sky, blue-black, the stars sparkled with a frosty light.

The broken gambler shivered under his furs, and began to walk, rolling over in his mind most desperate thoughts, and thinking more than ever of the case of pistols awaiting him in the old chest of drawers. But after going a little way he abruptly stopped before a heartrending sight.

On a stone bench, placed, according to ancient usage, close to the monumental door of a mansion, a little girl of six or seven years, barely clad in a black ragged dress, was sitting in the snow. She had fallen asleep there, in spite of the cruel cold, in a dreadful attitude of weariness and exhaustion, and her poor little head and dainty shoulder fell into an angle of the wall and rested on the icy stone. One of the child's shoes was detached from her hanging foot and lay lugubriously before her.

Mechanically Lucien de Hem put his hand in his pocket: but he remembered that an instant before he had not even found twenty sous there, and had been unable to tip the waiter at the gaming-house. Yet, impelled by an instinctive feeling of pity, he approached the little girl, and he was perhaps going to carry her away in his arms and give her a shelter for the night when he saw, in the fallen shoe, lying in the snow, something glittering.

He leaned over. It was a twenty franc piece in gold.

Some charitable person, a woman no doubt, had passed by that Christmas Eve, and seeing the shoe of the sleeping infant, and remembering the touching legend, had dropped from her kind hand a magnificent gift, so that the little abandoned one should still believe in the legend of presents made by the Child Jesus, and keep, in spite of her misfortune, some trust and hope in the bounty of Providence.

Twenty francs! It meant several days of rest and riches for the beggar girl: and Lucien was on the point of awaking her to tell her so, when he heard in his ear, in a kind of hallucination, the voice of the Pole, with his dragging and oily accent, murmuring softly the words:

"Look! for two days I have not left the club, and for two days the 'seventeen' has not come up. . . . You can cut off my hand if all at once, at the stroke of midnight, the number does not turn up."

Then this young man of twenty-three, sprung from a race of honest people, bearing a superb military name, who had never failed in a point of honour, had a dreadful thought. He was seized with a mad, hysterical, monstrous desire. With a glance, he made sure he was quite alone in the street, and, bending his knee, he put out a trembling hand and stole the gold coin in the fallen shoe. Then, running with all his strength, he came back to the gaming-house, went up the steps in a few leaps, pushed open the padded door of the accursed room with his fist, entered at the precise moment when the clock gave the first chime of midnight, placed the gold coin on the green cloth, and cried:

"All on the 'seventeen'!"

The "seventeen" won.

With a backward sweep of his hand, Lucien pushed the thirty-six gold coins on red.

Red won.

He left the seventy-two coins on the same colour. Red turned up again.

He risked the doubled stakes twice, thrice, with the same luck. He now had before him a heap of gold and notes, and he began to scatter them about the cloth madly. "The dozen," "the column," "the number," all his combinations were successful. It was unheard-of, supernatural luck. It seemed as though the little ivory ball, leaping in the divisions of the roulette, was fascinated by the glance of the gambler, and obeyed him. He had recovered in a dozen strokes the notes for some thousands of francs, his last resource, which he had lost at the beginning of the evening.

Then, punting on each occasion two or three hundred pieces of twenty francs, he set about recovering, by his fantastic vein of luck, the heritage he had wasted in a few years. In his eagerness to play, he had not taken off his heavy fur coat. Already, he had stuffed out the large pockets with bundles of bank notes and rolls of gold. And no longer knowing where to put his winnings, he was filling with money and paper the inside and outside pockets of his frock coat, his waistcoat pockets, trouser pockets, his cigar case, his handkerchief, everything that would serve as a receptacle. He played always, and he always won, like a madman! like a drunkard! throwing his handfuls of gold at hazard on the cloth, with a gesture of certainty and disdain.

Only there was something burning at his heart like a red-hot iron. He thought of the little beggar girl sleeping in the snow, the child he had robbed.

"She is still in the same place! Certainly, she must still be there! Immediately, as soon as one strikes—I swear it—I will leave, I will take her, sleeping, in my arms and carry her home and put her in my bed. I will bring her up, I will give her a dowry, I will love her as a daughter, and care for her, always, always!"

But the clock chimed one, then a quarter past one, half past, a quarter to two . . . and Lucien still sat at the infernal table. At last, at a minute to two, the keeper of the gaming-house rose up abruptly and said:

"The bank is broken, gentlemen. . . . It is enough for to-day."

Lucien sprang up. Roughly pushing aside the players who surrounded him and looked at him with envious admiration, he quickly departed, tumbled down the steps, and ran to the stone bench. In the distance, in the light of a street lamp, he saw the little girl.

"Praise God!" he cried. "She is still there!"

He ran up to her and seized her hand.

"Oh, how cold she is, the little darling!"

He lifted her up under the arms to carry her away. The head of the child tumbled backward, without her awaking.

"How these youngsters sleep!"

He held her to his breast to warm her, and seized with a vague anxiety, he tried to rouse her from her deep sleep by a kiss on her eyes. Then he perceived with terror that the eyelids of the child were half open, revealing the glassy, dulled, motionless eyes. A horrible thought crossed his mind. He put his mouth quite close to the mouth of the little girl, but no breath came from it.

While he was winning a fortune with the gold coin he had stolen, the shelterless child had died from the cold.

Caught in the throat by the most dreadful anguish, Lucien tried to cry out . . . and aroused by the effort he made he awoke out of his nightmare on the padded seat of the gaming-house, where the waiter, going round, last of all, at five in the morning, had left him sleeping out of kindness of heart for a broken man.

A misty winter dawn shone pallidly on the windows. Lucien went out, pawned his watch, had a bath and a breakfast and went to the recruiting office and signed on as a volunteer for the first regiment of the African light cavalry. To-day, Lucien de Hem is a lieutenant. He has only his pay to live on, but he manages on it, being a very steady officer who never touches a card. It appears he even finds a way of saving some money. For the other day at Algiers, one of his comrades, walking behind him down a hilly street of the Kasba, saw him give alms to a little Spanish girl sleeping under an arch. He was indiscreet to see how much Lucien had given. He was greatly surprised by the generosity of the poor lieutenant. There was a gold piece of twenty francs in the hand of the little girl.

AN ACCIDENT

FRANÇOIS COPPÉE

A MALE penitent! This was a rare and exceptional thing at Saint-Médard's; but in noticing by the red light of the lamp that hung from the pointed arch of the chapel the short workman's jacket and the large tacketty soles of the kneeling man, Abbé Faber thought that it was some workman who had kept his country beliefs and the good habits of religious practice.

Doubtless the confession he was just going to hear would be commonplace. So the vicar calmly entered the confessional, and, after having taken a liberal pinch of snuff, he opened, without emotion, the small green serge curtain that covered the opening.

"*Monsieur le curé,*" stammered a voice that was forcing itself to speak low.

"I am not the *curé*, my friend. . . . Say your *confiteor*, and call me 'My father.'"

The man, whose face, shrouded in darkness, the Abbé Faber could not see, mumbled the prayer slowly, which he seemed to remember with difficulty, and then continued dully:

"*Monsieur le curé,* . . . no, . . . my father. . . . Just excuse me if I do not speak as I should do, but I have not confessed for twenty-five years; yes, not since I left the country. . . . You know what it is . . . to be a man in Paris, . . . and then I was not more wicked than others; and I said to myself: 'The good God will be kind.' . . . But to-day I have something on my conscience that is too heavy to carry alone. You must listen, *monsieur le curé*. . . . I have killed a man!"

The abbé started on his seat. A murderer! That was something more than inattention during service, than wicked gossip about neighbours, and the other tittle-tattles of old women that he listened to with an inattentive ear, and for which he gave absolution with confidence.

A murderer! This head that was so near his own had conceived and carried out the thought of a crime; these hands clasped on his confessional were perhaps still stained with blood! In his agitation he was indeed just a little afraid. Abbé Faber could only find the mechanical words:

"Confess yourself, my son. . . . The mercy of God is infinite."

"Listen, then, to the whole story," said the man in a tone that vibrated with deep anguish. "I am a working mason, and came to Paris more than twenty years ago with a countryman, a companion of childhood. . . . We had harried nests and learned to read at school together. . . . He was just like a brother. . . . He was called Philippe, . . . and me, I am called Jacques. . . . He was a big, fine fellow; I have always been heavy and badly built. . . .

"No better workman than he, while I am but a 'bungler,' . . . and good and brave, with an open heart and hand. . . .

"I was proud to be his friend, to walk alongside of him—proud that he slapped me on the back, calling me a big blockhead; . . . in short, I loved him, because I admired him!

"Once here, what luck! We were both employed by the same master, . . . but in the evening he left me alone three-quarters of the time; he went to amuse himself with his companions. . . . It was indeed natural, at his age; . . . he loved pleasure, he was free, he had no burdens. As for me, I could not do it. . . . I was forced to save, for then I had still my invalid mother in the country, and I sent her my savings. . . .

"At that time I took my food at a fruiterer's, in whose house I lodged, and who cooked for the masons. . . . Philippe did not take his dinner there; he had arranged it different, and, to tell the truth, the cooking was not great. . . .

"But the fruiterer was a widow, not at all prosperous, to whom I saw that my custom rendered a service; and then, to be frank, I had fallen in love with her daughter immediately. . . . Poor Catherine! You will know at once, *monsieur le curé,* what came of it. . . .

"I remained three years without being able to tell her that I was in love with her; I have told you that I am but a middling workman, and the little that I earned was hardly sufficient for me, and with what I sent to my mother I had no means to set up house.

"At length my good mother was taken to heaven. I was less embarrassed, I put some money aside, and when I thought that I had enough to start housekeeping, I told Catherine my feelings. . . .

"At first she said neither yes nor no. Forsooth! I knew well that she would not fall on my neck all at once. I have not got a taking way. . . . However, Catherine consulted her mother, who considered that I was a steady workman, a respectable man, and the marriage was arranged. . . .

"Ah! I had some very happy weeks. I saw that Catherine did not accept me because she was drawn towards me; but as she had a good heart, I really hoped to make her love me some day. . . .

"Naturally, I told everything to Philippe, whom I saw each day in the shop, and when Catherine became engaged to me I wished him to make her acquaintance. . . .

"You have, perhaps, already guessed the result, *monsieur le curé*. . . . Philippe was a good-looking man, very gay, very agreeable, everything that I was not; and without doing it purposely, but innocently, he made Catherine mad about him. . . . Ah! But Catherine had a frank and honest heart, and when she found what she felt, she told me immediately. . . .

"But, all the same, I shall never forget that moment! It was Catherine's birthday, and, to wish her happiness, I had bought a little golden cross that I had packed nicely in a box with cotton-wool. . . . We were alone in the back shop, and she had just given me my soup. I drew the box from my pocket; I opened it, and showed her the trinket. Then she burst into tears.

"'Forgive me, Jacques,' said she to me, 'and keep it for the girl that marries you. . . . For I can never be your wife. I love another. . . . I love Philippe.'

"I was indeed vexed at this, *monsieur le curé,* I was, with all my soul. But what could I do, seeing that I loved both of them? As I believed that it was for their happiness that they should be married, and as Philippe had always made merry a little, and as he was short of money, I lent him my hoardings to buy the furniture.

"Then they were married, and everything went merrily at first, and they had a little boy, to whom I was made godfather, and I named him Camille, in memory of my mother.

"It was a short time after his birth that Philippe began to misbehave himself. I had been deceived in him; he was not made for marriage, he loved pleasure and going on the spree too much.

"You live in a district of poor people, *monsieur le curé,* you must know a story like this by heart. . . . A workman who slips gradually into idleness and drunkenness, who leaves his work for two or three days, who does not bring in his week's wages, and who only comes home in order to make a scene and to beat his wife.

"Very well, in less than two years Philippe had become one of these wretches. At the beginning I had tried to give him a lecture, and sometimes blushing at his conduct, he tried to amend. But this did not last long . . . and then my remonstrances ended by provoking him; and when I went to his house, and when he caught me looking sadly at the room dismantled by the pawnbroker, and at poor Catherine, quite thin and pale with sorrow, he became furious. . . .

"One day he had the cheek to be jealous, and made a scene with me about his wife, reminding me that I had been in love with her before, and accusing me of being so still. . . .

"Ah! We just missed jumping at each other's throats that day! . . . I did what I ought; I gave up seeing Catherine and my godson, and as for Philippe, I only met him by chance, when we worked in the same shop.

"But you will quite understand, I had too much affection for Catherine and for little Camille; I could not lose sight of them altogether. On Saturday evening, when I knew that Philippe had gone out with his companions to drink his pay, I prowled about the district; I would meet the child, I got him to talk, and, if there were too much misery in the house, he did not return with his hands empty.

"I believe that the wretch knew that I came to his wife's assistance, and that he shut his eyes, and found it very convenient. . . .

"But I must cut it short, for it is too distressing. Some years passed. Philippe sank deeper and deeper in vice; but I assisted Catherine to bring up her son as much as I could, and he is now a fine fellow of twenty years, good and courageous as herself. . . .

"He is not a workman; he is educated; he has learned to design in the night-schools, and is now with an architect, where he earns rather good wages.

"And although the home was still saddened by the presence of the drunkard, things were better, for Camille was very good to his mother; and for a year or two when I met Catherine—she was indeed changed, the poor woman!—on the arm of her boy dressed like a gentleman it warmed my heart.

"But yesterday evening, on leaving my eating-house, I met Camille, and in giving him my hand—oh, he is not at all proud, and he does not blush when he sees my blouse all stained with plaster—I felt something in the air.

"'Let us hear; what has happened?'

"'It was only yesterday that I took part in the lottery,' he replied, 'and I drew number 10, one of those that send you away to perish of fever in the colonies with the soldiers of the marine; and in any case I shall be there for five years, which will necessitate my leaving mother alone, without resources, with father—and he has never drunk so much, he has never been so unkind—and she will die of it, godfather, a curse rests on poor people!'

"And this morning I was bent like an old man by a sleepless night when going to the house that is in course of construction on the Arago Boulevard. Though one may be sorrowful, it is necessary to work all the same, is that not so? Well, I climbed up to the top of the scaffolding—we had already built the house up to the fourth storey—and I began to set my ashlar. All at once I felt some one tap me on the shoulder. It was Philippe. He only now worked by fits, and he had apparently just come for one day to earn something to drink. I had not seen Philippe for quite a long time, and I had difficulty in recognising him. Burned and withered by brandy, his beard quite grey, his hands trembling, he was not only an old man, but a wreck.

" 'Well,' said I to him, 'so the boy has drawn a bad number?'

" 'What about it?' he replied in a rough voice and with a nasty look. 'Are you also going to weary me with that, like Catherine and Camille? . . . God! I know well enough what's annoying them, my wife and son. . . . If I were dead, he would not need to go. . . . But so much the worse for them! I'm still firm on my pins, and Camille is not a widow's son.'

" A widow's son! Ah! *Monsieur le curé,* why had he the misfortune to say these words? The wicked thought came to me at once, and it did not leave me the whole morning.

" I imagined what poor Catherine was going to suffer, when she would be left quite alone with this miserable drunkard. . . . Eleven o'clock sounded from a neighbouring steeple, and our fellow-workmen descended for their breakfast. We were the last, Philippe and me; but on going to the ladder to descend in his turn, he was no more than on it when he looked at me sneeringly and said in a voice made husky with drink:

" 'You see, I've still got a foot like a sailor. . . . Camille is not near being a widow's son—bah!'

" Then there was a rush of blood and anger to my head! With both hands I seized the uprights of the ladder to which Philippe clung, screaming 'Help!' and, with one shove, I sent him flying out into space!

" He was killed on the spot, and they thought that it was an accident, but Camille is now a widow's son, and he will not need to go away! . . .

" That is what I have done, *monsieur le curé,* and what I must needs tell you and the good God! I repent of it, and I ask forgiveness for it, that is plain, . . . but I would not need to see Catherine pass, in her black dress, quite happy on the arm of her son; I should not be able to regret my crime any longer. . . . To avoid that, I shall emigrate and go off to America.

" As for penance. . . . See, *monsieur le curé,* here is the little golden cross that Catherine refused when she confessed that she was in love with Philippe. I have always kept it, in memory of the only happy days that I have had in my life. . . . Take it, and sell it, . . . and give the money to the poor."

Did Jacques receive absolution from Abbé Faber? So much is certain that the old priest did not sell the little golden cross. After having put the value, or thereabouts, into the poor's-box of the church, he hung the trinket as an *ex-voto* on the altar of the chapel of the Virgin, where he goes often to pray for the poor mason.

DIED AT SEA

FRANÇOIS COPPÉE

SOME years ago I passed several weeks in a fishing village on the Breton coast. What a hole it was, but how picturesque! A beach for ten boats at the most; a single street, very steep, and resembling the bed of a torrent; and up above, on the first plateau of the cliff, the church, a Gothic gem, in the midst of a cemetery full of wild oats, and commanding a view of the ocean. Finding myself situated favourably for work, I had lingered in this corner till the end of the month of September, which, by a chance rare enough in rainy Finisterre, was exceptionally clear and mild.

I was staying at the only inn of the village, and occupied a large whitewashed room, meagrely but neatly furnished, with the window facing the open ocean. Seated on a straw-bottomed chair, at a wooden table, I composed at that time a whole poem to the solemn and soothing noise of the great waves, which seemed to say to me incessantly that rhythm is a law of Nature.

But a man cannot always make verses or write, and long walks were my tonic and distraction. I used to go most often along the shore, having at my right the dry and monumental cliff, and at my left the tracts uncovered by the low tide, an immense desert of sand, spotted only by black groups of rocks. The solitude was complete. Hardly two or three times did I exchange a greeting with some patrol of the customs who was making his rounds with his gun slung over his shoulder. I was so quiet and peaceful a stroller that the sea swallows were not afraid of my red jersey, and hopped about a few steps from me, impressing their starry tracks on the damp sand. I used to walk in this manner four or five miles a day, and always returned with my pockets full of those delicate shells that one finds by excavating with the hand the little beach pebbles always wet by the tide.

This was my favourite walk. However, on the days when there was a high gale and violent surf, I used to leave the beach, and ascending the village street I would loiter about the moor. Or else I established myself with a book on an old bench in the cemetery, where I was sheltered from the west wind by the body of the church.

An ideal spot for melancholy and dreaming. Towards the autumn sky, where clouds were floating, rose the spire, devout and slender. The crows that nested there flew out and in, cawing, and the shadows of their great wings continually glided over the graves scattered in the tall grass. Between two half-ruined buttresses of the church, where the grey stone, eaten by the sea wind, supported here and there a waving cluster of little yellow flowers, there was picketed a black goat, which was almost terrifying, with its fiery eyes and satanic beard, as he bleated and pulled at his rope. In the evening above all, when, athwart the skeleton of an old dead apple tree, with rugged branches, one could see far away on the horizon the setting sun bleeding over the sea, this wild cemetery filled the soul with piercing melancholy.

It was on such an evening that, in wandering among the gravestones—many, below a sailor's name, bore the sinister inscription, " Died at Sea "—I read, on a cross still new, these words that astonished and touched me:—

HERE RESTS

NONA LE MAGUET,

Died at sea, October 26, 1878, aged nineteen years.

Died at sea! A young girl! Women, however, never embark on the fishing-boats. How had this misfortune happened?

" Indeed, sir! " said suddenly behind me a rough voice, " are you looking at the grave of our poor Nona? "

I turned, and recognised an old sailor with a wooden leg, whose good graces I had gained by a few glasses of brandy, offered in the public room of the inn.

" Yes," I answered. " But I supposed that all you fishermen refused to admit a woman on board. I have even been told that it brings ill luck."

" And it is the truth," replied the good man. " Likewise Nona never went on board a boat. You would like to know how she died, our dear one? Well, I will tell you about it.

" First of all I must tell you that her father, Pierre Le Maguet, was an old topman like me, an old comrade of mine. At Bourget, when the admiral, La Roncière, put his gilt-trimmed cap at the end of his sabre, and hurled us, our axes in our hands, against the fortified houses, Pierre and I marched shoulder to shoulder, and it was he who caught me in his arms when those cursed Prussians sent a bullet into my leg. That evening also, at the ambulance of the fort, Pierre held my hand to encourage me while the major chopped me up. And he was still there, the good Pierre, the day that the admiral brought my medal to me in bed. But, at last, those beggarly Prussians came out ahead. The treaty of peace was signed, and we were sent home. I, with my wooden leg, had nothing to do but to idle away my time like a worn-out dog. But Pierre, who had all his limbs entire, engaged in the fisherman's trade. Soon after, his wife died of an ague, and left him alone with this little Nona, who was nearly ten years old.

"Naturally, while the widower was at sea, it was I, the sailor, I, the old bachelor, who took care of the little girl. A good and quiet child, sir, very brave and very gentle. We used very often to go together over the shelving rocks at low tide, to gather large crabs, shrimps, and now and then a lobster. Oh! we were a pair of good friends.

"Things went on like this for two years. Nona had had her first communion and was growing like a sand thistle. But one tempestuous day the *Amélie,* the boat which carried Le Maguet, had great difficulty in getting back to the beach. The skipper did not haul down his jib and spanker in time, and was lost, life and goods, on that reef which you see from here—no, a little more to starboard. There were four men on board, the skipper, two sailors, of whom my poor Pierre was one, and the cabin boy. However, the sea did not wish to return but three of the bodies to the shore, and kept my comrade for its own. Now that Nona was an orphan, I of course did my best to take her father's place. But the child, even after the first shock of grief, would not be consoled. And can you guess why, above all? On account of an idea cherished by all the women of the place. They imagine, you see, that it is necessary to be buried in consecrated ground, lest the soul suffer in torment until the Great Judgment. We do not believe in all those stupid tales, we men, who know what takes place after there has been a death on board ship. I know the ceremony well: the body in a bag of tarred sacking, a cannon-ball at the foot, on a plank near the rail, and the commander bareheaded, the book in his hand, reading aloud the service for the dead. But the women about here are very religious, as you know well, and Nona began to burn candles in all the Pardons of the neighbourhood, that her father's soul might have repose.

"Still, in spite of all, time is a famous dealer in forgetfulness, and Nona, after several years had passed, seemed to me to be somewhat consoled. Moreover, her grief had not kept her from growing tall and beautiful; and it is not because I loved her like a father that I say so, but on my word of honour, she was the freshest and prettiest young girl in the parish. We lived so happily together! We were not rich, most assuredly, but we got along just the same. I have my pension and my medal, and besides, Nona and I used to go lobster-hunting among the rocks. The business is not a bad one, and there is only one danger, that of being caught by the rising tide. Alas! it is thus that she perished, poor little girl!

"One day that my rheumatism kept me chained in the house, she went alone for the lobsters, a day like to-day, with a clear sky and a high wind. But the other gatherers of shell-fish, coming back with full baskets, noticed that Nona was missing. There was no doubt possible, good God! She had delayed, she had been cut off by the tide, she had died at sea! Oh! what a night I passed! At my age, yes, old tough-as-leather as I am, I sobbed like a woman. And the thought kept coming back to me, of the poor girl's belief, that to go to heaven one must be buried in the cemetery. Therefore, as soon as the sea began to ebb, I dragged myself down to the beach, and set out with the others to search for the body.

"And we found her, my Nona," went on the old sailor, whose voice was breaking. "We found her on a rock covered with seaweed, where, seeing herself lost, the brave darling, she had made herself ready to die. Yes, she had fastened her skirts below her knees with her neckerchief for the sake of decency, and, still adhering to her old belief, she had tied her hair to the seaweed, her beautiful black hair, certain in this way that she would be found and buried in consecrated ground. And I can tell you, I, who know well what bravery is, there is hardly a man bold enough to do the like."

The old man ceased speaking. In the last gleam of twilight I saw two great tears roll down his tanned cheeks. We went down towards the village, side by side, without speaking a word. I was deeply moved by the courage of this simple girl, who, even in the agony of death, had preserved the modesty of her sex and piety of her race. And before me, in the distant spaces, in the sombre solitude of sky and sea, gleamed the lighthouses and the stars.

Oh! brave people of the sea! Oh! noble Brittany!

PAUL ARÈNE
1843–1896

UNCLE SAMBUQ'S FORTUNE

TROPHIME COGOLIN, generally known in the district as Master Trefume, had so often related the story of Uncle Sambuq and his fortune that he had finally come to believe it himself. The simple truth of the matter was that Peter Sambuq, a ne'er-do-well who had given his parents no end of trouble, had shipped as an ordinary seaman on a three-master one fine day in the year of grace 1848, and had never been seen or heard of since. These hard facts were too ridiculously simple for the worthy friends and relations of the vanished Peter; they could not understand how any one could set out for America without reaching that continent and making his fortune; so the worthy people gradually evolved the idea that Uncle Sambuq had gone and done likewise, and would one day return rolling in riches—of course, to die in due time and leave his fortune to them.

So the years rolled by, and Uncle Sambuq's fortune grew bigger in the imagination of his people. The older relatives died, and Master Trefume became heir to his uncle. Now, it happened one day that Trefume met a sailor whose acquaintance he had made a year or so previously. This man had just returned from a voyage to the States, and Trefume seized the opportunity to offer him a glass of brandy (contraband) and ask him if he had heard of Uncle Sambuq while on the other side.

The sailor, probably out of politeness, and in order to please Trefume and his wife, informed them that he had a distinct recollection of having on several occasions met an individual (on the quays of New York) who was undoubtedly very wealthy indeed, and was the exact image of Sambuq. That settled the matter; there could no longer be any doubt that Uncle Sambuq had reached America and made his pile, as any other reasonable person would do.

On the following day Trefume again met the sailor—or perhaps it was the sailor who made a point of meeting Trefume; be that as it may, the result of the meeting was another glass of brandy for the sailor, further questions about Uncle Sambuq, and a confidential communication to the effect that the stranger in New York was really the long-lost Peter, for he had spoken to the mariner concerning his relatives, and had dropped mysterious hints as to his intentions towards them.

The Trefumes became the envied ones of the neighbourhood. Uncle Sambuq and his fortune—especially his fortune—were the chief topic of conversation for many a day among the inhabitants of the whole district. The Trefumes lived happy and contented, patiently awaiting the time when they would have their share of the millions amassed by Peter Sambuq.

A few months passed away. One morning, when Trefume was least expecting it, he received a letter from New York. The letter bore the seal of the French Embassy. Trefume carried that precious letter about with him all day, without breaking the seal, in order to show it to his friends. Not till the evening, in the presence of his wife and children, his hands trembling with excitement, did he venture to open it. It was somewhat bulky—probably it contained banknotes. The papers were carefully taken from the envelope and proved to be—Sambuq's death certificate and a brief note from the Embassy.

" So he is dead? " said his wife.

" Of course he is," replied Trefume; " doesn't the Ambassador say so? "

There was silence. None of them had known the dead man, but they had thought so much about him that it seemed as though they had been on intimate terms with him, and they were able to squeeze out a tear.

" The Ambassador doesn't say anything about the fortune," observed Trefume's better half, wiping her eyes.

" I suppose you want him to tell us all about it straight off before the man is fairly dead," replied Trefume, sarcastically. " We can wait, and he knows it. He'll write again in a day or two."

He looked again at the envelope and noticed that it was addressed to " Monsieur Sambuq or Monsieur Cogolin." As all the Sambuqs were dead and he was the only Cogolin, it was natural that the letter should have been delivered to him, and the vagueness of the address did not inspire in the simple man any misgivings as to the fortune any more than did the brief note from the Embassy.

But, strange to say, the Ambassador omitted to write that other letter. As the time went on surprise deepened into anxiety; a veritable fever—a gold fever—took possession of them; they lost interest in everything, they could think of nothing but Sambuq's millions, and wonder what had become of them. At length their anxiety reached such a pitch that Trefume announced his intention of undertaking a journey to New York—a decision which met with the full approval of all concerned.

"I shan't be away more than a month—or two," said Trefume, "and the boy can look after the boat. A few hundred francs won't break us; besides, I know I shall be ill if I don't go and see what's going on over there."

I have said that every one approved the decision. I may add that had it been otherwise it would have made no difference. When Trefume got an idea into his head it wanted some getting out.

He travelled to Havre and embarked on a vessel bound for New York. He knew absolutely nothing of the great city which he was approaching; he could not speak the language—he was as helpless as a child in a wood. He began to get very anxious, and looked around for somebody to confide in and obtain assistance from. He tried the under-steward, a fellow-countryman, but the latter was too busy to be bothered. Trefume, however, refused to be shaken off, and the under-steward, in desperation, glanced about for somebody to whom he could refer the persistent fisherman, and so get rid of him.

"Here!" he said, pointing to two of the passengers; "those are the men to help you. They know New York so well that they could find their way blindfold anywhere in the city. Try them!"

Trefume looked at the men and thanked his compatriot heartily. He was delighted at the thought of meeting two people who were so well acquainted with New York. They were two shifty-looking Yankees, who had been left very severely alone on the voyage. He went towards the two passengers, who, after exchanging a word or two between themselves, walked away before he could reach them. Trefume walked after them, but they still avoided him and began conversing earnestly together. The fisherman hesitated; he thought they had something private on, and he did not wish to intrude. It never entered his head that they were avoiding him. He did not intend to lose his chance, so he continued to walk after them at a respectable distance. Two or three times, when he thought the moment opportune, he approached them hat in hand and attempted to speak to them in his best French, but was met with a scowl and a growl which made him retire. He put it down to American —or English—manners, and with a sigh he withdrew for a few minutes.

The two Americans were evidently much perplexed at the strange conduct of their fellow-passenger; they were worried about it, too; so, finally, they spoke to the under-steward concerning Trefume. The official was more busy than ever, but he was fond of a joke, and thought he might as well enliven the routine of the day by a little fun.

"You know that there has been a big robbery in Paris?" he said, in a confidential whisper. "Well, I wouldn't mind betting that this man is Jean Ernest, the cleverest detective in France, who is on the track of the thieves and has disguised himself as a fisherman from the South.''

The two men looked at each other, thanked the under-steward, and dived into their cabin, from which they only emerged when the ship was actually alongside the quay. Poor Trefume looked for them in vain; they got off the steamer unobserved by him, and he was left to find his way about New York as best he could.

How he went through the rest of that day, where he lodged at night, he never knew. He began again on the following day, looking for the Embassy, asking the way in his provincial French, and being laughed at and treated with contempt as an impostor, until, sick at heart, and thoroughly discouraged, he sat down on a doorstep and began to cry. Uncle Sambuq might have journeyed to his native country to die, and thus have made things easier for his heir!

After a few minutes he plucked up courage and determined to try again. He had just reached the end of the street when he saw one of the Americans to whom the under-steward had referred him on the steamer. He had changed his clothes and cut off his beard, but Trefume was positive that it was the same man.

'' Monsieur, monsieur! '' he cried, running towards the man.

Whether the man heard the words or not, he took to his heels as soon as he saw the Frenchman running.

'' What! '' said Trefume to himself, in an indignant tone. '' This man knows New York as well as I know Endoume, and he won't help me! I'll see about that.''

Away they went, the American and Trefume. In vain the former doubled this corner and that; his pursuer stuck to him until, thoroughly exhausted, the American took refuge in a bar and awaited the arrival of his pursuer.

'' So I have you at last! '' exclaimed the Frenchman. '' Why did you run away and give me all this trouble? Now you must——''

'' Hush! '' interrupted the American, turning pale in spite of the violent exercise. '' Don't make a fuss,'' he continued, in excellent French; '' that will be of no use. Come and sit down in this corner.''

'' Ah! that's better,'' thought Trefume. But he simply looked knowingly at the man and took a seat.

'' I know what you have come to New York for,'' said the man.

'' Good again! '' thought the fisherman; but before he could speak, the American continued:

'' We can arrange this little affair, can't we, without further bother? ''

'' Of course we can! '' exclaimed Trefume, thinking still that the man was talking about Uncle Sambuq's fortune.

" That's agreed. Now, how much do you want? "

" My fair share, of course! " replied the Frenchman.

" I'll give you this pocket-book—it has one hundred thousand francs in French notes—I have not had time to exchange them for American money. They are good, you need not be afraid that they are bad or stopped. Will that satisfy you? "

One hundred thousand francs! It was an immense sum; but was it a fair share? How much was Uncle Sambuq worth?

" Is that my fair share? " asked Trefume doubtfully.

" How much do you expect? " asked the other irritably. " It was a good thing, but it wasn't a gold-mine, and there are several to share it. It's either that or nothing! "

" Well! I'll take it! " said Trefume, beginning to fear that he might lose all.

" Very well! Now, you have this on condition that you go back in the *Bretagne,* and the *Bretagne* starts in two hours. And remember, you have never seen me! "

" Done! " exclaimed Trefume.

The pocket-book was handed to him, and he scrutinised the notes. They were all right. He tried to explain it all to himself; he was not clear on some points; but the more he tried to think it out, the more confused he became. Only one thing was clear: he had succeeded in getting a good slice of Uncle Sambuq's fortune and was now a rich man.

They remained where they were for an hour, then the American went with him to procure a ticket, saw him safely on board, and watched him until the ship started on its voyage across the Atlantic.

Thus it came about that Master Trefume, having had the good fortune to be taken for a detective, became the heir of Uncle Sambuq, who had died penniless in a hospital a few weeks before!

As to Trefume, he was never able to arrive at any proper understanding of the affair, but he did not worry himself much on that head. Later on, when he had given up work and donned a frock-coat, he used to shake his head and declare, with much gravity, that in business matters those American fellows were far ahead of any other people. See how quickly they settled that little matter of Uncle Sambuq's Fortune.

LÉON DE TINSEAU
B. 1844

THE BLACK PEARL

YOUR Parisians always make me laugh when, towards the end of August, they pretend—according to the newspaper reporters—that the "water-supply of the capital is inadequate." I know at the other end of the Red Sea a town of sixty thousand inhabitants called Aden, built on a promontory of cooled lava—imperfectly cooled. There, for all the wealth of the Indies, the detractors of our municipal authorities would not find a blade of grass, a leaf of salad, or a drop of water.

"But when it rains what becomes of the rain-water?" I asked my friend Pujol, the consul, who welcomed me on his rock one day as I passed there on my way back from China.

"When it rains the public cisterns are filled. But it is now five years since the natives have seen a cloud in the sky."

"Then where did the water come from that we drank this morning for lunch?"

"It comes from the factory. The English distil the sea-water and sell us, at the price of gold, an absolutely irreproachable product. But it is ruinous. My water bill comes to a hundred francs a month, including the bath-water for my wife, who cannot bathe in sea-water."

"The devil! How then do these poor Arabs get along. They don't seem to me to be able to afford twelve hundred francs a year for their drinking-water?"

"They are content with the water brought by camels every morning from those mountains you can see over there, twenty miles away. It is a disagreeable liquid, smelling of goatskin. But what is there to do? Distilled water is much too dear. Besides, a police regulation forbids its sale to the natives. It is exclusively reserved for European residents, for the British garrison, and for passing ships whose water-supply is quite exhausted."

I took these notes in my notebook, and we returned to the Consulate, where we were expected by Madame Pujol, a pretty Marseilles woman exiled in this desert, whom I had seen that morning for the first time, my friend having only lately married.

We talked about the country and its social attractions. Madame Pujol told me, with a sigh, that her visitors' list contained only two names, that of an old Englishwoman, who did not know two words of our language, and the landlady of the Hotel of the Universe, a worthy dame from the Champagne district, more used to wrangling with good-for-nothing Arabs and Somalis than to chatting with a fellow-countrywoman.

As I commiserated with the wife of my friend on her lonely way of life:

"Come, my dear," said Pujol to her, "don't dissimulate! Why do you hide the fact that you have a sweetheart in the Arab quarter?"

Madame Pujol seemed put out and shrugged her shoulders.

"A sweetheart as black as the inside of a chimney!" she said.

"Very black, but very handsome," Pujol insisted. "Black but comely, and very wealthy! The biggest coffee-merchant in Aden. I will take you to his place to-morrow. You will see his magnificent carpets and objects of art. A real bazaar! My wife spends hours there, and if I did not forbid it, this worthy Mulad would strip his house to furnish ours, under the pretext that the things that fill it pleased the white lady."

"What exaggeration!" said his wife, who seemed to grow more and more vexed. "Do not believe, sir, that I treat this negro as an intimate friend. It is a fortnight since I went to his house——"

"My wife is in a bad humour," explained the consul, "through the loss of a jewel this morning."

"Certainly I am upset about it," she said to me. "I have spent the whole day trying to find one of the two black pearls I wear in my ears. My husband bought them at Ceylon. You can judge how superb they were by the one that still remains."

I bent over to examine it and found that Madame Pujol had pretty ears and used a very pleasant perfume. Then the talk turned on other matters, and I went up to sleep on the roof of the house, according to the custom of the country.

The next day, accompanied by my friend, I went to the native quarter to pay a visit to "the sweetheart of Madame Pujol." Mulad ben Said is an Arab, as his name indicates. He is a millionaire of a coffee-merchant, and he sells the finest mocha in the world . . . after that of the grocers of Paris. But every traveller takes pleasure in bringing back some of his coffee. All considered, it is not very much dearer than that which you can buy in France.

In going to the great mocha man, we took with us a fellow-voyager and fellow-countryman whose name I forget, who had just done a tour of the world or thereabouts. He was what is called a learned man, a busy taker of notes, a great copier of inscriptions, a great writer of articles for the Academy, of which he said he was a corresponding member.

Mulad, who speaks English like a City man, is a superb specimen of the true Arab race, which is perhaps the most handsome on earth. He received us wonderfully well, and not only showed us over his shop but over his private apartments, which were far more interesting to us. Then at the end of the visit he served us with Oriental coffee, a fragrant beverage that resembles ours as champagne resembles gassy lemonade. It was accompanied by the inevitable chibouk and a jar of fresh water.

Water brought for seven leagues on camels' backs in leather bottles was not ideal. But I was dying of thirst, and, besides, I had drunk worse in the rice-fields of Lower China.

It was very strange! This water did not smell of goatskin; far from it. You might have said it was not absolutely limpid, but it had a decidedly agreeable savour. It smelt—by Jove! yes—it smelt of violets; violets in a spot facing Abyssinia!

The man of science perceived it as soon as I did. After smelling and sniffing it and tasting it in little gulps, he asked me, with a learned air:

"Don't you find this water has a particular flavour?"

"Yes," I replied, "it smells of violets."

"Exactly! Now, my dear sir, among the many derivatives of coal there are certain products with a smell resembling that of violets. Perfumers make use of it in adulterating their scents. So I conclude that this water is found in contact with coal. A coal-mine at Aden, sir! Do you see what that means. Think of the fortune there is in it! Every bit of coal burnt here has to be brought from England!"

Then he overwhelmed our host with questions about the exact site of the spring from which the camels came every day. He would have gone there at once, in spite of the distance, if the steamer was not leaving that very night. He wished at least to take a sample of the water in a flask, in order to have it analysed in the laboratories of Paris. I was astonished to see that his proposal caused an inexplicable anxiety in Mulad ben Said.

However, we were about to depart, and I poured out for myself a last glass of water, when I heard in my glass the noise of a hard body falling into it with the liquid. Oh, surprise! It was a black pearl, the sister of that which madame had shown me the evening before. And then that fragrance! I at once recognised it! I had smelt it, not without a little pleasant thrill, in examining the ear of my friend's wife, the vivacious lady from Marseilles.

He was a fool, the man of science with his coal-mines! And my poor friend Pujol . . . ! What I had just discovered did not relate to the mineral kingdom! I recollect him saying to me, the unhappy fellow:

"The climate of Aden is very curious in its action. It has a debilitating effect on men but an exciting action on women."

And in the home of this Arab, young, handsome, rich, and luxuriously housed, I had found the pearl that had fallen from the ear of Madame Pujol, with even the trace of her favourite perfume. What could I do? Absolutely nothing. The magnificent regarded me with a look I did not like, and the presence of the husband, the person most interested, prevented me from making any inquiries. I thought to myself sadly that if the great principle of consular inviolability is inscribed among the rights of nations, it seemed to be strongly denied in practice by Arabs.

While the man of science was corking his flask, I succeeded, by the pretext of pouring some of the water over my hands, in getting the pearl without being seen. At least Pujol should not lose everything. Then we left the Arab. The mineralogist went straight to the pier. I had to touch at the Consulate in order to restore the pearl. Very fortunately Pujol let me enter alone, while he walked to the steamer to have a chat with the captain.

"Before bidding you good-bye," I said in a pretty severe but quiet tone, "permit me, madame, to return you your pearl."

She gave a cry of joy.

"My pearl! What luck! Where was it?"

"*At Mulad ben Said's,*" I said, emphasising every syllable. "That is where I have just found it. Thank God, Pujol is not aware of my discovery!"

And as she displayed the deepest astonishment:

"I do not know anything more," I continued in the same tone, "and I do not wish to know more. Needless to say, I shall act like a gentleman and never speak to *any one* of this affair."

I went away, almost without touching her hand, showing her all my indignation in a single look. She should at least see that she had not deceived me. I found my friend on board. I embraced him with an outburst of feeling which amazed him. Poor Pujol. . . . An hour afterwards I was far away from Aden.

I last met Pujol and his wife on a Paris boulevard. They looked as though they were more tenderly united than ever. The two black pearls were hanging from the ears of the young woman. The three of us dined together and naturally chatted about Aden.

"By the way," said the consul, "you set our imaginations working finely for a week, thanks to your discovery of the pearl at the house of the worthy Mulad. Weren't you yourself perplexed about it?"

I was certainly very much perplexed about it at that moment, and I gave some answer without either head or tail.

"Just fancy," Pujol went on, "my servant had invented a singular means of increasing his income. He resold to the Arabs the water my wife had used for her baths. The pearl must have tumbled in the bath and have been carried in the water to Mulad ben Said. How did you find it there?"

"Heavens! I nearly swallowed it," I cried, looking at the pretty wife, who was blushing.

That did not prevent some one from reading before the Academy of Sciences a treatise on the coal-mines of Aden.

ANATOLE FRANCE
B. 1844

THE PROCURATOR OF JUDEA

AELIUS LAMIA, born in Italy of illustrious parents, had not yet left off the dress of youth when he went to study philosophy in the schools of Athens. He next settled in Rome, and led a life of pleasure with other young libertines in his house on the Esquiline. But charged with having illicit relations with Lepida, wife of Sulpicius Quirinus, a consul, and found guilty, he was exiled by Tiberius Caesar. He was then in his twenty-fourth year. His exile lasted eighteen years, and during this time he wandered through Syria, Palestine, Cappadocia, and Armenia, making long stays at Antioch, Caesarea, and Jerusalem. When, after the death of Tiberius, Caius was made Imperator, Lamia was allowed to return to the city. He even recovered a part of his property. His troubles had made him prudent.

He avoided all relations with women of free condition, did not canvass for any public position, sought for no honours, and lived quietly in his house on the Esquiline. Setting down in writing the remarkable things he had seen in his remote travels, he transformed, he said, his bygone pains into entertainments of his present hours. It was amid this tranquil work and in the assiduous study of the books of Epicurus that, with a little surprise and some sorrow, he saw old age fall upon him.

In his sixty-second year, tormented by a bad cold, he set out for the watering-place of Baiae. This shore, once the haunt of wild birds, was then frequented by wealthy Romans avid of the pleasures of life. For a week Lamia lived alone and friendless in a brilliant crowd, when one day, after dinner, feeling in good health, he had the whim to climb up the hills that, covered with vine branches like bacchantes, looked on the waves.

Having reached the top, he sat down beside a path under a terebinth, and let his eyes wander over the lovely landscape. On his left stretched, livid and naked, the Phlegræan fields as far as the ruins of Cumae. On his right Cape Misenum buried its sharp spur in the Tyrrhenian Sea. Under his feet, westward, rich Baiae, following the gracious curve of the coast, displayed her gardens, her villas peopled with statues, her porticos, her marble terraces, at the edge of the blue sea where the dolphins were gambolling. Before him, on the other side of the gulf, on the coast of Campania, gilded by the sinking sun, there shone the temples crowned in the distance with the laurel trees of Pausilypus, and in the depth of the horizon Vesuvius gleamed.

Drawing from a fold of his toga a scroll containing the *Treatise on Nature,* Lamia stretched himself out on the earth and began to read. But the cries of a slave warned him that he must rise to make way for a litter that was coming up the narrow path between the vines. As the litter approached, all open, Lamia saw lying on the cushions an old man of a vast corpulence who, his head in his hand, glanced about him with proud and moody eyes. His hawk-like nose came down to his lips, where a powerful jaw ended in a prominent chin. At once Lamia was sure that he knew this face. He hesitated a moment about the name. Then, suddenly springing towards the litter with a feeling of surprise and joy:

" Pontius Pilate! " he cried. " Thanks to the gods, it is given me to see thee again! "

The old man signed to his slaves to stop, and fixed an attentive look on the man who had greeted him.

" Pontius, my dear host, twenty years have so whitened my hair, altered my face, that you cannot recognise your Aelius Lamia! "

At this name Pontius Pilate came down from the litter as quickly as the fatigue of his age and the habit of his body allowed. And twice he embraced Lamia.

" It is very pleasant to see you again," he said. " Alas! you bring back the old days to me, when I was procurator of Judea in the province of Syria. It must be thirty years since I first saw you. It was at Caesarea, where you were dragging out the weary days of your exile. I was happily able to solace you a little, and out of friendship, Lamia, you followed me to that dreary Jerusalem where the Jews embittered and disgusted my soul. For more than ten years you were my guest and my friend, and both of us, with talk about the city, consoled one another, you for your misfortunes and I for all the worries of my position."

Lamia embraced him again.

" You do not say everything, Pontius. You do not recollect the generosity with which you opened your purse to me and the way you used your credit in my favour with Herod."

" There is no need to speak about it," replied Pontius, " for as soon as you returned to Rome you sent me a sum of money by one of your freemen that repaid me with interest."

"Pontius, money cannot repay my debt to you. But tell me, Have the gods fulfilled all your desires? Do you enjoy all the happiness you merit? Tell me about your family, your fortune, the state of your health."

"I have retired to my estate in Sicily, and there I grow and sell my corn. My eldest daughter, my dear Pontia, now a widow, lives with me and governs my household. I have preserved, by the mercy of the gods, my vigour of mind; my memory is as good as ever. But old age does not come without a long train of sorrows and infirmities. I am cruelly tortured by gout; and just now, when I met you, I was going to seek for a remedy from my disease in the Phlegræan fields. It is said that that burning soil from which flames come at night gives out acrid sulphur vapours that remove the pain and make the joints of the limbs subtle once more. At least the physicians say so."

"May you find it true in your case, Pontius. But in spite of gout and its fiery shoots of pain, you seem scarcely as old as I am, though you are really my elder by ten years. Certainly you have preserved more vigour than I ever had, and I rejoice to find you so strong. Why, my very dear friend, have you given up the public service before your time? Why, at the end of your government of Judea, have you lived on your Sicilian estates in a voluntary exile? Let me know what you did from the moment when I ceased to be a witness of your actions. You were preparing to put down a revolt of the Samaritans when I left for Cappadocia, where I hoped to make some money by breeding horses and mules. I have never seen you since then. What was the result of the expedition? Tell me. Everything that touches you interests me."

Pontius Pilate sadly shook his head.

"A natural solicitude and a sense of duty," he said, "led me to carry out my public functions not only with diligence but with love. Hatred has followed me continually. Intrigue and calamity have broken my life in its full vigour, and withered the fruits it should have born. You were asking me about the Samaritan revolt. Let us sit down on this mound. I will answer you in a few words. The events are as vivid to me as if they had happened yesterday.

"One of the natives, good at talking, like most of the people of Syria, persuaded the Samaritans to arm themselves and assemble together on Mount Gerizim which passes in that country for a holy place. He promised to discover before their eyes the sacred vases of an eponymos hero, or rather a native divinity, named Moses, in the ancient times of Evander and Aeneas, our Father. On this assertion the Samaritans broke out in rebellion. But, warned in sufficient time to forestall them, I had the mountain occupied by detachments of infantry, and had the approaches watched by horsemen.

"These measures of precaution were urgent. Already the rebels were besieging the town of Tyrathaba, lying at the foot of Gerizim. I easily dispersed them and stifled the rebellion at its birth. Then, to make a memorable example with only a few victims, I ordered the leaders of the sedition to be put to the torture. But you know, Lamia, how little scope I was allowed by the proconsul Vitellius, who, governing Syria not for Rome but against Rome, reckoned that the provinces of the empire were created to be farmed out by the tetrarchs. The head men of the Samaritans fell at his feet, weeping hatred to me. To hear them, nothing was farther from their thoughts than to resist the imperial power. I was a provocator, and it was to withstand my violences that they had assembled round Tyrathaba.

"Vitellius listened to their complaints, and handing over the affairs of Judea to his friend Marcellus, he ordered me to go and justify myself before the Emperor. With a heart heavy with sorrow and resentment, I crossed the sea. When I arrived at the Italian coast, Tiberius, worn out by age and empire, suddenly died at Cape Misenum, whose horn you can see from here lengthening out in the evening mist. I demanded justice from Caius, his successor, who had a naturally keen intelligence and understood Syrian matters. But wonder with me, Lamia, at the way in which my bad fortune worked my ruin. Caius then kept close to him, in the city, the Jew Agrippa, the friend of his boyhood, whom he loved more than his own eyes. Now Agrippa favoured Vitellius, because Vitellius was an enemy of Herod, whom Agrippa hated. The Emperor followed the advice of his darling Asiatic and refused even to hear me. I was compelled to abide under the blow of an unmerited disgrace. Swallowing my tears and consumed with bitterness, I retired to my Sicilian domain, where I should have died of grief if my sweet Pontia had not come to console her father. I have gone in for growing wheat, and I produce the heaviest ears in the whole province. Now my life is done. The future will judge between Vitellius and me."

"Pontius," said Lamia, "I am persuaded that you acted with regard to the Samaritans according to the uprightness of your soul and with sole reference to Roman interests. But were you not on this occasion carried away by that impetuous courage that always marked your actions? You know that in Judea when, being younger than you, I should have been more ardent, I often counselled you to be more clement and gentle."

"Gentle with the Jews!" cried Pontius Pilate. "Though you have lived among them, you do not understand these enemies of mankind. Proud and vile, at the same time uniting an ignominious cowardice to an invincible obstinacy, they wear out both love and hatred. My mind was formed, Lamia, on the maxims of the divine

Augustus. Already, when I was appointed procurator of Judea, the majesty of the Roman peace enveloped the earth. You saw no longer, as in the days of our civil wars, proconsuls enriching themselves by the sack of provinces. I knew my duties. I was tempted to use only wisdom and moderation. The gods are my witnesses. I am firm only in my gentleness. But what was the use of all my benevolent thoughts? You saw me, Lamia, when the first rebellion broke out at the beginning of my government. Need I remind you of the details? The garrison of Caesarea were taking up their winter quarters at Jerusalem. The legionaries bore on their ensigns the image of Caesar. This sight offended the people at Jerusalem, who would not recognise the divinity of the Emperor, as though, since it was necessary to obey, it was not more honourable to obey a god than a man. The priests of the nation came before my tribunal and begged me, with haughty humility, to have the ensigns carried out of their holy city. I refused, out of respect for the divinity of Caesar and the majesty of the empire. Then the people, joining with the priests, raised threatening cries around the Prætorium. I ordered the troops to form the pikes into fasces before the Antonia tower, and armed with rods like lictors to go and disperse the insolent crowd. But insensible to the blows, the Jews still adjured me, and the most obstinate of them laid down with outstretched throats and let themselves die under the rods. You were then a witness of my humiliation, Lamia. Under the order of Vitellius, I was obliged to send the ensigns back to Caesarea. This dishonour was not my due. In the face of the immortal gods I swear I have not once during my government gone contrary to law and justice. But I am old. My enemies and my denouncers are dead. I shall die unrevenged. Who will defend my memory?" He groaned and then kept silent.

"It is wise," said Lamia, "to have neither fear nor hope for the uncertain future. What does it matter what posterity will think of us? We have no other witnesses and judges except ourselves. Rest assured, Pontius Pilate, in the testimony you yourself give of your own virtue. Be content with your own esteem and that of your friends. For the rest, you cannot govern nations by gentleness alone. That love of mankind which philosophy counsels has little part in the actions of public men."

"Let us leave that," said Pontius. "The sulphur vapours have more strength when they come from the ground still warmed by the sunlight. I must make haste. Farewell. But since I have recovered an old friend, I should like to profit by my good fortune. Aelius Lamia, do me the favour of supping with me to-morrow. My house lies on the seashore, at the end of the town on the side of Misen. You will easily recognise it by the portico, on which there is a painting representing Orpheus among the lions and tigers, which he is charming by the sounds of his lyre."

"To-morrow, Lamia," he said again, getting into his litter, "to-morrow we will talk about Judea."

At supper-time the next day Lamia went to the house of Pontius Pilate. Only two couches awaited the feasters. Served without pomp, but honourably, the table carried silver dishes in which were prepared wrens in honey, thrushes, oysters, and Sicilian lampreys. Pontius and Lamia while eating talked to each other about their maladies, and described their symptoms at length, and communicated to each other various remedies that had been recommended to them. Then, delighted at having met once more at Baiae, they praised the beauty of its shore and the sweetness of its air. Lamia celebrated the loveliness of the courtesans who passed along the strand, adorned in gold and trailing cloaks embroidered by the barbarians.

But the old procurator deplored the passion for display which, for vain stones and cobweb tissues of man's making, sent Roman money circulating among foreign nations, and even among the enemies of the empire. Their talk then turned on the great works accomplished in the country. The prodigious bridge built by Caius between Puteoli and Baiae, and the canals dug by Augustus to carry sea-water to lakes Avernus and Lucrinus.

"I also," said Pontius with a sigh, "I also wished to carry out some great work of public utility. When I received, before my misfortune, the government of Judea, I sketched the plan of an aqueduct of two hundred stadia that should carry to Jerusalem a pure and abundant supply of water. Height of the levels, capacity of modules, the obliquity of the brazen unions into which the distributing nozzels ran—I had studied it all and, in the opinions of the engineers, worked it all out myself. I drew up rules for management of the water, so that no private person could obtain an illicit supply. The architects and the workmen were commanded, and I ordered the work to be begun.

"But far from seeing with satisfaction the erection of my aqueduct, which on its powerful arches would bring healthy water into their city, the Jews broke out into lamentable howls. Assembling in tumult and shouting of sacrilege and impiety, they fell upon the workmen and tore away the foundation-stone. Can you conceive, Lamia, more filthy barbarians? Yet Vitellius said they were right and commanded me to stop the work."

"It is a great question," said Lamia, "to decide if we ought to make men happy in spite of themselves."

Pontius Pilate went on without hearing him.

"What madness to refuse an aqueduct! But everything that comes from Romans is odious to Jews. To them we are unclean beings, and our mere presence is a profanation. You know they would not enter the Prætorium for fear of sullying themselves, and that I was obliged to exercise the office of magistrate in an open-air tribunal on that marble pavement your feet so often trod.

"They feared us and they scorned us. Yet is not Rome the mother and the guardian of nations which all, like children, repose in smiles upon her venerable breast? Our eagles have carried peace and liberty to the ends of the universe. Seeing only friends in those we conquer, we assure to the natives their customs and their laws. Isn't it only since Pompey conquered it that Syria, formerly rent by a multitude of kings, has begun to know repose and prosperity? And though Rome might sell her benefits at the price of gold, has she taken the treasures with which the barbarians' temples overflow? Has she stripped the Mother Goddess of Pessinus, Jupiter in Morimene and in Cilicia, the God of the Jews at Jerusalem? Antioch, Palmyra, Apamea, tranquil in spite of their wealth and fearing no more the Arabs of the desert, build temples to the genius of Rome and the divinity of Ceasar. Alone, the Jews hate us and defy us. We have to wrest the tribute from them and they stubbornly refuse military service."

"The Jews," replied Lamia, "are much attached to their ancient customs. They suspected you, without grounds I admit, of wishing to abolish their law and change their manners. Permit me, Pontius, to say that you did not always act in such a way as to dissipate their unfortunate mistake. In spite of yourself you took pleasure in exciting anxieties; and I have seen you more than once betray before them your contempt for their beliefs and their religious ceremonies. You particularly vexed them by having the sacred dresses and ornaments of their high priests placed in the Antonia tower and guarded by legionaries. We must recognise that, without being as advanced as we are in the contemplation of divine things, the Jews celebrate mysteries venerable by their antiquity." Pontius Pilate shrugged his shoulders.

"They have not," he said, "an exact knowledge of the nature of the gods. They worship Jupiter, but without giving him a name or a figure. They do not even venerate him under the form of a stone, as certain people of Asia do. They know nothing of Apollo, of Neptune, of Mars, of Plato, or any goddess. Yet I think that formerly they adored Venus. For at the present time the women present doves at the altar as victims. And you know that merchants, established under the portico of their temple, sell these birds in couples for the sacrifice. One day I was even told that a madman came and drove away these vendors of offerings and overturned their cages. The priests complained of it as a sacrilege. I believe that this custom of sacrificing doves was established in honour of Venus. Why do you laugh, Lamia?"

"I am laughing," said Lamia, "at a droll idea that has come, I know not how, into my head. I dreamt that one day the Jupiter of the Jews might come to Rome and pursue you in anger. Why not? Asia and Africa have already given us a large number of deities. We have seen temples raised in Rome in honour of Isis and the barking Anubis. We meet at the cross-roads and even in the race-courses the Good Goddess of the Syrians borne on an ass. And don't you know that, under the principate of Tiberius, a young knight passed himself off as the horned Jupiter of the Egyptians, and under this disguise ingratiated himself with an illustrious lady, too virtuous to refuse anything to a divinity? Beware, Pontius, that the invisible Jupiter of the Jews does not land one day at Ostia!"

At the notion that a god could come from Judea a swift smile flitted over the severe face of the procurator.

"But how could the Jews," he replied gravely, "impose their holy law on other nations when they themselves are rent apart over the interpretation of this law? Divided into twenty rival sects, you have seen them, Lamia, in the public places abusing each other and pulling at their beards. You have seen them on the stylobate of the Temple tearing their filthy robes, as a sign of desolation, round some miserable wretch given over to prophetic delirium. They cannot conceive that a dispute can be conducted peacefully and with a serene soul in regard to divine things, which, however, are covered with veils and full of uncertainties. For the nature of the Immortals is hidden from us, and we cannot know it. Yet I think it is wise to believe in the providence of the gods. But the Jews have no philosophy, and they will not admit a diversity of opinion. On the contrary, they consider those who profess in divine matters anything opposed to their law to be worthy of extreme torture. And as, since the Genius of Rome is above them and capital sentences pronounced by their tribunals can only be executed with the sanction of the proconsul or the procurator, they urge the Roman magistrate every moment to subscribe to their fatal sentences: they beset the Prætorium crying for men to be put to death. A hundred times have I seen them come in a mob, rich and poor, all reconciled round their priests, and madly besiege my ivory chair and drag me by the ends of my toga, by the straps of my sandals, clamouring, insisting on the death of some unhappy creature whose crime I could not discern and who merely seemed to me as insane as his accusers.

"What do I say—a hundred times! It was every day and every hour of the day. And yet I had to carry out their law as though it were ours, since Rome had appointed me not the destroyer but the upholder of their customs, and I was put over them with the rods and the axe. When I first began I tried to make them listen to reason. I attempted to rescue their miserable victims from execution. But this clemency only irritated them still more. They claimed their prey, beating with wing and beak around me, like vultures. Their priests wrote to Caesar that I violated their law, and their petitions, supported by Vitellius, drew on me severe blame. How many times I was seized with a desire to send altogether to the crows, as the Greeks say, the judges and their prisoners!

"Do not think, Lamia, that I cherish an impotent grudge and senile anger against this nation that conquered in me Rome and the peace of Rome. But I can foresee the extremity to which they will reduce us sooner or later. Not being able to govern them, it will be necessary to destroy them. Don't doubt it. Always unsubmissive, brooding over revolt in their fiery souls, they will break out some day against us in a fury, beside which the anger of the Numidians and the menaces of the Parthians are merely childish caprices. They foster in darkness the most insensate hopes and madly meditate our overthrow. And can it be otherwise, while they are expecting, on the faith of an oracle, a prince of their blood who shall reign over the world? You cannot manage this people. Jerusalem must be destroyed from top to bottom. Perhaps, old as I am, it may be given to me to see the day when its walls shall fall and fire shall consume its houses, when its inhabitants shall be put to the edge of the sword, and when salt shall be sown on the land where the Temple stood. On that day I shall be justified!"

Lamia tried to bring the talk round to a quieter tone.

"Pontius," he said, "I can understand, without any trouble, your old resentment and your sinister forecasts. Certainly what you know of the Jews is not to their advantage. But I, who lived at Jerusalem, an interested stranger, and mixed with the people, I have discovered in these men some obscure virtues that were hidden from you. I have known Jews full of gentle thoughts, with simple manners and faithful hearts that reminded me of what our poets sang of the old man of Ebalia. And you yourself, Pontius, you have seen, expiring under the rods of your legionaries, simple men who, without telling their name, died for a cause they believed just. Such men do not deserve our contempt. I speak in this way because it is becoming to observe measure and equity in all things. But I admit I have never felt any lively sympathy for the Jews. Jewesses, on the contrary, pleased me highly. I was young then, and the Syrian women worked on my senses. Their scarlet lips, their humid eyes, shining in the shadow, their long glances struck into me to the marrow. Painted and got up, smelling of nard and myrrh, macerated in aromatics, their bodies are rare and delicious."

Pontius listened to these praises with impatience.

" I was not the man to fall into the snare of a Jewess," he said, " and since you lead me to say it, Lamia, I have never approved your conduct in this matter. If I did not show you clearly in the old days that I held you a criminal for your relations in Rome with the wife of a consul, it was because you were then expiating heavily your fault. Marriage is sacred among the patricians; it is an institution on which Rome is founded. As for slaves and foreign women, the relations a man might have with them would be of little consequence if the body did not thus acquire a habit of shameful softness. Permit me to say that you have made too many sacrifices to the Venus of the crossways, and what I especially blame you for, Lamia, is not to have married according to the law, and given children to the commonwealth, as every good citizen should do."

But the exile of Tiberius was no longer listening to the old magistrate. Having emptied his cup of Falernian, he smiled at some invisible image. After a moment's silence, he said in a very low voice that little by little grew louder

" They dance with such languor, the women of Syria! I knew a Jewess of Jerusalem who in a low drinking shop, by the light of a small, smoking lamp, on a bad carpet, danced while lifting her arms to clash the cymbals. Her hips arched, her head thrown back, and as though drawn down by the weight of her heavy red tresses, her eyes swimming with passion, ardent and languishing and supple, she would have made Cleopatra herself pale with envy. I loved her barbaric dances, her singing, a little hoarse and yet sweet, her odour of incense, the way she moved about half asleep. I followed her everywhere, I mingled in the vile world of soldiers, mountebanks, and publicans that surrounded her. She disappeared one day, and I never saw her again. I sought after her a long time in dubious alleys and in taverns. It was more trouble to lose a taste for her than for Greek wine. After some months of inquiry, I learnt by chance that she had joined a little band of men and women who followed a young wonder-worker from Galilee. He was named Jesus: he came from Nazareth, and was put on the cross for I don't know what crime. Pontius, do you remember the man? "

Pontius Pilate knitted his brows and put his hand on his forehead like a man searching his memory. Then, after several moments of silence: " Jesus! " he murmured, " Jesus of Nazareth? I do not remember."

PUTOIS

ANATOLE FRANCE

"THIS garden of our childhood," said Monsieur Vergeret, "this garden that one could pace off in twenty steps, was for us a whole world, full of smiles and surprises."

"Lucien, do you remember Putois?" asked Zoe, smiling as usual, the lips pressed, bending over her work.

"Do I remember Putois! Of all the faces I saw as a child that of Putois remains the clearest in my remembrance. All the features of his face and his character are fixed in my mind. He had a pointed cranium . . ."

"A low forehead," added Mademoiselle Zoe.

And the brother and sister recited alternately, in a monotonous voice, with an odd gravity, the points in a sort of description:

"A low forehead."

"Squinting eyes."

"A shifty glance."

"Crow's-feet at the temples."

"The cheek-bones sharp, red, and shining."

"His ears had no rims to them."

"The features were devoid of all expression."

"His hands, which were never still, alone expressed his meaning."

"Thin, somewhat bent, feeble in appearance . . ."

"In reality he was unusually strong."

"He easily bent a five-franc piece between the first finger and the thumb . . ."

"Which was enormous."

"His voice was drawling . . ."

"And his speech mild."

Suddenly Monsieur Bergeret exclaimed: "Zoe! we have forgotten 'Yellow hair and sparse beard.' Let us begin all over again."

Pauline, who had listened with astonishment to this strange recital, asked her father and aunt how they had been able to learn by heart this bit of prose, and why they recited it as if it were a litany.

Monsieur Bergeret gravely answered:

"Pauline, what you have heard is a text, I may say a liturgy, used by the Bergeret family. It should be handed down to you so that it may not perish with your aunt and me. Your grandfather, my daughter, your grandfather, Eloi Bergeret, who was not amused with trifles, thought highly of this bit, principally because of its origin. He called it 'The Anatomy of Putois.' And he used to say that he preferred, in certain respects, the anatomy of Putois to the anatomy of Quaresmeprenant. 'If the description by Xenomanes,' he said, 'is more learned and richer in unusual and choice expressions, the description of Putois greatly surpasses it in clarity and simplicity of style.' He held this opinion because Doctor Ledouble, of Tours, had not yet explained chapters thirty, thirty-one, and thirty-two of the fourth book of Rabelais."

"I don't understand it at all," said Pauline.

"That is because you did not know Putois, my daughter. You must understand that Putois was the most familiar figure in my childhood and in that of your Aunt Zoe. In the house of your grandfather Bergeret we constantly spoke of Putois. Each believed that he had seen him."

Pauline asked:

"Who was this Putois?"

Instead of replying, Monsieur Bergeret began to laugh, and Mademoiselle Bergeret also laughed, her lips pressed tight together. Pauline looked from one to the other. She thought it strange that her aunt should laugh so heartily, and more strange that she should laugh with and in sympathy with her brother. It was indeed singular, as the brother and sister were quite different in character.

"Papa, tell me what was Putois? Since you wish me to know, tell me."

"Putois, my daughter, was a gardener. The son of honest market-gardeners, he set up for himself as nurseryman at Saint-Omer. But he did not satisfy his customers and got in a bad way. Having given up business, he went out by the day. Those who employed him could not always congratulate themselves."

At this, Mademoiselle Bergeret, laughing, rejoined:

"Do you recall, Lucien, when our father could not find his ink, his pens, his sealing-wax, his scissors, he said: 'I suspect Putois has been here'?"

"Ah!" said Monsieur Bergeret. "Putois had not a good reputation."

"Is that all?" asked Pauline.

"No, my daughter, it is not all. Putois was remarkable in this, that while we knew him and were familiar with him, nevertheless——"

"—He did not exist," said Zoe.

Monsieur Bergeret looked at his sister with an air of reproach.

" What a speech, Zoe! and why break the charm like that? Do you dare say it, Zoe? Zoe, can you prove it? To maintain that Putois did not exist, that Putois never was, have you sufficiently considered the conditions of existence and the modes of being? Putois existed, my sister. But it is true that his was a peculiar existence."

" I understand less and less," said Pauline, discouraged.

" The truth will be clear to you presently, my daughter. Know then that Putois was born fully grown. I was still a child and your aunt was a little girl. We lived in a little house, in a suburb of Saint-Omer. Our parents led a peaceful, retired life, until they were discovered by an old lady named Madame Cornouiller, who lived at the manor of Montplaisir, twelve miles from town, and proved to be a great-aunt of my mother's. By right of relationship she insisted that our father and mother must come to dine every Sunday at Montplaisir, where they were excessively bored. She said that it was the proper thing to have a family dinner on Sunday, and that only people of no breeding failed to observe this ancient custom. My father was so bored he could have wept at Montplaisir. His desperation was painful to contemplate. But Madame Cornouiller did not notice it. She saw nothing. My mother was braver. She suffered as much as my father, and perhaps more, but she smiled."

" Women are made to suffer," said Zoe.

" Zoe, every living thing is destined to suffer. In vain our parents refused these fatal invitations. Madame Cornouiller's carriage came to fetch them every Sunday afternoon. They had to go to Montplaisir; it was an obligation from which there was absolutely no escape. It was an established order that only a revolt could break. My father finally revolted and swore not to accept another invitation from Madame Cornouiller, leaving it to my mother to find decent pretexts and varied reasons for these refusals, for which she was the least capable. Our mother did not know how to pretend."

" Say, Lucien, that she did not like to. She could tell a fib as well as any one."

" It is true that when she had good reasons she gave them rather than invent poor ones. Do you recall, my sister, that one day she said at table: ' Fortunately, Zoe has the whooping-cough; we shall not have to go to Montplaisir for some time '? "

" That was true! " said Zoe.

" You got over it, Zoe. And one day Madame Cornouiller said to my mother: ' Dearest, I count on your coming with your husband to dine Sunday at Montplaisir.' Our mother, expressly bidden by her husband to give Madame Cornouiller a good reason for declining, invented, in this extremity, a reason that was not the truth. 'I am extremely sorry, dear Madame, but that will be impossible for us. Sunday I expect the gardener.'

"On hearing this, Madame Cornouiller looked through the glass door of the salon at the little wild garden, where the prickwood and the lilies looked as though they had never known the pruning-knife and were likely never to know it. 'You expect the gardener! What for?'

"'To work in the garden.'

"And my mother, having involuntarily turned her eyes on this little square of weeds and plants run wild, that she had called a garden, recognised with dismay the improbability of her excuse.

"'This man,' said Madame Cornouiller, 'could just as well work in your garden Monday or Tuesday. Moreover, that will be much better. One should not work on Sunday.'

"'He works all the week.'

"I have often noticed that the most absurd and ridiculous reasons are the least disputed: they disconcert the adversary. Madame Cornouiller insisted, less than one might expect of a person so little disposed to give up. Rising from her armchair, she asked:

"'What do you call your gardener, dearest?'

"'Putois,' answered my mother without hesitation.

"Putois was named. From that time he existed. Madame Cornouiller took herself off, murmuring: 'Putois! It seems to me that I know that name. Putois! Putois! I must know him. But I do not recollect him. Where does he live?'

"'He works by the day. When one wants him one leaves word with this one or that one.'

"'Ah! I thought so, a loafer and a vagabond—a good-for-nothing. Don't trust him, dearest.'

"From that time Putois had a character."

II

Messieurs Goubin and Jean Marteau having arrived, Monsieur Bergeret told them the subject of the conversation.

"We were speaking of him whom my mother brought into the world to be gardener at Saint-Omer and whom she christened. He existed from that time on."

"Dear master, will you kindly repeat that?" said Monsieur Goubin, wiping the glass of his monocle.

"Willingly," replied Monsieur Bergeret. "There was no gardener. The gardener did not exist. My mother said: 'I am waiting for the gardener.' At once the gardener was. He lived."

"Dear master," said Monsieur Goubin, "how could he live since he did not exist?"

" He had a sort of existence," replied Monsieur Bergeret.

" You mean an imaginary existence," Monsieur Goubin replied, disdainfully.

" Is it nothing then, but an imaginary existence? " exclaimed the master. " And have not mythical beings the power to influence men? Consider mythology, Monsieur Goubin, and you will perceive that they are not real beings but imaginary beings that exercise the most profound and lasting influence on the mind. Everywhere and always, beings who have no more reality than Putois have inspired nations with hatred and love, terror and hope, have advised crimes, received offerings, made laws and customs. Monsieur Goubin, think of the eternal mythology. Putois is a mythical personage, the most obscure, I grant you, and of the lowest order. The coarse satyr, who in olden times sat at the table with our peasants in the North, was considered worthy of appearing in a picture by Jordaens and a fable by La Fontaine. The hairy son of Sycorax appeared in the noble world of Shakespeare. Putois, less fortunate, will be always neglected by artists and poets. He lacks bigness and the unusual style and character. He was conceived by minds too reasonable, among people who knew how to read and write, and who had not that delightful imagination in which fables take root. I think, Messieurs, that I have said enough to show you the real nature of Putois."

" I understand it," said Monsieur Goubin.

And Monsieur Bergeret continued his discourse.

" Putois was. I can affirm it. He was. Consider it, gentlemen, and you will admit that a state of being by no means implies substance, and means only the bonds attributed to the subject, expresses only a relation."

" Undoubtedly," said Jean Marteau; " but a being without attributes is a being less than nothing. Some one once said, I do not remember who it was, ' I am, therefore he is.' Forgive my lapse of memory. One cannot remember everything. But the unknown who spoke in that fashion was very imprudent. In letting it be understood by this thoughtless observation that he was deprived of attributes and denied all relations, he proclaimed that he did not exist and thoughtlessly suppressed himself. I wager that no one has heard of him since."

" You have lost," answered Monsieur Bergeret. " He corrected the bad effect of these egotistical expressions by employing quantities of adjectives, and he is often spoken of, most often without judgment."

" I do not understand," said Monsieur Goubin.

" It is not necessary to understand," replied Jean Marteau. And he begged Monsieur Bergeret to speak of Putois.

" It is very kind of you to ask me," said the master. " Putois was born in the second half of the nineteenth century, at Saint-Omer. He would have been better off if he had been born some centuries before in the forest of Arden or in the forest of Brocéliande. He would then have been a remarkably clever evil spirit."

"A cup of tea, Monsieur Goubin?" said Pauline.

"Was Putois, then, an evil spirit?" said Jean Marteau.

"He was evil," replied Monsieur Bergeret; "he was evil, in a way, but not absolutely. It was true of him as with those devils that are called wicked, but in whom one discovers good qualities when one associates with them. And I am disposed to think that injustice has been done Putois. Madame Cornouiller, who warned us against him, and had suspected him of being a loafer, a drunkard, and a robber before she had seen him, reflected that since my mother, who was not rich, employed him, it was because he was satisfied with little, and asked herself if she would not do well to employ him instead of her gardener, who, if he had a better reputation, wanted more money. The time had come for trimming the yews. She thought that if Madame Eloi Bergeret, who was poor, did not pay Putois much, she herself, who was rich, would give him still less, for it is customary for the rich to pay less than the poor. And she already saw her yews trimmed in straight hedges, in balls and in pyramids, without her having to pay much. 'I will keep an eye open,' she said, 'to see that Putois does not loaf or rob me. I risk nothing, and it will be all profit. These vagabonds sometimes do better work than honest labourers.' She resolved to make a trial, and said to my mother: 'Dearest, send me Putois. I will set him to work at Montplaisir.' My mother would have done so willingly. But really it was impossible. Madame Cornouiller waited for Putois at Montplaisir, and waited in vain. She followed up her ideas and did not abandon her plans. When she saw my mother again, she complained of not having any news of Putois. 'Dearest, didn't you tell him that I was expecting him?'—'Yes! but he is strange, odd.'—'Oh, I know that kind. I know your Putois by heart. But there is no workman so crazy as to refuse to come to work at Montplaisir. My house is known, I think. Putois must obey my orders, and quickly, dearest. It will be sufficient to tell me where he lives; I will go and find him myself.' My mother answered that she did not know where Putois lived, that no one knew his house, that he was without hearth or home. 'I have not seen him again, Madame. I believe he is hiding.' What better could she say? Madame Cornouiller heard her distrustfully; she suspected her of misleading, of removing Putois from inquiry, for fear of losing him or making him ask more. And she thought her too selfish. Many judgments accepted by the world that history has sanctioned are as well founded as that."

"That is true," said Pauline.

"What is true?" asked Zoe, half asleep.

"That the judgments of history are often false. I remember, papa, that you said one day: 'Madame Roland was very ingenuous to appeal to the impartiality of posterity, and not perceive that, if her contemporaries were ill-natured monkeys, their posterity would be also composed of ill-natured monkeys.'"

"Pauline," said Mademoiselle Zoe severely, "what connection is there between the story of Putois and this that you are telling us?"

"A very great one, aunt."

"I do not grasp it."

Monsieur Bergeret, who did not dislike digressions, answered his daughter: "If all injustices were finally redressed in the world, one would never have imagined another for these adjustments. How do you expect posterity to pass righteous judgment on the dead? How question them in the shades to which they have taken flight? As soon as we are able to be just to them we forget them. But can one ever be just? And what is justice? Madame Cornouiller, at least, was finally obliged to recognise that my mother had not deceived her and that Putois was not to be found. However, she did not give up trying to find him. She asked all her relatives, friends, neighbours, servants, and tradesmen if they knew Putois. Only two or three answered that they had never heard of him. For the most part they believed they had seen him. 'I have heard that name,' said the cook, 'but I cannot recall his face.'—'Putois! I must know him,' said the street-sweeper, scratching his ear. 'But I cannot tell you who it is.' The most precise description came from Monsieur Blaise, receiver of taxes, who said that he had employed Putois to cut wood in his yard from the 19th to the 23rd of October, the year of the comet. One morning, Madame Cornouiller, out of breath, dropped into my father's office. 'I have seen Putois. Ah! I have seen him.'—'You believe it?'—'I am sure. He was passing close by Monsieur Tenchant's wall. Then he turned into the Rue des Abbesses, walking quickly. I lost him.'—'Was it really he?'—'Without a doubt. A man of fifty, thin, bent, the air of a vagabond, a dirty blouse.'—'It is true,' said my father, 'that this description could apply to Putois.'—'You see! Besides, I called him. I cried: "Putois!" and he turned around.'—'That is the method,' said my father, 'that they employ to assure themselves of the identity of evil-doers that they are hunting for.'—'I told you that it was he! I know how to find him, your Putois. Very well! He has a bad face. You had been very careless, you and your wife, to employ him. I understand physiognomy, and though I only saw his back, I could swear that he is a robber, and perhaps an assassin. The rims of his ears are flat, and that is a sign that never fails.'—'Ah! you noticed that the rims of his ears were flat? '—' Nothing escapes me. My dear Monsieur Bergeret, if you do not wish to be assassinated with your wife and your children, do not let Putois come into your house again. Take my advice; have all your locks changed.' Well, a few days afterward, it happened that Madame Cornouiller had three melons stolen from her vegetable garden. The robber not having been found, she suspected Putois. The gendarmes were called to Montplaisir, and their report confirmed the suspicions of Madame Cornouiller. Bands of marauders were ravaging the gardens of the countryside. But this time the robbery seemed to have been committed by one man, and with singular dexterity. No trace of anything broken, no footprints in the damp earth. The robber could be no one but Putois. That was the opinion of the corporal, who knew all about Putois, and had tried hard to put his hand on that bird. The *Journal of Saint-Omer* devoted an article to the three melons of Madame Cornouiller, and published a portrait of Putois from descriptions furnished by the town. 'He has,' said the paper, 'a low forehead, squinting eyes, a shifty glance, crow's-feet, sharp cheek-bones, red and shining. No rims to the ears. Thin, somewhat bent, feeble in appearance, in reality he is unusually strong. He easily bends a five-franc piece between the first finger and the thumb.' There were good reasons for attributing to him a long series of robberies committed with surprising dexterity. The whole town was talking of Putois. One day it was learned that he had been arrested and locked up in prison. But it was soon recognised that the man that had been taken for him was an almanac seller named Rigobert. As no charge could be brought against him, he was discharged after fourteen months of detention on suspicion. And Putois remained undiscoverable. Madame Cornouiller was the victim of another robbery, more audacious than the first. Three small silver spoons were taken from her sideboard. She recognised in this the hand of Putois, had a chain put on the door of her bedroom, and was unable to sleep. . . ."

About ten o'clock in the evening, Pauline having gone to her room, Mademoiselle Bergeret said to her brother: "Do not forget to relate how Putois betrayed Madame Cornouiller's cook."

"I was thinking of it, my sister," answered Monsieur Bergeret. "To omit it would be to lose the best of the story. But everything must be done in order. Putois was carefully searched for by the police, who could not find him. When it was known that he could not be found, each one considered it his duty to find him; the shrewd ones succeeded. And as there were many shrewd ones at Saint-Omer and in the suburbs, Putois was seen simultaneously in the streets, in the fields, and in the woods. Another trait was thus added to his character. He was accorded the gift of ubiquity, the attribute of many popular heroes. A being capable of leaping long distances in a moment, and suddenly showing himself at the place where he was least expected, was one of whom to be honestly afraid. Putois was the terror of Saint-Omer. Madame Cornouiller, convinced that Putois had stolen from her three melons and three little spoons, lived in a state of fear, barricaded at Montplaisir. Bolts, bars, and locks did not reassure her. Putois was for her a frightfully subtle being who could pass through doors. Trouble with her servants redoubled her fear. Her cook having been betrayed, the time came when she could no longer hide her misfortune. But she obstinately refused to name her betrayer."

"Her name was Gudule," said Mademoiselle Zoe.

"Her name was Gudule, and she believed that she was protected from danger by a long, forked beard that she wore on her chin. The sudden appearance of a beard protected the innocence of that holy daughter of the king whom Prague venerates. A beard, no longer youthful, did not suffice to protect the virtue of Gudule. Madame Cornouiller urged Gudule to tell her the man. Gudule burst into tears, but kept silent. Prayers and menaces had no effect. Madame Cornouiller made a long and circumstantial inquiry. She adroitly questioned her neighbours and tradespeople, the gardener, the street-sweeper, the gendarmes; nothing put her on the track of the culprit. She tried again to obtain from Gudule a complete confession. 'In your own interest, Gudule, tell me who it is.' Gudule remained mute. All at once a ray of light flashed through the mind of Madame Cornouiller: 'It is Putois!' The cook cried, but did not answer. 'It is Putois! Why did I not guess it sooner? It is Putois! Miserable! miserable! miserable!' and Madame Cornouiller remained convinced that it was Putois. Everybody at Saint-Omer, from the judge to the lamplighter's dog, knew Gudule and her basket. At the news that Putois had betrayed Gudule, the town was filled with surprise, wonder, and merriment. . . . With this reputation in the town and its environs he remained attached to our house by a thousand subtle ties. He passed before our door, and it was believed that he sometimes climbed the wall of our garden. He was never seen face to face. At any moment we would recognise his shadow, his voice, his footsteps. More than once we thought we saw his back in the twilight, at the corner of a road. To my sister and me he gradually changed in character. He remained mischievous and malevolent, but he became childlike and very ingenuous. He became less real and, I dare say, more poetical. He entered in the artless cycle of childish traditions. He became transformed into a Croquemitaine,[1] a Père Fouettard, or the sand man who closes the children's eyes when evening comes. He was the sprite that tied up the colts' tails at night in the stable. Less rustic and less charming, but equally and frankly roguish, he made

[1] The national "bugaboo" or "bogy-man."

ink moustaches on my sister's dolls. In bed, before going to sleep, we listened, and heard him cry on the roofs with the cats, howl with the dogs, fill the mill hopper with groans, and imitate the songs of belated drunkards in the streets. What made Putois ever-present and familiar to us, what interested us in him, was that the remembrance of him was associated with all the objects about us. Zoe's dolls, my school books, in which he had many times rumpled and besmeared the pages; the garden wall, over which we had seen his red eyes gleam in the shadow; the blue porcelain jar that he cracked one winter's night,—unless it was the frost; the trees, the streets, the benches—everything recalled Putois, the children's Putois, a local and mythical being. He did not equal in grace and poetry the dullest satyr, the stoutest fawn of Sicily or Thessaly. But he was still a demigod. He had quite a different character for our father; he was symbolical and philosophical. Our father had great compassion for men. He did not think them altogether rational; their mistakes, when they were not cruel, amused him and made him smile. The belief in Putois interested him as an epitome and a summary of all human beliefs. As he was ironical and a joker, he spoke of Putois as if he were a real being. He spoke with so much insistence sometimes, and detailed the circumstances with such exactness, that my mother was quite surprised and said to him in her open-hearted way: 'One would say that you spoke seriously, my friend: you know well, however——' He replied gravely: 'All Saint-Omer believes in the existence of Putois. Would I be a good citizen if I deny him? One should look twice before setting aside an article of common faith.' Only a perfectly honest soul has such scruples. At heart my father was a disciple of Gassendi.[1] He harmonised his own particular sentiment with the public sentiment, believing, like the countryside, in the existence of Putois, but not admitting his direct responsibility for the theft of the melons and the betrayal of the cook. Finally, while as a good citizen he professed faith in the existence of a Putois, he eliminated Putois from his explanations of the events that took place in the town. In this, as in everything else, he behaved as an honourable gentleman and a sensible man.

"As for our mother, she reproached herself somewhat for the birth of Putois, and not without reason. Because, after all, Putois was the child of our mother's invention, as Caliban was the poet's invention. Without doubt the faults were not equal, and my mother was more innocent than Shakespeare. However, she was frightened and confused to see her little falsehood grow inordinately, and her slight imposture achieve such a prodigious success, that, without stopping, it extended all over the town and threatened to extend over the world. One day she even turned pale, believing that she

[1] Gassendi (d. 1655), an exponent of Epicurus.

would see her falsehood rise up before her. That day, a servant she had, new to the house and the town, came to say to her that a man wished to see her. He wished to speak to Madame. 'What man is it?'—'A man in a blouse. He looks like a labourer.'—'Did he give his name?'—'Yes, Madame.'—'Well, what is his name?'—'Putois.'—'He told you that was his name?'—'Putois, yes, Madame.'—'He is here?'—'Yes, Madame. He is waiting in the kitchen.'—'You saw him?'—'Yes, Madame.'—'What does he want?'—'He did not say. He will only tell Madame.'—'Go ask him.'

"When the servant returned to the kitchen Putois was gone. This meeting of the new servant with Putois was never cleared up. But from that day I think my mother commenced to believe that Putois might well exist and that she had not told a falsehood after all."

IN THE REIGN OF TERROR

ANATOLE FRANCE

WHEN I entered, Pauline de Luzy gave me her hand. For a moment we remained silent. Her scarf and her straw hat lay carelessly on an arm-chair. On the spinet was open "The Prayer of Orpheus." Approaching the window, she looked at the sun sinking in a blood-red sky.

"Madame," I said to her at last, "do you remember what you said, two years ago this very day, at the foot of this hill? Do you remember how you raised your hands in prophecy and foretold these days of crime and terror? You stayed the words of love on my lips, and you said, 'Live and fight for justice and liberty!'"

Pauline de Luzy remained silent.

"Madame," I continued, "since your beloved hand pointed out the way, I have gone forward boldly. I have obeyed you, and done all I could by my writings and my speeches. For two years I have fought against the starveling agitators who seduce the populace by convulsive demonstrations of sham love, and the cowards who are ready to sacrifice everything to those likely to win power——"

She stopped me with a gesture and motioned to me to listen. We then heard, floating across the fragrant air of the garden, where the birds were singing, distant cries of death.

"To the gallows with the aristocrat! Get his head on a pike!"

Pale and motionless, she stood with her finger on her mouth.

"They are pursuing some unhappy man," I said. "Night and day these searches and arrests go on in Paris. Perhaps they are going to break in here. I must leave, or else I may compromise you. Although I am but little known in this part of the town, I am, as times go, a dangerous guest."

"No! Stay with me!" she said.

Again the shouts broke upon the quiet evening air. Mingled with the cries was the sound of marching feet and gun-shots.

The mob was coming nearer, and I could hear voices crying:

"Stop all the doors and gates so that the scoundrel cannot escape!"

Madame de Luzy seemed to grow calmer the nearer the danger approached.

"Let us go up to the next floor," she said. "We shall be able to see through the blinds what is going on outside."

But just as we opened the door we saw on the landing a man with a terrified face, his teeth chattering and his knees knocking against each other.

"Save me! Hide me!" he said in a stifled voice. "They are there. . . . They have forced open my gate and entered my garden. . . . They are coming. . . ."

Madame de Luzy saw it was Planchonnet, the old free-thinker, who lived in the neighbouring house.

"Did my cook see you come in?" she asked, in a low voice. "The woman belongs to the Terrorist party!"

"Nobody saw me."

"Thank God, my dear neighbour!" said Madame de Luzy.

She dragged him into her bedroom and I followed them. It was necessary to think of, it was necessary to find, a hiding-place in which she could shelter Planchonnet for some days, or at least for some hours, until those who were looking for him tired of their search. It was arranged I should keep a look-out, and that if I gave a warning our poor friend should at once leave by the side gate of the garden.

In the meantime he had not sufficient strength to stand upright. The man was broken and astounded. He tried to tell us that he, the enemy of all priests and kings, was now charged with having conspired against the Republican Constitution. It was a monstrous calumny. The truth was that Lubin had pursued him out of sheer hatred; Lubin, who had been his butcher, whom he had wished a hundred times to whip for selling meat under weight, and who was now the political chief of the district in which he used to keep a stall.

While murmuring the name of his enemy in a strangled voice, he thought he saw Lubin himself and hid his face in his hands. As a matter of fact some one could be heard coming up the stairs. Madame de Luzy bolted the door, and pushed the old man behind a screen. Some one knocked outside and asked to be let in. Pauline recognised the voice. It was her cook. The woman cried out that the municipal officers were at the gate with the National Guard, and wished to make a search of the house.

"They say," added the woman, "Planchonnet has fled here. I know he hasn't, and that you would not protect such a scoundrel. Yet they won't believe me."

"Very well, let them come in!" cried Madame de Luzy through the door. "Let them search the whole house from cellar to attic."

While this talk was going on, poor Planchonnet fainted behind the screen, where I had some trouble in reviving him by throwing water on his head.

"Depend on me, my friend," said Pauline to him very quietly, when he came to. "Remember that women are very resourceful."

And then, quite quietly, as though she were busy with some domestic, daily task, she drew her bed out a little from the alcove, and removed the bedclothes, and with my help arranged the three mattresses in such a way as to leave a space between the highest and the lowest, on the side against the wall.

As she was making these arrangements, a loud noise of boots and wooden shoes and musket butts and raucous voices broke out on the staircase. It was a terrible minute for the three of us. But the noise ascended little by little above our heads, and we understood that the National Guard, led by the revolutionary cook, had gone first to explore the attics. The ceiling cracked beneath their feet, and we could hear their threats, their kicks and bayonet thrusts against the partitions.

We breathed again; but there was not a moment to lose. I helped Planchonnet to slip in the space between the mattresses. But Madame de Luzy shook her head when it was done; for the bed thus upset, looked a very suspicious object.

"I must get in," she said.

She looked at the clock: it was only seven in the evening. She saw that it would not seem natural for her to be in bed so early. As for pretending she was ill, it could not be thought of: her cook would at once see through that trick.

So for some moments she remained sunk in thought. Then quietly, simply, with an august candour, she undressed before me and got into bed, and told me to take off my boots, my coat, and my cravat.

"You will have to be my lover and let them surprise us. When they come down, you will not have had the time to dress properly. You must open the door in your shirt sleeves, with your hair all disordered."

Just as our arrangements were complete, the troops clattered down from the attic, swearing and storming. The unhappy Planchonnet was seized with such a fit of trembling that he quite shook the bed. Moreover his breath so rattled in his throat, like that of a dying man, that they must have heard on the landing the sounds he made.

"It is a pity!" murmured Madame de Luzy. "I was so content with my little artifice. Still don't let us despair, and may God help us!"

A rough fist shook the door.

"Who is there?" asked Pauline.

"The representatives of the nation."

"Can't you wait just a minute?"

"Open the door or we will break in!"

"Go and unbolt it, my dear."

Suddenly, by a sort of miracle, Planchonnet stopped trembling and imitating the death rattle.

Lubin, the erstwhile butcher, was the first to enter, wearing his scarf and followed by a dozen pikemen. He stared alternately at Madame de Luzy and me.

"Pest!" he cried. "We have disturbed a pair of lovers! Excuse us, my dear!"

Then, turning towards the guards:

"You see how the aristocrats spend their time! Only the republicans have any regard for morality!"

But in spite of his virtuous attitude, the unexpected scene put him in good humour. Sitting on the bed, he took hold of the chin of my beautiful companion.

"Still," he said, "these lovely lips were not made merely to mumble prayers all day and night. That would be a shame. But the Republic before everything! We are searching for the traitor Planchonnet. He is here, I am sure of it. I must find him and guillotine him. It will make me!"

"Search the room if you like," said Madame de Luzy.

They looked under the furniture and in the wardrobes and chests, they stuck their pikes under the bed, and even probed the mattresses with their bayonets.

Lubin scratched his ear and looked at me from the corner of his eye. Madame de Luzy, fearing that I might be asked some awkward question, said:

"My dear, you know the house as well as I do! Take the keys and show Monsieur Lubin over the whole of it. Yes, show Monsieur the whole of it."

I led them down to the cellars, where they tumbled over the firewood and drank a pretty large number of bottles of wine.

After that, Lubin broke open, with the butt end of a musket, the full wine barrels, and, leaving the cellar flooded with wine, gave the order to depart. I went with them as far as the gate; then running back told Madame de Luzy that we were saved.

At the news, she bent her head over the space between the bed and the wall, and called:

" Monsieur Planchonnet! Monsieur Planchonnet! "

A feeble sigh answered her.

" Thank God! " she cried. " Monsieur Planchonnet, you gave me a terrible fright. I thought you were dead! "

Then turning to me:

" My poor friend, you who had such pleasure in telling me, from time to time, that you loved me—you will not tell me so any longer, will you? "

SPRINGTIME IN THE YEAR TWO

ANATOLE FRANCE

I

THE door-keeper shut the gate of the jail on the former Countess Fanny d'Avenay, " apprehended as a measure of public surety," as was written in the prison register, and in reality for giving shelter to some proscribed royalists. So there she was in the old building where, in bygone days, the recluses of Port Royal enjoyed their solitude in common; the revolutionaries had been able to turn it into a prison without changing anything.

Sitting on a bench while the recorder wrote down her name, she thought:

" Why do you let these things go on, O God, and what do you ask of me? "

The warder looked more surly than evil-hearted, and his daughter, a pretty girl, wore in a delightful way the white cap, with a cockade and a tricolour bow. The man led Fanny into a large courtyard, in the centre of which was a fine acacia. There she waited while a bed and a table were prepared for her in a room where five or six other women prisoners were already crowded. For the house was overfull. In vain it emptied every day its overflow into the revolutionary tribunal and into the guillotine. Every day the committees filled it afresh.

In the courtyard Fanny saw a young woman cutting some

letters on the bark of the tree, and recognised Antoinette d'Auriac, her friend from childhood.

"You here, Antoinette?"

"You here, Fanny? Get them to put your bed next to mine. We shall have much to talk about."

"Yes, many things . . . and Monsieur d'Auriac, Antoinette?"

"My husband? Faith, my darling, I had rather forgotten him. It was wrong of me. He has always been perfect in his treatment of me. I think he is in prison somewhere at this moment."

"And what are you doing there, Antoinette?"

"Hush! . . . What is the time? If it is five o'clock, the friend whose name I am uniting to mine on this tree is no longer alive. For he went at twelve to the revolutionary tribunal. He was named Gesrin, and was a volunteer in the army of the North. I got to know him in this prison. We have passed some pleasant hours together at the foot of this acacia. He was a young man of merit. . . . But I must see about your room, my dear."

And seizing Fanny by the waist she hurried her into the room where her own bed was, and induced the warder to leave the two friends together. They agreed to scrub the window down the next morning.

The evening meal, poorly prepared by a patriotic but wretched cook, was taken in common. Each prisoner brought a plate and a wooden fork and spoon (metal articles were forbidden) and received a portion of pork and cabbage. At this coarse repast Fanny saw women whose gaiety astonished her. Like Madame d'Auriac they had dressed their hair very carefully, and put on gay clothes. Overshadowed by death, they still took life pleasantly. Their conversation turned on matters of gallantry, and Fanny was soon acquainted with the intrigues that were woven and unwoven in the sombre prison courtyard, where love was goaded on by death. Then, possessed by an ineffable agitation, she felt a great longing to press some one's hand in her own.

She remembered the man who loved her and to whom she had not yielded, and a regret as cruel as remorse pierced her heart. Tears, ardent as passion, rolled down her cheeks. By the light of the smoky lamp that illumined the table, she saw her companions with eyes feverishly bright, and she thought:

"We are all going to die together. How comes it that I am sad and troubled at heart, and these women take life and death equally gaily?"

And she wept all night on her pallet.

II

Twenty long monotonous days passed heavily by. The courtyard, where lovers came in search of silence and shadow, was deserted in the evening. Fanny, who stifled in the humid air of the corridors, came out and sat on the grassy mound encircling the trunk of the old acacia tree that shaded all the courtyard. The acacia was in flower, and the breeze that caressed it came away sweet with fragrance. Fanny saw a paper nailed to the bark of the tree, below the letters cut by Antoinette. On the paper was written some verses by the poet Vigée, who was also one of the prisoners:

Here some hearts, exempt from hate,
Docile victims of dark fate,
Thanks to this protecting tree,
Forgot in love our misery.

Ye who live in sunnier hours,
Protect this tree of fragrant flowers!
Our griefs it soothed, our fears allayed:
And we were happy in its shade.

Having read these verses, Fanny remained full of thought. She looked back on her quiet, sweet girlhood, her loveless marriage, when her mind, entertained by music and poetry, was occupied only by a serious, passionless friendship. Then came the gallant gentleman who had enveloped her with his love without winning her, and for whom she now longed in the silence of the prison. And thinking she was going to die, a deep distress overcame her, and a sweat of agony broke out on her temples. In her anguish she raised her ardent eyes to the heaven full of stars, and murmured, while twisting her hands:

"My God! My God! Do not let me give way to despair!"

At this moment a light footstep came her way. It was Rosine, the daughter of the warder, who wanted to speak to her secretly.

"Citizeness," said the pretty girl to her, "to-morrow evening a man who loves you will be waiting for you, with a carriage, in the Avenue de l'Observatoire. Take this parcel, it contains some clothes like those I wear. You can put them on in your room at supper-time. You are about my height, and fair-haired like myself. In the darkness we might be taken one for the other. A jailer, who is my sweetheart and also engaged in the plot, will come to your room and bring you the basket with which I go marketing.

"You must go down with him by the staircase leading to my father's rooms. He will have the key to the staircase, and the door of our place is neither locked nor guarded. All you have to do is to avoid being seen by my father. My young man will lean with his back against a window and talk to you, as if he were talking to me. He will say, 'Don't be long, Rosine, and don't be naughty!' You must go quietly out into the street. Meanwhile, I will leave by the main gate, and we shall join each other in the cab that will drive off with us."

Listening to these words Fanny drew in a breath of springtime and the open fields. With all the force of her body, brimming over with life, she aspired to freedom. She saw and relished in advance her deliverance from death. And as the idea of love was mingled with the foretaste of an escape to a place of safety, she pressed her two hands over her heart to restrain her wild feelings of happiness. But little by little her high power of reflection dominated her emotions. Looking very attentively at the warder's daughter, she said to her:

"My lovely child! For what reason have you devoted yourself in this way to me? You do not know me!"

"Your friend," replied Rosine, "will give me a great deal of money when you are set free, and then I will marry my young man, Florentin. You see, I am working for myself. But I am more willing to save you than to save any other prisoner."

"I thank you for your kindness, my child, but why are you interested in me?"

"Because you are such a darling, and your friend is very sorrowful at being separated from you. Now, it is all agreed on, isn't it?"

Fanny stretched out her hand to take the parcel of clothes that Rosine offered her. But, suddenly drawing back her hand:

"Rosine, do you know it would be death for you if we were found out?"

"Death!" cried the young girl. "You make me afraid. Oh, no! I did not know that!" Then, quickly recovering her courage, "Citizeness, your friend will be able to find a hiding-place for me!"

"There is no certain hiding-place in Paris. Rosine, I thank you for your devotion to me, but I cannot accept it."

Rosine stood stupefied.

"You will be guillotined, Citizeness, and I shall not be able to marry Florentin!"

"Yes, you will, Rosine. I can help you there, without accepting your offer."

"Oh, no! It would be stolen money!"

The girl begged and wept and implored for some minutes. She knelt down and clutched at the hem of Fanny's dress.

Fanny pushed her off with her hand and turned her head away. A ray of moonlight illumined her calm, lovely face.

The night was charming; there was a light wind. The prisoners' tree, shaking its odorous boughs, scattered down pale flowers on the head of the voluntary victim.

THE JUGGLER OF NOTRE DAME

ANATOLE FRANCE

I

IN the time of King Louis there lived in France a poor juggler, native of Compiègne, named Barnabas, who went through the cities making tricks of strength and skill. On market days he extended on the public square an old carpet, all worn out, and, after having attracted the children and idlers by pleasing phrases, which he had learned from an old juggler and of which he never changed anything, he assumed attitudes which were not natural, and he placed a pewter plate on his nose and balanced it there. The crowd looked at him at first with indifference.

But when, with hands and head on the ground, he threw in the air and caught with his feet six copper balls which shone in the sun, or when, throwing himself backward till his neck touched his heels, he gave to his body the form of a perfect wheel, and juggled, in that posture, with twelve knives, a murmur of admiration rose from the spectators, and pieces of money rained on the carpet.

Nevertheless, like most of those who live off their talents, Barnabas of Compiègne had a great deal of trouble to live.

Earning his bread by the sweat of his brow, he carried more than his share of the miseries attached to the sin of Adam, our father.

Moreover, he could not work as much as he wished. To display his fine learning, as for the trees to give flowers and fruits, he needed the warmth of the sun and the light of day. In winter he was only a tree despoiled of its leaves and almost dead. The frozen earth was hard for the juggler. And, like the cicada whereof Marie of France writes, he suffered from cold and hunger in the bad season. But, as his heart was simple, he suffered his ills in patience.

He had never reflected on the origin of riches nor on the inequality of human conditions. He believed firmly that, if this world is bad, the other world cannot fail to be good, and this hope supported him. He did not imitate the miscreants who had sold their souls to the devil. He never took the name of God in vain; he lived honestly, and, although he had no wife, he did not covet his neighbour's; for woman is the enemy of strong men, as appears by the history of Samson which is related in the Scriptures.

In truth, his mind was not inclined toward material desires, and it would have cost him more to renounce mugs than women. For, although he never failed in sobriety, he liked to drink when it was warm. He was a good man, fearing God and very devout to the Holy Virgin.

He never failed, when he went into a church, to kneel before the image of the Mother of God and to address to her this prayer:

" Madame, take care of my life until it may please God that I shall die, and when I die let me have the joys of paradise."

II

One night, after a day of rain, while he was walking, sad and bent, carrying under his arm his balls and his knives hidden in his old carpet, and seeking for a barn where he might go to bed, without supper, he saw on the road a monk who was going the same way, and bowed to him courteously. As they were walking together they exchanged ideas.

" Friend," said the monk, " how is it that you are dressed in green? Is it to play the personage of a clown in some mystery-play? "

" No, father," replied Barnabas, " such as I am, I am Barnabas, and my profession is that of a juggler. It would be the most beautiful profession in the world if in it one could eat every day."

" Friend Barnabas," said the monk, " be careful what you are saying. There is no more beautiful profession than the monastic one. In it are celebrated the praise of God, of the Virgin, and the saints, and the life of the monk is a perpetual canticle to the Lord."

Barnabas replied:

" Father, I confess that I have talked like an ignorant man. Your profession may not be compared with mine, and, although there is some merit in dancing while holding a coin balanced on a stick on one's nose, this merit does not reach the height of yours. I would like to sing every day like you, father, the office of the Holy Virgin, for whom I have a special devotion. I would willingly abandon the art in which I am known from Soissons to Beauvais, in more than six hundred cities and villages, in order to embrace the monastic life."

The monk was moved by the juggler's simplicity, and, as he was not lacking in discernment, he recognised in Barnabas one of the men of good-will whereof our Lord has said: " Let peace be with them on earth." That is why he replied:

" Friend Barnabas, come with me, and I will make you enter the convent whereof I am the prior. The one who led Mary the Egyptian in the desert placed me on your path to lead you in the way of salvation."

It is thus that Barnabas became a monk. In the convent where he was received, the religious were devoted to the worship of the Holy Virgin, and each one used in her service all the learning and all the skill that God had given to him.

The prior, for his part, composed books which treated, in accordance with the rules of scholasticism, of the virtues of the Mother of God.

Friar Maurice copied with a learned hand these treatises on leaves of vellum.

Friar Alexander painted fine miniatures. One could see in them the Queen of Heaven, seated on the throne of Solomon, with four lions watching at the foot. Around her head, which has a halo, are seven doves, which are the seven gifts of the Holy Ghost: gifts of fear, of piety, of science, of force, of advice, of intelligence, and of wisdom. She had as companions six virgins with golden hair: Humility, Prudence, Retirement, Respect, Virginity, and Obedience.

At her feet two small nude and white figures stood in respectful attitude. They were souls that implored for their salvation and, certainly not in vain, her all-powerful intercession.

Friar Alexander represented on another page Eve with eyes toward Mary, so that one might see at the same time the sin and the redemption, the humiliated woman and the exalted Virgin. One could admire, moreover, in this book the Well of Living Waters, the Fountain, the Lily, the Moon, the Sun, and the Garden sung in the canticle, the Door of Heaven, and the City of God, and these were images of the Virgin.

Friar Marbode was, similarly, one of the most tender children of Mary.

He carved stone images incessantly, so that his beard, his eyebrows, and his hair were white with dust, and his eyes were perpetually swollen and tearful; but he was full of strength and of joy in his old age, and, visibly, the Queen of Paradise protected the declining years of her child. Marbode represented her seated in a pulpit, with a nimbus around her forehead, the orb of which was in pearls. And he was careful that the folds of her gown should cover the feet of the one whereof the prophet has said: "My beloved is like a closed garden."

At times, also, he represented her with the features of a child full of grace, and she seemed to say, " Lord, thou art my Lord! "

There were also in the convent poets who composed Latin hymns in honour of the Virgin Mary, and there was even a Picardian who related the miracles of Our Lady both in prose and in rhyme.

III

Seeing such a competition in praises and such a beautiful harvest of work, Barnabas lamented his ignorance and his simplicity.

"Alas!" he sighed, while he walked alone in the small garden of the convent, "I am very unfortunate not to be able, like my brothers, to praise worthily the Holy Mother of God, to whom I have devoted the tenderness of my heart. Alas! alas! I am a rough and artless man, and I have at my service, Madame the Virgin, neither edifying sermons nor treatises well divided according to the rules, nor fine paintings, nor statues correctly sculptured, nor verses in stately measure. I have nothing, alas!"

He moaned in this manner and yielded to sadness. One night when the monks were conversing, he heard one of them relate the history of a religious who could recite nothing but the Ave Maria. This monk was disdained for his ignorance: but when he died five roses came out of his mouth in honour of the five letters of the name of Maria, and thus his sanctity was manifested.

While he listened to this tale, Barnabas admired once more the kindness of the Virgin; but he was not consoled by the example of that death; for his heart was full of zeal, and he wished to serve the glory of his Heavenly Queen.

He sought for the means of doing this without being able to find them, and his affliction increased day by day; but one morning he awoke joyfully, ran to the chapel, and stayed there alone for more than an hour. He returned after dinner.

And from this moment he went every day to that chapel, at the hour when it was deserted, and passed there a great part of the time the other monks consecrated to the liberal and mechanical arts. He was no longer sad and he no longer complained.

A behaviour so singular excited the curiosity of the monks.

They asked themselves in the community why Friar Barnabas made retreats so frequently.

The prior, whose duty it is to ignore nothing of the behaviour of the religious, decided to watch Barnabas in his solitude. One day when he was closeted in the chapel, Father Prior came, accompanied by two elders of the convent, and observed through cracks in the door the things that were happening in the interior.

They saw Barnabas, before the altar of the Holy Virgin, head downward, his feet in the air, juggling with six copper balls and twelve knives. He was doing, in honour of the Holy Mother of God, those professional feats which had provoked the most applause. Not comprehending that this simple man thus placed his talent and his learning at the service of the Holy Virgin, the two elders cried that it was a sacrilege.

The prior knew that Barnabas's mind was innocent, but thought that he had fallen into insanity. They were preparing to drag him out of the chapel as quickly as they could, when they saw the Holy Virgin descend the stairs of the altar in order to wipe with a fold of her blue mantle the perspiration which fell from the juggler's forehead.

Then the prior, kneeling with his face against the marble slabs, recited these words:

" Blessed are the pure in heart: for they shall see God."

" Amen," replied the elders, kissing the earth.

CHRIST OF THE OCEAN

Anatole France

In that year several men of Saint-Valery, who had gone to the fishing-grounds, were drowned at sea. Their bodies were cast up on the shore with the wreck of their boats; and for nine days men carried the coffins on their shoulders up the hilly path to the church, followed by widows, weeping under their great black hoods, like the women of the Bible.

The skipper, Jean Lenoel, and his son, Désiré, were thus deposited in the great nave, under the vault from which there hung a full-rigged ship which they had presented as an offering to Our Lady. They were just men who feared God. And Father Truphème, vicar of Saint-Valery, after giving absolution, said in a voice trembling with tears:

" Never was there placed in holy ground, to wait the judgment of God, worthier men and better Christians than Jean Lenoel and his son Désiré."

And, while the fishing-boats and their masters foundered along the coast, great ships went down farther out at sea. Not a day passed without the waves throwing up some piece of wreckage. One morning, some children, who were working a boat along, saw a figure lying on the waves. It was an image of Christ, life size, carved out of hard wood, and painted in natural colours, and looking like an ancient work. It floated on the water with outstretched arms. The children dragged it on board, and took it to Saint-Valery. The head of the image was circled with a crown of thorns: the feet and the hands were pierced. But the nails were missing, together with the cross. With His arms still open in benediction and self-sacrifice, Christ appeared just as Joseph of Arimathea and the holy women had seen Him, when they were preparing the shroud and the tomb. The children gave the statue to Father Truphème, who said to them:

"This image of the Saviour is an ancient work, and the man who made it is, no doubt, long since dead. Although the merchants of Amiens and Paris now sell admirable statues for a hundred francs, or even more than that, we must recognise that the carvers of ancient times were also skilful. But I rejoice especially over the thought that, if Jesus has thus come with open arms to Saint-Valery, it is to bless our parish that has suffered so cruelly, and to announce that He takes pity on the poor people who go out to fish at the peril of their lives. He is the God who walked on the waters, and blessed the fishing-nets of Cephas."

And the vicar, having placed Christ in the church, on the altar cloth of the high altar, went to carpenter Lemerre and ordered a fine cross of heart of oak. When it was made, they attached God to it with bright new nails, and hung Him in the nave above the churchwardens' pew. It was then seen that His eyes were full of mercy, and as though moist with heavenly pity. One of the churchwardens, who helped to fix the crucifix, thought he saw tears running down the Divine face. The next morning, when the vicar entered the church with a choir-boy to say his mass, he was much surprised to find an empty cross above the church-wardens' pew, and the image of Christ lying on the altar.

As soon as he had celebrated the holy sacrifice, he had the carpenter brought before him, and asked him why he had taken the image down from the cross. But the carpenter replied that he had not touched it, and having questioned the beadle and the church-wardens, Father Truphème was certain that nobody had entered the church after the crucifix had been placed above the pew.

He then had the feeling that a marvellous thing had happened, and he thought on it with a prudent mind. The following Sunday he spoke about the matter in his sermon, and invited his parishioners to contribute by their gifts to the erection of a new cross, finer than the first, and more worthy of bearing the Saviour of the world.

The poor fishermen of Saint-Valery gave as much money as they could, and the widows brought their wedding-rings. Father Truphème was able to go straightway to Abbeville and order a cross of gleaming black wood, surmounted by a scroll with the inscription I.N.R.I. in letters of gold. Two months later it was fixed in the place of the first cross, and the figure of Christ was attached to it, between the lance and the sponge.

But Jesus left the cross as He had the other, and came down in the night, and stretched Himself out on the altar.

When the vicar found Him again there in the morning, he fell on his knees and prayed for a long time. The news of the miracle spread far around, and the ladies of Amiens made collections for the Christ of Saint-Valery. From Paris, Father Truphème received money and jewels, and the wife of the Minister of the Marine, Madame Hyde de Neuville, sent him a heart of diamonds. By using all the golden gems, a goldsmith of Rue Saint-Sulpice composed, in two years, a cross of gold and precious stones, which was set up with great pomp in the church of Saint-Valery, the second Sunday after Easter. . . . But He who had not refused the cross of sorrow rejected this cross of wealth, and was again found stretched out on the white linen of the high altar.

For fear of offending Him, He was let be this time, and He reposed on the altar for more than two years. Then Pierre, the son of Pierre Caillou, came and said to Father Truphème that he had found on the shore the true cross of Our Lord.

Pierre was an imbecile, and as he had not enough sense to earn his livelihood, he lived on the bread given to him in charity. He was liked because he never did any harm. But he talked in a mad fashion, and nobody listened to him.

But Father Truphème, who had not ceased to meditate on the mystery of the Christ of the Ocean, was struck by what the poor fool said. He went with the beadle and two churchwardens to the spot where the lad said he had seen a cross, and there he found two planks, nailed together and rolled about by the sea, that truly formed a cross.

It was a piece of wreckage. They could still trace on one of the planks two letters in black paint, a J and an L. There was no doubt it was the remains of the boat of Jean Lenoel who, five years before, had been drowned with his son Désiré.

At this sight the beadle and churchwardens began to laugh at the poor idiot who had taken the broken timbers of the boat for the cross of Jesus Christ. But Father Truphème stopped their jeers. He had meditated much and said many prayers since Christ of the Ocean came among the fishermen, and the mystery of infinite charity began to grow clearer to him. Kneeling on the sand, he said the prayer for the dead, and then ordered the beadle and the churchwardens to take the piece of wreckage on their shoulders and carry it to the church. When this was done, he lifted Christ from the altar, placed Him on the planks of the boat, and nailed Him there himself, with the nails that the sea had worn and rusted. By his order this cross was placed the next day above the pew, instead of the cross of gold and jewels. Christ of the Ocean has never stirred from His new crucifix. He has willingly remained on this wood, where men have died calling on His name and on the name of His Mother. And there, half opening His august and sorrowful mouth, He seems to say: "My cross is made of all the sufferings of men, for I am verily the God of the poor and the unhappy."

A GIFT OF DEATH

ANATOLE FRANCE

AFTER wandering for some time in the empty streets, André came and sat down by the bank of the Seine, and watched the water whitening against the hill where Lucie, his beloved, had lived in the days of joy and hope.

For a long time he had not been so calm. At eight o'clock he had a bath. Then he entered an eating-house at the Palais Royal, and, while waiting for his meal, looked at the public journals. He read in the *Courrier de l'Égalité* the list of condemned persons executed on the Place de la Révolution on the twenty-fourth Floréal.

He breakfasted with a good appetite. Then he rose and looked in a mirror, to see if his dress was in order, and if he had an easy air, and walked with a light step beyond the river, to a small house forming the corner of Seine and Mazarine Streets. There lived Citizen Lardillon, Deputy Public Accuser at the Revolutionary Tribunal, an obliging man whom André had known as a Capuchin friar at Angers, and as a violent Republican at Paris.

He rang. After some minutes of silence, a face appeared behind the grating of a peep-hole, and Citizen Lardillon, having prudently ascertained the name and bearing of his visitor, at last opened the door. He had a fat face, high in colour, brilliant eyes, a moist mouth and red ears. His appearance was that of a jovial but timorous man. He led André into the first room of his house.

On a little round table a meal was laid for two. André remarked a chicken, a pie, a ham, a pot of *foie gras,* and a galantine of cold meats. On the floor six wine bottles were cooling in a bucket. A pine-apple, cheeses and preserved fruits covered the mantelpiece. Flasks of liqueur were placed on a desk encumbered with bundles of papers. Through the half-open door of the neighbouring room an unmade bed could be seen.

"Citizen Lardillon," said André, "I have come to ask a favour of you."

"Citizen, I am ready to grant it, if it is not at the expense of the safety of the Republic."

" The service I ask of you," said André with a smile, " accords perfectly well with the security of the Republic, and with your own."

At a sign from Lardillon, André sat down. " Citizen Deputy," he said, " you know that for two years I have been conspiring against your friends, and that I am the author of a writing entitled *The Altars of Fear.* You will not do me any favour by having me arrested. You will only do your duty. So that is not the favour I ask of you. But listen to me: I am in love, and my sweetheart is in prison."

Lardillon bent his head to show he approved this sentiment.

" I know you are a man of feeling, Citizen Lardillon, and I beg you to unite me to her whom I love, and to send me at once to Port Libre."

" Ha! ha! " said Lardillon, with a smile on his lips that was both subtle and firm. " It is more than life you ask of me, Citizen: it is happiness! " Stretching out his arm on the side of the bedroom, he cried: " Epicharis! Epicharis! "

A tall dark-haired woman appeared, arms and neck bare, in a chemise and a petticoat, a cockade on her head.

" My nymph," said Lardillon to her, drawing her on his knee, " look at the face of this citizen, and never forget it. Like us, Epicharis, he has fine feelings; like us, he knows that separation is the greatest of all evils. He wishes to go to prison and to the guillotine with his sweetheart. Epicharis, can we refuse him this favour? "

" No," said the girl, tapping the cheeks of the Revolutionary monk.

" You have said it, my goddess. We must help these two true lovers. Citizen André Germain, give me your address, and you shall sleep to-night in prison."

" That is agreed on," said André.

" That is agreed on," replied Lardillon, giving him his hand. " Go and find again your sweetheart, and tell her that you have seen Epicharis in the arms of Lardillon. May this picture give birth in your hearts to radiant thoughts! "

André answered that perhaps they might find images more touching, but that he was none the less grateful, and regretted he could not hope to render him any service in turn.

" Humanity does not need any reward," said Lardillon. He rose, and pressing Epicharis against his heart, added, " Who knows when our turn will come? Meanwhile, let us drink! Citizen, will you share our meal? "

Epicharis said this would be gallant, and held André by the arm. But he slipped away, bearing the promise of the Deputy of the Public Accuser.

OCTAVE MIRBEAU
B. 1850

THE DEATH OF "TURC"

I

HIS master had called him Turc. He was miserably thin, yellow, sharp-nosed, with short, badly-formed ears—always bleeding, and a tail which stood mangy and erect in the form of a note of interrogation.

In summer-time Turc went into the fields, guarded the cows, and barked at the carriages and pedestrians passing along the highway, invariably receiving in return for his interest sundry hard kicks and stones.

His great pleasure was to chase a hare in a field of young clover, through hedges, fences, over brooks and furrows, to follow it in enormous bounds and eccentric gambols, which rendered him breathless and panting, the tongue lolling out of his mouth, running with perspiration.

In winter when the flocks and herds remained in the sheds, languid in their warm litter, Turc rested in a wretched broken barrel, at the end of which he slept the whole day through, curled up in a ball, or drawn out comfortably at full length.

His food consisted of a pittance of stale scraps and dirty water, which were brought to him each morning in a chipped sandstone dish; and whenever any one whom he did not recognise penetrated the farmyard, he sprang with one leap the length of his chain, displaying his fangs and growling fiercely.

Turc sometimes accompanied his master to market or fairs, when there was a calf to sell, a pig to buy, or other business to transact in the taverns of the town. He was ever resigned, faithful, unhappy, as is the nature of dogs.

II

One night, rather late, returning from one of these distant fairs, Turc missed his owner, who had entered a village cabaret. While the latter drank several little glasses of brandy, the dog roamed about in the neighbourhood, scratching with avidity among the rubbish in the hope of finding a bone, or some such delicacy.

Re-entering the tavern, somewhat ashamed of his escapade, and fully expecting to be cuffed, he found only two half-intoxicated peasants, quite unknown to him, who chased him away.

The village was planned in the form of a square, and Turc found himself at a point where six main roads converged. The poor animal was bewildered. He pricked up his ears to catch the sound of a familiar step, and sniffed at the ground to discover the still warm odour of a track. Uttering two little sighs, the dog departed hurriedly, but soon stopped short, uncertain and nervous. Proceeding now warily, nose to the ground, a few yards along a bypath which diverted from the main road, Turc climbed a bank, and once more scenting the drunken peasants, who were lying full length near the ditch, he turned again, still searching each cluster of trees, each tuft of furze, for trace of his master.

The night advanced. To the right and left of the route the fields were wrapped in violet shadows. As the moon rose in the cloudless heavens, Turc, seated on his hind legs, his neck and head strained towards the astral globe, whined continuously for his lost owner.

A great silence reigned supreme.

Only the dogs of the neighbouring farms responded from the depths of the night to the howls of the unhappy animal.

The moon, magic and radiant, rose higher and higher, and the dog's shadow lengthened on the whitened highway.

III

M. Bernard, the notary, ventured out at break of day, intent upon his customary walk. He was clothed entirely in black cashmere, as became a man of his profession, but as it was the height of summer, his sombre costume was relieved by a parasol of white alpaca. Every one in the little town was still abed. Only a few cafés had opened their doors, and some workmen shouldering their picks trudged lazily to their labour.

"Always early, M. Bernard," said one of them, respectfully saluting the notary.

M. Bernard was about to reply—for he was in no way proud—when he espied, at the end of the road, a dog, so yellow, so thin, so dirty, and apparently so fatigued, that the notary instinctively took refuge behind a plane-tree. The dog was Turc. Poor lamentable Turc.

"Oh! oh!" said M. Bernard. "Here is a creature that I have never seen before. Oh! oh!"

In such small towns one knew by sight every dog, just as one knew every human being, and the appearance of a strange animal was an event as important, as troubling, as that of a new visitor.

The dog passed in front of the fountain situated in the centre of the street without stopping.

"Oh! oh!" cried M. Bernard. "Why doesn't the creature stop to drink. Oh! oh! The dog is mad, obviously mad."

Trembling with fear, he picked up a large stone. Turc advanced shyly, with lowered head.

"Oh! oh!" cried M. Bernard, becoming pale. "He is foaming at the mouth. Oh! oh! Help! help!"

And, from behind the plane-tree, he threw the stone, but failed to hit the dog. Turc contemplated the notary a moment with his docile expression and then fled.

IV

The little town was at once astir with this novel excitement—a mad dog. Faces, still swollen with sleep, appeared at the windows. Inhabitants in their sleeping apparel gathered quickly on their door-steps. Some of the more intrepid armed themselves with pitch-forks, stakes, spades, billhooks and rakes. The carpenter gesticulated with his jack-plane, the butcher with his carving-knife, the shoemaker, a man slightly hunchbacked, with an obscene laugh, a great reader of bloodthirsty fiction, proposed torture exquisite and refined.

"Where is he? Where is he?" The whole town put itself in a state of defence, and everybody became courageous. M. Bernard had awaked the mayor and informed him of the terrible news.

"He flew at me, M. le Maire, foaming at the mouth. He all but bit me," cried M. Bernard, feeling his thighs, his calves, his stomach. "Oh! oh! I have seen many mad dogs in my life, but never one more enraged, more terrible. Oh! oh!"

The mayor, very dignified, but also very perplexed, looked up and reflected.

"It is a serious matter, very serious," he murmured. "But are you sure the dog was as mad as all that?"

"As mad as all that!" replied M. Bernard, indignantly. "If you had seen him—if you had seen the foam, the staring eyes, the bristling hair. It was no longer a dog, but a tiger . . . a tiger." Then, solemnly, he looked the mayor full in the face and continued slowly:

"Look here! This is not a question of politics, M. le Maire. It is a question of the safety of the inhabitants, of the protection—of the safety, I repeat—of the townspeople. If you divest yourself of the responsibilities which are incumbent upon you, if you do not take immediate action, you will soon regret it, M. le Maire. I tell you—I, Bernard, notary."

Now M. Bernard was Leader of the Radical opposition and the

mayor's enemy, so the latter, without further delay, sent for the village guard. Turc, having taken refuge in a place where nobody dared approach him, was tranquilly gnawing a bone which he held between his forepaws.

The village guard, armed with a gun confided to him by the mayor, and followed by a numerous procession, advanced to within ten paces of the dog.

From the balcony of the Hôtel de Ville, the mayor, who assisted at the spectacle with M. Bernard, could not refrain from saying to the notary, " Nevertheless, he eats," in the same voice that Galileo might have used when he uttered his famous phrase.

" Yes, he eats . . . the horrible, cunning creature," replied M. Bernard, and, addressing the village guard, he commanded, " Be careful. Do not approach too near."

The moment was tense. The village guard, helmet over the ears, his shirt-sleeves turned up, his face animated with an expression of heroism, loaded the gun.

" Don't push," said a voice.

" Don't miss fire," said another.

" Take aim at the head. No, rather at the shoulder."

" Take care! " said the village guard, who, doubtless hindered by his headgear, threw it violently before him in the dust. " Look out."

He took careful aim at the dog. The unfortunate Turc had deserted his bone, and regarded the crowd with a gentle frightened expression, appearing to realise instinctively its sinister intentions.

A great silence succeeded the tumult. The women stopped their ears in order not to hear the detonation, the men blinked their eyes. The crowd jostled one another. Anxiety was rife among the villagers, expectant of something extraordinary and terrible.

The village guard still took aim.

There was a loud report. And simultaneously a wail, rending and prolonged, echoed through the town. The dog jumped with pain, and limped away on three paws, leaving as he ran a little track of blood.

And while Turc slunk off to die in agony, the village guard, ashamed, stupefied, examined his gun; the crowd, amazed, regarded the village guard; and the mayor, open-mouthed, contemplated M. Bernard, seized with horror and indignation.

JACQUES NORMAND
B. 1848

THE P.L.M. EXPRESS

THERE was a general astonishment in our little circle of friends when we heard of the approaching marriage of Valentin Sincère. What! he?—the hardened celibate! the Parisian sceptic, rebelling against all matrimonial ideas!—the joyous free-liver who had a hundred times sworn that he would never have anything to do with it. Valentin, after all, was going to join the great brotherhood! And, of all women, whom was he going to marry?—a widow! We were bewildered.

So, the first time I met him, I buttonholed him, and demanded explanations.

" I've hardly time to speak to you—a heap of things to do. I have just come from the Mairie, and am on my way to Stern's, the engraver in the Passage du Panoramas, to get some invitation letters. If you'll go with me——"

" *If* I'll go with you! " I said.

We were in front of the Madeleine. We passed down the boulevards, arm in arm.

" The story's a very simple one," he said. " Commonplace to the last degree; but, since you want so much to know about it, here it is:

" In the month of February last I was going to Nice for the Carnival fêtes. I have the greatest aversion to travelling by night, and I therefore took the 8.55 morning train, due at midnight at Marseilles, where I proposed spending the following day with my friends, the Rombauds, who expected me to breakfast. The next morning I was going on to Nice, where I was to arrive at two o'clock in the afternoon.

" At the station there was an excited crowd; but, thanks to the proverbial obligingness of M. Regnoul, the station-master, I was able to secure a place in the only *coupé* in the train. The only other occupant was a gentleman with a red rosette in a buttonhole of his overcoat—a gentleman of severe aspect, and with an administrative air, whose luggage consisted solely of a portfolio.

Assuredly he was not going far with *that* outfit, and presently I should be alone. Alone! the only thing to make a railway journey supportable!

" All the passengers were in their places, and the train was about starting, when the sound of a dispute arose at the door.

" ' No, Monsieur, no! ' said the voice of a woman, fresh in tone, and with an almost imperceptible Southern accent. ' I ordered a sleeping-compartment, and a sleeping-compartment I must have.'

" ' But, Madame, I have told you, we haven't one! '

" ' You ought to have carried out the instructions in my letter.'

" ' We have not received any letter, Madame! '

" ' Have another carriage put on, then.'

" ' Impossible!—we have already the regulation number. Come, come, make haste; the train is about to start.'

" ' Well, I must have a place found for me.'

" ' I have offered you two, Madame, in the *coupé*.'

" ' There? '

" ' Yes, Madame—there! '

" A little dark-haired woman appeared in the doorway, and instantly started back, as if in alarm.

" ' There are two gentlemen in it! '

" ' Good heavens, Madame! I can't give you a whole carriage to yourself! '

" ' Very well, then; I will not go! '

" ' As you please. The train is off—I am going to give the signal.'

" ' Stay, Monsieur; stay. I *must* absolutely go; and since there is only this *coupé*—but you'll let me have a sleeping-compartment at the first station we come to? '

" ' Yes, Madame.'

" ' You'll telegraph for it? '

" ' Yes, yes, Madame.'

" ' You promise me? '

" ' Yes, Madame.'

" ' You are sure? '

" ' Yes, yes, yes, Madame! '

" The door was thrown open wide, and the little brown-haired lady, surrounded by half a carriage-load of parcels and wraps, entered the *coupé*; a shrill whistle, and—we were off.

" Gallantly the administrative gentleman seated himself by my side, so as to leave the opposite seat entirely at the service of the new arrival.

" Without even turning her eyes towards us, flustered and red with anger, she arranged her parcels around her with the ordinary haste of persons who have long hours to pass in a railway carriage.

" She had one bag, two bags, three bags, and—as to wraps—!

" Out of the corner of my eyes I watched these little proceedings, and I observed with pleasure that she was a charming little personage. I say with pleasure; for, in truth, it is always more agreeable to have a pretty woman for a travelling companion than an ugly one.

" It was very cold. The country, covered with snow, and lit up by a very pale-faced sun, flew rapidly by on either side of the carriage. The little lady, muffled up to her chin in rugs and other wraps, turned her gaze obstinately out of the farther window; the administrative gentleman put his papers, yellow, green, and blue, with printed headings, in order, and read them attentively; as to myself, comfortably installed in a corner with my feet on the foot-warmer, I waded through the file of newspapers I had bought at the station to pass the time.

" 11.21; Laroche. The train stopped. The administrative gentleman gathered up his papers, rose, bowed, and descended from the carriage. His feet had hardly touched the platform before he was received by the station-master, who called him ' Mr. Inspector.' The lady leaned out of the door:

" ' Mr. Station-master! '

" ' Madame? '

" ' They were to telegraph to you from Paris for a sleeping-carriage.'

" ' They have done so, Madame, and I have sent on the message.'

" ' Sent it on! Am I not to have a sleeping-carriage at once, then? '

" ' Impossible, Madame; we have no carriages here. They can only furnish you with one at Lyons.'

" ' At Lyons! At what o'clock? '

" ' At 5.45, Madame.'

" ' At the end of the journey! But, Monsieur, I can't remain in this *coupé* until that time! Impossible! I *won't*! '

" ' Take care, Madame, the train is starting! '

" It started.

" She threw herself into her corner again, in a furious pet, without casting a glance at me. I plunged once more into the contents of my newspapers—into the contents of the tenth, that is to say.

" Shall I confess it! That paper took me longer to read than its nine predecessors. Twenty times I began the same line; I believe that at least for some time the paper was upside down. Hang it, one can't be shut up for a long journey with a pretty woman without feeling *some* sort of emotion!

" I greatly wanted to enter into conversation with her, but what pretext for doing it could I find? The classic resources of putting up or down the windows, in such a state of the temperature, were non-available. What was there to do?—launch a commonplace remark of some kind? Better a hundred times keep silent than do that. My companion, I had seen at a glance with my Parisian eyes, was a woman of the best society. To speak to her brusquely, without being known to her, would have made me appear in her eyes no better than a vulgar commercial traveller. The only way of drawing her into conversation would be to find something strikingly original to say to her; but what?—what? I sought laboriously, but did not find.

"I was still continuing that search, when the train stopped suddenly, thanks to the powers of the new brake—so good against accidents, but so bad for passengers.

"'Tonnerre!—twenty-five minutes' stoppage!' cried a porter, opening the carriage door.

"My companion rose, threw off her rugs, which, with her three bags, she left in the carriage, and descended on to the platform. It was noon. Hunger had begun to make itself felt. She moved towards the buffet on the left, across the line.

"I followed her. I was then enabled to admire at my ease the elegance of her figure, well set off by a long fur mantle. I remarked also that she had a pretty neck, a grey felt hat, and very tiny feet.

"At the entrance to the buffet stood the manager. Wearing a velvet cap and bearing a striking resemblance to Napoleon III., he pointed out with his hand and with a napkin a long table to be taken by assault.

"I entered with a crowd of travellers—ruffled, hurried; in short, that stream of persons essentially grotesque and derogatory to human beauty, of an express train, bent all on devouring food of some sort.

"I seated myself and hastily swallowed the succession of dishes set before me: my lady traveller took some soup at a separate table.

"I was amongst the first to rise, and went out upon the platform to smoke a cigarette. The twenty-five minutes—reduced to twenty according to rule—were quickly spent. The passengers came in groups from the refectory and returned to their places in the carriages. I reinstalled myself in mine. My fellow traveller did not appear.

"I perceived her at the little bookstall on the opposite side of the line, looking over the volumes displayed. Although I could see nothing of her but her back, I easily recognised her by her pretty figure, her otter-skin mantle, and her grey hat. Her hair seemed to be a little less dark than I had imagined it to be; but that was the effect of distance, no doubt.

"All the passengers had resumed their seats, and the porters were banging-to the doors.

" 'She'll be left behind!' I thought. 'She's mad!—Madame! Madame!' I called to her out of the window.

" She was too far off, and did not hear me.

" The whistle sounded; the train was going to start. What was to be done? Prompt as a flash of lightning, an idea shot through my brain. She would be left there in the horrible cold without her luggage! Let her, poor woman, at least have her smaller belongings.

" I gathered up, in an armful, her three bags and her rugs, and threw the whole to a man in the uniform of the railway, who was on the line near the carriage.

" 'For that lady over there,' I cried.

" The man in uniform carried the articles in the direction of the lady at the bookstall. At the same moment the carriage door on the opposite side—the side next the platform—was opened, and my travelling companion, grumbled at by a station porter, hurried into the carriage, and the train started. Horror! I had mistaken the traveller. The lady at the bookstall was not the right one; the same mantle, same hat, same figure—but not she! It is perfectly absurd how much women resemble one another—the back view of them. I had made a pretty mess of it!

" She had hardly entered the carriage before she uttered a shriek.

" 'My parcels! Somebody has stolen my parcels!'

" And, for the first time, she turned her eyes on me, with a look —good heavens!—with a look never to be forgotten.

" 'No, Madame,' I stammered, 'your parcels have not been stolen; they—they have been left behind at Tonnerre.'

" 'At Tonnerre! How?'

" I explained all to her. By Jove! my dear fellow, I can't describe the second look she darted at me; but, I assure you, I firmly believe I shall remember it even longer than the first.

" 'I am distressed, Madame,' I further stammered, 'distressed exceedingly; but the motive was a good one: I thought that you were going to miss the train—that you would be cold—and—and I did not wish that you should be cold; in short—forgive me, and do not be uneasy in regard to your property, which is in safe hands—a man in uniform. At the next station you can telegraph—we will telegraph—and your things will be immediately sent on. Ah!—you shall have them, I vow, even though I have myself to go back to Tonnerre to fetch them.'

" 'Enough, Monsieur! I know what I have to do.'

" Stormily she rearranged herself in her corner, tugging pettishly at her gloves.

" But, alas, poor little thing! she had counted without the cold—she no longer had her warm rugs and wraps about her. At the end of ten minutes she began to shiver. It was in vain that she tried to huddle herself up, to draw her otter-skin mantle closer to her form: she positively shivered with the cold.

" 'Madame,' I said, 'I beg of you, on my knees, to accept my rug. You will catch cold—and it will be my fault—and I should never, to the end of my days, forgive myself!'

" 'I did not speak to you, Monsieur,' she said sharply.

" I was nervous—excited. In the first place, she was charming; in the next place, I was furiously annoyed with myself for the stupid blunder I had made: in short, I found myself in one of those predicaments that call for the taking of strong resolutions.

" 'Madame,' I said, 'accept this rug, or I swear to you I will throw myself out on to the line!'

" And flinging the rug between her and me, I opened the window and seized the outer handle of the door-lock.

" Was I determined?—between ourselves, not altogether, I think; but it appeared that I had the air of being so, for she instantly cried out:

" 'You are mad, Monsieur, you are mad!'

" 'The rug—or I throw myself out!'

" She took the covering, and in a softened tone, said:

" 'But you, Monsieur—you will catch your death of cold.'

" 'Do not be uneasy on my account, Madame, I am not in the least chilly—and, even if I should feel cold, it will only be a just punishment for my unpardonable stupidity.'

" 'Say your over-hastiness; for, as you have said, your motive was a good one. But how came you to mistake another lady for me?'

" 'Because she appeared to me charming!'

" She smiled. The ice was broken—the ice of conversation, that is to say; for, in other respects, I was shivering with cold.

" But how quickly I forgot the cold, the journey—everything! She was delicious, exquisite, adorable! She possessed a cultivated mind, keen, gay, original! She loved travel, like myself. In literature, in music, in everything in fact, we had the same tastes! And then—only imagine!—we found we had a heap of acquaintances in common; she was intimate with the Saint-Chamas, with the Savenois, above all with the Montbazons! Only to think that I had perhaps met her twenty times in their drawing-rooms without having noticed her! Good heavens! where had my eyes been?

" She spoke simply, amiably, with the frankness I so much love. A slight, very slight, provincial accent, almost imperceptible, a chirp rather, giving to her pronunciation something of the singing of a bird. It was intoxicating!

" But though I would have given all the world not to appear cold —great heavens, how cold I *was*!

" At Dijon (2.20) my right foot was half frozen. We telegraphed to Tonnerre for the articles left behind.

" Mâcon (4.30) it was the turn of my left foot. We received a message from Tonnerre, saying that the luggage would arrive in Marseilles next day.

" At Lyon-Perranche (5.48) my left hand became insensible; she forgot to demand her sleeping-carriage.

" At Valence (8.3) my right hand followed the example of the left; I learned that she was a widow and childless.

" At Avignon (9.59) my nose became violet; I fancied she had never wholly loved her first husband.

" At Marseilles (12.5 a.m.) I sneezed three times violently; she handed me back my rug, and said graciously: ' Au revoir! '

" ' Au revoir! ' Oh, I was mad with delight.

" I spent the night at the Hôtel de Noailles—an agitated night, filled with remembrance of her. The next morning, when I awoke, I had the most shocking cold in the head imaginable.

" Could I, in such a state, present myself to my friends, the Rombauds? There was no help for it; it was one of the accidents of travel; they must take me as I was, and to-morrow I would go and seek my cure in the sun of Nice.

" Oh, my friend, what a surprise! That good fellow Rombaud had invited a few friends in my honour, and among them was my charming fellow-traveller! my charmer!

" When I was presented to her, a smile passed over her lips; I bowed, and asked in a whisper:

" ' Tonnerre—your parcels? '

" ' I have them,' she replied in the same tone.

" We sat down to table.

" ' What a cold in the head you have got, my dear fellow! ' cried Rombaud, sympathetically; ' where the deuce did you pick it up—in the railway carriage, perhaps? '

" ' Very possibly,' I said, ' but I don't regret it! '

" Nobody comprehended the sense of this veiled reply; but I felt the tender glance of my fellow-traveller reach me through the odorous steam of a superb tureen of soup majestically posed upon the table.

" What more have I to tell you? Next day I set off for Nice; a fortnight hence I am to be married."

JEAN RICHEPIN
B. 1849

"BONJOUR, MONSIEUR"

"Modernity, the essence of inquietude!"—*Adrien Juvigny.*

FERDINAND OCTAVE BRUAT awoke one morning with an idea. Ferdinand Octave Bruat was what one commonly calls a man of letters. He had written verses that no one would publish, novels that all the publishers had returned unread, theatrical effusions that even the director of the Funambules had refused. However, he had, in default of talent, a theory, an ideal. He thought himself called to be a leader, and firmly believed that he had invented a modern school. He meant by that, all that constitutes our daily life, so bizarre on this side, so practical on that, so foolish on others. He maintained that the time had come to attack boldly all imitations, classic as well as romantic, and that he should ransack contemporaneous society to derive therefrom ideas, forms, a language absolutely new and original. He said that as each epoch had had its own expression so ours should have its own also.

He was not wrong. Unfortunately he had not the strength to carry to battle the standard he had raised, and all his valiance merely ended in debating much and haranguing in the cafés. He overthrew more fools than bigots and made more debts than masterpieces. But one morning, on rising, he found the masterpiece which he had sought. When I say he had found it, I am mistaken. *He had given birth to a title!* What to do with it? As yet he did not know. But the title seemed to him eloquent, sonorous, easy to remember, rich in variations, full of modernity, epitomising the whole century in a manner at once simple and complex. The title was the more wonderful that it was so common. It was a phrase of two words, spoken thousands of times each morning; a phrase without affectation, without pretence, without pedantry, neither classic nor romantic. It was simply, "*Bonjour, Monsieur!*"

Under this title he wrote first a sonnet. This sonnet was read to his friends, naturally accompanied by prefaces and commentaries, philological as well as philosophical, destined not only to make them the better enjoy its essence, but also to make them thoroughly comprehend its import. With one voice it was pronounced admirable. " It must be published at once," cried the most enthusiastic; " it will give the keynote to the poetry of the future."

One crabbed old fellow, who did not dare to give his opinion frankly, but who was irritated by this success, turned his criticism into a compliment. " As for me," he said, " I believe the subject demands greater development. Certainly the sonnet is beautiful; but does it not strike you that it is not sufficient for a subject of such importance? Think of it! A thing so profound, so varied, so complicated cannot be confined in fourteen lines. A thought so powerful breaks its mould. Were I Bruat, I would turn my sonnet into a drama."

The assemblage adopted his opinion, enchanted at heart to see the famous sonnet thus criticised. Bruat did not perceive the irony of the grumbler. " You are right," said he with an air of superiority. " I have compressed my idea into this narrow mould. Thanks for your criticism, which proves how much you esteem me. Truly my idea deserves more than fourteen lines. I will write a drama in five acts and nine tableaux." And, in spite of the hypocritical protestations of his friends, he tore into pieces his masterpiece of a sonnet.

He lived for five years on the memory of his sonnet. He was always promising the astonishing drama—" Bonjour, Monsieur! " He was becoming almost celebrated by this piece in embryo. They knew that he had but a few scenes to finish; they said that the work was advancing. The simple-minded and the prejudiced who had never seen the author were convinced of his genius and spread his renown. To believe them, there was a great future, a marvellous hope; one must wait for the thunderclap. No doubt he was taking his time; but do not aloes take a hundred years to flower?

At last the drama was finished. This was a great event for the daily papers. What theatre would be the battlefield of the new school? Without doubt the directors would dispute for the honour of presenting to the public the principal work of the nineteenth century? Would there be artists capable of interpreting it?

First of all, Bruat assembled his little court, wishing to give them the first-fruits of his victory. The drama did not meet with the success of the sonnet. Perhaps the wits had conceived in advance too high an idea of it. Perhaps Bruat had not been as brilliant as they had expected. Perhaps there was a little envy mingled with their judgment. Perhaps, also, the auditors were less young and therefore less enthusiastic. In short, the reading was a failure. The grumbler alone protested against the general coldness, and made a parade of an unlimited admiration. "Well and good," said he; "here is something that expresses the idea in quest, here is movement, life, research, keenness. Away with the sonnet! My friend, you have found the new drama, the modern drama, the drama of the future."

But Bruat was disheartened. At least he mistrusted the grumbler, who had counselled him to substitute the drama for the sonnet. He owed him a grudge because the drama had produced no effect in comparison with the sonnet. "Well," said he to the others, "where am I at fault?"

"Oh, in nothing, nothing at all," replied the chorus of friends.

"However, my drama does not meet with your approval; I see it clearly."

"Do you wish me to tell you the truth?" interrupted one, emboldened by Bruat's failure.

"Say it, my friend, for you know it is my principle to seek truth everywhere."

"Well, I think that modern life is too complicated for the drama. There are casualties, phenomena of the heart, complications of sentiment, descriptions material and spiritual, inquiries physiological and psychological, which cannot be expressed in action. You have striven against the difficulty. Sometimes you have avoided it, which has caused a lack of unity. Sometimes you have been overwhelmed by it, which has caused a lack of polish. In spite of all your talents you have not been able to control this monster. Your plot is obscure, your characters badly drawn, your conclusion unnatural. But, on the other hand, what observation! what brilliant analysis! what force of penetration! what language! Oh! to be inspired in spite of the obstacles, you must be a man of genius. What would you? The impossible cannot be achieved. In your case I would recast everything; I would expand, I would clarify, I would develop, I would take my time, I would enlarge my frame to the size of my idea, I would turn my drama into a novel."

"He is right," said the chorus, "he is right. That is the point. You must make a novel of 'Bonjour, Monsieur!'"

The opinion was unanimous. Bruat was too sincere not to be guided by it. Heroically he burned his drama, and set to work on his novel. In this work he spent ten years. To him it was the time of apotheosis. He had more prophets than God. Some exalted him from real admiration; others, because they thought he would accomplish nothing, and that, therefore, he would not be a dangerous adversary, spread his praises. Critics used his name to crush budding authors. Journalists filled up spaces with notices of his novel, with anecdotes of the labour in the thousand and one alterations in his work. The ignorant, the foolish, the gossips chattered about him without knowing why. He became as famous as the obelisk.

Nevertheless, they finished by waiting. The echo of his glory became fainter as it passed from one generation to another. At sixty he was about forgotten. He was only spoken of from time to time, and then merely as an eccentric, almost a lunatic. They remembered vaguely that he was working at a great novel, but they doubted whether he would ever finish it, or, rather, they were sure that he would never reach the end. They never spoke but with a smile of his gigantic undertaking, of the twenty volumes which would epitomise the nineteenth century, of this creation which would be the babel and pandemonium of modern life.

They would have laughed much more could they have known on what Bruat was engaged in his old age. The unhappy man had finished his formidable novel. He had written twenty-seven volumes under the wonderful title, " Bonjour, Monsieur! " But at the end of his labour, frightened at having spoken at such length, he did not dare the trial of the reading. Then he set to work to abridge, to cut, to condense. By this means he had, little by little, reduced the book first to ten volumes, then to two, then to one. Finally, he had epitomised everything into a story of one hundred pages.

Ferdinand Octave Bruat was then eighty years old. One friend alone remained to him, the confidant of his undying ambition.

" Publish your story," said his friend: " I assure you it will make a sensation in the world. It is the paragon of modernity."

" No, no," cried Bruat, " I have not yet condensed it sufficiently. You see, I know myself; I know the public. To hold it, to leave something to posterity, to create a lasting work, one must be intense. To be intense—that is everything. A hundred pages! That is too prolix. In my first inspiration I found the true form for my thought—a form short, precise, chiselled, straight, fitting the idea like a cuirass; I mean the sonnet. Oh! if I could recall the marvellous sonnet of my youth! But it has been abandoned too long. To-day I will do better. I will put into it my experience, my life. Could I but live ten years longer, men would see what fourteen lines could express, and posterity would know our modern life, so vast, in this poem so small, as one inhales a subtle essence prisoned in a diamond."

He lived those ten years, and the story was abandoned like the novel and the drama; and slowly, letter by letter, word by word, line by line, was written the colossal sonnet which was to contain everything.

At ninety-two Ferdinand Bruat lay on his death-bed.

His faithful friend was at his side, weeping, sobbing, in despair at seeing so high an intelligence laid so low.

"Weep not, my friend," said Bruat, "weep not. I die, but my idea dies not with me. I have destroyed by first sonnet, I have burnt my drama, I have burnt, one by one, the twenty-seven volumes of my novel; the ten, then the five, then the two, then the one and only, then the story. But, at last, I have created my masterpiece."

"The sonnet! the immortal sonnet! Give it me! You have not read it to me, but I know that it is a masterpiece. Give it me; I will publish it. If necessary, I will ruin myself that it may be written on gold in letters of diamonds. It merits it, it will dazzle the world. Give it me!"

"The sonnet? What sonnet?" stammered Bruat, gasping for breath.

"Your great sonnet!" sighed the friend, who saw the delirium of death approaching.

"Ah! yes, yes, the sonnet, the great sonnet. Too great, my friend, too long! It must be made more intense."

"What! have you burnt your last sonnet also?"

"I have found something better. I have found everything. Modern life, modernity, I hold it, I have it, I express it. It is not in a sonnet, nor in a quatrain, nor even in a line, it is——"

His voice grew weaker, became hoarse, wheezy, lost.

His friend, with bloodshot eyes, gaping mouth, leaned over the bed to drink in his last word, the word that would give the key to the mystery, the Open Sesame to art in the future.

"Speak, speak!" he cried.

"Everything in one phrase, everything in one phrase!" murmured Bruat. And the old man raised himself up in a paroxysm of agony. His look was ecstatic. One felt that over the threshold of death he saw his ideal. He made a terrible effort to express it, and the wondrous phrase fell from his lips with his last sigh. It was, "Bonjour, Monsieur!"

TOTOR'S DRUM

JEAN RICHEPIN

It is not necessary to see General X twice to know what to think of him. With his hawk-eyes and his tiger-cat moustache he is the accomplished and classical type of the gallant warrior, always in high spirits, with an inborn passion for war, with a courage not entirely free from ferocity. At the same time one can guess that he comes of old military stock and that it required long generations of cavaliers to arrive at this perfect product.

So I thought, very much infatuated, as we all are nowadays, with my ability to estimate and catalogue, attaching a tag to everything and judging everybody by appearances.

When I learned that the general was writing his memoirs I immediately thought of a collection of military proclamations, a monotonous list of brilliant charges, with a liberal admixture of haughty genealogies.

How easy it is to be mistaken! I append the first chapter of these memoirs.

What an erratic mistress is Fate! One would scarcely believe that I came of a family of silk-manufacturers and merchants.

Yet that is the truth. My father, my grandfather, and all my ancestors for a long way back, I believe, were silk-dealers in Lyons, and I was, of course, expected to succeed them.

If I have become a general, it is due to my mother's "blue devils," and especially to Totor's drum.

Totor was the son of our gardener at Montgain-sur-Saône, and mother's "blues" were the result of our residence in that country place, which bored her to death.

A widow at twenty-six years, left at the head of a great commercial and manufacturing house which she understood nothing about, she had retired for a time to Montgain to escape the importunity of her family, who wished to marry her again. This new union was, it seemed, necessary to her interests; there must be an experienced man in the business. This man was already picked out. His name was Monsieur Lematthieu. Thirty-five years old, a fortune equal to ours, a name well known in the silk industry; in short, the ideal husband. For the family, that is; not for mother. If the silk business would profit, her heart would suffer. Hence the blues.

I learned all that later. At that time, a boy of eight years and a half, I realised only one thing—that the house was sad. I stayed in it as little as possible, and passed my time playing with Totor.

I did not simply play with him; I took long vagabond journeys with him. It was not long till we left the garden and wandered into the village, then from the village into the country, with all the dirty urchins of the district. The gardener's wife was supposed to watch us, the gardener also. But the garden was so large, Father and Mother Barraud were so indulgent, the walls so easy to scale, and the alleys so tempting! And Totor was terribly clever.

Ah, what gay times we had! I remember them as if I were still enjoying them. And there is one in particular that I can never forget. As a matter of fact, I consider it my first campaign. My actual military service dates from then.

We were a regiment of soldiers that day, and we were recruited by the ingenious Totor.

He is eleven years old and he would have the right to command us—the other gamins and me. But he respects me and has named me chief. Our army is composed of a dozen troopers, among whom Totor has distributed guns of his own manufacture, to the detriment of certain vines which have lost their props and of certain brooms that miss their handles.

He has made a sword for me, not of vulgar wood like the guns of the men, but of real metal, with the help of a long frying-pan handle. On my cap he has planted the tail of a wretched rooster, reduced henceforth to hide his shame in the shadow of the cart-house.

Totor has supplied himself with a drum. This was not the easiest thing in the world. He had thought first of using a sauce-pan, but Virginie, the cook, had interfered. At last, in sheer desperation, Totor resorted to an old high hat, borrowed of his father and shorn of its brim. That makes a black drum, of muffled and cavernous sound. We are like a funeral procession.

No difference! Thus equipped, we set out for the conquest of pears and grapes, and I march proudly behind Totor, straight as a ramrod, my sword unsheathed and shining as bright as a greasy skillet can well shine. We cross the village and leave it, bent on pillage, excited by the furious rhythm of the black drum.

"Halt! Who goes there? Advance and give the counter-sign!"

It is an unknown and formidable voice that receives us thus at the turn of a sunken road.

A hostile army is in front! Composed of a single man, it is true, but what a man it is! A "real, right" soldier! More than that—an officer! Red trousers, a steel scabbard swinging from his left thigh, great up-tilted moustaches.

All is lost! Our army disbands, throws away its guns, and disappears in all directions like a flight of sparrows. I, the general, let my humiliated frying-pan fall at the feet of the victor. Totor alone keeps his courage, thrusts his drum on his head to inspire respect in the enemy, and retorts:

"France, Colonel!"

The colonel, who is only a lieutenant, begins to laugh.

"And where are you going like that, little warriors?"

"To war, of course, Captain," replies Totor, lowering the rank of the enemy, who is no longer terrible after he begins to laugh.

"Well," replies the officer, "will you serve under my orders? I am just looking for a dinner to take by storm. Show me where the nearest restaurant is, and I will treat you to a drop of something, my grenadiers."

Totor's nose expresses at this moment two conflicting emotions. He is allured by the prospect of the "drop," but he is disappointed in his heroic military projects. The enemy is too good-natured, entirely! Totor therefore preserves a contemptuous silence.

"You don't want to?" continues the officer. "Soldiers, and as timid as all that? What about you, little general? You're a nice-looking fellow."

And he taps my cheek with a wheedling gesture. He is very amiable, to be sure, and the more I look at him, the better I like him. Tall, slender, young, he has a fine open countenance, and his martial moustaches make the gentleness of his eyes seem gentler yet. It is a pleasure to think that his delicate hand has caressed me.

And all of a sudden, while Totor hesitates between his two conflicting ideas, I have an idea which seems to me admirable.

"Yes," I say, "I know a restaurant and I will take you there."

"Where's that?" demands Totor.

"Why, at our house."

Totor at once catches my idea and cries: "That's right! That will be great fun!"

The officer does not notice my dress, which is scarcely that of an innkeeper's son. He accepts my proposition and follows us.

"Well," he says on the way, "do you serve good meals at your place?"

"Pretty good," replies Totor, who has grown grossly disrespectful to an enemy that we seem to be bringing home prisoner.

Soon we reach the villa and enter the garden where mother, her hair down, dressed in a morning gown, is sadly giving her blue devils a little air and exercise.

At sight of the aristocratic cottage, the lieutenant sees his mistake. He excuses himself as well as he can: "He was out making topographical surveys, three leagues from the camp of Sathonay, too far to get back; and then, these little rascals——" He is charming in his excuses, confused without awkwardness, at the same time gallant and exquisitely polite.

As for mother, I see plainly that she has the same opinion of the officer that I have.

"It's this nice little fellow," he says, tapping my cheek again, "who got me into this difficulty. Pardon me, Madame——"

"But there is nothing to pardon," replies mother. "I am not at all angry with you, sir, nor with him either."

She even adds—for she is never able to conceal her thoughts: "Quite the contrary."

To make a long story short, the lieutenant is invited to dinner.

He even passes the afternoon with us. Mother seems enchanted with him, and I am, too.

It developed that our villa was a strategic point of the greatest importance; for from that day it became the centre of some very elaborate topographical surveys. And certainly the topography of the neighbourhood, and of our garden especially, must be very minutely described in the staff records; for the lieutenant soon acquired the habit of coming every day to study it.

It seemed, too, as if his red trousers frightened the blue devils, for they disappeared as soon as he arrived, from the first day.

Mother had become joyous again, and her joy kept increasing for three months, till the time when it reached its fruition, the day when mother dropped my father's name, but not to take that of Monsieur Lematthieu.

The business was sold. My ancestors blushed, no doubt, for us, their faithless descendants. As for me, I felt not the slightest remorse, nor have I ever felt any. I caught from my stepfather a love for his noble profession. In place of studying book-keeping, I learned fencing, riding, and the various other accomplishments which are necessary in order to enter Saint Cyr. And now, thanks to Totor's drum and mother's blue devils, I am a general.

Nevertheless, I have inherited one indelible mark of my ancestry; there is still one sort of silk with which I am somewhat familiar —the silk they make flags of.

RICHARD O'MONROY
B. 1850

THE FUGUE

I HAD made up my mind to spend the National Fête in some remote place in Normandy, and to that end was pacing up and down the hall of the Saint-Lazare station, when I heard an unmusical feminine voice calling me—unmusical certainly, but distinctly feminine.

" Monsieur Richard! Monsieur Richard! " I turned round. There was my friend Madame Manchaballe arrayed in a travelling costume of an ancient Surah dust-cloak—trimmed with black lace that had formerly seen service at Aix with Rebecca, I recognised it at once—and wearing a Leghorn hat with heaps of flowers and two pink ibis wings. Your imagination may be ever so vivid, but I defy you to picture to yourself Madame Manchaballe's head crowned with two pink ibis wings. It is a thing to be seen, and a spectacle once seen never—to—be—forgotten.

" And where are you bound for, my dear Madame? "

" I'm off to join Caroline, my youngest, at Houlgate: we have a little cottage there on the corniche."

" Caroline? Oh, yes! She is the singer. And are the Conservatoire examinations over? "

" They're over," Madame Manchaballe groaned, " they're over, but for us they never began."

" Oh! impossible! "

" Ah, it was outrageous injustice, Monsieur! We never even went in for them, though Caroline has a charming voice. You remember the night she sang the waltz from *Faust*?—

> Ah, how fine it is to see myself looking so nice in this mirror!

and then the great recitative?—

> How much I long to know who that young man was,
> If he is a great noble, and how much he pays!

" The words are not precisely like that, Madame Manchaballe."

" Yes, but that's what they mean. The words themselves don't matter at all in opera. I'm sure you remember how surprised you were, and how you said, 'The deuce! Your daughter has made tremendous progress; I will give her an introduction to my friend Victorien Sardou.'"

"It was Joncières I mentioned, Joncières."

"Well, they're both Victoriens, so where's the difference? I didn't waste any time about it. I not only got lessons for her from Madame Saxe, but I made her call on all the members of the jury. At first I thought I had better accompany her, but she said I made her nervous, and that she sang better when I wasn't there. So I didn't insist, but let her go by herself."

"Doubtless you were right, Madame Manchaballe."

"Yes, certainly. And besides I was so busy. I went to the meeting of the *Concert Vatoire*. That's a queer sort of concert, if you like! Such a funny room, half theatre, half study. The stage with its two chairs and a door resembled a porter's lodge, and a poor sort of porter at that. No furniture, no decorations, the walls painted red—the colour of raw meat—and not an ornament on them. They say that this plain and empty background makes it good for judging gesture, attitude, and the expression of the face. Well, I didn't mind. A long and severe-looking table took the place of the three boxes opposite the stage, and behind this table sat the jury, with the president in the middle; they were all getting old and short-sighted; not a handsome man in the lot. And such beards and heads of hair! Why do musicians always have such wonderful heads of hair? Perhaps music is good for the hair."

"But I want to hear about Caroline, Madame Manchaballe, and you are wandering from the point."

"All right, I am coming to that. Well, then, one day I got there late, at the end of the performance, and heard that Mademoiselle Ferville was to have the first prize for her Fugue—her wonderful Fugue, a fugue so marvellous and astonishing that it had literally carried the jury away. All round me I could hear the critics saying: 'What a fugue! My dear sir, what a splendid fugue!' As I did not want to seem out of it, of course, I said the same as others, and smiled like everybody else. But to tell the truth—now don't begin to laugh at me, Monsieur Richard—I hadn't a notion what a fugue was. Up till then, with Judith and Rebecca, I had only had to do with dancing. I knew all about pirouettes and such-like, but I had never heard tell of fugues. So presently when I got out into the vestibule I went up to Madame Chapuzot, Stella Chapuzot's mother. Stella was in the same class as Caroline, and Madame Saxe always said, 'If Stella doesn't make a hit at the opera first it will be Caroline.' Well, Madame Chapuzot was very jealous of us, and, of course, I ought to have been on my guard. But I thought between two mothers it would be all fair. So going up to her I said, ' Mademoiselle Jerville did very well with her Fugue; it seems a settled thing that she gets the prize. Now, as I wasn't there,' I went on, ' I should take it as a great kindness on your part if you would tell me what a fugue is, because then I could make Caroline get one ready.'

" Madame Chapuzot laughed so loudly when I said that, that everybody turned round to look at us. Of course I laughed too, for company's sake, though I didn't see exactly what there was to laugh at. All of a sudden Madame Chapuzot became quite serious, and said, ' A fugue, Madame Manchaballe, is to make yourself scarce just when no one expects it. For instance, suppose you are to sing in the evening at the Opéra Comique. Well, at eight o'clock you are off to Italy: that's a fugue. The directors are so frightened that to get you back they will decide either to raise your salary or give you a prize. That's what happened to Mademoiselle Jerville.'

" It seemed to me very odd. But that same evening I happened to meet at the Opéra an old tenant of ours, M. Jules Claretie, who is a member of the Academy, and therefore must know all about the French language. So I said to him: ' Monsieur Claretie, if a person who had to sing at the Opéra Comique at half-past eight went off to Italy at eight o'clock, would that be a fugue? '

" ' Certainly,' replied the Academician, with perfect politeness, ' that would be a fugue.'

" After that my mind was made up. I waited for the day of the competition, and then, without a word of warning to any one, I packed Caroline off to Houlgate. She objected, but I said, ' Leave it all to your mother, it's for your own good.' I went to the concert-hall, and when Caroline's name was called, I stood up and said, ' She's done a fugue. She's at her cottage at the seaside.' The president only said, ' Good,' and called on the next candidate, Stella Chapuzot. And she passed, and Caroline was ploughed. Now, wasn't that disgraceful, sir? I suppose I ought not to have trusted Madame Chapuzot; but, honestly now, how could I mistrust such a distinguished man as Monsieur Claretie? Put it into the papers, will you? Well, it will prove to the Government that whatever they say there's no equality yet; and that what brings success to one brings ruin to another. But there's my train. Good-bye, Monsieur Richard."

" A pleasant journey to you, Madame Manchaballe."

THE VIOLIN

RICHARD O'MONROY

I TOOK a stroll the other day down the *Rue de Provence,* and halted casually at a curiosity shop. Looking up I saw it belonged to good Madame Manchaballe, mother of the little Manchaballes of the *corps de ballet*. The second Manchaballe is slender enough, but Manchaballe the first is immense. However, it was not for that reason I turned the handle of the shop door. Not at all; I wanted to consult Madame Manchaballe about buying a bracelet. Instead, a violin of antiquated appearance caught my eye.

"Ah! Madame Manchaballe," I said, "so you sell musical instruments. Is that another string to your bow? But perhaps you are going to make Monsieur Pluque a present?"

"Nothing of the kind, Monsieur Richard, nothing of the kind. I am not one of those mothers who try to influence the professors in that way. I know the value of my Judith, and the promise there is in Rebecca, and I can wait quietly whatever fortune may have in store for my daughters. No, that violin represents a good deed I tried to do."

I stared at this. I don't know why, but somehow it was difficult to think of Madame Manchaballe doing a good deed; I couldn't realise her in such a position.

"Yes," madame continued, "I can quite understand your surprise. But, after all, my charitable deed was a failure, and I can promise you I am not likely to attempt another. How much do you think that violin is worth?"

I picked up the instrument. It looked to me like a child's plaything, rather the worse for wear, and I answered without hesitation:

"I should say it was worth twelve francs at the outside."

"Well, it cost me four hundred francs."

I jumped in my astonishment. It was evidently some little pleasantry. But then I noticed that behind her spectacles Madame Manchaballe's eyes were wet with tears, and as I am very soft-hearted, even the spectacle of a crocodile in tears, especially a lady crocodile, moves me. I grasped the old croco—I beg her pardon —Madame Manchaballe's hands, and said:

"Tell me all about it; you'll feel better then."

"Ah! Monsieur Richard, you make the wound bleed afresh, but I can refuse you nothing. Well, one cold winter's morning Judith and Rebecca had finished their breakfasts, and had gone off arm-in-arm to the eight o'clock class. I was dusting my china—I'm the only woman who really understands the art of dusting; it can't be taught, it's a gift. I think my light hand accounts for my daughter's light legs. Suddenly I see a little beggar-girl, ever so pretty, by Jove, in spite of her wretched rags. Ah! if young people but knew their own value! Well, she enters, violin in hand, and begs for a trifle, of course. It is a fixed principle of mine never to give to beggars whom I don't know, or even to those I do know. But the child starts crying——

"'Have pity, madame. It is only to buy sausage for mamma, who is so hungry. At ten o'clock, when more people are moving, I sing in the streets, and at mid-day I will certainly repay you. But I can sing, if you like, without any instrument; so, please, lend me twenty sous, and I'll leave my violin with you in pawn. It is a very old violin which belonged to my great-grandfather, and not for all the world would I part with it, so you need not be afraid.'

"Well, it wasn't much of a risk. I lent the twenty sous and retained the violin."

"I beg your pardon, Madame Manchaballe, but you said four hundred francs——"

"Don't be in such a hurry. About eleven o'clock a gentleman, who looked like some distinguished diplomatist, came into the shop. Ah! No one could have made a better impression. He gives an eye to my Renaissance Venus, to my Louis Quinze clock, and then comes to a sudden pull up at the violin.

"He takes hold of it, feels it all over, taps the case, and at last exclaims: 'This is a genuine Stradivarius!'

"'Impossible!' I reply.

"'It's possible enough for me to buy it from you for five hundred francs.'

"The thought of such a sum made me quite dizzy.

"'But the instrument isn't mine,' I pleaded. 'An artist left it here, and he declared he could not part with it. It seems he inherited it from his great-grandfather. Still he appeared to be very poor, and I lent him a few pence. Oh, I am sure the matter could be arranged.'

"'Pray attend to me, madame. You shall have two hundred francs commission if you get me the Stradivarius for five hundred francs. I shall have to pay thirty-five louis, but what of that? I can afford such follies; besides, I'm sure to make a good profit out of it.'

"'Very well, monsieur,' I reply. 'Please come back this afternoon; I will speak to the artist.'

"About mid-day my artist returns, and it is only fair to say that she brought me the twenty sous.

"'You see I am honest, madame. Here is your money, for which I thank you very much. Please give me my violin.'

"'My dear,' I said to her, 'I've an offer for you that will make you jump for joy. I know an old gentleman who will give you three hundred francs for your violin.'"

"I must apologise for interrupting you, Madame Manchaballe, but it was five hundred francs you said."

"Ah! truly, monsieur; but any of us may make a mistake even on our own side, and I couldn't help thinking that fifteen louis was a very large sum for this little good-for-nothing. Why, it would be a fortune from heaven for her, and I made sure she would be overjoyed at the proposal. Not at all! She made quite a fuss about it. Said the instrument was left to her by her grandfather, and that she must keep it. To my great sorrow I had to increase the price to four hundred francs. That still left me a little bonus of five louis."

"Without counting the two hundred francs commission?"

"Yes, without counting the commission. But business is business, and Rebecca and Judith are costing me more than they earn—at least just at present they are. At length my beggar-girl decided to sell, and as I, for private reasons of my own, did not want her to meet the diplomatist, I advanced her the four hundred francs and kept the Stradivarius."

"And is that all, Madame Manchaballe?"

"Monsieur, the whole affair was a swindle. *Bon Dieu!* Who is to be trusted if one can't have confidence in people who look highly respectable? That old gentleman was really a notorious thief, and the little beggar-girl was his accomplice. Neither of them have I seen again, and I still have the violin on my hands."

GUY DE MAUPASSANT
1850-1893

THE NECKLACE

SHE was one of those charming girls, born by a freak of destiny in a family of toilers. She had no fortune, no expectations, no means of satisfying her ambitions, except by a marriage with a rich and distinguished man, and, as she knew none, in order to escape from her surroundings, she married a clerk in the office of the Minister of Public Instruction.

She dressed simply, because she had no means of adornment; but she was as unhappy as though she had fallen from a high social position, for the women who have neither caste nor race use their beauty, grace, and charm as stepping-stones to those heights from which they are otherwise barred, their natural tact and instinctive elegance and quick perceptions being their only inheritance, and, skilfully used, make them the equal of their more fortunate sisters. She suffered incessantly when she glanced around her humble home, and felt the absence of all those delicacies and luxuries which are enjoyed only by the rich. In short, all the little nothings that another woman of her caste would not have seen, tortured and wounded her. The sight of the old Breton peasant woman who performed her simple household duties awakened in her vain longings and troubled dreams.

She dreamed of beautiful halls, discreetly lighted by candles in great bronze candlesticks, whose rich carpets gave back no sounds and whose walls were covered with silks from the Orient, and of obsequious footmen half asleep in their large armchairs, ready to attend to your every want at a moment's notice; of large salons draped in ancient silks; of " étagers " covered with priceless bric-à-brac. She thought also of coquettish small salons, made expressly for the " five o'clock," when one receives only one's intimates or distinguished men of letters, from whom it is every woman's ambition to receive attentions.

When she was seated at the table (whose cloth had already done duty for three days) or opposite her husband—who evinced his entire satisfaction with the evening's repast by such exclamations as: " Oh, the good 'pot-au-feu'! I know nothing better!"—her imagination carried her away to stately banquet halls, whose walls were covered with rich tapestries, portraying scenes in which ancient personages and strange birds were pictured in the middle of a fairy-like forest. She pictured the glittering silver, strange dishes, exquisitely served on marvellous plate, and gallantries whispered and listened to with the sphinx-like smile with which a woman of the world knows so well how to conceal her emotions, all the while eating a rosy trout or dallying with a wing of a lark. She had no toilets, no jewels, and it was for these things that she longed, as the fleet Arabian longs for his native desert. What pleasure to have pleased, been envied, to be seductive and sought after!

She had a rich friend, a comrade from the convent, whom she no longer visited, because she suffered from seeing the things she could not have, and on returning wept whole days for grief, regret, despair, and distress.

One evening her husband came home radiant, holding in his hand a large envelope.

" See," said he, " here is something for you."

She nervously tore open the envelope and drew out a card, on which these words were printed:

" The Minister of Public Instruction and Madame Georges Ramponeau beg the honour of the company of Monsieur and Madame Loisel for the evening of Monday, January 18th."

Instead of being wild with delight, as he had expected, she threw the invitation on the table, with an exclamation of disgust, saying sullenly:

" What do you wish me to do with that? "

" But, my dear, I thought you would be so pleased. You never go out, and this is an event. I only obtained it after infinite trouble. Everybody wants one; they are much sought after, and they are not generally given to employees. You will see all the official world there."

She looked at him with supreme disdain, and said impatiently:

" What would you like me to wear? " The secret was out. Manlike, he had not thought of that.

" But—the dress—that you wear to the theatre," stammered he. " You always look beautiful to me in that."

He stopped speaking, stupefied and dismayed on seeing his wife in tears. Two large tears trickled slowly down her cheeks.

" What is the matter? What is the matter? " asked he tenderly. By violent effort she conquered her grief and calmly said, while wiping her humid cheeks:

" Nothing; only I have no toilet, and, of course, cannot go. Give the card to one of your comrades whose wife is fortunate enough to have something suitable for the occasion."

Despairingly he said:

"See, Mathilde, how much will a dress cost to wear to this ball; one which can also be used for other occasions—something very simple."

She reflected a few moments, figuring in her own mind the sum she could ask without danger of immediate refusal and frightening her economical husband. Finally she hesitatingly said:

"I do not know exactly; but it seems to me I might manage with about 400 francs."

He paled a little, because he had been saving just that sum to buy a gun for the following summer, when he would go with some of his friends to the plains of Nanterre on Sundays to shoot larks. Stifling his regrets, however, he replied:

"Very well, I will give you 400 francs, but try to have a beautiful dress."

The day of the fête drew near; but Madame Loisel seemed sad, anxious, and uneasy. Her toilet was ready. What could it be? Her husband said to her one evening:

"What is the matter? You have been so queer for the last few days!"

She replied: "It worries me that I have not one jewel, not a precious stone to wear. What a miserable figure I shall be! I think I would rather not go at all!"

"You can wear natural flowers; they are all the rage this season, and for ten francs you can have two or three magnificent roses."

But she was not convinced.

"No; there is nothing more humiliating than to be poorly dressed among so many rich women."

"But how silly you are! Go to your friend, Madame Forestier, and ask her to lend you her jewels. You are friendly enough with her to do that."

She gave a cry of joy.

"Yes; that is true—I had not thought of it."

The following day she went to her friend and explained her predicament. Madame Forestier went to a closet and took out a large casket, and, opening it, said:

"Choose, my dear; they are at your service."

She saw first bracelets, then a necklace of pearls, a Venetian cross, gold and precious stones of exquisite workmanship. She tried them on before the glass, unable to decide whether to wear them or not.

"Have you nothing else?" said she.

"Oh, yes; look them over, I don't know what might please you."

Suddenly she opened a black satin case, disclosing to view a superb rivière of diamonds. Her heart beat furiously with the desire of possession. She took them in her trembling hands and put them on over her simple high-neck gown, and stood lost in an ecstasy of admiration of herself. Then, fearfully, hesitatingly, dreading the agony of refusal:

"Can you only lend me that?"

"Why, certainly; if it pleases you."

She fell on her friend's neck, embraced her tempestuously, and then left hastily with her treasure.

The day of the ball arrived. Madame Loisel was a success. Among all the beautiful women she was the most beautiful, elegant, gracious, and smiling with joy. She attracted the attention of some of the most distinguished men present, and on all sides was heard:

"Who is she?"

All the attachés of the cabinet sought her dancing card eagerly, and even the Minister himself expressed his approval. She danced with pleasure, thinking of nothing but the triumph of her beauty and the glory of her success. Intoxicated by all the admiration, she seemed to float through a cloud of happiness, intensified by her complete victory and the tribute paid to her charms, so sweet to the hearts of women. She left about four o'clock in the morning; her husband had slept since midnight in a small room, deserted except by two or three gentlemen who also awaited their wives.

He threw over her shoulders the modest cloak which she had brought, whose shabbiness seemed to mock the elegance of the ball toilet. She felt the incongruity, and walked swiftly away in order not to be seen by those whose rich furs were more in accordance with the occasion.

"Wait," said her husband, "you will take cold; I will call a carriage."

But she heeded him not, and rapidly descended the staircase. When they reached the street, there was no carriage in sight, and they were obliged to look for one, calling to the drivers who passed by, but in vain. Shiveringly they walked toward the Seine and finally found on the quay one of those nocturnal coupés one finds only in Paris after dark, hovering about the great city like grim birds of prey, who conceal their misery during the day. It carried them to their door (Rue de Martyrs), and they slowly and sadly entered their small apartments. The great night was ended for her, and he only remembered that he would have to be at his desk at ten o'clock.

She took off her cloak in front of the glass in order to admire herself once more in all her bravery, but, suddenly, she cried out: "The diamonds are gone!" Her husband, almost half asleep, started at the cry and asked:

"What is the matter?"

She turned toward him with a frightened air.

"I—I have lost Madame Forestier's necklace!"

He rose dismayed.

"What—how! But it is not possible!" And they immediately began to search in the folds of the dress, the cloak, in the pockets—everywhere, and found nothing.

"Are you sure that you had it when you left the ball?"

"Yes; I felt it while still in the vestibule at the Minister's."

"But if you had lost it in the street we should have heard it drop. It ought to be in the carriage."

"Yes; it is possible. Did you take the number?"

"No; and you have not looked at it, either?"

"No."

They looked at each other fearfully; finally Loisel dressed himself.

"I shall go over the whole ground that we travelled on foot, to see whether I cannot find it."

He went out. She sat still in her brilliant ball toilet; no desire to sleep, no power to think, all swallowed up in the fear of the calamity which had fallen upon them.

Her husband came in at seven o'clock. He had found nothing. He had been to the Prefecture of the Police, to the papers offering a reward, to all the small cab companies, anywhere, in short, where he could have the shadow of hope of recovery.

She waited all day in the same state of fear in the face of this frightful disaster.

Loisel returned in the evening pallid and haggard. No news as yet.

"You must write to your friend that you have broken the clasp of the necklace and are having it repaired. That will give us time to look around."

. . . . .

At the end of the week they had lost all hope, and Loisel, to whom it seemed this care and trouble had added five years to his age, said:

"We must try and replace the jewels."

The following day they went to the jeweller whose name was stamped inside the case. He consulted his books: "I did not sell that necklace, madame, I only furnished the case."

Then they went from jeweller to jeweller, racking their minds to match the jewels, both of them sick with grief and agony. At last, in a small shop in the Palais Royal, they found one which seemed to them like the one they had lost. With beating hearts they asked the price.

Forty thousand francs; but they could have it for 36,000 francs.

They asked the jeweller not to dispose of it for three days, and he also promised to take it back at 34,000 francs if the first one was found before the end of February.

Loisel had inherited 18,000 francs from his father. He borrowed the rest.

He borrowed a thousand francs from one, five hundred from another, five louis here, five louis there—he gave notes, made ruinous engagements, had recourse to the usurers, ran the whole gamut of moneylenders. He compromised his whole existence risking his signature, without knowing that it would be honoured, terrified by the agony of the future, by the black misery which enveloped him, by the prospect of all physical privations and moral tortures. He went for the new necklace and deposited on the counter his 36,000 francs.

When Madame Loisel returned the necklace to Madame Forestier, she coldly said:

"You should have returned it sooner, as I might have needed it."

She did not open the case, the one thing Madame Loisel had dreaded. What if she had discovered the change—what would she have thought? Would she not be taken for a thief?

. . . . .

From that time on Madame Loisel knew what life meant to the very poor in all its phases. She took her part heroically. This frightful debt must be paid. Her share of privations was bravely borne. They discharged their one domestic, changed their residence, and rented smaller apartments near the roof.

She knew now what the duties of the household meant, the heavy work of the kitchen. Her pretty hands soon lost all semblance of the care of bygone days. She washed the soiled linen and dried it in her room. She went every morning to the street with the refuse of the kitchen, carrying the water, stopping at each flight of stairs to take breath—wearing the dress of the women of the people; she went each day to the grocer, the fruiterer, the butcher, carrying her basket on her arm, bargaining, defending cent by cent her miserable money.

They were obliged each month to pay some notes and renew others in order to gain time. Her husband worked in the evening balancing the books of merchants, and often was busy all night, copying at five cents a page.

And this life they endured for ten years.

At the end of this time they had paid all the tax of the usurers and compound interest.

Madame Loisel seemed an old woman now. She had become strong and hardy as the women of the provinces, and with tousled head, short skirts, red hands, she was foremost among the loud-voiced women of the neighbourhood, who passed their time gossiping at their doorsteps.

But sometimes when her husband was at his office she seated

herself at the window and thought of that evening in the past and that ball, where she had been so beautiful and so admired.

What would have happened if she had not lost the necklace? Who knows? Life is a singular and changeable thing, full of vicissitudes. How little it takes to save or wreck us!

. . . . .

One Sunday as she was walking in the Champs Elysées to divert herself from the cares and duties of the week she suddenly perceived a lady, with a little child, coming toward her. It was Madame Forestier, still young, beautiful, and charming. Madame Loisel stopped short, too agitated to move. Should she speak to her? Yes, certainly. And now that the necklace was paid for she would tell her everything. Why not?

She walked up to her and said: " Good day, Jeanne."

Madame Forestier did not recognise her and seemed astonished at being spoken to so familiarly by this woman of the people.

" But—madame—I do not—I think you are mistaken."

" No; I am Mathilde Loisel."

" Oh!—my poor Mathilde, how you are changed! "

" Yes; I have had lots of trouble and misery since last I saw you—and all for you."

" For me! And how was that? "

" Do you remember the necklace of diamonds you lent me, to wear to the Minister's ball? "

" Yes; well? "

" Well, I lost it."

" Lost it! How could you, since you returned it to me? "

" I returned you one just like it, and for ten years we have been paying for it. You know, it was not easy for us, who had nothing —but it is finished, and I am very happy."

" You say that you bought a necklace of diamonds to replace mine," said Madame Forestier.

" Yes; and you never found it out! They were so much alike," and she smiled proudly.

Touched to the heart, Madame Forestier took the poor, rough hands in hers, drawing her tenderly toward her, her voice filled with tears:

" Oh, my poor Mathilde! But mine were paste. They were not worth more than 500 francs at most."

ULRICH THE GUIDE

GUY DE MAUPASSANT

SIMILAR to all the other little wood-built inns scattered here and there in the Hautes-Alpes, just below the glaciers in those bare, rocky pathways of the snow-capped mountain peaks, the Schwarenbach inn serves as a refuge for travellers through the Gemmi Pass.

During six months of the year it is inhabited by its owner, Jean Hauser, and his family, but as soon as the snow begins to get deep in the valley, so that the road to Loeche is only just practicable, the father and mother with their daughter and three sons leave their little mountain home in charge of the two guides, an old man named Gaspari Hari, and young Ulrich Kunsi, and Sam, the huge mountain dog.

The two men with their faithful keeper remain until the following spring in their snowy prison, having no other view than the immense white slope of the Balmhorn, surrounded by pale, glittering mountain peaks, until they are finally shut up, blocked, as it were, buried under the snow, which heaps itself up around them, and then presses close round the little house, bars the door, reaches the windows, and, in fact, wraps the inn round completely in its white mantle, and then falls thickly on the roof.

On the day when Hauser and his family set out on their journey back to Loeche, the winter had set in, and the descent was not without danger. The three sons went on first with the mules laden with luggage; then came Jeanne Hauser and the daughter, Louise, mounted on another mule.

The two guides walked behind with the father, for they were going to escort the little family to the beginning of the descent. They passed by the frozen lake which is between the great rocks near the inn, and then they continued along the valley, which looked like an immense white sheet, on each side of which rose the snowy peaks. A flood of sunshine fell on the white, shining, frozen desert, lighting it up with a cold, blinding flame. There was no sign of life in this ocean of mountains, no movement in this vast, measureless solitude, not a sound broke the profound silence.

Gradually the young guide, Ulrich Kunsi, a tall, strong-looking Swiss with long legs, got ahead of Hauser and old Gaspard Hari, and overtook the mule on which the two women were riding. The younger of them watched him advancing, and a happy light shone in her eyes. She was a pretty young girl, but her fair hair and her pale cheeks looked as though they had lost their colour through these long sojourns in the mountains surrounded by ice and snow. When Ulrich had overtaken them he slackened his pace and walked alongside of them, his hand resting on the crupper.

The Mère Hauser began at once to go over again all the details she had given him about the precautions necessary for the long winter season in the little inn. It was his first winter up there, whilst old Gaspard had for the last fourteen years spent his winter months under the snow in the Schwarenbach inn.

Ulrich Kunsi listened, but his eyes were fixed on the young girl, and he did not take in the sense of the words which fell on his ears. Every now and then he nodded his head and answered, "Yes, Madame Hauser," but his thoughts were far away, though his tranquil-looking face remained impassable. They arrived at the Daube Lake, the long surface of which, all frozen as it was, stretched out smooth and flat as far as the end of the valley.

On the right the dark rocks of the Daubenhorn rose up perpendicularly by the enormous moraines of the Lämmeren glacier upon which the Wildstrubel looked.

As they approached the Gemmi Pass, which is the beginning of the descent to Loeche, they suddenly came in sight of the immense horizon of the Valais Alps, from which they were separated by the deep, wide valley of the Rhône. It looked, in the distance, like a whole world of white, irregular mountain-tops, some flat and some pointed, and all glittering in the sunshine. There was the Mischabel, with its two horns; the huge mass of the Weisshorn; the heavy-looking Bruneck-horn; the high, formidable pyramid of the Matterhorn, the man-slayer; and that monstrous coquette, the Dent Blanche. Then, down below them in a hole at the bottom of a frightful abyss, they could see Loeche, the houses of which looked like so many grains of sand thrown down into that enormous crevice which the Gemmi Pass closes, and which begins over on the other side of the Rhône. The mule stopped at the beginning of the path which goes winding along, turning back and going on again, fantastic and marvellous the whole length of the mountain on the right until it reaches the almost invisible village at its foot.

The two women dismounted on to the snowy ground and waited until Hauser and Gaspard came up with them.

"Well, good-bye," said Hauser, shaking hands with the two guides, "and keep up your courage till we meet next year."

"Yes, good-bye till next year," said old Gaspard.

The Mère Hauser then shook hands with the guides, and then it was Louise's turn. Ulrich Kunsi whispered, as he held her hand in his: "Don't forget us up there under the snow," and she answered, " No; " but so quietly that he guessed what she said rather than heard it.

" Good-bye again, then," said Jean Hauser, " and take care of yourselves up there, you know," and shaking hands once more with the guides, he stepped on in front of his wife and daughter to lead the way down to the village. In a short time they were out of sight, hidden by the turn of the winding path.

The two men then retraced their steps and walked slowly back in the direction of the Schwarenbach inn. They went along, side by side, without speaking. They would be alone now—face to face with each other for the next four or five months.

Presently, Gaspard Hari began to tell about his life the previous winter. He had had with him Michael Canol, who was now too old to venture it again, as, of course, there is no knowing what may happen during those long months of solitude. It had not been so monotonous after all, for the chief thing is just to make up one's mind to it from the very first day, and then, too, they had found all kinds of things to do, and had played at various indoor games when they wanted a change.

Ulrich Kunsi listened mechanically to the old man's words, but his thoughts were with the little family on their way down to the village along the winding path of the Gemmi Pass. Soon the two men caught sight of the little inn, which was only just visible like a tiny black speck at the foot of the monstrous wave of snow. When at last they arrived at their destination and opened the door, the large dog with his curly hair began to jump up and frolic round them.

" Now, then, my lad," said old Gaspard, " we've got no woman here now to cook our dinner; you set to work and peel the potatoes, and we'll soon have something ready between us."

The following morning the time seemed to go very slowly; at least, so thought Ulrich Kunsi. Old Gaspard sat by the fire smoking his pipe, whilst the young man gazed out of the window at the dazzling white mountain opposite the house.

In the afternoon he went out for a walk and amused himself with following the tracks of the mule on which the two women had ridden the day before. When he reached the Gemmi Pass he lay down on the ground at the edge of the abyss, and looked down at Loeche.

The village in its rocky well was not yet hidden by the snow, which, however, had nearly reached it, but was stopped by the pine forests which sheltered the environs. Its low houses, as seen from that height, looked like so many stones in a meadow. Louise Hauser was down there now in one of those grey houses. In which one, though? Ulrich Kunsi could not tell, as he was too far away to be able to distinguish them separately. How he did wish he could go down to the village, now, before it was too late.

The sun had by this time disappeared behind the high crest of Wildstrubel, and the young man wended his way once more back to the inn. Gaspard was still smoking, but on seeing his companion he proposed a game of cards. They sat down to the little table facing each other and played for a long time, and then had their supper and went to bed.

The next few days were just like that first one—clear and cold, but no fresh snow. Old Gaspard would spend his afternoons looking out for the eagles and the rare birds which ventured on these icy summits, whilst Ulrich took his favourite walk down to the Gemmi Pass in order to have a glimpse of the village, and then on his return they would play at cards or dominoes, and stake some trifling object in order to add to the interest.

One morning Gaspard, who was up first, called out to his companion. A moving cloud, thick but light, of white foam was falling on them and all round them noiselessly, and was burying them gradually under a heavy, mossy mattress. This continued for four days and four nights, and the two men had, to keep the door and windows clear, to hollow out a passage and cut some steps in order to get up on to this icy powder which, after twelve hours' frost, was harder than the granite of the moraines. They had to live now almost like prisoners, scarcely venturing outside of their dwelling, and each of them accomplished regularly the everyday household tasks which he had from the first undertaken. Ulrich Kunsi did all the cleaning and the washing, and he also cut and carried the wood, whilst Gaspard's share of the work was the cooking and seeing to the fire.

Their regular, monotonous tasks were relieved by their games at cards and dominoes, and both of them being very quiet and placid, they never quarrelled by any chance. There were never any impatient or sharp words, and they were never even bad-tempered, for they had both taken in a good stock of resignation in order to be able to endure this winter sojourn on the top of the mountain. Sometimes old Gaspard would take his gun and go out chamois-hunting, and whenever he had luck there was great feasting in the little Schwarenbach inn.

One morning he set out on one of these expeditions. The thermometer was eighteen degrees below freezing-point, and as the sun was not yet up the wily huntsman hoped to surprise his prey round about the Wildstrubel.

Ulrich, finding himself alone, did not get up till towards ten o'clock. He was naturally a good sleeper, and would often have liked to stay in bed in the morning, but was ashamed to give way to his laziness when Gaspard was there, as the old guide was such an early riser and so energetic always. On the morning in question

Ulrich took his breakfast in a leisurely way and gave the dog his. Sam, too, spent nearly all his time now, night and day, in front of the fire sleeping.

When the young man got up from the table a strange, sad kind of feeling came over him, a sort of horror of the solitude, and he wished that Gaspard were there to have their customary game of cards. He missed it, as it had become quite a habit now to sit down after breakfast and have their game until it was time to prepare for the next meal.

Later on, as he could not settle down to anything, he set out to go and meet Gaspard, who was to be back home towards four o'clock. The snow had levelled the deep valley, filled up all the crevices, hidden the two lakes entirely from sight, and covered the rocks, so that there was nothing to be seen now between the two immense mountains but an enormous smooth white basin, all dazzling and frozen.

For the last three weeks Ulrich had not been down to the edge of the precipice to look at the little village. He wanted to go there before climbing the mountain slopes which led to Wildstrubel. Loeche was now also under the snow, and the houses were scarcely visible at all, buried as they were under this pale mantle. Turning to the right, Ulrich reached the Lämmeren glacier. He went on with his long, mountaineer strides, his iron-tipped staff striking the snow, which was as hard as stone, whilst, with his eagle glance, he looked round in search of a black moving speck in the distance on this measureless sheet of snow.

When he had arrived at the edge of the glacier he stopped suddenly, wondering to himself whether Gaspard had taken this road, and then he walked on along the moraines with a quicker step and a feeling every minute more and more anxious. It began to get dusk, a pink shade came over the snow, and a dry, frosty wind blew in gusts over its crystal surface. Ulrich called out in a shrill voice that vibrated through the air and broke the death-like silence in which the mountains were wrapped. It could be heard for a long distance over the deep, still waves of the frozen foam, just like the cry of a bird over the waves of the sea, and then it died away again and there was no answer. Ulrich walked on and on, and the sun was sinking gradually lower and lower behind the mountain crests, which were still purple from the reflection of the sky; but the deep valley itself was turning a leaden grey.

Suddenly the young man was seized with a strange, nameless fear. It seemed to him as though the silence, the cold, the solitude, and the winter death of these mountains were entering his very soul, and as though they would stop his blood and freeze it in his veins, as though they would stiffen his limbs and make him a motionless, frozen being. This idea took possession of him, and he set off running as fast as he could go towards their dwelling. "Gaspard must have come back by now," he said to himself; the old man had doubtless taken another road, and he would find him seated before the fire with his dead chamois at his feet.

Presently he came in sight of the inn. There was no smoke from the chimney. Ulrich hurried on faster and faster, but when he opened the door there was only Sam, who jumped up to greet him; Gaspard Hari had not yet returned. Terrified at the old man's long absence, Ulrich turned round as though he expected to see him hiding in one of the corners. He then busied himself with lighting the fire and making the soup, hoping that by the time the evening meal was ready Gaspard would be back. Every few minutes he would go to the door and look out to see whether he were not in sight.

It was night now, a pale, wan sort of night such as one has on the mountains, a livid dusk, lighted up from the edge of the horizon by a clear, yellowish crescent, which was just ready to fall behind the mountain-tops. The young man went back into the house, sat down and warmed his hands and feet at the fire, while he turned over in his own mind all the accidents which were possible.

Gaspard might have fallen and broken his leg, he might have slipped into a hole, or stumbled and twisted his foot. If so, he would be lying there in the snow, chilled through and through, and stiff with the cold; he would be in utter despair, shouting for help, calling out with all the strength he had left, and his voice would fall on the silent air, and there would be no one to answer him.

Where was he, though? The mountain was so vast, so rugged, and so dangerous to explore, especially at this season of the year, that ten or twenty guides might search in every direction for a whole week before finding a man in that immensity. Ulrich Kunsi, however, decided that if Gaspard Hari were not back by midnight, he would set out with Sam to search for him.

He began to make preparations for his expedition. He put enough food to last for two days in a knapsack, took his steel *crampons,* fastened a long, stout cord round and round his body, and examined his iron-tipped crook and his axe, with which he would probably have to cut steps in the ice. He then sat down and waited. The fire was blazing in the grate and the dog snoring away on the hearth, whilst the clock was beating time regularly within its wooden case like the heart of a human being. Ulrich sat there waiting, listening intently for any sound in the distance, shuddering when the wind rustled over the roof and against the walls.

The clock struck midnight, and the first stroke startled him. Then, feeling that he was all unnerved, he put some water on the fire to boil in order to make himself a cup of strong coffee before setting out. When the clock struck again he roused Sam, and then opening the door, started in the direction of Wildstrubel. For over five hours he continued his ascent, scaling rocks, cutting footholds in the ice, advancing slowly, and sometimes having to haul up the dog after him with his cord.

It was nearly six o'clock when he arrived on the top of one of the peaks where he knew Gaspard was in the habit of coming to hunt the chamois. Ulrich waited now for the daylight. The sky was getting paler over his head, and suddenly a strange light flashed over the immense ocean of the pale mountain-tops which stretched for a hundred leagues around him. It was as though this strange, weird light had risen from the snow itself, to fall again into space.

Gradually the highest peaks in the distance changed to a delicate, fleshy-pink hue, and then the red sun appeared behind the heavy giant heights of the Bernese Alps.

Ulrich Kunsi now started on his way once more. He walked along like a huntsman, with his head bent, looking out for tracks, and encouraging the dog every now and then with a "Search, Sam! Search! Good dog!"

He began to descend the mountain again, now gazing down at every precipice, and now and again calling out; but his voice always died away in the dumb immensity, and there was no answer on any side. Sometimes he would kneel down, with his ear on the ground to listen, and he would imagine he heard a voice, and would set off again quickly, calling all the way; but not another sound would he hear, and he would have to sit down to rest, exhausted and despairing.

Towards mid-day he took some refreshment and fed the dog, who was as worn out as his master, and then they started once more on their search. When night came on they were still going along, although they must have walked over thirty miles of mountain road. As they were too far from the little inn to think of getting back, and too tired to be able to continue their way, Ulrich hollowed out a hole in the snow and crouched down in it, with the dog, under a rug that he had brought with him slung over his shoulders.

They lay down together, the young man and the dog, trying to warm themselves by huddling close together, but frozen to the very marrow of their bones, both of them. Ulrich scarcely slept at all; he was haunted by all kinds of visions and shivering all over in every limb.

The day was just beginning to dawn when he got up. His legs were as stiff as bars of iron, and he was so low-spirited that he could have cried out in his anguish, whilst his heart beat so fast that he felt it would stop altogether at the slightest sound he might now hear.

The idea suddenly came to him that he too was going to die of cold in this terrible solitude, and the very horror of such a death roused him to action. He began to descend the mountain, this time in the direction of the inn. He stumbled and fell several times, and the poor dog lagged behind, limping along on his three paws. They reached Schwarenbach towards four o'clock in the afternoon, and found the house empty just as they had left it. Ulrich made a fire, and after he and the dog had eaten something, he was so worn out that he fell asleep, for he was absolutely incapable of thinking about anything.

He slept for a long time—a very long time—completely overmastered by invincible slumber. Suddenly the sound of a voice, of a cry of his own name, "Ulrich!" roused him, and he got up hastily. Had he been dreaming? Was it one of those strange cries which one hears in dreams when one's mind is ill at ease? No; he heard it again, now distinctly—that cry which vibrated, and which seemed to have entered into his very soul.

Most certainly some one had called, and it was his name he had heard—"Ulrich!" Some one was there near to the house, there was no doubt about it.

He rushed to the door, opened it, and shouted with all his might:—

"Gaspard, Gaspard, are you there?"

There was no answer, not a sound, not a murmur, not a moan, nothing. It was dark, but the snow could be seen as white as ever.

The wind had risen, that bitter, icy wind which cracks the stones and leaves nothing alive on those deserted heights. It swept along in sudden gusts, more withering and more deadly even than the fiery wind of the desert.

Ulrich cried out again: "Gaspard! Gaspard! Gaspard!"

Then he waited again and listened. All was dumb on the mountain. And now a mortal terror took possession of him, and he shook in all his bones. He rushed back into the house, closed the door, and fastened the bolts, and then sank down on a chair, shivering all over from head to foot.

He was certain, absolutely certain, that his comrade had just now called him with his dying breath. Of that he was sure, just as one is sure that one is alive or that one is eating a piece of bread. Gaspard Hari must have been slowly dying during two days and three nights down in some hole, in one of those deep, immaculate-looking ravines, the whiteness of which is more sinister than the dense gloom of the subterranean passages.

He had been dying during those two days and three nights, and now a few minutes ago he had drawn his last breath as he thought of his young comrade, and his soul was no sooner free than it had taken its flight towards the inn where Ulrich had been sleeping, and it had called him by virtue of that mysterious and terrible power which the souls of the dead have of haunting the living. It had cried out, this voiceless soul, to the soul of the young man as he slept; it had uttered its last farewell, or its reproach, or perhaps its curse, on the man who had not sought long enough on the mountain.

And Ulrich felt as though it was there with him, this soul, near him, behind the wall on the other side of the door which he had just bolted. It was roaming about like a night-bird which rustles against the lighted windows with its feathers, and the young man almost shrieked aloud in his awe and terror. He wanted to get up and rush away, but he dared not open the door; he dared not now, and he never would dare to from henceforth, for the phantom would remain there day and night, hovering round the inn, until the old man's body had been found and placed in consecrated ground in some cemetery.

It began to get light, and Ulrich felt more reassured at the return of the brilliant sunshine. He prepared his meal, fed the dog, and then he sat down again in despair and torture at the thought of the old man lying amongst the snow.

When once more the darkness began to cover the mountain, fresh terrors assailed him. He walked about in the dark kitchen, lighted only by one flickering candle. He walked backwards and forwards from one side to the other, taking long strides and listening—listening intently to hear whether the fearful cry of the previous night came across the gloomy stillness of the mountain. And he felt himself alone, the wretched man, more alone than any human being had ever been!

He was alone in the midst of this immense snowy desert, alone more than six thousand feet above any inhabited dwelling, right up above the world of human beings—alone in this frozen land. A wild idea took possession of him, to get away at all costs—to get away, no matter where, no matter how, to rush down to Loeche, to throw himself down the precipice! But, alas!—he did not even dare to open the door, so sure was he that the other one, the dead man, would bar the road for him, in order not to stay up here alone either.

Towards midnight, tired of pacing up and down, overwhelmed with anguish and terror, he sat down on one of the kitchen chairs, for he dreaded his bed just as one dreads a haunted spot.

Suddenly, once more, the strident cry of the night before fell upon his ears, and this time so piercing, so shrill, that Ulrich instinctively put up his arms to ward off the spirit, and in doing so lost his balance and fell over.

Sam, the dog, roused by the noise, began to howl, as dogs do when they are terrified, and began to walk round the dwelling to discover the danger. At the door he bent his head and sniffed along the ground, his ears pricked up and his tail straight out.

Ulrich, wild with terror, had risen from the ground and, holding the chair in his hand as a weapon, he called out, " Stay there! Do not come in: I will kill you if you come in." And the dog, more and more excited by his master's threatening tone, barked furiously at the invisible enemy who was daring to defy Ulrich.

Gradually, however, Sam began to calm down, and at last went back to his place on the hearth. He did not go to sleep again though, but just lay there looking anxious, his eyes shining, and growling every now and then. Ulrich, too, managed to master his terror, but feeling unnerved he opened the cupboard, and taking out a bottle of brandy, he drank several glasses one after the other.

His thoughts began to get confused, but his courage came back and a fever began to burn in his veins. The following day he scarcely touched any food; but he drank more brandy; and for several days he went on like this—drinking like some brute.

Every time the thought of Gaspard Hari came to him he would go to the brandy-bottle and drink until he fell down intoxicated. He would then remain there, his limbs feeble, his face against the ground, in a kind of drunken stupor.

No sooner, however, had the burning liquor lost its effect than the same terrible cry, " Ulrich! " roused him like some pistol-shot through his brain, and he would get up and stagger along, calling Sam to help him.

The poor dog seemed to be losing his senses too, like his master, for he would dart to the door, scratch with his paws, and gnaw at it with his long, white teeth, whilst the young man would go back to the brandy and drink a draught of it like water, so that it might once more deaden his terror and lull him to sleep. At the end of three weeks the stock of brandy had come to an end, and this continual intoxication had only calmed at intervals his terror, which now became more and more awful.

It had become a monomania with him, and his month's intoxication had exaggerated it so that now, in the midst of this absolute solitude, it increased day by day.

He paced up and down in his dwelling like a wild beast in his cage, putting his ear to the keyhole of the door at times to listen whether the other were still there, and defying him in angry tones through the wall. At night, no sooner did he begin tc doze, worn out as he was by fatigue, than the sound of the voice would make him spring to his feet.

At last one night, in sheer desperation, he rushed to the door and opened it, so that he might see who was calling him and oblige him to be silent. A gust of icy wind met him and seemed to freeze him through and through, and he banged the door to and bolted it again, without seeing that Sam had bounded out.

Then, shuddering, he threw some wood on the fire and sat down to get warm again. Presently he heard a scratching noise at the wall which made him start, and then there was a sound like a human voice wailing.

" Go away! " he shrieked, and a long, sad moan answered him.

All the reason which he had left gave way now in the face of this new horror.

He kept repeating his loud cry, " Go away," and wandered about looking for some corner in which to take refuge.

The moaning continued, and the other one wandered round and round the house outside scratching all the walls. Ulrich threw all his weight against the oak sideboard, full as it was of provisions and of china, and with almost superhuman strength he managed at length to push it against the door as a barricade. Then piling up everything that remained in the way of furniture, to the very mattresses off the beds, he stopped up the windows just as though the enemy were besieging the house. Some terrible, dismal groans were now heard from outside, and Ulrich answered by groans also.

Some days and nights passed like this: the one outside the house roaming round and round it, scratching at the walls and the door with such force that it seemed as though the wood-built building would be demolished; and all the time the other one inside the house listened to every movement and answered the terrible, lingering moans by fearful shrieks of terror.

At last one night there was silence again outside the house. Ulrich could hear nothing, and, thoroughly exhausted as he was, he lay down on the floor and fell asleep. When he awoke he had no memory of anything: not a thought came to him, it was as though his very brain had been emptied by that overpowering slumber. He was hungry, and he found some food and ate it.

Winter was over and the Gemmi Pass was once more practicable, so the Hauser family set out from the village to go back to their inn on the mountain. When they reached the top of the pass, the two women got on to their mule to continue the ascent, and they began to talk of the two guides who had been shut up on the mountain all the winter. As soon as the inn was in sight they saw that it was still well covered with snow, but there was smoke rising from the chimney, and this reassured Jean Hauser.

As they came nearer, they discovered on the very threshold of the inn the skeleton of an animal which had been torn to pieces by the eagles—a huge skeleton it was, and lying on its side.

They all examined it, and the Mère Hauser exclaimed, " It must be Sam! "

" Gaspard! " called out the father, and he was answered by a cry from inside the house, but it was a strange, piercing cry, and sounded more like the utterance of some animal than that of a human being. The Père Hauser called again, "Gaspard! Halloa!" and another cry like the first one was the only answer.

The father and sons then tried to open the door, but it resisted their efforts. They went into the empty stable and fetched a long piece of wood, which, with all their strength, they managed to push in. The door cracked and finally gave way, the wood breaking in pieces. Then there was a fearful noise, which seemed to shake the house, and there inside, behind the sideboard, which had turned over on to the floor, they saw a man standing up glaring at them—a man with long hair falling on to his shoulders and a long, wild-looking beard, and his clothes hanging in rags on his body.

The others did not recognise him, but Louise Hauser exclaimed, "Oh, mother, it's Ulrich!" and then the Mère Hauser saw that it was indeed Ulrich, although his hair was snow-white. He let them come up to him; he let them touch him; but he did not answer any of their questions.

They took him down to Loeche, and the doctors there pronounced him mad. His case, however, was not hopeless, though his recovery must of necessity be slow.

No one ever knew what had become of his companion, the old guide, Gaspard Hari. Louise Hauser nearly died that summer. She had a long illness, the cause of which was attributed to the cold on the mountain.

THE PRISONERS

GUY DE MAUPASSANT

THERE was no sound in the forest except the slight rustle of the snow as it fell upon the trees. It had been falling, small and fine, since mid-day; it powdered the branches with a frosty moss, cast a silver veil over the dead leaves in the hollow, and spread upon the pathways a great, soft, white carpet that thickened the immeasurable silence amid this ocean of trees.

Before the door of the keeper's lodge stood a bare-armed young woman, chopping wood with an axe upon a stone. She was tall, thin and strong—a child of the forest, a daughter and wife of gamekeepers.

A voice called from within the house, "Come in, Berthine; we are alone to-night, and it is getting dark. There may be Prussians or wolves about."

She who was chopping wood replied by splitting another block; her bosom rose and fell with the heavy blows, each time she lifted her arm.

"I have finished, mother. I'm here, I'm here. There's nothing to be frightened at; it isn't dark yet."

Then she brought in her faggots and her logs, and piled them up at the chimney-side, went out again to close the shutters—enormous shutters of solid oak—and then, when she again came in, pushed the heavy bolts of the door.

Her mother was spinning by the fire, a wrinkled old woman who had grown timorous with age.

"I don't like father to be out," said she. "Two women have no strength."

The younger answered, "Oh, I could very well kill a wolf or a Prussian, I can tell you." And she turned her eyes to a large revolver, hanging over the fireplace. Her husband had been put into the army at the beginning of the Prussian invasion, and the two women had remained alone with her father, the old gamekeeper, Nicholas Pichou, who had obstinately refused to leave his home and go into the town.

The nearest town was Rethel, an old fortress perched on a rock. It was a patriotic place, and the townspeople had resolved to resist the invaders, to close their gates and stand a siege, according to the traditions of the city. Twice before, under Henry IV. and under Louis XIV., the inhabitants of Rethel had won fame by heroic defences. They would do the same, this time; by Heaven, they would, or they would be burned within their walls.

So they had bought cannon and rifles, and equipped a force, and formed battalions and companies, and they drilled all day long in the Place d'Armes. All of them—bakers, grocers, butchers, notaries, attorneys, carpenters, booksellers, even the chemists—went through their manœuvres in due rotation at regular hours, under the orders of M. Lavigne, who had once been a non-commissioned officer in the dragoons, and now was a draper, having married the daughter and inherited the shop of old M. Ravaudan.

He had taken the rank of major in command of the place, and all the young men having gone to join the army, he enrolled all the others who were eager for resistance. The stout men now walked the streets at the pace of professional pedestrians, in order to bring down their fat, and to lengthen their breath; the weak ones carried burdens, in order to strengthen their muscles.

The Prussians were expected. But the Prussians did not appear. Yet they were not far off; for their scouts had already twice pushed across the forest as far as Nicholas Pichou's lodge.

The old keeper, who could run like a fox, had gone to warn the town. The guns had been pointed, but the enemy had not shown.

The keeper's lodge served as a kind of outpost in the forest of Aveline. Twice a week the man went for provisions, and carried to the citizens news from the outlying country.

He had gone that day to announce that a small detachment of German infantry had stopped at his house the day before about two in the afternoon, and had gone away again almost directly. The subaltern in command spoke French.

When the old man went on such errands he took with him his two dogs—two great beasts with the jaws of lions—because of the wolves who were beginning to get fierce; and he left his two women, advising them to lock themselves into the house as soon as night began to fall.

The young one was afraid of nothing, but the old one kept on trembling and repeating:

"It will turn out badly, all this sort of thing. You'll see, it will turn out badly."

This evening she was more anxious even than usual.

"Do you know what time your father will come back?" said she.

"Oh, not before eleven for certain. When he dines with the Major he is always late."

She was hanging her saucepan over the fire to make the soup, when she stopped short, listened to a vague sound which had reached her by way of the chimney, and murmured:

"There's some one walking in the wood—seven or eight men at least."

Her mother, alarmed, stopped her wheel and muttered: "Oh, good Lord! And father not here!"

She had not finished speaking when violent blows shook the door.

The woman made no answer, and a loud guttural voice called out: "Open the door."

Then, after a pause, the same voice repeated: "Open the door, or I'll break it in."

Then Berthine slipped into her pocket the big revolver from over the mantelpiece, and having put her ear to the crack of the door, asked: "Who are you?"

The voice answered: "I am the detachment that came the other day."

The woman asked again: "What do you want?"

"I have lost my way, ever since the morning, in the forest, with my detachment. Open the door, or I will break it in."

The keeper's wife had no choice; she promptly drew the great bolt, and pulling back the door she beheld six men in the pale snow-shadows—six Prussian men, the same who had come the day before. She said in a firm tone "What do you want here at this time of night?"

The officer answered: "I had lost my way, lost it completely; I recognised the house. I have had nothing to eat since the morning, nor my men either."

Berthine replied, "But I am all alone with mother, this evening."

The soldier, who seemed a good sort of fellow, answered, "That makes no difference. I shall not do any harm; but you must give us something to eat. We are faint and tired to death."

The keeper's wife stepped back.

"Come in," said she.

They came in, powdered with snow and with a sort of mossy cream on their helmets that made them look like meringues. They seemed tired, worn out.

The young woman pointed to the wooden benches on each side of the big table.

"Sit down," said she, "and I'll make you some soup. You do look quite knocked up."

Then she bolted the door again.

She poured some more water into her saucepan, threw in more butter and potatoes; then, unhooking a piece of bacon that hung in the chimney, she cut off half, and added that also to the stew. The eyes of the six men followed her every movement with an air of awakened hunger. They had set their guns and helmets in a corner, and sat waiting on their benches, like well-behaved school children. The mother had begun to spin again, but she threw terrified glances at the invading soldiers. There was no sound except the slight purring of the wheel, the crackle of the fire, and the bubbling of the water as it grew hot.

But all at once a strange noise made them all start—something like a hoarse breathing at the door, the breathing of an animal, deep and snorting.

One of the Germans had sprung towards the guns. The woman with a movement and a smile stopped him.

"It is the wolves," said she. "They are like you; they are wandering about, hungry."

The man would hardly believe, he wanted to see for himself; and as soon as the door was opened, he perceived two great grey beasts making off at a quick, long trot.

He came back to his seat, murmuring, "I should not have believed it."

And he sat waiting for his meal.

They ate voraciously; their mouths opened from ear to ear to take the largest of gulps; their round eyes opened sympathetically with their jaws, and their swallowing was like the gurgle of rain in a water pipe.

The two silent women watched the rapid movements of the great red beards; the potatoes seemed to melt away into these moving fleeces.

Then, as they were thirsty, the keeper's wife went down into the cellar to draw cider for them. She was a long time gone; it was a little vaulted cellar, said to have served both as prison and hiding-place in the days of the Revolution. The way down was by a narrow winding stair, shut in by a trap-door at the end of the kitchen.

When Berthine came back, she was laughing, laughing slyly to herself. She gave the Germans her pitcher of drink. Then she too had her supper, with her mother, at the other end of the kitchen.

The soldiers had finished eating and were falling asleep, all six, around the table. From time to time, a head would fall heavily on the board, then the man, starting awake, would sit up.

Berthine said to the officer, " You may just as well lie down here before the fire. There's plenty of room for six. I'm going up to my room with my mother."

The two women went to the upper floor. They were heard to lock their door and to walk about for a little while, then they made no further sound.

The Prussians stretched themselves on the stone floor, their feet to the fire, their heads on their rolled-up cloaks, and soon all six were snoring on six different notes, sharp or deep, but all sustained and alarming.

They had certainly been asleep for a considerable time when a shot sounded, and so loud that it seemed to be fired close against the walls of the house. The soldiers sat up instantly. There were two more shots, and then three more.

The door of the staircase opened hastily, and the keeper's wife appeared, barefooted, a short petticoat over her nightdress, a candle in her hand, and a face of terror. She whispered, " Here are the French—two hundred of them at least. If they find you here, they will burn the house. Go down, quick, into the cellar, and don't make a noise. If you make a noise, we are lost." The officer, scared, murmured, " I will, I will. Which way do we go down? "

The young woman hurriedly raised the narrow square trap-door, and the men disappeared by the winding stair, one after another going underground, backwards, so as to feel the steps with their feet. But when the point of the last helmet had disappeared, Berthine, shutting down the heavy oaken plank, thick as a wall, and hard as steel, kept in place by clamps and a padlock, turned the key twice, slowly, and then began to laugh with a laugh of silent rapture, and with a wild desire to dance over the heads of her prisoners.

They made no noise, shut in as if they were in a stone box, only getting air through a grating.

Berthine at once re-lighted her fire, put on her saucepan once more, and made more soup, murmuring, " Father will be tired to-night."

Then she sat down and waited. Nothing but the deep-toned pendulum of the clock went to and fro with its regular tick in the silence. From time to time, the young woman cast a look at the dial—an impatient look, which seemed to say, " How slowly it goes! "

Presently she thought she heard a murmur under her feet; low, confused words reached her through the vaulted masonry of the cellar. The Prussians were beginning to guess her trick, and soon the officer came up the little stair, and thumped the trap-door with his fist. Once more he cried, " Open the door."

She rose, drew near, and imitating his accent, asked, " What do you want? "

" Open the door! "

" I shall not open it."

The man grew angry.

" Open the door, or I'll break it in."

She began to laugh.

" Break away, my man; break away."

Then he began to beat, with the butt end of his gun, upon the oaken trap-door over his head; but it would have resisted a battering-ram.

The keeper's wife heard him go down again. Then, one after another, the soldiers came up to try their strength and inspect the fastenings. But, concluding no doubt that their efforts were in vain, they all went back into the cellar and began to talk again.

The young woman listened to them; then she went to open the outer door, and stood straining her ears for a sound.

A distant barking reached her. She began to whistle like a huntsman, and almost immediately, two immense dogs loomed through the shadows, and jumped upon her with signs of joy. She held them by the neck, to keep them from running away, and called with all her might, " Halloa, father! "

A voice, still very distant, answered, " Halloa, Berthine! "

She waited some moments, then called again, " Halloa, father! "

The voice repeated, nearer, " Halloa, Berthine! "

The keeper's wife returned, " Don't pass in front of the grating. There are Prussians in the cellar."

All at once the black outline of the man showed on the left, where he had paused between two tree-trunks. He asked, uneasily: " Prussians in the cellar! What are they doing there? "

The young woman began to laugh.

"It is those that came yesterday. They got lost in the forest ever since the morning; I put them in the cellar to keep cool."

And she related the whole adventure; how she had frightened them with shots of the revolver, and shut them up in the cellar.

The old man, still grave, asked, "What do you expect me to do with them at this time of night?"

She answered, "Go and fetch M. Lavigne and his men. He'll take them prisoners; and won't he be pleased!"

Then Father Pichou smiled: "Yes; he will be pleased."

His daughter resumed. "Here's some soup for you; eat it quick and go off again."

The old keeper sat down and began to eat his soup, after having put down his two plates full for his dogs.

The Prussians, hearing voices, had become silent.

A quarter of an hour later, Pichou started again. Berthine, with her head in her hands, waited.

The prisoners were moving about again. They shouted and called, and beat continually with their guns on the immovable trap-door of the cellar.

Then they began to fire their guns through the grating, hoping, no doubt, to be heard if any German detachment were passing in the neighbourhood.

The keeper's wife did not stir; but all this noise tried her nerves, and irritated her. An evil anger awoke in her; she would have liked to kill them, the wretches, to keep them quiet.

Then, as her impatience increased, she began to look at the clock and count the minutes.

At last the hands marked the time which she had fixed for their coming.

She opened the door once more to listen for them. She perceived a shadow moving cautiously. She was frightened, and screamed. It was her father.

He said, "They sent me to see if there's any change."

"No, nothing."

Then he in his turn gave a long, strident whistle into the darkness. And soon something brown was seen coming slowly through the trees—the advance-guard composed of ten men.

The old man kept repeating, "Don't pass before the grating."

And the first comers pointed out the formidable grating to those who followed.

Finally, the main body appeared, two hundred men in all, each with two hundred cartridges.

M. Lavigne, trembling with excitement, posted them so as to surround the house on all sides, leaving, however, a wide, free space round the little black hole, level with the earth, which admitted air to the cellar.

Then he entered the dwelling and inquired into the strength and position of the enemy, now so silent that it might be thought to have disappeared, flown away or evaporated through the grating. M. Lavigne stamped his foot on the trap-door and called, " Mr. Prussian officer! "

The German did not reply.

The Major repeated, " Mr. Prussian officer! "

It was in vain. For a whole twenty minutes he summoned this silent officer to capitulate with arms and baggage, promising him life and military honours for himself and his soldiers. But he obtained no sign of consent or of hostility. The situation was becoming difficult.

The soldier-citizens were stamping their feet and striking wide-armed blows upon their chests, as coachmen do for warmth, and they were looking at the grating with an ever-growing childish desire to pass in front of it. At last one of them risked it, a very nimble fellow called Potdevin. He took a start and ran past like a stag. The attempt succeeded. The prisoners seemed dead.

A voice called out, " There's nobody there."

Another soldier crossed the space before the dangerous opening. Then it became a game. Every minute a man ran out, passing from one troop to the other as children at play do, and raising showers of snow behind him with the quick movement of his feet. They had lighted fires of dead branches to keep themselves warm, and the flying profile of each *Garde-National* showed in a bright illumination as he passed over to the camp on the left.

Some one called out, " Your turn, Maloison."

Maloison was a big baker whom his comrades laughed at, because he was so fat.

He hesitated. They teased him. Then, making up his mind, he started at a regular breathless trot which shook his stout person. All the detachment laughed till they cried. They called out, " Bravo, Maloison! " to encourage him.

He had gone about two-thirds of the distance when a long flame, rapid and red, leapt from the grating. A report followed, and the big baker fell upon his nose with a frightful shriek.

No one ran to help him. Then they saw him drag himself on all fours across the snow, moaning, and when he was beyond that terrible passage he fainted. He had a bullet high up in the flesh of the thigh.

After the first surprise and alarm there was more laughter.

Major Lavigne appeared upon the threshold of the keeper's lodge. He had just framed his plan of attack, and gave his word of command in a ringing voice, " Plumber Planchet and his men! "

Three men drew near.

" Unfasten the gutters of the house."

In a quarter of an hour some twenty yards of leaden gutter pipe were brought to the Major.

Then, with innumerable prudent precautions, he had a little round hole bored in the edge of the trap-door, and having laid out an aqueduct from the pump to this opening, announced with an air of satisfaction, " We are going to give these German gentlemen something to drink." A wild cheer of admiration burst forth, followed by shouts of delight and roars of laughter. The Major organised gangs of workers, who were to be employed in relays of five minutes. Then he commanded, " Pump! "

And the iron handle having been put in motion, a little sound rustled along the pipes and slipped into the cellar, falling from step to step with the tinkle of a waterfall, suggestive of rocks and little red fishes.

They waited.

An hour passed; then two, then three.

The Major walked about the kitchen in a fever, putting his ear to the floor from time to time, trying to guess what the enemy was doing and whether it would soon capitulate.

The enemy was moving now. Sounds of rattling, of speaking, of splashing, could be heard. Then towards eight in the morning a voice issued from the grating, " I want to speak to the French officer."

Lavigne answered from the window, without putting out his head too far, " Do you surrender? "

" I surrender."

" Then pass out your guns."

A weapon was immediately seen to appear out of the hole and fall into the snow; then a second, a third—all; and the same voice declared, " I have no more. Make haste. I am drowned."

The Major commanded, " Stop."

And the handle of the pump fell motionless.

Then, having filled the kitchen with soldiers, all standing armed, he slowly lifted the trap-door.

Six drenched heads appeared, six fair heads with long light hair, and the six Germans were seen issuing forth one by one, shivering, dripping, scared.

They were seized and bound. Then, as a surprise was apprehended, the troops set out in two parties, one in charge of the prisoners, the other in charge of Maloison, on a mattress, carried on poles.

Rethel was entered in triumph.

M. Lavigne received a decoration for having taken prisoner a Prussian advance-guard; and the fat baker had the military medal for wounds received in face of the enemy.

A COWARD

GUY DE MAUPASSANT

HE was known in society as "the handsome Signoles." His name was Viscount Gontran Joseph de Signoles.

An orphan and the possessor of a sufficient fortune, he cut a dash, as they say. He had style and presence, sufficient fluency of speech to make people think him clever, a certain natural grace, an air of nobility and pride, a gallant moustache and a gentle eye, which the women like.

He was in great demand in the salons, much sought after by fair dancers; and he aroused in his own sex that smiling animosity which they always feel for men of an energetic figure. He had been suspected of several love-affairs well adapted to cause a young bachelor to be much esteemed. He passed a happy, unconcerned life, in a comfort of mind which was most complete. He was known to be a skilful fencer, and with the pistol even more adept.

"If I ever fight a duel," he would say, "I shall choose the pistol. With that weapon I am sure of killing my man."

Now, one evening, when he had accompanied to the theatre two young lady friends of his, whose husbands also were of the party, he invited them, after the play, to take an ice at Tortoni's. They had been at the café but a few moments, when he noticed that a man sitting at a table near by was staring persistently at one of his fair neighbours. She seemed annoyed and uneasy, and lowered her eyes. At last she said to her husband:

"That man is staring me out of countenance. I don't know him; do you?"

The husband, who had noticed nothing, raised his eyes, and answered:

"No, not at all."

The young woman continued, half smiling, half vexed:

"It is very unpleasant; that man is spoiling my ice."

The husband shrugged his shoulders:

"Pshaw! don't pay any attention to him. If we had to bother our heads about all the impertinent fellows we meet, we should never have done."

But the viscount had risen abruptly. He could not suffer that stranger to spoil an ice which he had offered. It was to him that the affront was paid, since it was through him and for him that his friends had entered the café, so that the affair was his concern, and his alone.

He walked towards the man and said to him:

"You have a way of looking at those ladies, Monsieur, that I cannot tolerate. I beg you to be so kind as to stare less persistently."

The other retorted:

"You may go to the devil!"

"Take care, Monsieur," said the viscount, with clenched teeth; "you will force me to pass bounds."

The gentleman answered but one word, a foul word, that rang from one end of the café to the other, and caused every guest to give a sudden start, as if moved by a hidden spring. Those whose backs were turned wheeled round; all the others raised their heads; three waiters whirled about on their heels like tops; the two women at the desk gave a jump, then turned completely round, like automata obedient to the same crank.

Profound silence ensued. Suddenly a sharp sound cracked in the air. The viscount had slapped his adversary. Every one rose to interfere. Cards were exchanged between the two.

When the viscount had returned to his apartment he paced the floor for several minutes with great, quick strides. He was too much agitated to reflect. A single thought hovered over his mind—"a duel"—without arousing any emotion whatsoever. He had done what he should have done; he had shown himself to be what he ought to be. His conduct would be discussed and approved; people would congratulate him. He said aloud, speaking as one speaks when one's thoughts are in great confusion:

"What a brute the fellow was!"

Then he sat down and began to consider. He must find seconds in the morning. Whom should he choose? He thought over those of his acquaintances who were the most highly esteemed and the best known. He decided at last upon the Marquis de la Tour-Noire and the Colonel Bourdin—a great noble and a soldier—excellent! Their names would sound well in the papers. He discovered that he was thirsty, and he drank three glasses of water in rapid succession; then he resumed his pacing of the floor. He felt full of energy. If he blustered a little, seemed determined to carry the thing through, demanded rigorous and dangerous conditions, insisted upon a serious duel, very serious and terrible, his adversary would probably back down and apologise.

He picked up the card, which he had drawn from his pocket and tossed on the table, and read it again, as he had read it in a glance at the café, and again in the cab, by the glimmer of every street-lamp on his way home. " Georges Lamil, 51 Rue Moncey." Nothing more.

He examined these assembled letters, which seemed to him mysterious, full of vague meaning. Georges Lamil! Who was this man? What was his business? Why had he stared at that lady in such a way? Was it not disgusting that a stranger, an unknown, should cause such a change in one's life, because it had pleased him to fasten his eyes insolently upon a lady?

And the viscount again exclaimed aloud:

" What a brute! "

Then he stood perfectly still, thinking, his eyes still glued to the card. There arose within him a fierce anger against that bit of paper—a malevolent sort of rage, blended with a strange feeling of discomfort. What a stupid business! He took a penknife that lay open to his hand, and stuck it through the middle of the printed name, as if he were stabbing some one.

So he must fight! Should he choose swords, or pistols?—for he deemed himself the insulted party. He ran less risk with the sword; but with the pistol he had a chance of making his opponent withdraw. A duel with swords is rarely fatal, mutual prudence preventing the combatants from engaging each other near enough for a point to enter very deep. With the pistol his life was seriously endangered; but he might in that way come out of the affair with all the honours, and without coming to a meeting.

" I must be firm," he said. " He will be afraid."

The sound of his voice made him tremble, and he looked about him. He felt extremely nervous. He drank another glass of water, then began to undress for bed.

As soon as he was in bed he blew out the light and shut his eyes.

He thought:

" I have all day to-morrow to arrange my affairs. I must sleep now, so that I may be calm."

He was very warm under the bed-clothes, but he could not manage to doze off. He twisted and turned, lay on his back five minutes, then changed to the left side, then rolled over on his right.

He was still thirsty. He got up again, to drink. Then a disquieting thought occurred to him:

" Can it be that I am afraid? "

Why did his heart begin to beat wildly at every familiar sound in the room? When the clock was about to strike, the faint whirring of the spring making ready made him jump; and then he had to keep his mouth open for several seconds to breathe, the oppression was so great.

He commenced to argue with himself concerning the possibility of this thing:

" Am I afraid? "

No, of course he was not afraid, as he had determined to carry the thing through, as his mind was fully made up to fight, and not to tremble. But he felt so profoundly troubled that he asked himself the question:

" Is it possible to be afraid in spite of one's self? "

And that doubt, that disquietude, that dread took possession of him; if some force stronger than his will, a dominating, irresistible power should conquer him, what would happen? Yes, what could happen? He certainly would go to the ground, inasmuch as he had made up his mind to go there. But suppose his hand should tremble? Suppose he should faint? And he thought of his position, of his reputation, of his name.

And suddenly a strange fancy seized him to get up, in order to look in the mirror. He relit his candle. When he saw the reflection of his face in the polished glass he could hardly recognise himself, and it seemed to him that he had never seen this man before. His eyes appeared enormous; and he was certainly pale—yes, very pale.

He remained standing in front of the mirror. He put out his tongue as if to test the state of his health, and of a sudden this thought burst into his mind like a bullet:

" The day after to-morrow, at this time, I may be dead."

And his heart began to beat furiously again.

" The day after to-morrow, at this time, I may be dead. This person in front of me, this I, whom I am looking at in this mirror, will be no more! What! I am standing here, looking at myself, conscious that I am a living man; and in twenty-four hours I shall be lying on that bed, dead, with my eyes closed, cold, lifeless, gone! "

He turned towards the bed, and he distinctly saw himself lying on his back, between the very sheets that he had just left. He had the hollow cheeks that dead bodies have, and that slackness of the hands that will never stir more.

Thereupon he conceived a fear of his bed, and, in order to avoid looking at it, passed into his smoking-room. He mechanically took a cigar, lighted it, and began to pace the floor anew. He was cold; he walked to the bell-cord to wake his valet; but he stopped, with his hand half-way to the cord.

" That fellow will see that I am afraid."

And he did not ring, but made the fire himself. His hands trembled slightly, with a nervous shudder, when they touched anything. His brain was in a whirl; his troubled thoughts became fugitive, sudden, melancholy; a sort of intoxication seized on his spirit as if he had been drunk.

And ceaselessly he asked himself:

" What am I going to do? What will become of me? "

His whole body quivered, shaken by jerky tremblings. He got up, went to the window, and drew aside the curtains. The day was breaking, a summer's day. The rosy sky gave a rosy tint to the city, the roofs, and the walls. A great flood of light, like a caress from the rising sun, enveloped the awaking world; and with that glimmer, a sudden, enlivening, brutal hope seized on the heart of the viscount. How insane he was to have allowed himself to be so struck down by terror, even before anything was decided, before his seconds had met those of Georges Lamil, before he knew whether he was really to fight!

He made his toilet, dressed himself, and left the house with a firm step.

As he walked, he said to himself again and again:

" I must be firm, very firm. I must prove that I am not afraid."

His seconds, the marquis and the colonel, placed themselves at his disposal, and after warmly shaking his hand, discussed the conditions.

The colonel asked:

" Do you desire a serious duel? "

" Very serious," the viscount replied.

" You insist upon pistols? "

" Yes."

" Do you leave us at liberty to make the other arrangements? "

The viscount articulated with a dry, jerky voice:

" Twenty paces, firing at the word, lifting the arm instead of lowering it. Shots to be exchanged until some one is badly wounded."

" Those are excellent conditions," said the colonel, in a tone of satisfaction. " You are a good shot; the chances are all in your favour."

And they separated. The viscount returned home to wait for them. His agitation, which had been temporarily allayed, increased from moment to moment. He felt along his arms and legs, in his chest, a sort of shudder, an incessant vibration; he could not keep still, either sitting or standing. He had only a trace of moisture in his mouth, and he moved his tongue noisily every second, as if to unglue it from his palate.

He tried to breakfast, but he could not eat. Thereupon it occurred to him to drink to renew his courage, and he ordered a small decanter of rum, from which he gulped down six little glasses, one after another. A warmth, like that caused by a burn, invaded his whole frame, followed as soon by a giddiness of the soul.

" I have found the way," he thought; " now it is all right."

But in an hour he had emptied the decanter, and his agitation became intolerable. He was conscious of a frantic longing to throw himself on the floor, to cry, to bite. Evening fell.

A ring at the bell caused him such a feeling of suffocation that he had not the strength to rise and receive his seconds.

He did not dare even to talk to them any longer—to say, "How do you do?" to utter a single word, for fear that they would divine everything from the trembling of his voice.

"Everything is arranged according to the conditions that you fixed," said the colonel. "At first, your adversary claimed the privileges of the insulted party, but he gave way almost immediately and assented to everything. His seconds are two military men."

The viscount said:

"Thank you."

The marquis added:

"Excuse us if we stay but a moment, but we still have a thousand things to attend to. We must have a good doctor, as the duel is not to stop until somebody is severely wounded; and you know there's no trifling with bullets. We must arrange about the place, too—near a house to which the wounded man may be taken if necessary, etc.; in short, we still have two or three hours' work before us."

The viscount succeeded in articulating a second time:

"Thank you."

The colonel asked:

"You are all right? quite calm?"

"Yes, quite calm, thanks."

The two men withdrew.

When he was alone once more it seemed to him that he was going mad. His servant having lighted the lamps, he seated himself at his table to write some letters. After tracing at the top of a page, "This is my Will," he rose with a jump and walked away, feeling incapable of putting two ideas together, of forming any resolution, of deciding any question whatsoever.

So he was really going to fight! It was no longer possible for him to avoid it. What on earth was taking place in him? He wanted to fight; his purpose and determination to do so were firmly fixed; and yet he knew full well that, despite all the effort of his mind and all the tension of his will, he would be unable to retain even the strength necessary to take him to the place of meeting. He tried to fancy the combat, his own attitude, and the bearing of his adversary.

From time to time his teeth chattered with a little dry noise. He tried to read, and took up Châteauvillard's duelling-code. Then he asked himself:

"Has my opponent frequented the shooting-galleries? Is he well known? What's his class? How can I find out?"

He remembered Baron de Vaux's book on pistol-shooters, and

he looked it through from end to end. Georges Lamil's name was not mentioned. But if the fellow were not a good shot, he would not have assented so readily to that dangerous weapon and those fatal conditions! As he passed a table, he opened the case by Gastinne Renette, took out one of the pistols, then stood as if he were about to fire, and raised his arm. But he was trembling from head to foot, and the barrel shook in all directions.

Then he said to himself:

"It is impossible. I cannot fight like this!"

He regarded the little hole, black and deep, at the end of the barrel, the hole that spits out death; he thought of the dishonour, of the whispered comments at the clubs, of the laughter in the salons, of the disdain of the women, of the allusions in the newspapers, of the insults which cowards would throw in his face.

He continued to gaze at the weapon, and as he raised the hammer he saw the priming glitter beneath it like a little red flame. The pistol had been left loaded, by chance, by oversight. And he experienced a confused, inexplicable joy thereat.

If he did not display in the other's presence the calm and noble bearing suited to the occasion, he would be lost for ever. He would be disgraced, branded with the sign of infamy, hunted from society! And that calm and bold bearing he could not command —he knew it, he felt it. And yet he was really brave, because he wanted to fight! He was brave, because—— The thought that grazed his mind was never completed; opening his mouth wide, he suddenly thrust the barrel of the pistol into the very bottom of his throat and pressed upon the trigger.

When his valet ran in, alarmed by the report, he found him on his back, dead. The blood had spattered the white paper on the table, and made a great red stain under the four words:

"This is my Will."

THE LITTLE SOLDIER

GUY DE MAUPASSANT

EVERY Sunday, as soon as they were at liberty, the two little soldiers would set forth.

They turn to the right on leaving the barracks, march rapidly through Courbevoie as if they are out for drill; then, as soon as they have left the houses behind, they follow at a more quiet pace the bare and dusty high-road that leads to Bezons.

They were short and spare, lost in their too long and too ample coats, the sleeves of which covered their hands; embarrassed by the red breeches, which were too large for them and forced them to stretch their legs apart if they would walk fast. And beneath the stiff, tall shakos one could see almost nothing of their faces—two poor Breton faces, with hollow cheeks; simple with an almost animal-like innocence, with soft, placid blue eyes.

They never spoke while they walked, but went straight on, with the same thought in their minds, which took the place of conversation; for they had found, on the edge of the little wood of Les Champioux, a spot that reminded them of their own country, and they felt at ease nowhere else.

At the junction of the roads from Colombes and Chatou, when they were under the trees, they would always remove the shakos, which weighed heavily on their heads, and they would wipe their brows.

They always stopped a while on the Bezons bridge to look at the Seine. They would stand there two or three minutes, bent double, leaning over the parapet; or they would gaze at the great basin of Argenteuil, where the bellying white sails of the clippers scudded by, recalling perhaps the Breton sea, the port of Vannes, which was near their homes; and the fishing vessels sailing across Morbihan towards the open sea. As soon as they had crossed the Seine, they would buy their day's provisions at the pork-shop, the bakery, and the wine-shop of the neighbourhood. A bit of pork-pie, four sous' worth of bread, and a litre of *petit bleu* constituted their provisions, which they carried away in their handkerchiefs. But as soon as they had left the village, they walked very slowly and began to talk.

Before them a barren plain, with a clump of trees here and there, led to the wood, the little wood that looked like that at Kermarivan. Wheat and oats lined the narrow road, which was hidden by the fresh young verdure of the new crops; and Jean Kerderen would invariably say to Luc le Ganidec:

"It's just like Plounivon."

"Yes, it's just like it."

They would walk on, side by side, their minds filled with vague memories of their own country, filled with reawakened images, images as naïve as the coloured pictures you buy for a sou. They seemed to see a corner of a field, a hedge, a bit of moor, a cross-roads, a granite cross.

And they always stopped beside a stone that marked the boundary of an estate, because it had a look of the cromlech at Locneuven.

Every Sunday when they reached the first clump of trees, Luc le Ganidec would cut a hazel switch and would gently set about peeling off the bark, thinking of the folks at home.

Jean Kerderen carried the provisions.

From time to time Luc would mention a name, or recall some incident of their childhood, in a few words which gave them food for long thought. And their own country, their dear, distant country, would gradually take possession of them, sweep over them, and send them across the intervening space its shapes, its sounds, its familiar landscapes, its odours—the odour of the green moor swept by the sea-breeze.

They no longer smelt the exhalations from the Parisian dunghill with which the soil of the suburbs is fertilised, but the sweet perfume of the flowering broom, plucked and whirled away by the salt breeze of the open sea. And the sails of the small boats, showing above the banks, seemed to them to be the sails of the coasting-vessels, seen beyond the broad plain that stretched away from their homes to the water's edge.

And Luc le Ganidec and Jean Kerderen would walk slowly on, happy yet sad, haunted by a mild sort of melancholy, the slow and penetrating melancholy of a caged animal that remembers.

And by the time Luc had finished stripping the slender switch of its bark, they would have reached the corner of the wood where they breakfasted every Sunday.

They would find the two bricks that they had hidden in the underbrush, and would light a little fire of dry branches, to cook their pork-pie on the point of a bayonet.

And when they had breakfasted, eaten their bread to the last crumb, and drunk their wine to the last drop, they would remain seated on the grass side by side, without speaking, their eyes far away, their eyelids drooping, their fingers crossed as during mass, their red legs stretched out beside the poppies; and the leather of their shakos and their brass buttons glittered in the hot sun and checked the flight of the larks that flew singing over their heads.

About noon they would begin to turn their eyes now and then towards the village of Bezons, for it was time for the girl who tended the cow to come.

She passed them every Sunday on her way to milk and house her cow, the only cow in the neighbourhood which was out at grass; it was pastured in a narrow field on the edge of the wood, farther on.

Soon they would spy the girl, the sole human being abroad in that part of the country; and their hearts were made glad by the dazzling reflection cast by her tin pail when the sun's rays fell upon it. They never talked of her. They were simply glad to see her, but did not understand why.

She was a tall, robust girl, with red hair, burned by the heat of sunny days—a great, plain-spoken girl of the environs of Paris.

Once, when she saw them seated in the same place, she said to them:

"Good day; so you always come here, do you?"

Luc le Ganidec, being the bolder, stammered:

"Yes, we come here to rest."

That was all. But the next Sunday she laughed when she saw them, she laughed with the patronising good-humour of a quick-witted woman who divined their timidity. And she asked:

"What you doing there? Watching the grass grow?"

Luc smiled back with unwonted animation: "Maybe so."

"Well!" she rejoined; "it don't grow very fast."

"That's so," he replied, still laughing.

She went on. But when she returned with her pail full of milk, she stopped in front of them again, and said:

"Would you like a drop? It will remind you of home."

With the instinct of a creature of the same race, and like them far from home, perhaps, she had divined truly and touched the right spot.

They were both moved. Thereupon she poured a little milk, not without difficulty, into the mouth of the bottle in which they had brought their wine; and Luc drank first, with little sips, stopping every second to make sure that he had not taken more than his share. Then he handed the bottle to Jean.

She remained standing in front of them, with her hands on her hips, her pail on the ground at her feet, well pleased with the pleasure she had given them.

Then she went away, shouting:

"Well, good-bye; till next Sunday!"

And they followed with their eyes, as long as they could see her, the tall, receding figure, which grew smaller and smaller and seemed to bury itself in the verdure.

When they left the barracks the following week, Jean said to Luc:

"Hadn't we better buy her something good?"

And they faced in dire perplexity the problem of choosing a delicacy for the girl with the cow.

Luc favoured chitterlings, but Jean preferred candy, for he was fond of sweet things. His opinion prevailed, and they purchased at a grocer's two sous' worth of white and red bonbons.

They breakfasted more quickly than usual, excited by anticipation.

Jean saw her first.

"There she is!" he said.

And Luc replied:

"Yes. There she is."

She laughed in the distance when she saw them, and called to them:

"How goes everything?"

And they replied in the same breath:

"How is it with you?"

Then she talked, talked of simple things that interested them—the weather, the crops, her employers.

They were afraid to offer their bonbons, which were slowly melting away in Jean's pocket.

At last Luc made bold, and murmured:

"We've brought you something."

"What is it?" she asked.

Thereupon Jean, blushing up to the ears, produced the little paper cornucopia and handed it to her.

She began to eat the bits of sugar, rolling them from one cheek to the other, so that they made lumps under her flesh. The two soldiers, seated in front of her, gazed at her, deeply moved and delighted.

Then she went to milk her cow, and again gave them milk when she returned.

They thought of her all the week and spoke of her several times. On the following Sunday she sat down by them for a longer talk; and all three, side by side, their eyes far away and their knees clasped in their folded hands, related trivial incidents and trivial details of the villages where they were born, while the cow yonder, seeing that the girl had halted on the way, held out its heavy head with its moist nostrils, and gave a long low to call her.

Soon the girl accepted an invitation to take a bite with them and drink a little wine. She often brought them plums in her pockets, for the plum season had come. Her presence enlivened the two little Breton soldiers, who chattered like two birds.

Now, one Tuesday, Luc le Ganidec asked for leave, a thing which he had never done before; and he did not return to barracks until ten at night.

Jean was disturbed, and tried to think what reason his comrade could have had for absenting himself so.

On the following Friday Luc, having borrowed ten sous of the occupant of the next bed, again asked and obtained a few hours' leave.

And when he set out with Jean for their Sunday walk, his whole demeanour was peculiar—excited and altogether different. Kerderen did not understand, but he vaguely suspected that something was afoot, although he could not guess what it might be.

They did not say a word until they reached their usual stopping-place, where they had worn the grass away by sitting always in the same spot; and they breakfasted slowly. Neither of them was hungry or thirsty.

Soon the girl appeared. They watched her approach, as they did every Sunday. When she was close at hand, Luc rose and walked towards her. She put her pail on the ground and kissed him. She kissed him passionately, throwing her arms about his neck, unmindful of Jean; she did not see him, did not think about his being there.

And there sat poor Jean, utterly bewildered, so bewildered that he could not understand; his mind in a whirl, his heart broken, but unable to grasp the situation.

Then the girl sat down beside Luc, and they began to talk.

Jean did not look at them; he divined now why his comrade had gone away twice during the week, and he was conscious of a sharp pang, a sort of wound—that rending of the fibres which is caused by treachery.

Luc and the girl rose together to go to change the position of the cow.

Jean looked after them. He saw them walk away side by side. His comrade's red breeches made a bright spot on the road. It was Luc who picked up the mallet, and who drove in the stake to which the beast was tied.

The girl stooped to milk her, while Luc with a distraught hand patted the animal's razor-like back. Then they left the pail in the grass, and went into the woods.

Jean saw only the wall of leaves where they had entered; and he felt so overwhelmed that, if he had tried to rise, he would surely have fallen flat.

He sat perfectly still, stupefied with amazement and distress, unaffected and profound distress. He longed to weep, to run away, to hide himself, never to see a human being again.

Suddenly he saw them come out of the wood. They walked slowly back, hand in hand, as betrothed couples do in villages. Luc was carrying the pail.

They kissed again before they parted, and the girl went her way with a friendly " good night " and a significant glance at Jean. She did not think to offer him milk that day.

The two little soldiers sat side by side, as usual, without moving, silent and calm, their placid faces betraying nothing of the perturbation of their hearts. The sun beat down upon them. The cow lowed now and again as she gazed at them from afar.

At the usual time they rose to return.

Luc peeled a switch, Jean carried the empty bottle. He left it with the keeper of the wine-shop at Bezons. Then they started across the bridge, and, as they did every Sunday, stopped in the middle to watch the water for a few moments.

Jean leaned over, leaned farther and farther over the iron railing, as if he had seen something in the stream that attracted him.

" Do you mean to take a drink? " Luc asked him.

As he uttered the last word Jean's head carried away his body, his legs described a circle in the air, and the little blue and red soldier fell like a stone, entered the water, and disappeared.

Luc, his throat paralysed with anguish, tried in vain to shout. He saw something move at some distance; then his comrade's head rose to the surface and instantly went under again.

Still farther away he saw a hand, a single hand, which came out of the water, then plunged back. That was all.

The boatmen who hurried to the spot did not find the body that day.

Luc returned alone to the barracks, running at full speed, like one distracted; and he told of the accident, his eyes and his voice full of tears, and blowing his nose incessantly:

"He leaned over—he—he leaned over so far—so far—that his head turned a somersault—and—and—he fell—he fell——"

He could say no more, for his emotion suffocated him. If he had only known!

THE BIT OF STRING

GUY DE MAUPASSANT

ALONG all the roads leading to Goderville the peasants and their wives were going toward the town, for it was market day. The men walked at an easy pace, the whole body thrown ahead at each movement of the long, crooked legs—men deformed by rude labour, by guiding the plough, which at once forces the right shoulder upward and twists the waist; by reaping, which turns the knees outward, for a sure foothold; by all the patient and painful toil of the country. Their blue blouses, glossy with starch, as though varnished, ornamented at the neck and wrists by a simple pattern in white, swelled out round their bony chests, like captive balloons from which heads, arms, and legs were protruding.

Some were leading by a cord a cow or calf, and their wives behind the animals were hastening their pace by the strokes of branches stripped of their leaves. The women carried on their arms great baskets, out of which hung, here and there, heads of chickens or ducks. They walked with shorter steps than their husbands, and at a more rapid pace, spare, erect, and wrapped in scant shawls pinned across their flat chests, their heads enveloped in white linen drawn closely over the hair and surmounted by a bonnet.

Now a pleasure waggon passed at a jerky pony trot, shaking fantastically two men seated side by side, with a woman at the back of the vehicle, all holding on to its sides to soften the hard jolts.

In the square of Goderville there was a crowd—a mass of mingled human beings and beasts. The horns of cattle, the high hats of the rich farmers, and the head-dresses of the women, emerged from the sea of people; and discordant voices, clamorous, bawling, kept up a continuous and savage babel, overtopped now and then by a shout from the robust lungs of a merry countryman, or the lowing of a cow attached to the wall of a house. All this mass was redolent of the stable and soil, of milk, of hay, of sweat, and diffused that rank, penetrating odour, human and bestial, peculiar to people of the fields.

Master Hauchecorne of Bréauté had just arrived at Goderville, and was going toward the square when he saw on the ground a bit of string. Master Hauchecorne, economist, like every true Norman, thought anything that might be of use worth picking up, and he bent down painfully, for he suffered from rheumatism. He took up the piece of string, and was winding it carefully when he noticed Malandin, the harness-maker, watching him from his doorway. The two men had long ago had a quarrel about a halter, and both being vindictive, had remained unfriendly. Hauchecorne was seized with a kind of shame at thus being seen by his enemy picking a bit of twine out of the mud. He quickly hid his prize under his blouse, then in his breeches pocket; then he pretended to search the ground again for something which he did not find, and he went off toward the market, his head in advance, bent double by his infirmities.

He was forthwith lost in the noisy, shufflng crowd everywhere in motion from innumerable buyings and sellings. The peasants examined the cows, went away, came back, hesitated, always fearful of being outwitted, never daring to decide, peering into the face of the vendor, endlessly searching to discover some trick in the seller, some fault in the beast.

The women, putting their great baskets down at their feet, had drawn out their fowls, which were lying on the ground, legs bound, eyes wild, combs scarlet. They listened to offers, held to their prices unmoved, their faces inscrutable; or suddenly deciding to accept an offer, cried out to the would-be purchaser slowly moving away.

"Agreed, Master Hutine; you shall have it at your price."

Then little by little the square emptied, and the Angelus announcing the noon, those who lived too far to go home dispersed to the various public-houses.

At Jourdain's the great dining-room was full of feasters, as the vast court was full of vehicles of every pedigree—carts, gigs, tilburies, pleasure vans, carioles innumerable, yellow with mud, mended, out of order, lifting to heaven their shafts, like two arms, or nosing the ground, rear in the air.

Opposite the tables of diners the great chimney-piece, full of bright flame, threw a lively warmth on the backs of the row at the right. Three spits were turning, weighted with chickens, pigeons, and legs of mutton, and a delectable odour of roast flesh and of juice streaming over its golden-brown skin escaped from the hearth, put every one in gay humour, and made mouths water. All the aristocracy of the plough dined there with Master Jourdain, inn-keeper and horse-dealer, a shrewd fellow, who had his money.

The platters were passed and emptied, and so were the tankards of yellow cider. Each one talked of his affairs, his purchases, his sales. The harvest was discussed. The weather was good for grass, but a little sharp for grain.

All at once the drum sounded in the court before the house. All save a few indifferent fellows were quickly on their feet and running to the door or the windows, their mouths full, their napkins in their hands.

When he had finished his roulade the public crier held forth in a jerky voice, cutting his phrases at the wrong place:

"It is made known to the inhabitants of Goderville and in general to all—the people present at market, that there was lost this morning, on the Benzeville road between—nine and ten o'clock, a wallet containing five hundred francs and important papers. You are asked to return—it to the town hall, without delay, or to the house of Master Fortuné Houlebrèque, of Manneville. There will be twenty francs reward."

Then the crier went on. One heard once more far off the muffled beating of his drum, and his voice enfeebled by the distance. Then they all began to talk of the event, estimating Master Houlebrèque's chances of finding or not finding his wallet.

And the meal went on.

They were finishing their coffee when the chief of police appeared at the door.

"Where is Master Hauchecorne of Bréauté?" he asked.

Hauchecorne, seated at the farther end of the table, replied:

"I'm here."

The chief proceeded:

"Master Hauchecorne, will you have the kindness to accompany me to the town hall? The mayor wishes to speak with you."

The countryman, surprised and disquieted, emptied at a draft his little glass of rum, arose, and, still more bent than in the morning, for the first movement after each relaxation was particularly difficult, he set out, repeating:

"I'm here, I'm here."

And he followed the chief.

The mayor was waiting for him, seated in his fauteuil. He was the notary of the vicinity, a big, solemn man, of pompous phrases.

" Master Hauchecorne," said he, " you were seen to pick up, on the Benzeville road, this morning, the wallet lost by Master Houlebrèque, of Manneville."

The peasant, astonished, looked at the mayor, frightened already, without knowing why, by this suspicion which had fallen on him.

" What! what! I picked up the wallet? "

" Yes; you yourself."

" Word of honour, I didn't even know of it."

" You were seen."

" Seen? What? Who saw me? "

" Monsieur Malandin, the harness-maker."

Then the old man remembered, understood, reddened with anger. " He saw meh, th' lout? He saw meh pick up that string! See here, m'sieu mayor," and feeling in the bottom of his pocket, he drew out the bit of cord.

But the mayor, incredulous, shook his head.

" You won't make me believe, Master Hauchecorne, that Malandin, who is a man worthy of credence, took that thread for a wallet."

The peasant, furious, raised his hand, spit, to attest his innocence, and declared:

" Yet it's the truth of God, the sacred truth, m'sieu mayor. On my soul and my salvation, I repeat it."

The mayor continued:

" After picking up the object you went on searching in the mud a long time to see if some piece of money mightn't have escaped you."

The old man gasped with indignation and fear.

" May one tell—may one tell lies like that to injure an honest man? May one say——"

His protest was vain. He was not believed. He was confronted with Monsieur Malandin, who repeated and sustained his former affirmation. For an hour the two men hurled insults at each other. Hauchecorne was searched, at his demand, and nothing was found on him. Finally the mayor, greatly perplexed, sent him away, warning him that he should inform the council and await orders.

The news spread. When he came out of the town hall the old man was surrounded and questioned with a curiosity, serious or mocking, but with no ill-will in it.

He began to recount the story of the string, but no one believed him—they only laughed.

He went on, stopped by everybody, stopping his acquaintances, beginning anew his tale and his protestations, turning his pockets inside out to prove that he had nothing.

" Move on, old quibbler," they said to him.

And he became angry, exasperated, feverish, sick at heart, at not being believed. He did not know what to do, but told his story over and over.

Night came. It was time to go home. He set out with three of his neighbours, to whom he pointed out the place where he had picked up the bit of cord, and all the way home he talked of his adventure. In the evening he made a circuit of the village of Bréauté to tell it to everybody. He met only incredulity. He was ill all night from his trouble.

The next day, toward one o'clock in the afternoon, Marius Paumelle, a farm hand, of Ymanville, returned the wallet and its contents to Monsieur Houlebrèque, of Manneville. The man stated, in effect, that he had found the wallet in the road, but not knowing how to read, had taken it home to his employer.

The news spread all about. Master Hauchecorne was told of it. He at once set out again on his travels, and began to narrate his story, completed by the dénouement. He was triumphant.

"It's not the thing 'at grieved me most, you understand," he said, "but it's the lie. Nothing harms you like being charged with a lie."

All day long he talked of his adventure. He told it in the streets to men passing, in the taverns to men drinking, after church the next Sunday. He stopped strangers to tell it to them. Now he was tranquil, yet something half disturbed him, without his knowing exactly what. People had an amused air as they listened to him. They did not appear convinced. He thought he detected whispers behind his back.

Tuesday of the following week he betook himself to the market of Goderville, driven there by the need of exploiting his case. Malandin, standing in his doorway, began to laugh when he saw him passing. Why? He accosted a farmer of Criquetot, who did not let him finish, but giving him a blow in the pit of the stomach, cried in his face:

"Go your way, humbug!"

Master Hauchecorne was dumbfounded, and more and more ill at ease. Why had be been called a humbug?

When he was seated at table in Jourdain's inn he again began to explain the affair. A jockey of Montivilliers cried to him:

"Come, come, old croaker, I know about your string!"

Hauchecorne stammered:

"But since it is found—the wallet?"

The other answered:

"Hold your tongue, father. One finds, another returns. I know nothing about it, but I have my suspicions of you."

The peasant was left choking. He understood at last. He was accused of having returned the wallet through an accomplice. He tried to protest. The whole table began to laugh. He could not finish his dinner, and went out in the midst of mockeries.

He returned home, ashamed and disgraced, choking with rage and confusion, the more overwhelmed because he was capable, with his Norman duplicity, of doing the very thing of which he was accused, and even boasting of it as a good stroke. Confusedly he saw it impossible to prove his innocence, his cunning being well known, and he felt himself cut to the heart by the injustice of the suspicion.

Then he commenced again to recount his adventure, lengthening each day his story, adding each time new reasonings, more energetic protestations, more solemn oaths, which he invented and arranged in his hours of solitude, his mind occupied solely with the story of the string. He was believed the less in proportion to the complication of his defence and the subtlety of his argument.

"That's the reasoning of a liar," they said behind his back.

He felt it, spent himself, wore his life out in useless efforts. He wasted away visibly. Wags now made him tell "the string" for their amusement, as one makes a soldier who has fought recount his battle. His mind, harassed and unsettled, grew feeble.

Toward the end of December he took to his bed. He died early in January, and in the delirium of his agony he attested his innocence, repeating:

"A little string . . . a little string . . . wait, here it is, m'sieu mayor!"

AMONG THE PEASANTS

GUY DE MAUPASSANT

I

THE two cottages stood side by side at the foot of a hill near a little watering-place. The two peasants laboriously tilled the unfruitful soil to rear their children. There were four in each house. All the little ones grubbed about the doors together from morning till night. The two eldest were six, and the two youngest about fifteen months; the marriages and then the births had occurred much about the same time in both houses.

Their mothers could hardly tell which were their own in the little heap; and the fathers mixed them up hopelessly. The eight names were jumbled together in their heads, and when they wished to call one of them they often tried several names before arriving at the right one.

The first house on the way from the watering-place of Rolleport was occupied by the Tuvaches, who had three daughters and a son; the other cottage sheltered the Vallins, who had one daughter and three sons.

All of them were brought up with difficulty on soup and potatoes and fresh air. At seven in the morning, at midday, and again at six at night, the mothers assembled their offspring to feed them, much as poultry-keepers collect their chickens. The children were seated in order of age before the wooden table, polished by fifty years of use. The mouth of the last little mite scarcely reached the level of the board. A big dish was put before them of bread soaked in the water in which some potatoes, half a cabbage, and some onions had been cooked, and all of them ate till they were satisfied, the mother feeding the smallest herself. A little meat in Sunday's soup was a treat for all, and the father on that day lingered over the meal, repeating, "I could do well with this every day."

One afternoon in August a light trap stopped before the cottages, and a young woman, who was driving herself, said to the gentleman at her side, "Oh, look, Henri, at all those children; aren't they sweet, grubbing like that in the dust?"

The man did not answer, accustomed to these bursts of admiration that were both a grief and a reproach to him.

The young woman continued: "I must kiss them. Oh, I wish I had one of them—that one, the tiniest!"

And springing from the trap she ran to the children, took one of the youngest, the Tuvache baby, and lifting it up in her arms covered with passionate kisses its dirty cheeks, its fair curly hair full of earth, and the little hands with which it was trying to ward off those troublesome embraces.

Then she climbed into the trap and drove off.

But she came back the next week, sat on the ground, took the little one in her arms, stuffed him with cakes, and gave them all sweets, playing with them like a girl, while her husband waited patiently in the light trap.

She came again, made friends with the parents, and returned daily, her pockets full of sweets and pennies.

II

Her name was Mme. Henri d'Hubières.

One morning when she came her husband got out of the trap also, and, without stopping to speak to the children, who knew her well by this time, she went into the parents' cottage.

They were in, busy splitting wood for the fire; they stood up surprised, offered their visitors chairs, and then waited. Then the young woman, in a broken, trembling voice, began: "My good people, I have come to speak to you because I would like so much—so much to take away with me your—little boy."

The peasants, stupefied and bewildered, said nothing.

She took a breath and went on: "We have no children; we are alone, my husband and I—we would adopt him—if you are willing."

It began to dawn upon the woman.

"You want to take Charlot from us? Ah, no, indeed; certainly not."

Then Monsieur d'Hubières intervened: "My wife has explained things badly. We wish to adopt him; but he will come back to see you. If he turns out well, as is likely, he will be our heir. If by chance we had children, he would share equally with them. But if he did not turn out well, we would give him on his majority a sum of 20,000 francs, which will be immediately placed to his credit with a lawyer. And as we have not forgotten you, a pension of 100 francs a month will be paid to you during your lifetime. Do you understand clearly?"

The woman had risen furious.

"You wish me to sell you Charlot? Ah, no, there are some things one does not ask a mother! No, indeed. It would be a crime."

The man, grave and thoughtful, said nothing, but he nodded his head to show he agreed with his wife.

Dismayed, Mme. d'Hubières began to cry, and turning to her husband, her voice full of tears—the voice of a child whose wishes are always gratified—she stammered: "They won't, Henri; they won't."

They made a last effort.

"But, my friends, think of your child's future, of his welfare, of——"

The peasant's wife, exasperated, cut her short.

"We understand, and we've considered. Go away and don't let me see you here again. That it should be allowed to try and take away a child like that!"

Coming out Mme. d'Hubières remembered that there were two little ones, and she asked through her tears, with all the obstinacy of a spoilt, headstrong woman who wants her own way: "But the other little one is not yours?"

Tuvache replied: "No, he belongs to our neighbours. You can go there if you like."

And he went back into his cottage, where his wife's indignant voice could still be heard.

III

The Vallins were seated at table, slowly eating slices of bread on which they carefully scraped a little butter taken with their knives from the plate between them.

Mme. d'Hubières began her proposal, but this time less bluntly and with more persuasion.

The two peasants shook their heads at first in token of refusal, but when they heard that they would have 100 francs a month they considered, looking doubtfully at each other, their resolution shaken. They remained silent a long time, worried, hesitating.

Finally the wife asked: " What do you think of it, my man? "

He replied in a sententious manner, " I think it is not to be despised."

Then Mme. d'Hubières, who trembled with anxiety, spoke to them of their little one's future, of his welfare, of all the money that he would be able to give them later.

The peasant asked: " This yearly pension of 1200 francs will be promised before a lawyer? "

Monsieur d'Hubières replied, " Certainly, to-morrow."

Then the wife, who had been thinking it over, said, " 100 francs a month is not enough to make up for the loss of our little one. In a few years he would be able to work for us. We must have 120 francs."

Mme. d'Hubières, full of impatience, agreed immediately; and as she wished to take the child away with her, she gave them a present of 100 francs, while her husband made out a deed. The mayor and a neighbour, hurriedly sent for, readily acted as witnesses.

And the young woman, radiant, carried off the child, howling, just as one might carry off some coveted trifle from a shop.

The Tuvaches from their doorstep, silent and severe, watched them set off, perhaps regretting their own refusal.

IV

And that was the end of little Jean Vallin. The parents went every month to the lawyer to get their 120 francs, and they were angry with their neighbours, because Mother Tuvache covered them with ignominy, saying everywhere how unnatural they must be to sell their own child; that it was a horror and a disgrace.

And sometimes she would take her own Charlot ostentatiously in her arms, saying to him as if he could understand, " I didn't sell you, did I? I wouldn't sell *my* little boy. I don't sell my children, no! I am not rich, but I don't sell my children."

And for years and years it went on daily, coarse allusions made outside her door, loud enough to be heard in the neighbouring house.. Mother Tuvache ended by thinking herself superior to all the countryside, because she had not sold Charlot. And any one speaking of her said, " I know it must have been tempting, but all the same she behaved like a good mother."

They pointed her out as an example; and Charlot, who was now eighteen, brought up with this idea continually before him, thought himself better than his companions because his parents had not sold him.

The Vallins lived comfortably, thanks to their pension, and this was the reason of the continued wrath of the Tuvaches, who had remained poor.

The Vallins' eldest son went to do his military training. The second died. Charlot remained to work with his old father, to keep his mother and his two younger sisters.

V

He was twenty-one when, one morning, an elegant trap drew up before the two cottages. A young man with a gold watch-chain alighted, giving his hand to an old, white-haired lady. The old lady said to him, "It is there, my child, at the second house."

And he went in as if he were at home in the Vallins' cottage. The old mother was washing her aprons; the father, old and frail, was sleeping at the fireside. Both looked up, and the young man said, "Good-day, father; good-day, mother."

They sprang up startled. The woman dropped the soap and stammered, "Is it you, my child? Is it you?" He took her in his arms and kissed her, repeating, "Good-day, mother." While the old man, trembling, said, with the composure which never deserted him, "So you are back again, Jean," as if he had seen him the month before.

And presently the parents wanted to take him out and show him off in the countryside. They called on the mayor, the priest, and the schoolmaster.

Charlot, standing at his cottage door, watched him pass.

That evening at supper he said to his father, "You must have been fools to let them take the Vallins' child."

His mother replied obstinately, "We wouldn't have sold our child."

The father said nothing.

The son went on: "It's not bad to be sacrificed like that."

Then Father Tuvache said angrily, "Are you going to reproach us because we kept you?"

And the young man answered brutally, "Yes, I do reproach you for it. You were idiots. It is parents like you that cause unhappiness to their children. I should leave you. That is what you deserve."

The good woman wept over her plate. She sobbed as she swallowed mouthfuls of soup, spilling half of it.

"What's the good of bringing up children?"

Then the son said roughly, "I would much rather not have been born than be where I am. When I saw young Vallin just now, my blood boiled. I said to myself, that's what I might be now."

He got up.

"It would be better if I didn't stay here any longer; I would only reproach you from morning till night. I would make your lives a burden. For you see I shall never forgive you."

The two old people said nothing, overwhelmed, in tears.

He went on: "No, the thought of it would be too hard. I'd rather go and earn my living elsewhere."

He opened the door. A sound of voices came in. The Vallins were celebrating their son's return.

Then Charlot stamped his foot, and turning to his parents, cried, "Wretches, that you are!" And he disappeared into the night.

TWO FISHERMEN

GUY DE MAUPASSANT

PARIS was blockaded—famished—at its last gasp. The sparrows on the housetops were few and far between, and even the rats in the sewers were disappearing. People ate anything they could get.

Early one bright morning in January, Monsieur Morissot, watch-maker by trade, was walking sadly along one of the outer Boulevards, his hands in the pockets of his overcoat, his stomach empty, when he unexpectedly ran into a friend, whom he recognised. It was Monsieur Sauvage, a riverside comrade of old times.

Every Sunday before the war Morissot started out at daybreak, a bamboo fishing-rod in one hand and tin box with bait and tackle on his back. He took the Argenteuil train as far as Colombes, and then went on foot to Marante Island. The moment he reached the river and had settled down at his favourite spot, he began to fish, and he went on fishing till nightfall.

There every Sunday he met Monsieur Sauvage, a linen-draper in the Rue Notre Dame de Lorette, a stout and jovial little man, as keen a fisherman as himself.

Often they spent half the day together, sitting side by side, their feet dangling over the water, hardly exchanging a word, and a friendship had grown up between them. Some days they were quite silent. Other days they talked; but they had so many tastes and ideas in common that they got on excellently without saying anything.

Often on a spring morning, when the sun's warmth was on their backs and a light mist hovered over the river, these two ardent fishermen enjoyed a foretaste of the coming summer. Then Morissot would say to his neighbour:

" Not bad this, hey! "

And Monsieur Sauvage would reply:

" I know nothing better."

No more words were needed for mutual understanding and appreciation.

Or in the autumn towards evening when the setting sun crimsoned the sky, dyed all the river with reflections of the fleeting clouds, lit up the whole horizon—so that the figures of the two friends were illumined as with fire—and tinged with gold the russet brown of the trees which already shivered at the first notes of winter—then Monsieur Sauvage would glance smilingly towards Monsieur Morissot and say:

" What a sight, eh? "

And Monsieur Morissot would answer, without taking his eyes off his float:

" Better than the Boulevards, isn't it? "

This morning no sooner had they recognised each other than they shook hands warmly; and quite overcome at meeting under such different circumstances, Monsieur Sauvage, sighing, muttered:

" A pleasant state of things! "

Monsieur Morissot, gloomy and depressed, replied:

" And what weather. This is the first fine day this year."

In fact the sky was clear and blue, and the sun was shining.

Pensive and sorrowful, they began to walk along together, and Morissot said: " And our fishing, eh? What good times we had! "

Sauvage answered:

" Ah, when shall we have such times again? "

They stopped at a little café, had an absinthe together, and then went on with their walk.

Presently they came to another café, and Morissot said abruptly, " Another absinthe, eh? "

" If you like." said Sauvage, and they went in.

When they came out they were a little giddy, as people are who take alcohol when they have been eating nothing. A mild and gentle wind caressed their faces, and Monsieur Sauvage, affected by the fresh air, said suddenly:

" Suppose we go, eh? "

" Go where? "

" Fishing, of course."

" But where? "

" Why, to our island. The French outposts are at Colombes. I know Colonel Dumoulin. He will let us pass through without any difficulty."

Morissot was excited with delight at the idea of going. " All right," he said, " I'm game." They parted to fetch their rods, and an hour later were walking briskly together along the high road. Presently they reached the villa where the Colonel was staying. With a smile he granted their request, and, supplied with the password, they went on their way.

Soon they were beyond the outposts, had passed through forsaken Colombes, and were in the little vineyards that slope down to the river. It was then about eleven o'clock.

The village of Argenteuil on the opposite side of the river seemed to be dead. The heights of Orgremont and Saumons dominated the whole countryside. The great plain that stretches as far as Nanternes looked like a desert. Bare cherry trees and grey earth were all that could be seen.

Monsieur Sauvage pointed at the heights and said softly: " The Prussians are up there "; and a vague sense of uneasiness fell upon the two friends.

The Prussians! Though they had never seen them, they had felt their presence for months past, encircling their beloved Paris, ruining their beloved France—pillaging, massacring, devouring; invisible and invincible. Something of a superstitious fear was added to the hate they bore to these unknown and conquering Prussians.

Morissot said quietly, " Suppose we meet them? " and Sauvage answered with the Parisian's characteristic gaiety, that could not be entirely suppressed:

" We should give them some of our fish—fried for supper."

At the same time, frightened by the silence and solitude all around, they both hesitated before venturing farther afield.

It was Monsieur Sauvage who after a time plucked up courage and said, " Come on, only let's be careful."

They went through the vineyard bent double, and taking cover from the bushes, while their eyes watched carefully on each side, and their ears were alive to every sound.

A stretch of open ground lay between them and the river. They crossed this at a run, and when they got to the bank hid amongst the dry reeds for safety. Morissot put his ear to the ground to listen if any one were coming, but could hear nothing. They were alone, absolutely alone.

Gradually reassured, they began to fish, the deserted island of Marante concealing them from the opposite bank. The little restaurant near by was closed and looked as if it had not been entered for years.

Monsieur Sauvage caught the first gudgeon, Monsieur Morissot the second, and after that they pulled up their lines every minute with a little silver fish wriggling on the hook. It was really a miraculous draught of fishes. As fast as the fish were caught they were placed in a finely meshed net which partly floated at the feet of the fishermen. The pleasure of enjoying a favourite sport, long forbidden, brought a positive happiness to the two friends. They no longer listened for strange sounds; they thought of nothing; they were dead to the world. In fact they were fishing.

Suddenly a tremendous noise that seemed to come from within the earth made the ground tremble. The guns had begun to thunder again. Morissot turned his head and saw above him, far away on the left, the great outline of Mont Valerien, with a cloud of thin white smoke from the gun, like a feather, on its summit. Quickly a jet of flame was seen, followed by another explosion. Then every minute from the mountain came a deadly breath, while the white smoke rose like a pall above it.

Monsieur Sauvage shrugged his shoulders.

"They are at it again," he said.

Monsieur Morissot, who was watching his float bob up and down, was seized with the rage of a peace-loving man against the combatants and growled out:

"They must be fools to kill one another."

Monsieur Sauvage replied:

"They are worse than the brute beasts."

Monsieur Morissot, who had just hooked a bleak, exclaimed: "And to think that it will always go on like this while we have such things as Governments."

Monsieur Sauvage corrected him: "The Republic would not have declared war."

Monsieur Morissot in his turn, said:

"A monarchy means foreign wars, a republic civil war."

And then in a quiet and friendly way, after the fashion of reasonable peace-loving men of common sense, they went on discussing and unravelling high political problems. On one point they were agreed, that no one would ever be free. And all the time Mont Valerien thundered unceasingly, demolishing French homes with its cannon, crushing out French lives ruthlessly, destroying many a dream, many a hoped-for joy, and bringing to the hearts of mothers and wives and daughters in France, and in other countries far away, sorrow and suffering which would never end.

"Such is life," said Monsieur Morissot.

"Say rather such is death," said Monsieur Sauvage.

The next moment they started, terrified, aware that some one was walking just behind them. Turning round they saw, standing beside them, four big, bearded men, dressed as livery servants, and wearing flat caps upon their heads. These four men covered the fishermen with their rifles.

The rods dropped from their nerveless hands, and floated away down the river. In an instant the fishermen were seized, carried off, flung into a boat, and ferried over to the island.

Behind the little restaurant which they had thought uninhabited were twenty Prussian soldiers. A gigantic hairy man, who was sitting astride a chair smoking a large porcelain pipe, asked them in excellent French if they had had good sport.

A soldier promptly placed at the feet of this officer the net full of fish which he had been careful to bring away with him.

The Prussian smiled: " Not bad, I see. But we have other fish to fry; listen to me, and don't be alarmed. You are evidently a couple of French spies sent out disguised as fishermen to watch my movements. Therefore I am taking you prisoners, and shall have you shot. You have fallen into my hands—so much the worse for you. It's the fortune of war. However, as you have passed through the lines you must certainly have the password. Otherwise you would not be able to return. Now tell me this password and I will let you go."

The two friends, pale as death, stood side by side, their hands nervously twitching, but no words crossed their lips.

The officer went on: " No one need ever know anything about it. You will go quietly home and the secret will go with you. If you refuse it is instant death for both of you. Take your choice."

They stood quite still without speaking.

The Prussian, pointing to the river, said calmly: " Consider, in five minutes you will be at the bottom of that water. I suppose you have relatives."

Mont Valerien still thundered unceasingly.

The two Frenchmen remained standing, perfectly silent.

The officer gave an order in German. Then he moved his chair so as not to be too near the prisoners, and a dozen soldiers with rifles drew up in line at twenty paces distance.

" I will give you one minute," said the officer, " but not a second more."

Then he got up from his chair and went up to the two fishermen. He took Morissot aside by the arm and whispered:

" Quick; give me the word, your friend shall never know; I shall pretend that I have yielded in pity."

Monsieur Morissot did not answer.

The Prussian took Monsieur Sauvage aside and made the same proposal to him.

Monsieur Sauvage did not answer.

The two men stood once more side by side.

The officer gave a word of command. The soldiers raised their rifles.

By accident Morissot caught sight of the net full of gudgeon lying on the grass a few yards away. A ray of sunshine lit up the mass of glittering fish, and a sudden weakness came over him, bringing tears to his eyes.

"Farewell, Monsieur Sauvage," he stammered.

"Farewell, Monsieur Morissot," replied his friend.

They gripped each other's hands, trembling from head to foot.

"Fire," called out the officer.

The twelve shots had the sound of one.

Monsieur Sauvage fell dead on his face. Monsieur Morissot, more heavily built, staggered, stumbled, and then fell across the body of his friend, his face turned upward to the sky, the blood spurting from his breast.

The Prussian officer gave more orders. His men dispersed, and then returned with cords and stones. They tied the stones to the feet of the two Frenchmen and carried them away to the river.

Mont Valerien still thundered unceasingly.

Two soldiers took Morissot by the head and feet, while two others did the same to Sauvage. The bodies swung to and fro, and then thrown far out, curved and fell feet first into the river.

The water rose, rippled, and then calmed down, while the ever widening circles, tinged with red, came in tiny waves to the banks.

The officer remarked in impassive tones: "The fish will have their turn now."

Then his eye fell on the net of gudgeon on the grass. He picked it up, looked it over, and smiling to himself called out, "Wilhelm!"

At once a soldier, in white cap and apron, came running.

The officer threw the catch to him, and said:

"Fry these little creatures for me at once, while they are still alive and kicking. They will be delicious."

Then he went on smoking his pipe.

MOONLIGHT

GUY DE MAUPASSANT

THE Abbé Marignan [1] bore his fighting title well. He was a tall, thin priest, always in a state of mental exaltation, and without guile. All his beliefs were fixed, with never a wavering. He honestly believed that he knew his God, that he could fathom His desires, His will, His purposes.

[1] Marignano (Melegnano), a town in the province of Milan, Italy, has been the scene of two great French victories: that of Francois I. over the Swiss in 1515; and of the French over the Austrians in 1859.

When he strode along the path of his little country rectory, a question sometimes arose in his mind, "Why did God do thus?" And he persistently sought the reason, mentally assuming God's place; and he almost always found it. He would not have murmured, in an outburst of pious humility, "O Lord, Thy designs are past finding out!" He said to himself, "I am God's servant; it is my duty to know the reasons for His actions, and to divine them if I know them not."

Everything in Nature seemed to him to be created with absolute and marvellous logicality. The "why" and the "because" always balanced. The dawn was made that our waking might be cheerful, the day to ripen the crops, the rain to water them, the evenings to prepare for slumber, and the dark nights to sleep.

The four seasons provided perfectly for all the necessities of agriculture; and the priest was utterly unable to harbour such a thought as that Nature acts without design, and that all living things are subjected to the stern necessities of time, of climate, and of matter.

But he hated woman; he hated her unconscionably, and instinctively despised her. He often repeated the words of Christ, "Woman, what have I to do with thee?" And he would add, "One would think that God Himself was displeased with that work of His hands." Woman was to him the "child twelve times unclean" of whom the poet sings. She was the tempter who had led the first man astray, and who ever continued her work of damnation; a weak, dangerous, mysteriously disquieting creature. And even more bitterly than her body of perdition, he hated her loving heart.

He had often been conscious that women had fixed their affections upon him; but, although he knew that he was impervious to attack, he was enraged by that craving for love with which they were always aquiver.

In his opinion God created woman only to tempt man and to put him to the test. One should not approach her without defensive precautions, and the same fear that one has of traps. In truth, she closely resembled a trap, with her lips open and her arms outstretched towards man.

He had no indulgence save for nuns, whom their vows rendered harmless; but he treated them harshly none the less, because he felt that, even in the depths of their fettered and humbled hearts, there still lived that everlasting affection, which went out to him, priest though he was.

He felt it in their glances, which were more melting with pious fervour than those of the monks; in those ecstatic transports in which their sex was wont to indulge; in their outbursts of love towards the Christ, which angered him because it was woman's love, carnal love; he was conscious of that accursed tenderness in their very docility, in the softness of their voices when they spoke to him, in their downcast eyes, and in their submissive tears when he reproved them roughly.

And he would shake his cassock when he went out of the door of the convent, and would stride swiftly away as if he were flying from some danger.

He had a niece who lived with her mother in a small house near by. He strove earnestly to make her a sister of charity.

She was a pretty creature, giddy and bantering. When the abbé preached at her, she laughed; and when he lost his temper with her, she would embrace him passionately, pressing him to her heart, while he instinctively tried to extricate himself from that embrace, which nevertheless caused him a delicious thrill of pleasure, arousing in the depths of his being that instinct of fatherhood which slumbers in every man.

He often spoke to her of God, of his God, as he walked by her side along the country roads. She hardly listened to him, but gazed at the sky, the grass, and the flowers, with a joy in living that could be read in her eyes. Sometimes she would dart away to catch some flying thing, and would exclaim as she brought it back, "See how pretty it is, uncle; I would like to kiss it." And that longing to kiss insects or lilac flowers disturbed, irritated, and disgusted the priest, who recognised therein that ineradicable tenderness which is always budding in a woman's heart.

And behold one day the sacristan's wife, who did Abbé Marignan's housework, informed him cautiously that his niece had a lover.

He was terribly shocked, and stood gasping for breath, with his face covered with lather, for he was shaving.

When he was once more in condition to think and to speak, he cried:

"That is not true; you are lying, Mélanie!"

But the peasant woman placed her hand over her heart:

"May our Lord judge me if I am lying, Monsieur le Curé. I tell you that she goes out every night as soon as your sister's gone to bed. They meet down by the river. All you need to do is just go there, and see for yourself, between ten o'clock and midnight."

He ceased to scrape his chin, and began to pace the floor excitedly, as he always did when he was engaged in serious meditation. When he concluded to return to his shaving, he cut himself three times, from nose to ear.

All day long he said not a word, bursting with indignation and wrath. His priestly rage, in face of love unconquerable, was intensified by the moral exasperation of a father, a guardian, entrusted with the keeping of a soul, who has been deceived, robbed, tricked by a mere child; the selfish, suffocating wrath of parents to whom their daughter declares that she has chosen a husband, without their help and in spite of them.

After dinner he tried to read a little, but he could not do it; and he became more and more indignant. When the clock struck ten he seized his cane, a formidable oaken staff which he always used in his walks at night when he went out to visit some sick person. And he glanced with a smile at the huge cudgel as he twirled it threateningly in his muscular countryman's fist. Then, of a sudden, he sprang to his feet, and, grinding his teeth, brought it down upon a chair, the back of which fell shattered to the floor.

He opened his door to go out; but paused in the doorway, surprised by such a splendour of moonlight as one seldom sees.

And as he was blessed with an exalted imagination, of the sort that the Fathers of the Church, those poetic dreamers, must have had, he suddenly became distraught, profoundly moved by the grand yet tranquil beauty of the pallid night.

In his little garden, bathed with soft light, his fruit-trees, set in rows, cast the shadow of their slender limbs, scarce clothed with verdure, on the gravelled paths; while the giant honeysuckle clinging to the wall of his house exhaled a fragrant, as it were a sweetened breath, so that a sort of perfumed soul seemed to hover about in the warm, clear evening.

He began to breathe deep, drinking the air as drunkards drink their wine, and he walked slowly, enchanted, wonder-struck, his niece almost forgotten.

When he had gained the open country, he stopped to gaze upon the broad expanse, all inundated by that caressing radiance, drowned in the soft and languorous charm of a cloudless night. The frogs at every instant threw into space their short, metallic notes, and the distant nightingales added their rippling music, which induces dreams without thought—that airy, vibrating melody, made to serve as an accompaniment to kisses, to moonlight seduction.

The abbé walked on, with a sinking at his heart which he could not understand. He felt as it were enfeebled, suddenly exhausted; he longed to sit down, and to remain there, in contemplation, marvelling at God in all His work.

Farther on, following the curving of the little stream, wound a row of white poplars. A fine haze, a white vapour through which the moon's rays shone, turning it to glistening silver, hung about and above the banks, enveloping the whole winding course of the stream with a sort of light, transparent down.

Again the priest halted, stirred to the depths of his soul by an increasing, irresistible emotion. And a doubt, a vague disquietude stole over him; he felt the birth within him of one of those problems which he sometimes propounded to himself.

Why had God done this? As the night was intended for sleep, for oblivion, for rest, why make it lovelier than the day, softer than the dawn and the sunsets; and why did that stately, seductive star, more poetic than the sun, and to all seeming (so discreet it is) destined to shine upon things too delicate, too mysterious for the broad light of day—why was it come to brighten all the shades?

Why did not the most talented of singing birds rest like the others, instead of performing in the disquieting darkness?

Why was this half-veil cast over the world? Why this fluttering of the heart, this emotion of the soul, this languor of the flesh?

Why this display of charms which men never see, because they are in their beds? For whom was this sublime spectacle intended, that profusion of poetic beauty cast from heaven upon earth?

The abbé did not understand.

But behold, at the end of the field, beneath the arched trees wet with glistening mist, two shadows appeared, walking side by side.

The man was the taller and had his arm about his sweetheart's neck; and from time to time he kissed her on the forehead. They animated suddenly the lifeless landscape, which enveloped them like a divine frame fashioned for them. They seemed a single being, the being for whom that tranquil and silent night was made; and they walked towards the priest, like a living answer, his Master's answer, to his question.

He stood there, overwhelmed, his heart beating fast; and he fancied that he had before him some biblical scene, like the loves of Ruth and Boaz—the accomplishment of the Lord's will in one of those magnificent settings spoken of in Holy Writ. The verses of the Song of Songs began to hum in his ears—the ardent cries, the cravings of the body, all the glowing poetry of that poem aflame with love.

And he said to himself, "Perhaps God has made such nights, in order to throw a veil of idealism over the loves of men."

He withdrew before this couple who went ever arm in arm. It was his niece, to be sure; but he asked himself if he had not been on the point of disobeying God. And must it not be that love is lawful in God's sight, since He visibly encompasses it with such splendour?

And he fled, bewildered, almost ashamed, as if he had penetrated into a temple where he had not the right to go.

THE DOWRY

GUY DE MAUPASSANT

THE marriage of Maître Simon Lebrument with Mademoiselle Jeanne Cordier was a surprise to no one. Maître Lebrument had bought out the practice of Maître Papillon; naturally, he had to have money to pay for it; and Mademoiselle Jeanne Cordier had three hundred thousand francs clear in currency, and in bonds payable to bearer.

Maître Lebrument was a handsome man. He was stylish, although in a provincial way; but, still, he was stylish—a rare thing at Boutigny-le-Rebours.

Mademoiselle Cordier was graceful and fresh-looking, although a trifle awkward; nevertheless, she was a handsome girl, and one to be desired.

The marriage ceremony turned all Boutigny topsy-turvy. Everybody admired the young couple, who quickly returned home to domestic felicity, having decided simply to take a short trip to Paris, after a few days of retirement.

This tête-à-tête was delightful, Maître Lebrument having shown just the proper amount of delicacy. He had taken as his motto, "Everything comes to him who waits." He knew how to be at the same time patient and energetic. His success was rapid and complete.

After four days, Madame Lebrument adored her husband. She could not get along without him. She would sit on his knees, and taking him by the ears she would say, "Open your mouth and shut your eyes." He would open his mouth wide and partly close his eyes, and he would try to nip her fingers as she slipped some dainty between his teeth. Then she would give him a kiss, sweet and long, which would make chills run up and down his spine. And then, in his turn, he would not have enough caresses to please his wife from morning to night and from night to morning.

When the first week was over, he said to his young companion:

"If you wish, we will leave for Paris next Tuesday. We will be like two lovers, we will go to the restaurants, the theatres, the concert halls, everywhere, everywhere!"

She was ready to dance for joy.

"Oh! yes, yes. Let us go as soon as possible."

He continued:

"And then, as we must forget nothing, ask your father to have your dowry ready; I shall pay Maître Papillon on this trip."

She answered:

"All right! I will tell him to-morrow morning."

And he took her in his arms once more, to renew those sweet games of love which she had so enjoyed for the past week.

The following Tuesday, father-in-law and mother-in-law went to the station with their daughter and their son-in-law, who were leaving for the capital.

The father-in-law said:

"I tell you it is very imprudent to carry so much money about in a pocket-book." And the young lawyer smiled.

"Don't worry; I am accustomed to such things. You understand that, in my profession, I sometimes have as much as a million about me. In this manner, at least, we avoid a great amount of red tape and delay. You needn't worry."

The conductor was crying:

"All aboard for Paris!"

They scrambled into a car, where two old ladies were already seated.

Lebrument whispered into his wife's ear:

"What a bother! I won't be able to smoke."

She answered in a low voice:

"It annoys me too, but not on account of your cigar."

The whistle blew and the train started. The trip lasted about an hour, during which time they did not say very much to each other, as the two old ladies did not go to sleep.

As soon as they were in front of the Saint-Lazare Station, Maître Lebrument said to his wife:

"Dearie, let us first go over to the Boulevard and get something to eat; then we can quietly return and get our trunk and bring it to the hotel."

She immediately assented.

"Oh! yes. Let's eat at the restaurant. Is it far?"

He answered:

"Yes, it's quite a distance, but we will take the omnibus."

She was surprised:

"Why don't we take a cab?"

He began to scold her smilingly:

"Is that the way you save money? A cab for a five minutes' ride at six sous a minute! You would deprive yourself of nothing."

"That's so," she said, a little embarrassed.

A big omnibus was passing by, drawn by three big horses, which were trotting along. Lebrument called out:

"Conductor! Conductor!"

The heavy carriage stopped. And the young lawyer, pushing his wife, said to her quickly:

" Go inside; I'm going up on top, so that I may smoke at least one cigarette before lunch."

She had no time to answer. The conductor, who had seized her by the arm to help her up the step, pushed her inside, and she fell into a seat, bewildered, looking through the back window at the feet of her husband as he climbed up to the top of the vehicle.

And she sat there motionless, between a fat man who smelled of cheap tobacco and an old woman who smelled of garlic.

All the other passengers were lined up in silence—a grocer's boy, a young girl, a soldier, a gentleman with gold-rimmed spectacles and a big silk hat, two ladies with a self-satisfied and crabbed look, which seemed to say, " We are riding in this thing, but we don't *have* to," two sisters of charity, and an undertaker. They looked like a collection of caricatures.

The jolting of the waggon made them wag their heads, and the shaking of the wheels seemed to stupefy them—they all looked as though they were asleep.

The young woman remained motionless.

" Why didn't he come inside with me? " she was saying to herself. An unaccountable sadness seemed to be hanging over her. He really need not have acted so.

The sisters motioned to the conductor to stop, and they got off one after the other, leaving in their wake the pungent smell of camphor. The bus started off and soon stopped again. And in got a cook, red-faced and out of breath. She sat down and placed her basket of provisions on her knees. A strong odour of dish-water filled the vehicle.

" It's further than I imagined," thought Jeanne.

The undertaker went out, and was replaced by a coachman who seemed to bring the atmosphere of the stable with him. The young girl had as a successor a messenger, the odour of whose feet showed that he was continually walking.

The lawyer's wife began to feel ill at ease, nauseated, ready to cry without knowing why.

Other persons left and others entered. The stage went on through interminable streets, stopping at stations and starting again.

" How far it is! " thought Jeanne. " I hope he hasn't gone to sleep! He has been so tired the last few days."

Little by little all the passengers left. She was left alone, all alone. The conductor cried:

" Vaugirard! "

Seeing that she did not move, he repeated:

" Vaugirard! "

She looked at him, understanding that he was speaking to her, as there was no one else there. For the third time the man said:

" Vaugirard! "

Then she asked:

" Where are we? "

He answered gruffly:

" We're at Vaugirard, of course! I have been yelling it for the last half hour! "

" Is it far from the Boulevard? " she said.

" Which boulevard? "

" The Boulevard des Italiens."

" We passed that a long time ago! "

" Would you mind telling my husband? "

" Your husband! Where is he? "

" On the top of the bus."

" On the top! There hasn't been anybody there for a long time."

She started, terrified.

" What? That's impossible! He got on with me. Look well! He must be there."

The conductor was becoming uncivil:

" Come on, little one, you've talked enough! You can find ten men for every one that you lose. Now run along. You'll find another one somewhere."

Tears were coming to her eyes. She insisted:

" But, Monsieur, you are mistaken; I assure you that you must be mistaken. He had a big portfolio under his arm."

The man began to laugh:

" A big portfolio! Oh, yes! He got off at the Madeleine. He got rid of you, all right! Ha! ha! ha! "

The stage had stopped. She got out and, in spite of herself, she looked up instinctively to the roof of the bus. It was absolutely deserted.

Then she began to cry, and, without thinking that anybody was listening or watching her, she said out loud:

" What is going to become of me? "

An inspector approached:

" What's the matter? "

The conductor answered, in a bantering tone of voice:

" It's a lady who got left by her husband during the trip."

The other continued:

" Oh! that's nothing. You go about your business."

Then he turned on his heels and walked away.

She began to walk straight ahead, too bewildered, too crazed even to understand what had happened to her. Where was she to go? What could she do? What could have happened to him?

How could he have made such a mistake? How could he have been so forgetful?

She had two francs in her pocket. To whom could she go? Suddenly she remembered her cousin Barral, one of the assistants in the offices of the Ministry of the Navy.

She had just enough to pay for a cab. She drove to his house. He met her just as he was leaving for his office. He was carrying a large portfolio under his arm, just like Lebrument.

She jumped out of the carriage.

"Henry!" she cried.

He stopped, astonished:

"Jeanne! Here—all alone! What are you doing? Where have you come from?"

Her eyes full of tears, she stammered:

"My husband has just got lost!"

"Lost! Where?"

"On an omnibus."

"On an omnibus?"

Weeping, she told him her whole adventure.

He listened, thought, and then asked:

"Was his mind clear this morning?"

"Yes."

"Good. Did he have much money with him?"

"Yes, he was carrying my dowry."

"Your dowry! The whole of it?"

"The whole of it—in order to pay for the practice which he bought."

"Well, my dear cousin, by this time your husband must be well on his way to Belgium."

She could not understand. She kept repeating:

"My husband—you say——"

"I say that he has disappeared with your—your capital—that's all!"

She stood there, a prey to conflicting emotions, sobbing.

"Then he is—he is—he is a villain!"

And, faint from excitement, she leaned her head on her cousin's shoulder and wept.

As people were stopping to look at them, he pushed her gently into the vestibule of his house, and, supporting her with his arm around her waist, he led her up the stairs, and as his astonished servant opened the door, he ordered:

"Sophie, run to the restaurant and get a luncheon for two. I am not going to the office to-day."

THE COLONEL'S STORY

GUY DE MAUPASSANT

Ma foi ! (said Colonel Laporte) I am an old man. I have the gout. My legs are as stiff as ramrods, and yet, if a woman, a pretty woman, ordered me to go through the eye of a needle, I believe I'd jump like a clown at the circus. I shall always be so—it's in the blood. I'm an old beau, you see; an old beau of the old school. The sight of a woman, a pretty woman, affects me clear down to my boots—*Voilà!*

Besides, we are all a bit like that in France, gentlemen. We remain cavaliers, cavaliers of love and adventure, even now when they have by edict suppressed God, whose sworn soldiers we used to be.

But woman, you see, they cannot take out of our hearts. She is there and she will stay there. We love her and we shall love her and commit all sorts of follies for her while there is a France on the map of Europe. And even if they wipe out France, there will always remain Frenchmen.

As for me, under the eyes of a woman, a pretty woman, I can do anything. *Sapristi!* When the sacred thought of her comes into my heart, it is like fire in my veins. I want to do something, I don't know what—to fight, to knock somebody down, to break the furniture, to show myself the strongest, the bravest, the most reckless and devoted of men.

But I'm not the only one. No, indeed. The whole French army is like that, I assure you. From the meanest private all the way up to the general, we are ready to go to the last extremity for the sake of a woman, a pretty woman.

Think what Joan of Arc made us do, long ago. Why, I bet you that if a woman, a pretty woman, had taken command of the army on the eve of Sedan, when Marshal MacMahon was wounded, we would have burst through the Prussian lines, *sacré bleu*! and drunk blood from their cannon.

It isn't a Trochu that we need in Paris, but a Sainte Geneviève.

I remember well a little story of the war which proves, beyond a doubt, that we are capable of anything in the presence of a woman. I was captain, then, only captain, and had command of a detachment of scouts who were fighting their way back through territory occupied by the Prussians. We were hemmed in, pursued, beaten, disheartened, and almost dead with exhaustion and hunger. Moreover, we must reach Bar-sur-Tain before morning, or we would be done for, cut to pieces, every one of us. How had we escaped so far? I'm sure I don't know. We had still twelve miles to make during the night, twelve miles in the snow and through the snow, with nothing to eat. I said to myself, "It's all up! My poor fellows will never get there."

The day before we had had nothing to eat. All that day we had remained hidden in a barn, close against one another, to keep warm, unable to speak or to move, sleeping by fits and starts, as men do when they are completely worn out. At five o'clock it was night, the pale night of a snowstorm. I roused my men. Many of them did not want to get up, they could not move or stand on their feet, so stiff were they with cold and lying down. In front of us was the open country, a great waste of country all bare, with the snow falling. It fell and fell like a curtain, the white flakes that hid everything under a heavy, frozen mantle, thick and dead, a mattress or cloth of ice. You would have said it was the end of the world.

"Forward, march, my children!"

They looked in front of them, at the white dust that fell from the sky, and seemed to be thinking, "What's the use? As well die here!"

Then I drew my revolver. "The first man who falters I'll shoot!" And they started to march, ever so slowly, like men whose legs can no longer support them.

I sent four ahead to show us the way, three hundred yards in front; then the rest followed *pêle mêle,* in a mass, according to the chance of fatigue and length of step. The strongest I placed in the rear with the order to hurry up the laggards at the point of the bayonet—in the back. The snow seemed to bury us alive; it powdered the caps and cloaks without melting upon them, it made phantoms of us, ghosts, the ghosts of dead soldiers, tired out.

I said to myself, "We'll never get out of this, except by a miracle."

Sometimes we stopped for a few minutes on account of those who could not keep up. Then we heard nothing but the vague whisper of the snow, that almost imperceptible sound made by the colliding and mingling of all the flakes that fell. Some of the men shook themselves. Others did not budge. Then I gave the order to move on. Muskets were raised once more to shoulders and in utter exhaustion we took up the march.

Suddenly the scouts returned. Something had alarmed them. They had heard voices in front of us. I sent forward six men and a sergeant and waited.

A moment later a shrill cry, the cry of a woman, pierced the heavy silence of the storm, and in a few minutes they brought back two prisoners, an old man and a girl. I questioned them in a low voice. They were fleeing from the Prussians who had seized their house that evening and at once invaded the larder. The father was afraid for his daughter, and, without saying a word to the servants, the two of them had escaped into the night.

I perceived at once that they were farmers, nothing but farmers.

" You will accompany us," I said to them, and again we started. As the old man knew the country, he was our guide. The snow ceased to fall, the stars came out, and it grew terribly cold. The young girl, who had her father's arm, walked with difficulty. She murmured several times, " I can't feel my feet any more," and I suffered more than she did to see the poor little woman dragging herself that way through the snow.

Suddenly she stopped.

" Father," she said, " I am so tired that I can't go any farther."

The old man wanted to carry her, but he could not even lift her, and she sank down on the ground, heaving a deep sigh. The men formed a circle about them. As for me, I stamped around the place, not knowing what to do and unable to make up my mind to leave them so, that man and that child. Suddenly, one of my soldiers, a Parisian whose name was " Pratique," spoke up, " Come, comrades, we must carry the young lady, or we're no Frenchmen, *nom d'un chien!* "

I believe, *ma foi,* that I swore with joy.

" *Nom d'un nom!* that's right, my children, and I'll do my part."

We saw vaguely, in the darkness on the left, the trees of a little wood. Several men went off and presently returned with a lot of branches tied together to form a litter.

" Who'll lend his cloak? " cried Pratique inquiringly. " It is for a pretty girl, brothers."

Ten cloaks tumbled at his feet. In a second the young girl was snuggled in the warm garments and lifted upon six shoulders. I placed myself at the head on the right, and was content, *ma foi,* to have my charge.

They started off as if they had had a drink of wine, more briskly, with more life. I even heard them cracking jokes. A woman is enough, you see, to electrify Frenchmen. The soldiers were all but marching in line, warmed and refreshed. An old sharpshooter, who followed the litter, waiting his turn to replace the first bearer that faltered, murmured to a comrade, but loud enough for me to hear:

" I'm not young any more, but it's all the same. A woman's the thing to put life into my heart! "

Until three o'clock in the morning, they marched almost without rest. Then, suddenly, the scouts returned once more, and in a moment the whole detachment had crouched down in the snow, making only a vague shadow on the ground. I gave the orders in a low voice and behind me I heard the dry metallic click of the loading of pieces. For down there in the middle of the plain a strange thing was moving. You would have said a great beast that ran, lengthened itself out like a serpent, or gathered itself in a ball, leaped quickly now to the right, now to the left, stopped and then moved forward again. Suddenly the moving thing drew nearer, and I saw approaching, at a good pace, one behind the other, twelve Prussian lancers who had lost their way.

They were so close now that I heard perfectly the loud snorting of the horses, the clanging of arms, and the creaking of saddles.

"Fire!" I cried.

And the report of fifteen guns broke the stillness of the night. Four or five shots followed, then one all by itself, and when the smoke cleared away we saw that the twelve men, with nine horses, had fallen. Three horses fled at a furious gallop, and one dragged behind him, hanging by the foot to the stirrup and bumping madly, the dead body of his rider.

A soldier behind me laughed, a terrible laugh. Another said:

"Long live the widows!"

A third added—he was married, perhaps:

"Not too long!"

A head was raised from the litter.

"What is it?" said she. "Are they fighting?"

I answered:

"It's nothing; we've killed a dozen Prussians"

"Poor men!" she murmured; but because she was cold she disappeared again beneath the cloaks.

We went on. For a long time we marched. At last the sky paled. The snow became clear, luminous, glistening; and a rosy glow showed itself in the East. A distant voice cried:

"Who goes there?"

All the detachment halted; and I advanced to tell who we were. We had reached the French lines.

As my men filed past the guard, a mounted officer, whom I had told, asked in a loud voice as the litter went by:

"What is that you have in there?"

Then a little blonde head appeared, dishevelled and smiling, with the ready answer:

"It's me, sir."

A laugh went up from the men and their hearts were gay. Then Pratique, who was marching beside the stretcher, flung up his cap and shouted, "*Vive la France!*"

And, though I don't know why, I was deeply moved; it was so kind and brave. It seemed to me that we had saved our country, that we had done something that other men could not do, something simple-hearted and truly patriotic.

That little face, you know, I shall never forget it; and if I were to give my opinion on the suppression of drums and bugles, I'd propose to replace them in each legion by a pretty girl. That would do more good than to play the "Marseillaise." *Nom d'un nom!* How that would put life into a trooper, to have a madonna like that, a living madonna, riding beside the colonel.

He was silent for a few seconds, then added with an air of conviction, nodding his head:

That's it, we love women well, we Frenchmen.

HOW HE WON THE LEGION OF HONOUR

GUY DE MAUPASSANT

SOME people are born with a predominant instinct, with some vocation or some desire which demands recognition as soon as they begin to speak or think.

Ever since he was a child Monsieur Caillard had only had one idea in his head—to be decorated. While he was still quite a small boy he used to wear a zinc Cross of the Legion of Honour on his tunic, just as other children wear a soldier's cap, and he took his mother's hand in the street with a proud look, sticking out his little chest with its red ribbon and metal star so that it might show to advantage.

His studies were not a success, and he failed in his examination for bachelor of arts. Not knowing what to do, he married a pretty girl, for he had plenty of money of his own.

They lived in Paris, and, as many rich middle-class people do, mixed with their own particular set, without going among other people, proud of knowing a deputy, who might perhaps be a minister some day, while two chiefs of division were among their friends.

But Monsieur Caillard could not get rid of his one absorbing idea, and he felt constantly unhappy because he had not the right to wear a little bit of coloured ribbon in his buttonhole.

When he met on the boulevards any men who were decorated, he looked at them askance, with great jealousy. Sometimes, when he had nothing to do in the afternoon, he would count them, and say to himself, "Just let me see how many I shall meet between the Madeleine and the Rue Drouot."

Then he would walk slowly, looking, with a practised eye, at every coat for the little bit of red ribbon, and when he had got to the end of his walk he always said the numbers out loud. " Eight officers and seventeen knights. As many as that! It is stupid to sow the Cross broadcast in that fashion. I wonder how many I shall meet going back."

And he returned slowly, unhappy when the crowd of passers-by interfered with his seeing them.

He knew the places where most of them were to be found. They swarmed in the Palais Royal. Fewer were seen in the Avenue de l'Opéra than in the Rue de la Paix, while the right side of the boulevard was more frequented by them than the left.

They also seemed to prefer certain cafés and theatres. Whenever he saw a group of white-haired old gentlemen standing together in the middle of the pavement, interfering with the traffic, he used to say to himself, " They are officers of the Legion of Honour," and he felt inclined to take off his hat to them.

He had often remarked that the officers had a different bearing than mere knights. They carried their heads higher, and you felt that they enjoyed greater official consideration, and a more widely extended importance.

Sometimes again the worthy man would be seized with a furious hatred of every one who was decorated; he felt like a Socialist toward them. Then, when he got home, excited at meeting so many Crosses—just as a poor, hungry wretch is on passing some dainty provision shop—he used to ask in a loud voice:

" When shall we get rid of this wretched Government? " And his wife would be surprised, and ask:

" What is the matter with you to-day? "

" I am indignant," he would reply, " at the injustice I see going on around us. Oh! the Communards were certainly right! "

After dinner he would go out again and look at the shops where all the decorations were sold, and examine all the emblems of various shapes and colours. He would have likec to possess them all, and to have walked gravely at the head of a procession, with an opera hat under his arm, and his breast covered with decorations, radiant as a star, amid a buzz of admiring whispers and a hum of respect. But, alas! he had no right to wear any decoration whatever.

He used to say to himself: " Is it really too difficult for any man to obtain the Legion of Honour unless he is some public functionary? Suppose I try to get appointed an officer of the Academy! "

But he did not know how to set about it, and spoke to his wife on the subject, who was stupefied.

" Officer of the Academy! What have you done to deserve it? "

He got angry. " I know what I am talking about; I only want

to know how to set about it. You are quite stupid at times."

She smiled. "You are quite right; I don't understand anything about it."

An idea struck him: "Suppose you were to speak to M. Rosselin, the deputy, he might be able to advise me. You understand I cannot broach the subject to him directly. It is rather difficult and delicate, but coming from you it might seem quite natural."

Mme. Caillard did what he asked her, and M. Rosselin promised to speak to the minister about it. Then Caillard began to worry him, till the deputy told him he must make a formal application and put forward his claims.

"What are my claims?" he said. "I am not even a bachelor of arts." However, he set to work, and produced a pamphlet, with the title "The People's Right to Instruction," but he could not finish it for want of ideas.

He sought for easier subjects, and began several in succession. The first was, "The Instruction of Children by Means of the Eye." He wanted gratuitous theatres to be established in every poor quarter of Paris for little children. Their parents were to take them there when they were quite young, and, by means of a magic lantern, all the notions of human knowledge were to be imparted to them. There were to be regular courses. The sight would educate the mind, while the pictures would remain impressed on the brain, and thus science would, so to say, be made visible. What could be more simple than to teach universal history, natural history, geography, botany, zoology, anatomy, etc. etc., thus?

He had his ideas printed in tract form, and sent a copy to each deputy, ten to each minister, fifty to the President of the Republic, and ten to each Parisian, and five to each provincial newspaper.

Then he wrote on "Street Lending Libraries." His idea was to have little carts full of books drawn about the streets, as orange carts are. Every householder or lodger would have a right to ten volumes a month by means of a halfpenny subscription.

"The people," M. Caillard said, "will only disturb itself for the sake of its pleasures, and since it will not go to instruction, instruction must come to it," and so on.

His essays attracted no attention, but he sent in his application and he got the usual formal official reply. He thought himself sure of success, but nothing came of it.

Then he made up his mind to apply personally. He begged for an interview with the Minister of Public Instruction, and he was received by a young subordinate, already very grave and important, who kept touching the buttons of electric bells to summon ushers, and footmen, and officials inferior to himself. He declared to M. Caillard that his matter was going on quite favourably, and advised him to continue his remarkable labours. So M. Caillard set at it again.

M. Rosselin, the deputy, seemed now to take a great interest in his success, and gave him a lot of excellent, practical advice. Rosselin was decorated, although nobody knew exactly what he had done to deserve such a distinction.

He told Caillard what new studies he ought to undertake; he introduced him to learned societies which made a point of taking up obscure points in science, for the sake of gaining credit and honours, and he even took him under his wing at the ministry.

One day, when he came to lunch with his friend (for several months past he had constantly taken his meals there), he said to him in a whisper as he shook hands, "I have just obtained a great favour for you. The Committee on Historical Works is going to entrust you with a commission. There are some researches to be made in various libraries in France."

Caillard was so delighted that he could scarcely eat or drink, and a week later he set out. He went from town to town, studying catalogues, rummaging in lofts full of dusty volumes, and was a bore to all the librarians. One day, happening to be at Rouen, he thought he should like to see his wife, whom he had not seen for more than a week, so he took the nine o'clock train, which would land him home by twelve at night. He had his latch-key, so he went in without making any noise, delighted at the idea of the surprise he was going to give her. She had locked herself in. How tiresome! However, he cried out through the door: "Jeanne, it is I."

She must have been very frightened, for he heard her jump out of bed and speak to herself, as if she were in a dream. Then she went to her dressing-room, opened and closed the door, and went quickly up and down her room barefoot two or three times, shaking the furniture till the vases and glasses sounded. Then at last she asked:

"Is it you, Alexander?"

"Yes, yes," he replied; "make haste and open the door."

As soon as she had done so she threw herself into his arms, exclaiming:

"Oh! what a fright! What a surprise! What a pleasure!"

He began to undress himself methodically, as he did everything, and from a chair he took his overcoat, which he was in the habit of hanging up in the hall. But, suddenly, he remained motionless, struck dumb with astonishment—there was a red ribbon in the buttonhole!

"Why," he stammered, "this—this—this overcoat has got the rosette in it!"

In a second his wife threw herself on him, and taking it from his hands, she said: "No! you have made a mistake—give it to me."

But still he held it by one of the sleeves, without letting it go, repeating, in a half-dazed manner:

"Oh! Why? Just explain. Whose overcoat is it? It is not mine, as it has the Legion of Honour on it."

She tried to take it from him, terrified, hardly able to say:

"Listen—listen—give it me—I must not tell you—it is a secret—listen to me."

But he grew angry, and turned pale:

"I want to know how this overcoat comes to be here? It does not belong to me."

Then she almost screamed at him:

"Yes, it does; listen—swear to me—well—you are decorated."

He was so overcome that he let the overcoat fall, and dropped into an armchair.

"I am—you say I am—decorated?"

"Yes, but it is a secret, a great secret."

She had put the glorious garment into a cupboard, and came to her husband pale and trembling.

"Yes," she continued, "it is a new overcoat that I have had made for you. But I swore that I would not tell you anything about it, as it will not be officially announced for a month or six weeks, and you were not to have known till your return from your business journey. M. Rosselin managed it for you."

"Rosselin!" he contrived to utter in his joy; "he has obtained the decoration for me? He! Oh!"

And he was obliged to drink a glass of water.

A little piece of white paper had fallen to the floor out of the pocket of the overcoat. Caillard picked it up; it was a visiting-card, and he read out: "Rosselin—Deputy."

"You see how it is," said his wife.

He almost cried with joy, and a week later it was announced in the *Journal Officiel* that M. Caillard had been awarded the Legion of Honour on account of exceptional services.

THE ACCURSED BREAD

GUY DE MAUPASSANT

I

DADDY TAILLE had three daughters: Anna, the eldest, who was scarcely ever mentioned in the family; Rose, the second girl, who was eighteen; and Clara, the youngest, who was a girl of fifteen.

Old Taille was a widower and a foreman in M. Lebrument's button manufactory. He was a very bright man, very well thought of, abstemious; in fact, a sort of model workman. He lived at Havre, in the Rue d'Angoulême.

When Anna ran away from home the old man flew into a fearful rage. He threatened to kill the head clerk in a large draper's establishment in that town, whom he suspected. After a time, when he was told by various people that she was very steady and investing money in government securities, that she was no gad-about, but was a great friend of Monsieur Dubois, who was a judge of the Tribunal of Commerce, the father was appeased.

He even showed some anxiety as to how she was getting on, and asked some of her old friends who had been to see her, and when told that she had her own furniture, and that her mantelpiece was covered with vases and the walls with pictures, that there were clocks and carpets everywhere, he gave a broad contented smile. He had been working for thirty years to get together a wretched five or six thousand francs. This girl was evidently no fool.

One fine morning, the son of Touchard, the cooper, at the other end of the street, came and asked him for the hand of Rose, the second girl. The old man's heart began to beat, for the Touchards were rich and in a good position. He was decidedly lucky with his girls.

The marriage was agreed upon, and it was settled that it should be a grand affair, and the wedding dinner was to be held at Sainte-Adresse, at Mother Jusa's restaurant. It would cost a lot certainly, but never mind, it did not matter just for once in a way.

But one morning, just as the old man was going home to luncheon with his two daughters, the door opened suddenly, and Anna appeared. She was well dressed and looked undeniably pretty and nice. She threw her arms round her father's neck before he could say a word, then fell into her sister's arms with many tears, and then asked for a plate, so that she might share the family soup. Taille was moved to tears in his turn and said several times:

"That is right, dear, that is right."

Then she told them about herself. She did not wish Rose's wedding to take place at Sainte-Adresse—certainly not. It should take place at her house and would cost her father nothing. She had settled everything and arranged everything, so it was "no good to say any more about it—there!"

"Very well, my dear! very well!" the old man said; "we will leave it so." But then he felt some doubt. Would the Touchards consent? But Rose, the bride-elect, was surprised and asked, "Why should they object, I should like to know? Just leave that to me; I will talk to Philip about it."

She mentioned it to her lover the very same day, and he declared it would suit him exactly. Father and Mother Touchard were naturally delighted at the idea of a good dinner which would cost them nothing, and said:

"You may be quite sure that everything will be in first-rate style."

They asked to be allowed to bring a friend, Madame Florence, the cook on the first floor, and Anna agreed to everything.

The wedding was fixed for the last Tuesday of the month.

II

After the civil formalities and the religious ceremony the wedding-party went to Anna's house. Among those whom the Tailles had brought was a cousin of a certain age, a Monsieur Sauvetanin, a man given to philosophical reflections, serious, and always very self-possessed, and Madame Lamondois, an old aunt.

Monsieur Sauvetanin had been told off to give Anna his arm, as they were looked upon as the two most important persons in the company.

As soon as they had arrived at the door of Anna's house she let go her companion's arm, and ran on ahead, saying: "I will show you the way," and ran upstairs while the invited guests followed more slowly; and, when they got upstairs, she stood on one side to let them pass, and they rolled their eyes and turned their heads in all directions to admire this mysterious and luxurious dwelling.

The table was laid in the drawing-room, as the dining-room had been thought too small. Extra knives, forks, and spoons had been hired from a neighbouring restaurant, and decanters stood full of wine under the rays of the sun which shone in through the window.

The ladies went into the bedroom to take off their shawls and bonnets, and Father Touchard, who was standing at the door, made funny and suggestive signs to the men, with many a wink and nod. Daddy Taille, who thought a great deal of himself, looked with fatherly pride at his child's well-furnished rooms and went from one to the other, holding his hat in his hand, making a mental inventory of everything, and walking like a verger in a church.

Anna went backward and forward, ran about giving orders and hurrying on the wedding feast. Soon she appeared at the door of the dining-room and cried, "Come here, all of you, for a moment," and as the twelve guests entered the room they saw twelve glasses of Madeira on a small table.

Rose and her husband had their arms round each other's waists and were kissing each other in every corner. Monsieur Sauvetanin never took his eyes off Anna. They sat down, and the wedding breakfast began, the relations sitting at one end of the table and the young people at the other. Madame Touchard, the mother, presided on the right and the bride on the left. Anna looked after everybody, saw that the glasses were kept filled and the plates well supplied. The guests evidently felt a certain respectful embarrassment at the sight of all the sumptuousness of the rooms and at the lavish manner in which they were treated. They all ate heartily of the good things provided, but there were no jokes such as are prevalent at weddings of that sort; it was all too grand, and it made them feel uncomfortable. Old Madame Touchard, who was fond of a bit of fun, tried to enliven matters a little, and at the beginning of the dessert she exclaimed, "I say, Philip, do sing us something." The neighbours in their street considered that he had the finest voice in all Havre.

The bridegroom got up, smiled, and, turning to his sister-in-law, from politeness and gallantry, tried to think of something suitable for the occasion, something serious and correct, to harmonise with the seriousness of the repast.

Anna had a satisfied look on her face, and leaned back in her chair to listen, and all assumed looks of attention, though prepared to smile should smiles be called for.

The singer announced "The Accursed Bread," and, extending his right arm, which made his coat ruck up into his neck, he began.

It was decidedly long, three verses of eight lines each, with the last line and the last but one repeated twice. All went well for the first two verses; they were the usual commonplaces about bread gained by honest labour and by dishonesty. The aunt and the bride wept outright. The cook, who was present, at the end of the first verse looked at a roll which she held in her hand, with streaming eyes, as if it applied to her, while all applauded vigorously. At the end of the second verse the two servants, who were standing with their backs to the wall, joined loudly in the chorus, and the aunt and the bride wept outright. Daddy Taille blew his nose with the noise of a trombone, and old Touchard brandished a whole loaf half over the table, and the cook shed silent tears on the crust which she was still holding.

Amid the general emotion Monsieur Sauvetanin said: "That is the right sort of song; very different from the nasty, risky things one generally hears at weddings." Anna, who was visibly affected, kissed her hand to her sister and pointed to her husband with an affectionate nod, as if to congratulate her.

Intoxicated by his success, the young man continued, and unfortunately the last verse contained words about the "bread of dishonour" gained by young girls who had been led away. No one took up the refrain about this bread, supposed to be eaten with tears, except old Touchard and the two servants. Anna had grown deadly pale and cast down her eyes, while the bridegroom looked from one to the other without understanding the reason for this sudden coldness, and the cook hastily dropped the crust as if it were poisoned.

Monsieur Sauvetanin said solemnly, in order to save the situation: " That last couplet is not at all necessary "; and Daddy Taille, who had got red up to his ears, looked round the table fiercely. Then Anna, her eyes swimming in tears, told the servants, in the faltering voice of a woman trying to stifle her sobs, to bring the champagne.

All the guests were suddenly seized with exuberant joy, and all their faces became radiant again. And when old Touchard, who had seen, felt, and understood nothing of what was going on, and pointing to the guests so as to emphasise his words, sang the last words of the refrain, " Children, I warn you all to eat not of that bread," the whole company, when they saw the champagne bottles, with their necks covered with gold foil, appear, burst out singing, as if electrified by the sight:

" Children, I warn you all to eat not of that bread."

OLD JUDAS

Guy de Maupassant

This entire stretch of country was amazing; it was characterised by a grandeur that was almost religious, and yet it had an air of sinister desolation. A great, wild lake, filled with stagnant, black water, in which thousands of reeds were waving to and fro, lay in the midst of a vast circle of naked hills, where nothing grew but broom, or here and there an oak curiously twisted by the wind.

Just one house stood on the banks of that dark lake, a small, low house inhabited by Uncle Joseph, an old boatman, who lived on what he could make by his fishing. Once a week he carried the fish he caught into the surrounding villages, returning with the few provisions that he needed for his sustenance.

I went to see this old hermit, who offered to take me with him to his nets, and I accepted.

His boat was old, worm-eaten, and clumsy, and the skinny old man rowed with a gentle and monotonous stroke that was soothing to the soul, already oppressed by the sadness of the land round about.

It seemed to me as if I were transported to olden times, in the midst of that ancient country, in that primitive boat, which was propelled by a man of another age.

He took up his nets and threw the fish into the bottom of the boat as the fisherman of the Bible might have done. Then he took me down to the end of the lake, where I suddenly perceived a ruin on the other side of the bank, a dilapidated hut, with an enormous red cross on the wall that looked as if it might have been traced with blood, as it gleamed in the last rays of the setting sun.

" What is that? " I asked.

" That is where Judas died," the man replied, crossing himself.

I was not surprised, being almost prepared for this strange answer. Still I asked: " Judas? What Judas? "

" The Wandering Jew, monsieur," he added.

I asked him to tell me this legend .

But it was better than a legend, being a true story, and quite a recent one, since Uncle Joseph had known the man.

This hut had formerly been occupied by a remarkable woman, a kind of beggar, who lived on public charity.

Uncle Joseph did not remember from whom she had this hut. One evening an old man with a white beard, who seemed to be at least two hundred years old, and who could hardly drag himself along, asked alms of this forlorn woman, as he passed her dwelling.

" Sit down, father," she replied; " everything here belongs to all the world, since it comes from all the world."

He sat down on a stone before the door. He shared the woman's bread, her bed of leaves, and her house.

He did not leave her again, for he had come to the end of his travels.

" It was Our Lady the Virgin who permitted this, monsieur," Joseph added, " it being a woman who had opened her door to a Judas, for this old vagabond was the Wandering Jew. It was not known at first in the country, but the people suspected it very soon, because he was always walking; it had become a sort of second nature to him."

And suspicion had been aroused by still another thing. This woman, who kept that stranger with her, was thought to be a Jewess, for no one had ever seen her at church. For ten miles around no one ever called her anything else but the Jewess.

When the little country children saw her come to beg they cried out: " Mamma, mamma, here is the Jewess! "

The old man and she began to go out together into the neighbouring districts, holding out their hands at all the doors, stammering supplications into the ears of all passers-by. They could be seen at all hours of the day, on by-paths, in the villages, or again eating bread, sitting in the noon heat under the shadow of some solitary tree.

Soon the country people began to call the beggar Old Judas.

One day he brought home in his sack two little live pigs, which a farmer had given him after he had cured the farmer of some sickness.

After that he stopped begging, and devoted himself entirely to his pigs. He took them out to feed by the lake, or under isolated oaks, or in the near-by valleys. The woman, however, went about all day begging, but she always came back to him in the evening.

He also did not go to church, and no one ever had seen him cross himself before the wayside crucifixes. All this gave rise to much gossip. One night his companion was attacked by a fever and began to tremble like a leaf in the wind. He went to the nearest town to get some medicine, and then he shut himself up with her, and was not seen for six days.

The priest, having heard that the " Jewess " was about to die, came to offer the consolation of his religion and administer the last sacrament. Was she a Jewess? He did not know. But in any case, he wished to try to save her soul.

Hardly had he knocked at the door when old Judas appeared on the threshold, breathing hard, his eyes aflame, his long beard agitated like rippling water, and he hurled blasphemies in an unknown language, extending his skinny arms in order to prevent the priest from entering.

The priest attempted to speak, offered his purse and his aid, but the old man kept on abusing him, making gestures with his hands as if throwing stones at him.

Then the priest retired, followed by the curses of the beggar.

The companion of old Judas died the following day. He buried her himself, in front of his door. They were people of so little account that no one took any interest in them.

Then they saw the man take his pigs out again to the lake and up the hillsides. And he also began begging again to get food. But the people gave him hardly anything, as there was so much gossip about him. Every one knew, moreover, how he had treated the priest.

Then he disappeared. That was during Holy Week, but no one paid any attention to him. But on Easter Sunday the boys and girls who had gone walking out to the lake heard a great noise in the hut. The door was locked; but the boys broke it in, and the two pigs ran out, jumping like goats. No one ever saw them again.

The whole crowd went in; they saw some old rags on the floor, the beggar's hat, some bones, clots of dried blood and bits of flesh in the hollows of the skull.

His pigs had devoured him.

" This happened on Good Friday, monsieur," Joseph concluded his story, " three hours after noon."

" How do you know that? " I asked him.

" There is no doubt about that," he replied.

I did not attempt to make him understand that it could easily happen that the famished animals had eaten their master after he had died suddenly in his hut.

As for the cross on the wall, it had appeared one morning, and no one knew what hand traced it in that strange colour.

Since then no one doubted any longer that the Wandering Jew had died on this spot.

I myself believed it for one hour.

JUDITH GAUTIER
1850–1917

ZIN-GOU

NIGHT reigns over the Imperial Palace, and all are asleep except the sentinels. No, not all, for a man creeps along by the walls and steals unseen through court and garden. He keeps on his noiseless way until he reaches the apartment where the Empress lies sleeping. Soft lamps shaded with silk are alight in the chamber, which is perfumed like a temple. The man advances unhesitatingly and stands beside the Empress. She springs up, but does not cry out.

She has recognised the intruder. He is the handsome leader of the army, General Také-Outsi-No-Soukouné. His uniform is soiled and dusty, and is stained with blood which is not yet dry.

The Empress throws aside the mosquito-curtain and springs to the floor. She is beautiful and graceful in her long flowing night drapery, although it is evident that she has the expectation of becoming a mother.

"You!" she exclaims. "What are you doing here? What has happened? Is all lost?"

"Worse than that, great Princess," he replies.

"What can be worse? Speak at once!"

"The Son of Heaven, the great Emperor, your august spouse, is dead. He was leading his troops to victory, but an arrow from the Coreans struck him, and—his great soul returned to the Heaven from whence it came."

"Ah, my presentiment was true, then!" the Empress wailed, clasping her hands on her long black hair. "My heart told me that Japan's Majesty should never risk his life in the field with those dreadful people. Tsiou-Aï-Teno would not listen to me! And now he is dead, my noble husband, son of the Prince of Warriors, whose piety made a home for a hundred thousand snow-white herons because his father's soul dwelt in one of them. Ah! where is his own soul now? Alas, where shall we seek it?"

Suddenly the Empress grew calm. She raised her hand with dignity, and signed to the General, who had fallen on his face at her feet, to rise.

"Tell me—is *all* lost? Has victory passed from us for ever?"

"Nothing is lost, my sovereign lady," replied Také-Outsi, rising to his knees. "I carried the body of my Emperor in my arms to his tent, placed it under the care of the most trusty guards, whose lives will answer for the least indiscretion, and spread the news that the Emperor was only wounded and would soon be well. Then I set out, riding all the way, and taking horse after horse as I came, and never stopped until I reached your side.

The handsome soldier raised his eyes to the face of the gracious lady who stood above him. She read in his gaze devotion, loyalty, admiration, perhaps even love. And she, so powerful a sovereign but so weak a woman, felt suddenly that here was a strong arm on which she could lean, a faithful heart which would give courage to her own. Her woman's vanity and her ambition sprang to life, and she felt that the spirit of her dead husband would approve her choice of a guardian for herself and for her unborn child, descendant of the Sons of Heaven.

"Thanks, noble chief," she said. "You have done well. The Emperor lives still; his wounds will soon be healed. To-morrow we will go to the camp together, and I will take his place. His child, who may some day be Emperor, will give me courage. The child shall lead the army through me. I will dress for the battle-field and for my child's protection, and will take the field with you. You, Také-Outsi, shall be my help and the support of the Empire. I give you the title of Nai-Dai-Tsin."

And now the great Empress Zin-Gou has for some days been on the march. Také-Outsi accompanies her, and new battalions raised to reinforce the army, follow them.

First of all come the lancers in bright armour, with visored helmets cut away at the back, and adorned in front with gleaming crescents of bronze. Lance in rest, a small flag waving at the end, they make a brave show. Next come the archers, their heads bound with white fillets with floating ends, their full quivers slung on their backs, the great bow balanced in the right hand. A second corps of archers comes with these; their bows are of a new shape, made for throwing stones of great weight.

Other soldiers follow in their order in the strange uniforms of old Japan. They wear grotesque black masks with bristling moustaches and red eyebrows, helmets with bronze horns or with real stag antlers at the sides. Some of them have chain mail helmets and masks from which only their eyes look out in a space between the meshes. And all kinds of flags and standards wave above this mass of marching men.

The Empress, on a fine horse whose mane is plaited so as to stand up like a crest, her feet resting on carved stirrups, rides at the head of the troops, and so they come to a stream called Matsoura-Gawa.

Then the beautiful Zin-Gou calls a halt. After all, she is only a woman, and she has taken a fancy that she would like to fish in the stream. Sitting on a little hillock, she casts the line, saying:

"If I am to succeed in my undertaking, the bait will be taken; but if failure awaits me, no fish will nibble."

There was silence for a time, while all eyes were intent on the light float swaying on the stream. Suddenly it became agitated; the Empress drew in the line quickly, and a silvery fish dangled from the hook, gleaming like a dagger.

Cries of joy were heard on all sides, and Zin-Gou exclaimed: "Forward, my men. The fleet awaits us and victory is certain!"

A tall and stately old man approached, bowing to the ground. He was a hermit who dwelt near the stream, and was greatly renowned for his virtue and learning. He presented the Empress with an amulet made from a blue stone, pierced with a hole.

"Wear this always, O Empress," said he; "and when the time comes for your child to open its eyes to the light, the war will be over and the sun of victory will shine on the infant's gaze."

Zin-Gou thanked the hermit, and aided by Také-Outsi, hung the precious amulet on her bosom.

They came to the harbour of Kasifi-Ne-Oura. The fleet was drawn up in fine array, the great junks looking like sea-monsters, and the sails like enormous wings. The sailors and soldiers greeted one another with cheers. The Empress dismounted and advanced to the water's edge. Taking off her golden helmet she loosened her long black hair, and bathed it in the flood. Then, after shaking it till it was dry, she twined it into a simple knot at the back of the head, such as was worn by men, and raising her battle-axe, went on board the noblest of the junks.

Zin-Gou stood above the crowd like a statue on a pedestal. Her armour was of black horn, fastened at the joints by cords of purple silk, falling over the wide trousers of white brocade with clouded pattern, caught in at the ankles. Her shoulder-straps were of black velvet, and the wide sleeves, falling to her feet, folded round her like a cloak of gold brocade, wrought with flowers, with a lining of plain white satin.

On the front of her corselet a gold chrysanthemum finely carved was fixed; and her helmet, tall and ending in a peak, was fastened under her chin by a silken strap. Two sabres and a battle-axe were carried in the girdle, and the warlike lady leaned on a long lance of ivory and gold.

The sails spread to the winds, the ships bowed to the waves, and Zin-Gou, gazing afar, cried aloud:

"See, the Ocean God! Foumi-Yori-Mio-Zin himself is our guide and will lead us to victory!"

She alone can see the god; but all acclaim her words, and victory is sure.

The King of Corea trembles and weeps in his palace, for his country has been invaded and his armies shattered. No resistance could withstand the indomitable valour of Japan, and he was certain of defeat even before he had gone into the field.

The conquerors have already taken the city. The warlike Empress is at the Palace gates. Hers is a truly heroic soul, for it is she who has inspired her army to victory, undaunted by every obstacle. She leads the attack, crosses the moat, and smites upon the Palace gate, crying aloud:

"The King of Corea is but the dog of Japan!"

The gates are opened and the victors pass into the Palace. The Empress hangs her staff of ivory and gold above the entrance doors, there to remain in sign of conquest throughout all succeeding time. All expect the signal for massacre and pillage; but first of all, the King of Corea comes forward to yield himself a prisoner. His hands are tied behind his back, and there is a chain about his neck. As he advances, he passes among heaps of dead and wounded.

"I am your slave!" he cries in despair, sinking at the feet of the lovely warrior.

But her woman's heart awakes beneath her coat of mail. Zin-Gou raises the poor King and removes his chains.

"Not my slave!" she says. "Still King of Corea, though my vassal!"

She straitly forbids the sack of the city, and orders the royal treasures alone to be collected and valued. Japan had then but little skill in art, and the Empress is fascinated by pictures and carvings brought hither from the workshops of China.

Joy succeeds to despair. The august lady is everywhere saluted as a conqueror, but finds her best reward in the praise and love of her intrepid General Také-Outsi, whom she raises to be her husband and the guardian of her heir.

More than sixteen centuries have gone by since this illustrious Empress returned to her capital in triumph, and there gave birth to a son, whose eyes, thanks to the magic stone, opened on the light of victory. Her reign was long and glorious. Her direct descendant holds the throne to-day; and Japanese soldiers and sailors of our time are as valorous as were those who fought under the brave Empress Zin-Gou.

PIERRE LOTI
B. 1850

THE WALL OPPOSITE

RIGHT down at the farther end of a court they lived, in a tiny set of rooms, the mother, the daughter, and a maternal parent already quite aged—their aunt and great-aunt—whom they had come to shelter.

The daughter was still very young, in the fleeting freshness of her eighteen years, when they were compelled, after a reverse of fortune, to withdraw there into the most secluded corner of their ancestral mansion. The rest of the familiar home, all the bright side that looked out on to the street, it had become necessary to let to some profane strangers, who changed there the old aspect of things, and obliterated the cherished associations.

A judicial sale had stripped them of the most luxurious furniture of other days, and they, recluses, had arranged their new little salon with objects a little incongruous: relics of ancestors, old things brought to light from the garret, the reserves of the house. But they fell in love with it at once, this salon so humble, which must now for years to come, on winter evenings, reunite all three around the same fire and around the same lamp. One found it comfortable there; it had an air cosy and intimate. One felt a little cloistered there, it is true, but without melancholy, for the windows, draped with simple muslin curtains, looked out on to a sunny court, whose walls, down at this farther end, were adorned with honeysuckle and roses.

And already were they forgetting the comfort, the luxury of other times, happy in their modest salon, when one day a communication was brought to them which left them in mournful consternation: the neighbour was about to raise his apartment two storeys; a wall was going to rise there, in front of their windows, to steal away the air, to hide the sun.

And there were no means, alas! to turn aside that misfortune, more intimately cruel to their spirits than all the preceding disasters of fortune. To buy that house from their neighbour, a thing that had been easy at the time of their past affluence, was no longer to be dreamed of! Nothing to do, in their poverty, but to bow their heads.

. . . .

And so the storeys began to mount, line upon line; with anxiety they watched them grow; a silence of grief reigned among them, in the little salon, the depth of their melancholy measured day by day by the height of that obscuring object. And to think that that thing there, higher and still higher, would soon replace the background of blue sky or golden clouds, against which in days gone by the wall of their comfort trailed off in its network of branches!

In one month the masons had achieved their work: it was a glazed surface in freestone, which was next painted a greyish white, resembling almost a twilight sky of November, perpetually opaque, unchangeable and dead; and in the summers following the rose trees, the bushes of the court, took on their green again more palely in its shadow.

Into the salon the warm suns of June and July still penetrated, but more laggardly in the morning, fleeing more hurriedly in the evening; the twilights of autumn fell one hour earlier, bringing abruptly down the dull, chill melancholy.

. . . .

And the times, the months, the seasons, passed. Between daylight and darkness, at the undecided hours of evening, when the three women left off one after the other their work of embroidery or sewing before lighting the evening lamp, the young daughter—who would soon be no longer young—lifted her eyes ever toward the wall, set up there in place of her sky of yesterday; often, even, in a sort of melancholy childishness that constantly returned to her like the sick fancy of a prisoner, she amused herself in watching from a certain place the branches of the rose trees, the tops of the bushes detach themselves in relief against the greyish background of the painted stones, and sought to give herself the illusion that the background there was a sky, a sky lower and nearer than the real one—after the manner of those who at night hang upon the deformed visions of dreams.

. . . .

They had in expectation a heritage of which they often spoke around their lamp and their work-table, as of a day-dream, as of a fairy tale, so far away it seemed.

But as soon as they possess it, that legacy from America, at no matter what price, the house of the neighbour shall be bought in order to pull down all that new part, to re-establish things as in times past, and to restore to their court, to restore to their cherished rose bushes of the high walls, the sun of other times. To throw it down, that wall, this had become their sole earthly desire, their continual obsession.

And the old aunt was accustomed to say at such times:
"My dear daughters, may God grant that I live long enough, even I, to see that happy day!"

. . . .

It tarried long in coming, that heritage.

The rains, and time, had traced on that glazed surface a sort of blackish stripes, melancholy, very melancholy to look at, formed like a V, or like the trembling silhouette of a hovering bird. And the young girl contemplated it wearily every day, every day.

. . . .

Once, in a very warm springtime, which, in spite of the shadow of the wall, made the roses more advanced than usual, and more spreading, a young man appeared at the farther end of that court, took his place for several evenings at the table of the three ladies without fortune. Passing through the village, he had been recommended by some friends in common, not without *arrière-pensée* of marriage. He was handsome, with a high-spirited face, browned by the great blowings of the seas.

But he judged it too chimerical, that heritage; he found her too poor, the young girl, in whom, besides, the colour began to fade for lack of sunlight.

So he departed, without return, he who had represented there for a time, the sun, energy, and life. And she who already looked upon herself as his fiancée received from that departure a dumb and secret feeling as of death.

. . . .

And the monotonous years continued their march, like the impassive rivers; there passed five; there passed ten, fifteen, even twenty. The freshness of the young girl without fortune vanished little by little, fading away, useless and disdained; the mother took on some grey hairs; the old aunt became infirm, shaking her head, octogenarian in a faded arm-chair, for ever seated at the same place, near the darkened window, her venerable profile cut out against the foliage of the court below that background of glazed wall where the blackish marbling accentuated itself in the form of a bird, traced by the sluggish gutters.

In the presence of the wall, of the inexorable wall, they grew old all three. And the rose bushes, the shrubs, grew old, too, with the less ominous age of plants, with their airs of rejuvenation at each return of spring.

"Oh! my daughters, my poor daughters," said the aunt continually in her broken voice that no longer finished the phrase, "provided I live long enough, even I."

And her bony hand, with a movement of menace, indicated that oppressive thing of stone.

. . . .

She had been dead a twelvemonth, leaving a dreadful void in that little salon of recluses, and they had wept over her as the most cherished of grandmothers, when at last the inheritance came, very upsetting, one day when they had ceased longer to think of it.

The aged daughter—forty years struck now—found herself quite young in her joy at entering into possession of the returned fortune.

They drove out the lodgers, you may be sure, they re-established themselves as before; but by preference they kept themselves ordinarily in the little salon of the days of moderate means: in the first place it was now full of souvenirs, and then besides it was again taking on a sunny cheerfulness, since they were to throw down that imprisoning wall which was to-day no more than a vain scarecrow, so easy to destroy by touch of louis d'or.

. . . .

It took place at last, that downfall of brick and mortar, longed for during twenty gloomy years. It took place in April, at the moment of the first balmy airs of the first long evenings. Very quickly it was accomplished, in the midst of the noise of falling stones, of singing workmen, in a cloud of plaster and of ancient dust.

And at twilight of the second day, when the work was finished, the workmen gone, silence returned, they found themselves once more sitting at their table, the mother and the daughter, bewildered at seeing so clearly, at having need no longer of the lamp to begin their evening meal. Like a formal visit from familiar days gone by, they contemplated the rose bushes of their court spread out once more against the sky. But instead of the joy they had looked forward to there was at first an indefinable uneasiness: too much light all at once in their little salon, a sort of melancholy splendour, and the feeling of an unaccustomed void out of doors, of limitless change. No words there came to them in presence of the accomplishment of their dream; rapt, the one and the other, held by an ever-increasing melancholy, they remained there without talking, without touching the waiting meal. And little by little, their two hearts pressing still closer, that grew to be a kind of grief, like one of those regrets, dull and without hope, which the dead leaves us.

When the mother, at length, perceived that the eyes of her daughter began to grow faded with crying, divining the unexpressed thoughts which must so perfectly resemble her own: "It can be built up again," she says. "It seems to me they can try, can they not, to make it the same again?"

"I, too, thought of that," replied the daughter. "But no, don't you see: *it would never be the same!*"

Mon Dieu! was it possible that such a thing could be; it was she, the very same, who had decreed it, the annihilation of that background of a familiar picture, below which, during one springtime, she had seen in high relief a certain fine face of a young man, and during so many winters the venerable profile of an old aunt dead.

And all at once, at recollection of that vague design in the form of the shadow of a bird, traced there by patient gutters, and which she would see again never, never, never, her heart was suddenly torn in a manner most pitiable; she wept the most melancholy tears of her life before the irreparable destruction of that wall.

AN OLD CONVICT'S SORROW

PIERRE LOTI

YVES told me this little story. He had gone into the Roads one evening with his gunboat to remove a cargo of convicts to the transport vessel which was to take them to New Caledonia.

One of the convicts was a very old man—seventy years old at least—who carried with him very carefully an unfortunate sparrow in a tiny cage. To pass the time Yves began to talk to this old chap, who had rather a good face, but was chained to a youth of mean appearance, short-sighted and sneering, who wore glasses on an insignificant nose.

The old man explained that he was an old highway robber now imprisoned for the fifth or sixth time for vagrancy and theft. "How can a man keep from stealing," he said, "when once he has begun, and when he has no trade of any sort, and nobody will have anything to do with him? He must steal, mustn't he? My last sentence was for a sack of potatoes which I found in a field with a carter's whip and a pumpkin. But couldn't they have let me die in France, I ask you, an old man like me, instead of sending me down over there?"

Comforted at having met somebody who would listen to him sympathetically, he showed Yves his most treasured possession in the world—the little cage and the sparrow.

The sparrow was so tame that it knew his voice, and had lived with him for more than a year, perched on the old man's shoulder in his cell. Only with considerable trouble had he procured permission to take it with him to New Caledonia. And then he had been obliged to make a cage for it that would serve for the voyage;

and that meant getting some wood, and an old piece of wire, and a little green paint to make it all look pretty.

I can remember exactly what Yves said at this point: " Poor sparrow! Although the food in its cage was just a morsel of that grey-coloured bread which is given to prisoners it seemed to be quite happy all the same. It hopped about as other birds do."

When the transport vessel was reached a few hours later, and the convicts were preparing to embark on their long voyage, Yves, who had forgotten the old man, again passed near him by accident.

" Here, take it," said the old convict in an utterly changed voice, holding out the little cage. " I give it to you. Maybe you will find some use for it; maybe it will give you pleasure."

" No, no," Yves answered. " I couldn't think of it; you must take it with you. It will be a little comrade for you over there."

" Oh! but he is no longer inside," replied the old man. " You didn't know that? You didn't hear about it then? He is no longer there." Two tears of hopeless, indescribable misery were on his cheeks.

The vessel had lurched and that had opened the cage door. The sparrow, frightened, flew out, and then, one of its wings having been cut, it fell right into the sea. Oh! that moment of terrible sorrow when he saw it struggle and die, swept away by the rapid current! And he all the time helpless, unable to rescue it! At first, by a natural impulse, he had thought of calling out for help; of speaking to Yves; of imploring him. . . .

But then he remembered his degraded position, and the impulse was checked at once. An old convict! Who would listen to the prayer of such a wretch? Could he suppose that the ship would be stopped to recover a drowning sparrow—a convict's poor bird? It was absurd to think of it. So he had stood there in his place without saying a word, watching the little grey body struggling to the end, till it finally was lost to sight in the sea-foam. And now he felt horribly lonely, now and for ever; and the great tears of solitude and of complete despair were in his eyes. But his companion on the chain, the youth with the eyeglasses, only laughed at seeing an old man weep.

Now that the bird was no longer there he had no wish to keep the cage—the cage which he had built with so much pains for that lonely dead bird. He offered it to the good soldier who had so kindly listened to his story, and he wished him to take it as a legacy from one just setting out on a long last voyage.

And Yves, because he was anxious not to cause any more pain to this depraved old convict, by seeming to despise a piece of work which had cost him so much trouble, sadly accepted the cage as a present.

It is plain to me that I have not been able to do justice to the pathos of this story as it was told to me.

It was quite late at night, and I was just going to bed. It amazed me to find my heart so torn by the distress of the old convict; and to realise that I, who in the course of my life have seen with hardly any emotion so many impressive sorrows, and dramas, and deaths, should be in danger of losing my sleep through that distress.

"Is it by any means possible," I said, "to send him another?"

"I thought of that too," Yves replied. "I thought of buying him a beautiful bird at a bird-fancier's, and bringing it back in the little cage for him to-morrow. That is if there's time before he sails. It would be a little difficult no doubt. Besides, you are the only person who could get into the Roads to-morrow and go on board the transport and find the old man. I don't even know his name. And then, don't you think people would think it very odd?"

"Why, yes, certainly. There can't be any doubt about its being odd."

For a moment I entertained the idea with pleasure, and laughed within myself, that happy internal laugh which rarely comes to the surface.

However I did not pursue the notion, and on awaking next morning, with the first impression gone, the whole plan seemed to me childish and ridiculous. A simple plaything could not bring consolation for a sorrow like this. This poor old convict, so utterly alone in the world! The most beautiful Bird of Paradise could never make up to him for the loss of that humble little grey sparrow with the broken wing, a bird reared on prison bread, which had been able to call up in him a tenderness of surpassing sweetness, and to bring tears from a heart hardened and well-nigh dead.

PAUL BOURGET
B. 1852

THE PORTRAIT OF THE DOGE

1

"You will be pretty comfortable," I said to Roger de Montfort as we came in sight of the magnificent villa erected by Joseph W. Bronson, of Philadelphia, upon that high cliff at Newport from which the grandest marine landscape in the world may be seen. "Poor old Joe," as he was still called, had not spent one hour in that palace of brick and stone, fashioned in the French style of the first half of the seventeenth century. This copper king, who began life by selling newspapers in the streets of his native city and had left a fortune of ten millions of dollars to his widow and an only daughter, had died some years ago, in his city office, from heart disease, killed by the cares of business before he had attained his fifty-fifth year. The indefatigable maker of millions had foreseen, when he brought over the Parisian architect to construct that gigantic bibelot of architecture, that he was preparing a summer residence for a son-in-law descended from the aristocracy of Louis the Thirteenth.

The young man of thirty-two years to whom I spoke so familiarly really belonged to the race of that Marquis de Montfort, grand master of the wardrobe and field marshal in 1637, who has left to us some curious and interesting memoirs of life at court and camp in the days of Cardinal Richelieu. The present marquis was not an unworthy representative of that illustrious ancestor, for he possessed a keen and intelligent mind, though lacking, it is true, a proper measure of pride and culture. But the enormous fortune which had belonged to the family from time immemorial had been almost entirely dissipated by his grandfather under the Monarchy of July. His father had continued the dissipation under the Second Empire, and the present marquis had followed their example under the Third Republic. The three of them had maintained a life of idleness and luxury; which is the reason why Roger had followed the beautiful and wealthy Jessie Bronson from Cannes to Paris and from Paris to New York and Newport. He had brought me to Newport to introduce me to her.

When I jocosely remarked to him, " You will be pretty comfortable," he replied in the same tone:

" Yes, it will not be too great a change from Montfort, which is of the same date and style; but "—with a shrug of his shoulders— " when I speak of the same style, you must remember that the copy of an ancient building, however exact it may be, is more or less a parody. It appears so easy to reproduce a façade, a roof, or a staircase! Ah! if you could have seen Montfort! But we will buy it and restore it, if——"

He did not finish the sentence, but smiled a peculiar smile as he always did when he spoke of his probable marriage with the heiress of Joe Bronson's millions. It is a French characteristic to laugh at oneself a little in order to disarm others. But Montfort was wrong in fearing my criticism. I considered it perfectly legitimate for him to offer the arms and coronet of a marquis to the charming American girl. As to her purpose in entering into this marriage, she very soon gave me a token of it.

Knowing the hour of his arrival, she was awaiting him in the garden. She saw him; she also saw me, and then her face assumed an air of disappointment. I understood that, in her opinion, Roger should have come alone on this first visit to Newport. But he had insisted upon my coming to Cliff Lodge with him, and I had a keen curiosity to visit one of those millionaires' villas at Newport which I had heard spoken of, sometimes in admiration—sometimes in derision. Fortunately, her look of disappointment was a momentary one; as soon as Montfort introduced me, she talked to me as familiarly as to an old friend, and questioned me, according to the custom of her country, concerning the impressions the New World had made upon me, a degenerate son of an ancient civilisation.

" You must have found New York very ugly," she said. " When Grand Duke Paul came over last year on Richard Martin's yacht, he would not stay in New York a day. So he came to Newport and liked it very much. To understand America you must remember that we have a great deal of liberty—too much liberty. Of course, in New York, as in all our cities, the men lead an active business life—nothing but business. That is why the streets are so ugly. Here we lead a social life—nothing but society. Oh, I know there are many crudities even here; but you will not find it wearisome. It is true we have no limit, even in our amusements. Lord Ronald Strabane—do you know him? He is a son of the Duke of Gairlock. He always said that the season at Newport, compared to the season in London, was like Niagara compared to a Scotch waterfall."

As she spoke her face wore a smile indicative of that defensive irony which I had already noticed in Roger's smile whenever he spoke about her. Yet I noticed, in their respective tones of raillery, a certain difference. Although the young American had a decided touch of international snobbishness, which displayed itself in the many references she made to the European nobility, she had also a sincere pride in her own country. If any one else had echoed the criticisms she permitted herself to make of her native land, her beautiful eyes would quickly have flashed with indignation. Montfort, on the contrary, in spite of his Parisian *blasé*, was rather ashamed of his efforts to contract this wealthy alliance, and his ironical tone seemed to savour of an apology for his mercenary act. He now replied to Miss Bronson with a complaisance that I knew to be only half sincere.

"But you malign New York," he said. "Do you not recall my impression of it on the day after my arrival, when you and your mother drove me to Central Park? I said then that in twenty-five years it will be one of the most beautiful cities in the world. Even now those great private mansions are superior to the ugly buildings of our Boulevard Haussmann. They constitute the first rough sketch of a new era in architecture. Am I not right?"

He appealed to me. I would not contradict him, but I was displeased to find him so supple and so prone to duplicity. My acquaintance with Roger had been only a superficial one, formed on the transatlantic steamer and not materially deepened by our sojourn in that bewildering New York where we had landed two weeks before; yet I felt grieved at his intended marriage, for I was convinced that he had no love for the girl. That was a matter of regret, for if ever an heiress deserved to be loved for herself and not for her fortune, it was that adorable young American. It may have been the great beauty of the girl that made so painful to me the idea that Roger entertained toward her only a mercenary interest. A marriage so arranged between a libertine and a very rich but very homely girl would probably not have touched my sympathy. But I was firmly convinced that this elegant young man saw in the charming young girl only a package of banknotes which he could distribute at pleasure; and that this charming girl saw in the elegant young man nothing more than a coat-of-arms on the panel of a carriage and a welcome to the Olympus of our Faubourg Saint-Germain.

"See what society makes of youth, love, and beauty!" I thought, as I observed the couple, whose marriage would be proclaimed by the public press of two continents. A royal list of wedding gifts would be published. They would be envied on both sides of the Atlantic, and the handsome young couple would be surfeited with everything that money can purchase; everything except the one thing that makes life worth living—true love.

II

I never knew whether or not I was deceived in my estimate of Miss Bronson's character. Was she, like so many girls in her country, at once sentimental and positive, romantic and practical? Although yearning to be called "The Marquise de Montfort," it is possible that she had a sincere attachment for the bearer of the coveted title. As to him, I obtained almost immediately, and in an unexpected manner, the proof that he was playing the part of a fortune-hunter; and, strange as the expression may appear, he acted from a sense of duty. Young Parisians of his class are sometimes *roués* from principle, cynics from a point of honour, and always on the watch to destroy, in a moment of compassion, the foundation of their own duplicity. Certainly he had no suspicion, any more than I, of the sudden change about to occur in his affairs. When we entered the hall of the villa he said to me, in a low voice, and with childish malice:

"To think that in two or three centuries my portrait, as an ancestor, will appear on one of those panels! What artist would you recommend?" Then, in a louder voice, he added, as the heiress returned from an adjoining room: "Miss Jessie, we were wondering where you had that beautifully decorated ceiling made."

"How—made?" replied the girl, with a slight display of indignation. "Why, it is a genuine work of art, dating back to the fifteenth century. We bought it in an old chateau in Touraine, and had it brought here, beam by beam, and put together again. Mama must have gone out. I cannot find her. However, I will show you some of our art treasures. They are not all so rare as this ceiling, but they are all genuine. Do you understand that, Monsieur de Montfort? You who have so little faith in the artistic judgment of the American barbarians."

"Barbarians who ravish everything that is beautiful in Europe," said Roger. "Ah! You have a perfect museum here. It is marvellous!"

I echoed his exclamation. Certainly, many of the curiosities hanging on the walls of that house should have been in the Louvre. The only defect in the collection was its incoherence; that betrayed its improvised origin. Pell-mell, the copper magnate had purchased two tapestries of the Middle Ages, worthy of a place in the Musée de Cluny; four antique sarcophagi; a bas-relief in terra-cotta; a *casson,* coloured in the Florentine style; and a miscellaneous collection of paintings by Philippe, Champaigne, Courbet, Perugino, and the most recent of our modern impressionists. Behind that assortment of incongruous objects one could divine the ill-considered travels through Europe and the thoughtless acquisition of a mass of art objects on the recommendation of some connoisseur who was earning a liberal commission. Many evidences of Napoleonic worship, so common among the citizens of the great republic, were to be observed in this collection of bric-à-brac; notably, a portrait by Robert Lefevre, hanging above a flag of the Old Guard. The discoloured and tattered silk standard was still clinging to its staff. The magic names of Marengo, Austerlitz, Jena, Essling, Wagram, were embroidered upon it in letters of gold. That tattered reminiscence of heroic France was such a striking commentary upon the remark just then made by Roger relative to the conquest of the Old World by the New, that I could not refrain from asking Miss Bronson where they obtained the relic.

"Oh, from a dealer in curios in Paris. You see, that standard has no history." She made the astounding remark in the most simple manner; then she added: "It is not like that portrait of the doge which you are examining so closely, Monsieur de Montfort. That is a Palma, dated and signed. Does it not interest you?"

"Very much," said Roger, who had been standing motionless for several minutes before the canvas of the Venetian master. "It is the portrait of a Navagero, if I read the inscription correctly?"

"Exactly," responded Miss Bronson; "and I bet you can never guess what we had to pay—but, no! you would lose. I will tell you the story. It was two years and a half ago, toward the end of the winter. Mama and I had left Rome to spend a few weeks in the north of Italy at a time when tourists and purchasers were not so plentiful. At Venice we were recommended to see an old priest, a certain Abbé Lagumina, who said mass in a pretty little chapel in which there was a portrait of the Virgin by Bellini—a veritable masterpiece. Mama offered him twenty thousand dollars for it; and I can yet hear him crying: 'If it were mine, *cara signora,* I would give it to you for nothing; but it belongs to God.' Then, after a moment's reflection, he added, 'But if your ladyship wishes a beautiful painting, I can take you to a place—only you must not tell any one that you were there.' We promised him to observe silence on that point. Then he said, 'I will see you at your hotel to-morrow. I will then know if *they* have anything to sell.'"

"Oh!" I said, laughing, "I know quite well whom they mean in Italy when they say *they*. You will be introduced into a family said to be most illustrious, and you will find on the third floor a dirty apartment inhabited by a gang of usurers who offer you some indifferent pictures at exorbitant prices."

"Yes, that is the case ninety-nine times out of a hundred," replied Miss Bronson, "but this was the hundredth. Do you know Venice? Well, imagine that abbé coming one evening about six o'clock, in a gondola, to the door of our hotel, and saying to us, in the tone and manner of a conspirator, that we could purchase a masterpiece if we would promise on our word of honour never to seek to discover the name of the seller or the palace to which he would conduct us. After making the promise, we entered the gondola, and the abbé gave his orders to the gondolier without mentioning any name. On the way, our guide said, 'It will be necessary to pay the money at once; if *they* did not require the money to-morrow, *they* would not sell.' After an intricate detour of the canals, we disembarked before a palace located on a narrow, unfrequented canal. We were introduced into one of those halls which had formerly echoed with the mirth of royal feasts, but was now in a ruinous condition. There we were met by a personage as fantastic as our priestly guide—a crippled giant with two squint eyes. He carried a copper lamp with three burners like those of ancient Pompeii. 'Ah!' he groaned, 'if the count would listen to me, he would not sell it. No, he would not sell it! Ah! I see I have forgotten the keys,' he added, when we reached the landing on the first floor. Then he entered another room, but, in his agitation, forgot to close the door. We remained upon the landing, and could not help overhearing a strange conversation. Evidently, the partly opened door led to the rooms occupied by the family. They spoke in the Venetian dialect, of which I understood sufficient to follow the meaning. 'There is yet time, my lord count,' said the voice of the giant, who, with the despair of an old servant, was seeking to prevent a sale which shocked his feelings. 'Father, do not listen to him,' said another voice—that of a young lady. 'If we do not give Bettina the money, she will not deliver our costumes. She will not give us any more credit, and it is absolutely necessary that Tea and I should go to this ball. What excuse can we make to the Countess Steno?' 'Then you wish me to sell the portrait?' said a third voice, that of the count. 'Sell the portrait to pay for a ball dress!' groaned the giant. 'Ah! Donna Laura, that will bring you misfortune.' 'To-day or to-morrow!' replied Donna Laura. 'We owe everybody; and, if we do not appear at this ball, people will say it is because we had no money to pay for our dresses. Other creditors will hear of it and come down on us. We can sell the picture at a sacrifice, as we did the last.' 'Do not listen to Donna Laura,' urged the giant; 'she wishes the dress because she thinks some one will be there. She knows who I mean. But he will never marry her.' During the progress of this conversation the good Abbé Lagumina made vain efforts to prevent the three speakers conducting their argument in such loud tones. But at least two of the speakers were too much interested in the issue to notice the sharp, short coughs by which the abbé sought to warn them of our presence. Finally, however, they closed the door, and we heard no more.

I shall never forget the scene upon the stairway of that ruined palace. The giant's copper lamp, placed upon the floor, shed a fantastic light about us, and we could hear the dull, monotonous swish of the waters of the canal lapping the wall beneath the window. The cries of the gondoliers were the only signs of life about us, until the giant reappeared, carrying the keys. He offered no excuse for his long absence, but at once opened a door and led us into an abandoned picture gallery, wherein we saw only a vast array of frames with green cloth taking the place of the absent pictures, until we were conducted to this masterpiece. That is how a noble family descended from the Doges of Venice sold one of their illustrious ancestors in order to pay for two ball-dresses. Don't you find the story very amusing? "

" I—I find it very sad," replied Roger, after a momentary silence. He spoke these words in such a strange, lugubrious tone that we both turned and looked at him in surprise. He noticed our action, and then quickly added, " It would have been sufficient for me to know why those poor people wished to sell this portrait; then I should not have had the courage to buy it."

" What would you have done? " I asked. The story related by the American girl had thrown Roger into a state of extreme agitation, which was as evident to me as it was unintelligible. I thought it advisable to change the conversation, so I said, " Everything has been for the best. Miss Bronson has her picture, which is admirable and well cared for. Donna Laura and her sister Tea doubtless obtained their ball-dresses and enjoyed themselves like the simpletons I presume they are. The creditors received their money. Come! Do not quarrel with the inevitable. Masterpieces of art must travel and carry their message of beauty to distant lands. That was Ruskin's idea—was it not, Miss Bronson? "

" Yes," she replied, with a forced laugh; " but it seems that Monsieur de Montfort is not a disciple of Ruskin. He appears to be sorry that he heard the story."

" Not in the least," said Roger abruptly. " To you, the affair was a lucky stroke of business. That is a very natural consideration in your country; but remember that I do not belong to your country nor to a race of mercantile people—that is all! "

III

" Certainly, you were not very polite to Miss Bronson," I said to Montfort fifteen minutes later, as we were leaving Cliff Lodge. After his rude and unwarranted remark, the conversation had lacked cordiality. On my part, I had a natural curiosity to learn what motive had caused Montfort to make such a curt reply to the young lady, so I said to him, "Miss Bronson said nothing to hurt your feelings?"

"No, she did not hurt my feelings," he replied. "I was nervous for a moment—that was all. Let us not speak of it."

So the conversation was changed, but I observed that his ill-feeling or irritation increased momentarily, and it ended by his quitting me with an abruptness that, in another person, would have given me offence. With him I was not offended. I considered that he had received a blow, the nature of which I did not understand. However, that same evening, as I was dressing for dinner, I received a solution of the enigma. Roger entered my room, in travelling costume.

"I have come to say good-bye," were his first words. "I shall dine on the train."

"Are you going away?" I asked. "Have you received any bad news?"

"No," he replied, "but I wish to catch the steamer for Europe to-morrow morning."

"You return to Europe!" I exclaimed. "Surely, you are not serious. And Miss Bronson?"

"Oh, she will find some French or English nobleman willing to marry her and become lord of the luxurious Cliff Lodge. I am now going to Europe to learn if my life's happiness has been irretrievably ruined through the most foolish and villainous of slanders."

The Parisian cynic who had accompanied me to Cliff Lodge that day had disappeared as he spoke. And I liked him better so, although I could not discover the connection between the young lady's story and Montfort's present trouble. My long experience should have taught me that in respect to unexpected events and incredible encounters real life surpasses the events of fiction. After a few adroit questions on my part, Montfort voluntarily told me the following story:

"The history of the sale of that picture, as told by Miss Bronson, interested you—it shocked me. It solved for me a mystery which has long been a burden and a torment to my soul. You are surprised to hear me talk in this tone. You have known me only as a man of pleasure, and, no doubt, you consider me incapable of any deep or lasting sentiment. That is only natural, and I do not blame you for holding that opinion. If it were not for the incident of to-day, would I not, without scruple, have entered into a marriage for money solely? I admit that I should have done so; because I failed to marry the only woman I ever loved, and the sale of that picture was the indirect cause of that failure. I will explain.

"Two and a half years ago, when Miss Bronson was in Venice,

I was there also. At that time I did not know her; but I was a frequent visitor at the Palazzo Navagero which she described, and every word she uttered awakened a bitter memory in my heart. The crippled giant, who served as Caleb to those ruined patricians, has, with his copper lamp, often conducted me to the little *salon* which opens off the first-floor landing. And that voice of the young girl whom Miss Bronson did not see—ah! how I loved its tender thrill and melodious accent as she spoke the soft dialect of the lagoon! It is a sweet but painful memory."

He ceased speaking, and I observed that his eyes were wet with tears. I pressed his hand, and this touch of sympathy caused him to open his heart to me without reserve. He continued:

"I hope you will not smile at my story. After hearing it you can judge for yourself if I am not right, if it is not my duty to go away—to go at once and ask forgiveness from one whom I have cruelly injured by an unjust suspicion. Donna Laura Navagero—for you will understand that it is of her I speak—was then twenty-two years of age. She had some Lombard blood in her veins, and, with her brown hair, rosy cheeks, black eyes and oval features, she had a delicious face, such as one sees in those old frescoes at Milan. She lost her mother when still quite young. Her only relatives were her father and her sister, Tea, who was one year older than Laura. Of the father I will say nothing, except that he inherited a meagre fortune, which he squandered in stock speculations. The sister was as homely as Laura was pretty. Between her father and her sister Laura lived without direction or surveillance, and it was inevitable that, being pretty and coquettish—with that coquetry of the twentieth year which is no more than a childish desire to please—she furnished food for gossip. I see that distinctly to-day, and I saw it even then; but when a man is in love he is not guided by reason, he is governed by emotion. That excuses, or at least explains, my conduct in believing so readily the evil that was said of her."

"Alas!" I said, interrupting him, "it is the eternal misunderstanding. In love, as in religion, those who are wise profess implicit faith. If they are deceived it is as if they were not, since they are ignorant of it; and they incur no risk of causing injury to a faithful heart by doubting it."

"Ah, you are quite right!" he exclaimed. "Why did I not think so before the occurrence of that little drama in which this portrait of the doge plays so prominent a part? I must first explain to you the relations which existed between me and Laura at the time the picture was sold. Although I may have seen Mlle. Navagero twice or even three times a day at her own house, on the promenade or in society, I had never told her of my love. Yet we were both well aware that we entertained for each other a tender feeling which required no expression in words. But from time to time certain disparaging remarks concerning her were made in my hearing, or came to my knowledge. Finally, by force of repetition, these remarks caused doubt and suspicion to enter my mind. How can I express to you the strange anxiety I experienced on her account, which, resulting sometimes in a conviction of her complete innocence and sometimes in a certainty of her guilt, finally caused me one evening to make a resolution that I would ask her hand in marriage? But on the following day I resolved to quit Venice for ever, without seeing her again."

"And she?" I asked, as he paused in his recital. "Had she any knowledge of your doubts and suspicions?"

"Alas," he replied, "her perspicacity greatly increased my anxiety and indecision! She appeared to read my mind like an open book. If I were sad and yet assumed an air of gaiety, she quickly divined the deception and questioned me until I invented some explanation, which she feigned to believe, but which never really satisfied her. One day, in one of my melancholy moments, she asked me, in a tone of deep earnestness and anxiety, 'Do you wish me to tell you what is wrong with you? Some one has told you wicked stories about me.' As she said this she looked at me so intently that I was forced to lower my eyes. 'Yes,' I replied, after an embarrassing pause. I resolved to equivocate no longer, but to tell her the truth, which course I deemed the better for both of us. She understood my intention and stopped me as I was about to speak. 'I don't wish to know anything about those slanders,' she said proudly and firmly. 'Look at me, and tell me if you believe that I have ever in my life done any act that I should not have done!'"

"But what had been said about her?" I asked Roger. "And who said it?"

"Who? Nearly every one in our circle of society in Venice. Laura had many acquaintances who envied her youth and beauty and the social success which those qualities insured. What did they say? Well, really, I am ashamed to repeat it. But I must confess that I believed it at the time. It was a base slander. It arose from her taste in dress and love for elegant costumes. Her gowns were as handsome and as stylish as those of the rich Austrian and Russian ladies who set the fashions in Venice. It was well known that the Navagero family was ruined; consequently, it was rumoured that Laura paid her bills through her lovers."

"And you believed it!" I exclaimed. "And you loved her! I understand it all. My God—the poor child!"

"But how could I know?" Roger cried, in a tone of supplication. "Why did the proud father conceal the fact that he was selling his pictures, one by one, to passing strangers? He was ashamed of his commerce. In sparing himself that humiliation, he never suspected that he was casting a cloud of suspicion over his daughter. Well, I will bring my story down to the evening of the ball given by the Countess Steno, for which occasion Laura had ordered a magnificent costume copied from Titian's painting of Queen Cornaro. Ah! how beautiful she was! So beautiful that her entrance evoked a murmur of admiration. And you can imagine my grief to see her, smiling, envied and admired, crossing the ballroom on the arm of a man whose name had been mentioned as a contributor to her toilets—a certain Marquis Vanini. He was older than she by at least twenty years, was married, and had enormous wealth; but he did not attempt to conceal his admiration for Laura. I can hear even now, and shall always hear, the voice of a Venetian whispering to a group of his friends, 'Vanini does things well. It appears that they owe everybody, and that Bettina, the costumier, was afraid to trust them. She would not deliver the costumes until she received her money.' In the light of that remark, which agreed precisely with many others I had heard as to the probability of Laura being able to appear at the ball, a horrible anguish rent my heart. I was overwhelmed by a dreadful suspicion; one of those insane suspicions in which one has an instinctive feeling that he must conceal himself in order that he may not do some irreparable injury to the object of his suspicions. So I retired to a corner of the balcony, whence I could see at my right the dark lagoon and the silhouettes of numerous gondolas; at my left, the ballroom, brilliant with lights. The dancers were whirling around to the music of an intoxicating Hungarian waltz under a ceiling decorated in a free and voluptuous manner by a pupil of Veronese. Suddenly it seemed as if the secret character of Laura Navagero lay fully revealed before me. Was not she the descendant of one of those patrician families in which there has been transmitted, as a secular heritage, an immoderate love of luxury and pleasure? While I was immersed in these bitter reflections, she was engaged in a dance, apparently happy, but, as I now suspect, awaiting my advances, having dressed herself to please me. That 'some one,' of whom the old servant spoke with a familiarity so characteristically Italian, was myself; and the first words she uttered, when I had emerged from my retreat and advanced to greet her, had no other meaning. Her success on that evening, the feverish excitement of the ball, the pleasure of feeling that she was beautiful, had illumined her sombre eyes and made her face radiant with ineffable joy, like a phosphorescence of happiness. It all vanished at my approach. Once more she read in my face that mental irritation of which she readily divined the cause. In fact, I did not try to conceal it. 'What is the matter?' she asked, in a low voice, as soon as we had gained a place where we could converse without being overheard. 'Do you not like my appearance?' She expected a friendly reply, but I said, 'What does it matter, provided the Marquis Vanini is pleased?' 'The Marquis Vanini!' she exclaimed. 'What do you mean?' 'You know very well. Adieu!' I replied. 'Do not go!' she urged. 'You owe me an explanation. Some one has told you some lie about me and the Marquis Vanini.' She paused a moment, and then abruptly said, 'And you believed it?' I replied, 'I believe that a young girl who wishes to avoid suspicion should not flirt with any man as you do with him, nor come to a ball in a dress which she is not able to pay for, as you have this evening. Such luxury costs very dear.' After I had uttered those shocking words, I saw her flush, turn pale again, then laugh convulsively; and, as the Marquis Vanini chanced to pass us at that moment, she gave me a terrible look and called to him in a loud voice, 'My dear marquis, do you wish to have this waltz with me?' and in a moment she was whirling away in the arms of that man, with an air of triumphant defiance."

"And what then?"

"I left the ball at once and quitted Venice the following day. I have never seen her since, but I have not forgotten her. Do you understand now why Miss Bronson's story so affected me, and what it suddenly revealed to me? Are you astonished now that I wish to go—where I wish to go?"

"To Venice?" I asked.

"To Venice."

"But you know nothing about the poor girl. She may be married."

"I can, at least, ask her pardon."

"But the other," I said. "Have you no feeling for her?"

"For Miss Bronson? Until to-day I thought she pleased me sufficiently to make the marriage endurable. Now, on the contrary, she gives me the horrors."

IV

Thus it was that the heiress of the copper king carried her immense fortune into the family of an English duke, who would be greatly astonished to learn that he owed his opportunity to the sentimental caprice of a little French marquis, who was at one time a great favourite in the contest for the heiress and her colossal dowry. From my French friend I have not heard since he told me his story some three years ago; but I have received information, indirectly, that when he arrived in Venice he found that the beautiful Laura Navagero was rich enough to repurchase all the portraits of the doges that her father had sold to American millionaires. She was married to the Marquis Vanini, who had become a widower—which proves that women frequently come to resemble that which we have thought them to be in certain moments in which they have placed their hearts in our hands. To suspect a young soul is an unpardonable crime, since it will venture much to justify the suspicion, when it despairs of eradicating it.

THE BROTHER OF MR. VIPLE

PAUL BOURGET

ONE of the most striking impressions of my childhood was the arrival in our country town of some Austrian soldiers, captured in the war of 1859. We were not spoilt by travellers in the sombre town of Clermont in Auvergne, where the railway had only come a few years before. The strangers consisted of a few sick people on their way to Royat or for Mont Doré and Bourboule, all difficult of access.

The arrival of the defeated soldiers, with their white uniforms dirtied by use, with their foreign faces, was an event for all the population, and particularly for boys of my age,—I was then seven. And we stared at the newcomers with an innocently cruel curiosity as they walked along the terrace of La Poterne, from which you can see the admirable line of the mountains from the table-land of the Côtes to the wooded mass of Grave Noire.

I do not know what war-like dreams fill the minds of the children who now roll their hoops on the terrace. The lads of the present day are sons of a nation living in the shadow of a great defeat, while we were children still touched with the glory of the heroic age of Napoleon. The old men who stroked our curly heads with their enfeebled hands had seen the victorious eagles defile on their return from Europe; and the legend of our ancient glory was still so strong that it was expressed in our childish imaginations by the most comical and touching fancies. We were convinced, for example, my four chums—Émile, Arthur, Joseph, and Claude, and myself—that a little French boy was stronger than two little boys of any other country. Great was our astonishment when we compared the brave and vigorous Austrian troops with our own soldiers walking on the same pavement and under the same trees. We stood amazed when we found that the foreigners were quite as tall and as muscular as our men. Such was the childish form of our faith in the superiority of our own race. Eleven years afterwards we had to pay too dearly for other and graver illusions founded on a faith almost as childish.

If I recall the short stay in our town of these prisoners in white uniform, it is because another recollection is attached to it. It relates to an anecdote that long remained in my mind before I was able to explain it, and which I always think of with passionate interest every time I listen to any discussion about the character of children. I must add that the man who told me the story stays in my mind as one of the most original figures I met in this country town. He was an old friend of my family, a retired school inspector, and he had the fantastic name of Optat Viple, and the man was as fantastic as his name. I can still see him, across the space of thirty years, as he came out of the church-yard to follow the Cours Sablon, his favourite walk when it was sunny. Very tall, very thin, hat in hand, with a bald pointed head, glasses on an infinite nose, his frock-coat tightly buttoned round his long figure, and his feet in heavy double-soled boots, which he wore winter and summer, indoors as well as out, for fear of catching cold.

He had kindly undertaken to teach me the rudiments of Latin and Greek, for the pleasure of using his own special method of instruction. Every morning at nine I came to work in his study for an hour before his dinner, which he invariably took at ten o'clock, supping—as we used to say in the country—at half-past five. Never once since the death of his wife had the retired inspector had more than these two meals a day, on a diet drawn up for him by one of his medical friends. Tobacco and coffee he regarded with horror. A single bottle of wine—obtained from his own vines—lasted him a week. But ten libraries would not have sufficed for his passion for reading. Anything in print attracted him, from our country newspaper to our local reviews, from the finest Latin author to the worst contemporary novels—all continually interlarded with a daily perusal of an edition of Voltaire that filled two enormous shelves in his study. Mr. Optat Viple was, I need scarcely add, outrageously irreligious and revolutionary.

This was explained by the fact that his uncle on his mother's side had sat in the Convention and voted for the execution of the King. How did he reconcile his republicanism with his passionate admiration for the first Napoleon? That was one of the mysteries of this worthy man.

When I come to think of it, it was scarcely a reasonable thing to entrust me to this Voltairian, even though he did not allow himself to contradict the religious instruction that I was receiving.

But young though I was, he used to speak to me with enthusiasm about the free-thinkers and the revolutionaries. Being appointed, on leaving the École Normale, professor at Langers, he had become acquainted there with one of Diderot's relatives. All the names of the writers of the eighteenth century occurred in the endless talks he had with me when we went walking together. For in fine weather he would join me at the house and lead me down the roads all littered with the scoria of the ancient volcanoes. We spent hours together, I questioning him about a thousand things, childish or serious, he answering me with unwearied kindness, while in the distance the domes stood out against the sky in the form of complete or truncated cones, and the vines spread all green around us, with their grapes tiny and green or big and black according to the season, and the brooks ran between the willows and unseen birds sang. Oh, the melancholy of bygone spring times.

I remember, as if we had been talking only yesterday, the day when my old friend told me the story I have alluded to. As the weather seemed uncertain, we set out to the Bughes, a kind of cross-roads planted with trees and neighbouring the town. As we were about to cross the terrace of La Poterne, we came upon one of the groups of Austrian prisoners in their white uniforms. Mr. Viple suddenly led me down a by-street to avoid meeting them. He kept silent for some time. I looked at his wrinkled face, and suddenly asked him:

"Don't you want to have a close look at the Austrians, Mr. Viple?"

"No, my child," he said, with a look I had never seen before on his face, a look full of gloomy memories. "The last time I saw their uniforms was very sad."

"And when was that?" I asked.

"At the invasion," he said. Then after a calculation, "That is forty-five years ago."

"Did they come as far as Issoire?" I said, knowing he was born in that town.

"As far as Issoire," he answered; and then as we were descending the road that leads towards the station he pointed to the parallel road that goes to Issoire, and added, "They came first to Clermont, and then straight on to us. Ah! Our house was almost burnt over our heads. It is true. We did not expect them. We knew that the Emperor had been beaten, but we could not believe that it was all over. That marvel of a man had always won in the end. And then we loved him, my father loved him. He saw him once holding a review in Paris after the campaign of Austerlitz. How often he spoke to us of the blue eyes of Bonaparte that compelled you to shout 'Long live the Emperor!' just by looking at you. Besides, he was a man of the Revolution, a revolutionary himself at heart, and he was not afraid of the black cassocks. Enough . . . enough."

"But why did the Austrians want to burn your house?" I asked, with the persistence of a child who scents out a story and does not mean to let it escape.

"The invaders came to us in the evening," continued the old man, who seemed to forget me and follow only the visions arising in his memory. "They were not very many—a detachment of cavalry commanded by a tall officer with an insolent face, quite young, with very long yellow moustache that almost waved in the wind. We had passed the day in the most frightful anxiety. We knew they were at Clermont. Would they come? How should we receive them? There had been a meeting at my father's house, who was mayor of the town at the time. Heavens! had he not been ill, he was the sort of man to barricade the streets and raise the people. Who knows? If all the villages had done as much, the allies would have suffered as our soldiers did in Spain. There is only one way out of it when you are invaded—guerilla warfare, hunting down the enemy head by head. Yes, we might have defended ourselves. We had food, and all the peasants keep a gun hanging up on a nail by the chimney.

"But the poor man was in bed, shivering with the fever caught while bird-shooting on the marshes. In short, counsels of prudence prevailed. A sound of trumpets was heard. It was the enemy. Ah! little one, may you never know what it is to hear buglers blowing a foreign march in the way they did. There was such insolence in the bugle-call, such contempt and hatred of us! I remember, I heard it in my father's bedroom, my face against the window, looking at the officer riding at the head of his men. When I turned round I saw my father crying."

"So it ought to give you pleasure, Mr. Viple, to see them now we have conquered them."

"Pleasure? Pleasure? I do not believe . . . but enough, enough."

This was what the old revolutionary used to exclaim when he did not wish to tell me anything that, repeated by me, would have displeased my family; and he went on with his story.

"Less than a quarter of an hour after the arrival of the Austrians, there was a loud knocking at our door. The handsome officer with the long moustache came to lodge with the mayor with two companions, and I was told to give up my room. I can still see myself storming against them, and hiding a pistol that I had loaded for our defence. I was angry at leaving my room, which was the prettiest in the house. It gave on a little terrace where I used to play, and from this terrace you could get into the garden by some stone steps, overgrown with grass. Underneath was the billiard-room, and above a kind of attic where I was sent until the officers left the house.

" They asked for dinner at once. They were fatigued with their ride, and everybody had to help in the kitchen to get the meal ready in time. Three of them, and six persons with them, that made nine, and it was very many. At last we completed the preparations for the meal, which my mother wished to make succulent.

" ' We must put them in a good temper,' said the poor woman, who compelled me to go to the fish-pond and catch trout for them. I had also to go down into the cellar to get some champagne, four of the bottles that my father used to uncork at the announcement of a victory by the Emperor.

" The stock was almost exhausted. I need not say how sad I was to have to prepare a feast for them with our things, in our house that began to resound with the noise of their violent gaiety, and this noise went on increasing, increasing amid the clinking of glasses and outbursts of laughter as the meal proceeded.

" They were giving toasts in a language I could not understand. For I listened to everything, sitting in the kitchen, where it had been arranged we should eat. To what were they drinking? No doubt to our defeat, and to the death of our poor Emperor. I was not more than twelve years old then, but I swear a man cannot suffer more from indignation and anger than I suffered, sitting on my little chair in a corner of the high chimney, face to face with my mother. As a good housewife, she was preoccupied with the breaking of the glasses and plates.

" ' Do they want anything? ' she anxiously asked our servant.

" ' They want this, they want that,' our worthy Michael replied. And we gave them that, and we gave them this, till Michael entered with a tragic air, and said:

" ' They want coffee.' "

" Surely it was very easy to prepare some for them," I interrupted.

" You do not know, my boy," replied Mr. Viple, " how rare sugar and coffee were at that time. You have been told, haven't you, that the Emperor had the idea of a continental blockade to prevent all commerce with England? It was a great idea though it did not come off; its immediate result for us was to diminish and almost to do away with certain kinds of goods that came to us from abroad. So when our servant brought this request to my mother, the unhappy woman was utterly upset.

" ' Coffee! ' she cried. ' But we haven't a grain in the house. Tell them so.'

" Two minutes afterwards Michael returned, his face quite pale.

" 'They are intoxicated, madam,' he said, 'and they say they will break everything if they are not given coffee.'

" 'Oh, my God!' said my mother, wringing her hands, 'and I have left my Sèvres service on the sideboard!'

"Meanwhile the uproar increased in the dining-room. The officers beat on the floor with their swords, and shouted enough to break the windows. Three times our good Michael tried to get them to listen to reason. Three times he returned to us driven out by volleys of insults.

" 'Coffee! Coffee!' they howled, and the simple words pronounced in German fashion took on a hoarse accent of cruelty. At last the tumult grew so loud that it mounted to my father's bedroom, and he appeared at the kitchen door, tall and shiny eyed, with a brown dressing-gown folded round him, a silk handkerchief knotted around his head.

" 'What is the matter?' he said, and I saw his lips trembling as he asked the question. Was it with fever? Was it with anger? We explained the situation to him. 'I will go and speak to them,' he replied.

"He walked towards the dining-room. I followed him. All my life I shall remember that scene. The Austrian officers in uniform, their faces illumined by drink, the bits of broken plates, the bottles thrown here and there on the floor, the stained tablecloth, and a cloud of tobacco smoke floating around these impudent conquerors. Yes, all my life I shall hear my father say to them:

" 'Gentlemen, I have not what you ask me for. I give you my word of honour in the matter, and I have got up from my bed of sickness to come to you and beg you to respect the house where you have been received like guests.' Before he had finished, the man with the long moustache, his blue eyes shining with malice, rose and, taking a glass of champagne, advanced towards us.

" 'Very well,' he said, speaking our language with a good accent, that showed he was better educated than his countrymen, 'we shall believe you, sir, if you will do us the pleasure of drinking the health of our master who has just saved your country. Sir, to the health of our Emperor!'

"I looked with anguish at my father, and, knowing him, I saw he was in a state of unspeakable fury. He took the glass, then, with a resounding voice, lifting the glass to a portrait of Napoleon on the wall, that these barbarians had not remarked, he said:

" 'Long live the Emperor!'

"The officer had followed the direction of my father's glance. He perceived the portrait, a simple engraving. He broke the frame into pieces with a blow of his sabre, and filling again the glass my father had taken, he said brutally:

" 'Come on, cry, " Long live the Emperor of Austria! " and do it quick.'

" 'Long live the Emperor!' said my father, taking the glass and raising it again.

" 'Ah! You French dog!' screamed the officer, and lifting up the chair that was near to him he struck the sick man full on the chest and knocked him down, and his head fell on an angle of the door. My mother, the servants and myself screamed with terror."

" Was he dead? " I asked.

" We thought so," replied Mr. Viple, " when we saw the blood staining the white silk handkerchief round his head. But he was not. Only it took him six months to get well."

" And what did you do? " I asked.

" I," said Mr. Viple, with some hesitation, " nothing, absolutely nothing. . . . But my brother . . ."

" You had a brother then? You have never spoken to me about him."

" Yes, he died when he was quite young. He was almost my age. Hardly a year older. When he went to bed that night in the attic—the same as mine—we shared the same room, and we had been exiled together—he began to think, to think. . . . Little boys of that time, you see, all wished to become soldiers. They heard so much talk of battles, dangers, cannon-balls and gun-shots, that they were not afraid of anything much. So my brother thought of all the events of that cruel day, the arrival of the enemy, their entry into the house, the preparation for their dinner. His father knocked down, the Emperor insulted. He saw the foreign officer sleeping in his bed, the bed that belonged to him, the son of the old sick man who had been wounded by the coward, and an idea of revenge began to grow in his little head. . . . He knew the old house as you know yours, in all its corners. It had been built at different times, and the window of the attic where the boy was lying opened on a roof with a slight curve which had a ledge. In walking along this ledge, you came to an ivied wall. In this wall were fixed bars of iron that formed a sort of ladder and led up to the chimney and down to the terrace that I have already mentioned.

" You will remember that it led to the bedroom where the officer was sleeping. . . . My brother arose, hastily dressed and glided like a cat over the roof, along the ledge and down the iron bars of the wall. Then dropping on the terrace, he approached the window. It was a very hot summer's night. The officer had merely closed the shutters without shutting the windows. My brother knew it at once by passing his little hand through a heart cut out of the wood of the shutter. Close to this heart there was a cord that served to open the shutters. He pulled it.

" 'The worst that can happen to me,' he thought, 'is to be found here. I shall say I overlooked something in my room.'

" It was a stupid excuse. But the child had an idea. The shutter opened with a grating noise: nobody stirred. The officer slept deeply, owing no doubt to the wine and the liqueurs. His snore filled the room like a kind of regular death-rattle. As wary as a thief, my brother went over the floor to the drawer where he had seen me hide the pistol. He took it. You can guess how quickly his heart beat at every movement.

He remained for perhaps a quarter of an hour, crouching on the ground, clasping his weapon without knowing what he was going to do. The moonlight illumined the roof just enough to enable him after a time to distinguish the vague form of objects. The officer slept on in a calm complete sleep with its regular snore. The boy thought of his father—the old man lifting his glass of champagne to the portrait, then the blow with the chair, the fall and the blood. The boy rose up and crept towards the bed. He could almost distinguish the features of the sleeper. He cocked the pistol. How enormous that little noise sounded in that minute. He put the barrel in the corner of the ear, there below the hair, and he pulled the trigger. . . ."

" And then? " I asked as he stopped.

" Then," continued the old man, " he ran like mad to the window, climbed up the irons in the wall, got on the roof and into the attic. He hid the pistol under his mattress and got into bed and pretended to be asleep, while a sudden tumult filled the house, showing that the pistol shot had awakened everybody, and that they were searching for the murderer.

" And was he found? "

" Never. . . . All the inquiries, all the threats led to nothing. They wanted to burn the house, arrest our servants, one after the other. But there was an alibi for everybody, happily, my brother included. And besides, how could they have suspected a child? And then, fortunately for us, the dead officer was detested both by his men and by his superiors. . . ."

" Ah! He was dead," I cried. " It was but justice! "

" Wasn't it? You think it was a simple act of justice? " asked the old inspector, his eyes glowing with a feverish light at this far-off and always present memory. . . .

" And your brother? " I insisted. " What became of him? "

" I have already told you. He died quite young," he replied.

Passing through Issorie, some years ago, I met at a distant relation's an old lady of eighty who was a cousin to my old friend the inspector. We talked for some time, and then I asked her:

" Did you know his brother? "

" What brother? " she said.

"The one who died quite young."

"You have made a mistake," she said. "Optat was an only child. I know it perfectly well. I was brought up with him."

So I understood why Mr. Viple did not want to cross the terrace where the Austrian prisoners were. He was the child who had avenged his outraged father, he, the old coddled professor, who perhaps had never touched a weapon since that time. What strange mysteries are at times hidden in the most peaceful and the most humble lives!

RENÉ BAZIN
B. 1853

THE RASPBERRY HARVEST

THROUGH the oppressive heat of the afternoon I have climbed to the entrance of the mountain glen. Now and again there is a touch of freshness, when breaths of air steal down from the Colère summit on my right and from the hill which bounds the valley on my left—two wooded declivities of exquisite curve. I feel that peace must surely dwell there, the peace which we always imagine to be where we are not. But where I stand, the peace is not yet perfect. Too many distant sounds still reach me, rising from the plain—vague phantom sounds, fading into this vast expanse. I hear the voice of a ploughman, shrill words of mothers scolding children at the farms, cooks heralding the hour of roosting, the grinding of a brake upon a cart-wheel, the rumbling of a train passing from Geneva. Yet of all this nothing is to be seen, neither the ploughman's team nor the mothers on their doorsteps, nor the flocks of poultry in the farmyards, nor the cart, nor the carriages of the moving train, which betrays itself only by the smoke, no bigger than a kerchief waving farewell. The plain beneath me is so vast, so profound! It is filled with a summer haze; and though all day its fields and woods and villages and meadows have been an immensity of green, it will soon become a lake of blue, and so remain till dawn. One might even fancy, as I did last night, that the lights of cottage windows, lost in this shadowy blue, are nothing other than reflections of the stars in heaven.

So I listen and feast my eyes, with that insatiate, and I believe infinite, joy of plunging more profoundly into the beauty of things. The landscape itself speaks in images and suggestions. All about me the grass is of a rich moist green which all the sun's power cannot pale, for its tufts reach down to water. The mosses make full, exuberant cushions, every little spike being tipped with gold; and if for a week there were a miraculous drought they would still quench the thirst of the scabious which crowd upon them. Everywhere is wild thyme. Hedges of mint and geraniums cover the tiny streamlets. You can trace their delicate arches wandering down the slopes, and their fragrance covers the hillside before the birth of the flowers and after their death. In the trees, and on the supports of the latest vines, I see blackbirds, linnets and goldfinches; but most of these are visitors, one imagines, resting on their journey. Except for the blackbirds, which plainly belong to the place and make their nests and rear their brood here, they show every sign of anxiety—flitting, searching, never resting. Plainly enough, this high glen is in winter a rude inhospitable region, where man and beast find but a scanty and precarious living.

Some of these flocks of linnets, I think, are coming down only because night is beginning to fall.

Men and women not very unlike them, gatherers of fruits as they are, and having scarcely more savings than the birds have, are at this hour coming homeward from the summits. These are the raspberry pickers. It is a delightful trade, which lasts all too short a time. They come down in merry companies and their clogs may be heard clattering through the streets of Belmont, the chief market of their industry. Last year there were sold there within a few days raspberries to the value of 10,000 francs. The workers emerge in long procession before the unsightly factories whose smoke-blackened arches open on the market-place. There are many women and children among them, and not a few men from this and neighbouring villages. Each carries a hamper, a wooden pail or a basket heaped with fruit. Hands, necks, women's bodices, men's shirts are all stained red. The broker, who has come up from the plain with his wain, swiftly weighs each labourer's gains and throws them into huge tubs whose staves seem to have been painted vermilion. A girl notes the weight of each and pays the current price. No other market in the world is fragrant as this. In an hour it is all over and the sweet fruit of the mountain is on its way to Marseilles to become jam or liqueur or syrup. And now these good people disperse and once more count their gains. I saw several receive as much as five or six francs, and one family with large baskets of fruit made fifteen francs. It is a strange source of wealth, for all these riches are due to a storm. Not long ago a hurricane swept down Mount Colère, devastating everything in its path, uprooting veteran pines, reaping avenues through the forest, so that two years hardly sufficed to clear these declivities of fallen timber. It meant bankruptcy for some of the proprietors, but brought good fortune to many a poor home. The sun and breezes touched the mosses with their magic. Vast fields of raspberry canes sprang up and filled the clearings, and there were fruit fields throughout the forest. But then once more the woods began to reclaim their own. From one season to another the pine-trees have shot upward and their shadows have become darker and closer. Soon the Belmont gossips will speak of the time when " there were raspberries on the hills," and there will arise a legend of the rosy treasure.

There is one man I know who will speak of those days, whom I see walking along these lanes with his staff on his shoulder and moving with heavy rustic step. His cheeks and chin are shaved, but a small ruddy moustache covers his lips. His expression is grave; his eyes are of the colour of gold, and are deeply shaded by his brow. Any one along the road will tell you, " 'Tis Joseph Samonoz, the quickest raspberry-picker of the countryside."

Not long ago all Joseph's wealth lay in his strong arms, his love of life, the habit of hard work learned of poverty, and a small and miserable field perched on a rocky ridge at the edge of the pine forest. Though Joseph's holding (or rather, I should say, the holding of the large family of which he was eldest) was high on the hill, there was another still higher up, a patch of two or three acres carefully levelled and cultivated to perfection, which belonged to a substantial owner, Philip Corrieu, who has meadows in every vale and groves of walnut on the foothills. Moreover—since 'tis a wicked world—it was whispered that Joseph Samonoz had the extraordinary impertinence to woo Rose Corrieu, the great man's daughter. This crime, you must understand, is as outrageous in the country as it is in the town. And it was all the worse in this case, because these two families living side by side had for many a long year been alienated by inveterate enmity. Old Corrieu had heard something of what was being said in the neighbourhood, and whenever he met Samonoz he contrived in one way or another to show his anger and contempt.

One morning, three years after the great storm, when the raspberry canes were beginning to yield their fruit, the old man met Joseph on the hill-path and gibed at him: " Aha, my good fellow, you won't make enough to marry on to-day, nor to-morrow either! "

Samonoz, who had long cherished a secret love for Rose, made no reply, but strode on and upward. For ten minutes afterward the sound of his empty pail clattering on the stick over his shoulder might be heard in the distance.

Rose's father then turned into his field and his heart rejoiced within him, so heavy were the oats and mighty in their straw. He reckoned up the price which they would yield this year and calculated at what date he might most profitably reap them. Then with vast contentment he returned homeward.

But that very night he had to hurry back again, under a blinding downpour of rain, against squalls which buffeted him till he staggered. With sodden garments clinging to his limbs, he fought his way up the hill, to witness the whole disaster which he had divined from his doorway. As soon as he reached the edge of the forest, he stood like one bereft of sense. What could have happened in the heights above? Had some dam or barrier formed by the fallen timber yielded all at once? Or had some landslide far above him changed a torrent's path? For of Corrieu's proud field of oats the greater part had been swept away and nothing remained but two wretched strips along the edges. A torrent was dashing downward, carving a deep bed, carrying away the ready harvest, and with cruel irony was dumping all Corrieu's treasure upon the land of the Samonoz. Boundary and partition were gone, and the fields of the neighbour-enemies were mingled in one confusion.

Turning his eyes away in despair from his vanishing wealth, Corrieu saw a man stumbling down the path, hurtled by the squall. He knew him well enough, but his need of help was more urgent than his hatred.

"Hullo, Samonoz! Come here!"

The young man took no notice, but went on his way.

"Samonoz, come and help me!"

The raspberry-picker did not hear, or did not want to hear, until the third appeal. He, too, was wet to the bone. Then might have been seen a strange sight. Amid the tempest of wind and hail and blinding rain these two men consulted for ten minutes on the devastated slope without thinking of shelter. Then at last together they sought the nearest pines.

No one ever knew exactly what was said. But we may form some conclusion when we consider that this was the very time when the raspberry harvest absorbs all available labour and when it is impossible to hire a working-man at any price. The villagers learned with growing astonishment three amazing facts: first, that Joseph Samonoz and Philip Corrieu had together on the very night of the hurricane succeeded in diverting the torrent which had ruined the field of oats; then, that Joseph Samonoz, renouncing his season of the raspberries, had laboriously carried back to its place on the height all the earth which had been swept away; and finally, in early autumn, that the two families, the poor and the rich together, had gone down to the town to buy gold ornaments for the betrothal of Joseph and of Rose.

The story of this raspberry-picker comes back to me as I watch him passing down the winding paths. Now he has disappeared behind the trees; again I see him lower down the hill. And now he is no more than a tiny shadow somewhat darker than the rest, gliding along the edge of the great blue gulf which is the valley. The sound of his clogs has died away. The farmyard sounds are silent. I know nothing more tender than that pale light which lingers on the western peaks when the heavens are wrapped in night.

THE SAVIOURS OF THE WHITE WINE

RENÉ BAZIN

"WHAT a goddess it is!" he said.

As he spoke, he waved his arm from the window to the hillsides before us clothed in vines.

"Ah, but what a beggar, too, she is!" he continued. "How many men she has ruined among both the great and the lowly! Yet confidence in her returns once more. All France is planting vines. In this very parish, famed for its white wines since the fourteenth century, and celebrated by Rabelais himself, where the people have all been vine-growers, forming a caste of their own, a parish of wine-presses, grape-thieves, drunkards and loafers, the dread phylloxera worked far more ruin than the war had done, and more indeed than two or three successive invasions would have brought about. Here the race of vine-growers disappeared almost altogether, and at least a third of the land lay fallow. From my parlour window where you stand I have looked out for more than ten years on a hillside covered with bracken. No plough passed over it, no stroke of the mattock, sharp as a pistol-shot, shook my window-panes. But to-day you see again the lines of the vine-props, as regular as the lines in an engraving, drawn across the landscape wherever the vine was cultivated before 1870. I think indeed that they have overstepped the ancient boundaries. And the same has taken place in every neighbouring parish. A new race of vine-growers has arisen, more skilled than the old race and better equipped, but less honest. They sugar, sir! None the less the change deserves to be noted and applauded for all time. The wine industry of France is re-established. A vast amount of capital is sunk in the enterprise. If you wish to get some idea of the sums we risk, let me tell you that every hectare I plant costs me upward of 3000 francs. I am one of the innumerable gamblers. I will even confess that I have thrown into the game all the passion that is left to me."

My host was an old doctor of the Saumur country, who after practising for many years in the city had done what is so very rare nowadays, in retiring to the country. He had the generous figure, brilliant complexion and keen eyes of the classic vineyardman; his white locks, dressed from right to left, then turned into a little curl above the ear, showed that the wearer had known the Government of July. The walls were covered with a quaint paper which simulated marble, and upon them engravings by Calamatta gave wan and stiff reproductions of crayon portraits drawn by Ingres of three ladies of the family and of my old friend's father.

"Yes," he continued, "my whole heart is in this vine-growing experiment, on which I see all the wealth of France is being staked. And I believe that we shall win. One of our great enemies is dead; the other is in a swift decline."

"And their names?"

"The first is the carelessness into which centuries of easy profits had thrown the earlier generation of growers. When there was a question of grafting the American vine, no one knew how to do it. For lack of specialists, ordinary gardeners were called in, men used to grafting pear-trees and apricots. But, my dear sir, what a hopeless mistake! What immense difference there is between arts which to you seem so similar! We learned this to our cost, those of us who set the example and were the first to replant. How many stocks of *rupestris*, how many of *riparia*, I have lost, for want of knowing the kind of soil suitable for each, for want of care, for want of enlightened love! Now, thanks to the schools of grafting, thanks to the competitions which the local authorities promote every year in one parish or another, there is not a county which has not its dozen or more graduates in the vine, simple peasants, who proudly show you their diploma as 'master grafters' —hasn't the title an old-fashioned air? These men know all about pruning and manuring, and saving the vine. When you take into consideration also the improvements in the presses, in the methods of making and storing the wine, you will understand what I meant when I said that one of the enemies of the French industry is dead. The grower is well-armed. But he has other enemies, and very formidable they are."

"What are they?"

When the old doctor smiled his thin lips lengthened until he seemed to me, for the moment, like the son or nephew of the fine ladies engraved by Calamatta.

"Yes, sir, the French vine has had many enemies and still has many, not to mention the ingratitude from which it has suffered. Many of my colleagues have been very unjust to the noble plant, which was indeed the first to give us alcohol, but which also is alone able to heal us of it. They do not consider what part it has chiefly played in the history of France. They cannot see that the French blood is neither Latin nor Celtic nor Frank, but is fundamentally the ruddy juice of the grape, and that this is the reason of its ardour. I used to think that in the end they would get the best of it. Although, in spite of my years, I am so full of hope to-day, I feared fifteen years ago that our white wine, our priceless treasure, the most inimitable, living, spiritual and lovable of our wines, whose fumes so quickly pass away and are forgotten, was doomed to perish under the calumny of the medical profession. No one was willing to buy from us those marvellous casks which have long ago disappeared and been broken up for firewood; or, at least, the middle-class customers were suspicious and gave our hillsides a wide berth. If we had not had——"

The maid opened the door of the room where we were talking, and said:

"The representatives of the 'Society,' sir."

"Good! I will come." He rose, and beckoning to me, said, "Come with me, and you shall see the men who have saved our white wine."

In the great cool vaults of my host's cellar, we found three peasants, dressed in their Sunday best, with clean-shaved, solemn, smug faces, having the clear complexion of the rustics of the Loire valley. They had a very important manner about them, and saluted us with a patronising air.

"We have come to buy," said the eldest, "if you have anything good."

The fellow's enunciation showed well enough that my friend's cellar was not the first which the deputation had sampled that day.

"Taste, gentlemen, taste; here are glasses, and twenty-seven casks of my best, among which you are very competent to select the finest. I leave the choice to you."

The envoy received the compliment as no more than his due; then, taking from the servant's hand a tin tube, plunged it through the opening of the cask by the wall, closed its upper end with his massive thumb, and raising the tube, filled his own and his companion's glasses with the golden liquor drawn from the very heart of the barrel. All three then raised their glasses to the level of the little window which lighted the cellar, and slowly, with all kinds of knowing tiltings and movements, let the rays traverse the virgin wine and judged of its tint. I could not yet tell their opinion, for each now put the glass to his lips with the same gravity, moved a mouthful of the wine about his cheeks, swallowed some of it, and turning aside politely ejected the rest, then drew himself up and gazed at his friends. Then followed little grimaces and shaking of the head, a faint sigh, but never a word. Judgment was evidently not to be pronounced until the twenty-seventh witness had been heard.

My old friend went out, after a bow to the three great men,

leaving his servant to do the honours of his vintage. He took a pathway leading to the vines.

"You have just seen," he said, "the delegates chosen by a general suffrage of the members of our village 'Societies.' These Societies, known respectively as the 'Cock,' the 'Joy,' the 'Union,' the 'Laurel,' and so on, are centuries old, and are very numerous throughout the valley of the Loire, as probably elsewhere also, though my knowledge does not extend beyond this region. The game of bowls is the occasion of these Sunday reunions, which the peasantry attend chiefly in order to talk and to drink wine of which the origin and price are well known to them, and whose soundness they know to be above suspicion. Yes, sir, these rural Societies of ours have remained faithful to tradition. However many faults of taste our people have committed—I would almost say faults of history—they have continued to choose the same wine, by means of the same estimable judges. These Societies have saved the white wine for us. They are the centre of its cult. Those deputies whom we have just left were chosen several weeks ago for the mission which they are fulfilling to-day. Entrusted with the choice of the wine for consumption in the present season, they ought to have made their purchases before this; and the green-keeper of their Society will soon bottle the seven or eight casks destined to cool the throats of the bowlers. And right well they earn their expenses. While they are on their quest, if any one comes to ask for them at home, Madame replies with free gesture, 'They are visiting the cellars.' They generally come to me last of all, and buy two or three of my best casks, which will furnish their sealed wine—wine distinguished by special label—which the wealthiest among them will taste with deference. Our three friends, the deputies, of whom one is a peasant landowner, another a veterinary surgeon, and the third a vineyardman, will themselves bottle this choice vintage, on a day when the moon is waning, and there is not a breath of wind, and when it is so clear that you can count seventeen steeples from our hilltop."

As he spoke we ascended between the ranks of vine-stocks, stretching away from us with amazing regularity, whose twigs, lately pruned, bore droplets of sap at every wound.

"My vines are weeping," said the doctor; "springtime is already moving in the soil." And with a charmingly youthful gesture he raised his hat to salute the coming harvest, even as the servant scrambled up the hill crying:

"Sir! Sir! I have sold the three best: two at 180 francs and the other at 210!"

THE FOURTH BEGGAR

RENÉ BAZIN

THE mother was lulling her child to sleep, singing, in low monotone, the refrain of an old folk-song which, like a pilgrim of old, has come we know not whence.

Beyond the threshold of the farmhouse a narrow strip of meadow land, grazed bare by the teeth of hungry sheep, stretched down to the sand dunes, all alike, solitary, untilled, shifting wastes, over which, when the wind blew in squalls, the thinly scattered clumps of rushes, bowing in unison, set silver ripples flickering to and fro. Far, far in the distance the sea could be seen on fine days, a band of light, the shipless sea, with shallow, treacherous coast.

It was not a gay landscape, but Julienne loved it, because it was home. The place would have been uninhabitable had it not been for the fields behind, hedged in with great stone walls, where oats grew fairly well and potatoes marvellously so. Is much more wanted for happiness? Julienne thought not, or rather, she never gave it a thought. She loved La Renardière, as this last farm, jutting like a spur almost down to the sands of the beach, was called; she loved her four children; she loved her husband, whom she had chosen poor, but who laboured with a will, whether digging the earth, gathering seaweed and wrack that washed ashore, or dragging the casting net with the help of Hervé, their eldest son. And besides, she felt great tenderness for all poor beggars who passed, and thus, with her six loves and her tender pity, Julienne's heart was full.

On this evening the sky was overcast; low hanging clouds shut out the horizon, hiding the sun which was near its setting. A fine rain was drizzling down the chimney, sputtering upon the cover of the kettle and on the hot coals. The husband was away at sea with Hervé; the wife was rocking the youngest child, chanting the vague song with long refrains:

> Not half-past seven, says the clock:
> How the wind beats on the pane,
> How it rattles at the lock,
> Oh, how heavy falls the rain!

The noise of the opening and closing of the gate of the adjoining garden made Julienne start. She listened. A single step resounded on the wet earth.

" It is not they," she thought.

The dark shadow of a man carrying a bundle tied to the end of a stick appeared in the opening of the door. Julienne felt afraid because she was alone. She could see only two red eyes looking at her and a tangled blond beard, roughened by the weather and matted by the rain.

" What do you want? " she asked. " Shelter for the night? "

For all reply the man nodded his head.

Julienne thought she recognised him, for, remote from market towns and villages as La Renardière was, they often lodged wandering tramps and travellers.

" Go to the barn; make yourself a bed in the loose straw. My husband will bring you some soup directly; I hear him coming."

It was her heart that she heard crying, " Come! Come! " but it made her more tranquil, and she began, when the beggar turned away, to follow again the lullaby of the hours:

Not half-past seven, says the clock.

Her face was thin, framed in with thick bands of chestnut hair half hidden by her coif, with dark eyes which easily filled with tears, easily became anxious, rarely smiling and then only for an instant. A maternal and primitive nature, which the solitude of the country had kept intact. When Julienne really wished a thing, her husband, the coarser and ruder nature, nearly always yielded; he felt obscurely the sentiment of profound peace in this home which, without respite and without noise, she kept in order, and after a long day out of doors, exposed to the wind of the beach or of the sea, he was disposed on returning home to show his best side.

The hand rocking the cradle gradually slackened the motion to a soft vibration, then gently let the willow go, which ceased to creak. The wind howled louder around the house, and the mother became again the timid woman, alone, watchful and anxious.

To give herself courage, she arose and began occupying herself with her household duties. A half hour passed; it was growing dark. All at once:

" Here we are! " cried the well-known voice. " We are hungry. A bad catch to-day."

A man, half peasant and half seaman, entered; he was dressed in coarse blue linen with a cap of yellow waxed linen. His long head, with its deep-set eyes, was bent forward searching in the shadow of the room for the mother, who was bending over the fire, skimming the soup. She looked up, nodding her head and smiling at the tall boy who, behind and towering above the paternal shoulder, was also trying to see her.

"*Bonsoir, m'man!*"

She embraced the stalwart boy, who offered his cheek, damp with salt fog and rain; then she lighted the candle which until then she had economised. The light flickering along the length of the wall rested on the hollow basket, where three fish with wrinkled, mud-coloured skin were squirming, still alive, under two crab-fish the colour of dregs of wine, their claws twisted like pebbles of marble.

"They will make the soup for to-morrow," said the man. "The sea was too heavy; come, let us eat."

They took their places around the table, when the door, which the son had barely closed, was pushed open from the outside.

"Can one come in?" a rough voice demanded.

"Where does one sleep here?" demanded at the same time a second voice.

"Out in the ditches of the fields!" cried the man. "You are a pretty pair of tramps, who do not know how to speak! Where does one sleep here? Do I keep an inn?"

In the foggy opening of the door, the two shadows, black in the demi-obscurity of the expiring twilight, fell back at the approach of the angry peasant. They thought him too big, his muscles too solid; and they lowered their voices:

"You would not turn us out of doors in such weather as this?" returned one of them.

"That I would, *tas de fainéants!* One sees no one else along the highways, where there is neither work to do nor to get. And we must work to give you what you want! Begone! Go sleep on the pebbles of the beach, the fish will not disturb you."

"I have already given one poor wanderer lodging in the barn," said Julienne, gently. "It is large enough for three, in my opinion." The man turned angrily around, seated himself and began eating without answering a word.

The wind howled; they could hear the flapping of the cloaks of the poor wretches against the wall outside.

"Show them charity," urged the wife.

"There are too many of them, when all is said and done! Every day and every day to open your house, to give your clean straw, which even the animals refuse afterwards, and to give warm soup! No, it happens too often!"

But as he grumbled these words, without ceasing to eat and rather as a regret for a weakness already consented to, Julienne said:

"Good people, follow along the house, and at the back of the court, after you have passed the stables, enter in our barn and dry yourselves. Presently I will bring you something to eat."

When the peasant, his wife and Hervé were alone in the closed house, with the three children asleep in the adjoining room, they began to talk about the fishing season, which was poor, and of the harvest, which had turned out badly. For two whole months, since the threshing of the grain, the two men had gone up and down the beach for nothing. *Dorados* and *lubrines* were scarce; the mullets appeared to have fled to the deep sea. The nets stretched to catch lobster caught nothing but crabs, and the few rock-fish caught by line on the pebbly flats of Faillebelle, were not worth a sou. They were fish of variegated colouring which none but fishermen would eat.

"Listen, Julienne," continued the farmer, "if this luck continues, I can no longer pay the rent of the farm, and the master will turn us out. Thou hast too tender a heart for idle beggars and tramps; beginning with to-morrow I am resolved to close the barn to them, and if they do not go away, I will drive them off, I and Hervé here, who is old enough to wield a pitchfork."

The youth smiled, showed his strong wrists, with their prominent bones projecting under the brown skin. The mother looked at the two with an air of reproach, sighed, arose, added the bread to the soup remaining in the saucepan, and went out into the night with the steaming porringer. In her left hand she carried a lantern, and, as she was feeling her way along the side of the house, she saw, in the stream of light which preceded her and penetrated the darkness, a moving form.

She stopped and with difficulty restrained a cry; she thought that it was another poor wanderer coming to ask for shelter, and she held up the light to make sure of it. It was, in effect, an old man, with beard curled like the tendrils of May peas, and wearing the hat of some Vendean ancestor, broad brimmed and out of shape from the wear of two or three generations. He advanced into the light and said:

"For the love of God, Mistress Julienne, do not leave me to sleep out of doors!"

"You speak as the other poor no longer speak," said Julienne. "I will lodge you to-night, but it will be the last time. My husband is going to close the barn. What is your name?"

"Poverty."

She looked at him and was astonished to find that his eyes were as soft and as blue as a child's. In spite of the wind which raged and of the rain which fell, Julienne felt in no more haste to return to the house than if it had been a day of brilliant sunshine in the happy summer time. She asked:

"Whether you have told me your true name or not, I know not; but where do you come from, Poverty?"

"From everywhere."

"And do people receive you well?"

"Less and less so."

"Then why do you continue wandering, never knowing where you may find a lodging?"

"To keep the hearts of men from closing up entirely. Where I pass I am alone: where I am received God gives his blessing."

Mistress Julienne of La Renardière looked searchingly at this poor wanderer. As she looked she was reminded of the apostles carved and painted in the church of her native village, and knowing well that the night is full of wanderers and one may never know who they are, she said:

"Come with me. The best corner is to the right, at the farther end; if you do not find fresh straw, take some down from the mow; I give you permission.

And when the four men were seated in a circle around the porringer, in the light of the lantern which the woman had hung from a nail in the wall, the black night settled down; the tempest redoubled its fury, the tide, rolling in, added such a roaring to the anger of the wind that one would have said that it was beating at the house and wished to destroy it.

Nevertheless, Julienne went in happy and she said:

"There are four now—as many as we have children!"

At daylight father and son rose to go and feed the cattle and to see whether the weather would permit them to venture out to sea. Scarcely had they crossed the threshold when they heard Julienne scream:

"Help! Run! Oh, what a misfortune!"

In an instant they were by her side at the end of the second room and, while she burst into tears, they saw that the drawer of the cupboard had been broken open, the drawer in which the savings of the whole year had been locked up. There was nothing.

The man grew furious; he blamed his wife, thanks to whom La Renardière had always been so prosperous; he made a terrible scene, overwhelming her with reproaches!

"Is it not all thy fault? Why didst thou receive the thieves? It is all of a piece with thy soft heart, stupid! Cry, run after them now! We are ruined, and it is all thy fault, hostess of brigands, tramps, thieves, tatterdemalions!"

Hervé grew pale with the shock of seeing his mother weep and his father in such a rage.

Half an hour passed before the angry peasant thought of going in search of the thieves.

He crossed the court, took his pitchfork from the stable and entered the barn.

His wife and son followed after him.

No one was there save the fourth beggar, who was asleep.

"*Hola!* Up, wretch! Where are your companions?"

Poverty opened his eyes without stirring. He was wrapped in a thick teamster's cloak, from which all the colour had long since faded; his face had the pallor of the dry wheat-straw which covered him.

"Dost thou pretend not to understand, *coquin*! Where are the others?"

The glance of this poor beggar was so serene, so deep, that it seemed to the peasant as if he were looking down into the depths of the sea into which he gazed every day over the side of his boat.

Beside himself as he was with anger, he yet dared not touch the beggar, and said less roughly.

"I don't accuse thee; I will not do thee any harm; only tell me where are the others, the thieves who have robbed me!"

"More than half an hour has passed, farmer of La Renardière, since I heard persons running past the door, but at the pace at which they were going, you will scarcely overtake them."

Without rising, resembling a statue in the calmness of his pose, speaking as one with authority, he demanded:

"What have they stolen from thee? Thy happiness?"

"No."

"One of thy children?"

"No."

"The consciousness that thou art an honest man, that thou hast always worked well and done thy duty faithfully?"

"No. They have stolen from me fifteen silver pistoles, which I had locked away in my cupboard."

"Then," said the beggar, "thou hast only lost what can be retrieved. What wilt thou give me if I enable thee to recover what thou hast lost?"

"Choose," said the peasant.

"I choose the key of thy barn," said Poverty.

"That thou mayest return?" inquired the other.

"I, or some other poor wretch, for thou wilt always lose more in closing thy heart and thy barn than in opening them both. Take down thy net—thy largest one—and follow me."

He arose, and the peasant, who was tall, remarked that the beggar was a head taller than he. He obeyed only the more quickly, and aided by his son and wife, he carried his great net along upon a hand-barrow.

Through the grass, wet and steaming in the morning air, and over the dunes, all four made their way to the beach. The tranquil sea was rolling up on the sands waves of violet, edged with a silver curl. Very slowly they advanced, skirting along the waves. Poverty spoke not a word, but looked into the hollow of the waves where the water was limpid, and, when they had arrived at the middle of the vast curve, he made a sign.

" Stretch here thy net."

The peasant and his son entered the water and the net rounded out over more than a hundred fathoms length. Whilst they were laboriously stretching it out, corks dancing through the waves, and while they were forming " *la bailée,*" the beggar went up on the nearest dune and stood there. The two men, harnessed to the sticks, their bodies thrown far forward, their limbs rigid, advanced with difficulty; it was as if some unusual weight from behind was pulling them back. The water remained transparent, and seemed empty. Nevertheless, the enormous circle began to contract little by little, and darts, as of fire, to shoot across it. The fishermen, divining the presence of the fish, turned now to the sea, and, stooping, seized the meshes above and below; then, as rapidly as they could, brought the pocket around. Soon they uttered a great cry; there was a moving mass of mullets in the net! They leaped up, they lashed the water with their tails, they dashed desperately against the meshes of the net, entangled themselves together, became wild with fright, until at last, enveloped by the folds of the net, they lay heaped up in a shining mass on the beach, like a reef all white with foam!

" Run, Julienne, run to the house! Harness the horse, bring the cart; there is a waggon load of them! Oh, the fine catch! *La belle journée!*

The peasant and Hervé sprang to right and to left, not to lose one of the catch, seizing the fish which were trying to escape down the wet slope.

When they stood upright, radiant, to look for Poverty, there was no one on the dune. Only the sand pinks were opening wide to the rising sun and they were alone.

Since that day, the barn of La Renardière has remained open. The key has never been brought back nor replaced. Never has the farmer counted the poor that his wife has sheltered there, and they have been many in the bleak winter months and in this out-of-the-way place. As for Julienne, when she tells the story to her children or to those of others, she never fails to add in her soft voice:

" My little ones, receive the poor, and be not frightened if they are many; it is not for us to choose. The first may be bad, and the second, and the third. It is often the fourth beggar who is good."

JULES LEMAÎTRE
B. 1853

THE SCULPTOR

It was a fine convent built on a high plateau. Above was the mountain covered with firs. The pointed roofs and turrets of the holy house stood out against this sombre background. Below was a large valley, with vineyards, cornfields, meadows edged with poplars, and a village straggling along a mountain stream.

The monks of this convent were good servants of God, great men of learning and excellent farmers. By day their white robes appeared here and there in the fields, bent over some work of agriculture. In the evening they could be seen passing from pillar to pillar, under the arches of the long cloister, with a murmur of conversation or prayers.

Among them was a young monk, of the name of Norbert, who was a very good sculptor. With wood or stone, or even with clay that he painted in vivid colours, he knew how to make such beautiful statues of Jesus and Mary and the saints that priests and pious people came from distant places to see them, and bought them at a high price for the adornment of their churches or their oratories.

Norbert was very religious. In particular he had an extraordinary devotion for the Holy Virgin. He would often remain for hours before her altar, motionless and prone under his cowl, the folds of his robe spread out behind him on the flagstones.

Norbert was given to day-dreams. Especially in the evening, as he watched from the terrace the sun sinking below the sky-line, he would become restless and sad. He wished to go far away, to see other parts of the world than that in which he lived.

"But what could you see elsewhere," the prior would say to him, "that you cannot see where you are? Here you have the sky, the earth and the elements. From them everything is made. If you were to see all things at once, what would that be but a vain vision?"

• • • • • • • • •

The good monks were very charitable; and as they were rich, the day came when there was not a single poor man living in the valley.

They resolved then to use their money in building a magnificent church close to their convent. Several hundreds of workmen were called in to help them. They dug out deep quarries, looking like white dazzling wounds on the mountain-side. They cut out, with great art, innumerable blocks of stone; and all the convent was enveloped in a white dust like flour.

On the wooded slopes above the monastery they hewed the finest oaks and pine-trees to make a timber roof for the church. When the trees were squared, they were then sawn by placing them on high trestles; and all the convent was enveloped in a yellow dust like gold.

Amid the immense solitude, the humming human hive pursued its work. Each quarryman, while cutting his stone for the future cathedral, was ignorant where the stone would be placed, and whether it would be seen by the faithful, but he knew right well it would be seen by God; and everybody rejoiced together in helping, each in his humble way, at the sacred work. And then, stone by stone, slowly, the cathedral rose up into the heavens.

. . . .

One of the old monks of the convent had written these words in a little book of religious meditations that he called *The Imitation of Jesus Christ:* "Do not dispute about the merits of the saints. These questions often lead to useless contests! they feed man's pride and vain glory, but give rise to jealousy and dissensions, this one preferring such a saint, and that one another. The starting of such disputes, far from leading to any good result, only displeases the saints."

The good monks did not follow this precept, when they were chatting together one evening on the terrace of the convent after the Angelus. Not only did they dispute about the merits of several saints, but even about those of the three persons of the Holy Trinity.

It was a question of deciding under what patron their church should be placed; and each expressed his own feeling in the matter, and supported it warmly. Perhaps if they had been persons of less piety they would have found it better to enjoy in silence the peace of the evening. Close at hand, the unfinished walls of the future cathedral surged up, dim and enlarged in the twilight, in such a way that the new structure was as beautiful and as majestic as a ruin. Below, the stream wound about like a thread of glazed silver. To the east, the trees of the plain took on a violet tint in the golden splendour of the setting sun; and now and then a solitary shout in the distance, or the creak of a home-coming cart, deepened the silence.

The prior, a man of tradition and authority, spoke the first: "It is becoming that our church should be placed under the patronage of our founder, Saint Eustace. Otherwise the faithful might believe that there is perhaps a greater saint than the illustrious hermit who instituted our Order."

"The most venerable saints," said the sub-prior, "are only pale reflections of Christ their model. Let us consecrate this church to Our Lord from whom salvation has come to men, and from whom all holiness proceeds."

Brother Alcuin, more than a hundred years of age and so thin and twisted by time that his white robe formed angles like linen left to dry on a knotted vine branch, spoke in his turn: "I propose God the Father. He is rather neglected. He would be quite forgotten, but for the custom of saying the Lord's Prayer. Yet it is He who created the world. For more than four thousand years men had no other God. At the present time many people adore Him who do not know His Son."

Father Theobald shrugged his shoulders. He was the most profound theologian of the abbey. He never went into the fields; he lived in the library, buried under parchments, deciphering ancient writings; and he was supposed to have opinions of his own about everything.

"It is to the Holy Ghost," he said, "that I wish to dedicate our church. His reign is to come. After the revelation of God the Father to Abraham, after that of Christ to the apostles, there will be the revelation of the Holy Ghost. It is necessary. For look how the world is! Impiety prevails and concupiscence, and the larger number of men continue to damn themselves. The Holy Ghost will complete the redemption of mankind. It is announced in the Gospel; only you must be able to read——"

At these words the prior frowned, and the sub-prior signed to Theobald to be silent. Then Eginard, a monk of thirty years, with strong, masterful features, said in a commanding voice:

"I would elect right willingly Pope Saint Gregory as the patron of our church. He dominated kings and emperors. He understood that physical strength, which like everything else comes from God, is still the most effective means of action in the hands of His servants, and that true charity consists in compelling men to be saved!"

"For my part," said the father gardener, "I prefer Saint Fiacre. In his mortal life he was only a poor man who did his work as well as he could, and had the fear of the Lord before him. But it happens that most men are only poor men, and we must set before them an example of virtues that they can understand and imitate."

At this moment a peasant, his mattock on his shoulder, passed along the path at the foot of the terrace. The prior said to him, "If you were rich enough to build a church, to whom would you consecrate it?"

" I have nothing to say against God or the Virgin Mary, or the other saints of Paradise," said the peasant, " but if you want to know my idea, I would choose Saint Evroult. It is in him I have most confidence, for he has cured my cow, and helped me to find three chickens that I lost."

A little while afterwards a young woman appeared at the bend of the path. Poor, but cleanly clothed, she carried a baby on her arm, and held another little child by the hand. The prior put to her the same question he had asked the peasant.

" I should dedicate the church to the Mother of God," she said.

" Why? "

" Because she is a mother."

Till then, Norbert had been silent. In thoughtful mood, he was watching the fading of the golden purple of the sunset. When he heard the woman's reply, he said:

" Oh, woman! you have spoken well. But it is not to Mary the mother of God that I would dedicate this temple, but to Mary the Virgin. It is because she was stainless that she was kind to all men. It was because she was sovranly pure and sovranly sweet that she deserved to be the mother of God. It is thus permitted, and I admit it is more pleasant to me to love her as a Virgin, and to honour her uniquely in her chastity and in her charity."

Suddenly the steward of the abbey, fat, high-coloured, with a large face and knowing eyes, strode into the middle of the monks, saying:

" My fathers, if you will believe me, it is not to God the Father, or the Son, or the Holy Ghost that you will dedicate your church. And neither Saint Gregory, Saint Eustace, Saint Fiacre, nor Saint Evroult will have anything to do with it. The good Saint Gengoul will be our patron! "

" And the reason? " said the prior.

" It is the name of the noble duke whose vassals we are. It will please him, and perhaps induce him to give up the idea of despoiling us under the pretext that we have become too rich. We must disarm men in power, if we can, by polite compliments like this. For times are bad, and people are beginning to have less respect for the clergy and the poor monks."

" But," said Father Eginard, " your Saint Gengoul is not a very illustrious saint. What did he do? What is known about him? "

" Very little, I am afraid; but we can be sure at least that he was a good man, since he appears in the calendar."

" That is no proof of his goodness," murmured Father Theobald.

" Anyhow," said the father steward, " I reckon that the greatest saint, for us, is the one who can serve us best. Besides, all the church is dedicated to God. You do not need to insist on that; and then, when you have honoured the patron of our worthy suzerain, there is nothing to stop you from putting up images of the Holy Virgin and all the saints that you like."

After keen discussion the advice of the father steward was followed. It was decided that the great porch should be surmounted by the statue of Saint Gengoul. A little way above the Virgin Mary would be placed, and, on the point of the gable, Jesus Crucified.

. . . .

Norbert was entrusted with the carving of these three figures. Without much zeal, he carved the figure of Saint Gengoul. Not knowing exactly what profession this saint had exercised in his lifetime, Norbert made a knight of him in order to please the duke. He thrust him stiff and straight into iron armour, and joined on his breast the enormous fingers of his gauntleted hands. This was soon done.

Then he carved, from a block of granite, a crucified Jesus, twenty-four feet high. Long, emaciated, with prominent ribs, knees like death's heads, the tension on the arms hollowing out great holes at the arm-pits, runlets of blood inter-crossing all down the body, meeting on the swollen feet, and dripping down between the soles, the head bent and swinging—this Christ truly seemed the incarnation of human misery, the despair of starving wretches, the distress of abandoned outcasts, the tortures of the sick, the possessed, the lepers, of those who are killed or tortured, of all those who suffer in their flesh. And at the same time the face was full of resignation, expressing the certainty of deliverance and repose; and while the bleeding body said "Suffering," the head, though crowned with thorns, said clearly "Hope."

But though Norbert brought to this work all his piety and all his craft, he thought without ceasing on the Virgin Mary whose image he must chisel next; and he reserved for her, without saying so, all the effort of his art and his love.

"And now, my son," said the prior to him, "may God guide your hand to enable you to give us a likeness of the Virgin Mary, holding the infant Jesus in her arms."

"But," said Norbert, "should I not represent her in the way that should give most pleasure to her?"

"Well!" said the prior, "is not her highest honour that of being the mother of God?"

"Yes," replied Norbert, "but to my way of thinking, I can honour her more by representing her, not in her glory, but rather in the attitude of virtue that won her such glory. If she shows herself to us carrying a God, even as a child, how can our prayers go to her without being arrested by Him? Then, what expression can I give to her face? It is difficult for me to imagine it. Perhaps she would feel for a God a true mother's love—tenderness over the fragility of such a little being, profound joy at having her child all to herself, and under her protection? But then if she loves her Son like a true mother with all her blood and flesh, it seems to me that she cannot love all men so much. But I know she loves us. Being closer to us than God, she understands us better. There are sins that God alone could never pardon, that He would not perhaps have the right to pardon. But the Virgin is there; she obliges Him to absolve the sin, saying, 'Pardon them! I take it all on me. If you only knew how unhappy these poor men are, how the clay out of which they are formed oppresses them, and how little their wishes enter into what they do! They would all be saints if they each had the special graces that I received.' She has an immense compassion and infinite mercy. This is her very essence and her true glory. Now, I ask you, is it on God that she lavishes her pity? I wish to represent her with her hands open and stretched out to mankind. How can she stretch them out, if she has a child in her arms?"

"My son, this talk of yours is strange and smacks of heresy. I command you to carve the statue of the Virgin Mother in the way I have told you."

. . . .

Norbert did not obey. All the time he was working on the statue he would not let it be seen, under the pretext that the remarks of the other monks would disturb and muddle his ideas. And, alone with his dream, he chiselled out the Virgin Mary such as he imagined her. Tall and draped in heavy folds, her head inclined towards men, the Immaculate One held out to them her two open hands in a gesture of forgiveness. The form of her body was scarcely shown; but the face was so lovely, the eyes had so tender a look, the mouth smiled with so sad a sweetness, the gesture of the hands so well expressed pardon to all the world that the sight of this image filled men with a desire to pray, to weep, and to become saints.

When the monks saw it, they cried out in admiration, and the prior himself declared it to be marvellously beautiful. But by reason of Norbert's disobedience, he condemned him to fast for a month on bread and water.

. . . .

Thus the Holy Cross, the statue of the Virgin and that of Saint Gengoul were placed in the positions that had been agreed upon. The church was almost finished. Two high towers rose on either side of the porch, in masses of slender columns crowned with bell turrets. Norbert, animated by a fervent zeal for God's house, spent his days on the roofs, amid an aerial forest of stone, along galleries of delicate open-work, and among the monsters of gargoyles, and under the arches of the flying buttresses. One evening he did not come down. He wished to dream there at ease all the night, and watch the fantastic play of the moonlight amid the lace-work of stone. He was standing on the top of one of the towers, on a platform, where the balustrade had not yet been built. He wondered if he would be able to see, from such a height, the statue of his beloved Virgin. He leaned over, and, very far beneath him, he thought he could distinguish the two hands stretching out beyond the niche. He leaned over a little more; his foot slipped; he fell with a loud cry.

In his fall he struck against the scaffolding, and, tumbling from the planks, shot down towards the gable of the front, from which rose the cross of stone. With his two hands, he clutched at the arms of the crucified Christ, and his body swung in empty space down the great cross. It was too big for him to grip it between his knees, and he was moreover embarrassed by the folds of his white robe.

There, face to face with Christ, his hair bristling with terror, he prayed Him humbly and madly to save him. Then he began to shout with all his strength; but the good monks, being at peace with God, slept so profoundly that none of them heard him. Scared night-birds circled above his head. His feet scratched the stone, searching in vain for a point of support. His fingers grew numb on the arms of granite; his finger-nails bled; he felt an enormous weight dragging him down. At one moment it seemed to him that the face of Christ, lit by the moon, drew back with a grimace of refusal and bitter irony. His fingers slipped . . . lost their hold. . . .

"Ah! Jesus, this is Thy vengeance! Help me, Virgin Mary!"

And again he fell. . . .

He fell, without hurting himself, on the two marble palms of the Virgin. Her merciful hands rose a little to retain him. He went to sleep like a child in a cradle. At dawn the monks perceived him. Long ladders were erected. When some one came up to rescue him, he was still sleeping.

"Why do you wake me?" he said.

He told no one the dream he had had in the arms of the Virgin, nor what she had said to him. But after that night he displayed a very exact devotion to Christ the Redeemer, and lived in the highest holiness.

THE SIREN

Jules Lemaître

Even as they drew near to the Isle of Sirens the breeze died away and the sea fell to a dead calm. The mariners furled the sails. Ulysses, bearing in mind the cautions which Circe had given, took wax and kneaded it in his mighty palms, and therewith stopped the ears of all his company; and they, obeying him, bound him to the mast with cords. Then they smote with their sweeps the foaming sea.

From the recesses of their sea-cave the Sirens had watched the ship's approach. As soon as it had come within range of hearing, they came down to the shore and took up their song:

"Hither, fair mortals, come hither. No mariner has ever passed our island without listening to our voice; and then he goes on his way with joy, having gained knowledge of many things. We know, we know all that is on Earth, mother of all."

Raising their sweet shining forms above the slumbrous swell, they waved their comely arms to invite and welcome. But far their subtlest charm lay in their voices, weird with all the magic of the sea, penetrating as the smell of seaweed, tender and a little hoarse as the voice of desire itself.

Ulysses struggled with his bonds; but his crew, forewarned, bound the thongs yet more firmly round his arms and thighs.

Nevertheless, one of the seamen, named Euphorion, reflected that songs which were so potent to move the wily Ulysses, master of wisdom, must be worth a man's life to hear.

He plucked the wax from his ears and listened; and such were the songs he heard that he leaned ever more eagerly over the bulwark, and in a brief space plunged into the bitter tide.

The mariners were loth to leave their shipmate to a dreadful death. But Ulysses commanded them, by his frowning gaze, to row onward and pass the island.

. . . .

With all the urgency of desire, Euphorion swam toward the voices. The water, glittering in the sunshine, swept darkening into the cool green cave. At its entrance were grouped the Sirens, seven in number. Downward to the middle they had the aspect of fair girls; their eyes were dark, their hair of greenish gold, their sharp teeth gleamed in somewhat large mouths; their features were strangely childlike. Below, their figures passed into a sheath of scales, and the swimmer nearing them saw the gorgeous colours of their tails moving awash with the water.

As soon as he had reached them, the song of the Sirens ceased; and throwing themselves with horrid cries upon the wretched man, they dragged him deep into the cave and thrust him naked upon a ledge of rock covered with bones. For the custom of these lovely creatures was to tear the bodies of the shipwrecked, and to suck the blood with their flowery lips.

Now, one of the Sirens had seemed to Euphorion even lovelier than her sisters, and her countenance not quite so pitiless as theirs. He turned to her and said:

"I die happy, in that I have heard the chanting of the daughters of the sea. But my joy will be complete if my death may come to me through you alone."

The Siren gazed upon him with surprise. Never before had she seen the face of man lit up by desire and by thought; for the eyes and features of her victims had hitherto expressed nothing but mortal terror, except when, worn out with effort, they were quite expressionless.

With a commanding gesture she bade her sisters keep away, saying, "The stranger is mine."

The other Sirens moved away. Perhaps the one who had spoken had some authority among them; perhaps they had some understanding among themselves, of which we know nothing, as to sharing the living flotsam of the sea.

And now, alone with the crafty Greek, she asked his name; and having learned it, spoke: "I love you, Euphorion. Deathless though I am, this is the first time that I have told my love, the first time that I have known what it is to love."

"And you?" said the Greek. "What is your name?"

"Leucosia."

. . . .

The other Sirens, faithful to the agreement which they had made, left Euphorion and Leucosia to live by themselves and as they pleased.

Landward the cave opened upon an undiscovered meadow where was a fountain of fresh water. With this Euphorion quenched his thirst, and lived on the shellfish of the rocks.

Leucosia never left him. Together they exulted in floating on the rhythm of the wave or in welcoming its huge caresses as it fell. Sometimes from a rocky pinnacle the Siren would swoop with rigid tail downward like an arrow; he would receive her in his arms, while both dived deep into the briny hollows. They rejoiced to play in the sunshine, sporting amid the lace-like foam of the beaches or spinning round in the whirlpools. Often they would join the games of the jolly dolphins and play all kinds of pranks upon them.

When night had fallen the other Sirens, lying on the turf, ranged side by side their heavy tails; but Euphorion and Leucosia found a secret corner of the meadow, and the seaman slept in the cold, cold arms of his little water-goddess.

They spoke rarely. Leucosia had words for everything essential to the life of a second-class marine divinity on a Mediterranean reef. She could name the sky, the sea, the sun, the moon, the stars, the rocks, all fishes and the various parts of the body. She could also say, "I see," "I hear," "I feel," "I love," "I want," "I hope," "I will." But these were the limits of her vocabulary.

Euphorion said to her one day, "When from the swift ship I heard you singing with your sisters, you vaunted that you knew many things of which men are ignorant. Will you not tell me of them, Leucosia?"

But she gave him to understand that in this matter the Sirens had spoken falsely, merely to excite the curiosity of those who heard them.

And in point of fact the words which they sang, and to which now he listened every evening, expressed no definite knowledge, but rather such feelings as answer to the wonder of the dawn, the majesty of sunset, and the immensity and beauty of the sea; or even quite simply the delight of having an agile body incapable of weariness; and sometimes the sting of a desire which these innocent singers could not define, but which was painfully clear to the heart of Euphorion, rich as it was in human memory and experience.

. . . .

Leucosia was well aware of her companion's sorrow and sought to console him with her fresh kisses. At sea and in the lake of the cave she was far stronger and suppler than he, and would help and protect him at every turn. But on the shore, and in the secret meadow she had only her hands to walk with, while her tail dragged uselessly behind; so that she admired and envied the able limbs of her companion. And then she began to feel that he had seen more than she had seen, and that his mind was furnished with images and thoughts of which she had no idea.

He therefore determined to teach her, and tried to give her a grasp of human life on the continents and in the larger islands. But he soon found that she understood nothing of it all, because the words which he used related to nothing which he could actually show her.

Then this life began to bore him a little. Leucosia had no longer the charm of novelty. She was too different from him and her soul was too elementary. Much which had fascinated him at first had now become wearisome. Leucosia's ignorance, and still more her clammy salt skin, got on his nerves.

He looked back on his former way of life with a regret which tormented him more and more. At night in the secret meadow, while the little scaly-tailed goddess slumbered at his side, his thoughts would turn to the fields and forests and rivers, the teams of oxen, the homes of men, the market stalls, the temples perched on promontories, the great ships by the quays, and then to the taverns where fragrant wine is on the table, and to the little dancing girls, blondes and brunettes, who stick red flowers in their hair, whose hands are hot, and whose legs——

It was about that time that a vessel, attracted by the siren songs, ran upon a neighbouring reef; and before Euphorion's horrified vision, these graceful girls fastened their sharp teeth into the shipwrecked bodies and gorged themselves like white bladders with human blood. Leucosia had refused to sing with her sisters or to take part in the horrid feast. Euphorion was thankful for this, but soon discovered that she had abstained merely in order not to displease him, and that although she had felt the touch of love, which is after all common to most animals, she was still a stranger to pity, which is the property of mankind alone.

. . . .

Sirens breathe with equal facility both under water and in the air. Under the tuition of his friend, Euphorion had learned to hold his breath longer under water than any diver could do. He delighted in swimming with Leucosia through groves of coral and gardens of bright seaweeds, and often wondered whether forms which he saw glimmering through the glassy translucence of the water were stones or flowers or beasts.

On one of these excursions he discovered at the bottom of a sea-glen the wreck of a ship; and among its planks and ribs were littered jars, cauldrons, cooking utensils, necklaces, jewels, girdles, mirrors of silver, painted panels showing divers scenes of human life, and lastly, a coffer filled with gold.

With Leucosia's help he fetched all these treasures to dry land. He adorned her neck with a necklace, her arms with bracelets, her waist with a finely-graven girdle, and placed a mirror in her hand. She was vastly pleased with herself, and smiled at her reflection. Then he explained the several uses of the other things, and showed her the meaning of the painted panels. And now at last Leucosia seemed to get some idea of a life different from her own, and said, with a touch of regret, "I wish I could see all that; but I am only a sea-goddess, and shall never know anything but the sea."

This suggested to Euphorion the plan of stimulating yet further her curiosity with regard to land life, and to make use of it to escape from the Isle of Sirens. He was thinking of leaving his friend at the very moment when she had taken a great step forward in intelligence, and had really begun to come closer to him. He never ceased tantalising her by delightful stories of the life enjoyed among men.

" If you would only come with me," he said one day, " we should be able to swim across the seas to a city called Athens, which is only three days' journey from here."

" But I should never be able to walk for any length of time on land! "

" I will help you," Euphorion replied; " and as soon as we get to the city a splendid carriage like those I showed you in the painted pictures will carry you wherever you want to go. And we will live happily with the gold out of our box."

But he kept back from her much that he was thinking.

. . . .

A three days' swim was nothing to the Siren, and swimming sometimes beside her, and sometimes supported by her, even Euphorion was not overtired when at last they reached the coast. They landed on a desolate shore, but a city could be seen in the distance, and the way thither lay by a long and dusty road.

Euphorion made a girdle of leaves so that he might appear respectably before men.

At first the Siren went bravely with her hands. But she scratched herself cruelly on the stones, and came near to fainting under the heat of the sun. Soon Euphorion had left her behind, but she called him back. " The human earth is very hard," she said. " I have carried you, my friend; do you in your turn, carry me."

He had not the heart to refuse her. He returned, and crouching, offered her his back. The Siren twined her arms round his neck; he rose and took his way along the road, while the tip of her scaly tail swept behind him in the dust.

Sweating under his burden, Euphorion muttered in irritation. He was wondering what in the world he could do with this woman-fish of his in the land of men. At last he rudely shook off Leucosia's arms from his neck, let her fall prostrate on the ground, and strode away rapidly in the direction of the city.

" Euphorion! Euphorion! " she cried plaintively.

It was such a pitiful cry that the man was touched and turned again. " Only be patient," said he. " I am going to the city to fetch a carriage for you."

" No, no," she moaned, " you will never come back; I know it well. You no longer love me because I am not in every respect like a woman. It is thanks to me that you are alive at all, yet you are going to be my death; for the gods will certainly have taken away my deathlessness to punish me for loving a man."

She wrung her hands, and for the first time the tears flowed from her weary eyes. Her dusty tail, all its lovely colours faded, flopped feebly on the roadway.

"Euphorion," she wailed again, "Euphorion, have pity!"

"Pity?" he cried. "You never said that word before!"

"Because I had never suffered," she said. "Listen, my friend. I can quite understand that I should always be a bother to you. And I, for my part, should always be anxious, because of the women who have feet. And then, all that I wanted so much to see only frightens me now. But I am far too weak to get back to the sea. If you will only carry me to the shore, I will return alone to my cruel sisters."

"Cruel?" cried Euphorion. "Another word which I had never heard from you!"

"Alas," she mourned, "it is you who have taught me its meaning."

Without another word, Euphorion raised her in his arms, and the Siren's hair streamed around him as they retraced their way. She smiled through her tears, and then moaned with so tender a voice that he felt all his resolution giving way. At length he laid her gently on the shore, quite at the margin of the wavelets.

"Good-bye, my friend," she said.

He sighed. "Ah, if only you had legs!"

"Well," she said, "I have no legs. And I shall not need them, after all, here in the watery sea. I shall try to forget everything and to become like my sisters again. If I were to remember, I should be too unhappy for having known you and for having learned so much from you. But shall I be able to forget? Alas, I am afraid that I am no longer anything but a poor little Siren outcast from all."

And now Euphorion wept aloud. "Be what you like," he said, "but as for me, I love you, and will not let you go without me. We will become whatever it pleases the gods to make us. Come! Into the water together!"

. . . .

The man would undoubtedly have committed this folly if merciful Thetis had not appeared to the two lovers at that very moment.

"You interest me deeply," she said, "and I am greatly concerned in your welfare. You, Leucosia, have been good to one of those who fought beside my son Achilles. And Euphorion, you have had pity on one of my sea-daughters just when you were about to realise your dearest wish. And both of you have raised one another, the one in knowledge and the other in goodness. Of course, I might reward you in any one of several ways. As for you, Leucosia, before sending you away home alone I might take away every memory of all you have learned, which could only cause you future suffering. On the other hand, Euphorion, I might give you the fins and body of a dolphin, while preserving to you your spirit and your human memories, so that you might live happily with Leucosia in the great and wide sea. But I wish rather to give you happiness in the way which you both are even now desiring. Leucosia, my darling, are you willing to give up immortality in order that you may live with him?"

"Certainly," said the Siren. "To enjoy immortality one would need never to think."

"Thank you for nothing," said Thetis.

"Oh," Leucosia exclaimed, "I did not mean you! I was thinking of a little goddess like myself."

"Don't apologise, child. It is clearly understood, then, that you consent to be mortal?"

"With all my heart."

"Be from henceforth woman, and follow the man you love!" With these words Thetis touched the Siren with her dainty trident and in an instant the transformation had come about.

"Now, my daughter," added the kindly goddess, "go to the priestess at that little temple which you see on the hill a hundred paces from here and ask her for a gown. Then the two of you go up to the city."

Euphorion and Leucosia beamed with joy. But there was a touch of melancholy in the smile of Thetis as she left them, for she was not quite certain, after all, that she had given them happiness.

WHITE MARRIAGE

JULES LEMAÎTRE

WHEN Jacques de Thièvres last winter took up his abode between Nice and Mentone in a quiet villa, he had no other purpose but to rest for a month or two, drinking in the sunshine and gazing upon sky and sea. He was forty-five years old, and felt himself very wan alike in body and in mind. His weariness arose not so much from the fact that he had loved, but because he had too often played at love, and always with a great expenditure of mental activity.

Jacques was far from being a professional Don Juan. He was

rather a distinguished amateur of somewhat original taste. Inspired by a genuine goodwill toward all women, he had always been difficult to please and particular in his choice. Among women, he sought above all else sentimental situations, ways of experiencing love which might seem new in some respect. But this is a matter in which unusual feelings are scarcely to be found except in unusual circumstances, so that his adventures had often brought him into difficulties from which it was not easy to escape. Sometimes the result had been that the others had suffered rather more than he would have wished, and that he had suffered himself more than he would have expected. For this reason he seriously intended to let his heart lie fallow throughout one season. And this indeed had been his doctor's advice.

. . . .

Almost every day he used to idle away the hours in the corner of a glen sheltered from the wind and descending to the sea. Whenever there was a warm sun he used to meet there a lady and a young girl. The lady seemed dignified, and the girl was pretty though plainly in a decline. Jacques got into the way of raising his hat and of exchanging a few words with them; and every time he left them he used to think with somewhat fatuous compassion, "Poor little girl!"

He learned that first the father and then a brother had died of this terrible scourge; that the girl's name was Lucie; that the ladies had only a very moderate income; that they occupied quiet rooms in a neighbouring hotel; that they had pleasant manners; that every one was sorry for them; and that no one had anything but good to say of them. He became more and more interested in the two women.

. . . .

When her daughter was not looking, the mother's face expressed unfathomable sorrow, the sorrow which neither hopes nor understands. The vigils by the bedside of her son and of her husband, the two deaths, the two burials, the certainty of very soon seeing all that for the third time, and of remaining alone in the world with all her heart in the past—Jacques understood it all and marvelled how she was able in the presence of her daughter to keep a brave show of wan smiles and even a pretence of gaiety, and while her thoughts were full of her dear dead ones to tend and adorn the dead that was to be.

White as a camellia, her eyes too big, her nose too thin, her voice too clear, her hair too heavy, blue veinlets showing on her waxen hands, so sweet and fragile as to compel your tears, with her graceful form smothered with cloaks and wraps, the little invalid, too weak to read, so that she let her book fall on the sand, or forgetting on her lap the pale water-colours which she had begun, in which the sails of the boats looked like flowers, would sit still for hours at a time gazing upon the horizon.

And Jacques used to wonder: "What is she thinking of, this little lass who is going to die, and most likely knows it?"

. . . .

One day Lucie, with pale long fingers and white silks and blue, was working at a little bit of crochet.

"That's a pretty little thing," said Jacques. "Is it a doll's cape?"

"No," Lucie replied. "It is for a friend of mine, who was married last year and expects a baby. She is very happy."

. . . .

The next day, seated beside her mother on the same bench, Lucie was reading. The page before her seemed to interest her deeply, for Jacques saw by the movement of her eyes that she read it several times. Then she fell into thought and forgot to turn the page.

Jacques passed behind the girl, and as he glanced upon the open volume, these lines met his eye:

> I have no fear of death, my God,
> If I might first have loved!

. . . .

Lucie was thinking:

"I shall not live long. They hide it from me; but I know it must be so, because I have the same trouble as my father and my brother had. Well, since it must be so, I do not mind dying young; but I wish I could first have lived, as other women do! Most of my friends are married, and those who are not yet married have men who love and court them. No one has ever loved or courted me. I shall never know what it is to be loved, to be a wife, to be a mother. Yet I am not plain. I have several times met men whom I certainly pleased, and who at first appeared to love me. And then all of a sudden their manner has changed, and they have stopped treating me as a girl; I suppose it was when they saw that it was not worth while; and after that their eyes showed only pity.

"I suppose that it must be plain to any one at once that I am going to die. That is the sad part of it! This man whom we meet here every day looks very pleasant and I am sure is good. But I scarcely dare to speak to him or look at him. I am afraid of discovering that for him, as for the others, I am only an invalid who must be treated very tenderly because she is going to die. Every one is so good to me; no one seems bothered by my fancies. But this very kindness, this air of pity which I see in every one, remind me at every moment of all that I would forget. Ah! If

I could only be loved in another way, even a little! How I should love any one who would love me for any other reason than my weakness and pale face!"

. . . .

On his side Jacques was thinking:

"The child is positively delicious! I know well enough that she might look insignificant without her illness. But this paleness, this weakness, the thought of inevitable death—— Yet no! I am sure that even in health she would be delightful. Poor little thing!"

Then he corrected himself. "Why 'poor little thing'? Is she so much to be pitied, after all? She will never grow old, nor know anything of the sordidness of life. She will have called out only the finest human emotions, sympathy and pity; and when she passes away she will be with us as the memory of a sweet flower."

But then the thought came, "Yes, it is well enough for us! But what about her? It is easy enough to guess what she is thinking of in these long silences. Well, what if one were to give her this joy? Why not give her the illusion of a woman's life, the illusion of love? Would it not be a charming deed of charity to let this little soul pass from hence happy and believing that she had lived? It would be a pious comedy to play—and who can tell that it would remain a comedy to the end?"

. . . .

Suddenly anxiety came to him with the question, "But what if she should not die?"

He took an opportunity of speaking to the doctor who looked after her.

"She is doomed," he replied. "There is no hope. I shall be greatly surprised if she has three months to live."

"Come on, then," said Jacques to himself. "This will probably be the best act of my life."

. . . .

He sought out her mother and asked for Lucie's hand. She thought at first he must be a little off his head; but he had one reply to every objection. "I love her," he said, and added, "You may be sure of my sincerity and good intentions, for I am very well off and ask no dowry with her. If, as you say, I am committing a folly, at least there is nothing dishonourable about it. But after all how can we be sure that it is a folly?"

He brought forward cases of incredible cures; he urged his case with eloquence, and woke in her mother's heart a gleam of hope.

"In any case," said he, "I am not a scoundrel, and as far as is necessary I will look after your daughter as if she were a little invalid sister. The two of us together will love and tend her—that is all."

At last the mother gave in.

. . . .

The first words of love which Jacques spoke to Lucie brought to her eyes a great light of joy.

" It is not, then, absolutely certain that I am to die? " she said.

" Surely my wish that you should be my wife is the best proof that nothing is less certain! I am a reasonable man, after all; and if I thought you were likely to leave me, you bad girl, should I prepare so great a sorrow for myself? You will live because I love you."

This reasoning seemed sound enough to Lucie. Moreover, Jacques was very well preserved, and when in his best form might still have passed for a young man.

Every morning for the next month he brought flowers for his betrothed, and they held long loving talks together. The radiant Lucie made all kinds of projects, and Jacques was clever enough to contradict her sometimes and even to scold her a little, just to show that he by no means thought of her as one at the gates of death.

. . . .

He prepared their marriage chamber. The walls were daintily hung with mauve and rose-coloured silks veiled with Indian muslin. Garlands of artificial hyacinths looped back the curtains of the windows and mirrors, and held the bed-curtains in festoons. The whole room was fresh and delicate in such a strangely fragile way that one felt that it was adorned only for a little time.

. . . .

Thither, after the ceremony, he brought Lucie, whiter than her wedding-dress and orange flowers, and almost dying of her great joy.

He took her on his knee as if she had been his little daughter, and undressed her slowly with the greatest care. Her breath came fast but gently, her pale lips, half opened, showed her little teeth, her frail arms were thrown round her husband's neck, and she gazed at him in ecstasy, forgetting all. And as he felt against him this little form, so slight, so supple, with so little substance in it, this form which would never have time to sin, but must so soon disappear in all its purity like a vision, Jacques was flooded with infinite tenderness.

Again it seemed to him that this was his little daughter whom he held against his heart. He dared not even kiss her lips. And when he had put on her the long nightdress adorned with lace and ribbons, he lifted her into bed like a child.

He passed the night seated beside her and holding her hand.

. . . .

So one week passed away.

On the eighth day, one hour before her death, Lucie breathed into Jacques' ear, " My friend, I know that I am soon going. But I am not dreadfully unhappy. I know that you will always remember me, always. And thanks to you, I have known like other women the joy of being a wife, and have been able to say, ' My husband! ' "

Through all the week-long duration of their marriage Jacques had sat beside her pillow, except one night when she was very restless, and without undressing he lay down beside her to support her head and to hold her in his arms.

. . . .

Jacques looked much older after this adventure. He had known for the first time, in all their fulness, love and suffering.

THE KHAN'S WIVES

JULES LEMAÎTRE

" WHAT I am about to tell you," said Mme. Latanief, " is certainly calculated to flatter the vanity of you men, and I have no doubt that you will think it reflects to the disadvantage of Western women. But I have a good heart, and you shall hear my little story all the same, especially as it will make no difference in our mutual relations. It will neither affect what you, gentlemen, are for us, nor what we do our best to be for you—or against you.

" When my husband was Governor of the province of Samarkand, I had the honour of being invited to visit the five legitimate wives of Khan ——, I have forgotten his name. I don't even remember whether he was Khan or held some other office. And I am not sure whether he was a Turcoman, or Kirghiz, or Usbeg, or to which of the terribly mixed races of that country he belonged. You see I have travelled so much and have seen such various and weird specimens of the human race, and so many scenes have passed like magic-lantern slides before my eyes, that I mix up everything.

" The Khan was at least seventy years old. He was a superb figure, with a long white beard and an air of grave sweetness, and had exactly the appearance which we imagine in the good viziers of the *Arabian Nights* and other tales of that kind.

" This venerable man had greatly enriched himself by brigandage and by deliberate extortion from the quiet agricultural Turcomans. Somewhere in the steppes he had magnificent tents of white felt round which hundreds of horses and thousands of sheep were pastured, and there he spent his summers. But for the winter he had a town house at Samarkand, and it was there that I saw his wives.

"He hesitated long before giving me permission to see them, and would certainly have refused if my husband had not been a very high official. In his opinion, intercourse with European women could only spoil his wives and put false ideas into their heads.

"The house was high and gaunt as a fortress, and had formerly been a great school in the days when they used to say that if Mecca was the heart of Islam, Samarkand was its brain. And, indeed, several centuries ago Samarkand was a notable intellectual centre. Poetry, astronomy, and mathematics were taught there, and explanations of the universe were given which were probably not more stupid than many others.

"I crossed a delightful court, like those of Moorish houses but more florid with ornament, surrounded by higher arcades and a more blazing symphony of colour, and was shown into the women's apartment.

"It was like every harem interior, but one is always surprised afresh in discovering behind the great white walls of Oriental houses these deep and wonderful retreats, where heaped-up carpets, fabrics richly embroidered with gold, enamels, mirrors, censers of finely-worked silver, and heavy jewels gleam with so sweet and warm and sumptuous a brilliance in a mysterious twilight. All this splendour is so hidden, so fugitive and unexpected that it has an air of unreality, like the heaps of precious stones, of which fables tell, discovered in massive wooden coffers.

"The five wives of the great man were there, seated or reclining about the room. The oldest, who received me,—we will call her Zétulbé,—was, I suppose, about forty years of age, of enormous bulk, her jet-black eyes glittering in her fat face; but she looked very kindly, and had certainly been a beauty. She knew a little Russian and I had a few words of Turkish, so that we were able to understand one another.

"Two other women were really nothing but bundles rolled up in pretty stuffs. But the two youngest, lasses of from twelve to fifteen years of age, were charming, with almond eyes, lips dainty as flowers, and slim little figures. Dressed in long red gowns, secured at the waist by a kind of shawl, their bodies had the slow and gliding movements of serpents and their arms the swift and cunning movements of little monkeys.

"Zétulbé showed me the most amazing collection of barbaric jewellery that I have ever seen. Some of it dated very likely from Gengis-Khan. But she said, 'That is nothing!' and then showed me with immense satisfaction bundles of imitation lace and handkerchiefs which must have come from Whiteley's or the Bon Marché, by way of the Nijni-Novgorod fair.

"The two little girls, though scared at first, soon became at their ease. And then with supple movements, laughter, and cries of astonishment, they amused themselves with gently undressing me. They were greatly excited over my corsets and other garments. And indeed, if you come to think of it, they are very singular objects.

"The dress of the women of the East respects the outline of the body, and does no more than veil it; if I may so speak, it leaves the woman always *there;* it is innocent of laces, hooks, and all other useless complications. The woman of the East adorns herself for man. But we, on the contrary, adorn ourselves for ourselves and against man. Our dress exaggerates all that is expressive in the outline which kindly Nature has given us, and at the same time uncompromisingly protects it. For us, dress is at once a meticulous cult offered to the whole of our precious person, a means of provocation and a rampart. It is our weapon and our armour. The two little monkeys could not recover from it.

"By reason of the universal freemasonry of women, I was soon talking almost familiarly with the good Zétulbé.

"I knew that the Khan was bound by the religious and the civil law alike—they are all one in the lands of Islam—to pay courteous attention to each of his wives at least twice in the week, and that if any consort felt herself neglected for a whole week she could justly complain and demand a divorce. I went so far as to ask Zétulbé whether the Khan honoured all his obligations. She passed on my question to her comrades.

"The two bundles scarcely smiled, but the two little monkeys broke out again into shrill laughter. And the prudent Zétulbé answered me very gravely, 'None of us has ever complained of our lord.'

"I really did not know whether to admire the grace which Allah had vouchsafed to my host or the discretion of these excellent wives. While I was pondering, a maid-servant brought in dates, conserve of roses, honey tarts, and coffee.

"I am not great at description, and all that I can say to you is that this servant was of an amazing beauty. There was nothing of the elephant about her, nor anything of the monkey. As she held, with upraised hands, her tray of little cups, she recalled the most graceful silhouettes painted on Greek vases, but with an added slimness and litheness reminiscent of Persian art. And what delicate vigour there was, what firm suppleness of line, under the great piece of striped silk which clothed her from neck to feet! And what a complexion of pale copper, what eyes, and on her rosy parted lips what a smile as of a little innocent queen unconsciously majestic!

" ' Heavens! ' I exclaimed, ' How beautiful she is! '

Zétulbé took me through the garden, then through a succession of little rooms with stained-glass windows, where beds were laid in recesses lined with tiles in designs as bright and almost as delicate as those of Kashmir shawls.

The servant raised the curtains as we passed, and at every one of her movements I cried out with admiration.

" ' She seems to please you,' said Zétulbé.

" ' Immensely.'

" ' Well, then, I hope you will accept her.'

" At first I thought this was a polite formula which was not to be taken seriously. But Zétulbé continued: ' She is mine. I bought her with my own money. My husband used to give me a great deal of money when I was younger. Do take her. I would like to give her to you, so that you may remember me. My husband will not mind, for he has great respect for the Governor's wife. I shall soon find a servant as pretty as Zorah, and in any case we have many others in the house.'

" ' Your generosity touches me deeply,' I replied; ' but the fact is—I can hardly——'

" Zétulbé thought that I hesitated, and would have persuaded me. ' The girl is very clever at making cakes and preserves,' she said, ' and sings well. She is a Persian, and was carried off in early childhood by Turcoman horsemen. She is very gentle and obedient.'

" ' Dear lady,' I said, laughing, ' nothing would please me better than to have such a pretty servant. But the fact is, she is far too beautiful. My husband might take a fancy to her——'

" ' Well? '

" ' Well, I would rather not lay myself open to any difficulty of that kind.'

" Zétulbé thought for a moment, and then, ' I do not understand,' she said gravely; ' I cannot understand what you say. How then do you women of Europe love your husbands? You are unwilling that they should be intimate with other women! The fact of the matter is that you do not love them. Otherwise you would wish to make them as happy as possible. For my part, I have taken some pains to bring here the youngest and most beautiful women I can find, so that my husband may still enjoy his life and forget that he is growing old. And my sisters,' she continued, pointing to the two bundles, ' have done the same. The fact is, we love our husband.' "

. . . .

Mme. Latanief paused, and tea was brought.

" Doubtless, Madame," said one of the men who had listened to the story, " you brought away Zorah with you? "

" I should rather think not! "

" Do you not then somewhat confirm Zétulbé's conclusion that you do not love your husband? "

" I will not say that."

" On the contrary, you love him? "

" Oh, I am not ready to say that either."

" Well, then? "

" Let us leave it at that."

GARNOTEAU'S THREE MANNERS

JULES LEMAÎTRE

WE were at the exhibition of pictures at the Salon, and I had stopped with one of my friends, a painter of advanced tendencies, before a painting by M. Garnoteau, a member of the Institute. It represented Diana and her nymphs enjoying graceful sports in the midst of a noble champaign.

Some of these figures were of a dark type of beauty, others fair, and the hair of one was frankly red. There were faces and backs and three-quarter views, full profiles, and one of the face almost turned away. Some lay on the turf, others crouched, and yet others stood up though leaning somewhat toward Diana. whose figure alone was quite upright. The composition was good, forming a pyramid of the approved kind; the colour work was powerful; and any one could see that it came from the studio of a master.

Yet one peculiarity struck me in this well-conceived and executed festival of the nude.

" It is most extraordinary," I said to my friend. " I cannot make it out. All these little women seem to me pleasant enough down to the waist. You have tints of white and pink, and plump and lissom busts, such as appeal to Americans. But do you notice how from the waist downward everything is thin and poor, and how scraggy all the legs are? All those pretty upper halves are perched upon the same support, which looks like that of a puritan old maid. What a joke it is! I wonder if it is a new case of some obscure defect of vision, and if old Garnoteau really sees like that? Or is it in the interest of morals that he has balanced the dangerous attraction of these breasts and arms by this austerity of the lower limbs? "

"You will find this absurdity," my friend replied, "in every picture that Garnoteau has painted in the last thirty years. But the explanation is the simplest which you could possibly imagine. Let me tell you a great secret. All these hips and all these legs are the hips and legs of Mme. Garnoteau, and of no one else, and you will not find in any one of M. Garnoteau's pictures other hips or thighs or feet than those of Mme. Garnoteau. But let us sit down, shall we? There is quite a story behind this odd practice of his."

Reclining on the circular divan in the centre of the great room, we let our glances drift, without alighting, over the immense glittering confusion of forms and colours, which is one of the best ways of visiting a picture show. Meanwhile my friend the painter confided to me as follows.

"You can guess the early stages of Garnoteau's career. Having won distinction in drawing at the school of the Brothers of Christian Doctrine, he was sent by Limoges, his native town, to Paris with a scholarship of 1200 francs. He worked like a horse, and after five or six years carried off the Prix de Rome with his 'Coriolanus among the Volscians,' or perhaps it was 'Themistocles among the Persians.'

"At last, one day, this great shy methodical lad discovered his vocation—figures in the nude, pictures of nymphs. The creature has never painted anything else. And as his nude figures have always been soapy and have never shown any trace of impropriety, they have carried him triumphantly to the Institute. Here you have an excellent fellow who has painted enough figures to populate a considerable number of harems, but has had from boyhood the gravity and strict morals of a solicitor. All his escapades have been on canvas. After all, this may have been the secret of his correctness; it may have acted as a safety-valve.

"Not long after his return from Rome, Garnoteau met in his native town a 'well-brought up' young person, as the phrase has it, neither good-looking nor too plain, but tall and hard. O mystery of the heart! Our painter of plump nymphs became enamoured of this maypole. Her father was a wealthy and respected hosier in Limoges.

"When Garnoteau asked for her hand, the mother raised some difficulties. 'An artist!' she exclaimed. 'And above all a man who paints only from the nude!' But Garnoteau urged that 'Art redeems all,' and, moreover, that his pictures sold extremely well. The hosier, on the other hand, was not averse to this style of painting. Célestine herself loved Garnoteau, and to marry an artist pleased her vanity. The wedding-day was fixed.

"One day Célestine took her betrothed aside and asked him with blushes, 'Is it true what they have told me, that you paint your pictures—from women—altogether undressed?'

"'Yes, dear, it is.'

"'But could you not paint—that—without a model, from memory?'

"Garnoteau explained that no one could do that.

"'Then,' Célestine continued, 'why not paint people in their clothes, scenes such as are often taken, pathetic subjects, like that picture "The Care of the Poor," or "The Return of the Soldier"?'

"'What an idea, my dear child! That would not be high art, and I dare not give up high art. And then, you must understand, the nude is my specialty. A man cannot change his specialty as easily as all that. It upsets the expectations of the public.'

"In a word, Garnoteau spoke so firmly that Célestine said no more, and seemed to have given in.

"But on the evening of their wedding day, when they were first alone together, Célestine, covering her blushing face with her hands, said to her husband, 'Promise me, dear, to do what I am going to ask you.'

"Garnoteau promised. It was one of those moments at which one would promise anything.

"'Well, then,' Célestine continued in low tones and broken sentences, 'I don't want to be unreasonable,—I am willing that other women should pose to you for the head, for the arms, and even—if it must be so—for the bust. But—as for the rest—I don't want you to have any other model but me. No, don't try to draw back! You have promised, and I am sure I should die of despair if you were to break your promise. It tortures me to think that you should be alone in your studio with a creature— Oh, I should die of it!'

"Garnoteau comforted her. He foresaw none of the dreadful consequences of their compact, and loving Célestine as he did, she seemed to him plump enough——" At this point I interrupted my friend. "But how can you have known all this?" I asked.

"Oh," he replied, "nothing could be simpler. Garnoteau himself one day, when he was rather jolly, told it to his best friend, old Petrus Carbonnel, who told it to Chichinette, a little model, who told me.

"Well," he continued, "Garnoteau was faithful to his promise; indeed, Célestine saw to that. She did not allow his models less than the costume of the Venus of Milo, worn rather higher up, and she kept watch on Garnoteau. She darted into the studio at the most unexpected moments, and on the two or three occasions when she found him trying to deceive her, she fell into such tantrums that the poor fellow thought it best to keep to his pledged word.

"Hence this interminable procession of nymphs, plump above and scraggy below, this weird discrepancy between blooming figures and the graceless ninepins which support them. Garnoteau's dryads were really rather like flowers blossoming at the end of thin stalks.

"While Célestine's youth remained, the results were not so bad. If she was not ample, she was at least fresh in colour. Moreover, Garnoteau managed to expand slightly all that he borrowed from his wife.

"Then his work became very popular, and the public were ready to take anything from his brush. The thinness of the lower half of his nymphs was accepted as elegance. People said that their legs were Florentine legs. One critic of great influence made the discovery that this was a very spiritual way of understanding and painting the female form, and that there was something poetic, subtle, simplified, and intellectual about these figures. He pointed out that Garnoteau's work was eminently fitted to chasten the heart and uplift the soul of the masses. Garnoteau was immediately received into the Institute.

"But with the passage of the years, Célestine became thinner still and the legs of Garnoteau's nymphs became also thinner. At the same time, by an unconscious desire for compensation, in proportion as his wife became thinner, Garnoteau chose more and more luxuriant models for the upper halves of his nymphs. At last the discrepancy became so obvious that even the public saw it; and then the sale of his pictures went steadily downward.

"Then Garnoteau had the idea of trying genre-painting. He painted little girls with their clothes on, but it was a failure. Then followed the ingenious idea of painting sirens and mermaids,—a method of escaping from the problem of the lower limbs. But these composite creatures passed unnoticed.

"At length Célestine herself recalled him to his nymphs. She had found pleasure in helping his work, and missed the occupation of a model. Things were now worse than ever, and the Florentine legs became little better than sticks. Still, inasmuch as nymphs were Garnoteau's specialty, as soon as he began to put nymphs upon the market again, the nymphs began again to sell.

"'Thanks to me!' said Célestine. And when people happened to praise her husband's work, she would lower her eyes and answer, simpering, 'The legs most of all! The figure up to the waist! It is, as you say, exquisite!'

"She was an excellent economist, and had enriched Garnoteau by stinting his food, depriving him of all amusements, and regulating even his tobacco. With the nymph-money she had bought two or three houses in Paris which brought in a good income; and, always convinced of her personal charms, she used to say, with a meaning smile, when Garnoteau's rents came in, 'To whom do you owe that?'

"Her avarice increased with age. Even while she was posing she would knit so as not to lose time. The unhappy Garnoteau, condemned to paint his wife incessantly, began to have a horror of her. And now, whenever he could get away, this man, formerly so correct, sought a solace elsewhere for this perpetual study.

"And now for the last phase."

My friend took me to a dealer's and showed me "A Dance of the Nymphs." They were all remarkable for the excessive development of the figure from waist to feet, and their thighs were like the pillars of a church.

"Whence," I asked, "whence this—meat?"

"They come from Garnoteau," he said, "whose wife died two months ago. The picture which you saw in the Salon was painted while she was yet alive. I think that Garnoteau, who is a good fellow at heart, regrets Célestine. At any rate, he wept copiously at her funeral. And he could hardly forget that she was the scaffolding with which he had built his reputation. But immediately afterwards he ran riot, and paints now as you see before you. No model is exuberant enough for him. He may be seen hunting the countryside around Paris for rustic figures comparable to those of his dreams, and whenever he persuades one of these to pose, he goes into it with all his heart. He paints limbs—deliriously! And note one singular and touching fact. It is now the upper part of the figure which has become more tenuous, more spiritual; it is from the waist upward that the nymphs have become modest and restrained, as if Garnoteau had in mind his Célestine!

"You know Raphaël's three manners: First, he seeks himself; secondly, finds himself, and thirdly, surpasses himself. And I think we may say that Garnoteau, too, had three manners. At first he painted well-balanced figures; then, those in which the upper half was expansive and the lower half starved; and finally, exuberant limbs joined to thin bodies above. Well, those three manners answer to the three periods of his life: before Célestine, under Célestine, and after Célestine."

THE FUNERAL OF FIRDOUSI

JULES LEMAÎTRE

I

WHEN Firdousi the poet was ninety-five years of age he stayed rather late in his little garden one cool evening, and, on going to bed, felt that he had taken a chill. The next morning, the doctor Thinini, called in haste by his old servant Zora, pronounced that the author of the *Book of the Kings* was ill of a sickness which the

Greeks called "pleurisy," that probably he would not be able to get over it, considering his great age, and that from all appearances he had only a few days to live.

The news, spread by word of mouth and by the written newspapers, profoundly stirred Bagdad and the whole kingdom; for Firdousi was more than a man, he was little less than a god.

The astonishment of the Persians was great when they heard he was going to die. They had regarded him as a prophet, but while they believed in his earthly immortality, Firdousi himself had often said that he would die.

He was ill three days and three nights. All the poets of Bagdad (fourteen of them) piously watched over him. But, at the bottom of their hearts, they found the time rather long. In the meantime, outside the house, waiting for the death of the old poet, were the men commissioned to collect the news, which was written down at once by hundreds of scribes, and in this way circulated through Bagdad. And to pass the time they rolled their fine tobacco into cigarettes. They had knocked so often at the door to ask, "Well, how is he?" that the old Zora would no longer open it, and several of these men, either from impatience or love of money, had already given out that Firdousi was no more, and the children, hugging in their arms huge bundles of written manuscripts, were shouting in the streets, "Death of Firdousi," and the good Persians who bought these gazettes, when they saw they had been deceived, were embittered against the dying man. At dawn on the fourth day the oldest of the fourteen poets opened the door and shouted from the top of the steps, "He is dead." "At last!" said the waiting ones.

II

Then it was decided to give the old poet such a funeral as had never been seen before. To give the deputations from the provinces time to arrive at Bagdad, King Ali-Rita decided that the funeral should not take place for seven days. They embalmed the body of Firdousi with myrrh, pepper, vanilla and other spices. They braided his long white beard, they put rouge on his cheeks, henna on his eyebrows, and antimony on his lips, gold chains round his neck, gold bracelets on his arms; they dressed him in a robe woven with gold, a present from the king, and the old poet looked like a sumptuous idol.

The ministers, generals, wise men, dervishes, and all people of note disputed the honour of watching beside the glorious corpse. Every one ordered wreaths from all the flower merchants. There were in Bagdad at this time a number of societies, members of which were accustomed to meet and sup together and to make speeches, societies of hygiene, of gymnastics, of rowing; societies for the spread of education, for the destruction of mosquitoes, musical and philosophical societies. All these had their presidents, vice-presidents, their commissioners, their rules, their banners, their insignia, and their periodical banquets; they answered the twofold need of men—to drink in company and to play a part in the world. There was a dispute among these innumerable " leagues " as to who would send the most beautiful wreath to the funeral of Firdousi. They gathered roses from the fields which make a girdle of colour and perfume round Bagdad, and it seemed that the earth would shower all her spring flowers on the poet who had so well sung her praises.

III

Every one laid claim to the honour of having known Firdousi. People of no importance before boasted in the newspapers of their intimacy with him, giving details of his private life and recalling his jests; one was surprised that the lonely man had had so many friends. Others, to appear important, busied themselves with the funeral arrangements, and went about with solemn faces. A great register was placed on a desk at the door of the dead man's house, and all who wished inscribed their names with suitable remarks and words of praise.

The poets and men of letters extolled him. But they placed him so high and apart, they made him so singular, so abnormal, so ignorant of his own powers, that no one could take umbrage, and by praising this unconscious monster his flatterers seemed to vaunt their own superiority. They appeared to say, " Firdousi was not cut out for a genius, while we——"

" He had no critical sense," said one.

Another added, " He was not witty."

And a third murmured between his teeth, " He was stupid as the Himalayas."

IV

The enthusiasm of the people, however, was simple and sincere, and so was that of King Ali-Rita, a young prince full of candour, who was deposed a few years later because he was too good and a little too thoughtless. This good young king asked himself what he could do to honour the poet. Just outside the walls of Bagdad, on the slope of a mountain, there was a marble monument of great height built by the wicked King Ali-Maboul for his tomb. This prince was deposed by the great-great-grandfather of Ali-Rita, and the tomb, abandoned for more than a century, was in ruins.

Ali-Rita commanded that the body of Firdousi should be transported to the tomb of Ali-Maboul, and in order that there might be time to make the necessary repairs, the funeral was postponed for seven days. At first every one approved of the plan, and the idlers went to watch the masons at work. But the wreaths prepared for the ceremony began to fade, for the weather was hot, and quarrels broke out between people who had ordered them and the flower merchants.

"They were for the funeral-day. We will not pay."

"It is not our fault that the fête has been postponed," argued the flower merchants. They began to swear and to fight; they pulled the wreaths to pieces, and for many days heaps of fading flowers were drifted down the streams of Bagdad.

The discontent grew worse. As the newspapers would speak of nothing but Firdousi, the writers who had been accustomed to narrate other matters began to find this glory too encroaching. Two or three rather important men had also died at this time and no attention was paid to them, and their families were angry with Firdousi for monopolising public attention. In short, these preparations, this turmoil, the cries of the pedlars who sold pictures of Firdousi, the noisy arrivals of the deputations from the provinces, greatly disturbed the peace-loving citizens and they felt in their hearts a growing hatred for this obstructive and obstreperous corpse, who was making their streets uninhabitable.

V

At this juncture a most extraordinary crime was committed in Bagdad in the Street of the Maple Tree. A family composed of father, mother and ten children were found murdered one night. Each of the twelve victims had the same little narrow triangular wound on the left side. Robbery was not the object of the crime. Nothing had been taken from the house. The people were lost in conjectures.

Suddenly Firdousi was forgotten.

Old Zora had noticed the number of those who came to watch beside the body growing fewer every day. The faithful servant, who had complained and grumbled to see her master's house invaded, was not angry at this desertion. She cleaned, swept, and polished the little apartment. Then for three nights she watched alone beside the great poet.

Towards the evening of the fourth day, when she was dropping from fatigue, a knock was heard at the door. A young girl entered, poorly dressed, but pretty, and with an innocent and gentle air. "Who are you?" "Zelulbe, your neighbour." "Ah, yes; the little dressmaker round the corner. And what do you want?" Zelulbe blushed and stammered. "I came to see—excuse me, but for several days no one has been, so I said to myself, 'There is perhaps no one to watch, and his old housekeeper may be wanting me.' " The old servant kissed Zelulbe, and for the three nights before the funeral the great poet was watched over by the little needlewoman.

She sat on a chair by the bedside of the dead man making garments for the poor, and singing Firdousi's little songs to prevent herself from falling asleep, and while she sang softly Firdousi seemed to smile under his braided beard.

The strange crime in the Street of the Maple still continued to occupy every one's attention. People kept saying that the murderer was found, and the stupid, curious crowd surged round the house night and day. As for the provincial deputies attending the obsequies of the poet, they spent their time in the taverns and houses of pleasure, and were taken up in the streets by the watchmen in a helpless state, quite forgetting why they had come to the city.

VI

At last the day was fixed, the funeral procession started, and the heat was terrific. Zora and Zelulbe went together. On the coffin were only two small wreaths, one of roses and the other of violets. Behind the two women there walked a magnificent officer sent by the king. After him fifty Persians dragged themselves along, very red, and perspiring under the vertical sun, their tongues hanging out and their arms dangling. Each of them was to read an address at the grave, and they fanned themselves with their manuscripts as they walked. Several slipped out of the route to stop at the taverns and refresh themselves, and thus the cortège became lamentably out of gear.

Behind the orators there followed a heavy carriage full of people who looked alive, but were quite motionless. These people were wax figures, and in the torrid heat they were slowly melting. They had been brought from the museum, and represented in wax the men of the day. Many of these, being high dignitaries, learned men, members of the various academies, were obliged by their office or their position to attend funerals, and had the ingenious idea of replacing themselves by their effigies in order to be spared fatigue and trouble. And the people did not notice this, for no one paid any attention to the meagre funeral. Not one of the fourteen poets came!

When the procession, dwindling at each street corner, arrived at the tomb of Ali-Maboul, nothing was ready. One workman was asleep, and the others were drinking. Zora awoke the sleeping one. "What a disgrace; what a shame!" she cried. "Get up and find one of your comrades and dig a little grave for my master under this palm tree, for we cannot take him back, you see."

Ten orators out of fifty were faithful; they read their addresses, and as soon as they had finished they went off to mop their faces. The tenth, a little old man, remained with the officer of the king, the two women, and the carriage of wax figures, and began imperturbably to read his manuscript: " Why this immense assembly? To whom are these enthusiastic praises made by this innumerable multitude? "

The good man, being only a person of very little consequence, had prepared a very long speech, so long it was that the two workmen who waited to fill up the grave grumbled impatiently. The old man was frightened, and sacrificed his peroration.

VII

Zora wept hot tears, Zelulbe sobbed. The king's officer approached the pretty girl, saying, " You are no doubt a relative of Firdousi."

" No, sir, but I was his neighbour, and watched beside him for three nights."

" I am not surprised," he answered. " Beautiful as you are, you must be kind. But do not cry, I beg of you; dry those pretty eyes."

The handsome officer talked for some time in this way, then he leaned over Zelulbe and kissed her pretty hair, and little by little the girl ceased crying, and, drying her eyes, she took the handsome officer's arm and they returned together to the city. When they passed through the great gate of Bagdad, Zelulbe's laugh was heard, clear as a bird. And from his place in eternity old Firdousi, perfectly wise and perfectly kind, looked after the amorous couple with a benevolent eye. It was the old servant alone who, on her knees by his grave, still wept for her master.

HENRI MALIN
B. 1852

THE FAMILY NAME

I

One afternoon, Mons. Sauvallier received from his younger son—a lieutenant in garrison at Versailles—the following letter:

"Versailles, May 25, 1883.

"My Dear Father—A terrible catastrophe has befallen me, one which will be a blow to you also. I am writing about it, because I dare not face you; I deserve never to see you again!

"Led astray by a companion, I have been gambling on the Bourse, and am involved in yesterday's crash, in which so many fortunes have been suddenly swamped.

"I scarcely dare to tell you how much I have lost. Yet I *must* do so, for the honour of the Sauvalliers is concerned. Alas! you will be all but ruined! I owe the sum of four hundred and sixty-eight thousand francs. Oh! what a miserable wretch I am!

"When I found that the smash was inevitable I went mad, and entered my room with the intention of putting an end to my wretched existence. But more sober thoughts prevailed; I changed my mind. I had heard that officers were being recruited for Tonquin, and I determined to volunteer for this service. My suicide would not have bettered matters; it would rather have left an added blot upon our family name. Out there, at all events, my death may be of use; it will cause you no shame, and may perhaps move you to a little compassion for your guilty, but most unhappy and despairing son, who suffers agonies at thought of the trouble he has brought upon you, and who now bids you an eternal farewell!

"Camille Sauvallier."

Mons. Sauvallier, who had been a widower for several years past, was one of the most respected business-men of Paris, the owner of a foundry, a judge of the Tribunal of Commerce, and an officer of the Legion of Honour. He had two sons: Camille, the lieutenant; and Auguste, an artist of some originality, who was the husband of a charming wife, and the father of a little six-year-old maiden named Andrée. Mons. Sauvallier had always deterred his sons from embarking in trade. He had shrunk from exposing them to the ups and downs of business life, its trying fluctuations, its frequent cruel mischances. He had arranged that at his death his estate should be realized; he did not wish the business to be sold outright, in case it should pass into the hands of strangers who might sully the hitherto unblemished name of Sauvallier.

And now, in spite of all his precautions, a disaster greater than any he had dreamed of had overwhelmed him.

Leaning back wearily in his arm-chair, with haggard eyes he re-read his son's letter, in order to assure himself that he was not dreaming. Yes! It was too true! Camille had ruined, perhaps dishonoured, him! It seemed as though the objects that surrounded him—the very walls and furniture—were no longer the same! As one staggering beneath a too heavy burden, he rose with difficulty, his limbs stiff, yet his whole frame agitated; then he sank back into his chair, with two big tears flowing down his cheeks.

By hook or by crook he *must* procure the sum, and the debt should be paid to-morrow. It would be a difficult task. The wealth of the manufacturer consists of material and merchandise. Would so hurried a realization yield the necessary amount? He could not tell. Again, when this debt was paid, would he be able to fulfil his engagements? Bankruptcy stared him in the face. A Sauvallier bankrupt? An officer of the Legion of Honour, a judge of the Tribunal of Commerce, insolvent? Never! He would die first!

But before it came to that, he would try every expedient: he would strain every nerve.

So all night long the poor man planned and calculated, and in the morning, with heavy heart, proceeded to put his plans into effect.

He visited his numerous friends and told them of his trouble, which elicited much sympathy. In order to help, some made large purchases of him, paying ready money, others advanced or lent him money. All day until the evening he was running about Paris collecting cheques, bank-notes, and orders.

In the evening, as he sat down to ascertain the result of the day's efforts, Auguste came in with his wife and Andrée. To help his father, the artist had parted with some of his pictures at a sacrifice, and he now brought the sum thus gained.

Andrée, unconscious of the trouble of her elders, began to play with her "Jéanne," a doll nearly as big as herself, which her grandfather had given her some time previously, and which she loved, she said, "as her own daughter."

But the child soon observed the sadness of her parents and her dear grandfather, and she looked with earnest, inquiring gaze from one to the other, trying to discover what was amiss. She saw her father lay down his pocket-book, she watched her mother place upon the table her bracelets, necklaces, ear-rings, and rings, while Mons. Sauvallier thanked them with tears in his eyes. With a very thoughtful, serious expression on her little face, the child turned towards her doll, embraced it with the emotional fervour of a last adieu, then carried it to her grandfather, saying, in sweet, resigned tones: " Take it, grandpapa! You can sell her, too."

Mons. Sauvallier wept upon the neck of his little granddaughter, murmuring: " You also, my angel? Oh, that miserable boy! "

II

Thus Camille's debt was paid, and the honour of the Sauvalliers was saved. But the father's fortune had gone!

He was able, however, to retain his business. He said to himself that he must work still, in spite of his threescore years; that he must labour incessantly, with the anxious ardour of those beginning life with nothing to rely upon save their own exertions.

He reduced his expenses, gave up his own house and went to live with his son, sold his carriage and horses, discharged his servants, and stinted himself in every possible way. Auguste became his designer, Auguste's wife his clerk. Each accepted his or her share of the burden bravely and uncomplainingly, as an important duty which must at any cost be accomplished.

The conduct of this old man, so jealous for his name, so upright, so courageous in misfortune, excited profound sympathy. All who knew him pitied him; orders flowed in, and soon a quite exceptional activity pervaded the establishment from basement to roof, inspiring Mons. Sauvallier with a little hope. But one persistent fear disturbed his sleep, and troubled his waking hours. It was that some day he might hear that Camille had been gambling again, and was once more in debt. He had forbidden all mention of his erring son, but the thought of him was ever present, and lay like an incubus upon his heart.

One year passed, then another. The foundry still flourished; work positively raged therein. It had no rest; it also, as though endowed with a conscience, did its duty nobly. Its furnaces glowed like ardent eyes; its mighty puffing and snorting shook the ground; the molten metal, red and fuming, flowed from its crucibles like blood from its body. At an early hour of the morning was heard its piercing summons to the work-people, and all night its glare illuminated the sky.

III

The campaign of Tonquin was in full swing. In the midst of an unknown country, harassed by innumerable difficulties, the French soldiers were contending painfully with an irrepressible, ever-rallying foe. The smallest success served to excite the popular patriotism, and all awaited impatiently the tidings of a decisive victory.

One morning, Auguste, looking very pale, entered his father's office, and handed him a newspaper. There, amongst "Latest intelligence," Mons. Sauvallier read the following:

"From the camp entrenched at Dong-Song, February 12th, 1885.—To-day Captain Sauvallier attacked the enemy with extreme vigour, fought all the day against considerable forces, and captured successively three redoubts. In attacking the last of the three, his soldiers, overpowered by numbers, were about to retreat; but, although seriously wounded in the head and thigh, the gallant officer, borne by two men, succeeded in rallying his company and leading them on to the assault. His conduct was admirable, but his condition is hopeless. I have attached the cross to his breast. This brilliant feat of arms will enable me to enter Lang-Son to-morrow.—General Brière de L'Isle."

Upon reading these words, Mons. Sauvallier felt a strange emotion, in which anguish mingled with joy. For a moment he was silent; then he said to his son, "You think that it is he? He is, then, a captain?"

He read the despatch again, then murmured softly: "The cross! Condition hopeless!" And a tear rolled down his cheek.

Two hours later the family received a formal intimation of Camille's deed and state from the Minister of War, and on the following day all the journals were praising Captain Sauvallier, son of the respected founder, of Grenelle. And now they gave details. Camille, it appeared, had been nominated captain a few months back. Throughout the campaign he had distinguished himself by his imperturbable coolness under fire, and reckless scorn of the death which he seemed to seek.

His act of heroic energy stirred the enthusiasm of Press and populace, and the name of Sauvallier was on every lip. Camille's portrait appeared in the shop-windows; the illustrated journals depicted him before the redoubt, carried upon the shoulders of two men, his sword pointed towards the enemy, encouraging his soldiers by his voice, gesture, and look, his forehead bound with a handkerchief, and his face bleeding.

Mons. Sauvallier could not go out of doors without seeing his son's presentment. From the news-stalls of the boulevards, the corners of the streets, the publishers' shop-fronts, a ubiquitous Camille watched him pass, and seemed to follow him with his eyes.

Almost at each step the father received congratulations, while complimentary letters and cards covered his table to overflowing. But, alas! the telegrams which he received daily from Tonquin left him little hope that he should ever again behold in the flesh his dear son, of whom now he was so proud.

One morning, three months later, Mons. Sauvallier was at work in his office, when the door opened softly, and disclosed Andrée's curly head. The little one seemed in high spirits, her eyes sparkled with glee. "See, grandfather, here he is!" she said, and led into the room Captain Sauvallier.

Auguste and his wife followed the pair. Mons. Sauvallier, taken completely by surprise, rose quickly from his chair, then stood motionless, overcome by his emotion. He saw before him Camille, with the scar upon his forehead, and the cross upon his breast—Camille, the hero of the hour, who had shed such lustre upon the family name!

Timid and embarrassed, like a child who has been guilty of a fault, Camille stood with bowed head, and when he saw how much his father had aged, he knew that it was his conduct which had wrought the sad change, and his contrition was deepened tenfold.

But as he was about to throw himself at his father's feet, Mons. Sauvallier, with a sudden movement, clasped him to his breast, exclaiming, in a voice full of tears, "No, Camille! in my arms! in my arms!"

Father and son, locked together in closest embrace, mingled their sobs, while Auguste and his wife, looking on, wept in sympathy.

The silence was broken by Andrée. The child had vanished for a moment, but speedily reappeared, fondling her precious doll, which, it is needless to say, had not been sold. Holding it out to the captain, she said in her liveliest manner: "Here is Jéanne, uncle! You remember her? Give her a kiss directly! Don't you think that she has grown?"

LÉON HENNIQUE
B. 1852

THE VIVANDIERE

It was about seven o'clock in the morning, during the terrible time of the Commune, when a battalion of Chasseurs captured the barricade of the Rue des Tournelles.

The sky was clear and sunny, and the morning breeze freshened the air, driving away the smoke and small flames which rose from the burning houses. Above the reports of the rifles, a mitrailleuse flung out the incessant noise of its horrible projectiles; the air was full of the smell of powder, and at some distance away the dull monotonous roar of the cannon could be heard.

After a short rest from the fatigue of the attack, to give time for the ambulances to come up and for some of the wounded to receive attention, two companies took to searching the houses in the immediate neighbourhood of the barricade. The soldiers became gradually separated, and the sound of firing was heard here and there where resistance forced the troops to make their way by violence.

An officer and a few of his men entered a large house with a coat-of-arms over the great dark doorway. Musket in hand, with bayonet fixed, each looked about cautiously, opening all the windows and examining all the corners. Not a sign of life was to be seen anywhere, and the soldiers were just about to leave the house and enter a desolate courtyard full of brambles and weeds, when they caught sight of the figure of a girl, a vivandière, evidently belonging to the enemy's side, running along by the wall toward a sequestered and shady park, evidently hoping to hide from her pursuers among its grand old trees. The six muskets were immediately levelled, and the six bullets aimed at the fugitive crashed into a window past which she was running at the moment.

Perhaps the men were excited by her sudden appearance; perhaps they fired without taking proper aim, or the reflection of the sun in the windows of the courtyard dazzled them; in any case, all the bullets missed their mark and the girl redoubled her pace as they whistled past her.

The six men hastened after her, loading as they ran, and just as she was about to climb a wall, the officer fired a second time.

"Now we have her!" they all cried with savage glee.

Indeed, the poor soul was wounded. She tried to drag herself to the foot of the wall, as the soldiers approached to put an end to her.

She looked round to see all six muskets pointed at her breast, and cried out in broken accents, "Oh cruel men! Has none of you a mother? If you have mothers, you will not kill me like this!"

Pallid with suffering she faced her captors, and her words had their effect on the officer. Some touch of pity, and of the natural reluctance of man to slay a helpless woman, made him hesitate and lower his bayonet, while he said, as if for his own encouragement, "Well, what have you to say?"

"I have to say," she replied in a sharp tone of rage and anguish, "I have to say that I have a bullet in the shoulder, and I should like to know the wretch who shot me!"

The soldiers muttered angrily, but they could not help being affected by the sweet face of the woman before them. No stain showed from her wound as yet, and they stood a little behind their officer, wondering at her as she faced them.

Then one of them growled, "You had better keep a civil tongue in your head, my girl!"

The sound of rapid firing was heard in the neighbourhood.

"Well," the girl exclaimed, "what are you going to do with me? Are you going to kill me like those poor people in the street?"

The officer threw an inquiring glance at his men, as if to ask their advice. He felt strangely though vaguely attracted by the wounded girl; and was conscious of a wish to save her, not so much from pity, as because, if he saved her life and had her wound looked after, she might bring some interest and hope into his lonely life.

The vivandière now spoke appealingly. "Please take me to a shop, or some other place of safety," she said. "Don't be too cruel to me. Look, I have some brandy still in my flask. Will you have some?"

The officer made no reply, but stood as if in doubt what to do. Then one of the soldiers whispered, "I think we might let her off."

"Yes," he answered, rousing himself, "we will let her off."

The poor vivandière shed tears of gratitude, and insisted on kissing the hands of all the soldiers, sobbing, "Oh! Thank you so much!"

They took her out of the courtyard by lifting her over the walls, and managed to get her unobserved into the house of a charcoal burner, who was persuaded by a gratuity from the officer to give her his own bed, and to look after her. If she should chance to die, he was instructed to say that she was his sister, who had been consumptive for many years.

The wounded girl undressed and lay down. Once safe in bed her strength gave way, and she fainted. After bandaging her wound the charcoal burner left her for a while, to hide her flask in a safe place under his store of charcoal.

The soldiers returned to their search in the Rue des Tournelles, and found some of the enemy in the deserted houses, so that several sharp encounters ensued. The officer fought as well as any, but his thoughts were all the time with the girl he had saved and hidden. He had promised the charcoal burner a handsome reward for his care and secrecy. He was impatient to go and see her again. His anxiety lent vigour to his arm, and before the fighting ceased, he had driven out the opposing force and had gained a step in rank.

He could not leave his post, nor court suspicion by going to the house where the girl lay hidden. Indeed, he could get no news of her; but day or night, whether fighting under a hail of bullets or resting in barracks, he wondered what was happening to the wounded vivandière with the dark flashing eyes and coal-black hair. "Hallo, Fabiani," said one of his comrades one day, as they were coming out of mess, "you don't seem to be half the man you were. Have the Communists got on your nerves, or what is it?"

When the barricades of Paris were overthrown, Fabiani's battalion was quartered in the Château d'Eau. After a fortnight of peace and quiet living the young officer decided one morning to fulfil the promise he had made to the charcoal burner, and donning his smart new uniform he made his way to the Rue des Tournelles.

After walking for quarter of an hour he stopped at a fruit stall, and bought some apricots for the invalid girl. He hurried along until he came in sight of the dingy abode of the charcoal burner. He suddenly stood still, overcome by a dreadful thought. His heart almost stopped beating. "Was she still alive? What if her wound had been mortal?"

Even while he asked the question he felt that he must have it answered without delay, and he almost ran until he had entered the doorway where the charcoal burner was emptying a load of fuel.

"The young woman," he exclaimed, "is she better?"

"Ah, sir! Of course!"

He followed the man to the room where he had last seen her. She was still in bed, and the not very clean sheets made her pale face seem livid. But she brightened at the sight of the young officer and exclaimed, "What! You here?"

He answered almost timidly, overcome by a new emotion, "Yes, I have come. You know I wished to see if they had been taking care of you. Are you better?"

She answered in a weary voice, but without complaining, that she was much the same, but that the doctor had some hope of saving her.

As she told him in detail all that had been done for her and all that she had suffered, Fabiani realised that her case was hopeless, and that his longing to see her well and bright as she had been when he first saw her was never to be satisfied. He could never hope to be her friend, perhaps her lover, as he had dreamed.

She ate an apricot and began to speak of other things; asking for news of what was going on in the town; of what was happening to the Commune; who was killed; which troops were victorious; and so on. "The charcoal burner knows nothing, nothing at all. He never goes anywhere, and never asks his customers anything."

Her voice trembled and broke, and at last she burst out, as if unable to restrain herself any longer, "And Rochefort? Has he been killed? Has he been taken prisoner?"

Fabiani did not know. And as he could not help noticing that she had received some of his news with impatience, and did not seem even now to be very favourably disposed towards himself, he said, "You seem to be very fond of the Confederates. How is that?"

She did not reply, and he went on, "Tell me why you became a vivandière for that battalion."

The wounded girl began to weep, and then told him everything. She had followed the regiment in order to be near her lover, who had been killed by one of the first shots fired in the Rue des Tournelles. But her tears only aroused in Fabiani a violent hatred of his dead rival.

The charcoal burner brought in a couple of glasses of liqueur, and after drinking to the health of the wounded girl, Fabiani rose and handed to the man a note for fifty francs—all the money he had—and was about to take leave, when the girl asked him suddenly: "Do you know which was the wretch who shot me?"

The young officer blushed and said: "No, I do not know. But I can easily find out, as there were only six of us altogether. Why do you want to know?"

"I want to tell him what I think of him, how I shall hate him for ever!"

Fabiani went away without another word, feeling thoroughly depressed and miserable. When he was back in barracks he gave way to a violent fit of anger, and swore that he would never do anything more for this woman, who had caused him nothing but trouble and disappointment. His annoyance lasted all day, and he even lay down at night cursing the vivandière; but when he woke next morning, the weather was so fine and everything looked so radiant that he was unable to nurse his anger, and, almost without meaning it, he found himself on his way to the charcoal burner's house.

The girl was better, and as she was much more friendly that morning, he was glad he had come to see her. Every day, now, he went to the Rue des Tournelles.

Not wishing her to know how deeply she attracted him, he pretended that he went to see her only out of charity, because she was ill and alone. But he often felt disgust and weariness at the thought that he was trying to win the heart of the woman whom he had wounded so cruelly. From time to time she would ask him, " Have you ever been able to find out who was the monster who put the bullet in my shoulder? "

Now, however, he blushed no longer. Indeed, he began to be rather amused by the energy and persistence with which she plied him with the question, and he was always expecting it.

Her state of health did not improve; on the contrary, she was daily growing weaker. At last he did not conceal his personal interest in her, and after a month of long talks on indifferent subjects, he admitted his passion, and she promised to return it as soon as she should be out of danger.

Nevertheless, they could never agree as to the Communists. " A worthless lot," he called them, while she declared that they were a noble army of martyrs. So they would argue until at last their dispute was stilled by a rain of ardent kisses. For now they were acknowledged lovers, though each was inflexible in his and her political opinion.

So things went on, and might have gone on indefinitely, if Fabiani had not had the misfortune to drink too much wine one night, contrary to his usual custom. His comrades urged him to go back to barracks, as he should have done, until his brain grew clearer; but he broke away from them, and went to knock at his sweetheart's door.

She greeted him warmly, too warmly for his state of mind; for throwing prudence to the winds, he clasped her in his arms so ardently that all the old pain of her wound came back. As he strained her to his heart, forgetful of the doctor's insistence that she should be kept quiet, she returned his kisses, and both repeated their vows of eternal love and fidelity. At last, recalled by her suffering to her old idea, the girl drew back and asked: " Have you found out yet who it was that wounded me? "

Fabiani replied, laughing foolishly, " It was I myself. What do you say to that? "

As she recoiled with a look of horror, the soldier went on: " It was I and no other who shot you. More than that, I hope and believe that it was I too who shot your lover! "

His wild laughter only ceased when he sprang forward to catch the dying girl as she fell, and to hear her last sigh as she died in his arms without speaking another word.

ANONYMOUS
1854

CAPTAIN OBSTINATE

ONE fine evening in the month of July, an old soldier of the "grand army," who had left one of his arms on the field of battle, was seated at the door of his pretty cottage.

He was surrounded by a group of young villagers, who were clamorously reminding him of his promise to tell them some of his military adventures.

After a moment of pretended resistance to their wishes, the old man took his pipe from his mouth, passed the back of his remaining hand across his lips, and thus commenced his tale:

"In my time, my friends, the French would have disdained to fight against Frenchmen in the streets, as they do in these days. No, no, when we fought it was for the honour of France, and against her foreign enemies.

"But my story commences on the 6th of November, 1812, a short time after the battle of Wiazma. We beat a retreat, not before the Russians, for they were at a respectful distance from our camp, but before the sharp and bitter cold of their detestable country, a cold more terrible to us than the Russians, Austrians, and Bavarians all put together.

"During the preceding days our officers had told us that we were approaching Smolensko, where we should get food, fire, brandy, and shoes; but in the meantime we were perishing in the glaciers, and continually harassed by the Cossacks.

"We had marched for six hours without stopping to take breath, for we knew that repose was certain death. An icy wind blew the drifting snow in our faces, and from time to time we stumbled over the frozen corpse of a comrade. We neither spoke nor sang; even complaints were no longer heard, and that was a bad sign.

"I marched by the side of my captain; short, strongly built, rough, and severe, but brave and true as the blade of his sword; we called him 'Captain Obstinate'; for when once he said a thing, it was fixed; he never changed his opinions. He had been wounded at Wiazma, and his usually crimson face was then ghastly pale, while a ragged white handkerchief, all stained with blood, was bound round his head, and added to the pallor of his countenance.

"All at once I saw him stagger on his legs like a drunken man, then fall like a block to the ground.

"'*Morbleu!* Captain,' said I, bending over him, 'you cannot remain here.'

"'You see that I can, since I do it,' replied he, showing his legs.

"'Captain,' said I, 'you must not give way.' Lifting him in my arms, I tried to put him on his feet. He leaned on me, and attempted to walk, but in vain; he fell again, dragging me with him.

"'Jobin,' he said, 'all is over. Leave me here, and rejoin your company as quickly as possible. One word before you go: at Voreppe, near Grenoble, lives a good woman, eighty-two years of age, my—my mother. Go and see her, embrace her for me, and tell her that—that—tell her what you will, but give her this purse and my cross. It is all I have! Now go.'

"'Is that all, Captain?'

"'That is all. God bless you! Make haste. Adieu!' My friends, I do not know how it was, but I felt two tears roll down my cheeks.

"'No, Captain,' I cried, 'I will not leave you; either you come with me, or I will remain with you.'

"'I forbid you to remain.'

"'You may put me under arrest then if you like, but at present you must let me do as I please.'

"'You are an insolent fellow.'

"'Very good, Captain, but you must come with me.'

"He bit his lips with rage, but said no more.

"I lifted him, and carried him on my shoulders like a sack. You can easily imagine that with such a burden I could not keep pace with my comrades. In fact, I soon lost sight of their columns, and could discern nothing around me but the white and silent plain.

"I still walked on, when presently appeared a troop of Cossacks galloping toward me with furious gesticulations and wild cries.

"The captain was by this time completely insensible, and I resolved whatever it might cost me, not to abandon him. I laid him down on the ground, and covered him with snow; then I crept beneath a heap of dead bodies, leaving, however, my eyes at liberty.

"Presently the Cossacks came up and began to strike with their lances right and left, while their horses trampled us under their feet. One of these heavy beasts set his foot upon my right arm, and crushed it.

"My friends, I did not speak, I did not stir; I put my right hand into my mouth to stifle the cry of torture which nearly escaped from me, and in a few minutes the Cossacks had dispersed.

"When the last of them had disappeared, I quitted my refuge, and proceeded to disinter the captain. To my joy he gave some signs of life; I contrived to carry him with my one arm toward a rock which offered a sort of shelter, and then I laid myself by his side, wrapping my cloak round us both.

"The night had closed in, and the snow continued to fall.

"The rearguard had long since disappeared, and the only sound that broke the stillness of the night was the whistle of a bullet, or the howling of the wolves feasting on the corpses that lay stretched around.

"God knows what thoughts passed through my soul during that dreadful night, which, I felt sure, would be my last upon earth. But I remembered the prayer which my mother had taught me long before, when I was a child at her knee, and bending low, I repeated it with fervour.

"My children, that did me good, and remember always that a sincere and fervent prayer is sure to comfort you. I felt astonishingly calmed when I returned to my place by the captain. But the time passed, and I had fallen into a state of half stupor, when I saw a group of French officers approach. Before I had time to speak to them, their chief, a little man, dressed in a furred pelisse, stepped forward toward me, and said:

"'What are you doing here? Why are you away from your regiment?'

"'For two good reasons,' said I, pointing first to the captain, and then to my bleeding arm.

"'The man says true, sire,' said one of those who followed him; 'I saw him marching in the rear of his regiment, and carrying this officer on his back.'

"The Emperor—for, my friends, it was he!—gave me one of those glances that only he, or the eagle of the Alps, could give, and said, 'It is well. You have done very well.' Then opening his pelisse, he took the cross which decorated his green coat, and gave it to me. At that instant I was no longer hungry, no longer cold; I felt no more pain from my arm than if that awkward beast had never touched it.

"'Davoust,' added the Emperor, addressing the officer who had spoken to him, 'see this man and his captain placed in one of the baggage-waggons. Adieu!' And making me a motion of the hand, he went away."

Here the veteran ceased, and resumed his pipe.

"But tell us what became of 'Captain Obstinate,'" cried many impatient voices.

"The Captain recovered, and is now a general on the retired

list. But the best joke was, that as soon as he got well, he put me under arrest for fifteen days, as a punishment for my infraction of discipline.

"This circumstance came to the ears of Napoleon, and after laughing heartily, he not only caused me to be set free, but promoted me to the rank of sergeant. As to the decoration, my children, here is the ribbon at my button-hole, but the cross I wear next to my heart."

And opening his vest, he showed his eager audience the precious relic, suspended from his neck in a little satin bag.

PONTSEVREZ
B. 1854

THE INGENIOUS REPORTER

"YOU see, gentlemen, this office is American; this typewriter, near me, is American, as well as the stand that holds it; this system of electric lighting is imported from America; even the pens that we use are of American make, and I propose to deal with politics and with advertising in the American manner. Yes, gentlemen, the sole method of being original, to-day, in Parisian journalism, is to run a paper on the American plan! No articles of literary value! The public does not understand literature, and it becomes irritated when we offer it material that it cannot comprehend and could never have conceived. It wishes to be informed of facts, of positive facts, gentlemen, for the public is positive. At the same time it has nerves and sentiments, and upon them we must play. Each day bring me a sensational fact! Let us be Americans!"

A group of editors sat in a large and beautifully appointed office, listening to the directions which fell from the lips of the proprietor of the *Voice of the People,* the most up-to-date and best informed journal of the day—"Special telephone connection with all parts of the world!"—"Special telephone connection with all parts of the world!"—this assertion appeared and reappeared in all its advertisements.

And when the proprietor had voiced his sentiments, standing erect at the corner of his American desk, his elbow posed on the top, he smiled in self-approval. He was proud of his powers of oratory, and thought to himself, "Bonaparte, at the foot of the Pyramids, may possibly have been more laconic; he cannot have been more eloquent, for true eloquence is the power of putting truths convincingly."

A few days later, one of his most modest reporters, Gaston Longouy by name, sent in a request to see the proprietor on urgent business. Monsieur Longouy was a young fellow neither handsome nor ugly, neither tall nor short, neither fat nor thin, neither dark nor fair, neither clever nor stupid; in another office where he had worked previous to this, a colleague who passed as a wit nicknamed him " The Midway."

In the eyes of the American proprietor of the *Voice of the People*, Longouy had one great merit. It was he who, at the time of the massacre in Belgrade, had conceived these thrilling headlines, which so impressed the populace:

SENSATIONAL INTERVIEW WITH PRINCE KARAGEORGEVICH!

He Refuses to Say Anything.

" He is capable of exhibiting real American genius," said the proprietor.

Consequently, he prepared himself to listen with interest and curiosity to the communication of his reporter. Assuming what he considered a very American air—hurried, cold and brusque, he greeted the reporter with:

" Well, you idiot, let us have it at once! Nothing but facts, if you please! "

" Sir," replied the reporter, copying the manner as nearly as possible; " at the entrance of Courgeville, principal town of Oise-et-Somme, thirty-eight miles from Paris, near the railway station in a little wood, a crime has just been committed."

" Crimes are committed every day," observed the proprietor phlegmatically.

" But this is not an ordinary crime. We can find material in it for a great sensation which will keep the public stirred up for many days and increase the sale of your paper tenfold. It has points particularly favourable to a plan which I have conceived.

" And what is your plan? Let us get to the point! "

" The victim is naked and mutilated beyond the possibility of recognition; the hands, the feet and the head have disappeared. Up to now, it has been impossible to establish the identity. The only thing that can be definitely known is that it is a woman, probably a young one. There is not the faintest clue to the assassin, and the police either can't find him, or don't want to."

" And your idea? "

" I will go to Courgeville; I will act suspiciously. I will make compromising remarks, as though they escaped me accidentally. They will suspect me, arrest me, imprison me and put me on trial. I will allow myself to be taken for the murderer, and each day, thanks to a fee paid to my keeper, I shall send to the *Voice of the People* an article on the impressions of a man accused of murder, without allowing the mystery to be cleared up. And you can open a great contest in the paper—a hundred thousand francs in prizes to those who will guess whether I am guilty or innocent, giving sensible reasons for their conclusions. Of course, it is understood that the prize-winners will be a half-dozen of our own people who will undertake the work for a few dollars apiece. That is American enough, don't you think so? "

" Longouy," cried the proprietor, " you are an ingenious reporter! Go to your adventure. During your detention, prior to trial, the office will assume the expenses necessary for a private room and all the comforts that can be procured for you. Good luck to the scheme! "

Longouy was not an entire stranger to the country around Courgeville; he was in love with a young and pretty woman of the middle class, who had originally come from there.

The preceding summer she had passed several weeks in her native town and had permitted him to visit her there several times, all in the most honourable way. Her husband had deserted her two years before, and none knew where he was, or even whether he was living or dead; and she had promised Longouy to be his wife when either a decree of divorce or a certainty of widowhood should make her free.

Less than a day after his arrival the reporter carried out his plans so well that he was seized by two detectives and dragged before the justice of the peace, who had been summoned in great haste.

Longouy was so delighted at this speedy success that he appeared before the magistrate with a malicious smile on his lips. The only thing that was really important was to prevent the mistake being manifested too soon, so that he should not quickly be discharged and sent back to the duties of a commonplace reporter. Accordingly, he assumed before the justice the English attitude—that every man is innocent until he is proved guilty.

"Monsieur," said he, " I shall not attempt to clear myself. You accuse me, and it is for you to prove your accusation."

" Still," insinuated the judge, "you would aid me very much with your explanations, in discovering whether the accusations are true or false."

" Not an explanation! " said Longouy firmly. " When you have collected all your information and all your proofs, I shall see what I have to say. If you have accused me rightly, I shall have nothing to reply. But if you are unable to find sufficient evidence to convict me, I should be very clever, shouldn't I, to furnish you with it? "

" That is equivalent to a confession! " said the judge.

" Not in the least," returned Longouy. " It is a simple precaution. Often perfectly innocent people may be harassed and worried under the strain of an examination until they let fall a remark which may cost them their lives. I shall be silent."

For three consecutive days Longouy preserved a stubborn silence in the face of all questioning. During this time the inquest had been in progress.

The moment he glanced at the judge, on the fourth day, Longouy felt sure that something new had transpired. "The judge looks very much pleased," he thought. "He has discovered my trick and is going to discharge me. It is too soon! What a nuisance!"

"To-day, Longouy," began the judge, "speak or not, just as you please; it no longer matters. We have now all our information in regard to you, the proofs are ready and I am about to propose your transfer in the court of assizes."

The reporter contented himself with a smile.

"You see," continued the judge, "one point alone has been holding me back, and that is the identity of the victim. It is difficult to accuse a man of killing a person when you don't know who that person was."

"It must be," smiled Longouy.

"And the identity of the victim is now known to us for the first time."

"So much the better. Would you be willing to confide it to me?"

"Presently; first I want to describe to you exactly what passed."

"I am extremely anxious to know," replied Longouy, assured and convinced that, at any moment, he could knock over this elaborate structure of evidence with the simple declaration: "This is all a farce; I have never killed any one. If you don't believe me, ask the proprietor of the *Voice of the People*."

"The unfortunate woman who found death where she looked for love—a guilty love, for which she was cruelly punished——"

"Ah," interrupted Longouy, "it was her lover, then, who murdered her?"

"Yes, Longouy, her lover. She was murdered on the evening of the tenth of October."

"I thought it was the evening of the twelfth."

"The body was discovered on the twelfth. The crime had been committed forty-eight hours earlier."

"And how do you know all this?" asked the accused man in the light inconsequent tone of one who interests himself in a matter from pure dilettanteism.

"Because on the night of the tenth you disappeared secretly from Paris, and since that same night no one has ever seen the woman who was your victim. The coincidence is convincing, and is insurmountable."

Longouy seemed to be thinking of something that had not hitherto occurred to him. Suddenly the judge asked him:

"What did you do on the night of the tenth of October?"

Apparently the question embarrassed the accused man.

"I have nothing to reply," he answered, resorting to his former plan; "it is for you to tell me what you claim that I did."

"Very well," said the judge. "Listen! You started from Paris at seven o'clock in the evening and arrived at Courgeville at nine o'clock; returning you took an express for Paris at half-past eleven and reached there at one, but you did not get to your home until half-past seven in the morning."

"Who saw me take this trip? No one."

"Because you disguised yourself—probably made yourself up in some way—and this precaution proves your guilt. When a man travels honestly he doesn't care who sees and recognises him. Two hours and a half would have been quite sufficient for you to kill and dismember your victim, who left Paris by the same train as you."

"It is prodigious what the police can gather in the way of positive information," said Longouy sarcastically. The magistrate's narration seemed to him absolutely grotesque.

But suddenly his irony gave way to an almost overpowering anxiety; the judge had continued:

"If you did not return to your house until half-past seven in the morning it was because you decided, on leaving the train, to finish the night at the hotel near the station." There the judge named the hotel. "And why this manoeuvre? It was to create an alibi. During the preceding day you had telegraphed to this hotel, under an assumed name, and reserved a room. In the evening you took possession of this room, when you came in company with a woman—the woman who is now missing. At one o'clock in the morning you allowed yourself to be seen around the hotel, as you had allowed yourself to be seen four hours earlier. You thought that in the interval no one would have remarked your departure; and you could thus deny the journey to Courgeville. All that was very well conceived, but your expenditure of imagination comes back upon you as proof of your guilt. An innocent traveller who has no necessity for wishing to be thought elsewhere than where he is, does not take such pains to make his presence noticed at certain hours, in a hotel. Now give me your own account of how you employed your time on the night of the tenth of October."

Longouy had turned very pale; it was impossible for him to explain definitely his actions on the date in question. As a matter of fact, the information which the judge possessed was largely correct. It was true that he had reserved and occupied a room in the hotel the judge had named; true, also, that he had gone there with a companion and dined with her, and it was with the sole idea of avoiding a scandal that she had not wished to show herself with him in the public dining-room or in a restaurant. And this was precisely what he could not tell. His reputation as a man of honour also precluded his telling the name of his companion. It was that of the lady whom he had visited at Courgeville in the summer.

She had accorded him this meeting, the most innocent in the world, in order to talk over with him the increasing probabilities of their early marriage, but her prudence had made her hesitate either to go to his house or to receive him at hers. Hence the room at the hotel. Let this woman now come forward and say: " From eight o'clock till eleven o'clock, on the night of the tenth of October, Gaston Longouy was with me in a room of such and such a hotel," and the accusation against him would melt into air, but this was neither possible nor necessary. Would it not be all-sufficient for the reporter to pronounce the word which would terminate what he still regarded as a comedy? Nothing was needed but that he should confess the fantastic plan which he had made and carried through in order to advertise his paper. He was about to have recourse to this method of ending the affair, when the judge, noticing his emotion, delivered the blow which he had been preparing in order to overwhelm the man and force from him an avowal of his guilt.

" This woman whom you turned from the path of duty, this woman whom you led first to a hotel in Paris and then to Courgeville to assassinate her, is now known to us. We have discovered her name, her position, everything pertaining to her. In spite of the horrible state of mutilation in which she was found, she has been recognised as Madame Ballestin, née Henriette Cardevache, of Trumot-lès-Courgeville."

" Henriette! Madame Ballestin! " cried Longouy. " Impossible! Impossible! Henriette is not dead! "

" Come, no more of this comedy! You know that she is dead, since it was you who killed her! "

" Ah, no, no! There is some mistake! It is too frightful! To imagine that I—I who loved her—could be her assassin! Ah, your honour, I was only pretending to be a murderer—experience of a reporter, and that sort of thing. The proprietor of the *Voice of the People* knows all about it; I told him of my scheme and arranged it all with him."

" There, there, that will do! You may tell all this wonderful fable to the jury."

" But assure me, your honour, that it is not true. Madame Ballestin is not really dead! "

" There is her death-certificate, made out after her disappearance was established. Her relations and her friends have been able to identify the sad remains."

" But then," cried the unhappy reporter, " it was later that she was struck down, the poor unfortunate! Find out if she did not take the midnight train for Courgeville instead of returning to her home! "

The judge shrugged his shoulders.

The next day the *Voice of the People* was able to publish an exceptionally sensational interview with the supposed murderer of Madame Ballestin. The sale was enormous and the proprietor delighted. Rarely, even in America, had the press been able to put up a better " bluff."

" My friend, you hold some excellent trumps in this game," said Longouy's lawyer to him, before the opening of the case in the court of assizes. "The prosecuting attorney is unable to produce any material proof; his whole case is built upon moral presumptions alone. It is a little chain of suppositions; I shall blow upon it and it will fall to pieces. But do not attempt to repeat to the court and the jury your ridiculous tale of simulated guilt, or you will turn them all against you. After such a recital I should not answer for anything."

The ingenious reporter was not willing to give up.

" But it is the truth," he cried, " and, furthermore, it is this brilliant invention which is going to establish my reputation as a successful journalist on the American plan. But it is impossible to describe to you my sorrow! Henriette dead! And I adored her! I wish I could torture the miserable being who murdered her! "

No sooner had he announced, for his line of defence, the plan which he had elaborated with a view to furnishing such sensational reports for his paper than the presiding judge admonished him. " Don't attempt to play with the law," he said, " or you will be guilty of contempt of court."

" There, what did I tell you? " murmured his lawyer. " You will spoil the whole affair. You will prejudice the jury against you, and they will give you the maximum punishment."

On the judge's bench and all through the court-room could be noticed the same incredulity.

The proprietor of the *Voice of the People* was sent for, came, and testified according to Longouy's expectations.

" Now, you see! " cried the latter exultantly.

" Monsieur," said the prosecuting attorney to the proprietor, " is it possible that a man of your perspicacity, a man with an American penetration, did not immediately discern that his exceedingly ingenious reporter was laying a pitfall for you by his very candour, and with an infernal astuteness, a diabolical audacity, planned to commit his crime with impunity and to invalidate the proofs which might be brought against him, by simply saying, 'They are fictitious; it was I, myself, who voluntarily assumed these fetters and forged them in order to do a good turn for justice, and prove to the public how easy it is for magistrates to deceive themselves?' "

The genial proprietor was rather taken aback by this view of the case; nothing was farther from his wishes than to look like a man who could be easily duped, and in order to prove his insight he replied quickly, "Oh, yes, certainly! I saw at once that there was something suspicious about this artifice of Longouy's, but I said to myself, 'If he chooses to throw himself into the jaws of the wolf——' Pardon me, I meant no disrespect to the law by this metaphor!"

"That is all right, quite right. You may sit down now," said the prosecuting attorney.

In the court-room indignation against the accused man was increasing every moment. His perverse audacity only inflamed it the more.

"Heavens, what a scoundrel!"—"Ah! these journalists!"—"Capable of anything!"—"To have cut and hacked that poor Henriette!"—"You knew her, didn't you?"—"Such a little thing—nothing but a charming child!"—"What a miserable brute!"—"Oh, the wretch!"—"And the effrontery of this ruse, to pretend to be playing at being a criminal!"—"To think that it is possible to behead such a man only once!"—"Even if they do condemn him to death"—"Why, is there a chance of his not being condemned to death? He may escape the guillotine?"

At this idea the popular fury mounted higher and higher, ready to go to any lengths in order to administer justice.

The hearing was over, the prosecution and the defence were deferred until the next day. When Longouy, surrounded by four guards, crossed the prison-yard in order to re-enter his cell, an enormous crowd pressed around him, and suddenly a cry was heard: "Hang him!" Twenty cries, a hundred, a thousand, repeated, "Hang him, yes, hang him!"

A howling mob of men and women threw themselves on the guards, surrounded them, forced them apart, and seized the miserable Longouy. In an instant they had bound his hands and feet; a rope was put around his neck; a street-gamin of sixteen years climbed a lamp-post, drew up the rope and knotted it firmly; the rest loosed their hold of the unfortunate reporter, who now was left dangling in mid-air, his eyes protruding and his tongue hanging from his mouth.

"They have lynched him!" cried the proprietor of the *Voice of the People,* turning pale at the horrible sight. " Well, at least, *that* is quite American! "

. . . .

The next day a woman dressed in black presented herself before the district attorney of the province of Courgeville: " Monsieur," she said, " I am Madame Ballestin, and I was never murdered. Five weeks ago, on the night of the tenth of October, on entering my house a little after midnight I found a cablegram from my husband, calling me immediately to New York, where he lay ill. Without losing a moment, without telling any one—I had given my servant permission to go out, and she had not yet returned—I rushed to the Saint-Lazare station, leaped into a train for Havre, and sailed for America the next morning.

" On arriving in America I was informed of the death of my husband; as soon as the necessary formalities would permit, I sailed again, to return. Newly widowed, I freely offer my testimony to save the life of Monsieur Longouy."

" In the name of heaven, madame," cried the district attorney angrily, " why could you not have managed to arrive twenty-four hours earlier? You put a very unsavoury affair on our hands! "

Madame Ballestin fainted dead away on hearing that she was twice a widow, once actually, and again prospectively!

Who was the victim? And who was the assassin? Justice, that blind goddess, knows the answer to the riddle, but she will never reveal it.

ALPHONSE ALLAIS
1855–1905

THE TELEGRAPH OPERATOR

I STEPPED upon the platform at Baisenmoyen-Cert station, where my friend Lenfileur awaited me with his carriage.

While on the train I suddenly recollected something that required immediate attention at Paris. Upon my arrival at Baisenmoyen-Cert, I went to the telegraph office to send back a message.

This station differed from others of its class because of the total lack of writing materials.

After a prolonged exploration, I finally succeeded in capturing a rusty pen, and dipping it in some colourless, slimy fluid. With heroic effort I succeeded in daubing down the few words of my telegram. A decidedly unprepossessing woman grudgingly took the despatch, counted it, and named the rate, which I immediately paid.

With the relieved conscience of having fulfilled a duty, I was about to walk out when my attention was attracted by a young lady at one of the tables manipulating a Morse key. With slight hauteur she turned her back towards me.

Was she young? Probably. She certainly was red-haired. Was she pretty? Why not? Her simple black dress displayed advantageously a round, agreeable form; her luxuriant hair was arranged so as to reveal a few ringlets and a splendid white neck. And suddenly a mad, inexplicable desire to plant a kiss upon those golden ringlets seized me. In the expectation that the young lady would turn round, I stopped and asked the elderly woman a few questions anent telegraph affairs. Her replies were not at all friendly.

The other woman, however, did not stir.

Whoever supposes that I did not go to the telegraph office the next morning does not know me.

The pretty, red-haired one was alone this time.

Now she was compelled to show her face, and, *Sapristi!* I could not complain.

I purchased some telegraph stamps, wrote several messages,

asked a number of nonsensical questions, and played the part of an ass with amazing fidelity.

She responded calmly, prudently, in the manner of a clever, self-possessed, and polite little woman.

And I came daily, sometimes twice a day, for I knew when she would be alone.

To give my calls a reasonable appearance I wrote innumerable letters to friends and telegraphed to an army of bare acquaintances a lot of impossible stuff. So that it was rumoured in Paris that I had suddenly become deranged.

Every day I said to myself, " To-day, my boy, you must make a declaration." But her cold manner suppressed upon my lips the words, " Mademoiselle, I love you."

I invariably confined myself to stammering:

" Be kind enough to give me a three-sou stamp."

The situation gradually became unbearable.

As the day for my return approached, I resolved to burn my ships behind me and to venture all to win everything.

I walked into the office and wrote the following message:

" Coquelin, Cadet, 17 Boulevard Haussmann, Paris: I am madly in love with the little red-haired telegraph operator at Baisenmoyen-Cert."

I tremblingly handed her the telegram.

I expected, at least, that her beautiful white complexion would effulge.

But no!

Not a muscle relaxed! In the calmest manner in the world she said, " Fifty-nine centimes, please."

Thoroughly nonplussed by this queenly serenity, I fumbled about in my pockets for the coin.

But I could not find a sou. From my pocket-book I took a thousand-franc note and gave it her.

She took the note and scrutinised it carefully.

The examination terminated favourably, for her face was suddenly wreathed in smiles, and she burst into a charming ripple of infectious laughter, displaying her marvellously handsome teeth.

And then the pretty young mademoiselle asked in Parisian cadence, the cadence of the Ninth Arrondissement,[1] " Do you want the change? "

[1] Paris is divided into twenty Arrondissements, or boroughs, each having its own mayor and borough hall; the 9th Arrondissement including part of the Grand Boulevards and the Opera House.

GEORGES DE LYS
B. 1855

THE ORDERLY

THE French had been driven from the park and were streaming across the level plain. They had held the position for two hours, standing stubbornly against all attacks, but had been forced to give way at last under a rush of fresh troops. Now all order was broken and they were scattering like whirling leaves swept by the wind.

A thin column of smoke was vanishing from the abandoned wall; other columns, still nearer, dragged along the ground and obscured the top of the walls here and there. The steady whistling of bullets had succeeded to the first scattering shots.

A grove stood in the midst of the bare fields, and the fleeing soldiers sought its shelter with mad, reckless dashes in which many fell, mortally wounded; those who survived rushed on in a still more reckless retreat.

Captain Revordy, hurried along with the others, did not waste his strength in struggling against the irresistible torrent. Every effort was strained to bring together the scattered soldiers, and he succeeded in placing himself boldly at the head of the retreat, in leading it to the friendly shelter of the trees, and in making a stand there where others might rally.

The soldiers reached the spot worn out, with hot throats, their heads throbbing from the tumultuous rush of blood. As soon as they reached the edge of the grove they threw themselves into the nearest thicket, keeping close to the ground and crawling along the hollows of the ditches. With shouts and gestures Revordy summoned the officers, and aided by a few brave men, he held back the rout, formed the ranks, assigned each one to his place, and prepared to make the last stand, the last defence.

A sergeant whispered something of importance in his ear; the cartridge-boxes were nearly all empty. The captain then gave the order: " Let no one fire until I give command! "

That calm voice aroused new courage in the men, for he breathed his own courage and energy into them. The captain was a short, thick-set man, with strong limbs. His face was burned by his many campaigns, for Revordy had fought from the Crimea to Mexico, and there was the dull red hue of copper under the brown tan, while from this glowing face blazed out a pair of large, clear, prominent eyes.

Some one shouted, " Here they are! " The enemy had formed under the shelter of the walls, and the defeated soldiers noticed that they were preparing for a new attack. The Germans drew closely together at the hoarse commands of their captains; then the line shook and moved forward.

Revordy watched the approaching enemy. They were moving straight toward the little silent wood, where there was no sound save the tense breathing of his men. They were scarcely three hundred yards from the first trees, advancing in dark, straight lines, making an easy target; then the captain gave the command, " Fire! " The edge of the grove seemed to burst out into sudden flame as it poured forth its volleys; then all was lost in smoke. But their ears told them what their eyes failed to see; they heard the hoarse shrieks and groans of the dying; then the frightened trampings of a disorderly retreat shook the frozen ground, growing more and more distant, until they ceased.

Then Revordy thundered out, " Stop firing! " The smoke passed away, entangling its spiral whiteness in the branches of the trees, and when it had grown clear they saw only a heap of brown bodies lying in furrows; the enemy had retreated to the park, and was already under cover of its walls. Other troops attacked them on the flank, and Revordy strengthened the position of his little company, grouping the squads about the sides. Then, encouraged by the support of the struggling companies who were gaining ground, the first assailants decided to risk another attack from the front. The volleys again made fearful havoc in the ranks; they wavered an instant, but the empty places were filled and the advance continued, for the men were encouraged, carried along by the enthusiasm of the German captain at the head of the line. But suddenly there was confusion. The chief had fallen, and the enemy had lost the soul which animated it.

" That's what you can call a true weapon! " shouted a proud voice. Revordy turned around and recognised his orderly:

" What! Did you do it, Fréchou? "

" Sure, Captain. I tell you that this primer can be depended upon! "

The officer smiled at the soldier, and the same thrill of pride warmed their hearts, united by a common danger and the love of a common cause.

Revordy's attention was soon turned to a new danger. On the left the enemy was invading the little grove and threatening to cut off the retreat. The firing was growing less frequent. Gloomy men were looking with desperate faces in their empty cartridge-boxes.

The captain shouted, " Bayonets to the cannon's mouth! " The soldiers rose, for they understood him. " Comrades, we must pass over the bodies of those men! Forward! "

Revordy raised his sword, and his soldiers advanced against the threatening wing. The brave captain staggered and fell with a bullet in his stomach. The impulse, however, had been given; the Frenchmen jostled, fell over, sprawled through the living lines of human breasts, until they had crossed the last one.

The Germans stopped to rest in the position they had so dearly purchased. Far off in the distance, the little company which survived their last volley was disappearing, while a few French stragglers were rallying about it. Suddenly they noticed that one of these isolated forms was growing larger, that it was approaching them, and making straight for the little grove. Soon the figure was clearly outlined, and the astonished victors saw that it wore the uniform of a French soldier.

In the meantime the major had collected the remnant of his battalion. When he saw the man approaching he gave orders to allow him to come past the range of their rifles—to capture him without injury. Soon they realised that the soldier was without arms, that he was advancing with a brisk step, a calm countenance, and with his head held high.

At the enemy's first challenge he answered simply:

" My captain."

The major had him brought before him and questioned him:

" Who are you? "

" Fréchou, Jacques Fréchou, soldier of the third regiment, Captain Revordy's orderly."

" What do you want? "

" My captain, who fell when we charged."

" What! You escaped, and have come back to us again? "

" The captain ordered us to force our way through your troops. We obeyed his order. I am his orderly. It is my duty to take care of him if he is sick, or to bury him if he is dead."

The Prussian looked at the man with a kindly eye: " Your captain is not dead. We have brought him in from the field, and you may take care of him. Müller, take this man to the French captain! "

Fréchou bowed low: " Thanks, Major. There's the making of a Frenchman in you! "

The major smiled and said nothing.

. . . .

The bullet which had struck down Captain Revordy had just

been extracted. Exhausted by the operation, crushed by the defeat, he lay with closed eyes, realising in the bitterness of his soul that he was vanquished, powerless, and a prisoner. Must he die here among the enemy without one word of farewell to those whom he loved?

"Captain!" The words sounded like a carol of joy in the ears of the wounded officer; he opened his eyes and saw his faithful orderly standing by his side.

"Is it you, Fréchou?" Then his happy cry of recognition was stifled by a sudden sadness: "They have captured you, too."

The soldier drew himself up: "Not a bit of it, Captain! We stepped right through them, just as you ordered. Sergeant Rastaire led the others back to the battalion. When I saw everything was all right, I came back to you."

The officer held out his hand: "Thanks, my brave comrade." Fréchou took it, overcome by his emotion. After a while he continued: "The Prussian commander—a decent sort of a fellow, if he *is* a Prussian—has given me the right to care for you. You will soon be cured now."

Revordy closed his eyes: "Cured! Yes, and for ever. Well, at any rate I shall not die alone."

"You must not talk like that," murmured the orderly, trying to keep down his own grief.

"Yes, my friend, I ought to talk about it. My wound is fatal. To-morrow you will bury me. Let my cross remain on my breast, and keep my pocket-book for old time's sake. Come, now, there isn't much in it!" he said, as Fréchou made a gesture of refusal. "I shall sleep on French soil, but it is still covered by the enemy! Oh, the cruellest part, Fréchou, of it all is that I can no longer help to chase them out of it!"

Revordy became silent, a mist swam before his eyes, and his mind began to wander. When he felt the end near he murmured, "Your hand, Fréchou!" He died, soothed by the brave, faithful grasp of his comrade's hand.

. . . . . .

Fréchou bought various pieces of cloth, red, white, and blue, with the money he found in Revordy's pocket-book. In rough soldier fashion, he sewed these strips together, so that the captain's winding-sheet was a flag. An armed German company attended his funeral and paid the last military honours to this officer who had died for his country. Fréchou followed the bier, upon which lay the worn, shabby coat whose gilt was all tarnished, and the soldier's cap, faded by the rain and the mud. Fréchou walked erect in his French uniform, trying to conceal his grief from the enemy's curious glances.

After the ceremony was over the major sent for Fréchou.

"My lad," he said, "I shall not take advantage of your noble spirit of devotion in coming here. You are now free to go when you please." At the same time he presented the French soldier with a safe-conduct.

"Thanks, Major," answered Fréchou, as he made him the proper military salute.

In a few moments he was on his way back to the French camp. Thanks to his safe-conduct, he passed through the enemy's lines without any difficulty, and once outside those lines he hurried on in his eagerness to join his regiment. On the way he thought of his captain whose body was lying yonder in the midst of the enemy. Oh, how gladly he would fight from now on to regain that bit of territory!

Then his mind dwelt on the German major. He was puzzled at the generosity of this Prussian. Could it be true that this officer had sent him back free, without one condition? That German was certainly a fine fellow! Fréchou had kept his safe-conduct in his hand all the time, and his curiosity was aroused to learn the name of this man who was so different from the other eaters of *sauerkraut*. He opened it and read the name, "Marchal."

The name astonished him. It was not German, and aroused none of the bitter hatred with which anything Teutonic filled the Frenchman. Who could this man be, commanding the troops of the enemy and yet bearing a French name?

And more than his name was French; there was something that had made the orderly, entirely ignorant of that distant Revocation of the Edict of Nantes, which drove so many staunch French Huguenots to other lands, utter the cry which the major had answered with a smile:

"There's the making of a Frenchman in you!"

JEAN REIBRACH
B. 1855

UNCLE TOM

THE excellent Simonnot couple were taken altogether by surprise when they heard one morning that Uncle Tom had just died, leaving them all his fortune. Their memories of Uncle Tom were so vague that they had to run over in their minds all their relatives before they could fix on the one who had brought himself to their notice in such an astonishing way.

When the first impression had passed off, husband and wife looked at one another and shook their heads. The husband's face expressed contempt as he said:

" It's a wretched little legacy; but still we must admit that we have got something without any trouble. Supposing it is only a few pounds, it will at least help us to paint the shop-front, to get the lamps in the warehouse mended, and to carry out the other repairs we have so often talked of."

By degrees Madame Simonnot's recollections began to grow clearer. She remembered Uncle Tom, who lived like a bear in his den, far away from all his relatives, who spoke of him with the greatest contempt. She counted the years back, and concluded that he must have been at least eighty when he died.

" I don't suppose the business of rag-dealer," she said at last, " can bring in very much money, but in spite of everything, if he worked all his life and did not spend much—well, you know how much those people save who have not to keep up appearances."

" Well, anyhow," replied the husband, " I can't help feeling amused at the idea of his leaving us all his ' fortun.' "

The wife went on calculating. " Let us suppose that it amounts to——"

After thinking hard for a moment, she said, not without some hesitation, as if fearing to mention such an immense sum, " A couple of hundred pounds, perhaps."

The husband shrugged his shoulders, but was deep in thought for a while, then began to smile and said cheerfully:

" Well, my dear, no one ever loses by being given something, anyhow. And if the old man was so miserly as you say——"

"Miserly he must have been, for he never seemed to have a single farthing."

"Well, in that case he may have left a good deal more than you think. Those eccentric old men have their own ways of saving money, and one never knows what they have hidden away. Indeed——"

He spoke so seriously and looked so wise that his wife was impressed. As he continued meditating, she said at last, "Do you really think, then that the old Uncle——?"

However, he would not answer definitely, but said, shaking his head like a wise parrot, "No, I cannot make a proper guess, but in any case one may hope for something. Do you remember what I read out of the evening paper to you the other day about an old rag-dealer, just like your Uncle Tom, finding twelve silver dishes in a lot of old rubbish which he was asked to clear away?"

Husband and wife looked at each other, and the gleam of untold gold seemed to sparkle in the eyes of both.

"Oh," said Madame Simonnot at last, "I am quite anxious to know the truth. Supposing the poor old man should have left a thousand pounds or so!"

"Well, why not? Those misers know how to get a good deal of money together."

Next morning Monsieur Simonnot woke his wife up very early and said, "Just listen. I remember having read in some newspaper, about a year ago, that an old rag-dealer had died leaving about a thousand pounds sewn up in an old mattress. Yes, a whole thousand pounds, all in gold."

Uncle Tom's humble calling had already begun to appear a respectable and interesting profession to the worthy couple.

"No one knows," went on Monsieur Simonnot, "what these rag-dealers can do. They find all sorts of things in the course of their trade: jewellery, purses full of money, pocket-books stuffed with notes, and all imaginable things which other people have forgotten."

However, he did not want his wife to think him a visionary or a crazy dreamer, so he added firmly, so as at least to appear sensible, "I expect we may count on getting eight hundred or a thousand pounds. We may be sure of so much. You will see I am right."

Pleased with the prospect of getting maybe a thousand pounds, they kept to this figure, and amused themselves by speculating as to what they would find the best way of using the money. First of all, their watchmaker's shop would be the better for being refitted and improved generally. They discussed all the details of this, and the thousand pounds or so on which they had agreed to count seemed a mine of inexhaustible wealth.

At the same time, the poor old Uncle began to assume a new importance in their eyes, and they sang his praises in the intervals of making suggestions and calculations. Their own laborious past began to fade away, and with it it carried away into the mists of forgetfulness the dingy past of the neglected poor relation.

" I am *so* sorry," said the wife; " we have not even got a portrait of him."

" No, indeed, and he was the best of the whole family," replied the husband.

For some days the watchmaker and his wife never sat down to a meal without murmuring, " Poor dear Uncle! If only we could have him with us now! "

" Yes, poor old man. How happy he would be to live with us."

They pictured the good old man working for them, saving that they might have plenty, living humbly and carefully amid privations and trials, so as to be able to leave them all he could gather together; and the thought of this was a new bond between them. The husband found himself growing daily more loving towards his wife. They often sat hand in hand like lovers, while they built castles in the air on the basis of the coming fortune.

When the shop was closed and they sat down to their evening meal, the wife's eyes would fill with tears as her husband raised his glass and said solemnly, " To the memory of poor dear Uncle Tom."

But Simonnot began now to make new calculations, for it seemed that eight hundred or even a thousand pounds would not go so very far after all. It would really be necessary for them to be exceedingly careful, and to treat this legacy only as a foundation on which they might build their future fortune.

Sometimes the wife spoke of giving up their small shop and taking a finer one in a fashionable part of the town. Then the husband would say, " My dear, my dear, we must keep within our means, you know! "

To this she would answer, " Well, but after all, why should he not have left us a thousand pounds at least? "

The watchmaker did not want to appear too sanguine, so he would shake his head and say nothing, but in his inmost thoughts he would repeat his wife's words, " Why should not he have left us a thousand pounds at least? "

And he would say aloud, " No doubt of one thing, he was a good old fellow, at any rate. One of the best of men! "

In the imagination of the excellent couple, never did a rag-dealer live fit to be compared to their lamented Uncle Tom.

. . . .

At last the eventful day came, which had been fixed by the lawyer for opening the will, and Monsieur and Madame Simonnot learned that Uncle Tom had left them eleven hundred pounds.

Both were taken aback, and when they got home the husband burst out, " What do you think of that? Eleven hundred pounds! What could we do with such a miserable sum? "

The wife sat down in silence, too dejected to reply, and the man, standing before her, and banging his hands together to give force to his words, went on: " Eleven hundred pounds, indeed! A man who could go about picking up jewellery and purses full of money all day long! A man who could live on so little, who had no appearances to keep up, who really wanted nothing at all for himself! What on earth did he do with his money? I am sure now that he was a worthless old rascal, drinking and loafing, instead of working and saving money for those who had a right to expect it from him. Oh, there is no doubt of it whatever! Your Uncle was a wretched old good-for-nothing. If you don't mind my saying so, darling; if your old waster of an Uncle were alive now, I would go and ram his miserable eleven hundred pounds down his wicked old throat."

After a pause he went on: " Yes, and I don't mind saying more than that. Not one of your whole family is any good. Except yourself, of course. All the rest are well known to be a bad lot. You must admit that your Uncle Tom behaved atrociously to us, and he must have been eighty at least. My dear girl, if a man has any decency at all, he does not go as your Uncle did. We owe something to our relatives in this world, even if we cannot make ourselves respected. Don't you agree with me? "

" Yes," replied the wife reluctantly. " I'm afraid it is true. And you know well that I never could bear the thought of that old vampire Uncle Tom."

" Well, it is very unfortunate, but the fact is that we have no remedy but resignation. We have both been the victims of a most vile piece of trickery at the hands of that wicked old wretch."

. . . .

The end of it all was that the Simonnot couple received their legacy with resignation, if not with satisfaction. They left their house and took a better shop in a fashionable street, where they made more than twice as much money as they had done formerly. They never mentioned the name of the wicked old Uncle at home, but they always thought of him with feelings of hatred and contempt. And when Simonnot closed his shop after a busy day and went to take a glass and play a game of cards with his friends in the café, he used to tell them how much better off he and his wife would have been if it had not been for that wretched old Uncle Tom, who had robbed them of the money which should have been theirs, and spent it all on drink and evil living.

PAUL HERVIEU
1857–1915

THE BULL OF JOUVET

I

On the Grande Côte, where no trees are able to grow, Hugues Barros keeps two hundred sheep, a quarter of which belongs to him.

It is already three months from Easter since he led his flock to the high, scattered pastures, that he has rented for the season, between the Mont des Archets, Combelouve, and the Lake of Jouvet.

To-day he is waiting for his weekly provisions—his store is exhausted—and he is hungry. In front of him the mass of his flock moves slowly; and a few brown fleeces creep in among the backs of white wool. Hugues Barros stands upright, leaning his long body on a thick branch of holly wood, the bark of which he has ringed with his knife. His broad shoulders are covered by an ample soldier's cloak that he bought last winter from one of those men who hawk goods from door to door and set up a stall at the fairs. When the keen wind shortens this good wrap of cloth, by blowing it into the small of his back, there can be seen the end of his breeches of chestnut velvet, screwed into gaiters of stout leather. The hard, rough face of the shepherd is sheltered by the wide brim of a felt hat, rusted by the sun, streaked by dust and rain.

Hugues frequently looks at the sky to see what the time is, and gets impatient, for hunger is gnawing at his bowels. At last his two dogs come growling to him, their pointed ears standing up. He shades his eyes with his callous hand, and he recognises his wife climbing slowly up the coombs of Lant Gelé. She carries a roomy basket in her left arm, and with her right hand she drags after her a lean bull with short legs, one horn broken and the other flat and black to the tip. At moments, by a simple backward movement of the head, the powerful beast stops the woman, and licks his dark flanks with his violet tongue.

"Aren't you ever coming?" cries the shepherd.

But his wife, her throat tightened by the high climb, does not reply.

"What are you bringing me there?" he goes on. "Where have you got that beast from?"

When his wife comes up to him on the height, she hastens to reply in a panting voice:

"It is this bull that has made me late. You must keep it for Tayot, until this heat is past. He won't stay either in the field or in the stable."

"How much will Tayot give me for my trouble?"

"He said to me that you could arrange it together, like."

"Na! Na! You tell him I want not less than twenty sous a week. I have to pay here ninety francs in rent!"

"I will tell him."

While the wife is unpacking her basket, her husband goes to his stone hut to get a stake and a mallet; some yards away he ropes the bull to the ground, and the beast looks at him with quiet, sly eyes.

When Hugues comes back and squats against a mound, he has the pleasure of looking over his provisions, spread out on the bald earth where the wind waves the rare tufts of grass. Very good! This time the loaf of bread is of the right size, and the blue cheese of cows' and goats' milk is also perfect. . . . And the bacon? Where the devil is it? Has it been forgotten? These blessed women! . . . But patience! His wife smiles! Here is the bacon and the salt pork, tobacco, and a couple of quarts of country wine that will give a sharp flavour to the raw spring water.

Without delay the shepherd appeases his appetite, and talks with his mouth full. Are the children all right? The eldest has begun his tricks. Yes, he is promising, but beware of the girls! And father? Won't he still have that gland taken out of his throat? He will be suffocated one of these fine mornings; but there, it will not be for want of good advice! Ah! the rural guard is going to summon Joseph Mabre about his geese! It was high time! And that gunpowder which the carter was going to bring from Albertville, when is it coming? For since last evening a couple of vultures have been sweeping around the Grand Rey, where a lamb had fallen. . . .

Hugues Barros finishes his frugal meal. He pulls out the wooden cork from the leather gourd that he carries over his shoulder. He lifts with both hands the goat's skin, and, pressing it, squirts on to his tongue a thin, cool jet of drink. Then, twirling his moustaches he leans over his wife and gives her, without having to hide it from anybody, a hearty natural kiss.

II

While the wife, lightened of her burden, goes down, light and firm of foot, the slopes that lead to the village of Longefoy, her husband, stretched out on his stomach and satisfied, puffs at his black pipe and sends out thick clouds of smoke. For another week he will not see a human figure. . . . Who cares! Under his half-closed eyelids he sees, in the valley of Aime, the twinkling waters of the Isère, cutting like a bright blade through woods and rocks. The houses of Centron, planted in the heart of the old forest, seem to him like yellow butterflies in a briar hedge; and the vines of Bellentre, in the distance, give a green tint to the earth like a low carpet of moss. Turning his face on the pillow of his arms, he distinguishes, at the bottom of the other slope, the green lakes of the valley of Tignes, that appear but little cattle ponds, with the waterfalls curling into them like the manes of white-haired horses. At last he grows drowsy with the sleep of noon, heavy and dreamless. . . .

Suddenly he is awakened by the barking of his dogs. The bull by a violent effort has pulled out the stake and drags it about, spreading panic among the pregnant ewes and the rams.

"On to the bull! Hss! Go for him!" Barros cries, with angry gestures.

But his dogs, unused to this work, howl on their haunches and refuse to attack.

"Wait, old broken horn, wait! I will settle you!" says the shepherd, stalking towards the bull.

The beast faces him boldly, lowering his threatening and mutilated head, but Barros strikes him across the muzzle with the mallet, and then, as the animal turns away bellowing, seizes the rope. With the other hand he drives the stake deeply into the ground, and picking up heavy bits of rock, he places them all along the rope till the nostrils of the beast are bent down to the soil.

"Fast a little," he says, "that will quieten you!" And he beats him on the back with his holly stick. Then he leads his flock towards a new pasture. As the hungry sheep spread out, they bite at the short roots of the exhausted grass; and, worried along by the dogs, their cloven feet break down the red and blue flowers of foxgloves, aconite, and the other unwholesome plants, which, in spite of their hunger, they have not bitten.

At the approach of twilight, Hugues returns with his sheep, which he pens, as they leap one over the other, between a gigantic rock and some hurdles. But the bull has again found a way of feeding himself, and he roves below, sniffing the wind, bellowing at regular intervals, and whipping his flanks with the lash of hairs at the end of the supple tail. The shepherd, stupefied, growls between his teeth:

"Ah! You are asking for it, you carcass, and you shall have it!"

He runs down, his gourd dangling from his neck by the strap.

The bull, waiting for him with a stubborn air, digs at the earth with his hoofs and throws it up in clods. Then, as the struggle is about to begin, the beast rolls his cunning eye and with a side spring dashes off by the valley of Armene. Hugues Barros pursues him in an angry chase across slopes of rock, patches of snow, screes of loose stones, and mountain torrents.

Close to the ruined farm of the Blancs the man succeeds in catching up with the brute. He tries to seize it from behind by the horns, and bring it down, as he had learnt to do, by a twist of the neck. But on one side his hand only meets with a stump and an ear. Yet he hangs there, kicking with his iron-shod boots at the shins of his adversary. The beast, however, by the advantage of his absent horn, escapes, and bounds away into the darkness that has swung up from the plains. Barros, who has rolled into a bog, gets up swearing. His palms and knees are skinned and bleeding and smarting. He finds his way through the gloom, and discovers in the last faint gleam of daylight the plateau on which his hut is perched. He painfully climbs up the Grande Côte, but just as he gets out on to it, the sound of something galloping behind him fills him with anxiety.

Something, darker than the shadows around him, rushes upon him. And, without even having the time to cry out, he is thrown down, senseless, his chest pierced by the single horn of the bull.

III

When he comes to, the round moon floats in the sky. Her fine, humid radiance washes on the surrounding amphitheatre of glaciers; and from the Col du Soufre as far as Mont Pourri the surface of snow shines as though a flora of sparks had blossomed out on the sheets of crystals.

Hugues Barros feels very cold. He tries to get up; but at this movement, an atrocious pain stabs him in the hollow of his stomach; and when he puts his hand there, it comes away all sticky, and, as far as he can see, covered with something red. Then he remembers what has happened. He gives a sigh that ends in a groan. He feels he is struck to the depths, and there comes to him in his loneliness a fear that he has never known before. A fever shakes his body and disturbs his vision. In front Mont Blanc seems to him to rise up to the moon, and on its flanks the Allée Blanche and the Glacier des Glaciers are dancing. He shouts madly. His broken voice, that frightens him, falls into the wilderness and the universal silence. The sheep are sleeping, and the dogs.

Slowly the night passes and scatters before the dawn. The sun surges up under his triumphal arch in supernatural colours of golden blues, red pearl tints and fiery greys. Dazzled with light, Barros tries by a side look to satisfy his terrified curiosity in regard to his wound. He suffers from a horrible pain. His resource is to press his fists over the gaping flesh, and the strength he thus spends relieves him for the moment. His blood, clotted on the grass, sparkles like the white frost around it. A dire thirst consumes him, but he cannot get his gourd, which has fallen under his back.

However, the dogs, surprised by his unusual lateness, begin to bark in chorus, and the hungry sheep, breaking through the light hurdles, scatter in a bleating crowd on the fresh grass. Very soon the flock will be no more than an imperceptible point fading away towards the Frasses.

Then the shepherd hears, a little way off, the bull heavily breathing in harsh sobs of ruttish passion. He is not alarmed by the return of the beast. On the contrary, he wishes the brute would rush on him again, and finish him. Without that, how long is it going to take him to die, twisting himself about in the agony of the damned?

But suddenly he is possessed by a new anxiety. Something is happening below. . . . A band of persons alight from their mules, and climb on foot the final cone of the Jouvet—four men and two women in bright dresses. Barros can clearly see their silhouettes outlined against the vacant air, with their arms directing their glasses towards the large features of the landscape. He is exasperated that they do not study his plateau, and he pities himself, while the immeasurably long shadows of these people, who had almost found him, retreat and vanish.

He implores them feebly with gesture and voice. But all in vain. The tourists depart without having seen him, and only the bull replies to his complaints by mournful lowings.

"Split them open too, then, you brute," he murmurs.

He reflects on the misfortune that has overtaken him. He has never been lucky. . . . Yet he has nothing to reproach himself with. . . . And the circumstances of his life defile before his mind. He especially remembers the time when they stopped him from remaining in the army, and the time when his three little ones were born. . . . He recalls the tranquil face of a neighbour whom he saw giving up the ghost with his relatives around him.

The day wears on; the sun clouds over. Thick mists enter France by their usual path of the Little Saint Bernard, where they condense; and, sliding quickly along, they arrive at the Grande Côte, and there they begin their interminable procession to the hymns of the wind.

Hugues Barros can no longer distinguish anything on earth. A slight froth rises from the corners of his lips; continual spasms shake his limbs. By a supreme effort he raises himself gradually to a sitting position.

And thus he dies, with vague eyes, like a man awaking.

THE SECRET OF THE LOWER GLACIER

PAUL HERVIEU

I

THE mysterious disappearance of Rudolph Schuchmann of Frankfort had caused a vast amount of excitement in the district of Grindelwald, where the banker was well known and liked on account of his wealth and sterling qualities.

For three years past he had come to spend the month of July in the "Grand Moine" boarding-house, where he was playfully known as Herr Schuch, an abbreviation of his full name.

Around the Scheideck district some accounted for his disappearance by the theory of crime, while others thought that he must have met with an accident. The inquiry was formally held on the 2nd of August, 1809, and a crowd collected round the Town Hall.

The party of guides were brought into court and sat in a row on the benches set apart for them. They were all young and hardy, inured by daily experience to all kinds of danger and anxiety, so that outwardly they seemed calm even to callousness. But their feelings found relief in the unconscious movements of their fingers, turning their hats mechanically like wheels.

The Mayor read out the names of the guides and found that all were present. Then he turned to a tall pale man who stood apart from the others, leaning against the door.

"Ulric Tagmer; give your statement."

The man came forward with hesitation, and leaning on the table spoke as follows, the court reporter taking down each word:

"We set out at five o'clock in the morning on Tuesday, intending to spend the day and night on the Schwarzegg Rock and to climb next morning to the Peak of Terror. I did not think it possible to get so high, but I was too proud to make any objection to the idea. Again, Herr Schuch"—he corrected himself—"Herr Schuchmann had promised to pay me fifty dollars whether we got there or not. We were three hours climbing the Lower Glacier without meeting with much difficulty. My employer was in high spirits and said: 'Ulric, I think we shall get up all right.' I replied: 'Perhaps; at any rate I hope so, Herr Schuch.' He laughed when I unwittingly used his pet name, as it were. Later he said to me: 'Ulric, I must get to that Rock; I am just starving!' After that he said nothing more, because the climb was so difficult that it needed all our breath. . . . When we passed the Zasenberg, I noticed that Herr Schuch—Herr Schuchmann—was leaving the path which I had cut in the ice. As I was walking in front, I did not notice this at first. When I saw it I called out to him: 'Take care where you are going; come back and keep behind me!' But for a few seconds he went on as he was going, saying: 'All right; but I just want to see this arch of red snow.' Then the thing happened——"

The speaker stopped dead in his story, which had been recited very slowly, and almost as if he had learned it by heart. His voice, which had trembled more and more, now failed altogether.

"Go on," said the Mayor, in severe tones.

Ulric Tagmer wiped his damp forehead, and with a violent effort resumed his statement.

"There must have been a bridge of fresh ice. I heard a crackling noise, an oath—and I saw no more."

There was a pause, and then the Mayor asked:

"Were you not roped to Herr Schuchmann? How could you have been so careless? After all, you are an experienced climber!"

After a moment's silence Tagmer muttered:

"He refused to be roped."

A murmur of astonishment broke from the guides on the back benches.

Ulric, very much annoyed, turned to them and cried out loudly:

"You all know very well how these things happen! When I went up to Herr Schuchmann, he pushed me away like this"—he made a gesture with his elbow—"saying, 'Don't come fooling about me with that confounded rope!' What would you have done? You know very well that a guide is only a servant, a helpless slave!"

These words were received with sharp exclamations and swift signs of dissent.

"Tagmer," said the Mayor, "every one with any sense will have the same impression as your comrades evidently have. If we are to believe your account, it does not speak very well for you. Tell us now what you did after the accident had happened."

Ulric tried to think for a few moments, and then said in a disheartened voice:

"I don't remember."

Then, seeing that his fellow-guides were looking at him in a threatening way, and meeting a very severe look from the Mayor, he pulled himself together and straightened up his athletic frame.

"Eh," he said, "eh—I went to the edge of the precipice and looked down into the crevasse. It was quite dark and cold, and there was a rushing noise like that of a millstream. I called about a thousand times: 'Herr Schuchmann! Herr Schuchmann!' I could hear my own voice reverberating from below, but no answer came up."

"How long did you stay there?"

"I don't know."

"Anyhow you did not come back until two days later. Every one has been struck by that fact. Why did you not go at once to inform the authorities?"

Ulric, overcome by emotion, replied in gasps:

"I—I was ashamed to come back. I was afraid to show my face. You know what people think of a guide who comes back without the tourist who has engaged him!"

This time his comrades agreed with him. Yes, it was a terrible position. Some of them had had the same awful experience.

After a pause the Mayor continued his questions.

"The day before yesterday four guides who were told off to inquire into the truth of what you stated were led by you to the spot where all this happened, and you were unable to point out to them the exact locality. That was surely a most extraordinary thing?"

Ulric could only stammer:

"It had snowed since then—I could not find the exact fissure in the ice——"

Then the Mayor rose.

"Tagmer, I must remind you of the very serious nature of the case. You are accused of having murdered the banker for the purpose of robbery, and of then having got rid of the body by throwing it into one of the precipices round the place where you were."

The witness grew still paler, and shrugged his shoulders in an effort to preserve his appearance of indifference.

The Mayor continued:

"Herr Schuchmann was always accustomed to carry a large sum of money about with him. The people in the valley often saw him take out a well-filled purse, and you knew that as well as the rest of them. Now, you know you contrived to go off alone with him——"

"No, no!" cried the other hastily. "I did not keep him from taking any one else with him."

"I can prove the contrary," said the Mayor. "I shall read you the sworn statement of the landlord of the 'Grand Moine.'

"'On the 28th of July Herr Schuch told me of his intention of going off next day to climb to the Peak of Terror. He seemed anxious, and he asked me if Ulric Tagmer was a man to be trusted. I advised him, seeing that he was going on such a dangerous climb, to take at least one or two additional guides. After some hesitation, Herr Schuch said: "Oh, no, I think that would annoy Tagmer, for he begged me not to take any of his comrades." That is all that I know about the business, and I make the statement with a clear conscience. Signed: MOEREN, landlord and owner of the "Grand Moine Hotel."' Now, what have you to say to that?"

Tagmer appeared thunderstruck. His laboured breath rattled in his throat. He muttered:

"I wanted—if luck was with us—to be able to say that I was the—first guide to climb with a tourist to the Peak of Terror, and that we did it alone together."

"So that it *was* your doing that there were only two of you on the mountain at the time. Let us suppose that what you say is true. The accident happened on Tuesday about ten or eleven in the morning, and it was only on Thursday, at six in the evening, that you came into Grindelwald in a state of great agitation, giving such incoherent accounts of the accident that before suspecting you of having committed a crime, people at first thought you had gone mad. You must admit that this behaviour was very suspicious. But there is more to be said. The evening before you set out you asked me to give you a certificate that you were destitute, to be shown to the local authorities."

"Here it is," interrupted the clerk of the court, waving a paper in the air in sight of all the guides.

The Mayor resumed:

"Therefore at that moment, Tagmer, you had no means of support. Now listen to the report of the municipal police constable:

"'Accompanied by the forester and the forest constable, I went to the house of Ulric Tagmer, who was absent. We proceeded to carry out the search for which we had a warrant in the room in which he lived. We searched the bed and all the furniture, and we turned over the litter used for the goats without finding anything of value. We were about to go away, when one of us noticed that the floor had recently been disturbed near the fireplace. When we examined the spot, we found twelve German gold coins. In testimony of which I the undersigned declare this to be the truth. Signed: HERMANN CLAUS, constable; PIERRE HIMGROUND, forest constable; JOSEPH-MARIE REDLINGER, forester.'

"Now, Tagmer, I must ask you to explain to us how you came to have this money."

A dull murmur passed along the bench where the guides were ranged, and for some moments the sensation in court prevented further comment.

Ulric Tagmer, overwhelmed by the authority of such testimony, kept a silence which was painful to every one.

The Mayor repeated his question, and the accused forced himself at last to utter a few sentences:

" I live on the road leading to the Lower Glacier. We stopped at my house on the way—just to get my ice-axe. Herr Schuchmann had pity on my poverty. He gave my wife a handful of gold pieces. She buried them at once, because our door has no fastening and we are always out."

" Well," replied the Mayor: "I must contradict, or at least correct, what you say. You are not married, Tagmer. You are living with a woman named Maria Müller, whose husband lives in Lucerne, and had to send her away on account of her bad conduct.

There was an angry murmur from the others in the court.

They all knew about the irregular association of the couple, but none of them thought it quite the right thing for the Mayor to bring it up against the accused at that moment. Their anger was directed against the Mayor for his lack of tact.

However, the Mayor soon made it clear that he had a purpose in what he had said. He continued:

" This woman whom you have taken to live with you is very handsome, as it seems. She is also very fond of pretty things to set off her beauty, but you, of course, are not in a position to supply these. I suppose you have heard the rumours which are going about?"

" No," replied Ulric, in a voice which had suddenly grown loud and strong.

" Well, it has been noticed that Maria Müller came in for a good deal of attention from the banker. It is even thought that for the last three years he came to this place regularly because of her. You have just said that he was very generous to you on her account, and that he gave her a handful of gold coins. Well, that gives colour to the general gossip about her. And I cannot help agreeing with what is the common belief in this place. You knew that Herr Schuchmann was about to leave, and you resolved by a bold stroke to get the money from him which you wanted before he left. This account seems much more probable than what you said about an accident, which was not at all likely to happen to such an experienced climber as Herr Schuchmann. Again, all the circumstances are against you; and I must add that the worst thing of all is the way in which you have given your evidence."

A most singular thing happened. The whole aspect of the accused changed. It was a very different kind of man who was now before the court. The dull, terrified Ulric had disappeared.

A sudden flame of passion glinted in his eyes, and he brought his closed fist down on the table, exclaiming, with the rage of those who have suffered in silence and unjustly for long:

" Let the people who have said that come and talk to me! I

shall know what to say to them. Maria is my wife in the sight of God, and she is a good and true woman. I love her and I will let no one insult her. I want to be brought face to face with those who tell lies, and then run off and hide like pigs in a sty."

The guides murmured their relief and approval of this outburst, for the whole scene from the beginning had been distasteful to them. The honour of the whole company of guides was at stake. After all, the accused was one of them, and if he disgraced his craft, the reputation of all must suffer.

The Mayor insisted no further. He thought that enough had been done; and, as a matter of fact, Ulric was far too excited to admit of further questioning. So the Mayor sent him into another room, to remain there under the charge of the clerk of the court, while the magistrates consulted together.

Outside the court there was a continual hum of voices, now and again broken by loud cries and arguments, while the dispute inside was no less violent.

There were several opinions to be gone into, and certain witnesses to be heard.

One of these was an uncle of the accused, his father's brother. This man, anxious for the honour of the family name, gave evidence as to the previous good conduct of his nephew, who had been a guide on the mountains from boyhood, but had never been accused of any misconduct, incompetence, or of anything to his discredit up to this, his thirtieth year. The only thing against him was this irregular intimacy with Maria.

After hearing all the arguments, the Mayor, wishing to shift the responsibility to a higher court, proposed to send the case for trial to the Assizes.

The guides protested vehemently against such a suggestion, and their leader, the oldest guide, appealed to the court in the following terms: If the case were sent for trial to the Assizes, what good would that do? The good name of all guides in that neighbourhood would be tainted; no one would have confidence in them; and yet, for all that, the real truth would never be found out. But if no crime had been committed, there had certainly been a grave error on the part of the accused. No one could understand how he had made such a mistake. Would it not be better that his comrades should be entrusted with the task of unravelling the mystery? In any case, Tagmer could no longer be considered a capable guide.

After every one had spoken, a vote was taken. A majority of eighteen out of twenty pronounced that Ulric Tagmer should no longer be a member of the Guides' Association.

He was led into court.

All present rose, and the sentence of his comrades was pronounced by the Mayor, solemnly as a sentence of death.

Ulrich listened calmly, pale and cold as a dead man.

The Mayor was evidently relieved. He had got rid of his responsibility, and saw his way to settle the matter without appeal to any other court and without further trouble. He spoke very kindly:

"I advise you in your own interest to leave this neighbourhood."

Tagmer only said:

"I am innocent all the same, and have no fear of anything."

They made him return his guide's portfolio, a large leather wallet containing pages for remarks. He handed this over with a sigh, while tears rolled down his cheeks.

His former comrades passed him coldly as they left the court. None of them bade him farewell, and when they appeared without him on the steps outside, there was a movement of relief among the anxious crowd awaiting their appearance. All crept nearer to the guides whose reputation had been re-established, and when the people learned what had happened, they separated in small groups whispering and wondering.

After dark, when the roads were deserted, Ulric Tagmer left the Mayor's court.

He crept through the village quietly, and plunged into the solitude of a marshy wood stretching from the village to the hermitage of St. Petronilla.

For half an hour he climbed up a stony path which had been made by the track of a brook, then, reaching a clearing and turning to the left, he stopped before a cottage near the Lower Glacier, gleaming white through the darkness. He had only to pull the string of the latch to enter his home.

A young woman sat there awaiting him. She was pretty, and wore the dress of the peasant girls of Lucerne. She sat with her elbows on her knees, and passed her fingers through her dark wavy hair. When the door opened, she looked up quickly.

"Well," she said, "what has happened?"

Her mouth was small and red; her eyes large and dark.

"It is all over," replied Tagmer, bursting into tears.

The woman watched him earnestly, trying to guess what he could not tell, and as she watched, she softened by degrees.

"Come here, Maria," he said, sinking on the wooden bench.

She came and sat beside him, and he told her just what had happened, stopping now and then, and only resuming his story when she coaxed him to go on.

When he had finished, he seized her in his arms and kissed her impetuously, uttering cries like a wounded animal. He became hysterical, and sobbed, laughed, and caressed her as if he had gone mad, holding her soft cheeks in his hands, and making no attempt to control his shattered nerves.

While he thus relieved his over-wrought feelings, so long cramped by silence and enforced calm, Maria uttered not a word. When he asked her to speak, to say anything to show he had not done wrong, she kissed him quietly and with apathy. He clung closely to her as if she could protect him from the misery of his grief. He forgot all except that she was his sole hope, all that was left to him in the world, as if he were a child and she his mother defending him against all outside the four walls of his dwelling.

Down in the village, his former comrades were talking about them both. They called him a criminal; and for her they had a fouler name. But up there in their cottage, near the shed where their goats slept, these two, alone and outcast, were happy in one another's company. All had fallen from them except each other.

All night they sat together, she soothing his grief, until he fell asleep in her arms. And when dawn broke, she laid him down to sleep and crept softly in beside him, while the goats in the shed awoke and went off to the mountain-side, with a chorus of jingling bells.

Nearly three years went by. Ulric and Maria had the money which they had acquired from the dead man, and lived quietly and in harmony together, though shunned by all. To eke out the little hoard, Tagmer kept a herd of goats and sheep on a small stretch of pasture which had belonged to his father at the foot of the Lower Glacier. The woman went from time to time to sell the milk and cheese, and to make her modest purchases in distant villages where she was not known, sometimes walking for eight or ten hours at a time, while her companion stayed with his flock. He never went far from his home, for he dreaded meeting some one whom he had known. Once or twice, when he did meet a former comrade and longed for a word, the other would abruptly turn his back on him, and would even retrace his steps or go a long way round so as not even to seem to see the lost outcast. No one wanted to know him, and even an utter stranger had a better chance of a greeting than he had.

He often met the Mayor who had condemned him to this dreadful fate, and always saluted him; but his salutation was ignored, and he never dared to open his lips to those who treated him as less than one of his own goats, for they were not criminals.

And so the years went by, until some sharp frosts set in, and strange news began to be spread about in the district.

The Lower Glacier *had begun to move,* and was coming down straight towards Tagmer's cottage.

There could be no possible doubt of this. Every one saw the moving glacier, and inasmuch as science had not yet reached this valley, there were many pious folk who recognised in this strange phenomenon a manifestation of the power of the Almighty, and of the impossibility of escaping from His justice.

Ulric had been the very first to see what was about to happen. He well understood the danger which threatened him.

Outside his cottage there was a budding lilac tree, and this was swept away by the melting snow. The young shrubs in the valley were powdered as in the depths of winter by particles drifting from the moving glacier. Often at night the crackling of the creeping ice could be heard, and Maria awoke him that he might share, and at the same time calm, her terror.

By degrees the slow mass of the icy torrent moved on. It covered Ulric's little grove of nut trees, and crept, slow as a snail but irresistible as death itself, along the mountain-side. Soon all his little property was swallowed up by the creeping monster.

Now he was reduced to sell his flocks. When the money which he had received from the sale of these was gone, he found an Alpine horn and took his stand among the mountain peaks where he could wake the echoes on the Black Lutschina in the direction of Interlaken. He became expert in calling out the sombre echoes of the rocky caverns and mountain walls, and the tourists passing on their climb were always willing to throw him a few coppers in return for his melancholy skill.

It was a miserable existence, and when the day was over, and he dragged his weary and discouraged steps back to his cottage, he received no welcome from Maria. She was always thinking, but never of him; she had not a kind word to throw to him, and if he spoke she did not seem to hear. Her mind seemed to have gone back to some distant period in her former life, and in her sleep she spoke of a man who worked alone and mourned the wife he had lost, who was still alive, and whose child believed himself to be an orphan.

The couple had lived so long alone that there was nothing more to be said to each other, they had already spoken of everything, and there was no longer any wish to repeat what had already grown wearisome to their thoughts. They had long since ceased to exchange affectionate words. What was the use of all that now?

Time went on, and still the glacier continued its steady march. Its outskirts spread so far now that the guides were obliged to take the tourists up the mountain by another route. Now, at last, Ulric's cottage was cut off by the creeping monster from all sign of other life. He was isolated by the glacier, buried and forgotten.

In the spring of 1850 the blocks of ice, breathing an appalling cold, crept up to within twenty feet of the cottage. Maria Müller was seized with a violent illness, beginning with icy shivers and ending with raging delirium, during which she died.

For thirty-six hours after her death the stricken man whom she had left behind her sat by the corpse without moving. When the moon rose on the second night he carried her corpse to the little cemetery on the mountain-side, where he dug a fresh grave under a rock and buried her beneath the Alpine flowers.

None of the neighbours troubled about her death. Most likely none of them knew of it.

At last Ulric could hold out no longer, and was obliged to go to some inhabited place to obtain food. The village was larger now; there were new roads round it, and additional houses had been built since he saw it before. He stopped for a long time before he could summon up his courage to speak to any one, but he need not have troubled. The misery through which he had passed, the hunger and cruel anxiety of his life had changed him so much that no one recognised him. Moreover, many changes take place in these mountain villages; young people grow up and leave, older people retire into the calm life of the plains, and many whom Ulric had known were now at rest for ever in the mountain graveyard.

Still, some curiosity awakes now and again in these quiet spots as to past days, and when Tagmer went into an inn to look for refreshment, he was questioned about his memories of former time. He was afraid to speak freely, so his dullness only made sport for the people there, and they gave him the playful greeting which one gives to half-silly old men.

As time went on he became a little bolder, and by degrees went more and more among his neighbours. He listened most attentively to all that they had to say, and by asking a stray question here and there managed to find out that there was now only one person still living who had taken part in the cruel tragedy of his life. It was the former Mayor, now a very old man who never left his room.

One day the sun was shining, and in the reflection of its rosy gleam on the ice Tagmer looked up and saw, looking down on him from an open window, the changed face of the man who had made him an outcast.

Still the glacier continued its slow course through the valley. Its corners had been broken or had melted away under the gleams of the Alpine sun, and fresh corners had come to replace them. These melted in their turn, mounds and hollows came and went, and still the mass of ice descended, stopping in the winter, resuming its progress as the spring advanced. At length it surmounted the last obstacle, and its frozen edge struck the foundation of Ulric's cottage.

He was now ninety years of age, and of these years sixty had been spent in hopeless misery. He was bent double, white-haired, a veritable skeleton with hollow eyes.

But his hearing, like that of all mountaineers, was still acute, and it was with joy that he heard the first crash of the ice-field against the masonry built on the solid rock close to his bed's head. He sat up and listened, awaiting the moment when the roof and all beneath it would be swallowed by the glacier.

To his great astonishment nothing more happened; the mass of ice had stopped again, and when the hot sun of July began to beat down on it, it melted rapidly.

One morning Ulric rushed from his cottage, and ran—if such a word can be used of his climbing and stumbling—to the village. His knees gave way, and he clutched at the bushes by the road to help himself along. When he reached Grindelwald he stopped in the main street, calling as loudly as he could:

"Herr Schuch has come back! Herr Schuch has come back!"

Outside the hotel of the "Grand Moine," which was now kept by Moeren's grandson, a party of tourists, who were just about to climb the mountain, greeted the poor old man with roars of laughter.

He certainly did look absurd with his floating white hair and beard, his excited manner, and his mingled laughter and tears. But he took no notice of the tourists. He continued crying:

"Herr Schuch has come back! Herr Schuch has come back!"

People began to crowd round and to ask who was this Herr Schuch, who seemed to cause such anxiety to the old man.

Still running, Ulric approached a pleasant little châlet set some distance back from the street. Looking up at the window he began to call out, "Sir! Sir!"

It was in vain that the people crowded round and told him that it was only a retired mayor who lived there, who could not do anything for him. The present mayor was in quite another part of the town. He insisted, most energetically, "It is my Mayor that I want to see, my own Mayor, the old one."

A few minutes later a window opened and a very venerable-looking man appeared.

"Good morning, sir. I am Ulric Tagmer. Please come at once to see Herr Schuch."

The old Mayor searched his memory. A melancholy smile crept over his features and he said, "I well remember those two names, and I can even remember the time when I heard them first. But what meaning can they have now?"

"I will tell you, sir. The Lower Glacier is melting and Herr Schuch, you remember him, Herr Schuch, you remember how he died when he was with me, Ulric Tagmer?"

"I remember it now," said the Mayor.

"Well, Herr Schuch is at my door. He is standing at it in the same precipice into which he dropped; his head is looking out. Oh,

I knew him at once, he has not changed a bit. Please come, I want you to see him."

The old Mayor stood as if reflecting, and gradually became more and more agitated.

" Herr Schuch? " he said. "Ulric Tagmer? But those are mere names. Names of ghosts and ghosts only. What can they want with me now? "

He stood reflecting, and said at last, " Well, I will go. Wait for me; I am coming down."

His old housekeeper grumbled and tried to prevent him from going out, but he took no notice of her. He went downstairs, took his old silk hat and the silver-topped cane which he had carried when he was Mayor, and went out amongst the group of people in the street.

Every one was asking what was the meaning of this.

The Mayor called to Ulric, " Can you show me the way? "

" Certainly, sir, I can show you the way. Oh, I was a guide on the mountain long enough."

His poor worn face was all lit up, and he continued to say, " Yes, I was a guide, I am still a guide, I can guide the Mayor now." He seemed to have been suddenly redeemed in his own estimation, and therefore in that of every one else.

He walked on as quickly as possible, resuming the ancient manner of a mountain guide, which seemed to have returned to him all at once. He looked neither to right nor left, nor would he answer any questions. The old Mayor kept pace with him, and these two seemed to leave the rest of the village behind them in living reality, as they had already left so many behind them in the course of those years which had passed over the heads of both old men.

The Mayor said not a word, nor did he pause until on the heels of his guide he stopped at last by Ulric's cottage. There a strange scene appeared. The ice was melting rapidly, the glacier was all torn and ploughed by the heat of the sun, and there, among bluish knots of ice, the head of a man appeared!

The cold had preserved the body from decay. Even the shape and expression of the features remained, and the fair whiskers were still in place as if the man were yet alive.

Ulric Tagmer seized a pickaxe, and rapidly freed the body from the ice, delivering the blows with certainty in spite of his age. Soon the whole body was set free, lying as if in a coffin in its bed of ice.

Then he cried:

" Now, sir, search the pockets yourself."

The Mayor obeyed without a word, moved by Ulric's insistence. With an effort he pulled apart the frozen flaps of the pockets of the dead man, and took from them one after another a bunch of keys, a handful of small coins, a purse full of gold, and a watch with the initials R. S., which proved the unmistakable identity of the corpse as that of Rudolph Schuchmann.

Then Ulric Tagmer drew himself up to what had been his former stature, and addressing the Mayor, who bent under the force of his calm words, he said:

"*Now* do you think that I am a thief? Will you still say that to the people here?"

The Mayor could not answer him. He staggered and nearly fell. At last, supported by those round him, he said:

"Poor Ulric Tagmer! Alas, my friends, I thought I had done my duty faithfully in my long life. Yesterday I thought I had nothing to do but to meet my end when it comes, free from care and with a clear conscience. Now, my latter days are clouded by remorse. Ulric, we have not long to live, either of us. On my knees, in presence of this man from the long-past days when we were both young, I beg you to forgive me if you can. I have done you a great injustice; if only you can forgive me, say so."

"Oh, sir!" murmured Tagmer in confusion, seizing the hands of the old Mayor stretched towards him.

The old Mayor had something else to ask.

"My poor old friend," said he, in a sort of helpless rage. "Why did you give in so easily? Why did you not appeal? Why did you not insist on a fuller trial? You took it all so quietly that no one could think you innocent!"

"What could I do?" said Ulric Tagmer dully. "I was always shy, and you were all so hard on me. Oh, I have lived so long and suffered so much! But you know the truth now!"

THE SILENCE OF THE BLOOD

PAUL HERVIEU

THE repast was over and the party were smoking and sipping their wine. The ladies in elaborate evening gowns fanned themselves indolently, with a lavish display of their charms. The men were quite at their ease, and talked freely. Young Cramant boasted that he, too, would give pleasant suppers like this as soon as he had the good luck to bury his father. Eloi de Norge declared that he had not been very sorry when his father died. Anne-Mimi said that people ought not to talk like that. But Coucy de Ripont insisted that no one ever really cared for his father. Biriboff alone did not join in the conversation, and at last the rest asked for his opinion.

" My Father? " he said, with an air of reflection. " Yes, I do remember something about him, but it is all very vague."

He continued: " It was in Petersburg a long time ago, when I was about twelve years told. I had always lived in the house of a good old priest, and one morning he came into my room looking as if he had something important to say.

" ' Listen, my boy,' he said. ' Put on your best clothes. You understand, the very best you have; and get ready at once.'

" I nodded, surprised at this unusual command; but after thinking for a moment he said very gravely:

" ' My boy, my dear boy, this is a great day for you. It will settle the whole course of your life. I am going to take you to see your Father! '

" I suppose I looked frightened. At any rate I felt faint, and he ran to my assistance, with a sharp cry.

" Until that moment I had believed myself an orphan. And now the very thought that I had a father overwhelmed me. A father! Like my friend Serge, who lived next door; *he* had a father who had given him a watch, and often gave him a thrashing.

" ' Oh dear, oh dear! ' moaned the old priest. ' Pull yourself together, sonny. I have tried to get this favour for you for ever so long. Lord, how I have prayed for it! Now, you are better, are you not? Heaven is on our side, at any rate. Come, you are all right now.'

" I clasped his hand earnestly."

" ' In the name of all the saints,' he went on, ' make haste and get ready. If he doesn't like you, it will be awful! I said you were so clever, so good, so perfect in every way.'

" I dressed as quickly as possible, and we set out along streets which were quite unknown to me. The old priest was more active than I had ever seen him, and he kept on murmuring words which I could not catch, but which sounded like prayers. We crossed several squares, and went along quays, avenues, canal banks, interminable streets. We were certainly going a very long way from where we lived.

" We crossed the Neva by a bridge. Not being able to keep up with the priest's long steps, I had taken to trotting at his heels. We passed a row of fine houses, and stopped before a magnificent building with heavy bars on the windows.

" ' Heaven be praised,' he sighed. ' Here is the place.'

" I was glad that my father lived in such a fine house, and still more pleased that we had reached it, for I was tired.

" However, my guide took me on again, past the front of the

fine building with its magnificent porch; then past other buildings, round a corner into a lane, and then round another corner into another lane. At last we stopped at a very humble side-door.

"A light knock at this door caused it to open, but I saw no one behind it. The priest, who seemed familiar with the place, led me along a dark passage with a ceiling so low that our steps on the flags sounded muffled. At the end of the passage another door, as heavy as the outer one, opened in response to a knock from the priest, but still no one appeared on the other side.

"Now we came into a small covered paved courtyard, with steps leading into a small round marble room, which seemed to have no door except the one by which we had entered. No one was to be seen.

"The priest walked straight on to the end of the room, licked his thumb, and pressed it strongly against a greenish spot in the wall, drawing it downward. The spot slid back, and in the space thus opened I saw the mouthpiece of a speaking tube, into which the old man began to speak softly. Then he listened, winking at me as if to convey to me what was going on. I felt frightened. Soon he winked and nodded faster than before, and exclaimed:

"'Heaven be praised! Your Father is expecting us!'

"He arranged my blouse and straightened the folds, took off my cap and smoothed my hair, put my cap in my left hand, and took hold of my right hand, giving me a kiss.

"I clung to him sobbing and imploring, 'Father, father, take me away. You are the only father I want. You have always been my father!'

"'Be quiet,' he replied. 'You are a good boy, and you must do as you are told.'

"I calmed down; and then I noticed that a space had opened in the marble wall, just large enough to admit us. We entered a dark corridor which seemed, from the sound of our footsteps, to be made of wood. Over our heads there was a rapid sound of steps, as if some one were going in front of us on the floor above.

"Another door brought us to the foot of a very steep staircase, the steps of which sloped downward like the teeth of a saw. It took us a very long time to climb this, and but for the help of my guardian I should have fallen several times, for I kept slipping back. The whole place gave me the impression of having been made for the purpose of discouraging visitors, or perhaps to keep intruders at bay.

"When we reached the top, a man who looked distinguished, though he wore only a simple peasant dress, told us courteously that his Excellency was ready to see us.

"'In there,' he said, pointing to a door overhung by a curtain on the right of the landing. On the left, another such curtain was moving its heavy green folds, as if some one were behind it. I watched the moving drapery timorously, peeping back over my shoulder.

"Two ladies dressed in mourning came out. One was young, the other elderly, and both seemed to be in the extremity of grief. A hand appeared behind them, through the curtain, making a gesture as if to wave them off. The elder lady sobbed in distress:

"'Ah, if your Excellency would only condescend to do it. He is not guilty, and he is so young! Oh, your Excellency!'

"I heard a door close heavily. It had fastened behind me, shut by the old priest whom I was following. I could still hear the lady sobbing. For a moment I thought that she must be speaking of me. I was so anxious about myself that I thought every one must think of me and of me only. She had said, 'He is so young!' And I was so young. Oh, how young I was! I was terrified to be so young among all these ancient things and beyond so many doors!

"The priest comforted himself with a pinch of snuff which made him sneeze violently. He tried to smile at me through the faces he made. I looked round the room where we were. A lot of garments were hung about on hooks as in a clothier's shop. Presently, the attendant came in and told us to follow him. The heavy green drapery on the landing began to tremble once more, and another attendant, similarly attired, came out. As soon as the curtain had fallen behind him, he began to laugh uncontrollably.

"Our guide shrugged his shoulders and whispered to his comrade as he passed him:

"'So you have settled matters this time with the governor? Well, you have got off all right, but I advise you to be more careful next time.'

"The other continued to laugh so happily that he stumbled against the top step of the dangerous staircase we had come up, and fell down the whole flight of stairs. He lay still at the bottom and laughed no more. Perhaps he was dead. I watched him eagerly to see if he would move, until my good old priest pulled at my sleeve.

"'Well, is it to be to-day?' called out a cracked voice impatiently from the room hidden from us by the heavy curtain, which the attendant had partly pushed aside.

"The priest seemed now as anxious as I was, and we both stood stockstill on the threshold.

"Two old men sat opposite each other in armchairs with leather cushions and enormous backs. They sat at each side of a huge log fire blazing in the great chimney. One of the old men wore a dressing-gown, and the other had a long white moustache, whose ends drooped like the whiskers of a seal. That was my first impression of both men.

" 'Go and speak to your Father,' whispered the priest to me.

" Not knowing what to do, I bowed to each of the strangers. Which was my Father? Was it the one who beckoned to me with a thin hand, which I recognised as the hand with a ruby ring, which had waved away those unhappy ladies in mourning? Or was it the one who looked so sad and kept on biting the end of a cigarette? I hoped this might be my Father. Why? I hardly know; I suppose one must always have something to hope for.

" 'Come here,' said the first. 'Are you frozen, that you can't move?'

" My guardian urged me on by a push from his knee. I managed to advance and stand between the two figures. I did not dare look at either of them. I was trembling all over, and in my nervousness I leaned against a small table and began to play with a paper-cutter whose carved ivory handle was topped with a skull and cross-bones.

" 'Drop that!' said the man with the cigarette.

" I obeyed, still without looking up. Suddenly, I shrank back. I felt a finger pressing on my forehead, and the cracked voice which I had heard as we came in said:

" 'Everything tastes bitter to him who has gall in his mouth.'

" Ought I to answer or merely to assent to this? The finger was removed from my forehead, leaving a cold spot behind it, and the other old man growled:

" 'That's the age when one is happy!'

" This was too much for me, and I burst into tears.

" Just then the attendant who had admitted us came in quickly, and announced a name which I did not catch.

" 'Send him in at once!' exclaimed both the old men. 'And go away, you two, if you please.'

" I hesitated, not knowing what to do, and the old man whom I had thought I would prefer bundled me off through a hidden door. The priest hurried after me, and we went down a winding stair into a basement where there were many servants. Thence we got out into the street by means of an iron ladder.

" The old priest raised his hands to Heaven, but said not a word.

" 'Well,' I ventured at length, 'which of those is my Father?'

" He trembled and moaned:

" 'Alas, alas, it is his own secret and not mine. It was for him to speak. Oh, blessed Lord, what a disappointment!'

" That," concluded Biriboff, " was the only time I ever saw my father in my whole life. And the only thing I can tell you about him is that he must have been the old gentleman on the right, unless perhaps he was the old gentleman on the left who sat and smoked his cigarette."

"Go and speak to your Father," whispered the priest to me.

Not knowing what to do, I bowed to each of the strangers. Which was my Father? Was it the one who beckoned to me with a thin hand, which I recognised as the hand with a ruby ring, which had waved away those [illegible] ladies in [illegible]? Or was it the one who looked so sad and kept on biting the end of a cigarette? I hoped this might be my Father. Why? I hardly know; I suppose one must always have something to hope for.

"Come here," said the first. "Are you frozen, that you can't move?"

My guardian urged me on by a push from his knee, and I managed to advance and stand between the two figures. I did not dare look at either of them. I was trembling all over, and in my nervousness I leaned against a small table and began to play with a paper-cutter whose carved ivory handle was topped with a skull and cross-bones.

"Put that down," said the man with the cigarette.

I obeyed, still without looking up. Suddenly I shrank back. I felt a finger pressing on my forehead, and the cracked voice which I had heard as we came in said:

"Everything tastes bitter to him who has gall in his mouth."

Ought I to answer or merely to assent to this? The finger was removed from my forehead, leaving a cold spot behind it, and the other old man growled:

"That's the one who looks hungry!"

This was too much for me, and I burst into tears.

Just then the servant who had admitted us came in quietly and announced a name which I did not catch.

"Send him in at once!" exclaimed both the old men. "And go away, you boy, if you please."

I hesitated, not knowing what to do, and the old man whom I had thought I would prefer bundled me off through a hidden door. The priest hurried after me, and we went down a winding stair into a basement where there were many servants. Thence we got out into the street by means of an area ladder.

The old priest raised his hands to heaven, but said not a word.

"Well," I ventured at length, "which of those is my Father?"

He hesitated and muttered:

"Alas, alas, it [illegible] and not [illegible]. It was for him to speak. Oh, blessed Lord, what a disappointment!"

"That," concluded Bertram, "was the only time I ever saw my father in my whole life. And the only thing I can tell you about him is that he must have been the old gentleman on the right, unless perhaps he was the old gentleman on the left who sat and smoked his cigarette."

ACKNOWLEDGMENTS

MOST of the translations in the Masterpiece Library of Short Stories have been made expressly for this work, but in several instances previously published translations have been reprinted, and among these the following acknowledgments have to be made:

To Messrs. GEORGE NEWNES, LTD., Southampton Street, Strand, London, W.C.,
In arrangement with whom the translations of "Catissou," by Jules Claretie, "Uncle Sambuq's Fortune," by Paul Arène, "The P.L.M. Express," by Jacques Normand, "Ulrich the Guide" and "The Prisoners," by Guy de Maupassant, and "The Family Name," by Henri Malin, are here reprinted from *The Strand Magazine*.

To the Editor of "EVERYMAN," London,
For permission to use the translations of "An Accident," by François Coppée, "Among the Peasants," by Guy de Maupassant, and "The Funeral of Firdousi," by Jules Lemaître, which originally appeared in the weekly review, *Everyman*.

To Messrs. G. P. PUTNAM'S SONS, New York and London,
By whose kind permission the translations of Guy de Maupassant's tales, "A Coward," "Little Soldier," and "Moonlight," are here reprinted from their series of "Little French Masterpieces."

The Editor's thanks are also due to the notable living authors of France represented in this volume, for the courtesy which has made its compilation possible.

VI
FRENCH AND BELGIAN

THE

Masterpiece Library of Short Stories

The Thousand Best Complete Tales of all Times and all Countries

Selected by

AN INTERNATIONAL BOARD OF EMINENT CRITICS

Sir William Robertson Nicoll, LL.D.
Sir Arthur Quiller-Couch
Clement Shorter
George Saintsbury, LL.D.
Richard le Gallienne
Brander Matthews, Litt.D.
Sir Frederick Wedmore
Sir Edmund Gosse, C.B., LL.D.
W. P. Trent, LL.D.
Carl Van Doren
Thomas Seccombe

Edited by

Sir J. A. Hammerton

VI. FRENCH AND BELGIAN

LONDON
THE EDUCATIONAL BOOK COMPANY LIMITED

Contents of Volume VI

THE FRENCH STORY-TELLERS

Alfred Capus and the Younger Generation

THE younger generation in France, in the eighteen-nineties, had much in common with their contemporaries in England. They were weary of the works of their elders, touched with despondency, and yet anxious to find new fields in art and letters. The end of the century was near, and for some inadequate reason this artificial division of time told upon the spirit of many of the new writers.

As a matter of fact, France, like Great Britain, was full of energy, and her younger men were acquiring a passion for sport unknown since the Middle Ages, while her inventors were developing new means of power and making an engine that could scale the skies. France should have produced somebody like Mr. H. G. Wells as interpreter of her new age. But the literary men of the younger generation rather affected a decadent mood, and left to Anatole France, Maeterlinck, and foreign writers read in translations, the task they pretended to be too weary to accomplish.

ALFRED CAPUS

Alfred Capus (1858–1922) was the representative of this strange young France. He became famous by his gospel of luck, by which it appeared that effort and sustained work were scarcely worth considering in comparison with the art of being born fortunate. His story of " Presence of Mind " is typical of his nonchalant, pleasant, easy-going way of looking at things. Smiling irony and witty depravity were the notes of his style and principal characters. The exquisite dubiousness he maintained in his study of crime in " The Marion Affair " remained characteristic of his art, until he became the political writer of the *Figaro* during the Great War.

GINISTY—REMY DE GOURMONT

Paul Ginisty (1858–1932), represented by a tale with an uncommon plot, " A Capitulation," also had an ironic touch, though he was on the side of honest men, instead of having been the apologist for amusing adventurers. In Remy de Gourmont (1858–1915) we come to the young master of French literature at the close of the nineteenth century. Gourmont began as an understudy to Anatole France, after dabbling in mediaeval mysticism. He adopted the Prussian philosophy of Nietzsche, and developed it at times in a coldly outrageous manner. In his principal works his race indeed seems to be utterly decadent, yet the man himself was one of the ripest fruits of French culture. His keenness of intelligence was extraordinary and his art, of which " The White Gown " and " The Magnolia " are examples, was perfect. His was the sweetest poison poured, just before the final struggle for life and death, into the brain of France.

BEISSIER—LE BRAZ

Ferdinand Beissier (b. 1858), in his comedy of love, " The Helmet," recovers the old gaiety of the Gaul, showing that the current of life still ran fresh and bright among the people. But Anatole Le Braz came to Paris from Brittany with a gift of poetic sadness derived from the new Celtic movement in the British Isles. Le Braz (1859–1926) was the disciple of Luzel, the Breton folk-lore gatherer, and he desired to found a French-Celtic movement on lines similar to those along which the Irish and Scottish schools were working. In his study in superstition, "The Blood of the Siren," he attained in a French way an effect like that which William Sharp produced by more archaic means.

"GEORGES COURTELINE"

With "Georges Courteline" (1860–1929) laughter is again heard. Courteline was one of the best of modern French humorists, but there is usually something serious beneath his fun. His farce of "A Gentleman Finds a Watch" is really a bitter thing. The class of officials that ran the French Republic before the war was generally bad. They owed their positions of authority to professional politicians, who shared the spoils of government among their immediate supporters in the manner of the old Tammany organisation of the United States. Courteline continually attacked the French bureaucracy in short stories and one-act plays, and his special weapon of ridicule told in the end with considerable effect.

LAVEDAN

Henri Lavedan (b. 1859) is a vivacious cynic engaged in painting fashionable life, until he was moved by fear of the abyss which his country seemed approaching. He wrote one of the greatest of sermons in his play, "The Marquis of Priola," which is pure literature and distilled worldly wisdom, yet ends in a tremendous moral effect. In his short tales Lavedan has a special love for the simple kindliness of French home life, as he shows in his exquisite picture of old age, "Years After." Quite as fine, original, and touching is his study of married life in "When He was a Little Boy." In the surprise story of "The Pocket-Book" he is still keen in seeing life's little ironies, and watching men and women sway under temptation.

PAUL MARGUERITTE

Paul Margueritte (1860–1918) was another remarkable writer of the modern French renaissance. Having been the son of one of the ablest generals in the war of 1870, he set himself to combat the early influence of Zola, and restore the spirit of heroism in literature. His curious tale of " The Dead Hand " is not only interesting itself, but symbolical of the author's constant view of life. For the dead hand that was an object of terror becomes an inspiration to healthy action.

GEORGES BEAUME

In his tale of French peasant life, " The Treasure," Georges Beaume (b. 1861) analyses the intense love of money prevailing, for both good and evil, in his country. It is a source of French power that enables the peasant to increase his hold upon the land and gradually break up the large estates into small holdings, and that gives the country its wonderful financial influence. It has made the French farmer monstrous in the eyes of Zola and Maupassant: yet without this national passion for saving, with all the laborious work it implies, France would never have maintained her greatness. During the war it was not until the hard, frugal peasants took the field that the fierce underlying tenacity of their race was fully revealed to the world.

DESCAVES

Though Lucien Descaves (b. 1861), one of the finest men of the realistic school, has never won the popularity of Mirbeau, his work has been appreciated by the best minds. In his apparently slight sketch, " An Interior," he lights up the main problem in modern French home life. The men are often sceptics of the anti-clerical sort, yet, despite all their efforts, their children continue to be brought up in the faith of their fathers. For the Frenchwoman cannot bring herself to follow the Frenchman, and wives, aunts, and grandmothers, even in the best political families, defeat the intentions of the Government.

FOLEY

Charles Foley (b. 1861) is not concerned with any important political or religious problem in his picture of the Avignon waiter " Pirotou." His tale is of an ironic character, yet expressive of sympathy with the unfortunate man who is so completely eclipsed by his wealthy, brilliant brother.

PRÉVOST

For long the fashionable novelist of his period, Marcel Prévost (b. 1862) deserves his position by reason of his subtle, ranging power of insight. In work after work he has illumined dim corners in modern French society. For example, the foreign reader will find nowhere else so concise and well balanced an analysis of the French *mariage de convenance* as in his " A Young Girl's Diary." The marriageable maiden is far from being a pawn in the affair. Her parents do the best they can to obtain a good match for her, and she is keenly alive to all the facts of the situation, and, with the special talent of her sex and race, plays the game for her future life with zest and skill.

In " Wolf-Solange " Prévost turns to the French peasantry for an example of the virile yet graceful type of womanhood he often celebrated in his longer works. For Prévost with all his faults is one of those energisers of modern France who were consciously or unconsciously preparing the people for the great ordeal. The strange ghostly tale of " Psyche " is not a mere essay in the uncanny. It is based on ordinary facts of life, the supernatural element being only a symbol of certain natural truths. The extraordinary plot of the next tale by the same author, " Mademoiselle Heudier's Husband," is again only an artistic vehicle for conveying one of Prévost's fine discoveries in psychology.

Although Prévost first appeared as a disciple of Paul Bourget, he is a more discerning student of human nature than his master. How slight is his material in his last tale, " The Beggar Child " : yet what a train of thought he suggests in it ! Doctor Johnson would have been pleased with this story, for he was given over to that curious kind of impulse that Prévost was the first to turn into the subject-matter of literary art.

D'ESPARBÈS

" The Butterfly " of Georges d'Esparbès (b. 1863) is a winged and iridescent idyll of studio life, that hovers daintily between the poetry and prose of the rather drab world of provincial competitive examinations. Perhaps it is the classic atmosphere of the most famous legend in Greek art, which the writer skilfully suggests, that makes his tale so charmingly distinctive. It is clear that " The Butterfly " is a remote descendant of the bird that came and picked at the grapes in the ancient Greek picture.

LÉON FRAPIÉ

Léon Eugénie Frapié (b. 1863) has classic qualities of a deeper character. Realistic in style, he is yet full of Virgilian tenderness. How vulgar is his title " The Missus," yet how beautiful is the idea and how fine the execution! As for Frapié's second tale, " A Simple Soul," which is written in a vocabulary befitting a music-hall sketch for a low comedian, the pathos and loving-kindness of it are incomparable. It is right to judge artistic works of art purely from an artistic point of view, but there is something larger than art in Frapié's tale.

PIERRE MILLE

Pierre Mille (b. 1864) scarcely believes in loving-kindness, as he shows in his dramatic story of " Mrs. Murray's Revenge." M. Mille began as a disciple of Mr. Rudyard Kipling, and developed into one of the ablest of the young professors of energy, with a fine, original vein of his own, until he put his literary work aside in order to labour at cementing Franco-British-American comradeship in feelings, ideas, and action during the war.

DE RÉGNIER—GEORGES RENARD

Henri de Régnier (b. 1864) is an extreme contrast to Pierre Mille. Régnier represents the old, idle, finely cultivated French aristocracy, and while composing volumes of poetry in a freshened classic mould, he returned in his stories to the traditions of the eighteenth century. By the pure grace of form of his works he won a position in the French Academy, and had the happiness of pleasing the men of the old school as well as the symbolists and other innovators. In his tale of " The Sign of the Key and Cross " Régnier executes a masterly variation upon a theme used by Poe and Villiers d'Isle Adams.

Régnier is usually derivative, yet his perfect art makes him seem less of an imitator than an eclectic master. In his gift for form he is practically equal to Anatole France, but his mind and spirit are those of an aristocratic dilettante. No fire from hell or heaven has touched him. There is far more feeling in the tale of the Franco-German war, by Georges Renard (1864–1930), " Jacques Brulefert's Death," the ending of which is one of the most magnificent things in the literature of the short story.

FERNAND VANDÉREM—PHILIPPE MONNIER

During the period immediately before the Great War, the French story-tellers of the younger generation appeared to lack the energy of imagination of the older men. They seemed rather to be training themselves for some national movement than bent on exploring new fields of individual art. Much of their work, however, was marked by qualities of high value. The curious study by "Fernand Vandérem" (1864–1911), entitled "Himself," has a fine originality of a subtle sort. "The Foolish Virgin," by the brilliant Philippe Monnier (b. 1864), owes its distinction to the way in which it is written. The idea of it is old, yet Monnier makes it new by means of his sympathetic and winning style.

GODARD—SCHWOB

"The Nona," by André Godard (b. 1865), is a surprise story, like Maupassant's "Necklace," depending entirely on skill and execution. The trick is often attempted, but the little masterpieces in the art of surprise remain small in number. Marcel Schwob (1867–1905), who follows Godard, was a master of all the effects of the short story, and as is seen in the strange, mystic tale of "The Wooden Star," he had a good deal in common with R. L. Stevenson. Schwob had a rich imagination, but lacked driving power of will, and the body of work he left behind him is as small as it is fine.

LICHTENBERGER—BRINGER

André Lichtenberger (b. 1870), on the other hand, is a profuse and varied writer. All his work is marked by distinguished qualities that would make the task of selection somewhat difficult, if it were not for the adorable "Trott." Trott is now the classic type of the French child living in pleasant circumstances, and the series of comedies in which he figures is a chain of delights. There is comedy also in "The Captain's Little Secret" by Rudolph Bringer (b. 1871). The idea of this story seems purely farcical, but it contains a telling satire upon a certain whim of pretension in oldish men, which, though especially noticeable in Frenchmen of the retired class, is not uncommon in other races.

LATER WRITERS

"Ashes," by Paul Renaudin (b. 1873), is a more serious work. Indeed, it is one of the most serious in the literature of its period. It marks the profound change that at the beginning of the century was taking place in the French conscience, owing to struggles of the new Labour parties in France. In the early work of Frederic Boutet (b. 1874), little of this new spirit of seriousness was to be seen, until the writer went into the fighting line. But his tale of "The Experiment" shows that Boutet was always a master of his art. He took little interest in the social study of human nature, and obtained nearly all his effects by means of situations in which some curious scientific idea was developed.

Paul Clesio, in his sketch "The Musgravius Monopoly," plays in an amusing fashion with those brilliant dynasties in the French world of science, resembling the Darwin dynasty, which is one of the glories of England. Jacques Constant goes far afield to Finland in his dramatic monologue "The Betrayal," while Georges Japy turns to Japan in his allegory of "The Mirror." With Marc Le Goupils, the neo-realistic movement greatly increased in strength, and, as is seen in the bitter tragedy of "The Cross-Roads," became one of the master currents in French literature of the twentieth century. During the war, this movement, with its union of French, Russian, and English elements, prevailed over all others; but in the years of troubled peace before the storm, there were many Frenchmen who, like A. le Hêtre in his poetic fantasy, "Tramp and Poet," continued to seek for delight and charm rather than for truth of facts.

Picturesque romance also attracted young writers, with a talent for pictorial effect, such as Georges Maurevert. His "Gold Chain" is a superb exercise in the art of painting with words, and carries on the traditions of Merimée and Barrés. His "Suicide," which by its alarming title promises to deepen the gloomy impression of his first story, really serves to show the suppleness of his mind, being only a brilliant farce, set in the scenery of Monte Carlo.

"A Silver Coin," by A. Roguenant, is an idyll of the Latin Quarter, original in idea and pleasantly maintaining the tradition established by Murger in his "Vie de Bohème." All oldish artists and literary men seem to think that Bohemia vanished when they became middle-aged;

but immortal youth meanwhile sweeps into the old streets of adventure, bringing with it perennial romance.

Maurice Saint-Aguet looks for romance in the age of Napoleon, in "The Croissey Yew." This is certainly the easier way, as in the moonlight of history everything seen in the past has a certain given picturesqueness. But M. Saint-Aguet's plot is so original and is told with such happy strokes that the little work deserves its position as an admirable example of the lighter historical tale.

"Nicette," by Saint-Juirs, is a bustling comedy of errors, compact with amusing situations. As Falstaff is as dramatic a figure as Hamlet, the art of the short story must also be allowed to range over the farcical side of life as well as the serious side. As Charles Lamb remarked, a laugh is worth a hundred groans in any market, and though the market price is not the only estimate of value, it represents often certain general human qualities overlooked by narrow-minded aesthetes. In striking contrast with the tale by Saint-Juirs is the study of Spanish court life, "The Princess 'Just Because'" by Raymond Schwab. This is a remarkable study of the blithe soul of a child, suffocated by the pomp and circumstance of royalty, and, as the Infanta Eulalie proves in her memoirs, Schwab penetrated closely to the truth in his portrait of his imaginary child princess in Spain of the old régime. E. W.

ALFRED CAPUS
B. 1858

PRESENCE OF MIND

LITTLE SERQUY and Jules Debot, whom his friends usually called Bobo, were completely stone broke from time immemorial. Such was their position that no one remembered having seen them with money in hand, except perhaps the oldest men of the Boulevard. They had arrived at this state of things by paths that were different but equally sure. Bobo had in a few years wasted a fairly small inheritance, and as for Little Serquy he had never possessed anything of the slightest value. The necessities of life had always prevented them from exercising any kind of profession. No one knew their families; but they lived very well, and always dressed in the best style. They also moved in the best society. They were about the same age, forty, and their reputation, without being the kind required in judges in affairs of honour, was still enviable.

A charming good humour and unalterable gaiety brought them frequent invitations, social successes and profitable friendships. Thanks to their pleasant personal qualities, everybody forgave them the incessant " touches " that constituted their only resource. For, in plain truth, they lived entirely on that delicate and Parisian variety of loan which has had to be distinguished by a special name. " Touching " a man is not the same thing as borrowing from him, and though it is a financial operation of the same family, it is distinguished by some essential features.

If, for example, you ask anybody for a sum of money, promising to repay it at a stated period, you contract a loan; if, on the other hand, you merely say to a friend or acquaintance, or to a stranger, " Lend me fifty pounds," without in any way undertaking to return it, that is a " touch." Men lend one another money in all countries and under all conditions, but " touching " only goes on in Paris among people of a certain class. A loan is often painful: it places you for the moment in an inferior and slightly humiliating position. It is not so with the art of " touching," which must be practised with a large easy air, as if the act of touching were a kind of homage to a chosen friend.

Bobo and Serquy excelled in this formidable art. They each had a fixed method, whose power they had proved by long use. The ability of Little Serquy consisted in a surprising tact that enabled him to divine the exact minute when anybody could be tapped. He knew when his victim had had a good day at the races or the card-table. He watched the play of his features, he never overworked him, and he used but little speech. He was like a discreet dentist who pulls out one of your teeth with a strong wrist at the critical moment without showing his instrument. His triumphs were beyond reckoning.

Bobo was a dentist with a gift of the gab who seemed to think it was a matter of no importance if you had one tooth more or less. At his genial good fellowship, his smooth and amusing flow of words, pockets opened naturally. Thus both men led an easy and joyful life, exempt from gloom, putting up with passing checks and trusting in the innumerable combinations of luck. They had even had brilliant times and periods of luxury. The months preceding the great panic were one of their bright memories, and also the period of the Rio Tinto boom. They were always hoping that such times would come again, for their destinies were based on the vagaries of the Public Funds. And after any great hit on the Stock Exchange you saw them hastening like gleaners in the track of their acquaintances.

But for several months Bobo and Serquy had been having a very critical time of it. Business was not moving, and they were the victims of a deplorable state of doldrums. They had just got through a week with small pieces of money, taking their meals in low-class restaurants, meeting at times at cook-shop tables on evenings when they had no invitation to dinner. They chatted to one another about the difficulties of life in Paris and the increased cost of living. Yet they maintained towards each other a perfect manner and affected merely to be living frugally until the money market improved.

By a sorry coincidence, most of their usual clients were down on their luck. Blache, who was always good for ten pounds, kept his pockets closed at the club. Dick lost an enormous sum at the races. Similar accidents struck their best chums. Never had they found themselves in such unfavourable circumstances.

At last one night, Bobo, coming into the card-room of the club, as was his daily custom, to gather news, learnt that Boisgenet, a very decent fellow, quite young, almost a beginner, had just made a splendid scoop in a flutter. After this great exploit, Boisgenet had immediately given up playing. Bobo hastened back to his rooms and left one of his cards on the hall porter's table, after scribbling on it that he wanted to be awakened at ten in the morning.

At half-past ten he entered Boisgenet's outer room.

"Master has gone out," said the servant.

Bobo murmured an "Ah!" of disappointment.

"But he is sure to be back before twelve. He has some friends coming to breakfast."

"That is all right," said Bobo, "I will wait for him in the smoking-room."

He began to read the newspaper in a tranquil frame of mind, but he had scarcely glanced at the headlines, when the servant opened the door again and introduced another visitor, brilliantly dressed, with light gloves, patent shoes and a smiling face. It was Serquy. Bobo and Serquy shook hands with an almost imperceptible frown.

"How are things going?"

"Not at all badly; and how are you getting on?"

"I say! How is it I did not see you at the club yesterday evening?" asked Bobo.

"I came rather late," said Serquy, "and I was told you had just gone."

"Ah!" An embarrassed silence followed. Bobo and Serquy knew too much about life to have the least doubt about the object of each other. On the other hand, they were too well mannered to indulge in untimely jests. Firmly resolved not to give way to each other, they stared coldly, gravely, attentively at one another. Then they began to chat about indifferent matters, avoiding the mention of Boisgenet, as though they were not in his house. Half an hour thus passed by.

Suddenly the features of Bobo relaxed. He called to the servant:

"Are you quite certain that Monsieur Boisgenet will return for breakfast?"

"Absolutely certain."

"Very well."

The servant retired. Bobo turned to Serquy.

"Just fancy, my dear friend . . . Yes, there is no harm in telling you. . . . You know Boisgenet well, don't you? What a charming fellow! And obliging. . . . You see, then, Boisgenet last month lent me a hundred pounds. . . . And with such a good heart! Ah! People who will lend you a hundred pounds when you are hard up are becoming rare! And I will admit to you that when I at last received my money this morning, I was vastly pleased to think I could go at once and return Boisgenet his hundred pounds. By Jove, he is making us wait a little, but I will stay here all the same. I should only gamble the money away this evening. . . . What a charming fellow Boisgenet is, eh?"

"Charming," said the other; and as he was somewhat cast down by having to wait so long, Serquy for a minute lost the keen edge of his intelligence. He thought innocently, "This is turning out very well. I will look in after lunch." And, getting up: "Faith! I merely came to get some information from him about the race to-morrow. I can see him this evening. That will be time enough. Good-day, old chap."

So it was Bobo who, on that occasion, touched Boisgenet.

THE MARION AFFAIR

ALFRED CAPUS

THE need for a quiet simple holiday led me one day to a little country town fifty leagues from Paris. At the inn where I left my luggage I asked if there was not some cottage I could take for the season. The innkeeper advised me to go and see Monsieur Marion, the owner of a pretty furnished villa.

"I don't think it has been taken this year," he added.

Monsieur Marion lived quite near to the town in a one-storeyed peasant hut. I found him smoking a pipe outside his door. He seemed from sixty to seventy years old. But his tall, upright figure, his big shoulders and lissom movements were those of a man full of vigour. He received me with the greatest civility.

"There is the villa," he said, showing me with his finger a square white building with green shutters. "If you like you can look over it at once. It is well furnished."

It suited me. Monsieur Marion put a very moderate rent on it, and I took it.

"You will be very comfortable here. The river flows two hundred feet away, and it is full of fish. Do you handle a rod?"

I admitted I had a passion for fishing. I settled in the house that day, helped by a servant whom my landlord was kind enough to get for me. And the next morning I began to fish with fervour. Angling did not seem to be the favourite sport in that part of the country. The banks of the river were deserted, in spite of their cool shadows, in spite of the slow deep water, in which big fish could at times be seen leaping. However, towards the evening, as I was returning for a second attempt, I heard the noise of branches moving behind me. Looking back I saw, box in hand, rod under the arm, an old little thin gentleman looking somewhat serious and slightly frowning. By these signs I recognised that not only was he a fisherman like myself, but that, in all probability,

I had taken his usual place. I rose up, excusing myself. At this mark of good-will, his face brightened.

"Don't disturb yourself," he said, "I will go farther up the river."

I replied I could not permit it, and that it was only because I was unaware . . . He insisted with a fine courtesy and bowed and went away.

I met him the next day, and little by little we began to chat together. He gave me special information about the best fishing places on the river, we lent each other tackle, and there was soon established between us the intimacy that comes of liking the same sport.

"It is you, isn't it, who has taken old Marion's villa for the season?"

"Yes. Is Marion one of your friends?"

"Not exactly," he said, with a smile; "but I have known him for a long time. . . . Yes, for thirty-eight years."

"He seems to be a decent man," I said.

"Yes, very decent."

"Have you lived for thirty-eight years in the country?" I asked.

"Much more than that. I have never left it. I was a notary, and I retired some years ago. My name is Lebrun."

"Possibly Marion was one of your clients?"

"Well. . . . Somewhat."

These evasive answers in regard to my landlord began to puzzle me in a vague way, but I could not obtain any more precise information. A few days afterwards, as we were fishing side by side, I again mentioned the name of old Marion. Monsieur Lebrun had just caught a perch that leaped and twisted at the end of his line. He placed it carefully in his box, then said abruptly:

"How is it that you never heard of the Marion affair? It is true you were young at the time. But it excited so much . . ."

I leant over to listen, and he continued in a low voice so as not to disturb the fish:

"It was in 1855 a terrible crime was committed in the parish: a woman and a child had their throats cut—Widow Berez and her little boy. Don't you remember it?"

"Not at all."

"Suspicion fell on Marion, who was then a man of about thirty-two. I ought to tell you that there was a good deal of evidence against him, but I will spare you the details. He was only condemned to penal servitude, benefiting by certain points that could not be cleared up. He was taken to New Caledonia. Then, five years afterwards, in 1860, a rumour was started that Marion had been wrongly condemned. The real criminal, it was said, had confessed on his death-bed. That created an enormous scandal. It was observed that up to the moment of the crime Marion had always behaved well. Public opinion was very strongly moved. The Emperor took part in it, and after all the proceedings had been revised, Marion came back here. Since then, I must add, his life has been very honourable. He inherited the property of some relation and became a man of leisure. All this story is now forgotten. Most of the witnesses are dead. No one in the place thinks of making the slightest allusion to it."

I asked for details.

"Ah! It has all got mixed up in my mind. . . . Besides, to my way of thinking—and I was present at the trial—the case was extremely perplexing."

"But he is innocent . . . the confession of the criminal . . ."

"Clearly, he is innocent. There is nothing to say about that. The confession of the guilty person was made in legal form. I stand on settled things," added Monsieur Lebrun with a smile. "When Marion was condemned, I believed in his guilt. When the authorities decided that he was the victim of a mistake, I immediately believed in his innocence."

"But what is your own sincere opinion in the matter?"

"My opinion is that it is forty years since all that happened." And without another word, the old notary cast his line again into the river.

You always end by getting somewhat bored on a quiet holiday in the country. In one of those hours when idleness weighs as much on the mind as heavy work, I determined to find some occupation by getting old Marion, if possible, to tell me his story. I often met him, either at his door, or on the path by the river. He wished me a good catch, and I asked him about his health, and there our talk came to an end. After the revelation of the old notary, I tried to get on a more intimate footing with my landlord, whose case had excited my curiosity. One day I offered him some fish. He accepted it on the condition that I drank some plum brandy that he made himself with fruit from his garden. Then I invited him to dinner. It was only then a question of finding an opening. "You have struck up a friendship with the notary?" said old Marion. "I noticed it. He is just as mad about fishing as you are. I know him of old."

"Yes," I answered, "we are good friends. He is a delightful man." And I added rapidly, "We have talked . . . about you. I already knew about . . . your terrible affair . . . before I came." I shook him by the hand, saying, "My poor Monsieur Marion!" And I thought to myself, "I have got him."

But far from being astonished or putting on a serious air as I expected, old Marion began to laugh.

"Ha! Ha! I don't doubt it. It made some noise at the time, that affair. It is well known in Paris, eh?"

"Very well known," I affirmed.

The ice was broken. Old Marion filled his glass with plum brandy, then, still smiling with winning good nature:

"Eh! Yes, that was an amusing story. . . . At first, when I returned they carried me shoulder high in triumph. Next they tried to get me into politics on the side of the opposition. I refused. I was always afraid of politics. Then I had scarcely been back six months when they began to say that my judicial error was a government invention, and that I had got off by intrigues and backstairs influence. Men shunned me in the street, although I didn't care a button. Some of our local newspapers attacked me, others took my part. It was comical! For six months I was innocent, then crack! I again became a great criminal, after I had spent half a year in being a martyr whom everybody honoured. Travellers had begun to ask to be introduced to me. But one fine morning all that changed, without rhyme or reason. I was nothing more than a monster of hypocrisy who had cheated the guillotine. Isn't it funny? At last, everything was forgotten; is it not so? Just imagine, on the fourth of last September . . ."

Old Marion expanded with jollity, as though he were recalling a merry past.

"On the fourth of last September, as my name was very well known—they did not remember why—they came and asked me to stand as mayor. . . . Ha! Ha! You will guess I declined the honour. . . . Now it is all finished, finished. . . . It is a legend. . . ."

Such nonchalance and gaiety strangely surprised me. What especially astonished me was that old Marion did not display the slightest animosity against his persecutors, that he never spoke of his sufferings at Noumea, that he never appeared to retain the least grudge against his country for the horrible adventure of which he had been the victim.

As for myself, I inclined from one extreme to the other. Sometimes, looking at his white beard, his fine figure of robust old age, I took him for a philosopher, superior to common men by his simplicity, his pride of soul, his gentleness and resignation. At other times, seeing his clear cold eyes and thin lips, I conceived the most abominable suspicions.

Naturally I never dared ask him the question that was on my lips: "You are innocent, aren't you?" It was extremely curious, for during the three months that we chatted together he never said to me in a downright positive way, "I am innocent." On the eve of my departure for Paris we dined together. Then I went back with him to his cottage. We shook hands. Then looking me in the face, with a smile that seemed to me at the moment diabolical but may have been only a delicate and ironic allusion to the unjust suspicions he had divined in me, he said:

"Would you like me to tell you something quite extraordinary? To-day I am exactly sixty-eight years old. It doesn't matter now who committed or did not commit a crime in 1855. Well, they have told me so often that I was guilty and that I was innocent that, on my word of honour, I don't know myself what I am." And he disappeared into his cottage, giving me, behind the door, a friendly good-night.

PAUL GINISTY
B. 1858

A CAPITULATION

" Oh dear, oh dear! " exclaimed M. Amalfi, after reading the letter which he had received.

As he always did when a matter seemed very important, he took off his glasses, blew on them, wiped the lenses with his handkerchief, and put them on again. This operation gave him time to think.

He was sitting at his study table, which was covered with documents, papers, cases full of written sheets, all of them heaped in a disorder which only he could regulate. An old bachelor, he never allowed a woman's hand to put his papers straight, and his servants were ordered not even to disturb the dust which gathered on his desk.

" Oh dear, oh dear! " he said again. " This is a trifle strong, all the same! "

M. Amalfi was a man about fifty years of age, who had been gifted by Nature with a ferocious-looking moustache, though he was really of a very pacific temper, thinking of nothing but his work as a historian, which had gained him a reputation for scrupulous accuracy, the result of his inflexible conscientiousness. When he had pronounced his decision, it was as certain as Holy Writ; for every one knew how careful he was, how scrupulously he verified every single source of information, and how anxious he was that there should not be a single error, however slight, in his facts. Then large volumes, consecrated to the Wars of the Royalist Insurgents, bore witness to the admirable precision of his method, by which not a single word was written without absolute proof of its truth.

Yet this hard-working historian, whose eyes were worn by the constant examination of the manuscripts which he had laboriously got together, was not altogether devoid of feeling. He was impartial, but could at the same time feel sympathy for one side or another. A stranger to the present day, hardly knowing what was going on in the world around him, or at least not troubling about it more than he could help, M. Amalfi lived in the past. For the dead he felt pity, admiration, affection, just as he often felt for them anger and disapproval; he seemed to live in the lives of those whose deeds he described, and belonged only to the past which he evoked.

Being naturally kind-hearted, he was often sorry to have to fix irrevocably in print matters which he had so laboriously discovered. Thus, he had been known to visit a cemetery in the suburbs of Paris, where one of the heroines of the Vendéan War lay buried. She had died in the odour of sanctity, but he sought her tomb to ask pardon of her memory for the revelations which truth compelled him to make concerning her private life, for these revelations ill consorted with her virtuous reputation. On that occasion the good M. Amalfi was profoundly regretful. Nevertheless, the profession of historian has its own unalterable obligations, which may by no means be evaded.

The letter which he held in his hand referred to an important recent research, which he had lately had published in a magazine. He had been led by degrees, though not at first without surprise, to a conviction of the double part played, during the Royalist Insurgent War, by the Marquis de Villeroc. This warrior had been regarded by the Royalist party as one of the most faithful comrades of Larochejaquelein, and had received great honours and rewards under the Restoration, not for his own merit alone, but also for that of his former companions-in-arms, whom Fate had not spared to reap the final success of their cause. As a last recompense for his devotion to his King, he became a peer of France in 1827. Villeroc, one of the most celebrated leaders of the Catholic Royalist Army, one of the most active agitators of the Vendée, convicted of disloyalty! At first, M. Amalfi felt ashamed of harbouring the least suspicion of the man's probity, and accused himself of a lack of charity; for in his absolute regard for truth he never believed harm of any one, except when it was quite impossible to doubt it. But this mystery, upon which he had come, occupied his thoughts for a time, and ended by absorbing all his attention. In his usual scientific method, yet not without anxiety, he devoted himself to the study of the problem. If Villeroc had been a traitor—the ugly word must be faced—a careful examination of all the facts must some day show the truth.

When once he had set out on the trail, M. Amalfi never turned aside; and in the present case he was more than usually tenacious. He never allowed the doings of Villeroc to escape him for a single moment, and conviction soon followed what had begun as no more than suspicion. He grudged neither the journeys he had made nor the most patient inquiries, nor the most elaborate researches; and at last, in the face of the world's opinion, he was absolutely convinced that what he stated was the astounding and lamentable truth. The hand of Villeroc, the " glorious Villeroc," was clearly to be traced in many of the disasters of the Royalist Army. He had played a double game. While leading the peasants of the West, and swearing all the time by God and King, he had kept the enemy informed of the movements of the Army to which he belonged, and had indicated at the same time the weakness of its positions. The " heroic Villeroc " had been the miserable agent of the destruction of his brothers-in-arms, whom he had basely sold. A dastardly hypocrisy had won his reputation for valour and loyalty.

Once sure of his facts, M. Amalfi had no fear of their refutation, for he had only too many proofs of the truth of his discovery. He therefore set to work at once, and wrote an article for a magazine, embodying the substance of the book which he was preparing, and unmasking with avenging indignation the Villeroc who had been so unjustly honoured.

The letter which he had this morning received was from the present Marquis of Villeroc, who bore the title with all the tenacious pride of a man who has done little himself, and is therefore all the more indebted to his ancestors. By universal consent, his manner was perfect, and he was a notable ornament of the French nobility. His hereditary title gave him the distinction of being one of the Councillors of the Royalist party, though it must be said that his counsel was rarely asked. In a word, he represented traditional loyalty, unshakable faith in the monarchy, and chivalrous devotion to the Royalist cause, though he had never had occasion to prove his fidelity.

His letter contained a lofty protest. In a few dry lines, in which there were two mistakes in spelling, the Marquis spoke out his mind to the crazy historian who dared to upset history, and demanded a withdrawal of the facts which had been advanced. It was this that had caused M. Amalfi's exclamations. The tone of the letter was haughty. " As the guardian of an inheritance of glory," wrote the Marquis, " as the descendant of a hero, it is impossible for me to permit such an absurd attack on his memory."

" Very well," said M. Amalfi, " I will just go and show you what your hero was really like! "

An idea came to him. He took a case of papers out of the drawer of his desk, folded it in a rather worn leather cover, which had seen much service on the tables of public libraries and record offices, and though he was not as a rule very careful of his appearance, he put on his best overcoat. As he went downstairs he smiled and whistled, with the air of a man who knows what he is about. A cab was passing, and hailing it, he told the driver to go to the Rue de Varenne.

The Villeroc town-house was a magnificent building. Impressed by the noble lines of its architecture, M. Amalfi looked at it for a moment before entering. He was still smiling. He gave his card to the servant and was admitted into an immense drawing-room, looking out on a fine garden, and seeming as if it could not have changed much since the Restoration. The first thing which attracted his attention was a huge portrait, by Gérard, of the great Villeroc, in his robes of a peer of France. In another and smaller portrait, he appeared in his uniform of General of the Army of the Vendée, sword in hand, dealing out death to the enemy. Everything in this great room recalled him; everything was eloquent of his glory. The two autograph letters of Louis XVIII, in which he called Villeroc his " dear and faithful friend," were mounted in gold on either side of a sword of honour, which he had received from the former soldiers of the Royalist side, when he was created a peer. A glass case contained his plumed hat, with the white cockade. All spoke of the heroic past, and of the honours paid to the illustrious ancestor.

The Marquis at length appeared, after keeping his visitor waiting for a long time, no doubt to put him in his proper place. He was tall and thin, and singularly like Gérard's portrait.

" Sir," he said, without any other salutation: " I have seen your article."

" It is only an abstract of a large volume I am bringing out," interrupted M. Amalfi, whom the sight of all these souvenirs, impressive to others but not to him, inclined to obstinacy.

The Marquis shrugged his shoulders. " You ventured, sir," he continued severely, " to make most unwarrantable attacks. We despise them, sir, we despise them. Understand that clearly. They do not touch us at all. Still, we have the right to exact——"

M. Amalfi had been carefully studying the Marquis. He was very solemn, but was evidently sincere.

" My Lord Marquis," said he, " I never write anything of which I am not certain. Will you please look over some papers which I have brought with me? "

" We despise them, sir, we despise them," repeated the Marquis.

" Very good," replied M. Amalfi, with annoyance; " despise them if you like; but do look at them all the same."

Very carefully he took from his case about twenty different papers which he spread out one by one in due succession before the Marquis. The first was a letter from the Prior of the Marne to the Adjutant-General Savary, dated the 22nd of Frimaire (November-December) of the year II. In this letter the position of the Royalist camp was given, and certain information which came from " an unexpected source " in that very camp. The papers were full of details as to the occupation of Le Mans by the

Catholic Royalist Army, and as to its defeat in 1793. A note from Villeroc, in a scarcely disguised hand-writing, gave all particulars of the celebrated Council of War, held in the Hôtel de la Biche, between the two parties of Talmont and Larochejaquelein, under the presidency of the Bishop of Agra; and mentioned the indecision of the Vendéan leaders. Then there were a few lines from Maignan, Commissioner of the Revolutionary Police, plainly stating the name of Villeroc as a man overwhelmed with need of money, and capable of doing anything to obtain it. Nothing was lacking to complete these successive revelations, graduated so as to admit of no doubt whatever. The travelling case of Garnier de Saintes, a member of the convention, lost by him at Pont-Lieu, forgotten for a hundred years in the garret of a farmhouse, but the contents of which had at last been carefully collated and examined by M. Amalfi, left no room for the slightest shadow of doubt. For the sum of 500,000 francs, Villeroc had betrayed the Army which he served, pointing out the points at which it could most easily be attacked and routed. There was even an order from Turreau for the payment of the sum in question, confirming the shocking fact of the betrayal. And before that, there was a long correspondence with General Rossignol; and a letter from him, describing in his coarse way and in cynical terms, the intrigues in which Villeroc had engaged with him.

It was all quite undeniable. The gorgeous legend faded pitiably. Villeroc had made use of the favour which he enjoyed with the Royalists only to betray them. And mark—it was not a moment of madness, a sudden impulse, but a long premeditated and steady course of treason, for the basest motives; an appalling duplicity. It was infamy of this kind, which Villeroc had believed to be for ever concealed, that had been so splendidly rewarded by the foolish and ignorant gratitude of Louis XVIII; it was this tissue of crime and felony which had gained for the Vendéan leader the admiration of a deluded posterity.

The Marquis was stupefied. He could not speak. His face was flushed; he wrung his hands in distress which could find no other expression. M. Amalfi, in absolute certainty of his facts, had proved the authenticity of these terrible documents, brought to light to show the truth which had been so long hidden.

" You see," said the historian, " Kléber and Marceau won the Battle of Le Mans; their forces gave them the victory; but knowing, as they did, what was going on in the town, they could easily have won it three days sooner."

Tears rolled down the thin face of the poor Marquis. M. Amalfi, who had been speaking quite absorbed by his subject, suddenly stopped and looked at him. He now felt very sorry for him. The blow had been a severe one.

"Permit me, sir," said the Marquis de Villeroc at last, wiping his forehead, "to go and consult my wife."

He went out. M. Amalfi, who was also very much upset by this too sharp revenge for doubt thrown on his good faith as a historian, began to arrange the papers in his case. A quarter of an hour went by. The Marquis returned, accompanied by the Marquise, a woman who had been very beautiful and was now very dignified. There had been a hasty but serious conversation between the husband and the wife.

She did not beat about the bush, but went straight to the point.

"Sir," she said, "you are bringing dishonour on our house."

"Madame," replied M. Amalfi, who began to feel very uneasy, "I am only an historian. It is a painful task sometimes."

"Sir," she said, "you are in possession of secrets which until now were unknown to us. I assure you on my honour that we knew nothing of them. If you make them known it will kill us; I implore you not to publish your book."

"But it has been announced and is expected! I also have my duty to do."

The Marquise was really tragic and imposing in her grief. M. Amalfi felt for the agony which he had inflicted on this family. In spite of his uncompromising reply, he felt softened. Moreover, the Marquis had lost all his former haughtiness, and was now only a poor man who saw all his great position taken away. M. Amalfi was overwhelmed; he was sorry he had come.

"Sir," said the Marquise, "perhaps you will listen to a mother. We have a daughter who is about to be married to the heir to one of the greatest titles in France. Who knows what terrible consequences may result from the dreadful scandal which you will cause in our circle?"

She stretched out her hands toward him in appeal—she who was so proud, and had lived all her life in the prejudices of caste; and the downfall of her pride made her distress all the more pitiable.

Troubled by his innate kindness of heart, M. Amalfi murmured words of consolation, expressing his sympathy and sincere grief at having ever undertaken these researches, the result of which had been only too certain from the beginning. He excused himself humbly, and endeavoured to restore the courage of those on whom he had inflicted so deep an injury.

The Marquise saw that he was shaken in his resolution, and that he was truly grieved; and believed that only one last effort was necessary in order to obtain the victory.

"Be generous," she urged. "Our gratitude will be everlasting."

A struggle evidently took place in the mind of the honest historian, who had never in his life dreamed of tampering in the least with the truth, but had weighed so carefully every one of his words, and had given chapter and verse for every statement. And yet, he was miserable at the thought of the deep humiliation which he had inflicted on the Marquis, in spite of his arrogance at the beginning of their interview, and on his wife, who was plainly suffering acutely.

"Well?" asked the Marquise, anxiously.

"Well!" replied M. Amalfi, convinced in all good faith that he was about to make the greatest possible concession, and feeling rather uncomfortable in his conscience, which he was forced to bend before the pity which overpowered him: "I am so touched by your grief that I will give way. I will make a great sacrifice."

"And——?"

"Instead of saying in my book that Villeroc betrayed his party for five hundred thousand francs, I will say that in fact he only received half that sum."

REMY DE GOURMONT
B. 1858

THE WHITE GOWN

AH! How sorry I was to leave the corner of the railway carriage, where I had sat dreaming of views more interesting than the silent mills, the solitary spires, the gnarled apple-trees, and the melancholy hovels we passed, seeming, under the evening mist, to sleep the weary sleep of Nature freed at last from light and gaiety, from labour and from tears.

I had been invited to be present at the wedding of my friend, Albert de Courcy, whose best man I had agreed to be. I gave this promise with polite indifference, for I make it a principle never to seem to take too great an interest in other people's joys or sorrows. I maintain an air of dignity combined with friendliness, and the calm and somewhat melancholy smile which I bestow on my friends wins forgiveness for the flash of resentment which I sometimes cannot repress when it gleams for a moment in my eyes.

No one came to meet me, for I was not expected until the following day. I set out on foot, and walked through the woods for three-quarters of an hour, avoiding the open spaces and the moonlight, which bored me.

I did not feel anxious about the late hour of my arrival, for I had been here before and knew the ways of the house. The gate was unlocked; no dog made a sound; I entered as silently as a thief.

I crossed the smooth lawn so as to cut short the way by the winding avenue, and as I passed a group of syringas, whose poignant odour was spread around, I saw two windows lighted up in the dim white façade of the house.

These two bright windows were beside one another on the ground floor. Before tapping at the glass, I made bold to stop and look in.

In the midst of a small room littered with many garments, three women were gazing at a white gown which lay on an arm-chair, a gown white as the souls of the Holy Innocents. They were Rosa, a trusted maid of the family, Madame de Laneuil, and a girl whose face recalled my playmates of long ago, the little maidens with whom Alberic and I had sported; I remembered how they had pretended to be our brides, giving us flowers from their bouquets to wear as favours, and gravely posing in that marriage ceremony which is so dear to the heart of feminine childhood. How many years ago was that? A good many; perhaps ten. How many days had passed since those childish games! How many times since then the thrushes had sung in the tall chestnut trees round the house!

The place had been shut up ever since the death of M. de Laneuil, and had only been reopened now that Alberic was to take away a bride from here. My part was to lend to the marriage the indispensable stamp of social approval. Edith and Elphège had been our playmates, and now he was to marry Edith. The girl whom I saw before me, fair and pale, paler indeed than if she herself had been the bride, must surely be Elphège, my little sweetheart of other days. Elphège had always been fair and pale, and at the sight of her my boyish affection revived and my heart went out to her. Of course, she would be bridesmaid to her elder sister.

I yielded to the fascination of her charm and dreamed of the happiness of a double wedding, if that could be; two couples kneeling at the feet of the priest, two wedding rings instead of one. Of course it was Elphège who stood there, and I felt that I had loved her all through these years unconsciously, and had come here now just to fulfil my destiny.

Yes, I had loved her, though far away! My love had grown, even as I grew from boyhood to manhood, as the laughter of childhood softened into the serious smiles of youth, as the first gaiety of life melted into the dreams and strivings of manhood. And I seemed now to live those lost hours over again, and to listen once more to the songs of the thrushes every morning in the chestnut tops as they greeted the rising of the sun.

The perfume of the syringas was wafted on the night air, and went to my head like wine. I tapped at the window. The three women started, and after a pause and a word from the elder lady, Rosa pulled aside the curtain, and shading her eyes with her hands, asked who was there.

I spoke my name; Madame de Laneuil disappeared; the young girl smiled to me with the smile I knew of old, Elphège's smile; and all hastened to unbar the door and welcome the midnight visitor.

My old friend greeted me warmly, and raising the lamp examined me closely, exclaiming, " How pale you are! "

I hastened to assure her that I was very well, and that the moonlight made every one look pale; it seemed to have had a special effect on me that evening.

" You find us in a great difficulty, my dear," she said; " we hardly know what to do. Every one went to bed early. Elphège seems unwell; she has that mysterious depression which attacks girls whose sisters are being parted from them by marriage. I wished Edith, before going to rest alone for the last time, to come with me and join me in prayer. We were just going upstairs when the wedding gown arrived from Paris—that white gown. We thought of making some alteration in the trimming of the bodice, and Rosa pinned it on. Imagine our horror when we found that it will not fit at all! It is much too wide. Far too wide. We do not know what to do. We have been arguing and thinking; each of us in turn took up the scissors, but we dare not touch it for fear of spoiling it. Still, we must do something, even if we have to stay up all night."

My voice was as lifeless as the white gown itself, as I said, vainly attempting a tone of indifference: " When I tapped at the window, I happened to see one of your daughters, and I supposed it was Elphège. I took for granted that it was Elphège."

" They are very much alike; you might easily mistake one for the other, especially as it is so long since you have seen them. But come in; perhaps you will be able to help us. Men often have good ideas as to these things."

I stood still, and she repeated, " Come with me."

As I followed her into the little sitting-room, Edith looked at me with some surprise; but Madame de Laneuil explained who I was, and how I came to be there at such a late hour.

I vaguely heard her talking and laughing through the tumult of my thoughts. It was indeed Edith; Edith, pale and fair, the bride of to-morrow. And it was Edith whom I loved, whom I had always loved. The force of passion so overwhelmed me that if I had been alone with her I could not have restrained myself; I must have told her my mad desire to have her for my own, and to carry her off even at that hour, though against her will.

Madame de Laneuil continued to talk and laugh, explaining an idea which had come into her head.

And now I grew calmer; I mastered my emotion and looked at Edith, for I felt that she was looking at me and never once took her gaze from my face. I looked at her, I say, and in that look I saw that my passion was returned. Our eyes met for a second, which might have been eternity, so much was felt, so much conveyed in that glance of mutual understanding and consent.

Then I heard Madame de Laneuil saying, " Well, what do you think? Give us your advice."

I pulled myself together, trembling all over, and radiant with the happiness of the discovery I had made. Even my hostess noticed the change in my manner.

" Come," she said, " you look brighter already. A wedding is always a happy time, isn't it? "

Edith smiled sadly.

" First of all," I said, trying to appear business-like; " first of all, Edith must put on the dress."

" That is true; of course she must."

I shaded my eyes with my hands like Rosa, and looked out of the window, while the change was being made. The moon was high, throwing the shadow of the great manor-house across the courtyard. I saw nothing outside; another vision filled my brain, called up by the rustling of the silken fabric as they fastened the gown—the vision of the white throat and dainty form of my dear one, as she raised her arms, and from all her being a perfume was exhaled, sweet and poignant as the syringas in the night air outside. But now the white gown fell like an avalanche over all and blotted out my vision.

Edith still smiled sadly.

We talked like dressmakers. I gave my advice, which was taken. Rosa undertook to make the necessary alterations in the gown, and I saw by the way she looked at me that I had risen greatly in her estimation.

Madame de Laneuil took me to my room. Before leaving I said good-night to my love, just found and lost again, the bride of another. As we parted a sad sympathy welled up between us, the consciousness of a fatal secret shared by both. Her eyes followed me as I went out—her clear blue eyes now dimmed with tears.

The thrushes had long been singing to the dawn from the tops of the mighty chestnut trees. Alberic came into my room to talk of the morrow. He spoke of his bride, of his wish to make her happy, of his fear that he was not good enough for such a perfect creature. He rambled on like a good fellow who wants others to reassure him of what he tries to believe. I let him talk. It did me good to listen to him, for when one is unhappy there is consolation to be found, as Scripture tells us, in the anxieties of our friends. But all the time I thought, and thought incessantly, of the felicity which was not for me.

" The bride is coming! " A murmur went round the great drawing-room as Edith entered, fair and pale, beneath the pictured gaze of generations of her ancestors. She had not wept, neither had she slept; there were heavy shadows beneath the sapphire of her eyes. Her slender form was outlined by the white gown whose defects I had been called on to correct, and the virginal white veil fell over all.

Turning aside from the others, she approached her grandfather, who leaned against the mantelpiece, evidently deeply touched by the scene. As she passed close to me, barely moving her lips, her breath coming as in a sigh, her eyes cast down, these words reached me, so faint as to be no more than uttered—" Too late! "

I, too, lowered my eyes, thrilled once more by the forbidden joy of a secret understanding.

She offered her fair cheek to the old grandfather's kiss, and resting her two hands on his shoulders, she smiled up at him. But the smile was sad. The old man's kiss seemed to bring a blessing from all her ancestors on the nuptials of this daughter of their race.

I stood so near that the ample veil floated round my head, wafted by the breeze from an open window, and it seemed as if a breath of love came in to bear us, my Edith and myself, to the Paradise of parted lovers.

When she had again reached her mother's side, she looked at me for an instant fixedly, and then the white veil fell between her eyes and mine and hid them from my gaze—for ever! The perfume of the syringas, cruelly poignant, floated in through the open window. She was a wife!

During the ceremony, I repeated in my heart the bridegroom's replies to the questions of the priest, and when the nuptial blessing was pronounced, I bowed my head at the solemn words which bind together man and woman with an indissoluble bond.

I remembered my college days and the theological studies in which I had delighted, and I knew that in every sacrament there are two parts, the essence and the outer form, the true spirit and the manner in which the hidden blessing is imparted to those who await it. That spiritual essence of marriage—what is it? Not the blessing of the priest, nor the outer rites and ceremonies: but the union of hearts, the mutual consent of the lovers, and—that alone.

" My Edith," I thought, " bride of another, in this world you can never seem to be mine. But in reality you belong to me as you can never belong to him who outwardly possesses you, for his is only an apparent possession. You are mine in very truth. God knows of our mutual consent. *That* is His sacrament, and that alone."

I felt a bitter joy, as the priest spoke the solemn admonition to the wife—" Forsaking all others, she shall cleave to him and be faithful to him until death. And those whom God has joined together, let no man put asunder."

Silently I slipped away, and left the house as I had entered it —silently as a thief.

The thrushes had ceased their song in the tops of the high chestnuts, and the poignant syringas hung their perfumed heads, already faded, faded as the memory of a childish love.

THE MAGNOLIA

REMY DE GOURMONT

THE two orphan sisters came forth from the house where they lived —the young and beautiful Arabella and the old and ugly Bibiane. Arabella was like a daughter and Bibiane like her mother.

They came out of their sad dwelling and stopped under the magnolia, the magic tree which no one had ever planted and which grew so gorgeously in the garden of the melancholy house. It bloomed twice in the year: in the spring, before the green spikes had opened into leaves, and in the early autumn, before the great green leaves began to fade. In autumn, as in spring, the noble form of the magic tree was laden with chalice-shaped, lotus-like flowers, their waxen petals white as death, with a tiny crimson spot symbolical of life.

Leaning on the arm of her sister Bibiane, who was always kind to her fancies, Arabella stood under the magnolia, thinking, " He will die with the second blooming of the magnolia—he, whose blood should make me live, flower that I also am! Now I shall be pale for ever and must also die! "

" There is still one blossom left," said Bibiane.

It was only a bud, whose white unopened beauty showed bright amid the setting of deep green leaves.

" The last! " said Arabella. " It will be my sole bridal adornment. The last? No, there is still another, but it is faded and almost dead. Symbols of both of us! Oh, I fear and tremble at the sign, for what could more clearly show what we are than these two flowers? I pluck the one which is myself, Bibiane. Look, here I am. If I should have to die too? "

Silently Bibiane caressed her trembling sister, and, in fear herself also, led her from the sorrowful garden, and from the magnolia stripped of its last beauty.

They entered the house which was the abode of lost happiness and of early grief.

" How is he? " asked Bibiane, taking from Arabella's shoulders the white scarf of the bride.

Arabella sat down to contemplate the unopened blossom which she held in her fingers, and the mother of the dying man continued, " We must make haste, for he is dying and his last wish must be accomplished before he goes. Come, my Arabella, my daughter, bride of a dying man, whose beauty will lighten the last sad prayers, softening Death with Love. It is Death which awaits you, alas! my child; the nuptial kiss pressed on your forehead will come from one who is already claimed by the cold tomb, who will pass from your arms into a darkness which will fall for ever between you both, a darkness which the light of your eyes will never pierce, my Arabella. My son will die; he is already numbered among the dead, and you, so fair, so bright, so fitted for the joy of life and love, must be united to the endless gloom and corruption of the grave. Alas! Alas for both of you, my child!"

They wept together as the witnesses came in, to attest the union of Death with Life. The priest followed, prepared for two sacraments, that which should bless the ring of marriage and that wherein holy oil should ease the passage of the parting soul.

All went up in silence, their steps sounding dull and solemn as those of the bearers of a bier, to where he lay prepared for the sacrament of Life and the sacrament of Death. The nuptial couch and the coffin, how could they differ now?

They ascended in silence, unbroken except by the words of the mother, repeating, "We must make haste, for he is going to die, and his last wish must be accomplished."

In the chamber of the dying man all knelt, except Arabella, who stood by the nuptial couch, her white robe falling round her like a shroud; and when her turn came to kneel too, her face pressed on the pillow, all the company trembled, as if she too were claimed by Death. Her soft white hand was laid on the thin wasted hand of the dying man, lying outside the coverlet, and in her other hand was the unopened magnolia bud, symbol of virginity, which she pressed to the dying lips.

The solemn words of the service alone broke the stillness. All watched the son supported by his mother, fascinated by the expression of his face. No resignation, no peace of love fulfilled was there; but the rage of despair, of passion unaccomplished, of struggle to retain the life which was fleeting away, of hatred and envy of the life which remained. The flame of his hollow eyes gleamed on Arabella as though in withering jealousy of her fresh young beauty, and all present thought, "How dreadfully he must suffer!"

He raised himself with a supreme effort. He murmured with livid lips, over which the tint of death was stealing, amid the strained silence of the men and the low sobs of the women:

"Farewell, Arabella; you are mine for ever now. I must go, but you must follow me. I shall be there. Every evening I shall await you under the magnolia, and you shall know no other love but mine. No other, Arabella. You shall have proof of my love; yes, proof indeed, for yours is the soul which I must have!"

And with a smile which gleamed like that of a satyr or a devil across the gathering shadows of his wasted face, he hoarsely repeated these words, which sounded like wanderings, but had the deep significance of a warning from beyond the tomb:

" Under the magnolia, Arabella, under the magnolia! "

All day, and almost all night, Arabella sat and watched the magnolia, its blossoms all gone, its discoloured leaves ready to fall; and at night, when the wind rustled through the stiff dry foliage and the magic tree stood tall and noble in the moonlight, which gleamed fitfully from among October clouds, Arabella trembled and cried, clasping Bibiane, " He is there! "

He was there, under the magnolia, in the masses of the fallen leaves, like a shadow waved by the wind.

One evening she said to Bibiane, " We loved one another. Why should he do me harm? He is there, and I will go to him! "

" The wishes of the dead must be obeyed," replied Bibiane. " Go, and fear not. I will leave the door open and will come if you call. Go; he is there."

He was there indeed, among the dead leaves rustling in the wind, and when Arabella reached the magnolia, the shadow stretched out its arms, twining them about her like cold and slimy serpents, writhing and hissing on her fair shoulders like snakes of hell.

Bibiane heard a stifled cry. She ran to where her sister lay dead, and carried her back to the house. On her neck were two livid marks like the pressure of thin and bony fingers.

Her eyes still kept an expression of anguished horror, and her hands were clasped on something dry and brown. It was the withered flower which they had seen on the tree on her wedding day, the last pitiful dead bloom which they had left there in compassion, the flower which had symbolised the other, the one who had passed beyond the grave.

FERDINAND BEISSIER
B. 1858

THE HELMET

" BUT, uncle—I love my cousin! "

" Get out! "

" Give her to me."

" Don't bother me! "

" It will kill me! "

" Nonsense! you'll console yourself with some other girl."

" Please——"

My uncle, whose back had been towards me, whirled round, his face red to bursting, and brought his closed fist down upon the counter with a heavy thump.

" Never! " he cried; " never! Do you hear what I say? "

And as I looked at him beseechingly and with clasped hands, he went on:

" A pretty husband you look like!—without a sou, and dreaming of going into housekeeping! A nice mess I should make of it, by giving you my daughter! It's no use your insisting. You know that when I have said ' No,' nothing under the sun can make me say ' Yes '! "

I ceased to make any further appeal. I knew my uncle—about as headstrong an old fellow as could be found in a day's search. I contented myself with giving vent to a deep sigh, and then went on with the furbishing of a big, double-handed sword, rusty from point to hilt.

This memorable conversation took place in the shop of my maternal uncle, a well-known dealer in antiquities and *objets d'art*, No. 53 Rue des Claquettes, at the sign of the " Maltese Cross "—a perfect museum of curiosities.

The walls were hung with Marseilles and old Rouen china, facing ancient cuirasses, sabres, and muskets, and picture-frames; below these were ranged old cabinets, coffers of all sorts, and statues of saints, one-armed or one-legged for the most part and dilapidated as to their gilding; then, here and there, in glass cases, hermetically closed and locked, there were knick-knacks in infinite variety—

lachrymatories, tiny urns, rings, precious stones, fragments of marble, bracelets, crosses, necklaces, medals, and miniature ivory statuettes, the yellow tints of which, in the sun, took momentarily a flesh-like transparency.

Time out of mind the shop had belonged to the Cornuberts. It passed regularly from father to son, and my uncle—his neighbours said—could not but be the possessor of a nice little fortune. Held in esteem by all, a Municipal Councillor, impressed by the importance and gravity of his office, short, fat, highly choleric and headstrong, but at bottom not in the least degree an unkind sort of man—such was my uncle Cornubert, my only living male relative, who, as soon as I left school, had elevated me to the dignity of chief and only clerk and shopman of the "Maltese Cross."

But my uncle was not only a dealer in antiquities and a Municipal Councillor, he was yet more, and above all, the father of my cousin Rose, with whom I was naturally in love.

To come back to the point at which I digressed.

Without paying any attention to the sighs which exhaled from my bosom while scouring the rust from my long, two-handed sword, my uncle, magnifying glass in hand, was engaged in the examination of a lot of medals which he had purchased that morning. Suddenly he raised his head; five o'clock was striking.

"The Council!" he cried.

When my uncle pronounced that august word, it made a mouthful; for two pins he would have saluted it bareheaded. But, this time, after a moment's consideration, he tapped his forehead and added, in a tone of supreme relief:

"No, the sitting does not take place before to-morrow—and I am forgetting that I have to go to the railway station to get the consignment of which I was advised this morning."

Rising from his seat, and laying down his glass, he called out:

"Rose, give me my cane and hat!"

Then, turning towards me, he added, in a lowered tone and speaking very quickly:

"As for you—don't forget our conversation. If you think you can make me say 'Yes,' try!—but I don't think you'll succeed. Meanwhile, not a word to Rose, or, by Saint Barthélemy, my patron of happy memory, I'll instantly kick you out of doors!"

At that moment Rose appeared with my uncle's cane and hat, which she handed to him. He kissed her on the forehead; then, giving me a last but eloquent look, hurried from the shop.

I went on scouring my double-handed sword. Rose came quietly towards me.

"What is the matter with my father?" she asked; "he seems to be angry with you."

I looked at her—her eyes were so black, her look so kind, her mouth so rosy, and her teeth so white that I told her all—my love, my appeal to her father, and his rough refusal. I could not help it—after all, it was *his* fault! He was not there: I determined to brave his anger. Besides, there is nobody like timid persons for displaying courage in certain circumstances.

My cousin said nothing; she only held down her eyes—while her cheeks were as red as those of cherries in May.

I checked myself.

"Are you angry with me?" I asked tremblingly. "Are you angry with me, Rose?"

She held out her hand to me. On that, my heart seething with audacity, my head on fire, I cried:

"Rose—I swear it! I will be your husband!" And as she shook her head and looked at me sadly, I added: "Oh! I know that my uncle is self-willed, but I will be more self-willed still; and, since he must be forced to say 'Yes,' I will force him to say it!"

"But how?" asked Rose.

Ah! how? That was exactly the difficulty. But, no matter; I would find a way to surmount it!

At that moment a heavy step resounded in the street. Instinctively we moved away from each other; I returned to my double-handed sword, and Rose, to keep herself in countenance, set to dusting, with a corner of her apron, a little statuette in its faded red velvet case.

My uncle entered. Surprised at finding us together, he stopped short and looked sharply at us, from one to the other.

We each of us went on rubbing without raising our heads.

"Here, take this," said my uncle, handing me a bulky parcel from under his arm. "A splendid purchase, you'll see."

The subject did not interest me in the least.

I opened the parcel, and from the enveloping paper emerged a steel helmet—but not an ordinary helmet, oh, no!—a superb, a monumental morion, with gorget and pointed visor of strange form. The visor was raised, and I tried to discover what prevented it from being lowered.

"It will not go down—the hinges have got out of order," said my uncle; "but it's a superb piece, and, when it has been thoroughly cleaned and touched up, will look well—that shall be your to-morrow's job."

"Very good, uncle," I murmured, not daring to raise my eyes to his.

That night, on reaching my room, I went at once to bed. I was eager to be alone and able to think at my ease. Night brings counsel, it is said; and I had great need that the proverb should prove true. But, after lying awake for an hour without receiving any assistance, I fell off to sleep, and, till next morning, did nothing but dream the oddest dreams. I saw Rose on her way to church in a strange bridal costume, a fourteenth-century cap, three feet high, on her head, but looking prettier than ever; then suddenly the scene changed to moonlight, in which innumerable helmets and pieces of old china were dancing a wild farandola, while my uncle, clad in complete armour and with a formidable halberd in his hand, conducted the bewildering whirl.

The next day—ah, the next day!—I was no nearer. In vain, with clenched teeth, I scoured the immense helmet brought by my uncle the previous evening—scoured it with such fury as almost to break the iron; not an idea came to me. The helmet shone like a sun: my uncle sat smoking his pipe and watching me; but I could think of nothing, of no way of forcing him to give me his daughter.

At three o'clock Rose went into the country, whence she was not to return until dinner-time, in the evening. On the threshold she could only make a sign to me with her hand; my uncle had not left us alone for a single instant. He was not easy in his mind; I could see that by his face. No doubt he had not forgotten our conversation of the previous evening.

I went on rubbing at my helmet.

"You have made it quite bright enough—put it down," said my uncle.

I put it down. The storm was gathering: I could not do better than allow it to blow over.

But suddenly, as if seized by some strange fancy, my uncle took up the enormous morion and turned and examined it on all sides.

"A handsome piece of armour, there is no doubt about it; but it must have weighed pretty heavily on its wearer's shoulders," he muttered; and, urged by I know not what demon, he clapped it on his head and latched the gorget-piece about his neck.

Struck almost speechless, I watched what he was doing—thinking only how ugly he looked.

Suddenly there was a sharp sound—as if a spring had snapped—and—crack!—down fell the visor; and there was my uncle, with his head in an iron cage, gesticulating and swearing like a pagan!

I could contain myself no longer, and burst into a roar of laughter; for my uncle, stumpy, fat, and rubicund, presented an irresistibly comic appearance.

Threateningly, he came towards me.

"The hinges!—the hinges, fool!" he yelled.

I could not see his face, but I felt that it was red to bursting.

"When you have done laughing, idiot!" he cried.

But the helmet swayed so oddly on his shoulders, his voice came from out it in such strange tones, that the more he gesticulated, the more he yelled and threatened me, the louder I laughed.

At that moment the clock of the Hôtel-de-Ville, striking five, was heard.

"The Municipal Council!" murmured my uncle in a stifled voice. "Quick! help me off with this beast of a machine! We'll settle our business afterwards!"

But, suddenly likewise, an idea—a wild, extraordinary idea—came into my head; but then, who ever is madder than a lover? Besides, I had no choice of means.

"No!" I replied.

My uncle fell back two paces in terror—and again the enormous helmet wobbled on his shoulders.

"No," I repeated firmly, "I'll not help you out, unless you give me the hand of my cousin Rose!"

From the depths of the strangely elongated visor came, not an angry exclamation, but a veritable roar. I had "done it"!—I had burned my boats!

"If you do not consent to do what I ask of you," I added, "not only will I not help you off with your helmet, but I will call in all your neighbours, and then go and find the Municipal Council!"

"You'll end your days on the scaffold!" cried my uncle.

"The hand of Rose!" I repeated. "You told me that it would only be by force that you would be made to say 'Yes'—say it, or I will call in the neighbours!"

The clock was still striking; my uncle raised his arms as if to curse me.

"Decide at once!" I cried, "somebody is coming!"

"Well, then—Yes!" murmured my uncle. "But make haste!"

"On your word of honour?"

"On my word of honour!"

The visor gave way, the gorget-piece also, and my uncle's head issued from durance, red as a poppy.

Just in time. The chemist at the corner, a colleague in the Municipal Council, entered the shop.

"Are you coming?" he asked; "they will be beginning the business without us."

"I'm coming," replied my uncle.

And without looking at me, he took up his hat and cane and hurried out.

The next moment all my hopes had vanished. My uncle would surely not forgive me.

At dinner-time I took my place at table on his right hand in low spirits, ate little, and said nothing.

"It will come with the dessert," I thought.

Rose looked at me, and I avoided meeting her eyes. As I had

expected, dessert over, my uncle lighted his pipe, raised his head, and then——

" Rose—come here! "

Rose went to him.

" Do you know what that fellow there asked me to do, yesterday? "

I trembled life a leaf, and Rose did the same.

" To give him your hand," he added. " Do you love him? "

Rose cast down her eyes.

" Very well," continued my uncle; " on this side, the case is complete. Come here, you."

I approached him.

" Here I am, uncle," and, in a whisper, I added quickly: " Forgive me! "

He burst into a hearty laugh.

" Marry her, then, donkey—since you love her, and I give her to you! "

" Ah!—uncle! "

" Ah!—dear papa! "

And Rose and I threw ourselves into his arms.

" All right! all right! " he cried, wiping his eyes. " Be happy, that's all I ask."

And, in turn, he whispered in my ear:

" I should have given her to you all the same, you big goose; but—keep the story of the helmet between us two! "

I give you my word that I have never told it, except to Rose, my dear little wife. And, if ever you pass along the Rue des Claquettes, at No. 53, at the place of honour in the old shop, I'll show you my uncle's helmet, which we would never sell.

ANATOLE LE BRAZ
B. 1859

THE BLOOD OF THE SIREN

SHE was a very young woman, Marie-Ange, and as fresh and as gracious as her name; she was like a water nymph risen from the waves as she seized the ladder of the *Louise* and slowly climbed on board.

" How is Jean? " was the captain's question. " How many lobsters did he catch this season? "

It seemed as if the question had disappeared far back in the depths of her sea-green eyes as she answered:

" There has been a wonderful catch this season. We had one hundred and fifty for our share alone; and that is why Jean could not come with me to the christening. He had to sell them in the Isle of Saints. They pay more there."

I had listened enchanted. Her voice was pure music. She did not speak; she sang. She was sitting on the bench beside me, her hands joined in a gesture of adoration. She crossed herself in silent prayer.

" It is because we enter Fromaveur," she said.

Suddenly the waves became choppy and rough and threw themselves against the sides of the ship and I remembered the old story I had heard in my youth. Here, they had told me, the sirens have their palaces, tormented by endless desires which they endeavour to quench in vain; for the lips of the sons of men from which they wish to drink love are frozen by death under their kisses. Disappointed one day, they begin the next.

" Do you believe in sirens, Marie-Ange? " I asked idly.

She grew pale, her lips compressed, and a shadow crept into her eyes at the question.

" Why do you ask that? " she said fiercely.

" Only that the country people have told me such stories of this Fromaveur," I answered.

" From what part of Brittany do you come? " she said, smiling once more.

Then we entered one of the two harbours of Ouessant. She flew up the rocky path like a bird and laughed as she watched my slow and awkward ascent. Each note of her laugh was like a pearl.

"You must have a charming voice, Marie-Ange. I should like to hear you sing," I said.

She became serious at once. "In our island the women never sing after marriage, except in church."

A delicious perfume spread about us, subtle and penetrating, made up of a thousand little secret odours.

"Do not look for it," she said. "That is the aroma of Ouessant. It fills everything here, even the stones of the old houses."

Then came the parting of the ways and she went to Cadoran, the oldest house of this island, the cradle of the clan Morvarch. She went down the hill and away from me.

Suddenly, as I walked along toward my destination, a sharp voice called behind me:

"Won't you ride, sir?"

She who called was a little old woman with a fresh face framed by a small black hood from which escaped some locks of white hair like bits of uncarded wool. She crouched in the little waggon, drawn by a tiny horse.

"Nola Glaquin, sir—at your service."

I asked her abruptly: "Tell me, who is this Marie-Ange?"

"Aha!" she said. "Another one bewitched by the beauty of Marie-Ange! There is a spell over that woman. She is married to Jean Morvarch, a fine fellow, a pilot and also a lobster fisher." Nola Glaquin made the sign of a cross and I heard her say under her breath: "God keep the dear fellow!" Then she said: "They have a child, a perfect cherub."

"But what is it that is strange about her?" I asked. "She seems unlike all the rest of us."

"Will you believe me if I tell you?" said the old woman.

"Yes, because you believe," I answered.

"A long time ago, sir," she said, "twelve virgins, as lovely as angels in body, but demons in soul, had their summer home down there in that basin where the water of the sea comes in among the rocks. In winter they followed the storms, no one knew whither; but as soon as the sunshine reappeared, they came back. They never came out of the water, for they could not walk on land; and at night they sang. The young men of the island grew wild. Many lost their souls because of these sirens and many ruined their parents, too, for these wicked ones. Then God took pity on the island and sent good St. Veltez, who was the bishop. He gave them his ring to kiss and they burned their lips fearfully and fled away, crying."

The little old woman shivered under her thin cape.

"They appeared here no more, but across there on the other

coast you can hear their cries on clear nights. There are only eleven now."

"Where is the other one?" I asked.

Then she looked at me. "Will you believe me if I tell you?"

"Because you believe," I said.

"The old men who are older than I am," she said, "tell how the head of Cadoran was fishing one morning, and one of the sirens was resolved to have him, for he was the proudest and most handsome man in the island. When he had drawn her out of the water, she said to him:

"'Let me be your wife after the manner of men, and I will make you king of the sea.'

"She spoke very sweetly, and he wanted to be king of the sea.

"'But you are only half a woman,' he said.

"And she replied, 'Carry me in your arms to the door of your house.'

"She was as cold as ice when he took her up, but as they travelled the road to Cadoran she became warmer and warmer and the scales fell from her limbs. And when he reached the door and opened it, she walked in by herself."

The little old woman watched me to see whether I believed. Then she went on:

"She could only belong to him at night, and a little before dawn she always crept back to the sea. He became king of the sea, as she had said. The winds and the waves obeyed him. He was happy and rich, and a beautiful child came to them. One morning he said to her as she rose to leave:

"'I need you by the light of day.'

"And she was sad. 'Do not ask such a thing. It would ruin us both and all our posterity.'

"'If you refuse,' he said, 'it is because you do not love me!'

"And the words hurt her so that she fainted, and when she opened her eyes again it was day.

"Since then"—the old woman spoke very softly—"trouble follows the race of the siren. In each generation her blood runs in a woman irresistibly charming, whose voice and face show the unquiet of the siren's soul, and an implacable destiny watches over her from the depths of the sea. In the midst of her joy, soon after her marriage, the blow falls. One fine day the husband goes out as usual to fish; evening comes and he does not return. Once more those eleven sisters have punished the offence of the twelfth, and while the widow cries from the rocks to him who never will return, you can hear afar off the light voices laughing. Marie-Ange is one of these."

I heard Marie-Ange sing the next day in church, and I could

see her. And her face showed that she was the inconstant, divine being born of the dreams of primitive humanity in the illumined depths of the sea. The music of the waves trembled under her lightest note and her eyes shone with the mysterious fire of the sea. Her heart exhaled its perfume, her flesh reflected the morning and the evening glow, and the breath of the ocean breeze swept about her.

I asked where Jean was, her husband. He had stayed overnight, she thought, at Saint Isle. "He will probably return to-night; the winds are fair."

That night, when the breath of the sea came hot from the furnace of the tropics, we sat in the window of the Hôtel Stephan. The bells in the little church tower had rung for curfew, and there was one among us with his pipe to his lips who was telling the story of a shipwreck. "Do you recall the speech Nola Glaquin made that night before we got the news?"

"Who is Nola Glaquin?" I asked.

"An old fool. She pretends that she knows the misfortunes that are coming a couple of days before the rest of us. They nicknamed her the Death Gull. The people here swear that the gulls talk to her and she understands them. It is true," he went on, "that the hearth of her house is covered with the feathers of these birds, and when they are wounded they come to her and are cured; and in return for this attention they are said to bring her tidings from the sea."

"Yes," said another of the group to me; "one day she passed our house. My mother asked her if she would not come in and light her pipe."

"'Alas,' she replied, shaking her head; 'do not jest, Renée-Ann! You will have me in your house sooner than you can possibly expect!'

"And that same evening I went for her, for my father was drowned; and she is a watcher with the dead in this village."

At this moment the hotel-keeper's youngest daughter came in in great excitement, followed by a man of enormous stature. His jacket was too short for him, the sailor's clothes hung in rags about him. The schoolmaster recognised him first.

"It is Mauet-Euss, the mate of Jean Morvarch."

The man looked like a frightened animal.

"What has happened?" we asked.

He bowed his hairy face over his herculean breast and sobbed like a child. The air in the hotel office suddenly thickened with the sea-fog; and the lamp burned with a green light over the face of our companion. The schoolmaster gave him a drink of brandy, and he told us, brokenly, his sweat and tears flowing together, of what had happened to his master.

He had started the night before for home, very gay, for his pockets were full of money and the sea was as still as a pond. And Jean Morvarch had sent his mate to sleep and had sung an old song as he stayed by the helm. And then the mate heard a voice and awakened suddenly. He jumped up and ran to the helm—there was no one there! The sky was clear, and the sea even clearer, and it seemed as if there were lights under the water, and he called, "Morvarch! Jean Morvarch!" And the call had echoed as in a church, and then from the distance came a long, sad call, ending in laughter. And the laughter was all about the boat; and although they sought for hours, until the sun was high, they could find no sign of him.

The next day I saw Nola Glaquin as she stood before a table. In front of her rose the catafalque, upon which rested the waxen cross that represented the body of the one who could not be there. Marie-Ange was sitting by the oaken cradle where lay the baby.

"GEORGES COURTELINE"

B. 1860

A GENTLEMAN FINDS A WATCH

FROM the top seats of L'Étoile tram-car I perceived my friend Bréloc, who was just crossing the Place Blanche in such a state of excitement that I got down from the car on purpose to question him.

"Hey! *mon Dieu!* what is the matter, Bréloc? What is the meaning of this face of yours, more mournful than a shop closed on account of a death in the family?"

"Please don't mention it," he replied; "I've just had a narrow escape from being put in gaol."

Which led me to think that he had committed some dishonest action, and I began to ejaculate rather loudly, when he, guessing the turn of my thoughts, exclaimed: "You don't seem to understand! I was very nearly being put in gaol through an unlucky watch that I picked up last night on the Boulevard Saint-Michel, and which I honestly deposited in the hands of the commissaire (police inspector) of our district. Pretty rough, hey? I feel almost ill from astonishment and fright. But you can judge for yourself. Have you five minutes to spare?"

"Certainly. Why not?"

"Then listen, and I hope you may profit by my experience.

"About 9 A.M. I presented myself at the police station in the Rue Duperré carrying said watch—a beautiful timepiece, by the way, with gold case and platina monogram—and I asked to be shown to the commissaire. That gentleman had just finished drinking his cup of chocolate, when he gave orders that I should be admitted to his presence, and without deigning to say good-day or offer me a seat, he began:

"'What do you want?'

"I had composed my features for the occasion, with the smile of a man who accomplishes a meritorious act for which he expects to be almost crowned with glory. So I answered, 'Monsieur le

Commissaire of Police, I have the honour of depositing in your hands a watch that I found last night, and——'

"Without letting me finish the sentence, the commissaire sprang up, repeating the words:

"'A watch! A watch!'

"The gendarmes were playing cards in the next room.

"He hallooed to them:

"'Hey! you there! Close the street door! There is more draught here than in a windmill!' And he remained grumbling until his order had been executed.

"Then, resuming his seat, he proceeded:

"'Please give me that article.'

"I handed him the watch, which he began to turn about, examining and turning the winder, opening the case and the chain swivel.

"'Yes,' he said gravely, 'it is indeed a watch, there is no denying.'

"Saying which, he deposited the watch in the depths of a very large safe, closing its three locks.

"I looked on with astonishment, and he resumed:

"'And where did you find this valuable article?'

"'Boulevard Saint-Michel, at the corner of Rue Monsieur-le-Prince.'

"'On the ground?' asked the commissaire; 'on the pavement?'

"I answered in the affirmative.

"'It is very extraordinary,' he said with a suspicious look at me; 'the pavement is not the usual place to leave a watch.'

"I remarked smilingly:

"'If I may call your attention——'

"Drily the commissaire said:

"'That will do! You may omit all remarks. I know my business.'

"I stopped talking and smiling.

"He resumed, 'In the first place, who are you?'

"I gave my name.

"'Where do you live?'

"'I have already said that I live at the Place Blanche, 26, second floor.'

"'What are your means of living?'

"I explained that I had an income of twelve thousand francs.

"'At what time, as near as you can tell, did you find the watch?'

"'Three o'clock A.M.'

"'Was it not later?' he remarked ironically.

"'I don't think it was,' I said candidly.

" ' Well, I congratulate you,' he said ironically. ' It seems to me that you are leading a somewhat singular existence.'

" As I was rather warmly protesting my right to live according to my fancy——

" ' Admitted! ' said the commissaire. ' But I have a right to know what the deuce you could be doing at that hour on the Boulevard Saint-Michel, corner of Rue Monsieur-le-Prince, you who *say* that you are living at the Place Blanche? '

" ' What do you mean by that, I *say*? '

" ' Well, you do say so.'

" ' If I say so, it is a fact.'

" ' That is what we must have proved. Meanwhile, please do not wander from the conversation, and answer courteously to all the questions that I feel it my duty to put to you. I am asking what were you doing at that unearthly hour in a neighbourhood that was not your own? '

" I explained (as was true) that I was coming from the house of a lady friend.

" ' What does she do, your lady friend? '

" ' She is a married woman.'

" ' Married. To whom? '

" ' To a druggist.'

" ' What is his name? '

" ' That is none of your business,' I answered impatiently.

" ' Do you dare to talk like that to me? ' bawled the commissaire.

" ' Of course.'

" The commissaire's face became purple.

" ' Well, my man! you will have to alter your tune; that strain of yours does not suit me. And—I fancy that I recollect your features.'

" ' Oh, nonsense! '

" ' Yes—I do have a recollection——'

" There was a moment of silence. Then:

" ' Have you ever been committed for trial, Bréloc? '

" This exhausted my patience.

" ' Have you? ' said I.

" The commissaire sprang to his feet.

" ' You are a blackguard! ' he cried.

" ' And you are an idiot! ' I retorted.

" At that moment I thought my last hour had come. The commissaire bounded toward me, flushed and foaming with rage. Under his bushy eyebrows I could see the glistening of his wild eyes.

" ' What did you say? ' he stammered. ' What did you say? '

" I attempted to utter a word, but he did not give me a chance.

" ' And I say that I am going to send you to gaol; and it will not take very long! It is just the hour for the patrol waggon! Ah! you are going to put on airs! Ah! you want to jeer at me, and at the law that I represent! Very well! you came to the wrong place!'

"He brought down his fist violently on the papers lying on his table with each of his sentences, adding:

"'Do I know you? Do I know who you are? You say that your name is Bréloc; I don't know anything about it! You say that you live at the Place Blanche. Where are the proofs of it? You say that you have twelve thousand francs income. Am I bound to believe you? Show me your twelve thousand francs! Hein! you would have a hard job to show them to me.'

"I was stunned.

"'All this is not very clear,' he concluded violently. 'I say—do you hear?—that it is not very clear, and I don't know that you did not steal that watch!'

"'Steal it!'

"'Yes, steal it! Anyhow, I am going to find out.'

"The gendarmes, hearing the noise, had come into the room. He called out to them:

"'Search this man!'

"In a second they undressed me completely, even down to my socks.

"'Ah! you think you are smart!' the commissaire repeated mockingly. 'Ah! you mean to trick us! Look well under his arms,' he said to the gendarmes. 'Search him thoroughly!'"

At the recital of these indignities Bréloc's voice became over-excited. But I was laughing, nodding my head approvingly, because I could recognise in his story the two implacable enemies of honest folk—the administration and the law.

"Catch me finding another watch!" roared my unfortunate friend, with a closed fist as if threatening the future.

HENRI LAVEDAN

B. 1860

YEARS AFTER

Between 1850 and 1855, in a little provincial town, in a deserted quarter, in an old room that was full of memories of the past, two old people, a man and a woman, sat before the fire on a Christmas night at a late hour.

Their hair was as white as the winter's snow that was falling without in slow flakes like little pieces of moonlight. Their faces were spiritual, tender, fine, full of charm, and goodness. Sometimes a smile, like a pale ray of the late season's sun, lit up their faces, which one could see had in former days been very kindly. Even now they retained traces of their former beauty. One had only to see them seated there side by side in their well-worn arm-chairs, their knees almost touching, to be sure that they had loved each other very much.

They did not speak. They watched the fire flare up and die down again. The flames, short or high, rose and fell, dancing a little ballet in their red, blue, and green skirts. The old couple followed them with their eyes, and one could well imagine that they were looking through the dancing flames in the old cast-iron fireplace at the long scroll of their youth. It was just because, if they had opened their mouths at all, they would have had thousands of things to say that would have taken them days and weeks, that they were silent on this Christmas night. But it is possible to understand one another without the aid of speech. Silence is the language of golden hearts, and this old married couple did not need to use words and phrases to question one another and reply. They knew beforehand, once for all, what they thought of themselves and of this world—and of the other, in which they both believed. They knew each other so well! Never had a cloud, however faint, dimmed the azure of their happiness; never had they had a secret from one another for forty years. They had had a secret all their lives, to tell the truth, but it was a mutual secret that they bore lightly, that of their quiet and delightful happiness, which they had guarded and concealed as best they could, because they knew that too great earthly happiness is lost as soon as one boasts of it or even tells of it in confidence. Tell your best friend under the seal of secrecy that you possess a treasure, and it is already stolen.

But it had been easier for them than for ordinary people of the regular world to conceal, and it may be forgiven them, for at that time they were both members of that free-mannered, slightly suspect, amiable, dangerous, madcap, unreflecting, rich and poor craft, whose vices honest people copy and in which virtue is so often to be found, that is called the guild of actors.

Yes, this couple of worthy and delightful old people, married hard and fast years ago by mayor and priest, before God and before man, as seriously as a grocer or a marquis could be—they were a couple of old play-folk, former treaders of the boards, beings created in the image of God—born on this very night—who had rouged their cheeks and blacked their eyes, who had recited verse and prose of which they were not the authors, on the stage, and all for money to make a living! And they were there, in the venerable white hair that was their own, dreaming before the hearthfire—their last footlights—on their return from the midnight mass to which they had gone, arm-in-arm, to wonder at the scenes of that adorable play, so simple and so popular that the number of its performances can no longer be reckoned, that has made the world weep and laugh, in which the principal actors are Joseph, Jesus, the Virgin, and the Ass, and, in the secondary rank, the Kings, who, with their poor offerings of gold and precious stones, play only secondary rôles. The husband was called Valère and his wife Lise. These were their stage names, the names they had had the modesty to assume to avoid dishonouring the excellent families to which they belonged and which included among their forebears a Roman prince, two barons, three generals, a king's favourite, a bishop, many bankrupts, a roué, and one man who had been hanged.

Their sentimental history was as simple and naïve as the intrigue in a curtain-raiser, as the dialogue in a piece for school children. One evening, as they told each other their love on the stage, they had had a revelation of their own mutual love and had married soon after, like the end of one of Scribe's plays. They had had no children, but in spite of that they had been very happy. For five and twenty years they had played together in more than a thousand comedies, tragedies, farces, and dramas. They had great talent. They had laughed, wept, and portrayed adorably emotions that were at once sincere and simulated. They had died in a hundred different ways; from joy and from sorrow, by cold steel and by poison, by fire and by shipwreck; they had gathered bravos and laurels, celebrated their silver wedding and then retired to a little country town, as prettily planted and swept as a stage-scene, of which they had preserved a specially tender recollection ever since they had passed through it in the mail-coach while on tour, and where they had sworn by the prompter's box to come back and end their lives playing over their old parts. They were playing them over now in the mild calm and happiness of an eternal vacation, remembering the repertoire of their happiness that had been so pure, so complete, so rare.

As the hour sounded from a clock that was still older than they and had been saying the same thing over and over again since the days of Louis XIV., Valère, smothering a slight cough in his silk handkerchief, said to Lise:

"We are very silent, my Chloe."

She gave a slight nod of the head—if it was not the little perpetual trembling, the sad yes-and-no of old age—and sighed: "That is true, but I was thinking."

"Of what?"

"Of something that it will cost me dear to tell you of, and yet I must tell you. I have a confession to make."

"A confession to make to me?"

"Yes, and a very serious one."

"Does it concern love?" and his eyes shone with a Don Juan flame.

"Yes."

"Bah! Another?"

"Alas!"

"Why alas?"

"You shall see," and she began: "You suppose I have always been faithful to you, do you not?"

"Assuredly, and I suppose it still. By the devil who made woman!" That was an oath from a romantic play in which he was inimitable.

"You are mistaken."

"You have deceived me?"

"Yes."

"You?" He sat up in his chair. "You, Lise, in whom I have placed the blindest confidence! What! You have—wicked and sacrilegious—you have thanked me in this way for the marked favour I have shown you by choosing you from among so many other princesses to elevate you to my rank and seat you on the throne of Spain!"

In spite of himself he was wandering and repeating to her passages that had formerly won him applause, and this last phrase that he had just uttered, tongs in hand, had come back to him from *The Caverns of Grenada,* in which he had electrified the house.

"Yes, sire," she answered, in a low tone. Then, returning to a more natural language, she went on: "I have deceived you without deceiving you, my friend, but it is almost worse and uglier than if I had deceived you by actually deceiving you."

"Explain yourself clearly, gypsy, or be on your guard!" Another sounding phrase, in spite of himself.

"Here it is. You know when you confessed your love to me——"

"Yes, and you to me——"

"Yes. You know that I was sought after?"

"Oh, Lord, do not remind me of it! I suffered enough through it. I was jealous—jealousy, infernal gnawing that——" He was going on with one of Othello's tirades, but she stopped him.

"You were wrong."

"Undoubtedly. But can a man control his impulses to mistrust and anger when he is in love? And I loved you! I love you still. Ah, you were so beautiful then, you are beautiful now!"

"Hm!" she observed. "The play has grown stale."

"How could I not have been jealous?" he continued. "You see, instead of being wrong, I was right, for this evening, forty-five years afterwards, you inform me that——"

"Do not be so quick to accuse me. Let me go on to the very end."

"Go on, my Celimène."

"Do you remember, one of the things that used to put you beside yourself in the height of our passion was the letters, the declarations, I received every day after the performance?"

"Ah, yes. They rained down on you from all directions, from all sides at once! They were from young fops."

"From old ones, too, and middle-aged."

"From poets and military men——"

"I had only to choose."

"And did you make a choice?"

"Do not interrupt me. Do you remember, too, that these burning love-letters, whose number was considerable, even when it was well known that we were madly in love with each other, fell off and became much more infrequent as soon as we were married?"

"We loved each other even more, however, if that was possible."

"Yes, but, as a lawful wife, I did not move the public to such extremes, I did not seem to promise so much, and, while I was resolved never to deceive you, while I loved you more than the richest and most fashionable man on earth, must I tell you?—well, I suffered from this falling off of homage and pursuit. All those false and high-flown declarations that I received, of course, I did not believe in in the least. I laughed at them——"

"As for me, I wept over them."

"Wait. We read them together. Really, I quite enjoyed it;

it became a delightful habit that I could not do without, a divine tobacco whose smoke-wreaths I missed."

"Is it possible?"

"Yes, indeed. And didn't you ever notice it, Scapin?"

"Never."

"You have forgotten. You used often to ask me, 'What is the matter with you, Marinette? Why are you so sad? You never say anything. Your mind is wandering. What are you thinking of?'"

"Perhaps—yes—vaguely. So that was it—the rarity of those strange declarations?"

"Yes, that was it. But do not say the rarity, say the cessation, the total disappearance, for at the end of six months of married life I was not getting a single one. What a humiliation it was for me! The door-man at the theatre, the dressers, the stage-hands, who only a year before had been accustomed to deliver whole shovelfuls to me at all hours from my generous admirers, were never charged with the least clandestine message for me, and I could feel their pitying contempt in their looks. I grew thin. I contemplated the river, like Ophelia."

"And all this time I never noticed anything!"

"Men never notice those things, my lord, especially husbands."

"You should have told me."

"What could you have done? Nothing."

"That is true."

"I had arrived at that point of anger, humiliation and concentrated distress, when one morning, one fine morning—ah, Valère! Ah, Fantasio!"

"A letter?"

"Yes."

"Oh, Lise, that is what I feared. A love-letter?"

"Yes, and such a letter! I was happy again. And the next day another!—and the day after, and every day for a month. At last, I was beloved once more, I was courted, I was not looked upon as a strait-laced wife, married, settled down, finished, so to speak, having renounced the pomps and vanities of this wicked world——"

"Well, and afterwards? Go on."

"Afterwards the letters became less frequent."

"Ah, good!"

"But they continued to come with faithful persistency, sometimes every five or six days, sometimes every fortnight."

"For a long time?"

"For two years."

"The deuce! And who was it wrote them?"

"An unknown."

" A nameless admirer? "

" Yes, he never told his name."

He poked the fire, humming to himself, " And he never was seen any more."

" I have always thought," she observed, " that it was some great personage who wanted to preserve his incognito, for the writing was always disguised, as if he had written with his left hand."

" The sly dog! And so you have never spoken to him? "

" Never! "

" If that is the case, then you have never deceived me? "

" Oh, yes, I did! "

" How was that? "

" At first his letters were so ardent, so beautiful, so delicate, so tender, so subtle, so delicious—oh, you could not imagine them! "

" Have you kept them? "

" Yes, for a long time—and hidden them."

" Where? "

" I will tell you that—later."

" When? "

" When you are a hundred. Then, as my lover—my lover on paper, but he was my lover all the same, wasn't he?——"

" Well, I must certainly make up my mind about that. He was a lover after a fashion, there's no getting around that."

" As my lover had given me a mysterious address, where I could write to him——"

" Ah, the scoundrel! You replied to him? You have replied to him? "

" Yes, often and so ardently! "

" Oh, Jacqueline! Oh, Rosamonde! "

" Do not scold. If you could only imagine how imperious and charming his letters were! It was impossible to leave them unanswered. A heart of stone would have taken up the pen! What do you think of that metaphor? "

" It is like yourself, bold. And did the other man speak ill of me in his letters? "

" No, never. On the contrary, he besought me to respect your honour."

" Come, come. That is stranger still. And what did you reply to him? "

" Follies, the greatest follies! "

" Oh! "

" What would you have? It was better than to commit them."

" I do not deny that. All the same——"

" I repeat, if you had been able to read his letters, you would understand, you would forgive me."

"That is not so sure. But, more than the letters, what I would have liked to see—ah! how I would have liked to see them—was your replies. They ought to be still more interesting!"

"Enough, Horatio. Yes, unfortunately, or rather fortunately, he has carried them off or destroyed them. They belong to the things that will never be known this side of the other world!"

"So be it. We shall wait. But while we are on these confidences of long ago, you wicked little old woman, tell all to your knave of hearts. Did you never seek to learn who was writing to you?"

"Never."

"Did you never feel a temptation, a curiosity, to see him, to speak to him, to know him?"

"No."

"Strange! You never longed for the reality?"

"The unreal was too beautiful. I thought of it sometimes, but I was afraid, if I found myself face to face with my unknown, I would fall from my pinnacle. That was all. The lamp—don't you remember? I played Pysche when I was fifteen."

"Perhaps you were right. Even in their folly women are wise."

"Well, it is finished—there is my confession—and I am over sixty. I have deceived you, poor Organ, by correspondence. Do you forgive me?"

He took her hands in his: "Yes, madame," he said, in a gently tragic voice, "if you will give me the letters."

"Very good, sir; if you are going to use force, you shall have them."

She released herself with a smile, rose, and opened her large armoire, with its piles of linen bedecked with ribbons from old bouquets, and, away at the back, on the middle shelf, thrusting her little hand under a mass of fine chemises and gewgaws, she drew out a packet of faded letters, tied with an old gilt string from a bonbon box. She inhaled their perfume, looked at them, raised them to her lips, shrugged her shoulders, smiled with a little pout, and murmured:

"How silly we are when we are young!"

"And when we are old too," he replied.

She handed them to him with the air of a duchess, saying, "Here, sir!"

"Very good, madame."

They were amusing themselves, they were playing comedy, they were doing "the big scene in the fourth act."

"You will allow me to read them?"

"Yes, sir. But not before me—I should be too embarrassed. No, not until I have withdrawn to my apartment."

"Her apartment," which she indicated with a wave of her hand, was her own little twin bed, which stood side by side with his.

"Turn around, sir."

He pivoted in his chair. "I have done so. I am not looking. But do not forget to put your slipper in front of the fireplace—it is Christmas Eve."

"Just as you please. But what shall I find in it?"

He made an evasive gesture. She brought over one of her little velvet slippers, on which the light of an old jewel sparkled in the buckle, and laid it on the hearthstone.

Then with three sighs and a faint rustling, she was in bed, with the linen sheet under her chin. In a voice that was already drowsy, she said, "Good-night, dear old friend."

He leaned over her and tucked her in. "Good-night, my life, my soul," he said.

The clock struck the half-hour. Two kisses passed between them, one from her on his cheek, one from him on her ivory forehead, and then she fell asleep, breathing regularly, one, two, one, two, like a child.

He listened to her, laughed to himself, and with tender mischievousness went softly on tiptoe over to the Louis XIV. marquetry secretary, pulled out a deep bottom drawer, thrust his arm into it, mysteriously drew forth a packet of faded letters tied together with an old silk cord, and, stooping down at first and then on his knees, deposited it in the rose-coloured slipper, murmuring to himself in a low tone:

"The answers. What a surprise it will be for her to-morrow!"

WHEN HE WAS A LITTLE BOY

HENRI LAVEDAN

MADAME DE PRÉCY said to her husband: "You wish to know what is the matter? Oh! I will tell you, if for a few moments you will condescend to lend me your attention."

In an icy tone he answered, "I will not lend, I will give it to you."

"Well, then, the matter is"—and a trembling voice betrayed her excitement—"that life with you has become unbearable and that I have resolved no longer to try to endure it. You are, I admit, an honourable man, and have, I believe, been a faithful husband. I, on my side, have never forgotten my marriage vows. Here we stand on the same ground. The trouble is that we are uncongenial. Everything I do annoys you, and to me all your ways are insufferable. What I say always vexes you, and your laugh drives me crazy. Even when silent, we provoke each other. About the merest trifles we have frightful scenes—about a hat, a dress, whether it will be best to carry a cane or an umbrella, or whether the meat is overdone or not—in short, everything—and everything makes us quarrel! Then, at home, either you talk so much that I cannot put in a word or else you do not open your lips, and you look about as cheerful as a mortuary chapel. I must be happy when you are happy, sad when you are sad. Your temper is changeable, odd, quick; you do not allow the slightest contradiction; if I begin to speak of something which does not interest you, I am not allowed to finish my sentence. For me to express an opinion suffices to make you take an opposite view. You insist that you understand music, and that I know nothing about politics, while, in point of fact, the contrary is the truth. You scold my maid until she cries, and your disgusting valet drinks all the wine in my cellar. You forbid me to smoke, and insist that my dresses shall not be cut too low. And when we quarrel, even about some very ordinary matter, instead of its being over in five minutes, it lasts for hours, and we try to outdo each other in saying bitter things which neither of us forgets. In short, everything about me is disagreeable to you. I feel it, and I know it: you hate the tone of my voice, the sound of my step, my gestures, even my clothes; do not deny it, at this very moment I can read in your face that you would like to pitch me out of the window."

"Therefore?" said Monsieur de Précy.

"Therefore I conclude that it is wiser for us not to prolong our experience of married life. Its having proved a failure is neither your fault nor mine, or rather it is the fault of both; at any rate it is a fact. We were not made to live together; until we cease to do so, neither of us will be happy. After all, there is nothing to prevent us from amicably parting. Fortunately there is no child to quarrel about, we have each an ample fortune, so I really cannot see why we should remain any longer on the same perch, pulling out each other's feathers. As for me, I have had enough of it, and you have had too much. I am quite sure you will be happy. Sometimes in the morning, while you are shaving, you will think of me; and for my part I shall always remember you as a perfectly honourable, thoroughly disagreeable man. But for that I bear you no ill-will, because it is in your blood, all the Précys are so, and your own father and mother, as you have often told me, could never contrive to remain together for more than ten days at a time. However, I will waste no more breath in talking about the matter, but will now, Monsieur, retire to my own rooms, where until to-morrow I shall pass my time in thinking over the most practical way in which to arrange our separation."

Monsieur de Précy had received this avalanche of reproaches in silence, but his lips twitched, once or twice he sighed, sighed deeply, and toward the middle of the discourse he had begun to pace the floor. When his wife ceased speaking he stopped before her, and, looking at her with an expression which he strove to render as dignified as possible, said in a sad, somewhat victimised, tone of voice:

"Have you finished?"

"I have finished, and it is finished."

"So be it, my dear; the book is closed, and I, like you, think it best not again to open it. As you wish it, we will separate to-morrow and each try solitude."

"Oh, I permit you to enliven it!"

"Thanks, and I forbid you to do so."

"Gracious! I do not dream of such a thing. When I leave you, it is to become my own mistress, not to change masters. You can be quite easy; to marry again would be a folly I shall never commit. Have you anything more to say?"

"No, except that if we take this step without knowing to what it may lead . . ."

"Oh! I know. First to peace, then to old age, finally to Père Lachaise."

"Do not joke, but please allow me to finish. We will do as we wish, but it is not necessary that the world should be at once enlightened as to our disagreements. That is my opinion, and I think you will agree with me."

"I do not know, because, of course, people cannot long remain ignorant . . ."

"Yes, but for a time. Later the same objections will not exist. In short, this is what I ask: before taking any measures to obtain a divorce, let us separate by all means, but under special conditions which will save appearances, and excite no suspicions in the minds of our friends."

"What, then, is your idea?"

"As you wish to leave to-morrow, do so; but instead of taking refuge with some friend in the country or abroad, as is probably your intention, go to Meneaux, my château in Brittany, and as long as you can endure it—two months, if you have the courage—remain there. Madame Bénard, my parents' old housekeeper, who brought me up, is in charge. She will receive you, and in every way look after your comfort. You can tell her that I will soon join you."

"That, I imagine, will not be the truth."

"No, but you had better say so. The house is well furnished, pretty, and not more than four miles from Guérande. Under the pretext that Brittany is too far away from Paris, you have always avoided setting foot upon this family estate where my childhood was passed. This, before we each go our way in life, is a good opportunity to look at it. If you let this chance escape, you will never have another. Now can I count upon you? Do you consent?"

"You have made your request with civility, and I consent. I will go to Meneaux, and will remain there for two months. You may send a telegram to Madame Bénard."

Then a few words more were exchanged with a coldness too intense to be quite genuine. "Thanks—good night—good-bye! yes, good-bye!" Their voices did not tremble, oh no; but their hearts, their poor hearts, ached! Each one privately thought, "What? Can it be true we are to part—and for ever? That is what we shall see, my wife! I'm not quite sure about that, my husband!"

But, nevertheless, the next day Madame de Précy departed.

. . . .

On a clear, fresh May morning the young woman arrived at Meneaux. It is at the seaside, a delightful place when spring, like a tiny child on its uncertain legs, hesitatingly treads there. The sparse, backward vegetation is more rugged than elsewhere, the blue of the sky has a deeper tint, and in the salt air there is something bracing and healthful which brings red to the cheek and peace to the soul.

For Madame de Précy's occupation, Madame Bénard had prepared, on the second floor, a large bedchamber, wainscoted in oak and hung with old sulphur-coloured damask; on one side it overlooked a wide expanse of flat country, broken only here and there by a rock or a thin cluster of reeds; and on the other a pine wood ceaselessly murmuring in the breeze.

After she had emptied her trunks and made herself at home in her room, Madame de Précy found plenty of time for reflection. Nature offers many consolations to those who at a moral crisis fly to her. By a sort of reflex action, she deadens pain, soothes and cheers. Her immutability, her apparent egotism, are good advisers. Before her who does not pass away one learns to see that everything else will do so, our little happinesses as well as our great sorrows; and the order which she observes in everything incites us to order also our hearts and minds. Madame de Précy began to think, and more seriously than for many and many a long day before. She reviewed her entire past life, beginning with the first white pages of cradle, dolls, first communion, long skirts and balls, next turning to the chapter of marriage. Her life had not been a romance, scarcely even a story, but very ordinary, without great joys, great catastrophes, or anything striking. Every night she had gone to bed with the secret hope that the next day something might happen. During the nine years of her married life, the sun had risen many times, but never had anything happened. Little by little she and her husband had become embittered, and perhaps he also, without being willing to admit it, had suffered from that monotony to some beings so irritating—monotony of things, hours, events, crimes, heroisms, vices, seasons, rain, sun, admirations, and anticipations. Her husband was not a man to be despised: cultivated, distinguished, honourable, sometimes (only sometimes) tender-hearted—in fact, admirable—yet impossible to live with. So, while deploring her fate, in the bloom of youth finding herself thus alone and in a false position, she did not, however, regret the impulse to which she had yielded. She would not know happiness, but she could have peace. One cannot expect everything at once. Without feeling that her dignity was compromised, she gladly accepted the society of Madame Bénard, the old housekeeper in charge of the château, and yet, as a rule, she was haughty. But Madame Bénard had brought up Monsieur de Précy, and moreover the country equalises; its solitude brings together human beings, raising a little those who are below, and lowering a little those who are above, so that Madame de Précy and the good old lady—for a lady she really was—soon became friends.

On the day Madame Bénard took Madame de Précy through the château, she went first to a large room on the third storey, and, as she pushed open the door, said:

"I want to begin by showing you everything connected with Monsieur's childhood. This is the room where Monsieur played and amused himself when he was a little boy."

Then she opened closets where lay balls, drums, trumpets, boxes of tin soldiers, games of patience, draughts, and dominoes, saying as she fingered them one after another:

"These were Monsieur's playthings when he was a little boy."

And suddenly she pulled from a heap a doll with a broken nose.

"See, Madame! he even had a doll, that boy; he called her Pochette, and when he kissed her he used to say, 'She shall be my wife!' Was it not ludicrous? Well, he would not say that now. He has something better."

Madame de Précy did not reply.

The housekeeper questioned: "It must move you to see all these things?"

"Yes, Madame Bénard."

Then the old lady took her to see the room where Monsieur used to sleep; sometimes forgetting herself, instead of Monsieur, she said Louis; and Madame de Précy was strangely moved at hearing pronounced by another that name she had so often said, but might never say again. The room where her husband used to study was next exhibited, with its shelves still filled by his old school-books and copy-books. One of the latter was seized by Madame Bénard, who, tendering it to Madame de Précy, cried, " See how well Monsieur wrote when he was a little boy." And traced in large, uncertain letters she read, " Let us love one another." Then she exclaimed, " I should like to go out into the air; I do not feel quite well."

They went out of doors, and for some moments silently walked about. When a large pond, on which floated two beautiful white swans, was presently approached, Madame Bénard announced, " Here is the pond where Monsieur kept his boat when he was a little boy. One evening he came near drowning himself. I shall never forget that."

When, a few steps farther on, they reached an old straight-backed, moss-grown wooden bench, on either side of which stood a tall earthenware vase, she cried, " This is the bench where Monsieur used to sit and read when he was a little boy."

Next they entered the vegetable garden, and Madame Bénard, walking at once toward a little plot, enclosed by a hedge of box, said again, " This was Monsieur's garden when he was a little boy."

As they afterward crossed the servants' court, a glimpse of the farm horses in their stalls, afforded by widely opened stable doors, caused Madame Bénard to exclaim, " Oh, Boniface used to be kept there! "

" What was Boniface? " asked Madame de Précy.

" Boniface was Monsieur's pony when he was a little boy."

So clearly had Madame Bénard brought before Madame de Précy a little Louis who studied, read, wrote, laughed, and played, that she almost saw him now, in short trousers with sunburnt legs and bare head, running across the garden.

When later in the day they were both seated in the dining-room near a large window overlooking the sea, Madame Bénard began in a simple way to relate the story of Monsieur when he was a little boy. It was not very cheerful.

" I must tell you, Madame," said the old woman, " that Monsieur's parents were very peculiar. You never saw them, but I knew them well.

" Just imagine, they actually disliked each other, and without any good reason. That they were not ' congenial ' was the only excuse they could give for living almost always apart; but think how wicked that was! If the father was in Paris the mother travelled, and when she returned he went away. They both loved Monsieur Louis, but rather than share his society preferred entirely to deprive themselves of it. So he was sent here to me, and I had to be to him both father and mother. That is the way I happened to bring him up, and I did my best. His parents both died quite young and he, poor child, wept as bitterly as if he had known them. I can forgive him, but I'm quite sure that when I die he will not grieve as much.

" I tell you all this, Madame, because perhaps he has never done so, and also that you may be able to make allowance for him if sometimes he appears nervous, quick-tempered, or moody. It is not his fault; it is the fault of old times when he was a little boy. Had it not been for his deserted, lonely childhood, he would have grown up quite a different man."

All this Madame Bénard said and much besides, telling many anecdotes, and giving a mass of details, so that the conversation lasted until evening. Neither of the two women thought of ringing for a lamp, and darkness enveloped them. Therefore Madame Bénard did not observe that Madame de Précy was furtively drying her eyes. When she rose it was to say:

" All you have related about my husband has interested me very much, dear Madame Bénard," and she warmly pressed the good old woman's hands. This did not astonish Madame Bénard, nor was she surprised when the young woman handed her a telegram for Paris to be sent to the office at Guérande. What did the telegram contain?

What is sure is that it was sent that night, and the next day Monsieur de Précy arrived.

THE POCKET-BOOK

HENRI LAVEDAN

MONSIEUR CERVEAU crept cautiously, like a mouse, the whole length of the Rue d'Assas. As he was coming out of his office some of his friends had prevailed upon him to go to a café, and he had lost nearly three francs at dominoes. Now he was hurrying home, having learned by former sad experience that Madame Cerveau expected him punctually at her dinner-hour. He grew even more timid as he reached the door. What a scene there would be!

He climbed the stairs slowly, for he was covered with perspiration, and was breathing heavily. When he reached the second storey he heard a cough above him. Raising his head he saw his wife bending over the railing with a light in her hand, and he trembled still more. He continued climbing, however, trying to conceal his fear under the mask of a smile. She was standing on the landing, and the lighted lamp she held in her hand gave her the appearance of a vestal virgin. Monsieur Cerveau had already bent his humble head ready to submit to all her reproaches, to endure all her scoldings; but to his great astonishment she only said:

"Here you are at last! I have been watching so impatiently for you!" Then seizing him by the arm: "If you only knew! I have such a wonderful thing to tell you. Come!" They entered their room, and Madame Cerveau closed the door, repeating: "You will see, you will see!" Then she laughed, a forced, nervous laugh.

"You worry me, Léonie. What is the matter with you?" cried Cerveau.

"Why, nothing is the matter, but listen. Such an extraordinary thing happened to me an hour ago. You have read novels, haven't you?"

"Of course. What do you mean?"

"Can't you guess? Just try to guess."

"Tell me what it is, I beg. You are torturing me."

"Yes, that's true. No one could guess it. Well, as I was coming back from the Faubourg St. Honoré, this is what I found while crossing the Champs Elysées." With some difficulty she drew forth from the depth of her pocket a black stuffed thing which she held for a moment as though trying to decide how much it weighed. Then her face grew grave, as if she were about to do something important, and she held the object toward her husband with a gesture that said, "Look, and give your opinion."

Cerveau took it and said, after he had turned it over and over again: "It's a pocket-book."

"The inside—look inside!" commanded his wife.

He opened it carefully. Several slips of paper dropped out. As he was not examining it quickly enough to suit her, she snatched it from his hands. "Give it to me. There!" She opened the first piece of paper her hand grasped. "Do you understand? These are foreign shares. I don't know how much money each one represents, but I'm ready to wager they mean quite a sum."

"Yes, yes, they do," stammered the amazed Cerveau. "It is very strange. They are certainly foreign shares. And you found this?"

"Yes. In the Champs Elysées. I stepped on it. I almost fell over it."

"Somebody must have lost it."

"Of course."

"If you like, we will take it to police headquarters after dinner.

It will give us some place to go for our evening walk. What do you say?"

"Why, of course. I had no idea of keeping it," she answered impatiently.

They sat down at the table, both out of temper, like people who have a disagreeable task to perform. Suddenly she said to him: "Morin, who is at the Bourse, is going to lunch with us to-morrow. I am rather curious to find out through him the value of those papers. Suppose we wait a while before we give them up. There is plenty of time."

He was overjoyed at finding her so willing and readily consented.

They told the story to Morin the next day, and after he had carefully examined the papers, he exclaimed: "Russian—Austrian railways. This is luck! They are worth at least forty thousand francs!"

Forty thousand francs! They both jumped to their feet. Why, that was a fortune. "And you know," continued their friend, "in a few years they will double their value. I'm well acquainted with these things." Then he laughingly added: "Heavens! if I were only in your place!"

Cerveau was thoroughly shocked and interrupted him: "Oh, Morin!"

"Well, you may be right after all," answered the man from the Bourse. "Honesty is too complicated a thing for me to understand."

He seized his hat and left them somewhat coolly.

In the afternoon they went to headquarters, gave up the pocket-book, and returned relieved and pleased with themselves. Then life resumed its ordinary course, and eight monotonous months passed by. Toward the middle of the ninth month, Madame Cerveau gleefully said to her husband, "Would you believe it? The other day I went to find out who had called for the pocket-book. It has not been claimed! It is still there!"

"What difference do you suppose that makes to me?" he asked.

"Don't you know? The difference for you, the difference for us is, that if nobody appears within four months, as one year will have passed since we gave it up, the money will belong to us."

"Is that true?"

"Of course!" And she clapped her hands.

From that moment they lived in the most painful and continuous excitement. Cerveau would mutter each morning as he dressed, "If only the owner does not put in an appearance!" And each evening, on returning from his office, he would say, "Has he shown up?" They made so many visits that the chief grew weary of seeing them. They began to think that Providence was working for them as time went on, and they would startle each other by declaring together, "We shall have it!"

They could not sleep at night. They would seat themselves by the bed, and by the dim light of their candle they would build air-castles. They wavered between a farm in Beauce or a villa by the seashore. They had already decided to name the latter "Villa Léonie." In any case they would have a man-servant; they would buy a great deal of silverware. They would live to be very old, and would never be ill. Then, when they suddenly realised that this precious treasure did not yet belong to them—that they might lose it at the last moment, they would become furious, as if they were under the immediate danger of being betrayed, of being robbed. At times they would grow tender and would say with tears in their voices: "Our poor money!"

One evening, in a confiding moment, he said to his wife: "At any rate; we shall not have stolen it."

Only one week remained before the end of the time so ardently desired. Cerveau resigned his position. What was the use of working, now that he was rich? He saw on the fourth page of a newspaper, "Swiss chalet for sale at Petites-Dalles." He bought it for ten thousand francs, and promised to pay in fifteen days.

At last, on January 12, which was the happy, the blessed day, dressed in their best they both went to police headquarters and, after having signed their names, tremblingly received the pocket-book from the officer. The long waiting was over, and they went to the church and offered thanks by lighting a candle in that sacred place.

They had invited Morin to dinner, planning to surprise him, and if the truth must be told, in no wise sorry that they had an opportuity of crowing over him.

They gave him no hint of their good fortune until the dessert was brought on, and then they gave full vent to their joy, telling the good news with joyous, excited cries. Cerveau brought forth the pocket-book, which was hidden behind the handkerchiefs in a bureau drawer. Morin took it and cast his eyes over the papers.

"Russian and Austrian railway shares!" he exclaimed. "They've gone down during the last six months, my poor friends. Why, you will be lucky if you get three hundred francs for them now! Didn't I tell you that would happen?"

PAUL MARGUERITTE
B. 1860

THE DEAD HAND

I

RENÉ D'YONS came home at four o'clock in the morning. Since his mother's death he had lived alone in the great house, which now seemed so lonely. Its blank white face looked out over the dark garden, and there was no homeliness in its aspect. He pushed the key into the lock of the side door, and entered the gloomy house with a feeling of repugnance and dejection.

He had been to a party, which had not amused him. For one thing, there had been high play, and he had lost a good deal of money. He had also drunk too much champagne, which had depressed him, and he had been obliged to come home in a crawling night cab, which shook all his bones and set his teeth on edge. He pictured the uses of the cab when it was not taking fares. It served as a bed for the cabman, and as a granary for his horse. That was certain, for it reeked of tobacco and stale hay. And he also thought of its other possible uses—to take patients to the fever hospital, and all sorts of people to see them afterwards. He checked his thoughts with a shudder.

Since his mother had died and left him to his own devices, he had run after pleasure. And now, after all, what pleasure had he got? An intolerable weariness and disgust, and the certainty that he could never pay the debt of honour which he had incurred under the promise that it would be paid by noon next day. He was the most unhappy and pitiable of creatures. That was what his pursuit of pleasure had done for him.

He went up the dark silent staircase. No one waited for him; no one greeted him on his way. The two old servants who had remained with him after his mother's death had long since gone to bed, for he had told them never to sit up for him. He lit the gas in the passage and went into his bedroom, passing in haste the dark rooms which had never been opened since his mother's death. He shivered with cold, the cold of a sleepless night and the deadness of the time before the rising of the sun, that mysterious hour when all Nature seems to be at her lowest ebb, and to have resigned all part in the lives of men.

He had lighted the candle which was always left for him outside his bedroom door, but the draught blew it out as he entered his room, just as if it had been purposely extinguished by human means. He thought, " They always leave my window open, and of course the wind has grown stronger during the night."

Ten minutes passed while he hunted for matches. He did not like to wake the old servants, and he had to search through his cupboard, for his match-box was empty.

He succeeded at last in relighting his candle, and saw all the familiar objects of his bedroom. There were the bed, the sofa, the wardrobe with the long mirror in which he could see his form reflected. It was not a very nice reflection, for he was weary, dispirited, and untidy. His face was drawn and sallow after his night's exhaustion in search of pleasure.

Looking away from the mirror in disgust, his glance fell on the carpet in front of the wardrobe, and his complexion changed from sallow to green. He stood staring at the spot on which his eyes had rested. What did he see?

There, on the thick red carpet just in front of him, lay a human hand. The fingers were spread out and slightly curved; the wrist was cut short off, and still red as if from recent bleeding. It was unmistakably a hand cut from a person who had been alive only a short time before. What did it mean? Why was it there on his carpet, in his bedroom, mute evidence of a crime of which he knew nothing? No other trace was there. The ghastly hand lay before him, unconnected with any other object in his well-ordered chamber.

Certainly he was not dreaming. The horrid thing lay there so near him that he could just touch it by moving the toe of his patent leather boot. Who could have put it there? Was this a practical joke played on him by one of his friends? Was the hand made of wax, or was it some anatomical preparation?

He reflected for a moment, and then, wishing to reassure himself, he gave it a little push with his toe, but without being able to repress a shudder of disgust. The object which he touched was soft and rather elastic, and he recoiled from the contact. The thing was flesh and blood. It had been alive a few hours before. When he became convinced of this, René trembled from head to foot, and the candlestick rattled in his hand like the little bell of a sacristan.

II

After some hesitation the young man ventured to look more closely at the object on the floor. Then he cast a glance round his room. He saw the bed, the wardrobe, the long heavy window curtains, and holding his breath he listened attentively. His open window admitted a breeze from the garden below, bearing with it the odour of moist earth. He went over and closed the window, shivering as he did so lest a dagger stroke between his shoulders should stretch him lifeless against the iron balcony. Taking a revolver from his pocket, he continued examining his bedroom so as not to leave a single nook or corner out of consideration.

Now a new fear assailed him, and he crept upstairs to the second storey as softly as possible to make sure that nothing had happened to the old servants who slept there. He listened at the door until their heavy breathing reassured him; and not seeing anything unusual in the appearance of the passages, he went down again, stopping at intervals on the stairs to listen. He descended to the lower floor, and opened the doors of the rooms which had formerly been used by his mother. All of these rooms had a damp and musty odour; and as nothing had been disturbed in them for a long time past, the carpets were covered with fine dust. The clocks on the mantelpieces had stopped, and everything spoke of the silence and immobility of death.

René returned to his own room. He felt terribly uneasy, but was a little reassured when he saw that the hand was still lying in the same place. He could not conquer his repugnance, but his anxiety to solve the mystery caused him to approach the object more closely, and he stooped to examine it by the light of his candle.

III

The hand was small, white, and delicate, and must have belonged to a woman or a youth. René began to picture to himself the actual commission of the crime. He seemed to see the blood flowing and the victim dying while the murderer prepared to cut the still warm body in pieces. The idea made him tremble, and he tried to banish it from his mind and to regain enough self-control to inspect the object calmly and with lucid judgment. That hand was too dainty not to be the hand of a woman; it had been very well cared for, but the points of the fingers were slightly darkened as if they had touched soot or ashes. René looked toward the fireplace, in which the fire had gone out some time ago. There could be no doubt whatever that the hand had fallen down the chimney, having been dropped from the roof by the crafty murderer, who was anxious to get rid of the proofs of his crime as easily as possible. It must have rebounded on striking the burnt-out coals, and fallen on the hearth-rug.

It was plump, fresh, and of youthful smoothness. It was the left hand. Where was the other, the right one? Perhaps he would find it in the garden during the coming day. Or was it also in his room? No, he dismissed that idea; he had searched too minutely. The third finger had a small white swelling at the base of the finger, evidently the mark of a ring which had been forcibly pulled off by the murderer. There was a scratch on the soft palm. The nails were prettily cut in almond shape.

That poor hand was still attractive-looking, dainty, and inviting, as it had been in the owner's lifetime. He looked at it closely and was able to see that it had belonged to a woman of the demi-monde, for it had been manicured with the aid of specially perfumed ointments such as were fashionable among some of those women whom he knew. He ventured to touch it gingerly, and found it soft as velvet, but cold as marble. He lifted it and was surprised to find it unusually heavy, with the heaviness of dead flesh. He tried to stretch it out flat, but the fingers contracted. He shuddered at what he was doing, which seemed indeed a sacrilege, but he could not help it; his curiosity was stronger than his self-control. Finally he stood up and faced his own reflection in the mirror, which gave him back a look of perplexity and alarm. What was he to do?

Well, first of all he had to wait for the daylight to come. He could not very well run off just then to rouse up the officers of the law, or wake the poor old servants to go hunting about in the dark garden or to help him to try to find the murderer in the deserted streets. The crime might have been committed somewhere very near his house, yet the criminal himself might now be very far off. It might even be that the murder had been committed at the other end of the town and the fragments of the corpse distributed broadcast. But in any case it could not be long since it had happened; and René, sitting by the window with his revolver within reach of his right hand, remained staring at the poor dead thing lying before him, admiring its fine delicate outlines, and trying not to see the ghastly stump in which it ended.

He tried to sleep, but found it impossible. First of all he thought he would hide the thing, and he picked it up in a towel and laid it on his dressing-table, carefully covered. Now he could not see it, but he knew it was there, and it was impossible for him to take his eyes away from its vague outlines. He put a screen before the table and looked at it. He felt a great pity for the poor creature who had met with a fate which is unfortunately not an uncommon one for women of the class to which she had belonged. His imagination pictured the details which the newspaper would publish with regard to this nameless and mysterious hand. He ran over in his mind all that was going to happen when day should come and he must go to the police station, where the tale which he had to tell and the interviews which would follow with the reporters of the daily papers would bring his name into every one's mouth for a short time at any rate. His pity for the victim of the crime was succeeded by a sort of vanity at his own share in the discovery, and at the attention which he was certainly about to attract.

A breath of air shaking the window frame caused him to start and grasp his revolver. He looked round with a shudder, and a cold perspiration stood out on his forehead. The question occurred to him: " Was it after all only by chance that his room had been selected as the spot into which the hand had been thrown? Was there any idea of revenge in this apparent chance, any hint of the cruel reprisals of which we read in annals of bygone days? "

The more he pondered on this, the more insistent the idea became, even when he felt its absurdity. He began to wonder if he had any special reason for being so much interested in that hand; if it had even belonged to some one whom he knew. He was fascinated by the idea, and he thought: " I know now. I have seen that hand before. I know the girl it belonged to. I will think of her name presently, when my mind is less confused." He began to run over in his mind the personalities of the men and women with whom he had spent the evening at the supper party from which he had just returned. At last, by a violent effort of will, he drove away the terrible idea which was beginning to dominate his mind, and which, if he continued to entertain it, would end by driving him mad.

IV

He took up a book and tried to read one of the stories which used to interest him so much in former days. Impossible to keep his mind on it. Every sentence, every line, every idea, seemed to contain some one of the two words which hammered incessantly on his brain, " hand " and " death." At last he got rid of the thought of the first word, but the second became more insistent, and flooded his imagination with sinister thoughts. What was there real in this life except death? Visions of it flooded his mind: the death of his mother; the death of this unknown woman; perhaps his own death soon. When would that take place? Life is short, very short at best, and the end comes much sooner than any of us expect. How many things may lead to death! Illness, an apparently trifling accident, a chance cold, a whiff of foul air, a fall from a horse. All these things lie in wait for us at every moment of the day. And then there are other dangers which we bring on ourselves: the vengeance of a neglected woman or an angry husband, the murderous blow of one whom we have perversely made our enemy. René looked back into the years which had gone by, the years which he had wasted in the pursuit of his own idle pleasure. In his mother's lifetime, out of respect for her goodness, he had restrained his mad impulses. But since his death, what had been the case? He said with conviction:

"My present way of life is an insult, not merely to the memory of my mother, but also to the invisible presence of her spirit, which may be watching over me at this moment. This hand, a poor fragment of the mystery of another life, may have been sent into my presence to warn and advise me. Never could the thought of the unceasing menace of death have been brought so forcibly to my mind in any other way, or under any form so terrible and so insistent. I must make a better use of the days of my life which still remain to me, if I am not to be for ever lost to all possibility of good. I must try to control myself, to make some good use of what capacities I possess, to believe in something or in some one, to serve my fellow-creatures, to love those who deserve to be loved, to obtain the love of those whose love is worth having. Nothing else can make life endurable or the thought of death a matter to be borne with calmness. I see it all now. That poor hand which lies so cold, so lifeless, has served the purpose for which it was mysteriously sent to me; pulseless and still though it lies, it has pointed out to me the writing on the wall."

René sat absorbed in these reflections until the rays of the new day poured over roof and steeple, falling all about him, and lighting every corner of his room. He seemed to be suddenly delivered from the agony of gloomy thought which had weighed him down through the night, and without casting another glance at the screen beyond which he had placed the table with its ghastly burden, he rose from his chair and rang for his servants to give them the orders which would mean the end of this nightmare.

GEORGES BEAUME
B. 1861

THE TREASURE

I

FOR a long time Roch had lived alone with his son, in his house, built of reeds and stones, by the roadside, under the hill overlooking the far-off little town. He was the owner of rich lands, planted with vines, both on the hillside and in the plain. Only on rare occasions he quitted his own paths to climb into the mountain woods, to shoot the hare, or gather mushrooms and salads.

People sometimes came to see him, mostly on the eve of the vintage, to treat for the purchase of the fruit, which he sold on the vines for ready money, and on no other terms. At those times, after business, he would invite the dealers or his comrades to drink a bottle of wine, over which he would gaily talk about the doings of his youth, his health; all the while laughing the laugh of the master, sitting at his door in the sun, his fowls picking and scratching in the straw and dust around him.

His son Michel resembled him closely—blonde, square-shouldered, with beard and hair tufted like the brambles in a ravine.

The old man was becoming grey, and bushy eyebrows protected his keen little eyes, which took a dreamy expression when, at the close of the day, he sat upon his stone bench and saw the trembling sea of darkness overspread the plain. He was a miser. He mended his own clothes, repaired his own ploughs, replastered the worn-out walls of his house and trimmed the hedges on his domain. He and his son, without any beast of burden to help them, did all the work. They dug deep, and opened out their cultures to the sun with energy and confidence. Their vines were the best in the country. They never quitted them—never ceased thinking of them day and night; and so, lived by them.

Roch took pleasure in this kind of existence. He loved money—religiously, with all his strength. He hungered for gold, more and more gold, that he might handle it, imbibe its powers, hide it in corners, at the foot of trees, under heaps of rock.

On sunny Sundays he collected his fortune from its hiding-places, and heaped it on his table in front of his door, in the midst of his fowls, alone, and counted his silver and his gold pieces, making them glitter in the sunlight, and fall through his horny fingers in a clattering shower. Near him, within instant reach, he had his double-barrelled gun. And he laughed and fed his eyes with his large fortune. A glory sang within him, he swelled with the pride of being rich. He thought of Michel, of the happiness which this treasure, amassed with so much fervour and patience, would give him at some future time, when he would no longer be there. At ease in his solitude, he gave himself up to this enjoyment; he enjoyed his lands, still full of riches, while his son, down yonder, behind the trees, dug bravely at the foot of a vine.

Then, suddenly, overtaken by terror, he hurriedly returned his gold to a canvas bag and bore it away; made a fresh hole in the ground, no matter where, sometimes in the most open and noticeable spots, so as to ward off suspicion. And when he had thus buried his treasure, the old man stood powerless, oppressed with remorse, as if he had buried his happiness, his eyes lost in an ecstasy: he planted himself for a moment before his cottage, lifted his eyes towards the blue sky, scanned the high road along which were passing the dull and indifferent waggoners, and ever fearful of having been watched, he looked for his son, still working yonder behind the trees.

When he returned to labour and health, the joy of the soul came back to him abundantly. Yet he was pursued by an anxiety, a miser's care, a peasant's pride in his lands. After him what would become of the patrimony? What would become of his gold? He had confidence in his son—who resembled him; but his son would not remain alone. He ought to be married already. And the young wife and the new relatives would, perhaps, destroy the order and prosperity of his possessions. He would himself choose a wife for his son.

Michel bowed humbly before his father, whom he regarded as a superior being, since, out of nothing, from the depths of poverty, Roch had raised himself to opulence. They went forth together, at dawn, one Sunday in spring. The clear sky hung over all like a robe of innocence. Fresh voices murmured in the solitude.

"We will not go into the town," said the old man. "We shall not find there what we want: the girls there are too fond of luxury and amusements. Let us try what we may see in the villages."

Michel followed him, his hands in his pockets, his head bent downwards, not daring to turn his eyes on the country, agitated by happiness and weakness, troubled in his virgin nature as a brooklet by the storm.

They went on for a long time without speaking: they were

thinking of the old woman who, for five years, had slept at the foot of an oak, and for whom, at sunset, they said a prayer. She was wanted now. She would have given her advice, and Roch, supported by her, would have been enabled to maintain his authority; as it was, he, for a moment, mistrusted his experience.

They visited the hamlets and villages, to the surprise of those who lived there, and were taken to the café, to the skittle and racket grounds, and to the spots where the crowd was promenading. They refused to drink, and walked about slowly, considering the girls.

Michel tired of these proceedings after a while: none of the girls pleased him. He thought them all too much dressed up and too forward in their bearing. The father grumbled at the young man's ill-humour and exaction. With quickening steps they made their way into the open country.

In the evening they returned home tired out. On the way the old man, angrily and with flashing eyes, attacked his son.

"What do you mean by all this?" he demanded. "Don't you want to marry? Are you hoping to find a princess, blockhead?"

Michel shrugged his shoulders.

"I know nothing about it—only that I love the land—and that a girl who has sprung from it might please me."

The old man, dumbfounded by this reply, bit his lips. He wished to get at the full meaning of what his son had said, suspecting that they implied the existence of a love as yet unknown to him. Something like a feeling of joy dawned upon him, but coupled with the agony of a fear, lest he might be deceiving himself.

But, blunt and rough as he was, he dared not ask any questions, conscious of his inability to touch the desire which, like a flower under water, was waking in the young man's simple soul.

II

On the farther side of the mountain, on the border of a torrent and shadowed by trees, stood a farmhouse, poor and isolated, the only house to which Michel sometimes paid a visit. Its inhabitants were a man named Bruno, taciturn, always at work, rusted by the sun; the wife, Olympe, a dried plant of the mountain, burned up like a cinder, like her husband, for ever at work, sewing, and tending the flowers and vegetables; then the daughter, a tall, brown-haired girl, sweet-smelling as the grass about a spring, the pure and caressing growth of the peace of the fields.

This was Justine, the sunshine of the hearth, the pride of her parents. For her sake Bruno put off his taciturnity after the day's work, and on Sundays went to the town and to the fêtes, exhibiting his heiress dressed in bright-coloured gowns, with gold chains about her neck—the jewellery of a long-forgotten grandmother. Justine was not yet twenty, and there had been no thought of marrying her.

Michel sometimes went to the farm, and he and Justine chatted, standing by the well, or, more often, under the mulberry trees, breathing the freshness of the leaves in the hours of rest and when the heat was too oppressive, looking through the hanging branches away to the far-off hills and the wide-stretching plain.

Then Michel returned home in company with Justine's father, examining by the way the vineyards, meadows, and olive gardens of their neighbours, comparing them with their own. But only Michel entered the enclosure. Occasionally Roch, putting down his spade, came forward, and he and Bruno, in their shirt sleeves, with their arms resting on the barred gate, chatted for a while, but in a tone of no great intimacy. Bruno never entered the gate, which Roch never opened, seeming to guard his domain on the threshold.

Sometimes Bruno received commissions from him which he executed in the town on Sundays; these were the only confidences between Roch and him. The old miser had never been across the mountain, and had only by chance seen Olympe and Justine as they passed along the hedges; when that occurred they only said " Good day " and smiled, without stopping to converse.

Michel and Justine had grown up together on the same soil. They regarded each other as if they had been old people, talking and laughing together without restraint, their conversation always turning on the same subjects, their labours and the seasons.

On the evening of the day following that on which he had been with his father on that strange excursion to the town and the adjacent villages, Michel met Justine; they looked at each other—then suddenly flushed, and their eyes grew moist with fondness.

They walked side by side.

At length Michel, with a thrill of contentment, clapped Justine on the shoulder.

" Are you going home? " he asked.

" Yes, I am returning from the town—tired. Where are you going? "

" I'm on my way home, too—but I'll go with you; I have not seen your parents for a long time."

They walked on slowly up the hill.

As they went down the other side, the fresher evening breeze fanned their faces, and they were penetrated by a glory of health : a pleasure of calm and purity united them. Their eyes turned together to the same objects of interest. They had one and the same soul, and the same feeling of life.

When they were near the farm, already dim amid the shadows that were creeping to the brow of the hill, Justine asked:

"You and your father were away from home yesterday—why?"

"Oh, yes!—Fancy!"

And with laughter and abrupt gestures, fearing to offend Justine by ideas forbidden to her modesty, Michel related to her the story of the pilgrimage in search of a wife.

"It was all nonsense," he added; "I don't know what my father has been thinking of lately. I have constantly seen him, spade in hand, removing his treasure from one place to another. And now he wants me to marry—a thing I never thought of," a look of dreamy helplessness in his eyes.

"Well, don't worry yourself about it, stupid!" cried Justine. "One would think you were going to cry!"

She bantered him noisily; but he stopped and gazed at her in surprise, that she should mock instead of console him. They entered the farmyard. The young man's gravity had touched Justine; she went to him with downcast eyes, vexed at having hurt his feelings. They went on to the house in painful silence. In the kitchen the mother was setting the supper table; Bruno was sitting by it more than half asleep.

"Oh! there you are!" cried Olympe, putting down a glass and a yellow plate before her husband.

Bruno lifted his elbows, rubbed his heavy brow, admired his daughter; the two young people seated themselves somewhat uneasily in front of the father.

"What is the matter with you?" asked the mother, laughingly; "have you two been fighting?"

"No," murmured Michel.

"No," repeated Justine.

She sighed, and in turn recited in a breath, and forcing herself to smile, the quest of Michel and his father about the country in search of a wife for the young man.

The old people were taken aback, painfully disturbed, as if threatened with the deprivation of something. They looked at the young people. A heavy silence fell upon the hum of life which came from without. They were afraid to think, and the same idea, as by a miracle, entered and haunted their minds.

"I'm going," said Michel, abruptly. He rose from his seat. The silence still continued. Michel repeated: "I'm going."

"So soon?" And Justine involuntarily held him, with a longing to ease her heart and win his forgiveness.

"Stay!" commanded Bruno.

Michel resumed his seat beside Justine. They all looked at him. He blushed, dared not speak, bit his lips, and drummed on the table with his finger-nails.

"Do you want to get married, Michel?" asked Bruno.

The young man blushed redder still, shrugged his shoulders uncomfortably, and replied:

"My father has ideas—stupid ideas that come into his head—and insisted on going about the villages——"

"But—what need was there to search so far away?"

And Olympe, with her large hands widespread, boldly indicated her daughter. It was Justine's turn to blush.

"Why not?" continued Bruno. "We are fond of you, Michel. But it was not for us to say anything: your father has money."

"Oh!"

This question of money shamed the young man.

"My father would like it," he said, resolutely.

Justine raised her eyes to him, took his hands between hers, and extended them on the table. It seemed like an oath taken, and a bright vision passed before all of them in silence. Justine moved nearer to her lover, pressed closely against him, and encouraged him to trust and to will.

"Now I shall no longer dare to come to your house," she said.

"Nor I," added her father.

The anxious mother turned away, stirred the fire on the hearth, and made the soup ready.

"Already such big children," murmured Bruno.

This speech made them smile. Michel drew his hands from those of Justine, slowly, uneasily. She contemplated him as if she had found him again, after a long separation, grown, and handsomer, and better.

He went away, filled with regrets, tormented by a remorse. All accompanied him to the threshold, Bruno in advance. Then, with a movement of courage and will, Michel said to the master of the farm:

"My father esteems you: he will only do what I wish."

And he departed. Justine saw him, through the shadows, mounting the hill path. He walked quickly, agitated by his new emotion. For the first time in his life, he thought things no longer appeared to him as they had hitherto appeared. A voice spoke to him confusedly, awaking dreams in his soul, a joy in his flesh. He also felt a fear. He tried to drive away the memory of Justine; but this memory clung to him, went before him, shining like a tender light. In his absorption he went by the gate of his father's enclosure.

On discovering what he had done he ran back, entered the cottage hurriedly, and, face to face with his father, felt as if he had suddenly been turned into a block of ice. Roch was grumbling.

"Where have you come from?—from Bruno's?—Oho!" And bursting into a loud laugh, he added: "By your hang-dog look one would imagine that you have been up to some mischief. What ails you? "

The old miser then tranquilly seated himself at table and helped the stew. While they were eating, Michel eyed his father furtively, watching for the moment to explain himself.

" Well—what's the matter with you? " repeated the old man.

" I daren't——"

" I know: you need not tell me. It is this marriage business that worries you, and you have some notion of your own."

Michel nodded.

" Justine pleases you, then? "

The young man looked at his father, and resolutely replied: " Yes."

" What about me? "

Michel was silent; his weakness and cowardice came back; he was afraid of offending the miser.

" Don't be uneasy," said the old man. " Justine is to your taste, but what dowry will she have? Her parents are not rich, I believe, while you will have money and rich lands, you know."

" Yes."

" Oh! I know that they are honest people, and that with them my vines have nothing to fear."

Filled as he was with anxiety, Michel knew not what to say: his heart was overflowing with love and entreaty.

" You are an odd fellow; but well, after all, why should I not accept Justine? I prefer people who have surmounted privation and poverty." And with a decided tone and gesture he added: " Well, we'll see about it—that will remind me of past happiness and of your poor mother."

He scratched his forehead, dried his eyes: big tears were running down his cheeks.

" I'll have it so—but on one condition. It's a fancy of mine."

Michel turned pale and his lips quivered, and he leaned back a little in his chair, as if terrified by these strange exuberances.

" What is this condition? "

" You will marry—that is settled; but I'll not give you the money till you have given me a grandson—an heir to my name." And he laughed boisterously, Michael observing him dubiously.

" So be it, father—I accept! "

They struck hands on the bargain made.

Three months afterwards Michel and Justine were married and living at Bruno's farm by the torrent. Michel still worked at his father's vines, but Justine never went beyond the enclosure. All were happy. The miser's fortune slept tranquilly underground in some unknown nook.

But, near all this happiness and hopefulness, death was keeping watch.

One evening the miser, while doing something in the interior of his cottage, slipped, fell on his head, and expired. When he was found—the next morning—his body was cold and rigid. Naturally, the old man's treasure occurred to the minds of all: had he been murdered by some robber? Everybody on the farm, including Olympe, set to searching the whole of Roch's land; but nothing was discovered. The cottage, with its barred door, would speedily have fallen into ruins under the beating of the rain; but they kept it intact, as a sacred altar.

The spring arrived, and Justine became a happy mother. With the spring, too, came a long and heavy downfall of rain. Michel, Bruno, and the women, who sometimes tremblingly entered the dead man's domain, went to see what effect the deluge had had upon the empty cottage. They opened the door: a breath as from the tomb exhaled from the deserted dwelling. They sounded the walls: the rain had eaten into them on every side—the shattered building of stones and reeds was ready to fall at any moment. Michel sadly and vaguely gazed on the ruin.

But the clouds had passed to the far end of the plain; the sky cleared, and suddenly a flood of sunlight spread over the lands of the departed miser.

Then from the highest part of the roof of the desolate cottage broken tiles began to fall, and a shapeless something was laid bare to the sun—a coarse canvas bag, which moved and burst: the miser's treasure! The peasants sprang back, and pieces of money, white and yellow, poured down in a torrent.

Ah!—old Roch might well have laughed to himself! Vainly the domain might have been searched till Doomsday! Doubtless he met his death in the act of forming that final hiding-place for his beloved treasure. And still the shower of gold continued—slowly now—now at intervals—now drop by drop.

Michel collected the whole—thousands upon thousands of gold and silver pieces. Silently he and Bruno heaped the treasure upon a hand-barrow, covered it with a blouse, and wheeled it to the farm through the livid half-light of the evening.

Nothing was said of the dead miser, but the thoughts of all turned to him—a little more lovingly. Their wealth was great enough for them to have enjoyed ten years of luxurious life in the great cities far away; but Michel and Justine, in spite of their opulence, determined to live in the farm, to change nothing in their way of life—in the peace of their hearts and the joy of their love, and in the delight of dreaming of amassing a great fortune for their children. Who shall say what constitutes the *summum bonum* of human happiness?

LUCIEN DESCAVES
B. 1861

AN INTERIOR

MY old pal Rondeneux looked in to see me this evening, and we had a pipe together.

I have a great affection for him, going back to the days when we were in the army together, fifteen years ago. Even then I was able to appreciate the great qualities of his heart, which have never changed, although he has veneered them with a hateful covering of republican humbug. He has a rare native goodness, which always makes me think of some exquisite tropical plant dragging out its existence under glass at the door of a low public-house. He is a thoroughly good chap, absolutely straight and unselfish, and would certainly go gaily to death if he thought it would do me any good.

We disagree upon every subject under the sun, and on politics most of all. I cannot help pulling his leg when I see his name on the municipal posters asking for every one's votes. He takes the matter absolutely seriously, all the same. He revels in committee meetings and demonstrations, and in all occasions when the " representatives of the people " give an account of the " trust which has been reposed in them." I happen to know that he has given away much of his small savings to help toward the election expenses of the stupid old buffers who stand for our borough in the House and the County Council, and cannot help chaffing him. " Does not the collector of rates and taxes take enough off you already? " I say. " My dear old boy, you must have lots of time and money to chuck away." But his answer is always ready. I do not " fulfil the duties of citizenship."

" Don't you understand," he says, " that it wouldn't matter a bit if you voted absurdly or on the wrong side? But the dreadful thing is that you don't vote at all. What would become of us if every one was as careless as you? Nemesis will fall on you and your children, and you will only have yourself to thank for it."

But there is one matter above all others on which we fundamentally disagree. Rondeneux simply cannot stand the sight of a priest's cassock. I know quite well the origin of this, though he is always ready with other explanations. When he was a little lad he was indiscreet enough to imitate the cawing of a crow behind the back of a pompous priest, who turned and went for him. He has never forgotten that experience; and from the day when that great formula appeared, "Clericalism is the enemy," he adopted it as his war-cry. He uses it in and out of season, and is always ready to hurl it at the head of an opponent. But I am not without my own stock answer, and I think that he gets as good as he gives. My point is this: "Look here, old chap, you are a back number; that kind of sentiment is really out of date. The enemy is not Clericalism, but Capital, which is a long way more dangerous and subtle." Now, Rondeneux is an employer and has at least a dozen workmen. So my attack in flank is unwelcome and always puts an end to our discussion.

Of course he often has his revenge, and enjoys it thoroughly. When we are invited together to a wedding or funeral conducted under the auspices of the Church, he waits for me near the door to gibe at me: "Of course you will go in. When you have quite finished with all that play-acting, you will find me in the pub round the corner. So long!" Good old Rondeneux!

He came in to-night when we were just leaving the table. My younger kiddie, a little white bundle in his high chair, was trying bravely all kinds of words, practising his lips and tongue upon them, and executing a design upon the tablecloth with a spoon. The elder, now six years old, was mad with excitement and jollity, as he always is after a meal, and was disciplining with hearty blows the beasts of his toy menagerie.

In a word, the noise was such that we could no longer hear one another. But a familiar voice came upon their games like a curfew bell. It was Granny, come to put them to bed. She brought them both up to be kissed, the eldest, still shaking from his interrupted activity, and the little one, whom she held out to us like a beaker of fresh water to the lips of a thirsty traveller.

Rondeneux really loves these babies, and is proud of having witnessed their entrance into the world. This means that he went with me to the registry office on the days of their birth to make the usual declaration. He is proud of having acted in this capacity. It would give him no pleasure, on the other hand, to have held them at the font. He gave expression to his inveterate dislike for these venerable rites when he said, as Granny carried the two away to their bedroom, "So that's the little kitten whom you had baptized last month?"

"The very same," I replied.

"Do you know, there is something I cannot understand about you," he said. I saw the squall ruffling the waters in the distance, and took down a reef in my sail.

"What is it you don't understand, old man?" I said.

"Well, you know," he made answer, "you have nothing to do with religion, or its dogmas or practices!"

"That is true enough."

"I know very well," he continued, "that you regard baptism as worse than useless; it is even ridiculous. You cannot feel the need of washing away the stain of original sin when you don't believe in original sin. And then again, even if you were to take your stand by baptism as it was administered to the early Christians, full-grown men and women and full of faith, you cannot believe, any more than I do, in administering it in this way to these unconscious little wretches."

"I cannot deny it," I said.

"Let us be quite frank," he said. "You do not believe in the existence of Our Lord?"

"Very true."

"And yet—you baptize your children?"

"True, old man, I do."

"And then you will have them make their first communion?"

"Perhaps. I don't deny it. It all depends."

"And nuns will drill them in the Catechism! The Catechism—!" The smile of my friend—I should have told you he is a cabinet-maker—was notched as a plane is when it meets a nail in the plank. And then he added: "Do you know from what book my children learned to read?"

"I can guess," I said. "Out of one of those lovely illustrated alphabet books, with a long-necked giraffe beside the letter 'G,' and an elephant twining his trunk round the 'E,' and monkeys doing acrobatic tricks on the 'M.' It is a good enough beginning."

Rondeneux made a little gesture of annoyance, and said: "On the whole, I would rather talk seriously. My boys began with Paul Bert's *Manual of Moral and Civic Education*. I have used that wonderful little book in bringing them up, so that they shall be soundly formed in every way. Ask them any question you like on patriotism, taxation, property, justice, republican principles, military duties, universal suffrage, Léon Gambetta, and they will answer you straight off. If you have to carry a cargo of knowledge through life, that sort of stuff is infinitely better than the commandments of God and the Church. And now, if you do not mind my coming to the point, I have known you for a long time, you did not baptize your children because you were a hypocrite; you did it because you were weak. The fact is you have fallen under the influence of women; your will has been weaker than theirs."

"All that is perfectly true," I replied. "I plead guilty to weakness, an absurd tolerance, and even cowardice. The burden of your charge is that I was accessory to a solemn rite which I believe to be nothing more than an empty formality. Can you not understand that it is precisely because this rite has no meaning for me whatever, that I could not see my way to deny the pleasure of its performance to these women, tender-hearted and devoted people, for whom this trifle has such extraordinary value. I justify myself on the ground that I did not give way to them either for any personal advantage, as for money or a bequest, or anything of the kind. I took into account nothing but questions of love and esteem. You ask my reasons, Rondeneux. Listen! "

The muffled voice of the old grandmother came to us through the half-open door.

" In the name of the Father——" she whispered.

" In the name of the Father and of the Son and of the Holy Ghost. Amen," the two babies repeated, with folded hands.

" O Lord," suggested the old lady, " bless——"

The tiny lips babbled after her, " O God, bless Daddy, and Gran, and my brother, and the servants, and people who are unhappy and ill——"

" And grant, O Lord——"

" Grant, O Lord, that Daddy may be able to get us our daily bread; and that dear little Mummy, who has gone away from us, may rest in peace with You."

Was that profound silence which followed in the house and the world outside or in our hearts? Were those footsteps, which I think we both heard and knew so well—Whose were they?

Rondeneux rose and looked at me, as I at him, through a mist of tears. And inasmuch as there is no nonsense about him, he took my hand, and his grip said all that there is to say. And then he left.

Poor old chap! I can still hear him stumbling down the stairs, sounding as if he had a bad cold, caught in my house.

CHARLES FOLEY
B. 1861

PIROTOU

EVERY time I stopped at Avignon and spent the night at the little hotel, I found the same waiter there. Pirotou—for that was his name—seemed to do all the work of the place, and, I suppose, was the only man they kept. He used to meet the trains with the omnibus, carry the luggage upstairs as if it were as light as cork, sweep and dust the rooms, polish the shining floors, and twice every day, well-groomed, would act as waiter in the coffee-room.

The man always looked so genial and happy that he greatly attracted my interest. When he laughed, it was not with his lips alone, but with his dark bright eyes, his expansive nose, and even with his close-cropped hair and young moustache. He was the most obliging waiter I have ever seen, and was popular not only with the guests of the hotel but with every one in the vicinity. When he was perched high up on the bus, driving between the hotel and the station, he used to nod or wave his whip or smile to almost every one he passed. Indeed, he was pleased with all the world, and every one had a good word for him. Being so popular he had, of course, unusual privileges. He loved the sound of his own voice, and his manner was more intimate than one cares for in a waiter; but he was such a simple and natural fellow that no one could be offended.

When the dinner things had all been taken away and almost every one had left the room, Pirotou loved a chat with any one who had remained behind; but these conversations were brief, for the proprietor or one of the guests would always cut them short, when Pirotou was wanted to do this or that. Nevertheless, he managed to give me a good deal of information on my very first evening in the hotel.

"Just imagine!" he exclaimed. "My brother is an army officer. It is remarkable, is it not? One brother to be an officer and another a waiter! Yet it is true enough; my brother——"

"Pirotou, the lady in No. 10 wants her luggage." "Pirotou, take up coffee to No. 5." "Pirotou, get out the bus immediately."

And the astonishing fellow would whip out of the room and with swift good temper carry out all these orders.

After a time I discovered that his brother was his only subject. He did not know much about him, but was very proud of him, and might even be said to worship him. Just as a farmer is always talking about the weather and the sunshine, Pirotou was always talking of the brother whose image ruled all his life. But it was a little perplexing that, after dropping the conversation at one point, he would take it up again at the same point on the following day, just as if we had never been separated.

" I fancy you would like to know how it happened? " he suddenly remarked to me one day.

I was at a loss to know what he was talking of, and said as much.

" I mean, how my brother came to be an army officer."

" Yes, indeed; how did it happen?"

" Near our village there was an old lady, very rich, whose son had died. My brother and I were orphans, and she took an interest in my brother, for he was a handsome boy and about the same age as her son who had died. She supported him at school in Paris, near her house, and then sent him to the army school at Saint-Cyr. A few months ago she died, and very sorry I was to hear it, because my brother——"

" Pirotou, where are you? There's a bell ringing! "

Next day Pirotou's story was continued.

" The old lady—— " he said.

" Whom do you mean? " I inquired forgetfully.

" The old lady who looked after my brother," he replied, a little annoyed that I had not remembered. " When she died she left him a large sum, so that he has now a good income. It was a great comfort to me that he should have an income suitable to his rank, for I had been somewhat anxious about him."

" And what did she leave to you? " I asked.

" To me? " he exclaimed with astonishment. " Nothing to me, sir. It was all to my brother, who was of the same age as her boy."

" Does he come here to see you? " I said.

" Oh, yes, he came five or six years ago, when he was on furlough. The governor gave me four days' holiday, and we went together to our old village. Four days seemed a very short time to have with him, but our holiday did not even last four days. I was here again for the third night. My brother could not give me more than two days, after all, for he had been invited to two or three big houses. And I think, though he did not say so, that our old village bored him. Of course, it was to be only expected that it should bore him—an army officer! "

" Does he do anything to help you? " I inquired.

The question gave Pirotou vast amusement. "Help me, sir? Why, no, sir. He is not used to the kind of work I do."

"Of course I don't mean that," I said. "As he is well off, does he not send you money?"

"Oh, no," said Pirotou; "and if he did, I would not accept it. I have good wages, and gentlemen are very kind in the way of tips, and I have no expenses such as he has; if you think of it, sir, you will see that I am as well off as he."

"And has he not visited you again?"

This question made Pirotou somewhat uncomfortable. He answered shyly: "He has promised to come soon at the time of my marriage. I am going to be married, you understand."

"Indeed? I congratulate you."

"Thank you, sir. I am sure I thank you. Yes, sir, it is time that we should be married. I shall soon be twenty-four years old, and the young woman belongs to this neighbourhood, and we have kept company for three years. We have not been able to see much of one another, all the same, as she is maid in a family in Paris who come down here for three months every summer. I can only see her every Sunday after mass; so we shall both be glad to get married."

"I suppose you will then take up some other occupation?" I suggested.

"Not as yet, sir; not for a time. We have not saved enough yet to set up in business. With luck we may do that in five or six years. But when we are married, I am to have a place in the house where Louisette is engaged. Louisette, sir, that is her name. My brother is coming to the wedding," he continued with enthusiasm. "Everything will be very well done, sir, as it would need to be, he being an officer of the army!"

"Pirotou, where are you? Fetch the key of No. 50."

. . . .

Several months elapsed before I visited Avignon again, and then I was painfully struck by the change for the worse which had taken place in poor Pirotou. His manner was dull and dispirited, and he could hardly call up a smile when he greeted me. It was evident that he wished to speak to me, but as usual he was wanted on every hand, and the proprietor was always shouting: "Quickly, Pirotou! Quickly!"

Pirotou sprang to the call, but not with the joyous alertness of old days. I remembered how he used to toss the trunks about as if they were empty, but now they seemed to be filled with lead. I remained at the dining-table when every one else had left; my anxiety to hear about Pirotou's marriage surprised me. He joined me as soon as he was at liberty, but did not stand beside me with his old intimate manner. He stood before me looking very depressed, and I guessed what had happened.

"Did not your brother come to the wedding, after all?" I inquired.

"Oh, yes, sir, he came. But let me tell you all that happened. On the first day, I was sure that he would take a room here, at our hotel, so that I might spend the time with him when I was free. I was very sorry, sir, to hear that he had gone to the Hôtel St. Yves, at the other end of the city. And even then, he did not come to see me, but sent a note telling me to meet him at a café, and that I was to remember to take off my apron and put on a coat and hat. It was perhaps well that he reminded me to make myself tidy, because I was so anxious to see him that very likely I should have run down the town just as I was. When I got there he looked so handsome, and his uniform was so fine, that I felt very proud of him, and would have embraced him; but he only held out his hand, and asked whether I would take wine or absinthe. He spoke very kindly and explained matters to me. He gave me to understand that he could not come to see me, but that I could meet him there. He was anxious that people should not know he was in the town; for the fact is, sir, I had stupidly talked about him a great deal too much, and he did not want to exhibit himself like a show. It was all quite right, of course; he is an officer, after all. I asked him if he would not come once and see the governor here; that seemed to me natural; but he pointed out that this would put him in an awkward position; and, of course, I saw that he was right. But you will understand, sir, that it has made it a little uncomfortable for me, because my employer and all the others think I must have asked my brother not to come, and that I was ashamed of them."

"It was, indeed, uncomfortable for you," I said. "But how about the wedding, Pirotou?"

"I am coming to that, sir," he replied; "there is not much to tell about the wedding. At the café I told my brother about Louisette, and, of course, he wanted to see her. I said that she and her mistress would be at church next day, and he promised to meet me there. He came; and when Mme. Dalbert came in, followed by Louisette, I whispered to him who they were. 'She is pretty, is she not?' I said; and he nodded. I saw, however, that his eyes never left Mme. Dalbert, and that when we left the church he still stood watching her, and at last went away without giving me an opportunity of introducing him to Louisette.

"Next day I met him again at the café, but this time he was accompanied by friends of his, officers whom he had met accidentally. When he saw me coming, he left them and came forward to meet me, knowing that I should be uncomfortable among these friends of his.

" 'Did you say that Mme. Dalbert was the name of the lady where your Louisette lives?' he asked me; and when I said that was so, he continued: 'This is very awkward, very awkward! That you should be engaged to her maid! Whatever shall we do? These friends of mine are going to a shoot at Mme. Dalbert's and want to take me with them. You would not mind?'

" Of course I laughed at the idea that I should mind, and gave him a message for Louisette.

" Two days afterwards I met him again, but his manner had changed. I asked him about Louisette, but he explained that as he had gone there with these friends he could not speak to the maid. 'I said nothing about you, either,' he added; 'I am sure you will not misunderstand——'

" All this seemed very strange to me, but I said nothing, and he continued speaking while stroking his moustache.

" 'Mme. Dalbert is a very charming woman,' he said.

" I did not reply; indeed, I had never noticed her, for my eyes had always been fastened on Louisette.

" 'If this engagement of yours were broken off,' he inquired, 'should you feel it a great sacrifice?'

" I could only answer that we had waited three years for one another, and that both of us had desired nothing so much in the world as our marriage.

" He frowned and chewed his moustache, and I soon went back to my work. For one reason and another, I did not see him for a week afterwards, and then went up to his room at his hotel, a fine big room on the first floor. He was in a great state of excitement, and paced the room impatiently. At last he came to a stand before me, and said: 'Can I trust you? Have you courage to bear it?'

" 'What is it?' I asked anxiously, seeing as I did that something had happened, and wishing to be worthy of his trust.

" He turned his head away as he spoke. 'The fact is that I have fallen in love with Mme. Dalbert and have spoken to her, and she returns my love. But I am so, so sorry for you, old man,' he continued, laying his hands on my shoulders.

" 'Why should you be sorry for me?'

" 'Great Heavens! Surely you understand? Now that we are engaged you cannot possibly marry her maid! It would be too absurd, too humiliating, that you should come to our house as a servant.'

" I shivered with cold, and I think my face turned pale, for he seemed to relent, and said: 'Well, well, let us wait and see if something cannot be done; perhaps the matter can be arranged——' "

Pirotou stopped abruptly in the midst of his story and two great tears stood in his eyes. He winked desperately to keep them from falling.

" What about the wedding? " I said, after a pause.

" Well, sir, the fact is, there has been no wedding," he said, looking on the ground. " Perhaps there will never be a wedding. I try to be patient, but my brother never writes, and Louisette has not written for a long time. Perhaps they have persuaded her that it would not do. Perhaps they have forced her to give me up. I know nothing about it; except that they are now in Paris.

" It was hard for me, sir, for we had loved one another so long and waited so patiently, but in his case it was just a fancy for a pretty face. But there was no way out of the difficulty. I could not humiliate my brother, you know. He is older than I am, and he is all that I have in the world. And then, sir, remember—he is an officer! Still, it is very hard! "

With these words, as the tears came again to his eyes, the unhappy Pirotou moved away to the window.

MARCEL PRÉVOST
B. 1862

A YOUNG GIRL'S DIARY

WHEN I was going up to my room, last Monday night, mamma kissed me, and said, in the severe tone which she reserves for communications touching my marriage: "Juliette, two gentlemen will dine with us Thursday. Consider it settled. You know what you must do."

I considered it settled, certainly; but mamma was mistaken in one thing—I was in absolute ignorance as to what was expected of me. What is expected between a Monday and a Thursday of a young girl who is to be inspected by two suitors for her hand? One cannot change one's face or figure, and there really isn't time to learn a new language, one of those tongues which possess, so mamma says, such a powerful attraction for marriageable men! Nor have I even the time to order a new gown. I have decided, therefore, to remain just as I am, and to present to those gentlemen on Thursday evening the Juliette of Monday, with her pink and white complexion, her five feet four of stature, and the two poor little living languages which she murders atrociously.

Who are these gentlemen? I have a faint suspicion. Mamma will not tell me their names, for she fears my preliminary criticisms. Usually I sit upon her candidates so thoroughly beforehand that she dares not exhibit them. "They are charming men," she declares; "charming, that expresses it. Much too good for a madcap like you. One of them is no longer young; but the other is not yet thirty." That mamma of mine has such an adorable way of putting things! She regards my suitors collectively, offsetting the faults of the one with the good qualities of the other. Would she like to have me marry all of them at once, I wonder?

Papa gave me more information. I do anything I choose with papa by a walk to the Champs Elysées in the morning, or a stroll on the boulevards about five o'clock. I walk along with my hands clasped around his right arm, clinging to him, my large grey eyes raised to his white beard as if in adoration. People nudge each other as we pass, and then how papa straightens up, and how happy he is! In these moments, if I were not a good girl, I could have my allowance doubled; or buy all the diamonds in the shop windows.

It was after one of these strolls that I questioned my dear old papa about the two musketeers who are to open fire next Thursday. Immediately he grew grave and answered:

"They are charming fellows—charming, that expresses it. Much too good for a——"

"Madcap like me. Agreed. Why do you let mamma put things into your head, you, who have such sound judgment? It is shameful!"

Now, nothing irritates papa so much as the discovery of mamma's exaggerated influence over him.

"Put things into my head! Put things into my head, indeed! I will not permit you to say that your mother put things into my head. I can judge men at a glance. The duke" (papa was a prefect under the Empire) "used always to say: 'Givernay—he is my hand and eye.' Do you know that, little one?"

I should think I did know the saying of the duke. At the age of three I had already heard it told so often in the family that I never said "papa" without immediately adding "hand," "eye."

"Why, papa dear, you know very well that I am of the duke's opinion, and that is the reason I want you to guide me a little with your experience. I am not a judge of men myself, and suppose both these gentlemen should please me next Thursday?"

Evidently this contingency had not been thought of. And, nevertheless, suppose I should be smitten with both of them, with the one who is no longer young, and with him who is not yet thirty? Papa's eye, celebrated by Morny, grew large and round. He looked thoughtful.

How amused I was!

"These two gentlemen," said he finally, "are certainly both capable of pleasing. However, I know one of them better, and therefore am disposed to favour him. He is a companion of the Imperial, Monsieur de Nivert, forty-three, cultured and high-spirited."

"What does he do?"

Papa wrinkled his brow and racked his brain in an endeavour to think what Monsieur de Nivert could possibly do; after which he concluded, pitiably enough:

"I believe he doesn't do anything!"

And then he immediately resorted to mamma's mode of defence; he considered the two collectively.

"But on the other hand," said he, "the other gentleman is a young man with a brilliant future. He is Judge of the Exchequer, and not yet thirty. Just think of it! Gaston Salandier will be director-general of a great administration some day, or a minister perhaps. And then he is very good-looking."

Poor Monsieur de Nivert! It seems after all that his most brilliant qualities are possessed by Monsieur Salandier! This freak of Dame Fortune begins to make me sympathetic.

"But," said I, after a few moments' reflection, "it seems to me that mamma was hesitating among four possible matches for me, and not between two."

Papa smiled.

"Yes; but after thoroughly considering the candidates, we have decided that two only are worthy of the prettiest girl in Paris. For," he added kissing me, "you are the prettiest girl in Paris."

Poor papa, I wish I could have a husband like him. And just think how desperate mamma makes him!

Let us sum up the situation: Fate decrees that I shall become the wife of a serious young man, or of a middle-aged fashionable man of the world. Let me think a moment. No; I have never seen even the picture of the brilliant Judge of the Exchequer, who may, perhaps, be minister. But I think I noticed Baron de Nivert at a club entertainment. It seems to me that he has not much hair, but, by way of compensation, as mamma would say, he has a small stomach—oh, quite small. On the whole, he is not distasteful to me, for the baron, if I remember rightly, is very elegant and stylish in his dress.

Well, the die is cast! Idle nobleman or plebeian with a future, it is one of you two, gentlemen, who will wed—in January—Mademoiselle Juliette Givernay.

It is over. The presentation took place last night, and I must jot down the story of that memorable evening for the amusement of my old age.

Well, last night, at five minutes to eight, when my maid had assured me that all our guests had arrived, I made my appearance in the drawing-room. Entering a room is my strong point. I don't think I have often failed at it. I walk straight ahead, gazing steadily before me over the eyes of those present; I do not see, nor do I wish to see any of those who are looking at me. I choose, on the contrary, as a point of direction, some old lady settled comfortably in an armchair, or some inoffensive old friend of papa's, or simply mamma. Invariably all conversation ceases at once, and all eyes are centred on me. What wonderful tact I possess, and isn't it a pity to be compelled to exercise it in such a limited sphere?

Besides my parents, my suitors, and myself, the diners yesterday were Count and Countess d'Aube, nobility of the Empire, whose combined ages would make a century and a half—insufferable bores, but fine people withal; Madame Salandier, the mother of the young Judge of the Exchequer, bourgeoise, with a protruding forehead, round eyes, and a ridiculous toilet, quite out of place in our society.

At table Monsieur de Nivert sat on mamma's right and Monsieur Salandier on her left. I found myself seated between Madame Salandier and Monsieur de Nivert. Madame Salandier immediately began talking to me in quite a patronising tone that quickly irritated me. She extolled the serious character of her son, whom she proudly called "my own." "My own" retires every night at ten. She also offered me a few cursory glimpses of the qualities she expected her future daughter-in-law to possess—her deportment, economy, and domestic habits—"with occasionally a reception or an evening at the theatre, of course; that is necessary in the position which 'my own' occupies."

In the meantime "my own," quite at his ease and stroking from time to time his pointed beard (he is really very handsome), was holding forth on the reduction of the public debt.

Papa, mamma, Monsieur d'Aube, Mademoiselle Espalier and even old Madame d'Aube, who is as deaf as a post, listened with open mouths, and Madame Salandier whispered in my ear:

"Listen to him. Not a minister is there that knows as much about it as he does——"

I looked at Monsieur de Nivert. He met my glance with one of discreet irony, and immediately we felt like comrades, two exiles from the same country who had fallen among barbarians.

Monsieur de Nivert is not handsome, but it is astonishing what an immense advantage he has gained over his rival by simply not saying a word about the public debt. In pouring me a glass of wine he paid me a neat compliment upon my gown, noticing that there was something really graceful and out of the common about it. And then we began to talk of "chiffons" in a low tone, while "my own" continued his harangue for the benefit of papa and mamma, who do not know how to add up the household accounts, and of Monsieur d'Aube, who is an old imbecile, and of Madame d'Aube, who is deaf. The handsome judge, however, is not stupid if he is pedantic. In a few moments he saw that he was boring us.

"This conversation," said he, "must be quite tiresome to Mademoiselle."

"Oh, no," I replied artlessly; "I was not listening."

And I had the joy of seeing a look of dismay spread over the countenances of my parents and the good Espalier, while Madame Salandier glared at me like a bonze who has just seen a street arab of Paris make a face at his Buddha.

Monsieur de Nivert smiled.

A little piqued, I think, "my own" replied:

"Indeed, such a conversation is beyond the depths of the young girls of our continent. In America they willingly take part in such discussions. Is there not some State in the North where women have the right to vote? "

" Do you hear, Juliette? " said mamma.

Did I hear? I should think I did! He wearied me, this economist bent on matrimony, and I let him see it very plainly. I took up the accusation of frivolity implied in his sentence, but I took it up as a banner. Proudly I declared my right—the right of a pretty woman, to be ignorant, frivolous, and whimsical. I argued the advantages of frivolity over seriousness, and of spirit and dash over dignity.

Oh, papa's expression and that of the two relics of the Empire and the mother of " my own "!

" My own " seemed perfectly amazed at discovering a young girl capable of giving him a retort that took the wind out of his sails.

Nivert alone encouraged me with smiles and whispered bravos.

The dinner ended in confusion.

In the drawing-room, in order to serve the coffee, I became a very proper young lady again; but the company had not regained its wonted composure. Madame Salandier could find nothing better to say than to ask:

" Isn't Mademoiselle Juliette going to play something for us? "

" Certainly," said mamma.

" Ah," thought I, " you want some music; well, then, you shall have it. Wait a moment."

I seated myself at the piano and played—and I played without stopping. I played everything that I could remember, for striking upon the little black and white keys soothed my nerves a little. Ah, you want some music! Well, listen. Take some Massenet, a little Mozart, some Serpette, some Wagner, and some Beethoven, some Lecocq, and some Berlioz, some Tchaikovsky, and some Nimporteki, one after another haphazard, pell-mell; one hour and three-quarters at the piano without stopping. After which I turned round and looked at my auditors. They resembled a plantation after a hail storm—they were simply annihilated. They took immediate advantage of the lull in the storm and fled. I was still caressing the keys with my right hand, they trembled lest I should begin again. In a few minutes the drawing-room was empty.

Mamma came toward me:

" Will you tell me now, Mademoiselle——"

But I stopped her short.

" Listen, mother. You know that I am usually very amiable and seldom nervous, but this evening I am very nervous. Don't worry me, please. We will talk to-morrow as much as you like."

And I ran lightly up to my room.

This morning, on coming down to breakfast, I expected to find my parents with long faces, but oh, what a surprise! they smiled upon me, they kissed me, and were as sweet as could be.

The key to this mystery? It is this: papa rejoined the baron at the club last night about midnight, and Monsieur de Nivert said to him:

"My dear Givernay, your daughter is adorable! You will, I hope, permit me to call upon the ladies again as soon as possible."

But what is even more surprising is, that an hour before breakfast a letter came from Madame Salandier, in which that former chestnut vender declared that "her son had been deeply impressed by the wit and grace of Mademoiselle Juliette," etc., and finally asked if my mother could receive her on Monday to have a serious talk with her.

My friend Pepita was evidently right when she said:

"Little Juliette, there are two classes of men that you must trample upon in order to make them respect you—servants and suitors."

WOLF-SOLANGE

MARCEL PRÉVOST

THREE of us, with our packs on our shoulders and staff in hand, had tramped all the afternoon through the forest—that wonderful forest of Tronçais, covering half of Saint-Amand and half of Nevers. The little village of Vigne, nestling on the bank of the Cher, marked the end of our day's tramp, and having dined with our friend, a modest country doctor, we were seated at his door, peacefully smoking.

About us, over the blue forest that shut in the horizon, the darkness was slowly gathering. The flight of the swallows streaked the sky, and in a little tower that rose above the roofs of the village a clock was striking nine.

A woman, still young, dressed in a bright red flannel skirt and white blouse, came out of one of the houses near the doctor's, and went down to the river. On her left arm she carried a baby in long clothes, and with the right hand led a little boy, who himself had a still smaller boy by the hand. Arrived at the river bank, she seated herself on a large stone, and while the two little fellows undressed and ran into the water, splashing and shouting with laughter, she began nursing her latest born.

One of us, a painter, remarked, " There is a picture that would take in the *Salon*. She is well set-up, that young woman, and in a beautiful light! And what a fine splotch of red that skirt makes against the blue background! "

A voice behind us said, " Are you looking at Solange, Wolf-Solange, young men? "

It was our host, detained a moment in his office by a patient, who now rejoined us.

And when we asked who this Solange, Wolf-Solange, was, and how she got her strange surname, he told us this story:

" Wolf-Solange, whose real name is Solange Grillet, *née* Tournier, was the prettiest girl in all the country of Tronçais ten years ago. To-day, the hard work of the country—and she has had five children—has worn her out a bit, but in spite of her thirty years, she is still looking as you see her.

" At the time of the adventure to which she owes her surname, she was living with her parents, small farmers of Reiu-du-Bois, a few miles from here, near Lurcy-Lévy. Although poor, she was much sought after by the young men, even by the rich. But she paid no attention to their advances, except those of a certain Laurent Grillet, whom she had chosen, as a little girl, when the two of them tended their flocks in the pastures of Reiu-du-Bois.

" Laurent Grillet was a foundling, and his only fortune was his hands. Solange's parents had no notion of marrying their daughter to a poor man, especially when her hand had been sought by wealthy suitors. So they forbade Solange to see her friend. Of course the little girl met Laurent just as before. Living in the same neighbourhood, with the forest close at hand, they had every opportunity for meeting. When papa and mamma Tournier discovered that neither their scolding nor their schemes had any effect, they decided on a grand stroke. Solange was put out to service at Vigne, on the model farm of M. Roger-Duflos, our deputy.

" You suppose, perhaps, that our two lovers no longer saw each other on that account? Not a bit of it. They saw each other at night, instead of sleeping. As soon as it was dark, they both left the farms where they worked and walked toward each other by a cross cut shorter than the main road. Meeting, they stayed together until the first light of day in the sheltering forest.

" This was in 1879. The summer passed and the autumn. Then came winter. It was a terrible winter. The Cher was filled with ice and then froze over solid. The forest of Tronçais bent under its weight of snow like a heavily laden roof.

" All the roads became well-nigh impassable. The forest was deserted. Little by little, abandoned by men, it was reconquered by the beasts. And, a thing that has not happened since that terrible year, the wolves came.

"Yes, young gentlemen, wolves. They disturbed the outlying farms of Lurcy-Lévy and Vigne. They were even encountered in the streets of Saint-Bonnet-le-Desert, a wretched village close to the forest. It was necessary to organise bands to hunt them, and a price of fifty francs was placed on a wolf's head. I myself saw three, two of them huge fellows, prowling on the other side of the Cher, one morning when I went out in my buggy to see a patient at Saint-Amand.

"Neither the winter nor the wolves prevented Laurent and Solange from meeting each other. They continued their nightly expeditions in the face of a thousand dangers. It was the dead season in the country—the time when the peasants are no longer at work. Every evening Laurent left Lurcy-Lévy, his gun under his arm, and walked with a quiet step through the forest, all black and white. Solange, too, left Vigne about nine o'clock. They met a little way from here, near a clearing which cuts the forest road and is called *La Decouverte*.

"Well, one evening Laurent Grillet, on reaching the rendezvous, slipped and fell on the ice, breaking his right leg and spraining his right wrist. Solange tried to lift him, but she could not; she could only drag him to a great elm and prop him up against it, wrapping her own cape about him.

"'Wait for me here, my poor Laurent,' she said; 'I'll run as fast as I can to Vigne to the doctor's, and he'll come and take you back in his buggy.'

"She started off, but had not more than passed the first turn in the road when she heard a gunshot and the cry, 'Come to me!'

"She hurried back and found her friend trembling with pain and fear, his hand clutching his gun as it lay on the ground. She asked, 'What is it, Laurent? Was it you that fired?'

"He answered, 'Yes. I saw a creature with red eyes and a strong smell. He was like a big dog. I am sure it was a wolf.'

"'And you fired at him?'

"'No, I can't raise my gun on account of my arm. I fired along the ground to make him afraid. And you see, he's gone.'

"Solange thought a moment. 'Will he come back?' she asked.

"'I am afraid he will,' replied the young man. 'You must stay here, Solange, or I shall be eaten by the creature.'

"'Of course,' answered Solange, 'I'll stay. Give me the gun.'

"She took it, threw out the old cartridge and put in a new one. And they waited.

"An hour went by, or two; perhaps more. The moon, still invisible, had risen above the horizon, because the sky at its zenith reflected a faint glow that grew every moment more intense. Laurent had fever; he shivered and moaned. Solange, as she stood leaning against the tree, chilled through and through, began to feel drowsy.

"Suddenly a kind of snort, a growl, as of dogs surrounded, in the night, made her start. In the darkness, growing gradually brighter, she perceived two red eyes that looked at her. It was the wolf. Laurent tried to rise, to seize the gun, but the pain made him fall back with a cry.

"'Raise the gun, Solange,' he said. 'Don't shoot too quickly. Aim between the eyes.'

"She lifted the gun to her shoulder, aimed, and fired. But the recoil swerved the gun aside and the beast was unharmed. It disappeared, however, down the road. A little while after, they heard it howling in the distance and other howls answered it.

"The moon rose higher. Suddenly it passed above the dark mass of underbush and lighted the whole forest as the lamp on a gate lights the road. And then Solange and Laurent saw a terrible sight: a gunshot away, five wolves were seated on their haunches like dogs, across the road, and another, more courageous, was slowly advancing.

"'Listen,' said Laurent to the girl. 'Aim at the nearest one. If you can bring him down the others will eat him and leave us in peace for the time.'

"The wolf kept advancing by short steps. Now his bloodshot eyes were clearly visible, the bones of his back and of his whole body, his dull coat, and the long tongue hanging out of his mouth.

"'Take a good aim at the hollow of his shoulder, and fire.'

"The report sounded. The beast leaped to one side and, without a cry, fell dead. The rest of the pack galloped off and disappeared in the underbush.

"'Run quickly, Solange,' cried Laurent, 'and drag him as far from the road as you can. The others will be back in a little while.'

"She went, but he called her back.

"'You must cut off his head for the prize.'

"'You have a knife?' asked Solange.

"'Yes, in my belt.'

"It was a knife with a short handle and large blade—a hunting-knife. She took it, ran to the beast, and plunged it into his throat, the hot blood gushing over her hands, her clothing, her face even. She severed the head from the still quivering trunk, then dragged the body by one leg over the slippery snow as far away as she could, and came back with the shaggy, bleeding head.

"What Laurent had predicted came true. The wolves, at first terrified by the death of their companion, were drawn back by the scent of blood. They returned, the whole five. By the light of the moon, the young people saw that terrible group coming nearer over the echoing snow, saw them leap on their fresh prey, pushing each other aside; saw them quarrelling over it, tearing it in pieces, devouring it, till there remained not so much as a tuft of hair, not so much as a single bone.

"Meantime, the boy began to suffer more than ever from his broken leg. Solange, whose strength was completely exhausted, struggled vainly against fatigue and drowsiness. Twice the gun she held fell from her hands. The wolves, having finished their repast, began to approach. The young girl fired one shot, then two into the pack, but her numbed fingers trembled so that she shot wild. At each report the pack turned tail, trotted off down the road a hundred yards or so, stopped a while, then came back.

"At last the poor children understood that it was all over; that they must die. Solange let go the gun. Not for one instant did she think of trying to save herself, of abandoning her wounded friend. She lay down beside him under the same mantle, she put her arms round him and laid her cheek against his, and both of them, their flesh chilled by the cold, their blood burning with fever, waited for death. Before their misty eyes rose strange pictures. They thought the sweet nights of summer had returned, when the forest, clad in its green robe, sheltered their peaceful meetings. Then, suddenly, the trees and bushes were stripped of their leaves and covered with a glistening mantle of snow and peopled with moving forms, red-eyed and open-jawed, that multiplied, that drew nearer, that were about to devour them.

"But, happily, neither Solange nor Laurent were destined to perish in this frightful way. Because Providence—I believe in it, young men—permitted that on that very morning I should return in my buggy from Saint-Bonnet-le-Desert, where I had been up all night with a sick patient. I had the reins, my servant had the gun and kept a sharp look-out down the road. Undoubtedly our bells alarmed the wolves, because we did not see one of them. But, in front of the elm at whose foot the two lovers were lying, my mare gave a start that attracted our attention. I jumped out, and, with the aid of my servant, I got the poor children, numbed and unconscious, into the buggy. We wrapped them up as well as we could with all the rugs we had, and we brought also the bleeding head of the wolf.

"It was about seven o'clock in the morning when we got back to Vigne. The sun rose on a country of threaded glass and white velvet. The farm-hands of M. Roger-Duflos and half the people of the village, alarmed by Solange's disappearance, came to meet us. And it was in that great kitchen where we dined this evening, in front of a roaring beech-fire, that Laurent and his friend told us about their terrible night."

One of us asked, " And after that, doctor, were they married? "

" Yes," answered our host. " What had happened seemed to show the will of Providence so clearly that the least discerning were struck by it. After the adventure with the wolves Solange's parents consented to the marriage of their daughter to Laurent Grillet. The wedding took place in the spring, and the fifty francs' reward for the wolf went to pay for the bridal gown."

The story-teller ceased. Night had fallen. The sky of turquoise-blue with its first stars was reflected in the river. The masses of trees, ink-black and motionless, looked now like black mountains. We saw Solange, Wolf-Solange, dressing the two children and returning to her house, the baby asleep in her arms. She passed close to us and, in passing, smiled at the doctor, who smiled in return and said, " Good evening, Solange! "

PSYCHE

MARCEL PRÉVOST

LIKE a wounded animal seeking cover in its wonted haunts, Ludovic Ambrus fled from Paris to his estate at Hourquet, in the depths of the Gascon country, there to exchange his poignant grief for an anguish attended by the luxury of memories.

Wrapped at that time in the fogs of winter, Hourquet was the spot where he had passed his childhood, and where, two years earlier, he had brought his bride. He had returned thither with her the September previous, more a lover still than a husband. And now he came alone—Paris held his dead.

But the dead woman had left too many souvenirs in this honeymoon spot. Her sunshade and straw hat, relics of the summer, met his eyes in the vestibule; in the deep closets were hanging gowns, still fragrant with the perfume she had used. On the table lay a book, the place where she had closed it marked with an envelope bearing her name. A withered bouquet she had hung over a window-seat made one fear to open the window lest the flowers should shower down in dust.

Ludovic could not understand why these tokens of a vanished life did not cause the cruel heart-pangs that similar personal belongings, encountered in the apartment in Paris after Louisette's death, had given him. It almost seemed as if all the things Louisette had left at Hourquet suggested sleep rather than death. The Louisette of this place seemed still to be alive; she was only away and the things she had lately touched slept in her absence. By and by she would come back and all would awaken. She would come back. . . .

Ludovic was undergoing that crisis which follows all very painful separations. He would have given the remainder of his days to see his wife again, if only in a dream or a hallucination—even in aberration of mind. Every night he tried to evoke this dream by calling up the features, the dress, the gestures of Louisette. Alas! Sleep dissolved the beloved image. Ludovic would dream of morbid things; he would see himself wandering in a cemetery, talking with men in mourning garb; he would imagine himself composing answers to the letters of condolence from his friends. But the phantom Louisette was persistently absent from these dreams.

"Is there not," thought Ludovic, "some way of compelling it? Has not modern science, with its power of causing slumber by powerful drugs, the faculty of conjuring up images during this artificial sleep?"

He asked this question of the only neighbour whom he ever admitted to his retreat—an old physician who no longer practised, and who occupied an unpretentious dwelling about two miles from Hourquet. Himself a widower of many years' standing, Dr. Séjour lived alone with his daughter, Martha, a beautiful and reserved woman of Junoesque appearance who, in spite of her twenty-seven years, did not appear to think of marrying. Intelligent but timid, the country doctor passed his life in ineffectual studies; for want of learning painfully arriving at results which, unknown to him, others had achieved before him.

"Friend," he replied to the question hesitatingly propounded by Ludovic, "do not give yourself up to the hope of a dream. I, too, experienced that haunting desire when, like you, I lost an adored wife. But, mark me, never have I seen her since her death. And if you have, as I believe, a healthy and well-balanced mind, you will never see your wife again. Believe me, it is better so. Let us do as the Scriptures tell us—leave the dead to bury their dead. Do not let us live in contradiction to Nature. Memory fades; time obliterates the images we call up. Let us be resigned to this. As for me, I have lived for my daughter and for my humble labours. You are not yet thirty years old; you will marry again and your life will readjust itself."

"Never!" replied Ludovic emphatically. His glance met the great black eyes of Martha Séjour. "I have a vague feeling," he said to himself, "that Martha, good and beautiful as she is, is not indifferent to me, that my sorrow interests her. But my whole being revolts at the idea of introducing her or any one, no matter whom, into the place which Louisette filled in my life."

He continued to yield himself up to the luxury of grief steeped in the memory of the dead woman. Although completely idle, he was not a prey to ennui. He meditated ceaselessly on sad themes. His days did not differ materially from his nights: the enervation experienced at night was deeper and less voluntary; that was all. He grew weaker physically, however, and observing this began to hope for death.

One night as he entered his sleeping-room to go to bed, with the lamp in his hand, he saw, the instant he opened the door, in the cheval-glass standing next to the window, the figure of his wife. Yes, for an instant Louisette was there, her image reflected clear and vague at the same time, in the half-light—Louisette, just as he had so often seen her last autumn, in a costume of some light material.

A second more and the image disappeared. The cheval-glass, when he approached it gave back only his own reflection.

The apparition had not causd him the slightest fear. On the contrary, the presence which had at last benignantly appeared brought him serenity. He spoke to it, he thanked it, he begged it never to forsake him. He went to bed and slept peacefully. For the first time since coming to Hourquet he was unable to recall his dreams.

All the next day an impatient desire for the coming of night consumed him. Would he see Louisette again? He had a strong premonition that he would. He went up to his room exactly at the same hour as the night before. He took the utmost pains to open the door with precisely the same movement, holding the lamp at the same angle. The shaft of light which entered the room by the open door reached the cheval-glass, revealing, as on the night before, the rapidly disappearing vision of the well-remembered light dress, the dear, smiling face of Louisette.

From that time the life of Ludovic Ambrus was concentrated on the moment of happiness accorded to him every evening by merciful fate. The days were insufferably long. He was like a lover who, having a rendezvous after sunset, could willingly insult the sun for still remaining above the horizon. The hours of anticipation were withering his heart; he could no longer, as before, dream of Louisette in a sort of calm torpor. He went in search of distraction, to shorten the endless days. Spring drew near, and with it the labours of country life recommenced. He applied himself to working actively on his estate. He visited his neighbours, the doctor and Martha; he received them at Hourquet. But while engaged in all these duties of real life, his soul was apart; he really lived only in the ineffable moment when, every night, the face of the dead woman would smile at him from the dimly lighted mirror.

Spring came, and with it cool nights, warm days, and sharp showers, bringing the renewed youth of the earth. Ludovic became animated by a peculiar feeling. He experienced a passionate desire for that phantom which, up to now, had satisfied him simply by its fugitive apparition. He supplicated the dead woman as if she were a saint, a Madonna. He begged her to leave those regions whence she smiled, and, if only in a dream, brush lightly by him, let him touch her. Alas! again were the dreams inexorable. Louisette would not, even in a dream, vouchsafe him the kiss which he entreated. But she continued to appear every night, verifying for an instant the lifeless mirror with her apparition.

The recluse of Hourquet wasted away. His neighbour, Séjour, expostulated with him.

"You must be insane to bury yourself in this manner with your grief. What a life for a man of your age! You will fall a victim to some nervous disease. Get away from here as quickly as possible; travel, get out of yourself."

Ludovic shook his head. "No, I am well here."

But he felt that Séjour was right; that in living only for a phantom he was slowly destroying himself. He was dying by inches of this longing; the endless repression was becoming unbearable. "And since I shall never love any woman except Louisette," he thought, "there is no remedy."

Towards the end of March the doctor and his daughter dined one day at Hourquet. Their host was seeing them to the front door when Martha found that she had forgotten a black lace fichu which she wore over her head and shoulders on the cool spring evenings. Ludovic went back to the drawing-room to fetch it. As he was long in returning, Martha went to help him find it, while Séjour lighted a cigar in the vestibule. For some minutes the fichu could not be found. Then Ludovic saw it on the rail of a chair where it had slipped half out of sight. He held it out to Martha. Was it she —was it he—or was it a force outside their own beings that threw them into one another's arms? Their lips met without having uttered a word. Forgetting all else, their lips still meeting in a long kiss, they were suddenly startled by a peculiar noise which caused them to draw apart. It sounded like the click of a ringed finger on glass.

"What was that noise?" murmured Martha.

"I do not know. . . ."

The voice of the doctor called: "Well, my children!" They joined him. Martha hid her flushed cheeks in the folds of the lace. Séjour pressed his host's hand. They departed.

Left alone, Ludovic locked and bolted the door behind them. The hour was at hand when it was his custom to go up to his room for the mysterious meeting. Anxious and uneasy, he awaited that hour, face to face with the lamp which glowed softly in the silence.

" Louisette will not come to-night," he thought. " I have been untrue to her. Oh, why did I do it? " He went slowly upstairs. With the accustomed movements, which he repeated each night like a religious ceremonial, he entered the room. The light of the lamp shone on the blank surface of the mirror. Was it true? Had Louisette fled?

He drew near to the cheval-glass. His own reflection confronted him, cut in two as by an iridescent blade.

Straight across it the mirror was traversed by a crack.

MADEMOISELLE HEUDIER'S HUSBAND

MARCEL PRÉVOST

I

I DON'T think I shall encumber this valley of tears much longer. There was only one interest in my life of an old maid, resigned, and, after all, happy enough, in spite of age and loneliness. Now this interest has gone; it no longer exists, it never did exist; it was a mistake. There remains my dog Moustache, my harmonium, and the preparation of my soul for eternity. . . . Hum! it is pretty thin. If I were a young girl in some love trouble, I could at least find relief by writing my secret sorrows in a little copy-book prettily bound. . . . But one does not form new habits at forty-three.

I have loved and been loved from the age of fourteen till forty-three until yesterday at half-past two. Are there many professional beauties in Paris or London who could boast as much? And never a quarrel nor infidelity, twenty-nine years of perfect love.

II

This is how it began.

My father was a humble Excise man, one of those who never attain a high post, because every time such a post is vacant another less timid or with more influence steps in. He vegetated all his life in the canton of Sarthe, where he had been appointed on his marriage, and where I was born and brought up.

It was there, at Givry, that I met " my husband "—his parents and mine and myself, we all called him that—little Lucien, who came and spent two months every vacation with his parents, our neighbours. He was the son of a Comptroller of Customs, a worthy man with a numerous family, who found it no easy matter to support on his poor pay a wife and five children. In comparison with the Letertes, my parents, with their small independent income and one child, seemed almost rich. My ready consent to the " marriage " with Lucien was therefore prompted by no interested motive; besides, we were both fourteen—he was two months older than I. At that age money seems of little importance.

We were nice sweethearts, Lucien and I. . . . He was very timid and gentle; I did what I liked with him. I had made him believe he was my husband, and he accepted the situation.

To be my husband meant, between the ages of fourteen and eighteen, running at my heels like a little brother during his holidays. We kissed each other sometimes, which caused us about as much emotion as the knocks and slaps that we also exchanged. . . . (I begin to think, after forty-three years, that I must be of a cold nature; as for Lucien, until the time he left me, he was like a little girl, even more innocent than I.)

At eighteen we were parted. The Letertes, thanks to influence, had got an unexpectedly good post for Lucien. He went as travelling companion to a very rich Englishman, who, having spent his life travelling for business, now wished to travel for pleasure. He wanted a young Frenchman to keep him company, knowing that the conversation of the French is particularly charming and amusing. Lucien, in spite of the real sorrow he evinced in parting from me, seemed delighted with the idea of seeing the world. . . . Our plans for the future were not forgotten. " As soon as the old soap merchant (that was the Englishman—' Robinson's Soap ') has given me enough money, I shall leave him and come back to you. . . ." How long would it take to make enough money? We were not sure, but evidently it would not be long, and our marriage seemed only an affair of months. I shared Lucien's enthusiasm, and there was laughter mingled with our tears when we bade farewell.

III

All that happened twenty-five years ago. Twenty-five years! It is long enough for an ordinary woman to found a family, and often to see another generation succeeding her own children. I had waited for marriage and family life for twenty-five years. I know if I confided this to any one they would not believe me; they would think me mad. All the same, it is the truth. For twenty-five years the only thing that has made life pleasant has been that I loved some one and that some one loved me. Fate has not been over kind to me. I lost my father, then my mother; the little money I had was reduced to half one day by the roguery of a lawyer; all the same I never lost hope, confident in the happiness that the future held for me. . . . Without having once in all those years seen Lucien?

Yes, without having seen him again. I believed implicitly all that he wrote me, for during these twenty-five years I received letters regularly enough from Lucien, in which nothing gave the lie to our hopes of the future, and which all seemed to me stamped with the same affection that I put in mine. He was seeing the world during those years, my little Lucien: Egypt, North Africa, Russia, India, America—he travelled widely in company with "Robinson's Soap." . . . Now and then he passed through France, but so quickly, so hurriedly, that he never had the necessary twenty-four hours to spare to come to Givry and see "his wife." His wife, that is what he always called me in his letters. And I replied, "My dear husband."

IV

Yesterday, about two o'clock, when I was practising on the harmonium some music that I was going to play next Sunday, my little maid came and told me that a lady had called to see me. It was an old friend of my parents who had become a fairly important person in the scholastic world—general inspector of primary schools, I think. She had come back to Givry very well pleased to show her success to those who had known her as a young girl. We talked about half an hour, recalling in turn all our old acquaintances. At last she said to me:

"And Monsieur Leterte, do you keep in touch with him?"

"Lucien Leterte?"

"Yes; the one who is married in England, in Derbyshire?"

I managed to answer: "No, I have lost sight of him . . ." and I asked more details. She gave them to me readily.

Having been sent to England recently to study the organisation of the Board Schools, she had spent some days in the manufacturing districts. And whom had she met at Derby in the manufactory of "Robinson's Soap" but "my husband," Lucian Leterte, old Robinson's heir, married, and the father of three children. . . .

V

When I found myself alone I wept a little, then I laughed at myself for being such a fool as to think that any man could remain faithful to a memory for twenty-five years. It is true that I had given to this very memory all my youth and a certain beauty that might have found me a husband, perhaps. . . . I began to write in this tone to Lucien, reproaching him especially for the useless deceit of his letters. Then I began to think. Thanks to this deceit I have spent twenty-five almost happy years. I have been married for twenty-five years. What would those years have been without the illusion that Lucien has given me? Perhaps he understood that himself. That is what kept him from saying nine years ago when he married: " My poor Adèle, you must not think of me any longer. . . ."

So, courage!—and no more tears. For twenty-five years I have believed myself married; to-day I am widowed or divorced, that is all. And then . . . when I think of it, he has three children. If I were to write him a nice affectionate letter and ask him to send me one of them, one that I could bring up here, less luxuriously, perhaps, than in England, but as a little Frenchman, speaking the same language his father spoke when he was in love with me? Surely Lucien will not refuse me that, and to bring up this little one will perhaps help me to follow with patience the road that leads from my house to the cemetery. . . .

I am quite cheered at the idea of it. Come along, foolish old Adèle Heudier, take your glasses and your best pen and write to the heir of " Robinson's Soap."

A little courage and goodwill is all that is necessary to overcome cruel fate. You will be a mother as you have been a wife—in imagination.

THE BEGGAR CHILD

MARCEL PRÉVOST

IT is a little story, very slight and delicate, so slight, indeed, so delicate, that I am afraid the very act of putting it into words on paper may destroy its fragile grace, its faint perfume. Why, then, when it was told us one evening in the midst of the complex luxury of a modern dinner, by the charming woman who is its heroine—why did it make upon us all so lasting an impression that it has become, in this corner of the Parisian world, one of those classic stories which are the inheritance of each group of society and to which an allusion is always understood and welcomed? Perhaps because it was like a ray of light shed for a moment on our frivolity and cheapness; perhaps because, just as a movement, a gesture is sometimes enough to reveal the whole of a beautiful form, so, too, sometimes it only needs a few sincere words to lay bare the whole of a pure heart.

We had been speaking of the mysterious impulses, already classified and named by science, from which so few people are exempt. These mysterious forces compel one man to count the flowers on the wall-paper, the volumes in a bookcase, everything he sees that can be counted. They impel another to set himself the task, as he walks along the street, of reaching a particular lamp-post before the cab coming up behind overtakes him, or, if a clock is striking, before the last stroke has sounded. They make still another go through a set round each night before retiring, arranging certain objects, and examining certain pictures and boxes. They are the slight maladies of our modern brains, germs of monomania and madness transmitted from one generation to another, until they finally become a part of human nature itself.

We were all confessing our weaknesses, our absurd superstitions, reassured by the confessions of the others, charmed to find them like ourselves, or even worse than ourselves. But one young woman had said nothing. She listened to us, a little surprise on her beautiful face, framed in its set bands of dark hair. Some one asked her:

"And you, madame, are you exempt from our modern aberrations? Haven't you the least little peculiarity to avow?"

She seemed to be searching diligently in her memory.

"No." She shook her head. "No!"

And we felt that she spoke the truth, for everything that we saw and knew of her, her gentle poise, her spotless name, set her apart from the worldly dolls who had just confessed their shortcomings. But evidently her modesty took fright at claiming an immunity so complete, when all those about her were confessing their troubles. She changed her mind:

"Really, I'm afraid I can't say that I am in the habit of counting the cabs, or that I look through my boxes every night before going to bed. But still, the other day I had an experience that seems quite like what you have described—if I understood you—a sort of impulse from within, a force that peremptorily commanded me to do a certain trifling thing, as if it had been a matter of life and death."

We asked for the story, and she told it with a charming air of excusing herself for occupying the general attention with so unimportant an experience.

"This is what happened, in a few words. It was five or six days ago, and I had gone out with my little daughter Suzon. She is eight years old, you know. I was taking her to her lecture, for, if you please, the little lady already attends lectures. The day was so fine that we decided to walk along the Champs Elysées and the boulevards to our destination, a house in the Rue Laffitte. We were going merrily along, chatting together, when a cripple, a mere boy, dragged himself in front of us and held out his hand without saying a word. I had my sunshade in one hand and was holding my gown in the other, and I confess I didn't want the bother of stopping and looking for my purse. So I went on without giving to the beggar.

"We continued our walk down the Champs Elysées, Suzon and I. The little one had suddenly stopped talking, and I, too, without knowing very clearly why, no longer had anything to say. We reached the Place de la Concorde without having exchanged a word since our meeting with the beggar. Little by little I felt growing up in my heart a sort of uneasiness, the feeling of having done an irreparable mischief, and of being menaced, on account of it, by some vague danger in the future. I always try to look squarely at what I have done; so as I walked I searched my conscience.

"'I, certainly, have not committed a very grave fault against charity,' I said to myself, 'in not giving to this beggar. I have never pretended to give to every one that I meet. I shall be more generous to the next, and that ends it.'

"But all my arguments failed to convince me, and my distress increased, became a sort of agony. Time and again I was on the point of turning round and going back to the place where we had met the child; but, if you will believe it, a sort of false pride kept me from doing so in the presence of my daughter. We have sunk pretty low when we hesitate to do right because of what others may think of us!

"We were almost at the end of our walk, and had just turned the corner of the Rue Laffitte, when Suzon touched me gently on the hand to attract my attention.

"'Mamma!' said she.

"'What is it, baby girl?'

"She raised her big blue eyes to my face and said gravely:

"'Mamma, why didn't you give to that poor beggar in the Champs Elysées?'"

"Like myself, she had thought of nothing else since our meeting; her heart was oppressed as mine was; only, being better than her mother and more sincere, she confessed her trouble quite simply.

"I did not hesitate a moment. 'You are right, dear,' I said to her.

"We had walked more rapidly than usual under the obsession of our fixed idea, so we had still twenty minutes before the time set for the lecture. I called a fiacre, got in with Suzon, and the driver started toward the Champs Elysèes, roused to his best speed by the promise of a generous tip. Suzon and I held each other by the hand, and I can assure you that we still felt very uneasy. What if the crippled boy had gone? What if we could not find him again?

"Arriving at the corner where we had passed him, we jumped out of the fiacre and looked up and down the avenue. Not a sign of the poor little fellow! We questioned a woman who hires out chairs near by. She remembered seeing the boy. He was not, she said, one of the usual beggars at that corner. She did not know in which direction he had gone. Our time was short, and we were just about to give up in despair, when all of a sudden Suzon spied the little cripple, squatting under a tree, fast asleep, with his hat between his knees. Suzon went to him on tiptoe, and slipped a small gold piece in the empty hat; then we returned to the Rue Laffitte. I know well enough it was absurd, but we hugged each other as if we had escaped a grave peril."

The young woman ceased speaking, covered with blushes to have talked so long of herself with everybody listening. And we, who had heard her reverently, felt as if we had breathed a purer air, had drunk from a stream of fresh water at its very source.

GEORGES D'ESPARBÈS
B. 1863

THE BUTTERFLY

THERE was unusual gaiety in the little dwelling. Aline had never laughed so gleefully as on that morning.

" I can't understand you! " her grandmother complained indignantly. " How can you be so frivolous only an hour before the competition? "

Aline only laughed the more. " Oh, Granny, Granny, you surely don't want me to go before the gentlemen with a face as long as yours! And, dear, just think what Queen Rose would say, the rose that we are all to paint, if I looked glum and solemn! "

There was nothing solemn or gloomy about Aline! Her hair shone like silk threads in the sun, her mouth was adorable in every mood, her brown eyes shone with youth and almost seemed to tinkle like little bells, their glances ringing music in the hearts around. In a word, Aline was a darling, dear to every one in the little Gascon town, where she taught painting to a class of schoolgirls. It was an old, shabby little town, and it wore Aline as an old coat is brightened up by some sweet spring flower. And Aline was as clever as she was pretty.

The competition for which she was entered had been founded by an obscure painter lately dead. His bequest provided an annual prize of 3,000 francs to be competed for by youths and girls between the ages of fifteen and twenty-five, and the subjects chosen were to be landscape or still life, flower or fruit. Thus the good man had made sure that his name should ever be held in pleasant memory. This was the first year of the competition; a great man had come down from Paris to preside; and notices had been sent to every village in the county calling the young painters to come up. The town was keenly interested. " Fifty artists," they said, " coming to paint one little rose! Poor little rose! "

But Granny went on complaining. " I never felt being poor so much before! " she said. " Ah, if your poor, dear father had not been so fond of his dinner and his wine, you would have had at least enough to pay for a Sunday frock. But you keep dancing about there! Do stand still till I get a look at you! Deary me! Yes, there's something on my bonnet that will do for your hat!"

She trotted with her tiny steps into her bedroom, and Aline's hat was soon the brighter for a tulle rosette—a lovely little rosette fit for a fairy's cradle. "Now, what about your frock? Turn round. That's better! Now walk a little. It is badly creased here; wait while I smooth it. Now put out your foot. There; that will have to do." The girl still crowed with glee.

"Your shoes and stockings are all right. Don't laugh, you silly child. Be quiet! You get on my nerves! The competition is a serious affair; but you—you are as pert as a sparrow!"

The old lady's quaintness upset Aline again. "You might have stepped out of one of the old masters, you old darling!" she said. "But don't be afraid; I shall not laugh up at the hall; I shall put on my best smile!"

"How many kinds have you?"

"Two at least, Granny; one for home and one for company!"

"You ridiculous mite," said Granny, "whoever taught you——" But the cathedral bell boomed through the noonday air, and the fragile old woman raised her arms aloft. "The clock has struck," she cried, "and you are not ready! Your easel, brushes, box of paints; are you sure you have everything? What it is to have to think for two! Have you got everything?" And she sank excitedly on the sofa. "A kiss, sweetheart!" she said.

The sun without was calling Aline. The girl gathered up her things, and drew down her veil over firm lips which seemed to say, "These judges shall see what I can do!" In a moment the grandmother was alone, a pathetic, dispirited figure.

"After all," she said, "a rose cannot be so hard to paint! If only Aline could tell the flower how lovingly we care for our own flowers here in the garden, it would surely do everything it could to help her. How noble it would be of that rose to save her and me!" Alas, Granny spoke none too strongly; "save" was exactly the word. And then the 3,000 francs would be only the beginning; the prize would lead to all kinds of honours. Aline, first among women painters of all the countryside; pupils thronging to the bright flowery studio—Oh, this prize would be far more than a fortune; it would mean a future!

Crouching in a corner of the sofa, with her hands clasped on her knees, the old lady murmured her dreams all through the drowsy afternoon. "Will to-day," she asked, "be the turn of our fortune? Will to-day repay me for taking to the peasant life and putting on this black apron and these clumsy shoes? How young I was when I lost family and fortune, never to dance or hunt any more, nor wear pearls, nor even taste sweets! And for ten long years my darling fairy and I have eaten nothing but scraps of bread!" The wrinkled lips moved feebly and Madame de Colainville almost slept, then muttered again: "And then one day she wanted to teach painting. Aha, I drew the line at that! Fancy a de Colainville earning her bread! And she—what did she say, the minx? 'Times are changed, Gran,' she said; 'the king is dead. We are just common people, you and I. Let me work like all the rest.' I had to give way to her. And how she has worked! Surely those judges must give her the prize: she is so good, so good." And then Madame slept till her darling's return.

In the evening Aline could not hide her anxiety; and when the old lady pressed her: "I have no chance," she said. "The model was a great, lovely Gloire-de-Dijon, a perfect flower; and I am sure my work was true; it looked a sweet little study. But the judge passed me three times without stopping to look, though he often stopped behind others of us. He seemed specially struck with No. 34. I was No. 9. I could have cried."

"Don't be silly, No. 9," said her grandmother sharply; "come and have supper. We may be poor, but there is a special supper for to-night. Your judge is a stupid. I should like to give him a bit of my mind!"

"Ah, but he was not the only one," Aline continued with troubled voice, while a tear hung on her lashes. "Other judges passed and they did not stop either. I hate No. 9! I hate her! She can't paint a bit!"

"Now, girlie, have some custard. I have no doubt at all that any king would delight in your rose, No. 9. You will have the first prize; don't fear. Our 3,000 francs will buy food for a year! We shall be rich; oh, so rich! And you will live long and happy in the dear old place where you were born. Stop crying, Aline; stop it, I say! I never was so angry in my life! Judges fit to judge turnips, not paintings! What are their precious names?"

"Monsieur Duran is the chief; but he is too big a man, and is not likely to come. Then there are President Baconel, Monsieur de Saint-Felu, Monsieur Prades the florist, and Monsieur Lambeye the land-agent. I don't know the others; there are more."

"I have a good mind to go and see them this minute!"

"Ah, don't! Please, don't! They will meet to-morrow to settle who is to have the prize."

"Mark my words: you will get it!"

"No such luck for me. I know very well what will gain it—a sickly, washed-out rose, done by a pretty blonde girl third from me on my left. It seemed to fascinate the judges; I heard Monsieur de Saint-Felu congratulating her."

"Poor child!" said Granny. "Your silly little head is full of nonsense; nothing but talk, talk, worry, worry. To-morrow Monsieur de Saint-Felu will choose No. 9. There is the moon above the elm; little girls should be in bed."

Next day at ten, in a great bright room, the judges gathered before the fifty studies of the rose. They eliminated the worst, and it was not long before fifteen canvases were set aside as hopeless. Then twenty others, neither very good nor very bad, shared their fate. From the fifteen which remained, the judges chose first seven, and then from the seven, three. Between these it was indeed difficult to choose.

"For my part," said the land-agent, "I am quite sure that the greatest of our painters, if he were here with us, would vote for No. 22."

"It is weak in drawing," said President Baconel. "On the other hand, this very excellent No. 9 is too gloomy, too heavy. Perhaps I should rather say it is too simple and natural. It lacks something. Now, this No. 18 is a picture. I vote for No. 18."

The gardener and florist, with a peasant's diffidence, had no remarks to offer. Bending forward, with his great gnarled hands resting on his knees, he studied the three roses with breathless attention.

"The fact is," exclaimed Monsieur de Saint-Felu at last, "that all three are quite charming. In my opinion we ought to split the prize. Give no first prize; but, instead, give two seconds and one third. That is my view."

At that very moment a little white butterfly fluttered in at an open window, darted about above the heads of these elderly gentlemen, alighted on one of the roses, and caught its feet in the wet paint.

The gardener stood erect at once. "No. 9 has won!" he cried.

So No. 9 won the great prize; no one could question the butterfly's choice. Granny, all joy and pride when she heard it, clapped her hands and sang that a butterfly had brought to Aline fame and a fortune. The young painter tried to free her benefactor, but found him dead. Mounted in a bracelet-medallion, he still hovers on the wrist of Mademoiselle de Colainville; and when she paints, she gently invokes his aid.

LEON EUGENIE FRAPIÉ
B. 1863

"THE MISSUS"

WHENEVER Dubour mentioned "the missus," every one in the office shook with suppressed laughter, for his large clean-shaven face took on such a ludicrous expression of obedience, compunction, and respect. How touchingly submissive that big man must be at home! He was generally known as "the good little boy." Not that the others were all masters at home! Oh, no! Vanard, for instance, had to light the fires because the maid used too much wood and madame could not think of spoiling her hands; and Bijou was forbidden to smoke, as snuff was much more economical. But once away from the domestic tyrant, none but Dubour maintained that attitude of respectful obedience, not one adhered so religiously to the home regulations. Dubour's housewife evidently made him regard her as infallible, and certainly held him well in hand. No wonder he was in such good health; not the slightest excess, not the smallest caprice did she allow him. Sometimes at luncheon he would sigh: "I have too much meat, but I would rather force myself to finish it; the missus knows better than I what I should eat, and she would scold if I left any."

Before going home in the evening he was often pressed to come and have a drink, simply for the pleasure of hearing his frightened refusal: "Oh, no, thank you, I can't; it is impossible. I am expected. I must not be late."

It was evident that, office work excepted, he did nothing without the approval and consent of his petticoated government. If, for instance, a subscription list happened to be brought round, for a funeral wreath or a presentation, he asked for it again the next day; then he always gave generously, but it was clear that the amount had first to be discussed with "the missus."

Dubour was no talker. Little was known about him and speculation was difficult, for he had entered the service late in life, after several unsuccessful attempts at business. At the end of two years the most inquisitive had extracted only a few bare allusions to his failure and to family sorrow; details as to the awe-inspiring missus were entirely wanting, so that chatterers had to content themselves with feeble jokes, such as, "She must have a moustache," or, "Surely she is always armed with a poker."

Although holding merely a modest post in a government office, Dubour was always well, even fashionably dressed. This proof that he must still have a remnant of his former fortune added to the consideration which his forty years compelled. Moreover, his never-failing kindness and willingness to oblige had made him justly popular. But he was really too much "the good little boy."

It was partly owing to the affection his colleagues felt for him that they concocted the plot to make him late, and thus disobedient to the commands of his dreaded missus. They wanted to break through his ridiculous submission, and felt convinced that it only needed one determined effort to shake off the yoke. The cleverest attempts had failed one after another; but at last Leflot proposed a sure plan for his birthday.

On that evening, five minutes before the office closed, Dubour's colleagues pressed round him with such beautiful flowers and such hearty good wishes that only a boor or a coward could have run away on the plea that it was time to go home. At the same moment Leflot ran out shouting: "I will just send a wire to your home," and gave no time for objection. Then bottles of champagne were brought out of a kit-bag and glasses were set out on the table.

"Silence," some one cried, "silence! What has Leflot to say?"

That conspirator, who had only pretended to run to the telegraph office, reported; "That's all right! Your people will have the message in a minute or two!"

Reassured on this point, and touched, flattered and dazed by the many speeches and incessant handshaking, Dubour drank several glasses of champagne, and before he knew where he was, had become more than a little merry. Unprotesting, he accompanied his gay comrades to the restaurant and joined them at a dinner in his honour. There, as the hours fleeted past, the company nodded and grinned with glee. What a dressing-down poor old Dubour was in for! And worse than the late hours was the fact that he had spent ten francs of his salary; for every penny of it went every week to the missus.

Near midnight came the question how this good little lad was to be taken home. No one wanted to carry the joke too far, and every one felt that a reporter must go to witness the rage of the domestic tyrant. Yet it was difficult to find any one ready to take the risk; for doubtless the virago would be waiting with a broomstick, and whoever should accompany Dubour might easily come in for some of its blows.

There was long and furtive discussion on this point, and at last

Leflot was forced to volunteer. After all, he carried with him authority, logic, and strength, for he was at once head clerk of the office, a trained lawyer, and had formerly held the amateur championship in fencing.

The unlucky Dubour was perfectly helpless. The gorgeous bouquet dangled from his neck by a string; a card bearing the legend "Leave till midnight" was pinned conspicuously to his coat; the ends of his tie floated in the breeze, and fragments of song issued from his wavering voice. Leflot, still fairly sober, led his victim by the arm.

At last they arrived, and Leflot was struck dumb with astonishment. Dubour had stopped before a poverty-stricken tenement of flats, and the glimmer of the matches which they struck showed a steep, narrow, ill-tended staircase.

Dubour was instantly seized with his inveterate instinct of submission. He whispered "Hush!" at every step, and muttered, "I'll slip into my room and shut the door; the missus won't see me at all. Here we are!"

The door of the flat was ajar and a narrow gleam of light came through. After a moment's hesitation Leflot, conscious of his standing at the office and other qualifications, stepped confidently in. There was no lobby; he found himself at once in the dining-room.

O surprise of surprises! Here, too, was to have been celebrated this happy festival, but the missus, worn out with waiting, slept in a chair beside the feast which she had prepared in vain. On a round table, covered with oilcloth, was a leg of mutton now quite cold. One place showed that a child had supped; the other two, quite undisturbed, proved that the missus had gone without her dinner. Before one of these there stood a little bunch of wallflower in a glass, and a new pipe. How sweet, humble, homely a life stood revealed at a glance!

And the missus? Dubour's little girl; no more than twelve years old, yet a perfect housewife, with this serious little face, neat dress and blue apron. She woke as in a dream, yet seemed to grasp at once the whole pitiable story. Her first thought was one of courtesy to her guest.

"Please sit down," she said. And then, anxiously, to her father, "Have you dined, Daddy?" Then a loving kiss, and one more from the little brother who had at last been put to bed and had sobbed himself to sleep, at not having been able to say the little verses he had learned for Daddy's birthday.

Dubour had taken his easy chair, and in spite of the fumes of wine, showed vast satisfaction in being home again. Sitting near, Leflot tried to construct a plausible explanation.

"I am sure you will understand," he said to the waiting child,

" that this irregularity of to-night is due to an old custom of ours at the office. It is an old custom from which none of us can escape. I can assure you," he continued, glancing doubtfully at Dubour, "that he has—there has been nothing—nothing excessive." And so he stumbled on, hardly knowing what he said; only conscious that all his special pleading was lost on the grave little maid before him.

Ah, but he was touched! All these so-loving preparations had been wasted; all this happy anticipation had been rudely shattered and changed to a solitary, anxious vigil. All the time, while he spoke those measured phrases in which he was so expert, his eyes were on the little gift bought with money saved, penny by penny, where every coin meant another self-denial, the little gift at which for weeks past she had gazed in the shop windows. Then he studied this mistress of the house, whom they had pictured as a termagant, and saw in her a child who ought to have been playing with dolls, but with rare devotion preferred this brand-new pipe to any toy. She was slight, with transparent complexion of a delicate flush; her fair hair was done up in a tight little knot; there she stood in the homely frock, smiling kindly to him, and apparently accepting the " custom of the office " and the " nothing excessive." " Of course, monsieur," she said, " what must be, must be; and Father isn't more tired than usual."

And all the time, while listening to the stranger and approving what he said, the missus was at work so quietly that it was hardly noticed. She seated her father more comfortably, gave him a cup of cold coffee, arranged his tie, and removed the flowers from his neck and the hateful card from his coat. Not one proof of the excesses which she so indulgently denied escaped her.

Seeing all this, Leflot was struck with a kind of fear. The child's gentle, simple mind was quite ready to agree with his argument. " Certainly, monsieur, you are quite right." But there was also in her mind another faculty, though inarticulate, which judged matters from a higher standpoint. There was that clear calm vision of the housewife, which assures the well-being, security, and regularity of every family; the directing love which watches and repairs and cares for all; that recall to wisdom and temperance to which even the strongest and most favoured at times must listen. Without this strict and loving protection who can live?

The dainty, kindly little housekeeper came downstairs with Leflot, to light his way; serious, calm, and reserved, she thought of everything, without a trace of ostentation. " I beg your pardon," she said, " the lining of your pocket is pulled out; you might lose your purse. Take care, there is one more step. At the end of the street you will get a bus; it's not yet half-past twelve."

When the heavy door had closed behind him Leflot, the head

clerk, lawyer, and fencing champion, still stood there gazing at the house with a sad and tender smile. He was conscious that he himself was only " a little boy."

A SIMPLE SOUL

LÉON EUGÉNIE FRAPIÉ

WHAT do I want, sir? I beg your pardon, sir. I'm his mother, sir. Yes, sir, his mother. Mother of my boy; him as was shot by mistake.

I beg your pardon, gentlemen, I'm a little hard of hearing. Were they sorry for it? Oh dear, yes, sir, yes indeed. They couldn't understand how it could have happened, and begged my pardon, and said that no such thing should ever occur again. Oh, they were very kind indeed, most kind and considerate they were. Terrible upset they were and said there should be handsome compensation.

Don't you remember about it, sir? It was this way, gentlemen. If I may make so bold, sir, do you mind if I sit down? I'm that tired, having been on my feet since nine, and running this way and that over half the town. I went to the police station down our way, and they sent me to the head office, and a gentleman there told me to try the solicitor in charge of the case. I forget his name, but he wrote it down, and his clerk—the gentleman was busy—told me to apply to the magistrate, and there the officer said I ought to come here, gentlemen. What with walking, and missing my way, and buses, I have been half over the town. But if you're in a hurry it is quicker to walk than to take those buses, especially when the heart is sad.

The accident? Yes, sir, I'm coming to that. There were burglars who had broken into a house, the family being away, and the police were on the look-out for them, and had an idea, the burglars not being in the house, that they had got away by the roofs; and as I say, they were on the look-out for them all down the street. It was a Saturday afternoon, a fine day of sunshine it was, and my Henry, being a slater by trade, was doing a job on one of the roofs, and the police, thinking the burglars were on the roof and seeing them, though indeed I was told in the following week that they hadn't seen any one but just fired to scared them, and so my Henry got the bullet through his head.

You may well say so, sir; it was terrible indeed. When they brought him home to me he still had the bit of lilac in his coat. Oh, it was a sad, sad day!

He was a good boy, was Henry. Always lived with me and hardly ever went out in the evenings, and was as handy as a woman about the house. And then came this dreadful accident; it was just the week after I finished a new dress, black with red spots, to please him.

Oh, yes, every one was very kind in my trouble. One gentleman wrote out a petition for me, and it was sent in, and after a time a messenger came and took me to the President himself. Ah, he's a kind good man! Directly I went in at the door of his room he got up, and as soon as I began to speak he said: "Dear lady, I know everything, and I promise you that everything shall be done for you. You shall have a life-pension." Those were his very words. Only, he said that I must give the Government time. I was not in his room more than a minute. And since then I have waited, waited; it is almost a year now!

But how I have been worried about the boy's death ever since, gentlemen, you would never believe! Called to one enquiry after another, questioned this and questioned that! They were set on showing that the police must not shoot innocent boys, and set on finding out who were guilty.

Well, four weeks ago they found them out, Victor and another, and sent them off to gaol.

Victor has the heaviest sentence of the two; and begging your pardon, gentlemen, I have come to see you about him. They say you can do something—— It being our trouble and me being the mother I must ask you, gentlemen—— Every one in our street knows that the President was good enough to say, "Why, certainly, my good woman, you shall have all you want!" They all know me; I have lived there for upwards of forty years; and in these last months they have all been so kind! They nod so friendly when I go down the street, and the shopkeepers behave as if I was a lady almost, as if I was rich. Well, so I am, when the President has promised!

But Victor's friend—she is called his wife—came to me and asked if I could do anything. And I thought and thought, but could not see how I could help them——

Gentlemen, please let me make an exchange. Only an exchange. If you can do it, please let me not have the pension which the President promised, but let Victor have a pardon instead!

I'm a useless old woman, anyway. I am over sixty—so old that I need hardly anything. Money? What should I do with money? I do very well as I am, with three hours' work in the morning and five in the afternoon, at threepence an hour. And sometimes a special job like a dinner, with plates and dishes to wash until midnight, and extra pay. Don't you see that I have everything I need? Besides, I am getting old and stiff, and if I should stop work I should soon not be able to do anything at all.

I'm not saying, gentlemen, that the people in our street will be quite as respectful when they find out that I shall have no pension; but there, no one ever paid much attention to me before, anyway.

And Victor, he's not a bad man. It was only his carelessness. He was never in trouble before. And he told the truth in court; he didn't lie like the others; that is why he came off worst. He is sorry about it, truly sorry. Then he has promised to marry the girl as soon as he comes out. She has a baby girl now; and Victor is just as old as my poor boy would be; and I sometimes think that when they are married they may look in on me sometimes. There isn't a living soul to care for me.

Are you going away, gentlemen? Office hours over? I must ask your pardon for taking up your time so long. I have been on my feet since nine this morning and had no idea of the time.

You took notes, then? On everything I said? And you will really do your best? I shall not need to come back, then, but only wait? How can I thank you for your goodness? Thank you very, very truly.

That door, do you say, sir? I came through so many doors and passages that I am confused; and my eyes, too, are getting weak.

You, sir, are the clerk here, are you not? Now, please remind the gentlemen sometimes, so that they will not take too long in——

Oh yes, please, do take it for your trouble, though it's only a trifle. It is because I am the mother, you know.

PIERRE MILLE
B. 1864

MRS. MURRAY'S REVENGE

"MRS. MURRAY! Madam! I have to tell you—— there has been a terrible accident—— Mr. Murray——!"

The veteran servant of the Bank of Messrs. Murray and Co. of Singapore could hardly speak for emotion. His eyes were red; he had run up from the town, weeping, and had wondered all the way how to tell the dreadful news. He had arrived without having made up his mind. Under the blazing sun the steep road from the Bank, near to the docks, up to the Murrays' country house, had quite exhausted him. And now, under the pale brilliant sky, he looked afar over the native fields rich with intensive cultivation; over the homes of wealthy Englishmen, of very British architecture, though smothered in exuberant southern vegetation, like European girls dressed in tropical raiment for a fancy dress ball, and saw stretching far below him the immense seaport and harbour full of steamships and sailing-vessels, and further still, among all the little islands, ships in full steam and full sail, Chinese junks and Malay boats, all meeting there at the crossways of three worlds.

Mrs. Murray, very pale, came quickly to his cry. "Is my husband ill?" she said. Her book fell from her hand, and the cashier raised it with habitual respect. Her next words were in a very low tone. "Is he—— Is he dead?"

"Yes, madam," he said. But knowing that he had not told all, the confession brought him no relief. She, who had loved her husband deeply, stood beside the man wondering why she suffered so little. The name of "death" seemed quite meaningless. She might have wept, but it would have been sheer affectation; she could not conceive that her husband could be dead, because every impression she had ever received of him was one of life and joy and vigour. But all at once a dreadful thought struck her, and she whispered hoarsely, "He did not—take his own life?"

"No, madam," said old Jim Stevens. "He was killed. We found him by the open safe with a knife between his shoulders. He had evidently just opened the safe, as he did every evening since the illness of the head cashier, to put away the coin and takings of the day. But we found nothing in the safe. They must have taken everything."

"Who?" cried Mrs. Murray, with great excitement. "Do you know who?"

"Yes," he replied. "It was Weldon, the head clerk, and his friend Nathan, the little cotton-broker. It is they who did it. Nathan had called to see Weldon, and we suppose that one of them caught his arms and the other did it." And then, so as to finish his story, he added, "They have escaped. We have not been able to find them. They must have got away from the town."

All this time Mrs. Murray was thinking, in shame and distress, "I cannot feel; I cannot suffer; I cannot understand."

She could not even see her husband Alfred except through her accustomed view of him, and this dreadful shock had not disturbed her memory of the quiet, silent, powerful man of command, to whom she had given herself entirely as wife and housekeeper, and whose service was the joy of her life. She strove in vain to picture him lying prostrate and motionless in the little strong-room of the office, with a dark stain on his coat and on the floor. Yet she felt fierce anger at the horrid deed, and a great desire to act, to do something. And now she saw the open safe, and experienced for a moment the suffering and rage of the betrayed and dying man. If he had still lived he would have had no thoughts but those of the living; he would have made swift pursuit to regain the wealth with which he had been entrusted. This seemed so clear, so certain, and so luminous, that Mrs. Murray nearly cried aloud, "He is in my heart and brain; this is he who insists on action!" And indeed, the impulses of man or woman are sometimes so strong, that it is impossible to believe that they do not come from another.

Five minutes later she was swinging downward towards the city in a palanquin carried by two Chinese porters, straining the muscles of their goat-like legs, while the bewildered Stevens ran behind them. There was a great crowd around and within the Bank; the clerks in the office were talking excitedly, while a police-inspector was interrogating them individually, insisting on every detail of the afternoon's events, whether important or not, with an invariably careful and calm manner. The dead banker, almost forgotten, lay on a long bamboo lounge, with a handkerchief over his face. Flies had gathered in troops on the handkerchief; it was this which first struck home to the mind of his wife, and taught her that here indeed were death and dissolution. She fell to sobbing by the body, and all around kept an uncomfortable silence.

Suddenly she rose and quietly asked how much had been stolen. The question was put in such an unfeeling way as to be almost shocking, especially as the woman was quite free of avarice, and hardly knew the value of money. Some one replied that the books had not been fully examined, but that the booty of the thieves might amount perhaps to 300,000 dollars in banknotes, and in securities to perhaps twice as much again. The murderers must have booked their passage beforehand on one of the ships which ply from Singapore to Yokohama and thence to San Francisco. A steamer of this line was the only one which had left the port since the hour of the crime.

"We have telegraphed," said the inspector, "and shall ask for their extradition."

Mrs. Murray shrugged her shoulders. "I know nothing about all that," she said; "but I know that Weldon and Nathan are Americans, and that the United States are not in the habit of giving up their subjects. As for seeing them in their own country, you know very well that they have plenty to buy the jury with. We must go after them; that is all!"

The inspector started with amazement. "Go after them? But how should we do that? And why? That does not lie within our powers. We communicate with the foreign authorities and give them all possible information. My duty ends there!"

"I said nothing about you," she replied; "*I* am going after them. It is *my* husband whom they have murdered."

The dead man seemed to her like a leader fallen in the fight, whose place must be taken by the next in command. She told Stevens to have his body carried in the litter to her home, to watch over it, and to make every arrangement for the funeral, as she was going away that very night. To every one present she seemed to have taken leave of her senses; but they let her do what she would, because her force of will was positively formidable, and it was evidently useless to waste time in meddling with her affairs. They thought, indeed, that she would be unable to leave Singapore, and would be stopped by the practical difficulties of her project. But eagerly, swiftly, without a moment's hesitation, she forced her way through every obstacle.

All along the quays the long ranks of steamers slumbered, silent and cold, with great funnels and tall naked masts, while hordes of coolies were incessantly throwing coal into their bunkers. Of all of them only one was under steam; it was a long, swift, narrow vessel of cunning aspect, its steel hull painted a dazzling white. It was loaded with grapes, peaches, and a whole cargo of other fruits, destined for an Indian port. This was the product of the ingenious enterprise of a Yankee; and the ship had been built for great speed, in order to transport undamaged these perishable goods.

Mrs. Murray chartered the steamer, and having purchased its cargo, unloaded it at any price it would fetch on the Singapore market. She raised money by pledging her house and jewels, and emptied her current account at the Bank. At eight o'clock that evening she set out, armed with a copy of the inspector's report, and accompanied by two of her husband's clerks to serve as witnesses. The people of the town were standing all along the quay, gazing with silent curiosity, for it was generally believed that she had gone off her head.

The Yankee skipper had laid his course and pressed his engines to the utmost. He was eager for the chase. "There's a woman for you!" he said; "I guess she's as real as they make them!"

She stood beside him, with every nerve bent on her enterprise, and questioned him about their course. She was a tragic figure in the white gown which she had not had time to change. She heard how they must keep free of Saïgon and pass round Manilla; and the throbbing of the screw, shaking all the hull, was like music in her heart. And now the skipper had the fires banked up, skirted dangerous shoals, cut every corner; he pored over the chart with her, and was amazed how tireless she was and never thought of sleep. At last, under the lee of Formosa, they saw the smoke of a great steamer, and knew that this was their quarry.

The two clerks, who had suffered pitiably from the sea and took little pleasure in their present mission, now came upon the bridge. The crew, who had gathered something of the object of their chase, were howling like dogs, while the skipper could not contain himself for joy, and spoke of using the little quick-firing gun in the bow, which was mounted there as a protection against Chinese pirates. The *Sunbeam* cut the water so swiftly that you would have thought it was about to leave the surface like a flying-fish. The roar of its syren cleft the air and spread far across the wide spaces of the sea. The *Swan of Japan* thought that a pirate was in pursuit, and held all the more swiftly on its way.

"Give her all you can!" shouted the skipper down to the engine-room. "We are gaining."

And indeed, they gained at last!

Two hours later the *Sunbeam* was within fifteen fathoms of the liner's quarter. On the latter, expecting an attack, women were weeping aloud, while the captain mounted the bridge with his megaphone. "What do you mean by pursuing an honest ship?" he cried. "Put down your helm or I will ram you and sink you."

The Yankee skipper, taking his own megaphone, began by showing him that an American can swear more roundly than any other on sea or land. To tell the truth, too, he did not find it very easy to explain why he had pursued "an honest ship," and only swore the more.

"Give me your speaking-trumpet," said Mrs. Murray. Raising it, she called across the waters: "You cannot sink us because we are swifter than you. I am the wife of Alfred Murray, who has been murdered by two passengers on your vessel, Weldon and Nathan, who booked with you under false names. I have come to identify and arrest them, and to get back the money they have taken. We want you to lower a boat."

The captain's voice came back to her, "You must be mad! In any case it is none of my business. You must apply to the authorities in Japan or in the United States. And now, go to the devil!"

"Stop and lower a boat," Mrs. Murray replied; "I will explain everything. If you do not stop I shall follow you to the end of the world. We are well armed. I do not say that we shall sink you, but we shall bring down any one who remains on your bridge, and shall begin with you. Please lower a boat."

At this moment Weldon and Nathan, white with fear, were to be seen climbing the steps to the bridge.

"There they are!" shouted the woman. "I know them. They want to buy you off. If they go up another step, I fire."

The captain of the *Sunbeam* was already at his gun, and a loud report followed. The passengers on the other vessel thought that their last hour had come; but their captain, to whom the whole episode was merely absurd, now brought it to an end.

"We are lowering a boat," he shouted, "but I may tell you that you will have to pay heavily for all this."

The boat came alongside the *Sunbeam*, and Mrs. Murray entered it with her two witnesses. As they did so, Weldon was heard to say in shaking accents, "It is all up, old man; we shall have to settle the bill, Nathan."

"True enough," the other replied. "Good-night and good-bye." Thereupon two revolver shots followed closely on one another, and the murderers fell to the deck.

"Oho!" exclaimed the captain. "So your story was true! I don't mind admitting that this alters the appearance of affairs." And while he gazed curiously at the two criminals, Mrs. Murray came on deck.

She pointed to her companions. "These gentlemen," she said, "have come with me——"

"Oh, my dear lady," answered the captain, "I have no need of witnesses! These wretched fellows have not gone out for nothing. Where is the purser?"

The purser came slowly up, shaking with terror. Shudders ran down his back all the time that he was searching the trunks of the two wretches. All the same, he recovered the whole of the money stolen from the Murrays, and in addition 15,000 dollars which represented the savings of the two murderers.

"Keep the whole of it, Commodore," said the captain, giving

to the young woman in all seriousness the highest title in the American navy. "Keep it all; it will pay for your little expedition."

She handed him the inspector's report.

"Whatever do you want me to do with that?" said he. "We like to look after justice ourselves, especially in these latitudes, and you have had good reason to do so, in all conscience. But you are very pale; will you have a glass of champagne?"

The poor woman was, in fact, at the end of her strength, and now that her end was attained, collapsed altogether. The champagne quite knocked her over; she had to be carried up to the *Sunbeam*.

The steamship passengers, fully satisfied now of their safety, shouted, "Hurrah for the lady commodore!"

But she heard nothing. During the whole of the return journey she lay in her cabin in utter prostration, and weeping bitterly. She felt that she had not done what it was her duty to do, that she ought to have stayed beside her husband's body, to have watched over him, to have buried him; that she should, in short, have acted as a woman and have been a woman. Most of all, it was a real torture to her that she was not in mourning; this fact was even a cause of the acutest physical distress. The sound of those two revolver shots made her head turn giddy continually. She seemed always to see before her those two figures with their writhing limbs stretched out in the noontide glare, those two faces on which death had fixed their last convulsions.

"And it is I who did it all," she told herself; "can it be that I am still a woman?" She suffered horribly from the sense that she had divested herself of sex.

And now they were steaming toward the quays of Singapore. The Yankee skipper signalled the news by semaphore, and shouted to surrounding boats the story of their success, of Mrs. Murray's courage, and of the death of the two fugitives. The mad, romantic, incredible tale intoxicated him, and he used the bombastic words of journalism, exaggerating all. He was more and more impressed by the sensational drama in which he had played a foremost part; and while he admired himself, he admired more the indomitable lady.

"Listen to me," he said to her. "I want you to take back your money. I have said it before; let me say again—you are indeed a woman! And will you let me say this too. I hardly know how to say it—— But you know how men in love with an actress love and desire her with the strength of all the thousands of hearts who long for her. I want you; I beg you to be my wife. The seas will be ours, if you like, from China to San Francisco; ten years would be enough to capture all the shipping companies, so that not a vessel would ply on the Pacific without our permission. Or let us go to the States, if you prefer, and gamble with land and gold and all that is human; let us found cities and reign as queen and king over great areas where everything shall be ours, where none shall live but by our consent, nor traffic except under our licence. We might pour the population into moulds of our own design, so that all human life should be stamped with the mark of our absolute will."

The woman stood with her face covered by her hands, trembling a little, and answered not a word. As the *Sunbeam* glided past the little island off the port, thousands of voices were raised in acclamation, and countless yachts, boats, and other craft surrounded her. All the ladies of the European colony were gathered at the Victoria Docks with huge bouquets of brilliant and fragrant flowers. It was a reception that could only be compared to apotheosis. Jason returning with the Golden Fleece, or Columbus bringing to Cadiz the glory of the New World, or Nelson coming to Naples and the arms of that terrible lover, Lady Hamilton, was not welcomed so splendidly as Alfred Murray's widow. The gangway was thrown out to the quay, and down it there glided humbly an unhappy woman, her face lined with fear, her hair nearly white, whose crumpled gown of white silk seemed to fill all her mind with shame. " For the love of Heaven," she said, " give me a black dress! I cannot show myself like this! "

The report spread that the unhappy woman, who had set out in madness, had returned in dementia. This belief was, however, unfounded. She was the same courageous little English wife who had lived obedient to her husband, securing his comfort in every way and controlling his household efficiently; who had never missed going to church, and had obeyed all the world's laws, respecting all that she had been taught to respect. And now her lord was dead, and she had broken the world's law by doing something immoderate, something unfeminine. She suffered mentally because she could not recognise nor understand herself. She was desperately conscious of inability to carry the enormous load of her renown. People struggled to get a glimpse of her; she was mobbed by her adorers; all eyes and voices reproduced the glances and the tones of the Yankee captain; every one took for granted that she was an exceptional woman, of formidable will, whereas in fact she was weaker than she had ever known herself to be. All her commonplace and tenuous will had been squandered in one swift act of violence. Yet henceforth people would always expect from her that which she could not give; she had left the feminine herd, and there was no more place for her in the world. No man would ask for her in marriage except it were one of brutal ambition such as this seaman, whom after all to have married would have been to have deceived, because she had no more spirit to bring him than that of a feeble and affrighted child. But still they spoke with enthusiasm of her courage and of the grand characteristics of her race; and with all her heart she desired nothing so much as to die.

Yet in spite of her prayers death was refused to her. When her lawyers had paid the liabilities of the Bank and had sold the home and business, and even the very name of the man to whom she had given her life, there was left to her a tiny income, just enough to eke out a miserable existence. She left the tropic scene and returned to England, a lonely mourner estranged from her sex. It was in those unhappy days that I saw her in a London boarding-house of mean aspect, where other poor, melancholy, dull women were passing their declining years. Mrs. Murray looked exactly like any one of the others, so that her story, when recited by a friend, who had compassionately looked in upon her, was received with incredulity. As for herself, she holds all those memories in horror, and cannot be induced to speak of them. Little wrinkles have gathered round her eyes, her nose is sharp and white, and the saddest thing of all, I think, is the delusively youthful flush of her cheeks, the thousands of tiny injected vessels of her skin. It is as if her form were withered and her soul were dead.

HENRI DE RÉGNIER
B. 1864

THE SIGN OF THE KEY AND THE CROSS

As I walked through the streets of the city I kept thinking of one of the stories which Monsieur d'Amercœur had told me. Without having named the place where the circumstance occurred he described it minutely, so that I seemed to recognise everything. The old city, noble and monastic, crumbling in its dismantled ramparts beside the yellowish river, with, beyond, the mountains piled against the horizon; the narrow streets, half shade, half sunshine, the old walled-in houses, the churches and numerous convents, each with its chime of bells—all was familiar.

I seemed to find it again exactly as he described it, this city, an old pile of stones, sombre or luminous, wrapped in warmth and solitude, and the dusty ossification, retaining for such of its monuments as were yet standing the skeleton of past grandeur. In the centre the houses were crowded in a compact mass, still vast, outside of which the buildings were scattered, while over all a sleep or torpor seemed to hover, broken suddenly at times by a tolling or a merry clang of bells.

The streets, paved with flat stones or hardened with gravel, cut across each other oddly to open into squares where the markets were held. The flocks of the country-side gathered there to go away dispersed, according to their sale. The auction and the church service were, turn about, the sole occupations of the inhabitants. The place remained rustic and devout. The quick trot of the sheep pattered over the pavements, which echoed with the sandals of the monks. Pastor and flock jostled each other. The odour of the shearing mingled with the smell of woollen cloth. The air was redolent of incense and tallow; of shorn and tonsured; of shepherds and priests.

I arrived at the angle of two streets. A fountain was flowing into a time-worn basin. I remembered the fountain; Monsieur d'Amercœur had praised the freshness of its water. The street to the right ought to lead to the Close of the Black Friars. I followed its windings, which led into the very heart of the city. A few poor shops displayed their wares. Rosaries hung beside horsewhips. The street suddenly grew wider. The high frontage of an old mansion appeared. I had seen several others of the sort here and there, but this one was particularly noticeable. It was built on a battered stone masonry. The windows, high above the soil, were grated. In former times they must have used those foundations for the present building, which was of severe architectural design. At the corner of the structure the street turned abruptly and descended by steps, gradually encircled the back of what proved to be an ancient castle—a stronghold, with its blocks of stone laid into the living rock.

I recognised the mansion d'Heurteleure. The street ended; before me I saw an avenue of poplars. Old stone sarcophagi, now empty, stood in rows amid the long grass where a pathway had been worn. To the right stretched a wall with a low door at the side. I started as I perceived it. It opened into the herb garden of the monks, the portal of whose convent could be seen at the end of the walk. I paused and approached the little mural door. It was massive and iron-bound. The keyhole was shaped like a heart.

Continuing, I reached the convent porch and rang. The porter admitted me. Immense corridors led to vast halls. We ascended stairs, my guide gathering up the skirts of his frock as we mounted. We met no one. From the chapel, which I did not enter, came the droning chant of psalms. I was shown through several cloisters, one of them charming, square, full of flowers, and habited by doves, grouped on the cornices like a natural, graceful bas-relief. From a church spire, visible in the distance, the horologe was ringing the hour. A great yellow sunflower was looking into the deep water of a well and reflecting there its golden disc, like a monstrance.

Nothing had altered since Monsieur d'Amercœur visited the city. The same aspect proved the duration of the same habits. The cracking of horsewhips still mingled with the clicking of rosaries; the convent bells clanged their chimes together as of yore, when Monsieur d'Amercœur, in frock and cowl, his bare feet sandalled, his staff in hand, came knocking at the door. He asked to see the prior, which office was at that time held by Dom Ricard, whose tomb I was shown among the anonymous sepulchres surrounding it. The prior had preserved powerful links with the world from which he had retired, keeping one hand open there for alms, and lending it, at need, in exchange for delicate enterprises, which might be aided by his prudence and wisdom. Monsieur d'Amercœur explained to him the meaning of his dress, the motives for his coming, and the details of his mission.

After twenty years of high service in the army, a gentleman of the country, Monsieur d'Heurteleure returned to settle. He married shortly after Mademoiselle Callestie, a poor girl of good family and great beauty. The wedded pair lived at the d'Heurteleure mansion. The nobles of the city frequented the house, the most assiduous in his visits being Monsieur d'Aiglieul. He had served under and was related to Monsieur d'Heurteleure, who was very fond of him. Life at the mansion was very simple, no pomp, very few domestics; the dignity of rank was upheld by the vast proportion of the apartments, the width of the stairways, and the general aspect of antiquity.

Whether they grew weary of the dull existence in this old town after the excitements of a military life, or were seized suddenly by a spirit of adventure, or from whatever cause it might be, Monsieur d'Heurteleure and Monsieur d'Aiglieul disappeared one day, no one knew whither. Time passed. The searches were fruitless. Some mystery was hinted at. Madame d'Heurteleure wept. All sorts of singular suspicions were afloat, which finally reached the Court, where these two gentlemen were still remembered. One day the double disappearance was mentioned in the hearing of Monsieur d'Amercœur, who determined to solve the enigma. He was empowered with full authority to act, and at once he set about it.

His first care was to assume a monastic frock, certain with this attire to penetrate everywhere, through half-opened doors as well as through the fissures of conscience, and Dom Ricard helped him to the best of his power. For a while his researches were without result; but aided by the disguise of his costume and his apparent calling, his inquiries were patient and diverse. He hovered about the d'Heurteleure house, scrutinised the people and the habits, studied the life. He listened to and weighed all the still vivacious rumours. In vain. He wished to see Madame d'Heurteleure. He was told that she was ill. Every day he passed the house; following the street which rises around the sub-basement, he reached the front, pausing sometimes to slake his thirst at the fountain. Returning, as he descended the steps, he examined the enormous foundations of stone and solid rock, longing to apply his ear and listen to their mystery, for it seemed to him that the flanks of the old castle contained the phantom of the secret, which he had come to evoke from silence before it passed into oblivion. At last, discouraged, he was on the point of giving up. He would have taken leave of Dom Ricard but for the old monk's urgent advice to remain. The venerable prior enjoyed the society of this sheep, so dissimilar to the members of the flock which his wooden crook conducted in the monotonous paths of the Order.

One day toward five o'clock in the afternoon, Monsienur d'Amercœur went out by the old portal and strolled amid the tall grasses of the avenue. The moment was melancholy and solemn; the trees threw their shadows across the funereal path, the lizards ran over the warm stones of the antique tombs and in and out of their fissures. With one hand Monsieur d'Amercœur held up the long monk's frock, with the other he held the key to open the heart-shaped lock of the medicinal garden, where he loved to wander. He wished to visit it once more before he went away, to hear once more the soles of his sandals scraping over the gravel, while his frock brushed the borders of boxwood. The symmetry of the plots pleased him; their squares contained delicate plants and curious flowers; little pools nourished aquatic specimens which plunged their roots into the water, flowered, and mirrored their bloom. At the intersection of the paths stood porcelain urns painted with emblems and pharmaceutical designs, with serpents twisted about the handles, and these urns contained varieties rare and precious. Above the walls waved the tops of the poplars; from the kitchen gardens off to one side, separated by high green trellises, came the sound of a rake, the striking of a spade against a watering-can, the little sound of shears clipping the young shoots; in here all was silence; a flower bent, flexible, under the weight of an insect; swallows darted about; dragon-flies flitted across the greenish water; heavy plants and delicate vines twined and intertwined.

Monsieur d'Amercœur was going toward the door of this odd little enclosure when, at the end of the avenue, he saw approaching a woman dressed in black. She walked slowly with faltering steps. By some inner revelation he knew at once that this was Madame d'Heurteleure. He slackened his own pace, so as to meet her at the moment when he stopped before the door. Arrived there, he put the key into the lock. At the sound the lady started and hesitated. He stooped as though trying to turn the key. She wished to profit by this moment to pass; but found herself face to face with him as he suddenly turned. She stood with one hand pressing down her palpitating heart. He saw a face pale and lovely, though haggard from grief and insomnia, with troubled eyes, half-parted lips. Then he entered quickly, closing the door and leaving in the iron heart of the lock the key.

The next day he was meditating in the little cloister when a messenger came to tell him that a veiled lady desired to speak with him. She was admitted. He recognised Madame d'Heurteleure, and invited her to be seated on a stone bench. The doves cooed softly on the capitals of the quiet cloister, their murmurs mingled with the sighs of the penitent. She sank on her knees, and with bent head and hands folded in his wide sleeves Monsieur d'Amercœur listened to her dolorous confession. It was a horrible and tragic story. Why relate it to him? Because her secret seemed to have been laid bare. When she saw a monk holding a key to open that heart-shaped lock, she felt as though he meant to force open her conscience. Their meeting seemed like a decree of fate, his gesture a mysterious allusion to the deliverance of her soul imprisoned in the horror of its silence.

Her marriage with Monsieur d'Heurteleure was loveless. She esteemed, while she feared his noble character, the hardness of which intimidated her confidence and discouraged her tenderness. Years passed. One winter Monsieur d'Aiglieul appeared and called frequently. He was handsome and still young. She yielded to his love. Then followed days of joy and terror; a dread of discovery and an agony of remorse. Monsieur d'Heurteleure seemed unaware of their perfidy, though he grew suddenly old and another deep line was added to those already furrowing his brow. He was as usual often absent. One evening Madame d'Heurteleure retired to her room about midnight. She felt depressed. Monsieur d'Aiglieul had not appeared and he seldom missed a day. As she was combing her hair before a mirror she saw the door open, and her husband entered. He was booted, but his boots bore no trace of outdoor mire; his coat looked dusty, a long spider web hung from his sleeve, and in his hand he held a key. Without speaking he went directly to the wall of the chamber where a nail fastened an ivory crucifix, which he tore off and broke upon the floor, while in its place he suspended the heavy, rusty key. Madame d'Heurteleure gazed for a moment without comprehending, then all at once her hands clasped her heart, she gave a cry, and fell unconscious.

When she came to herself the whole affair was clear to her. Her husband had allured Monsieur d'Aiglieul into some trap. The old mansion in its invisible depths contained dungeons, chambers of eternal oblivion. A cry, his, vibrated still in her ears. It seemed to come from below, deafened by the piled-up stone, piercing the super-imposed arches, reaching her from those lips for ever separated by the thickness of the walls. She tried to get out; the door was fastened, the windows were padlocked, the domestics occupied another part of the house and were beyond her call. The next day Monsieur d'Heurteleure came to bring her food. Each day he came. The spider's web still hung from his dusty sleeve, his boots creaked on the tesselated floor, the great line on his forehead deepened in a pallor of sleepless misery. He went away silently, and to her tears and supplications he replied only by a brief gesture, showing the key hung against the wall.

During those tragic days the wretched woman lived with her eyes fixed on the horrible key, which grew larger to her vision, became enormous. The patches of rust looked like red blood.

The house was still as death. Toward evening a step was heard. Monsieur d'Heurteleure again entered bearing a lamp and a basket. His head had grown white, he did not now so much as glance at the unhappy being who grovelled at his feet, but he never failed to stare greedily at the key. Then at last Madame d'Heurteleure understood the desire which gnawed, which was devouring him—to see his rival in death, to gloat over his vengeance, to feel of the corruption that had once been flesh and blood, to take down that key he had hung on the wall in place of the Sign of Pardon, the ivory emblem of which he had shattered to substitute an iron symbol of eternal rancour. But alas! vengeance never is satisfied, always she craves for more; frenzied, insatiable, she feeds on her own vehemence to the very dregs of memory, until the end of life.

Monsieur d'Heurteleure felt that she guessed his morbid longing and that added to his torture. The adamant pride was streaked with veins of blood. One night when Madame d'Heurteleure slumbered, stretched on her bed, she heard her door open softly and saw her husband on the threshold. He carried a lamp with the flame turned low, and walked as lightly as a shadow without a sound, as though the sombre somnambulism of his fixed idea had made of him an imponderable phantom. He crossed the room, reached up, took down the key, and went out again. There was a dead silence. A fly awakened by the light buzzed for an instant and then ceased. The door remained on the latch. Madame d'Heurteleure bounded up. In her bare feet she slipped into the hall. Her husband was going downstairs; she followed him. At the ground floor he continued to descend; the stairway plunged into gloom, but she could hear along the subterranean corridors the steps which preceded her. They were now in the ancient substructures of the castle. The walls sweated, the ceilings were vaulted. A last stairway twisted its spiral into the rock. At its base the light of the vanishing lamp still glimmered on the slimy pavement. Bending forward, Madame d'Heurteleure listened. A grating sound reached her and the light disappeared. At the foot of the stairs she found a circular chamber. An opening in the wall revealed a shallow bay; she still crept on, until, at the end of the passage, by feeling her way, she recognised a door very slightly ajar. She pushed it open. In a sort of square hole, vaulted above and tiled below, Monsieur d'Heurteleure was seated beside his little lamp. He was motionless, staring with wide-open eyes. He looked at his wife without seeing her. A nauseating odour came from the cell, and beyond the shadow spread over the tiles lay a fleshless hand already greenish in hue.

Madame d'Heurteleure did not scream. Should she waken the wretched somnambulist, whose frenzied sleep had drawn him to this tragic dungeon? Was she capable of inflicting this degrading shock upon his pride? No. The vengeance of the outrage was just. She felt pity for those wild eyes, which stared at her without seeing her, for the tortured visage, for the hair blanched by such poignant anguish, and it seemed to her best to protect the secret of this nocturnal adventure, so that he might never discover his self-betrayal. He must, she deemed, be allowed to satisfy his terrible craving in the eternal silence of the tomb, without ever knowing whose unseen hand walled him in face to face with his sacrilege.

Monsieur d'Heurteleure still gazed blankly at her. Very calmly she knelt and clasped the greenish palm which stretched its fleshless fingers over the tiles, and then from the outside she closed the door. Walking away on tiptoe, she slid the bolt of the vault which closed the passage. She ascended the spiral stairs, the subterranean steps, the stairways of the upper house, and on the rusty nail of her chamber wall she suspended the tragic key, which balanced itself an instant, and then hung motionless to mark an eternal hour.

The doves passed to and fro as they flew below the arches of the little cloister. The hour rang out simultaneously from all the belfries in the city. The miserable woman sobbed and offered Monsieur d'Amercœur the great key, letting it fall at his feet. He picked it up; it was heavy, and the patches of rust were red like blood. He walked away. Madame d'Heurteleure, still kneeling, supplicated wildly with her hands joined convulsively. He descended toward the little garden, which embalmed the centre of the cloister with its fragrant flowers, which grew in beds equally divided by boxwood. Great roses engarlanded the well with its stone circle; their thorns clung to the monastic frock as he bent over to drink; the water spurted out. A tall, golden sunflower mirrored its honey-laden monstrance. A dove cooed faintly, and Monsieur d'Amercœur, returning to his still prostrate penitent, murmured in her ear the words of an absolution which, if it lost nothing in heaven, gave at least on earth peace to a tortured soul.

GEORGES RENARD
B. 1864

JACQUES BRULEFERT'S DEATH

I WAS on my way to the village, toiling up the old, paved road on a slope, known for miles around as the stiffest climb in the neighbourhood. It was a hot August day, and as I stopped to take breath, old Sauvage, the owner of the "Rising Sun," an inn most discreetly perched at the top of its thirsty summit, came up behind me, and accosted me with a cordial "Good-day!" We went on together, glad of each other's company; and at last arrived at the very steepest part of the way, a sheer incline, abutting on a ravine, thickly clad with undergrowth, at the bottom of which flowed the river; and bordered by a green hedge, the only protection against a fall over its side. Right in the very middle of this hedge was a great gap, which seemed as though some massive weight had crashed through it.

"Has there been an accident here?" I asked my companion.

"Better than that," was his answer. "That hedge still wears the scars of war, like a disabled warrior. A terrible thing happened there."

I scented a story.

"Tell me about it," I begged; and, as we advanced slowly under the burning sun, he began:

"It was the 17th of December, in the year of misfortune 1870—a date I have good reason for remembering.

"On the afternoon of the day before, a troop of German soldiers had arrived among us. No one thought much about it at first: we had grown accustomed to such visits by then, for our village is on the road to Germany, and for the last three months, Heaven knows, we had seen nothing but Prussians and Bavarians, Uhlans and artillerymen, cuirassiers and foot-soldiers passing through—a never-ending stream. They did not stay long, but managed to consume everything they could get hold of; they devoured our corn, our oats, our cattle, and our sheep, which they were brutes enough to kill before our very eyes, and left us in their stead little scraps of paper with I don't know what sort of unintelligible stuff written on them. Afterwards they would go on down the hill, through the valley, and forward to Paris. At night, when the wind blew from the west, we used to hear dull, heavy sounds which were the voice of the cannon—Paris calling for help. But Paris called in vain, and in vain we hoped; the *pantalons rouges* never came, and always, always there arrived fresh troops of Germans. I would wager more than a hundred thousand have been over the old, paved road where we are. But we could do nothing, and had to watch them go by in mournful helplessness, as you might watch the course of a river that had overflowed its banks.

"This time it was only an infantry battalion. It halted up there, in front of our place, by the church. But evidently something extraordinary had happened. The soldiers stood at attention; their officers were in a group, gesticulating, shouting, swearing. I could hear them at it from the house. The commandant was the most furious of all. I can see him still—a long, lean old fellow, with a red scar on his white face, a great white moustache, with occasional reddish hairs in it, and the very oddest way of walking I ever saw—just as if he were walking on egg-shells, and was afraid of breaking them—and a way of swinging himself about that made me think of a poplar swaying in the wind.

"While he was raging up and down, a captain pointed out to him the house opposite to ours. And at once he seemed overjoyed; he called out some order in his lingo; four men came out of the ranks, and followed by them and the captain, he marched forthwith to the house pointed out to him, looked at its signboard, and read aloud: 'Jacques Brulefert, Engine and Machinery Mender'; then he opened the door and entered with the officer.

"I wondered what the Prussians could be wanting with Jacques, and said to myself: 'Look out for squalls!' for I must tell you Jacques hated the Prussians, and he was a hot-headed fellow. He had served with the army in Africa, and though now he was well past forty, had courage and daring and strength enough for a much younger man; he was not tall, nor by any means a beauty. By much fighting against Bedouins he had got almost as swarthy as they are, but he was as agile as a cat, and dexterous as a monkey, while he was as sound as only an old Zouave like himself could be.

"Ah, there was no lack of fire in him, eyes or heart, I can tell you! His rage had known no bounds ever since the campaign had begun. You should have heard him storming against the Emperor in the big room at the inn, for a coward who couldn't even die when he ought to, and against the townsfolk, who were cowards too, and the Germans who could only fight three to one.

He banged on the tables as if they were Prussians. He was mad about it all. Why, I myself, sir, as true as I'm here speaking to you, I saw him cry like a child when he heard that Bazaine had surrendered Metz.

"At every fresh disaster (and, Heaven knows, there were enough of them) he wanted to be off, wherever the fighting was, and take his share of it; he said that the others had got the very job he wanted, and he would have gone, over and over again, in spite of his age, if he had not had to stay and take care of his wife and his little boy, a lad of ten years. So he stayed behind, but as if he felt disgraced, and ready for any desperate deed. Every time the Germans came through, he shut himself up so as not to see them, and if by chance some of them were billeted on him, he would rather pay to send them to the inn, than himself lodge the sauer-kraut gobblers, as he called them.

"So I said to myself, when I saw the two Prussian officers going in to friend Jacques: 'There'll be a row, I warrant.' And I wasn't far out, as you'll see. They had hardly been inside for three minutes when I heard a great uproar of doors banging and shouting. Then out came the commandant, as red as a cock's-comb, and shouted out some rigmarole to the four men who had stayed outside; they rushed into the workshop, and I knew that they must have had orders to fetch out Jacques. But not a bit of use was it, for while they were turning the house upside down, I saw a man suddenly leap out of the loft, and run for dear life along the road. It was Jacques; and he went like a runaway horse; but a few minutes after, a Prussian showed his ugly face at the very window Jacques had jumped out through. You can imagine his looks when he saw Jacques had been under their very nose all the time. And the officers, too! They swore like anything, and the commandant looked as black as thunder.

"*He* didn't jump out (it was too far from the ground for that), but he rushed down the staircase with his men, called up the others, and set them like dogs on the track of the runner. Ah, so he did —but there was no Jacques to be seen! Every trace of him had disappeared! He was nowhere to be found, and they searched everywhere in the bushes, the corners behind the church, and the little wood! And bare and level before them stretched the road. Where the deuce could he have got to? The night was beginning to fall; in vain the men searched everywhere round; in vain the commandant swore and raged and fumed like a madman: the soldiers had to come back jabbering and empty-handed. All the village had assembled up there at last, looking as though they understood nothing, you can imagine, but bursting with laughter to see them so dumbfounded.

"Everyone knew already what had happened. My wife had

been up to Jacques's house to see what had been done, and she has a tongue of her own, you know, a regular woman. She found the poor wife frightened out of her wits, and crying with fear. It seems that the commandant had wanted Jacques to go with him at once, without a moment's notice. He wanted him to repair a great steam-engine he was escorting with his battalion, and that he had had to leave behind a mile back. The night before, the engineer had been killed as they came through a wood, by a *franctireur*; and he wanted someone to replace him in bringing along the machine which was stuck there. You can guess it was pretty serious for him. The machine was dragging along a great cannon destined for the bombardment of Paris. And the commandant had come to requisition Jacques for the job, as if he had been a Prussian soldier, at the least. He had come to the wrong shop this time. Jacques got white as a sheet, and said: 'Supposing I won't do anything of the kind?' The commandant told him, with a sneer, 'Then you'll be forced to,' for he spoke French like a schoolmaster, the great, lanky lout. But he did not know Jacques. With one bound the fellow skipped through the door behind him, and once out of their sight, got away as I told you.

"We thought that was the end of it. But there's no dealing with these obstinate folk. A few minutes after there wasn't one among us inclined to laugh, for the commandant announced to the Mayor that he would now spend the night in the village; and soon we each had our share of Prussians to lodge. And to see them there, strutting about in one's own house, stretching across the fireplace or the table, and talking a jargon no one could understand, while the very rifles they carried had probably shot down more than one brave fellow from our little village, was enough to take the laugh out of one for ever, I can tell you.

"Up at the inn, of course, we had the commandant and two captains to provide for gratis, and didn't feel particularly flattered by the honour. The commandant was striding up and down, and looking very furious. Suddenly I saw him stop and rub his hands. 'A bad sign,' thinks I. And, sure enough, he calls his men and talks away to them, pointing every now and then to Jacques's house. I didn't know yet what he was up to, but I hadn't long to wait. Outside in the street we heard a noise, loud laughs, and the cries of a woman and a child; then our door was pushed roughly open, and a woman was just thrown into the room by four great ruffians, who pushed, and dragged, and hustled her in. It was that old wretch's idea. The cunning old thing said to himself: 'If you want to take the male, the surest way is catch the female.' And he had Jacques's wife arrested.

"As for the boy, a regular son of his father, as bold as a lion, he tried to resist; yelled and screamed, fought and kicked, and was trying to bite the hand which had grasped him cruelly by the wrist. Poor little lad! they wouldn't even let him stay in with us, but kicked him outside, and for a quarter of an hour or more we heard him sobbing with rage and cold out in the dark night. The mother was like a creature possessed. She struggled until she was in such a dishevelled state you wouldn't have known her, and screamed insult after insult at the commandant, calling him 'cad,' 'villain,' 'coward.' He cared no more than if he had been a log; but laughed mockingly at her, the heartless beast, and said, quietly, 'Come, come, behave yourself! You shall be set free when your husband returns. If he doesn't come back, so much the worse for you. You will be our prisoner, and will have to come with us. That will teach your man to refuse us his services.' And while the poor woman, over whom two soldiers mounted guard, was crying quietly in a corner of our big dining-room, the commandant and two captains, seated at the other end, ate enough for six, and drank enough for ten, because they knew they were not going to pay for their dinner."

By this time we had climbed the hill, and reached the inn, where I had invited Père Sauvage to drink a glass of wine with me, and it was over a venerable bottle in a cool corner of the big room, looking on to the sunny highway and the delightful view beyond, that he continued: "Well, the Prussians were gobbling at the very table we are sitting at now, and I was serving at the bar, when Jean Lacroix, the mason, came in. He had come to fetch a pint of wine; but he looked as though something was up; so when he made me a sign, I pretended that I had to go down to the cellar, and went into the kitchen with him.

"'I've seen Jacques,' he said softly.

"'Where?' I asked.

"'Quite close. He has hidden under the road. I found him crouched up in the little tunnel that takes off the rain-water in bad weather. The Prussians must have passed over his head at least a dozen times when they were looking for him. Wasn't it a trick to play them? But now he is cold and hungry. He whistled softly to me as I was coming in from the fields. He wants something to eat, some sort of wrap, and a little money, then he is going off to his Uncle François—who lives three leagues off. I wanted to tell his wife, and knocked at her door; but there's no one there. What am I to do?'

"I told him the Prussians had arrested her, and meant to take her off with them; that she was up there in the dining-room, and that we must let Jacques know somehow; but it was easier said than done, as one ran the risk of being caught in the act, and betraying his hiding-place. Then I thought of the boy, who was bold enough for anything, and an intelligent little fellow. It was a pitch-dark night; he could creep along and hide himself in the ditches more easily than a man; and then, once with his father, he would at least have someone to defend him.

" 'He can't be far away,' I said to Jean Lacroix. 'We must find him, and send him.'

" It seemed the best thing to do, sir, and yet I have often thought, since then, that without meaning to, I was doing just what that old wretch of a commandant wanted. No one will ever persuade me that that wasn't the idea he had in his head when he let the child go: he thought he would get at the father through the child. What do *you* think? Jean Lacroix was of the same opinion as myself, that it was the only thing to be done, and he went off to see after it all.

" The Prussians had done their dinner, and were smoking like a factory chimney. Jacques's wife was still crying silently in her corner; she would neither eat nor drink; and it was heart-breaking to see her so wretched and know that we could do nothing for her. The sentinels in the street could be heard calling 'Wer da?' (who goes?), and no one was allowed to enter or leave the village without the commandant's permission. The officers and men came in from time to time to report to him. But on the stroke of seven, Jacques's wife sat up straight, and gave a loud cry. Her husband and her little boy were being brought in by the patrol.

"Jacques was quite pale and very calm, but his jaw was set, and his look ugly. When the commandant said, with a laugh: 'I knew we should catch you, my fine fellow,' he replied, looking straight into his eyes:

" 'I was not caught at all. I knew that you had arrested my wife, and that she would be set free if I came back. So here I am. But all the same, you have acted like a coward.'

" The commandant grew quite white, then quite red, as if he were nearly choking; his hand felt for his sword, and I thought he was going to fall upon Jacques, who stood before him with folded arms. But he contented himself with swearing big oaths, which I didn't understand; but he must have been wild, to judge by his men, who were trembling in their shoes. Ah! if they had not had need of Jacques Brulefert and his skill, the poor fellow would have had a bad time of it. At last, when the commandant could control himself sufficiently to speak, he said:

" 'You are going to sleep here, you dog of a Frenchman. Your tools will be brought to you, and to-morrow, off you go with us. The least attempt to get away, and you'll be shot at once.'

" Jacques did not flinch. He sat down quietly at a table in the corner, while four great Germans settled themselves at the next table, with their guns loaded and bayonets fixed. His wife brought him food and drink. He supped as though nothing was the matter, without saying a word; then asked for his tool-bag and a blanket; sent home his wife and the little lad, who didn't want to leave him; after which, like the old veteran he was, he rolled himself up in his blanket, stretched himself out on his table, with his box for a pillow, and went to sleep.

"The next day, at dawn, a whole company stood at attention in front of our door, sent to fetch away Jacques. He had already jumped down from his table, and stretched his limbs by a turn round the room, so he took a glass with me and was ready to go.

"He chaffed and joked his four guardians, who would not let him out of their sight for a single moment, but seemed afraid that he might vanish up the chimney. All the same, there was something very queer-looking about him. Sometimes he would stay for a whole minute staring and frowning, as if he was looking at something a long way off, and then he would suddenly rear up his head, as if he was defying some one.

"At about eight o'clock his wife and the child came to see him. The poor woman was crying so, that she was pitiful to see.

"'Listen, Catherine,' he said; 'you must promise me to leave the village at once, and go to Uncle François.'

"And when she objected, he spoke lower still. My own opinion is that the four soldiers didn't know a single word of French; but they may have been shamming, and anyway it was wiser to speak softly. So he whispered into her ear:

"'You see, I mean to try and escape on the way. But if you are still here, they will arrest you again to get me back. I shall not feel safe, unless I see you away. Go and get your things ready, and don't be afraid, dear wife. I'll get out of it, you'll see.'

"He kissed her affectionately, almost cheerfully, to inspirit her a little, and pushed her towards the door. The boy stayed behind, sobbing—naturally enough. But Jacques caught him between his knees and said:

"'Little man, you must be brave, and not cry; those cads are only too pleased if they see you cry. Think that I am going off to the war, and shall be coming back again. If by chance, though, things go badly with me, and I never come back any more, you must love your mother, my boy. You must love her for two. And when you are a big man, remember to be a good soldier, so that the Prussians may get back from you some of the harm they have done us. Now, laddie, don't cry, whatever you do.'

"And the little fellow nearly choked himself in his efforts not to cry, and said:

"'You see, father, I'm not crying now.' Only the words

sounded very shaky, and two great tears ran down his cheeks. Jacques sent him off after his mother. Ah! he couldn't manage to look cheerful any longer, just then, poor Jacques! His voice was trembling when he said to me:

" 'It's cold this morning, Père Sauvage. Let's have one more drink together—perhaps it's for the last time.'

" 'The last?' I said to him. 'Why, man, it's not the first time you've been in the wars: you'll come back to us, never fear!'

" He smiled without speaking, but I saw he had got something planned out in his head.

" The commandant had just come out from his room, and he was no sooner downstairs than he gave the word 'March!' Jacques took his box and followed him outside. All the village was there, sir, to see him off, and everyone had a good word for him and insisted on shaking him by the hand: he had never had so many friends. He kept looking anxiously towards his house, but when he saw his wife come out holding the boy by one hand, and in the other her bundle of things, he seemed relieved. Only, as all the good-byes were being said, and everyone wished him *au revoir* and *bon voyage*, the commandant asked, roughly: 'Where is she going?' He was a sly old thing, that commandant, to be sure; and was suspicious about this departure of hers. But Jacques replied, as quiet as you please:

" 'I shall be away some time, it seems. She is going to stay with our uncle as long as you need my services.'

" The commandant was quite taken in.

" 'That's right,' he said, slapping Jacques on the shoulder. 'You are sensible this morning; and that's better all round, my lad. In a week you'll be back here. It's not so bad after all, is it?'

The wife and the child started off as he said this. Jacques followed them to the next turning with his eyes, threw them a kiss from where he stood, and gave a great sigh; but as soon as they were out of sight, sir, you would hardly have believed it was the same man: his expression changed as you might change your shirt, saving your presence. It was our Jacques at his very best; laughing and joking and snapping his fingers at the Prussians; whom he called old slow-coaches, telling them they never would get anywhere at that rate. A regular 'gamin,' sir, but a true Frenchman too, who meant to show these lanky Germans that there was nothing in *them* to frighten an old soldier of the African army.

" At last the column began to march. Jacques, who was placed in the middle, walking along quite gaily, called out to us, 'I shall see you again soon! You'll be having news of me before long.' I assure you, sir, he could not have gone off holiday-making more gaily, and more than one of the village folk were surprised, and didn't quite like to see him so soon going quietly with the Prussians. But I knew my man, and could have sworn he had in his head some trick to play them and their machine.

"The place where the Prussians had left it was not half a league away, upon the plateau above us; and, faith, we were curious to see this engine which had come from so far. 'Well,' said I, 'let's go along; the Prussians won't eat us'; and five or six of us followed after the column that was taking off Jacques.

"Soon, in the middle of the road, we saw a great black object, guarded by a little detachment that had had to camp out round it. It was that brute of a machine: a traction-engine, it was called, I think; and behind, on two great carts, themselves a mass of iron, was the gun and the carriage! Ah, sir, if you had seen the creature! A monster of a cannon! Heavens, how is it possible such engines are invented? Two men could have lain down in its mouth, and goodness knows how many tons it weighed! It could discharge shells that would demolish a whole house from garret to cellar. And when we thought that a piece of that calibre could carry two leagues at the least, we said to each other, gloomily enough, that the Parisians weren't exactly going to have a gay time of it. Only you will guess a mass like that wasn't easily conveyed about; it would have taken thirty horses at least just to move it. Steam alone could drag along such a monument, and just in the very nick of time the engine-driver had been killed, and the machine got out of gear. 'Ah!' we said to each other, 'what a pity Jacques got taken prisoner! If only he could damage its inside a little, so that it couldn't be got to move.'

"But nothing of the sort; he just gave a look to its works, and in a few minutes had put everything right, for he was a rare workman, I can tell you. Then, while they were getting up steam, we heard him giving a heap of explanations to the commandant. The old man was afraid of the incline it had to descend. But Jacques reassured him; he understood quite well how to manage it; he would slow down at the entrance to the village; he would put on the brake; he would shut off steam; if necessary, he would reverse the engines. 'You needn't be afraid of anything,' he said. 'I'll answer for it all. It'll answer to my hand, an engine of that kind. Only, send some men on first to clear off the snow which is drifted up on the hill-side. That might make us slide down.'

"For I must tell you there had been a heavy snow a week before. Since when, though it had been trodden into mud by the passers-by, some still lay between the paving-stones, and as it had frozen hard during the night, the road shone in the morning sun like a mirror. The commandant had noticed it. 'You're right,' he said to Jacques, and some minutes after, the Prussians who had stayed in the village were clearing the highway with picks and brooms, like so many road-labourers, and spreading shovelfuls of earth from top to bottom of the incline.

"All this time Jacques was waiting. The machine was ready, he was seated on it, and smoking his pipe as calmly as if he had been at home. The commandant, however, did not yet feel quite safe about him. At the moment of starting he called a lieutenant and said something that I couldn't understand, though I heard him plainly. The lieutenant answered: 'Ja, commandant. Ja, commandant.' Then I saw him take a revolver from his belt, and climb up on to the locomotive by Jacques; and the commandant called to Jacques from his horse:

"'Understand, you engineer fellow, at the first attempt to escape, you'll be shot.'

"'You'll be shot,' seemed to be the words that came most natural to him. Jacques shrugged his shoulders.

"'I've no wish to get away,' was his reply. But in spite of that, for greater security, the commandant had a double file of men posted alongside, to the right and left of the machine; then he himself went to the head of the column, calling out first something in German, and then in French for Jacques, 'Forward, march!' The engine panted and snorted and tugged with all its might; the cannon jerked off with a clash of iron; and between the two rows of soldiers who accompanied it, it all proceeded slowly along the level highway.

"We had run on to the village to announce the approach of the wonderful machine, and all our folk, men, women, and children, were out in the road to see it pass by. Soon were heard cries of 'It is coming! It's coming!' and there it appeared, clearly outlined against the sky, all black and smoking. Lean this way a little, sir: you can see the place from here. It was about ten feet from our house. You can see, just where the cobble-stones stop and the paving begins. That's where the incline begins; there's a little slope before the big one.

"At that moment the commandant, who was prancing along on horseback, turned round to Jacques, and called out, 'Attention!'

"'Don't be alarmed,' sings out Jacques. 'I'm going to put the brake on.'

"Ah, sir, if I live to be a hundred, I shall never forget what happened then; no, nor will any one who was there, and saw it all. Then I understood why Jacques had sent off his wife and the little one. Such a sight would have driven them crazy.

"Instead of slowing down, he put on all possible speed, jumped at the lieutenant, twisted his arms, so that the revolver fell out of his hands, and kept him fastened to the spot, shouting all the time,

'*Vive la France!*' And the engine began to rush on down, leaping over the paving-stones; and the gun rushed after it, gun-carriage and all, making a very deuce of a noise. The commandant only just got out of the way in time to escape being crushed. He was yelling like a madman, and shouting out orders to his Prussians; which I expect meant: 'Stop him! Kill him!' But, all the same, they stood still, stupid with astonishment and terror. They might as well have tried to stop an express at full speed. The machine sped straight on, like a flash of lightning. The houses shook; the paving-stones were crushed under it, and sent out showers of sparks; it was a whirlwind crashing down the street with thunder and lightning. Jacques, clinging to his Prussian, looked a regular demon. Once more we heard him shout, '*Vive la France!*' Then, at the turn of the road, in a single bound through the hedge, everything rolled over into the ravine below. It was an awful crash. To have any idea of it, you must imagine a thunderbolt falling into the midst of this room. And then immediately there came a great silence. No one could speak; the women covered their heads with their aprons; we felt sick at heart.

"Can you believe it, sir? I can't think of it, even yet, without creeping all over. And yet it's fifteen years now since then. I expect you'll despise me. But I can't help it.

"Well, to cut a long story short, the Prussians were more than six weeks over fishing up their big gun. At the bottom of the ravine was a horrible mess of twisted iron-work, dislocated wheels, ploughed-up soil, broken trees, and shattered stones. When at last it was all got up out of the débris, it was too late to be of any use in the bombardment—the siege of Paris was raised.

"Good old Jacques! That was what he had wished. And to think that we could never even give him a hero's funeral.

"He had been so completely crushed that nothing of him was found but a few mangled scraps of flesh some days after—one couldn't even tell if they belonged to him or the Prussian. Everything was carried off to the cemetery, almost without ceremony, for the Prussians were still in the village and furious after the smash. Later on we put up a little headstone over the grave, with the inscription, 'Died for his country,' under his name, then the date, and that was all. Thirty years hence, no one will remember who it was. The wife is dead, the house sold, the boy has gone for a soldier—now he is a sergeant in the line, and the Prussians will catch it pretty hot if ever he has a chance of getting at them. But he doesn't often get back to his old home; and with the exception of himself and a few old folk like me, who will remember Jacques Brulefert?

"I have it, sir: you, who are a scholar—you should write his story. It would only be justice to him. I tell you, spite of their great battalions, and their great guns, the Prussians would have had a bad time of it in 1870 if there had been many Frenchmen like our Jacques.

"And now, sir, I've been talking long enough. I must get to my work. Your health, sir!"

"*A la santé de la France, père Sauvage,* and the memory of Jacques Brulefert. I promise you to write his story."

"FERNAND VANDÉREM"
B. 1864

HIMSELF

"No, sir, I am sorry that there is not an unoccupied table. But if you don't mind waiting five minutes, sir, there is a table, this one just behind you. You see, sir, they are finishing their coffee."

In no very good humour I looked all round the many tables of people dining in the dim evening about the garden, and the little lights of gilt candlesticks which made the tablecloths gleam in the twilight. A voice sounded close to me, "So it is you, is it?"

I turned and recognised my friend, Lacquin. Perhaps I should hardly call him my friend; for our friends, after all, are people like ourselves, are they not, who have to bear the same anxieties and sufferings and weaknesses as our own, and whom we love with that strange mixture of pity and tender devotion which we have for ourselves. No, I can hardly say that Lacquin was my friend, but he was something really very much more pleasant and soothing than a friend. I had struck up a kind of acquaintance with him the year before, when away on a holiday, and his frank, jolly, debonair way pleased me; there was something delightfully careless about his way of thinking and acting. He had no ambition, because he was in the happy circumstance of succeeding his father in a huge leather business. Of course, he had no bother about money, for the profits of the business were very large indeed; and then again he had no social worries, because, like myself, he could not stand the humbug either of a drawing-room or of a club. He was really a happy creature, being quite free from all those little torments with which people spoil their lives and stultify their minds. Now, that is the kind of man I love to spend my leisure with; a man like that is a great rest from those dreadful creatures whose faces are always white and drawn with the love of money or of notoriety, or of getting on in some way or other; he is a rest, I say, from those who are always chewing hatred and rancour as you might chew a poisonous drug.

"Well," he said, "how are you, after all this time? Share my table, will you not? I have hardly begun." "Thanks," I replied, "I shall be delighted," and ordered my dinner.

I found that Lacquin had lost nothing in this last year of that radiant good humour, and natural delight in life and wisdom of the man of the world, which had so attracted me. He was the same fine fellow, careless of all humbug and nonsense, the same brilliant talker, who never said a fatuous word, and was extremely well-informed on every subject. He was just the same as I had known him a year ago, only that he was even more genial and jovial, from the fact that he was in better health. But all of a sudden, when he was in the middle of a hunting story, he stopped and threw me a glance of pointed meaning, and then turned it on a big fair-haired woman who was followed by a big man with light moustache. The head waiter was just taking them to a table near our own.

"What do you think of her?" Lacquin whispered, in a very confidential way.

I looked at her with the eye of a critic. "She's a bit of all right," I said. "Good deal of swank about her!"

"I should jolly well think so," he said. "She's a high-stepper, isn't she? Well, old chap, that's my wife."

"Good gracious," I said, "you don't say so! The lady, as you say, is very attractive——" but here I stopped, not knowing exactly what he wanted me to say. I did not want to put my foot in it. The only thing I had ever heard about his marriage was the fall of the curtain, the divorce. When Lacquin told me one day that he lived alone and had been divorced two years before, I could hardly ask particulars, and he offered none. As usual in such cases, there was a moment of silence, and then we went on to another subject. But there is rarely much mystery about these unhappy affairs; very likely she was a wanton trifler, or he was tired of her, or both, and they had agreed to separate. When I had met him in the country, I came to the conclusion that it was he who had been unfaithful, but I was far from sure of that when I saw her in the garden of the hotel. No, the fault,—if fault there had been,—had lain with those great blue eyes, those heavy eyelids, and that astonishing burden of golden hair. And then I saw her taking off her gloves with the languid and supple manner of women who never, even in public, can throw off the sleepy grace of the lover. I nodded so as to say, "Yes, she is lovely indeed."

Lacquin kept his eyes upon her until her gaze met his, and then turned quietly to me. "She's a beautiful woman; I will say that for her," he said; "but Lord, how I have suffered through that hussy! She gave me three years of it; three appalling years! You know I am not difficult to get on with. Well, sir, in those three years I became a cruel, hateful creature, whom it is horrid to think of. I was like a wild beast. There was nothing ordinary about our divorce. From seedtime to harvest, it took no less than three years. By James, what a time it was!"

I kept silence so as not to seem to invite the secret of his life. He continued, after a pause:

"After all, why should I not tell you the story? I don't know the lady. I shall never know her again. She is nothing to me. She is no more to me than she was before her marriage, a pretty figure in the street, a certain Mlle. Legoin."

He moved a little on his chair and leaned his arms upon the table, evidently recalling the past. "Yes," he said, "it must have begun about five years ago. One day, about three o'clock, I came home much earlier than usual so as to give Marie a surprise—that is her name. I thought of taking her for a drive in the Bois, or spending the afternoon in chatting or playing with her—anything. I loved her more than I can say. I do not mean as you love a mistress, of whom you can never see enough, but with the ordinary good honest love of marriage, which in two years had never weakened nor been shaken. Quite apart from her beauty, Marie had really been very good to me. I had never cause to notice her attentions to others, and she had the prettiest way of trying to give me pleasure. No, in those days I had nothing against her. Possibly, it is true, I might have wished that she had been a little more intelligent, though, again, 'intelligent' is hardly the right word. She might perhaps have had a finer insight, a finer judgment about the world and its people. But that is not what you have a wife for; there are plenty of friends if you want serious talk. When you set up house together, all you want is to live quietly with a dear, good woman. Is that not so?"

I nodded, and he continued:

"Well, sir, I got to the house and opened the door and came quietly up the stairs. I stole furtively into the drawing-room to give her a surprise. What do you think I saw? Marie was standing close to the window reading a letter. At every moment she stopped to kiss it, and then read again with a mad joy, and then lavished on it kisses such as you can hardly imagine. Certainly she had never given me the like. In a few swift paces I was at her side, and tried to seize the letter. She crushed the paper in her hands and tried to hide it away, crying, 'O Henri, Henri, please don't.' But I had set my mind on having it, and after a moment's struggle it was in my hand, and I began to read: 'My sweet Beloved.' I could hardly believe my eyes! The pages, from beginning to end, were in my wife's handwriting! It was a love-letter which she had written to herself! It purported to come from a man who said here an infinity of sentimental and disgusting stuff. He had wept incessantly through the last twenty-four hours, and wanted to plunge his face into the river of her golden hair, and would suffer any torment to be allowed to bite her tiny coral ear. And here she was sobbing beside me with her head buried in her hands. 'O Henri, you are cruel, are cruel,' she cried. I was like one bereft of his senses. The most frightful and horrible thoughts swept through my mind like dead leaves driven by the wind. But I bent over her and schooled my voice to its tenderest and most kindly tones. 'Come, Marie,' I said, 'why don't you trust me? You know how truly I love you. Do tell me the meaning of this letter and of all its absurdities.'

"She had not a word to say, and indeed her voice was broken by great sobs. 'No, no, no,' was all that she could murmur. Then all of a sudden she made up her mind, rose and fetched from her desk an envelope addressed to herself in her own handwriting, to 'Mme. Henri Lacquin, 27 Rue Lafayette.' As well as she could speak for weeping, she implored me, 'Do not be angry, do not laugh at me. I wanted so badly to have a love-letter. And then—and then—I thought I would write one to myself.' Just imagine it, she had written to herself that she loved herself! What do you think of that?"

I could hardly say for the moment, and besides, her act appeared to me to have a certain charm about it. I told him so, but Lacquin interjected:

"Yes, that is just what I thought at the first moment. I took Marie on to my knee and into my arms and comforted her and kissed her and gave her a playful little scolding, chaffing her about her friendship with this ardent correspondent. Then I rang for the carriage, and we drove to the Bois. She was now quite happy and pleased, and often laughed with that sweet voice of hers which did me so much good to hear. 'I am a silly little thing,' she would say, 'am I not?' and I would answer, 'You are silly enough for two.' But then there was a change. When we were returning in the twilight she became very thoughtful, so thoughtful indeed as to forget my presence. I wondered what in the world she was thinking of, and then a thought struck cold to my heart. Of course, it was plain as the sun in the sky. She was thinking of Him! She must always now be thinking, quite naturally and inevitably, of Him and Himself alone, the unknown lover whom all her romantic being was for ever awaiting. On this there followed the certainty that she had no love for me. If she had loved me she could never have thought of writing that detestable letter, with its very unpleasant imaginations, so as to voice the lover who was so much desired but who still had never come nor written. Oh, it was horrible! My impulse was to tell her how I hated it all; but it seemed wiser to be silent, lest any incautious words should clothe this imaginary person with more reality than he had yet achieved.

"I could only study her face and wonder what those great eyes of hers were meaning. But in the evening after dinner I could not resist chaffing her as in the afternoon. I asked her whether He was dark or fair, if He was a good sort, if He smoked, if He rode in the Bois, and so forth. At first she was reproachful, pleading that I had given my word not to laugh at her; but soon she entered heartily into the joke and became radiant under the influence of the delightful game, which surely had long been the secret felicity of her life. She drew a picture of Him for me, describing in the minutest detail His character and appearance. I managed to laugh, though my heart was tortured to hear her so ready with an answer to every question about the man who was yet to come. I knew all the time that He was bound to come; He would certainly come and rob me of my Marie's heart.

"From that day forward this pitiful jest continued. Every morning I would ask her whether she meant to meet Him that day, and every evening when I came home from the office I asked how He was and whether she had any letters from Him. Of course you will say that this was a stupid and fatal thing to do, and so it was. But somehow I could not help it. The fact is that He was stronger than I. At home, at dinner, even in our own room, wherever I was with Marie, I felt Him always there. Try to imagine the situation. Realise what it was to be jealous of and to hate with all one's heart an intangible being who did not yet exist, but was unquestionably coming into existence, and who—I knew it with absolute certainty—must some day turn up and take away my wife, who was all the time waiting for Him, and had already saved Him the trouble of writing to declare His love."

Lacquin dropped his voice, saying with a bitter smile, "Aha, my voice has startled you. That is the voice, you understand, which belonged to those dreadful and horrible years. When I look back on them I become once again that insane beast that I was all that time. But let me finish. This life of hidden torture and suspicion went on for two years, until I happened to make some joke about Him in very bad taste indeed. Marie no longer laughed as she had done before. Instead, her face darkened. I insisted on an answer, but she quickly put me in my place. 'My dear boy,' she said, 'surely this comedy has lasted long enough. For my part, I really find it rather dull. It may be your idea of humour, but will you try to understand that it is not mine?'

"So, all this nonsense no longer amused her! You can hardly imagine what an enormous relief her confession was to me. Anything said against Him, any joke at His expense, no longer pleased my lady. I knew what this must mean. At last He had taken to Himself existence, and had really arrived. She had a lover at last. In place of that awful suspense there was now the peace and relief of accomplished and final ill. From this time forward I had no interest in life but to get hold of the brute and to strike Him to the earth—the scoundrel who at last had found courage to appear in the flesh, instead of lurking as a cowardly fugitive phantom in the eyes of the woman I had loved.

"I need not go into all the miserable story: how I put detectives on their track, made out a case, and got my divorce. It is enough that my long martyrdom came at length to an end. For two years I had no longer loved my wife. I was now able to return to the good old way of living which I had followed before the nightmare of my marriage.

"By the way, there is one rather curious thing that I forgot to tell you. My wife had always described Him as having a short brown beard. This had always been a fixed idea with her. But see how wide of the mark we shoot when we try to foresee our fate. That man there is the man in whose arms I found her when——"

Lacquin nodded toward the man with the long fair moustache who was now dining with the late Mme. Lacquin. As I looked from him to her I noticed that her face was slightly turned in the direction of her former husband, and that it wore a pensive little smile.

"Surely," I remarked, "she is smiling at you! Can it be that it is you who have now become Himself?"

Lacquin's reply was given in a tone of derision. "Oh dear no. That would indeed be a waste of her favours. No; it is not she who is destined to be my love, but another for whom I shall indeed be—Himself. There is some 'Himself' for every one in this world. Not one of us but is that incomparable treasure—to Someone!"

PHILIPPE MONNIER
B. 1864

THE FOOLISH VIRGIN

It happened when we were seated round a table in a restaurant of a town of which I will not give the name. It was when we were happy boys, each with hardly a moustache, but with a grandiose future. When we laughed we made such a noise that the windows shook. It was awfully cold; it was winter, and the wind was scurrying down the streets. And it was then that she came in.

She was just one of those poor women who go round from door to door singing tiny songs, wearing a threadbare shawl, and carrying a guitar. Some of us knew her, and others did not know her, but we were all of one voice in crying, "Put her out!"

Our wish that she should not enter was due to the fact that we very much valued these evenings together, and did not want either the botheration of a beggar or the unpleasantness of looking upon unhappiness.

All the same, she came in. Shivering with cold, humble, simple, and poor, one of life's victims, she came in. She was certainly Italian, having that weird, wicked air of an old sorceress who is always ready to tell your fortune. You see, our old women, even the poorest of them, have always got something, a shawl or bonnet, which is a link with happier days; when they are almost starving they still make a point of keeping up appearances. But this poor old thing was a derelict of improvidence, and as useless as a broken pitcher. But you could see very well that tears were no strangers to her cheeks, for her pathetic face looked like marble polished by a stream.

Our disgraceful reception did not put her out. She came quietly up the room with that contrite little smile of hers and that look of aged resignation, as if she was quite accustomed to this kind of welcome. She took all our silly noise as a joke; and this was all the more courageous of her, because she was quite conscious that the charm of womanhood had left her long ago.

Young dogs that we were, we shouted all the more; we beat our feet and sticks on the floor, and whistled and made every kind of zoological noise. Really it was a tremendous row, and our only excuse must be that we were very young. The effect was overwhelming, and she suddenly stopped affrighted. Her hands were trembling, and her eyes, unseeing, opened widely, reddened by light and fatigue and tears. She was suddenly aware that we really meant that she should go, and what a helpless, lonely, poor old thing she was. She stayed quite still while you might count sixty, and then her poor little mechanical smile went out. Without a word she turned and went toward the door.

Well, we had gained our point and were alone. The wretched old woman had departed. But as soon as the door had closed behind her and she was out in the inclement night, we all became very silent and rather uncomfortable.

Then Blaise,—I can see Blaise as if he was here,—he had a wonderful voice and his eyes lit up with spontaneous goodness. I remember that when he used to sit down in country inns the dogs and children from all around used to come to him. He has gone over to the majority, and on that day when we laid him under ground, I think we buried our youth with him.

He got up and walked quietly out; and then we heard him calling in that silver voice of his to the poor old lady; and they came in together, she with her hand on his arm. They were a picture, the two of them: he was young, in glorious health and joy of life; she was old and worn, and had one foot in the grave.

Partly because of the curiosity of the picture before us, but I think even more because we were thoroughly ashamed of our scandalous conduct, we gave them a rousing cheer. It was a far worse noise than we had made before. We clinked our glasses and raised a cloud of dust from the floor, and a waiter ran in to implore us to be quiet.

The old lady sat down with us, and Blaise did his best to serve her. He seemed happy, eager, and respectful. He called her "Madame," and fished for the best bits of lemon in the punch. But Blaise was always well-behaved to women, even to housemaids and peasants and beggars; we often used to joke him about it.

Of course I must confess that we were very young, and therefore rather coarse. Moreover, this unhappy person now seated with us had been dragged through the gutter, had fallen down into the pit of life, had lent herself to the most degrading uses, and at the last was gaining a crust here and there by a crazy song to the sound of her guitar. She had fallen very low, and I think we had fallen a good deal lower, but as soon as she had taken her seat at our table we became more collected in spirit, and felt that we had a certain bond with her. After all, she was a woman.

She bravely drank the punch, hot and strong as it was, so that it made her cough. She was a little frightened, as if surprised at kindness to which she had been so long unaccustomed. Her fingers were very thin, and she sat just at the very edge of her chair. It really made quite a jolly picture—all these happy boys crowding round the poor old singer. Then some one said, "Won't you sing?"

And then she sang. She sang the music of old Italy, those melodies for ever sweet and fresh, which leave behind them joy upon the soul as a boat leaves its wake upon the summer seas. One could tell, too, that she had had the best of schooling in the art. I wondered even at what theatre she had burned the hearts of men. But now it was a tiny thread of a voice, like the voice of one of the kids you hear singing when you pass the day school. And these tender little songlets, coming from her dried and ancient lips, touched us with the strangest sense of I know not what. I suppose it was the first time that any of us had realised that nothing lasts in this world, that roses wither and birds fly to other climes, and understood, too, that this youth of ours was fleeting as the roses and the birds, and that even if we should remember it in days to come, it would be but as the echo of a song.

Poor grasshopper of forgotten summers! She had sung all her life long through. Any one could tell that she had never known how to do anything else but sing. She had sung her breath and life away. Doubtless she had sung before kings and princes, in great halls shining with fair women and lights and jewels. Doubtless she had been worshipped like a goddess. No doubt that when she was young and lovely the applause and the gaze of men went up to her like incense. All summer she had lavished her trills and smile, and had laughed in the insolence of beauty and the carelessness of the morrow. Her radiant and prodigal youth had been spent on every comer, and every drop from her flask of oil had been consumed in midnight revelry. Then, at last, had fallen the shades of night, and—there was no more oil. The cutting winds had come upon her, and no store was in her larder. With nothing but an old guitar she trailed the streets and begged a livelihood, and boys howled upon her when she came into the café.

I wonder whether she thought of all this, child of joy that she was, who had lived for joy alone and had survived it! O, foolish virgin, who had not learned to die when spring was dead! The myrtles had faded, the song of the birds was done, the laughter of happy couples had ceased from the countryside, but this touching old wretch had gone on, lost in the maze of years and the snows of winter, with no longer an excuse but her misery. She sang with so frail a voice that the noise of a cab would have drowned it. Hers was not the rich fruit of autumn, but the white peace of winter. As for us, on the other hand, we were boys rejoicing in the dawn of life, racing one another up the steeps of hope. All the sky was fair above us, and all our youth was laughing in the sun.

And here, all at once, we were touched by a fellow-feeling for this weird old crone, who had refused to take anything from life but just exactly those things that we ourselves were after, love and laughter, wine and song. She was actually just as old as we were, and our sister. She was just ourselves grown old. And she was a symbol, too, a moral of a kind, to show us at the beginning of joy's path what was its end.

Reflecting many things, we listened in silence with a rich and pleasing melancholy, while the lightsome and florid arias followed one another from her tiny voice.

Whence had come this child of Italy, whom chance had made our guest? What had been the unhappy story of her life? What had been the cost of those fire years, when she had learned that sorrow was no longer her servant, but had become her master? If only she had been able to tell you! If only she had known! But the fact is that she did not know. She had never learned anything except to sing and to be pretty and to please her lovers; and the day had come when she could no longer please any one. To tell the truth, she was no more than a bundle of bones, and retained nothing of her former splendour but a pair of rather too gaudy earrings, which were doubtless the memory of an ancient love. Not so very long ago it was she who had graced the tables of others, but now it was only by grace of the others that she was received at their table. Why was all this? Surely neither her heart nor her manner had changed. Surely it was not her fault. No; the world was visiting her age and ugliness upon her as if they had been sins.

Contemplating her white hair and all the misery of this playmate who had grown old and could no longer play, we could not but think of other aged women, as, for instance, of our mothers. They were not in the least like this. They were not tossed about at the mercy of fate, but lived in venerable repose. They were comfortably and decently dressed, and were firmly established upon their honourable record. Look into the eyes of any one of them, whether rich or poor, and you will see the same profound and chaste tranquillity, the same sweet and recollected mother's love. But this poor old grasshopper, on the other hand, had no son to dream of or to bless; even lads like us were men to her, not children.

That was plain enough when she had finished singing, and, thinking to please us, ventured on certain jests which are supposed to appeal to careless manhood. This was quite the saddest thing of all. Her risky playfulness and double meanings were infinitely sadder than those old-world love-songs of hers, or than her miserable life itself. None of us said a word in reply, and the poor old thing was evidently thoroughly ashamed of herself, for she looked round us with so pitiful a gaze that I thought she would break down.

And now she sat quite motionless, her hands clutching at her guitar as if she were afraid that it would be stolen. She was like some wild creature not quite sure that any kindness was not a trap. She said not a word, and was intently awaiting some horrible jest to be sprung upon her. A few minutes ago, when we were hissing and jeering at her, she had smiled from force of habit; but now that we were altogether friendly she was every moment on the watch. Her eyes and head were lowered, and she sat silent before an empty glass. It was then that Blaise spoke to her with his honest and good-hearted voice. He clothed her with his interest and sympathy. He tried to assuage this horrible fear of hers.

For some time she was unable to reply. It seemed to me that she could find nothing, though she raked in the ashes of her memory. But those bright eyes of his, and his honest smile, and that voice which always touched one like a caress, began to do their work. And when she spoke, it was not of her loves or her successes, nor of the sand or mud which the flow of time's river had washed upon her shores, but of the days when she lived at home a little girl, and herded geese along the green hillsides. This was what she treasured—the fact that she had been loved, that her nurse had put her to sleep cuddled in her arms and singing to her. This alone had survived the shipwreck of a life. This fact of love was the luminous and lovely truth. This was what came to the memory of this ancient hag of the gutter.

As if no time had flowed away, and as if everything which separated her from blissful childhood had been nothing but a dream or an illusion, she told us boys a thousand absurdities of those days so long ago, which came quite fresh and sweet from under the ruins of her memory. There was a boy who had made her such a clever bird-trap. That day when her brother went away on horseback to the wars, how his sword shone and how brave his plume! And you should have seen those Corpus Christi processions, especially one when she had led the way, a tiny white-robed child, candle in hand. And then she told us of her first communion in the parish church, which smelt that day, oh, how sweet, of branches and of herbs.

Strange, simple soul, had she ever since then received the Sacred Host? And had Its merciful miracle worked in this queer old body any cleansing or renewal? Not many months could pass before again the priest should bring to her the Blessed Sacrament, to where she lay in some hovel or infirmary. And then, this flighty songful soul, forgetting all her sins and all the wearisome paths of error, would go all white and clean to heaven. God would forget those passing adventures of hers. Indeed, would she herself remember them? Had not her forgetfulness and unconsciousness of evil already brought her back to that white little girl, candle in hand? I tell you that in this restaurant, where we ourselves were quite far enough removed from the realities of life, we felt a sudden unity, we young men, with this ancient child. She spoke a language which we altogether understood. We had exactly the same feelings and had the same stories to tell. Our hearts came together with hers, and we drew our chairs nearer; and we were very happy indeed, let the wind blow never so wild and cold outside.

All of a sudden she smiled rather wonderfully. Something had come into her memory and had evoked a whole world of long-forgotten images. It was a song; might she sing it? Of course we said " Yes " and " Hurrah! "

Doubtfully at first, but soon with growing certainty, she sang this song to us. It had nothing in common with those gay lyrics of hers all flowery with spring and love, which were, after all, the songs of her profession. It was an old, old peasant chanty, so good, so elemental, one of those dear old grandmother songs which you may find in any land the world over, and which teach you how like all peoples are. God knows when or where she had picked it up. She had forgotten it, and across this great space of time had recalled it, with us—and may I not say, perhaps because of us?

As she sang she slowly swayed and nodded, moving her head to right and left, her trained voice doing it every justice. There were no more trills or flourishes; she only remembered the countryside of long ago. This ancient ditty had some kind of refrain, and Blaise soon joined in it with a sweet tenor. All of us followed him. And then, at the end of this chorus, we were silent, while her thin, feeble, but now joyous voice renewed its antique strains.

The old girl was smiling all over. She was happy and calm. We had all of us found our real point of contact. There was no longer the poor old wandering beggar and a few smug youths; all our spirits were united in one sympathy and intention. It is the fact that there are eternal realities which bring all men together, whether they be learned or simple, rich or poor, strangers or dwellers in the same house, and these are the things which lie at the root of all humanity and at the source of every life and being. Why do we not, in brotherly fashion, seek those things which are the same for all of us, instead of seeking, as we are so apt to do, every possible point which may distinguish and separate and make us envious?

And now the singer was ready to go. She was warmed and comforted. She could take out into that dark winter night a new peace and happiness. Not the drinks we had given her nor the contagion of our youth, but our sympathy had done her good. We had really subscribed for her a little of our hearts.

She got up to go—and when in this city shall we see her again?—and one of us took off his hat and took it round the table. We threw in everything we had, copper and silver, the coins which by some miracle remained in our trousers pockets, and the cash had a jolly tinkle and laugh as it fell into the hat. The old lady was in an ecstasy of delight, and I verily think believed she had got to heaven.

Many years have passed, and yet I remember that hat going round the table. It collected little, and there was nothing very noble about our impulse. But when I look back on our unprofitable youth, wherein there was so little good of any kind and so many scandalous extravagances, I sometimes think that this absurd boyish act of generosity is after all the thing which it is pleasantest to remember.

ANDRÈ GODARD
B. 1865

THE NONA

COUNT RAYMOND DE VILLEMÈRE woke at last from the heavy stupor of unconsciousness which had lain so long upon him, and slowly stretching his limbs, murmured, " Thank Heaven, I am safe! "

But his eyes suddenly met those of the doctor, fixed upon him with an expression of profoundest sorrow, as the old man exclaimed, with a deep sigh, " My poor, dear friend! "

The Count was startled by his alarming tone.

" If you will brace yourself to hear it," the doctor continued, " I will tell you the whole truth."

" Whatever are you talking about? "

" You have all the symptoms of nona."

" What do you say that I have? "

" It is a mysterious and dreadful illness, which begins with a period of deep unconsciousness. This is followed by an interval of brightness and apparent health, lasting for three hours. But at the end of that time the patient suddenly—expires! "

" Good Heavens! "

" Why trouble, after all? " the doctor resumed. " Is life really worth while? And you, I know, are a brave man, and need have no fear of death. Good-bye, dear friend! Good-bye! "

With these words the doctor left him alone, in order that he might settle up any business that might have to be done in the short time still left to him. The Count presently rose from his couch and began to dress with the most scrupulous care. After arranging his hair and putting the finest polish on his dainty nails, he got into a soft smoking-jacket, and, choosing a good cigar, sank down into the sofa-cushions to smoke and meditate. Ah, for all those many cigars which he might never smoke!

The Count was a brave man; the thought of death had no terrors for him; but he might be excused for thinking that fate had dealt with him in a particularly cruel and unfair way.

Yesterday he had been convinced that he was about to die; and when he felt the fever taking hold upon him had called in priest and lawyer, and had burned all his correspondence. And when all this was finished, he lay back upon the pillows, believing in his heart that he would never wake again on earth.

He felt now as a criminal must feel who has been sentenced to death and has then been reprieved, but finds himself at last cheated of his hope, face to face with the gallows.

It was mid-June. The world outside was all brightness, colour, and joyous movement. The gay-liveried equipages of the wealthy passed in endless procession along the Champs-Elysées, and the streets were crowded with people enjoying life to the full. At this moment he felt in as perfect health as any one of them; and yet, if he was to believe the doctor's verdict, long before to-morrow's dawn, all this gay crowd would for him be no more. The only procession left for him was the rumbling, slow ride in a sombre hearse, with the silent, black-robed mourners, ending at the newly dug grave, and the muttered prayers above it. All that he had loved in life, its dearly loved faces, its pleasures, its romance, its emotion, would be never any more.

And now, in the curling smoke of his half-consumed cigar, he seemed to be reviewing the whole drama of his life. Ancient memories of childhood came back with all the vividness of a dream; and then he saw, following one another in swiftest images, the faces which had figured in all those many love-romances of his youth; and at last he lived once more through that first sweet month which had followed his marriage.

Raymond remembered every moment of those wonderful days of cloudless bliss. What a gay and glorious holiday their honeymoon had been! What fun they had had, and how jolly and bohemian they had been! They had made quite a stir, and some of their escapades had come near to providing society with scandals. Everywhere they had gone his wife had been the centre of admiration, and he had rejoiced in her and had loved her more passionately every day. With what bitterness he reflected upon the stupid misunderstanding which had shattered their happiness! A mad blunder on his side, the carelessness of high spirits on hers, and the Count and his little Countess had agreed to part for ever!

They lived apart, indeed, and met only as chance acquaintances; but in their hearts they loved one another as passionately as before; and those who knew them best had least belief in their comedy of indifference. So it was to the Countess that the dying man's thoughts were turned in these last moments that he had to live. He *could not* die without seeing her once more! Surely at a solemn time like this, neither of them could persist in an attitude of relentless pride!

Raymond decided at least to make the attempt. After all, if it should fail, he had nothing now to lose by it. Rising hastily, he seized a telegraph-form and wrote a few words, then rang for his servant, and told him to send it off at once.

He took out his watch. Two hours still remained to him! There was yet time for her to come!

But would she come? Would this appeal, though sent in the hour of death, succeed in moving her woman's heart; or would her woman's pride, looking only on her private injuries, still refuse to relent, even at this awful crisis?

His heart was torn by the conflicting emotions of hope and despair, and in spite of his resolve to face with calm resignation everything that must come, his nerve began now to give way. As his few brief moments passed so swiftly into death, he found himself watching the clock with a dreadful fascination. One precious hour had flown! He sat at his desk and wrote to his mother, telling her all, and recalling a chain of tender memories.

He was brushing away the tears which could not be kept from his eyes, when the door-bell rang sharply, and before he had time to rise, his heart beating furiously with excitement, the servant announced the Countess of Villemère!

His face went dead white. "Odette!" he cried hoarsely, springing up from his chair.

But the visitor did not move a step. She stood just within the door; and as she looked at him a flame of anger kindled in her face.

"How dare you deceive me so cruelly?" she said, in tones of deepest indignation.

"Deceive you? How?"

"Your wire said that you were ill and dying, yet here you are writing letters, as well as you have ever been. Good afternoon!"

"Odette! Odette! Listen for one moment! Let me explain!"

She turned angrily to leave the room, but the Count seized the letter to his mother which was lying on his desk, and thrust it into her hand. "At last," he cried, "read this!"

She took the letter and scanned its earliest sentences; then, unable to read any further, she threw herself weeping into his arms.

"My poor darling! Oh, it is true, then, true!" she cried.

He clasped her more closely, and for a long time they forgot all else, locked in the embrace of utter suffering and of bliss. Thoughts of their happy life together passed unspoken between them; and passionate regrets for the wasted year of foolish pride thrilled their repentant hearts.

He drew her down beside him on the sofa, and with clasped hands they sat in silence, too deeply moved for words.

Once the Count ventured on a jest, evoked by the memory of an ancestor who had gone to the block humming an operatic air. "I suppose I should be proud," he said with a smile; "doubtless I shall be a leader of fashion, and to-morrow all Paris will have this new disease." But Odette could not bear this ghastly humour, and when he saw that he had pained her, he spoke no longer in that strain.

After a time they fell to talking of the old happy days. They spoke at first hardly above a whisper, and with the sense of being in a death-chamber; but gradually this excessive awe receded before the train of memories conjured up by all the familiar furniture of the room, and they began to smile as they recalled to one another details of their many adventures, and of those sweet times now gone for ever. A hunting picture made them think of the first day on which they had followed the hounds together; and they seemed to hear again, as on that misty November morning, the cheery horn of the huntsman and the crisp rustle of dead leaves beneath their horses' feet. They handled the dust-begrimed little favours which brought them together in a cotillon of long ago, and remembered the tender gay coquetry amid the palms of the conservatory that evening.

How many wonderful mornings had seen them out early on horseback, cantering under the trees in the Bois, and enjoying existence like a couple of truant schoolboys. Then they would breakfast at the Pavilion, and return home by way of the Champs-Elysées. Then for a few hours they had to part, each to endure a round of tiresome social functions; but in the evening they would meet once more, perhaps at the Opéra, but oftener quietly at home.

Living over again in memory those happy days, Raymond and Odette forgot all else, even the fatal shadow which had brought about their reunion, until the sound of the bell suddenly startled them into recollection. They looked at one another in terrible anguish.

The servant entered. "Doctor Darlois!" he announced.

"What!" cried the astonished doctor. "You are still up? Why, I called to——"

"You called to—what?"

"As I seem to have made a mistake, I may as well tell you the truth. I thank God that I was wrong. I came round to convince myself that you were really dead."

"You are very kind," said the Count with a smile.

"Is he—going to live?" asked the anxious little wife.

"Certainly. There is no doubt now. I don't understand it at all. He had all the symptoms of nona, as described by the highest authorities. Let me assure you that I am overjoyed to find——"

No doubt it was indeed a joyful surprise to the worthy physician.

But perhaps there was also in the depth of his heart just a tinge of annoyance at his failure in diagnosis.

" Don't you think, Odette," Raymond whispered, smiling, " that it would be a good idea to ask him to dine with us this evening? "

MARCEL SCHWOB
1867–1905

THE WOODEN STAR

I

Alain's grandmother was an old charcoal-burner, who lived in the heart of the forest. This forest was immemorially old, and so dense that its paths were merely clearings through the trees, which opened from time to time upon little green lawns surrounded by giant oaks; or, again, upon a moveless sea of bracken, and above it the impenetrable interlacings of delicate twigs. Here, through the ages, these majestic trees reared their mighty colonnades, among which the fugitive leaves held counsel, their branches forming window-frames through which one looked upon an immense sea of green, with its deeps of heavily scented shade and its pale rays of light from the hidden sun. Here was all the magic of a bank of purple heath or a flaming river of gorse among the trees; the wonderful filigree of glimmering lights and shadows; the freshness of young pines and oak trees springing up in the natural clearings, and swaying lightly in the soft breezes; the great forked mossy roots of the ancient trees plunging deep into their beds of red-brown pine-needles. Squirrels had their homes in the tree-trunks, adders in the rich earth beneath them; myriads of insects darted and circled in the spaces, and the leafy galleries were filled with the songs of countless birds.

In the heat of midsummer the forest was alive with humming, like a mighty ant-hill; and whenever there was rain, it continued for long afterwards a rain which was quite its own, falling slowly and aimlessly from the tree-tops, and dripping sadly on to the dead leaves. It seemed, indeed, to breathe and to sleep, at times even to snore; and again, held in a profound silence, to be watching intently, without so much as the rustle of a snake or the warble of a bird. What was it for which the whole forest was waiting? No one could say. This forest was like a feminine creature of moods and fancies; now throwing out a strong line of birch trees, straight as the flight of an arrow, then ending it tremblingly in a cluster of aspens; now advancing a step beyond her boundaries, right out into the open plain, and, again, repenting of such temerity, seeming to flee back to the cool, sombre depths of her ancient woods, into the everlasting night at her heart. All sorts of wild creatures lived in peace and unmolested within her boundaries; but there was something inimical to man in this tremendous palisade of inexorable trunks, stretching out on all sides like huge petrified lightning flares thrown up by the earth.

The forest was not unfriendly to Alain; but it had, in fact, hidden the heavens from him. The little boy had so far known no other light than the dim confused greenness which pervaded it, and in the evening he used to see the stack of charcoal glowing with little red points here and there. He had never seen the procession of gold and silver lights across the spangled night sky. His little life had been passed with the good old charcoal-burner, whose face, like the bark of a tree, had settled into the deep lines of patient and peaceful old age. He helped her daily to cut down branches, to pile them up into stacks, to cover the piles with earth and with turves, to see that the fire burned slowly and gently, to pull out the pieces into black heaps, and to fill the sacks of the charcoal-heavers, whose faces were almost indistinguishable in the forest gloom.

But Alain had many joys and delights of his own in this deep old wood. He loved to lie at mid-day under the tall bracken and listen to all the forest sounds, watching the tiny dancing circles of sunlight, and drowsily meditating upon the fact that his grandmother and he were neither green like the world nor black like the burnt charcoal, until he would fall asleep and dream that the old woman was a twisted oak tree, and that the trees were seated at table sharing their soup. He liked to watch the saucepan boiling on the fire, and would wait expectantly to sniff up its delicious smell; and he delighted in the gurgling of the water when he thrust his little stone jug into the spring, where three big stones held it as in a cup. Sometimes a lizard would dart across the foot of an elm like a wavy flash of green light, or in a hollow on the trunk of the tree a huge flaming toadstool would form.

Many such delights the forests had for Alain, and at ten years old he had a heart and mind filled with the dreams which it gave. In the autumn of that year a great storm swept over the forest. The mighty trees groaned and creaked, as the torrents of rain pelted down through their thick foliage, and squalls of wind came swirling among their tops; the noise of the tempest became deafening; it crashed through the wood, carrying destruction before it, and many veteran trees received their death-blow. The great trunks fell headlong to the ground, carrying with them masses of shattered branches, twigs, and foliage; the wonderful forest roof lay in fragments beside its fallen columns, and through these yawning gaps the unwonted daylight penetrated into its scared depths.

In the evening, when the storm had subsided and peace reigned once more in the forest, Alain went out into the glorious freshness which follows upon a long and fierce tempest, to dip his basin in the little pool of the spring. As he stooped down to the water he saw in it brilliant points of light, glittering, shaking, and dancing, as if in sparkling laughter. He thought at first that they must be sparks of fire like those which glowed in the charcoal piles; but when he tried to touch them with his fingers they did not burn him, and always escaped his grasp, glancing hither and thither, and returning defiantly to their first place. These were cold and mocking bits of fire. Then, leaning over further, Alain saw among them the reflection of his own face and hands. So he looked up above him.

There, through a great rent in the curtain of foliage, shone the radiant sky, no longer hidden or veiled by the forest. Alain had a sense of sudden confusion, as if he had been discovered naked, for from this vast distant blue vault thousands of bright eyes were shining steadily down upon him, twinkling and sparkling, piercing the distance with their myriad glancing rays. Thus Alain saw the stars for the first time in his life, and they smote his heart with a wonderful joy and an immense desire.

He rushed in to his grandmother, who was gently stirring the pile of charcoal, lost in thought, and asked her how it came that there were a lot of shining points of fire shimmering among the trees and reflected in the little pool.

" Those are the bright stars of heaven, Alain," she told him. " Above this forest there is the sky, and the people who live outside in the open country see it all the time. And every night God lights His stars in the sky."

" God lights His stars in the sky," repeated the boy. " And could I light stars, too, grandmamma? "

The old woman stroked his head with her hard wrinkled hand. " You are too small," she said. " We are all of us too small. Only God Himself can light His stars in the dark night."

And again the boy repeated her words, " Only God Himself can light His stars in the dark night."

II

From this time a certain restlessness tinged all Alain's former delight in his forest life. There was a jarring note in the sounds which had sung him to sleep, and the lacy bracken was no longer a protecting nest. The sunlight seemed to die off the mosses with disappointing quickness, and he grew tired of living in these gloomy green shades. He longed for light, for something far beyond the glistening of lizards or the heavy vividness of toadstools or the red glow of the charcoal. Before going to bed he stole out to the little pool and looked up to the glittering face of the sky. His whole soul went out in a great yearning to be beyond the dark gloom shut in by these beeches and oaks and elms, and always more and more of them, an impenetrable night of great forest trees. He remembered his grandmother's words, and his pride was stung by them: "*Only* God Himself can light His stars in the dark night." He thought, "I, too, might be able to light my stars if I could go into the open country outside the forest. Oh, I must go; I *will* go!"

Nothing any longer pleased him within the forest, which seemed to besiege him like an entrenched army; which held him as in a harsh prison, where tree-gaolers in ever-increasing numbers barred his escape, holding out threatening arms in all directions, rearing themselves like huge, terrible, silent ogres, supported by knotty buttresses and by forked barricades, and with enormous unfriendly hands. The forest now seemed to him to be hostile to all that was not part of itself, to anything that was not one with its own dark and gloomy heart. It would soon close up again the rents which the storm had made and by which the light had entered, and the little pool would once more become shrouded in darkness, unable to see or reflect the dancing lights of the sky.

But Alain dreamed of stars which were always dancing. And one night, while his grandmother was asleep, he escaped from the little hut, taking with him some bread and a hard end of cheese.

The charcoal piles gave out a few quiet glimmers of dying light. What a miserable light beside the living sparkles of the sky! In the night the great oaks were only like huge shadow forms blindly groping in the dark. These grim gaolers were, like his grandmother, asleep, but they slept standing at their posts, each trusting to the others to keep watch, and Alain knew that they would remain thus silent and still until the first fresh breath of dawn stirred among their leaves. But by that time he would already be beyond their power. When all the birds chirped out their warning, Alain would already have slipped through their hands, out into the open plain where they dared not follow him. They might threaten as much as they liked from a distance, this army of dark giants, but it would be in vain; they could only gather themselves together in ever thicker ranks, spread out their forked palisades and their silent tentacles, thrust forward their great heads or their horrible club-like branches; but at the edge of the plain they became powerless, held in a sudden enchantment, dazzled into stupor, as it were, by the light.

Once safely out in the open, Alain dared at last to look round. The great black giants seemed to look after him sadly. Then he looked up. Surely a miracle had appeared in the sky. The whole vault of heaven was studded thickly with stars, twinkling and flashing, dying out and rekindling, growing larger and smaller, shining red or gold or steely-blue or silvery-white, uniting and separating again. Sometimes they shone with piercing radiance, painful to the eyes, but again took on a softer light, then became misty and blurred, shone clearly again, and glanced through the air with the sharpness of a stiletto. Alain began to discover all sorts of figures among them—houses, carriages, animals—and the light gleamed first on one feature and then on another. Now it sparkled on the roof, now on the doorway, now on the end of the carriage-pole, and then it disappeared from all, and in the changing brilliance all the forms he had seen became confused.

The boy stretched out his arms into the night, longing to seize these lights and to shape them into new forms of his own. He wanted to find out what their fires were like, and whether there were up there great piles of blue charcoal studded with points of flame.

He looked about him over the plain. Flat, bare, and formless it stretched away to the horizon, with no stir of life amid its low vegetation. In the distance wound a slow-moving river, showing only as a vague white ribbon upon the plain; and Alain crossed to this river that he might see the stars in it. Here they seemed to be flowing with it, to have become fluid changing things, now distorted in shape, now round, and again divided into a crowd of fine glittering lines. Sometimes they came to the water's edge, strayed into a backwater, and died, stifled among the bunches of weeds.

All night long Alain walked up and down the river bank. The coming dawn threw a shroud of pale grey over all the stars, shot with pink and gold. Alain sat down under a small tree with silvery quivering leaves, and munched his bread, drinking from the running stream. He was a little tired; but he walked on all day, and at night slept in a hollow in the steep river-bank. The next morning he started walking again.

And now the river became much wider and the plain more colourless; the air was damp and salty, his feet sank in the sand, and a tremendous murmuring sound seemed to fill the space in front of him. White birds were sweeping and circling, uttering shrill and mournful cries. The water turned yellow and green, swelled up and became foamy. The river's banks gradually disappeared. Soon Alain could see nothing but a vast stretch of sand, across which in the distance ran a long dark streak. Here the river was stopped by a barrier of foam, against which its wavelets seemed to dash themselves in vain; it spread itself out into a great flood, sweeping over the sandy plain as far as the eye could see.

Alain saw tufts of sea-pinks and of dry yellow reeds dotted over the sands. A ceaseless tumult was all about him. The fresh salt breeze played over his face. The water rose and fell in perpetual rhythm, the white-crested waves breaking on the shore like dark yawning mouths closing down to swallow it up. As they fell they cast up along the sand a line of slime and bubbling foam, and amid it all sorts of strange and beautiful fragments; shining shells perforated with tiny holes, wonderful fossil flowers, bright crinkled cornets, weird, soft, transparent things which moved with quaint and rapid motions, indeed an extraordinary mass of debris. The low roar of the waves was sad and soft; they did not groan like the forest trees, but in another voice of more gentle complaint. But they, too, must have been jealous and insensible as the forest; the light could never penetrate into the deeps of the rolling purple billows.

Alain ran along its margin, delighting to draw his feet through the wet foam. The sun had set, and for a moment red flares from the western sky took fire in the shining waters and glowed there. Then night covered the ocean's face and reigned supreme, silencing the rolling of the waves, and in the sky above the stars shone out. But the ocean did not mirror the stars. Impervious as the forest, its cold dark heart resisted their radiant beauty by the ceaseless movement of its surface. The mountainous waves heaped themselves up, and in the same moment were again dissolved; they advanced in armies at a furious gallop, only to fall in a moment utterly lost to view.

A dancing light appeared at the base of a jutting cliff, and Alain advanced to examine it. At the water's edge were a group of children, moving busily about, examining the treasures left on the beach by the sea; one of them was carrying the unsteady light. Alain joined them, and saw that they were gathering up little star-shaped things full of wonderful lights and colours—rosy, violet, shimmering blue, spotted vermilion, touched with phosphorescence. They looked like the palms of unearthly hands, with shrivelled fingers curling round them, or like fleshy leaves of some sea plant, endowed with life and movement, or like starry beasts which belonged to the deeps of a dark firmament.

"Sea stars! sea stars!" the children shouted gleefully.

"Ah," said Alain, "stars!"

The boy who held the light turned to Alain. "I will tell you the story of the stars," he said. "On the night when Our Lord was born, who is the children's God, a lovely new star was born. It was a great big blue star; it followed Him wherever He went, and He loved it. When wicked men killed Him the star wept tears of blood, and three days after His death it died too. It fell into the sea and was drowned. At the same time a great many other stars drowned themselves in the sea for grief at His death. The sea, being sorry for their unhappiness, would not let them lose their beautiful colours, and every night gives them up to us in this sweet way so that we may keep them in memory of Our Lord."

"But can I not light them again?" asked Alain.

"They are dead," said the boy. "They have been dead ever since Our Lord died."

When Alain heard this he turned away, his head bent down, and left the little band of torchlight seekers. He had no desire for a dead, drowned star, whose light was put out for ever; he wanted to light a star, even as God does, to rejoice in its brilliance, and to see it rise through the clouds, far beyond the shadows of the forest which shut out the stars, far from the deep glooms of the great sea which drowned them. These children might collect dead stars if it pleased them, might keep them and cherish them, but he had no use for them. He had no idea where he should find his own particular star; but he was certain that he would find it. It would be wondrous lovely; he would light it himself and it would belong to him; perhaps, even, it would follow him everywhere, as the glorious blue star followed Our Lord. God, who had so many stars, could not grudge this one to little Alain; he wanted it so badly. How astonished his grandmother would be when he went back home and the whole terrible forest was lighted to its darkest corners by his star! He would say to her then, "It is not only God who can light the stars. Here is a star which is all mine. Only Alain lights this one, to shine amid these old trees. This is my star, my own star of fire!"

The dancing light of the children's torch moved hither and thither, reddening as the night grew misty, until it died away in the darkness, and with it the shadowy forms of the children. Alain was alone again. A fine drizzling rain began to fall, chilling him to the bone, and shrouding him in a delicate network of tiny drops, which filled all the vast space about him. The unceasing sea now murmured gently, now grew to a deep roar, while at times a huge wave would dash with a loud report against the cliff, and, scattering into spray, would rise like a great foam-spectre into the black night. Gradually it settled down into a low monotonous plaint, like the sighs of a sick person whom sleep evades, or the gentle strife of light breezes. Then all became still for Alain.

III

Day followed day, and Alain watched the rising and the setting of the stars; but still he had not found his own star. He had reached a countryside where everything was dried up, and the autumn grass had turned yellow over the fields, while the vine leaves were reddening on the stems before the sour and thickly clustered bunches of immature grapes. Long lines of poplars stretched across the plain, and clumps of oak trees made dark spots upon the bleached meadows of the gently sloping hills, while the steeper hills were crowned with dark, gaunt pines. On the vast uplands the trees stood in open and formidable array, amid which the little clusters of fir trees made by contrast quite a cheerful note.

Across this barren plain a clear, pebbly little stream wound its way, leaping gently down a hillock, its bed half dried up below the first of its falls, then making itself two arms to encircle the base of flower-covered ruins of old wooden houses. The water was so transparent that the backs of the shining, speckled fishes, lying in close, motionless groups on the bottom, were clearly seen, and the pebbles made a bright mosaic of its bed. At night Alain saw cats crouching on both its banks, intent on catching fish.

In the distance, where the stream became a river, a charming little town nestled on its low banks, whose tiny houses had pointed roofs and many grated windows, and wonderful chimney-pots painted blue and yellow. There was an old wooden bridge and an old monastery, a great ruddy, shadowy edifice, with the sign of Saint George in the act of thrusting his lance into the jaw of a huge red sandstone dragon.

The shimmering green river swept in a broad curve about the little city. On the one side of it, in the distance, rose great snow-capped mountains, and on the other side the pleasant hills, up which the streets of the town sloped gently, each bearing its own signboard painted in colours—the "Helmet Road," the "Crown Road," the "Swan Road," and the "Wild Man Road," which was near the Fish Market, with its great stone lion, from whose mouth issued a fountain of crystal water. There were homely inns, where jolly-faced girls poured out the sparkling wine into tankards of pewter. In the centre was the town hall, where the magistrates held their courts of justice, arrayed in a cloak of fine cloth over a shirt of unbleached linen, and wearing the gold ring of office on their second finger; and in the narrow streets surrounding it one might see stalls full of inkhorns and parchment for the use of the lawyers and their clerks. The women of the little town had wonderful blue eyes in patient faces full of love and gentleness; they wore veils of tulle over their heads, and sometimes the mouth was covered with a band of fine white linen; the girls, in their white dresses, with slashed sleeves and gay-coloured girdles, carried distaffs, upon which they seemed to be spinning their long golden hair, and the little children had glorious red locks and the fairest of skins.

Alain passed under a low, thick-set arch into the Old Market, a rambling square encircled with small houses, hunched up under the slated roofs like old women squatting over a fire. The parish church, with its monstrous gargoyles bearded with heavy mosses, was built about a great square tower, tapering away into a long pointed spire. Close by was the barber's shop, whose thick bulging windows, round as bubbles, were flanked by green shutters, on which were painted in red, designs of scissors and lancets. In the centre of the square was the well, its kerb worn away by the steps of the thousands who had used it, its opening guarded by a dome-shaped lattice of iron against the barefooted urchins who were always playing about it, some running, some engaged in a game of hopscotch, and one fat little boy with a treacly mouth sobbing quietly by himself. Alain tried to talk to them; but the children ran away and stared furtively at him, without answering a word.

The night dew began to fall through the smoky air, and candles shone in the thick window-panes with deep ruddy light. Doors were fastened, shutters closed, and the bolts were drawn. The signboard of the inn creaked on its iron support, and through the half-open door Alain could see the light of the great log-fire, could sniff up the good smell of the roasting joint, and hear the wine being poured out; but he was afraid to go in. Then a woman's gruff voice announced that it was closing time, and Alain slipped into a narrow by-street.

In this inhospitable town he could find no shelter from the cold night air. The forest at least offered the hollows in its cloven trunks and the river the little pits in its banks; on the plain one could creep into the furrows of the stubble-fields, and by the sea find shelter in the angles of the cliff; even the parched countryside of yesterday had given him a ditch under a hedge to sleep in; but this sullen, bleak-hearted town, with its many rows of tightly closed doors, had not a friendly corner to offer the little wanderer; even the stalls were all dismantled and stowed away. In every direction it raised hostile barriers across his path, throwing out suddenly posts or planks from side to side of the winding passages and alleys. Without any warning a house would thrust out its turrets into the street, or another overhang it darkly with its gables, so that the ways of the town were everywhere dark and forbidding; its buildings, like gloomy sentinels, cast over all an inhospitable silence and a thick pall of night. Alain trudged up and down and found himself wandering in circles, till he arrived once more in the Old Market square. All the windows were dark and shuttered up, except one small round window, where the light of a candle still flickered feebly.

This gleam of hope shone out from beside one corner of the church tower, and Alain found a door opening upon a spiral staircase which led right up to it. He plucked up courage and started to mount it. Half way up a cresset was burning, casting a dim light on to the staircase, and when he reached the top he found a weird-looking door studded with bronze nails. He stopped to take breath, and from within came the sound of an old yet piercing voice speaking in short, broken phrases. As he listened Alain's heart began to beat rapidly, and he felt as if he must choke. The strange old voice was talking about the stars! Alain put his ear to the iron-bound keyhole and waited, entranced. The voice went on:

"Stars which are baneful and of bad influence for the night, for this hour, and for those who inquire of them, write:—Sirius, showing blood red; the Great Bear, hidden by clouds; the Little Bear, veiled in mist. The Pole Star is brilliant and of warlike aspect. To-night, Tuesday, Mars red and fiery, in the eighth house, the house of the Scorpion, signifying death by fire, battle, slaughter, and consuming flames. At this third hour, injurious in its essence, Mars is in conjunction with Saturn in the house of fear, signifying death, calamities, and failure in all undertakings. Mars and Saturn are in union, signifying fire during the night and alarms while men sleep. The aspect is contrary, for the Bull enters into the Upper Circle and the Scorpion into the Lower Circle. Jupiter in the second house is in opposition to Mars in the eighth, signifying the ruin of all wealth and glory and might. The fiery Mars rules over all the buildings and life which belong to Saturn, signifying the city in flames and deaths by fire. In the third hour of this night of Tuesday, God is about to turn His eyes from His stars, and to deliver the souls of men to the flames."

As the voice of the old wizard finished dictating these words, the door was burst open by excited little hands and feet, and Alain drew himself up on the threshold, indignant, erect, and with blazing eyes.

"It's a lie!" he cried. "God never forgets His stars. Only God can light His stars in the dark night!"

An old bent man in a long sable robe, who was stooping over an astrolabe made in the form of an armillary sphere, raised his head, blinking his red eyelids like some ancient night-bird startled from its hole. A thin, pale little boy, who was seated at his feet writing down on parchment the horoscope, dictated by the old wizard, dropped the reed from between his fingers. The flames of two great wax candles waved and flared up in the draught. The old man stretched out his arm, showing at the end of his furry sleeve a hand as skinny as the hand of a mummy.

"Oh, unbelieving and untutored child," he said, "in what dark ignorance you live! Listen, this child here will teach you. Tell him, my child, what is the nature of the stars."

The thin, pale little boy recited as out of a lesson-book:

" The stars are fixed upon the crystal vault of heaven, and revolve so quickly on their own axis that they become ignited by their own motion. God is only the prime mover of these orbs, and the first cause of the revolution of the seven spheres; but since this first moving the sphere of the stars obeys only its own laws, and rules according to its inclination the events on this earth and the destinies of men. Such is the teaching of Aristotle and of Holy Church."

" It's a lie! " reiterated Alain. " God knows all His stars, and He loves them. He has shown them to me in spite of the big trees in the forest which used to hide the sky, and He has made them float along the river and dance so jollily over the great plain; and I have seen, too, the stars that drowned themselves when Our Lord died, and soon He will show me my own star."

" My child, God will show you your own star. So be it! " said the old man.

Alain was not sure whether he meant what he said. He heard nothing more, for at that moment a sudden gust of wind blew out the candles. He groped his way along the wall to the stairs, and, growing bold, seized the little copper lamp with its floating wick, and bore it off, thinking he would punish the horrid old man for his lies about the stars.

The whole place was in black darkness, but Alain came safely out into the street by the light of his lamp. The night sky was covered with a lattice-work of stars, crossed by the finest airy threads with sparkling knots, and with a network of limpid fire hung upon it. Alain raised his face toward this radiant spectacle. The stars seemed to laugh at him with their sparkling, frosty laugh. There was no pity for him in their glance; indeed, they did not know him, since he had been all his life hidden from them by the horrid forest. These lofty and dazzling gems of beauty could only laugh at him, small as he was, with his flickering smoky lamp; but they would laugh, too, at the old wizard, with his lies and his extinguished candles. He looked at them again, wondering whether they laughed in pleasure or mockery, and thinking that they must be happy because they danced so joyously. Did they know that some day Alain would light one of them, and had God told them, perhaps, which it was to be? Surely, one night, this little star would come down to him and he would only have to pick it like a ripe fruit; or, if it would not let him touch, it might fly in front of him with its wings of fire, laughing with him and making him laugh, till the gloomy old forest should be sprinkled all through with tiny lights which were just sparkling gleams of laughter.

Alain had reached the old bridge, which trembled on its carved pillars as he walked. Between its great girders the water could be seen. Half way across was a watchman's box covered all over with blue and yellow tiles, but the watchman had deserted his post, or he would not have let Alain pass with his lamp. The boy walked very quickly past it, not daring to let the light shine into its dark opening. Across the bridge were the humbler streets, whose houses had none of the coloured coats-of-arms, nor the carvings of dragons and monsters for waterspouts and window-frames, nor of snakes about the doorways, nor of hideous, unshining suns at the gable-ends, which decorated the prouder houses of the other side. These little houses were quite simply made of squared planks, without even tiles or slates on their roofs.

Alain raised his lamp above his head in order to see the road. Then, suddenly he stopped, trembling all over. There was a star right in front of him, hardly higher than his head!

It was a dark star, indeed, for it was made of wood; but it was perfect in form, and was nailed to the end of a pole which projected over the roadway. Alain let the light fall on it and examined it. It was already old and cracked, having waited a very long time; perhaps God had forgotten it in this out-of-the-way little town, or perhaps, rather, He had just let it stay there, knowing that Alain would come. The house was a poor one, with no shutters, and within its lower windows Alain saw strange figures made of wood, with stiff straight gowns, dull round eyes, rigid lips, and crossed hands; all stood upon a plank, as if to look out of the window. There were an ox and an ass, too, with straight, spread-out legs, and there was a cross with a pitiful figure nailed to it, and then, over a wooden manger, there was a little star just like the one in the road.

Alain knew now that he had found it at last. This was his star, made out of wood from the forest, and waiting to be lighted. It had been waiting for Alain. He put his lamp to the star, and the red flame licked the wood until it crackled. There were little glimmerings of blue, and then the star really took fire and flared up, a wonderful sphere of red. The child clapped his hands and cried, "My star at last! My star is burning!"

Then he heard a coming and going in the house. The upper windows opened, and Alain saw little scared heads with long untidy hair, the heads of children in their night-dress, who had waked and were looking out to see. He ran to the door and went into the house, exclaiming, "Children, come and see my star, my star on fire! Alain has lit his star in the night!"

But the flames spread rapidly and sparks were thrown around; the dry wood took fire, then the thatch caught, and flames raged upward from the house. There were cries of fear, cries for help, loud wailing cries. The house had become a furnace. Its structure fell, huge flames roared upward through the smoke, there was a dreadful confusion of red and black, and all soon ended in a fiery pit full of burning embers.

Then, the bell of fire's alarm tolled heavily.

At that very same moment the old wizard in the church tower was aware of a new red star in the sky. It mounted in what he called " the Heart of Heaven," which is the House of Glory.

ANDRÉ LICHTENBERGER
B. 1870

THE SNAIL

MAMMA had gone out for the whole day. In the morning a party of ladies and gentlemen had called for her in a grand carriage to take her out. M. de Veler was driving and M. de Thilanges blew great resounding blasts on the coach horn. It was all very jolly indeed. Of course Trott stayed at home; he was much too small to go with them! Mademoiselle had been asked instead to come and spend the day with him so that he should not feel lonely. Trott would much have preferred to have been left alone with Jane, but then who would ever have thought of asking a small boy about his likes and dislikes?

Mademoiselle was seated on a rustic bench at the foot of the garden reading an English book. She wore spectacles on her very imposing nose, and never moved a muscle of her face. With automatic regularity she turned over the pages of her book. Trott had tried to amuse himself in ever so many ways, but nothing seemed to come right all day; and at last he went to the corner where his own tiny garden was, to see if it needed any attention. He found it in a terrible state of untidiness; it was nothing but a wilderness of pebbles, rubbish, weedy-looking turf, and twigs —all of which made the garden look very far from beautiful. All the same, it contained one redeeming feature—there was a small rose-bush growing in the centre. Trott had not planted it himself, yet to him it was a superb achievement of gardening, and sometimes it even grew roses. To-day, as it happened, one had just budded out. Trott looked at the rose from every point of view with the greatest pride and delight. Oh, it was a ravishingly beautiful rose!

Suddenly Trott's eyes grew as round as saucers and were transfixed with horror, his mouth formed a round O! and his face crimsoned. What was this ghastly sight before him? Climbing over his lovely rose was a snail, a villainously ugly snail, that left behind it a slimy track. It turned its head from left to right, drew in its horns, put them out again. It didn't seem to be much embarrassed by Trott's gaze.

For a moment or two Trott watched it, and then he called out in a shrill voice, "Oh, Mademoiselle, please come here!"

Mademoiselle lifted her big nose from her book. She then closed the book, put it under her arm, and in four strides was beside Trott.

"What is the matter?"

Trott pointed one finger at the snail in disgust; he hated creeping things.

Mademoiselle fixed her eyes on the creature.

"Why, it is only a snail!"

Trott was not in the least convinced.

"This mollusc is harmful to vegetation," Mademoiselle continued; "you must destroy it."

Trott was pleased to have such permission, but a shiver of repulsion went through him at the thought of touching the animal.

"Mademoiselle, won't you do it for me, please?"

Mademoiselle looked at him sternly.

"Why should I kill it and not you?" she asked him severely. "It is on your property, and you ought to defend your own possessions."

Trott sighed deeply. He knew that whenever Mademoiselle spoke in that final way it was no earthly use for him to protest. He put out his hand, then drew it back again. At last he touched the shell with one finger. What a stroke of luck! The snail was afraid! It had withdrawn itself altogether into its house. Nothing further happened. Trott began to breathe more freely. But all the same he did not like these creatures; in fact, he hated them. What was the poor boy to do? Ah, what a splendid idea! he would throw it over the garden wall into Madame Ducrieux's flower-beds. Trott lifted up his arm ready to throw.

But Mademoiselle seized it just in time.

"You must never seek your own good at the expense of other people," she said sternly. "This mollusc would eat your neighbour's plants. It would be wrong for you to throw it into her garden."

"Then what am I to do with it?"

"Crush it under your foot," she answered.

Trott looked at the snail in great perplexity. Crush it under his foot? Pah! The very thought of hearing the shell crack under his foot and then of feeling beneath his sole the soft body of the animal sickened him. There must be other ways of killing it; why, he might even throw it down a well. Yes, that would be ever so much better.

Trott began to put his plan into execution. But still he was not satisfied. After all, the poor snail had not done anything very wrong. Would it not be wrong to kill it for no offence?

It had been wandering about in an aimless way, and perhaps it had been very happy indeed walking about and dining on his beautiful rose tree under the golden sun. Yes, but it was destroying the tree; it was eating it, and ought to be punished. But why punish it? Surely the snail had a right to eat if Trott had. It was only eating its natural food. It had not been crawling about the rose out of spite or to do it any harm, but simply because it was hungry and had to find food for itself. Would Trott be justified in killing it for doing this?

But still, didn't people kill cows and sheep, calves and the poor little lambs that bleat so sadly, as well as the lovely birds that sing joyously in the woods? They were much more interesting than a snail, and no more wicked than this creature. Perhaps, though, they killed them humanely. Then so would he! Trott lifted up his arm to throw down the snail. But again he lowered it slowly, though he still held the enemy in his hand.

Yes, it was true that all these animals were killed, but that was in order that they might be eaten, and human beings had to have them as food. Trott remembered how once he had seen his father box the ears of a little street urchin who had stoned a bird to death. How angry papa had been then! And yet the birds pecked at the fruit and spoiled it; cows and sheep browsed on grass and pretty flowers. It was only the other day that Trott had seen a cow root up at least fifty marguerites at one time. In spite of that, though, it would have been very wicked to kill the cow, and the snail was guilty of no worse crime than the cow.

Poor Trott, perplexed by all these difficult problems, began to feel very restless. He felt very much inclined to cry. It seemed to him that he would be committing a very great crime if he made the snail the scapegoat of his anger. And yet at the same time he knew he could not leave his flowers to be at the mercy of this ugly brute. What was he to do? His mind was in a ferment.

Then at last some ideas began to shape themselves into something definite. It was wrong to kill a sheep for nothing, but not to kill it to eat. It was wrong to kill a snail, but——

He faced the creature in terror. No, truly, such an idea was impossible. Mademoiselle was watching him from a distance and grinning at him. She had let her book slip down upon her knees, and her open lips showed the yellow teeth that looked like an antique set of dominoes. She was laughing at Trott while he was in trouble. What was to be the end of his cogitations?

Suddenly Mademoiselle jumped up from her bench as if some one had pricked her sharply with a pin. She uttered one shrill cry and ran forward, leaving her treasured book where it had fallen on the grass.

What had happened to rouse her like this? Automatically, with a swift and unexpected movement, Trott had thrust the snail into the back of his mouth, then, closing his eyes tight, he had swallowed it.

"Oh, Trott! for shame! How could you do it? What a disgusting thing to do! You naughty boy! Oh, how horrible!" The words of Mademoiselle fell over one another in her haste.

Trott stood still in the midst of this outward storm. He was far too much engaged by internal troubles to listen to her. He was inwardly in a very uneasy state. He could hear a curious sound—surely the snail must be walking about inside him! The thought made him feel horribly queer!

But no, it was all over now; he must have digested it by this time. So Trott went back to his garden, and, with an increased tenderness, he looked at his rose, his heart beating high with pride because he had protected its beauty so carefully, yet without making a needless sacrifice of the life of its lowly enemy.

TROTT'S CHRISTMAS

André Lichtenberger

"It's Christmas Day!" Trott was only half awake when something whispered this to him, but the whisper wakened him completely. Last night he had lain in bed for hours, thinking tomorrow would never, never come; but now that it was actually here he jumped quickly out of bed and ran over to the fireplace to look inside the two little yellow slippers that he had purposely left there. When he saw them he gave a little shout of joy, and for a minute stood looking at them in delight: a drum, a sword, a gun, four boxes of soldiers, two picture-books, a box of chocolates, and other smaller things overflowed from his shoes—and they were all for Trott! Turning his head, he found that his pretty little mother was watching him from the door, and in his happiness he ran up to put his arms around her. She stooped to kiss him, and said gently:

"You won't forget that it's the child Jesus who gave you these toys, will you, my dear?"

Trott had seen pictures of the child Jesus and knew Him quite well, and he could not help wondering how any one so small could carry such a heavy load, and how He could still look rosy after He had climbed down so many chimneys. A feeling of awe stole over Trott, and he thanked the child Jesus from the depths of his heart. He hurried somewhat over his prayers, nevertheless, and resumed the enjoyment of his new treasures.

Jane, Trott's English nurse, opened the shutters. It was a beautiful day, and the bright sun of Nice peeped in at the window; the sea was a brilliant blue, and the very air seemed full of joy. Such a beautiful and sparkling Christmas made Trott's happiness all the greater. He felt he could hardly stand still to be washed and dressed, and he had to be coaxed to eat his breakfast. But at last he was sitting on the floor beside his mother's chair playing with his toys. He examined them on this side and that, and admired them greatly in every position. Suddenly he said:

"How I wish poor papa were here!"

Mamma gave a little sigh in reply to this. Papa had gone away in a big boat, and at that moment was sailing, far away, on the other side of the round globe.

A bell rang, then Jane came in, carrying a large bouquet and an even larger toy, Punchinello. She handed the flowers to mamma and Punchinello to Trott, saying, "They're from M. Aaron."

Mamma uttered a cry of delight, blushed, and hid her face in the beautiful flowers. But Trott felt displeased, and eyed his Punchinello askance. Trott didn't like M. Aaron. M. Aaron was very rich; he was handsome and fairly young; he had always been kindness itself to Trott, had taken him out driving in his carriage with mamma, had brought him sweets, and called him his fine boy. All the same, Trott did not like him: he took his dear little mamma away from him too often, and frequently, when Trott came home from a walk he would find M. Aaron sitting close beside her, and he would be sent away with Jane very quickly. And beside all this, M. Aaron was a Jew. Trott knew that the Jews were the people who had put the poor little child Jesus to death when He had grown up. Trott remembered a picture which showed Christ hanging upon a cross, and near Him was a man in fine clothes who was very much like M. Aaron. Trott knew that M. Aaron went to Mass, but in spite of this he was still a Jew. Teresa, the cook, said so, and Trott agreed with her. . . . What right had *he* to celebrate Christ's birthday?

Mamma spoke at last:

"What a lovely Punchinello, Trott, darling! Our friend, M. Aaron, spoils you terribly!"

"I don't like Punchinello," Trott answered sullenly.

Mamma was astonished, and began to praise its good points. Trott scowled while she spoke, and then replied: "It has an ugly hooked nose like M. Aaron's, and I don't like it." Mamma laughed at this and made fun of Trott, but he felt hurt and ignored her remarks. In revenge he put the Punchinello in the corner, with its ugly nose facing the wall, and every now and then he looked at it threateningly.

But Trott's bad temper did not last. Eleven o'clock struck. Since it was a feast-day, Trott went to church with his mother. Dressed in his coat with the velvet collar, his fine yellow gloves, and his new cap with silk ribbons, he carried mamma's prayer-book and walked along by her side. At the door of the church a gentleman spoke to them. It was M. Aaron. Mamma thanked him for his present. Trott refused to open his mouth. Mamma made some excuse for her boy, and then, to soothe M. Aaron's wounded feelings, invited him to her house to tea. Trott was furious, he had never heard of such a thing happening before. M. Aaron seemed delighted; putting his hand up to his mouth, he said something to mamma in a low voice which made her laugh and even blush slightly.

They entered the church. Trott sat down and listened attentively to the singing, the liturgy, and the sermon. The priest told the story of Christ's birth in the stable where the cow and the ass were kept; he spoke of His grievous death, and he begged the congregation, in honour of the feast, that each one should try to give happiness to his fellow-beings, especially to the poor and humble.

Trott drank in the words of the preacher, and his mind was disturbed by conflicting emotions: he felt his hatred for the Jews and M. Aaron become intensified, and yet he felt a wonderful tenderness for the child Jesus, and he wished to show this in the way that had been pointed out to him. But there——! Trott was too unimportant to make other people happy; every one gave things to him, but he had nothing to give. Who could find any one humbler than Trott, and who was so poor that he could not help him better on Christmas day?

When he had reached home Trott began to meditate on this serious matter. His mother spoke to him, but he did not hear her, and she, too, fell into a reverie. At last a sound broke in upon his dreams and made him lift up his head; it was the voice of a little girl who always stood on the beach beside a grey donkey, ready saddled, on whose back Trott was sometimes allowed to ride. No, Trott told her, he would not go out to-day. The donkey began to bray its morning greetings to him, and the little girl struck it sharply to silence it. The sight of the blow made Trott most unhappy, and suddenly a light came into his mind. Was it not the little Jesus Himself who was showing him a humble creature he could succour? This poor beast was the only friend of Trott who was not feasting to-day; he was the only one who had no reason to be happy. Now, Jesus was born near an ass and a cow. Trott knew no cows, but he did know a donkey—a donkey like the one that had witnessed the birth of Christ. And besides, perhaps this was that identical donkey! Teresa had told him how very old it was! Trott was all a-tremble now with joy, and yet felt a little abashed to think that he had ridden on the back of an animal which might possibly have been the first comrade of the infant Christ.

During luncheon Trott thought out his plan of action. After lunching, his mother left him in order that she might write some letters and prepare herself to receive M. Aaron. Trott slipped out at the front door and ran down towards the beach: he meant to look for the animal and give it some dessert from the dining-room table. The little girl consented to entrust her charge to Trott, and they returned to his home together, Trott leading the animal respectfully along, and, in spite of his impatience, not daring to hurry it even when it paused to chase a fly from its bald flank. Trott made the donkey stand still before the dining-room window, and said to it: " Wait a minute! " then rushed into the room. Alas! while he had been out Louisa had cleared the table and there was nothing left. Trott would have gone to the kitchen to ask for some bread, but he knew that good works must be done in secret. He was heart-broken. He went to the window and saw the ass waiting outside. Seeing him, it raised its head and came closer with short steps and an expectant air. It stood in front of Trott, and seemed to look at him first in astonishment then with reproach. What! had he been deluding the unhappy creature with false hopes? It gave vent to its disappointment by loud braying. The harsh sounds smote Trott like a cry of despair and of sorrowful reproach. Tears came into his eyes: had he nothing to give to this friend of baby Jesus?

All at once Trott's eyes fell on the flowers which M. Aaron had sent and were now arranged in a vase on the mantelpiece, and again, as in the morning, Trott had an inspiration. He understood in that moment that it was his duty to please Christ by punishing one of His murderers and helping one of His friends at the same time. Seized with an almost apostolic fervour, Trott took the flowers in his hand, ran to the door, down the steps, and stood still in front of the ass. For a moment it smelt the flowers, then it tried them with its teeth, and ate them greedily. Trott watched it in ecstasy, his heart beating with delight. So absorbed was he that he did not hear the window of the drawing-room open, nor saw his mother, who had heard the braying, put out her head to see what was happening.

" Trott, what *are* you doing? "

Trott's ecstasy suddenly vanished. He raised his eyes. His little mother was frowning, and her voice was angry. Trott stood still, feeling vaguely that something was wrong.

" Come in at once, and bring me my flowers! "

Trott went into the house and showed her sorrowfully a shapeless bunch of headless stalks. Mamma cried out:

" Oh, my poor flowers! Trott, how could you do that to them? "

Trott was greatly troubled to hear mamma speak like this.

" You have done it to revenge yourself on kind M. Aaron and to hurt me. Oh, you bad, naughty boy! "

Trott, overwhelmed with these reproaches, stammered out:

" I wanted to please the ass. Our priest said we should think about the humble people. I didn't know you loved M. Aaron so much."

But instead of appeasing mamma, the last sentence made her angrier than ever.

" I don't love M. Aaron. I have a great respect for him, and he deserves it. He's a very good friend." And mamma began to scold poor Trott so very hard that his heart felt like breaking, and the tears began to flow. Even then she did not soften. She sent him into a corner of the drawing-room and ordered him to stay there quietly, so that he should be kept from committing other follies, if that were possible.

It was too much. Trott hid his face in his hands.

" Mamma, mamma, you have never scolded me like this before, —not even when I broke the beautiful locket poor papa gave you when he went away."

The little boy broke into a storm of sobs. For a long time he cried; then, little by little, his tears ceased, but a horrible, sceptical idea took root in him. He no longer believed in good or evil. The child Jesus had deceived him; the ass was treacherous; he must ask M. Aaron to forgive him; he had hurt his dear little mother, and she had scolded him, oh, so hard! Another sob, which he could not repress, rose in his throat.

" Trott! " said a changed voice.

Trott dared not take any notice of it.

" My own little Trott! " said the voice, even more gently.

Trott turned his head a very little, looked over his shoulder, and saw that his mamma was smiling to him. His dear mamma was angry with him no longer.

" Come here and kiss me, Trott, darling," she said, her lips trembling a little.

Trott flung himself into her arms; she drew him up on to her knees and covered his face with kisses. Trott closed his eyes and was carried away with joy. When he opened them again he saw that his mamma's eyes were laughing. Would he ever again be able to hurt her without knowing? . . . No, surely not, for mamma began to laugh, and then, gathering up what was left of M. Aaron's bouquet, she said:

" Bah! since it is spoilt, it may as well be finished completely. Take it to your donkey and let him eat the rest of the flowers."

Trott hurried off in high glee.

" After you have done that," mamma called out to him before he had gone out at the door, " when it has been eaten up altogether, run and bring me my writing-case. I shall write to M. Aaron to ask him not to come to tea to-day because I have a headache. You shall take it to him yourself with the donkey."

That night Trott said his prayers as usual, with his little mother standing by his bedside. And when he came to the clause, " Lead us not into temptation but deliver us from evil," something warm fell upon his forehead. But Trott did not feel it, for he had fallen asleep already.

M. AARON, PHILANTHROPIST

ANDRÉ LICHTENBERGER

TO-DAY such a jolly thing happened. Mme. Ray came to see mamma to ask her to take a walk with her as far as the Winter Gardens. Mamma hesitated a little, saying, first, No and then Yes, and when she had finally consented, Mme. Ray said with her slightly American accent, " Let us take Trott with us."

First of all mamma said, " Oh no, he'd be so much bother," and then Mme. Ray answered, " I'm sure he won't; he'll follow us about like a little poodle, won't you, Trott? " And Trott had looked pleadingly at mamma while he echoed, " Yes, I'll follow like a little poodle; really, I will, mamma." Mme. Ray began to laugh at his answer, and called him a darling, and this made mamma laugh too. He was hastily thrust into his blue jersey and his fisherman's cap with a big tassel. Then they set out in great style!

You can imagine how proud Trott felt as he marched along the road! With one hand he swung his beautiful cane, which had a bulldog's head in place of a knob; with the other he grasped tightly a ten-centime piece that Mme. Ray had given him to buy a cake or some barley-sugar. It was a brand new copper coin, and Trott felt certain that for such a bright piece he could purchase a particularly large cake or an extra long stick of barley-sugar. From time to time he half opened his little fist to see how shiny his penny was. He felt tremendously happy. And all the time that he trotted along behind the two ladies he was murmuring to himself that he was not really a little poodle at all, but a big, strong man, whose business in life it was just now to take care of the ladies and protect them from any unexpected dangers. His companions were quite unaware of Trott's important position, but he realised it thoroughly.

Oh, what a stroke of bad luck! There was M. Aaron coming out of a shop! As he stepped out into the street he was in the act of replacing in his waistcoat pocket a beautiful purse made of gold meshes. He recognised the ladies at once, and showed his teeth in a pleased smile. He hastened forward to meet them, raised his soft hat, and bowed so low that he displayed the back of his shiny black head, just as though he were at the hairdresser's. Trott suddenly grew very sulky. His eyes had a malevolent gleam as he took in all the details: M. Aaron had on a pearl-grey suit; his collar was a dazzling white, accentuated by the blackness of his beard; he wore a flower in his buttonhole; his tie was of tartan; his boots were immaculate; and in his left hand, on which two enormous rings were sparkling, he swung a silver-headed cane. Mme. Ray looked at mamma in a quizzical way, as though she wanted to laugh, while mamma looked rather displeased, and was blushing a little.

Were they never going to say good-bye to this gentleman? It didn't seem like it, from the way they stood there talking about all kinds of things. M. Aaron gesticulated and smiled, scratched the earth with the end of his cane, and puffed out his chest; he looked exactly like one of the fat pigeons that coo and bow in front of the stable that belongs to the Cosmopolitan Hotel. At last they had resumed their walk. But M. Aaron, instead of taking the outer edge of the pavement, walked beside mamma and continued his conversation with her. Surely that was not the right thing to do!

Evidently Mme. Ray thought this as well as Trott, for in a few minutes she dropped back a step and walked with Trott.

Suddenly she said, "*Look*, Trott!"

As soon as she had said this she put out her tongue and made a fearful grimace at M. Aaron's back. Trott laughed out loud, and at this mamma and M. Aaron turned round sharply. Then very calmly Mme. Ray told them a little story which she said had made Trott laugh, and the little boy could not restrain his mirth. He knew that it would have been a very ill-bred thing for a small boy to do if he had made a face like that, but it was most amusing in a grown-up person. Really Mme. Ray was very amusing!

They spoke about many things which were of no interest to Trott, but having nothing better to do, he listened to their conversation in a dreamy way. He heard Mme. Ray ask M. Aaron for some details of a fête that had been held in aid of the St. Mary's Hospital for Sick Children. Poor little children! Sometimes Trott had seen them when he had passed very close to the hospital garden: they always looked thin and pale, and were always coughing. He hoped that people had collected a great deal of money for them.

M. Aaron shrugged his shoulders scornfully. He didn't approve of fêtes like that: they were an excuse for providing amusement for the idle rich rather than a source of profit to the poor children. At least half the money, he declared, was frittered away in needless expenses. It was an extremely silly habit to clothe charity in this garb of amusement. When people wanted to have a little excitement, let them take it openly; but, when they were busy helping the poor, they ought to take their work seriously and give themselves up entirely to it, without considering themselves or their own enjoyments in the least.

Trott had only half understood M. Aaron's speech; but one thing was clear to him, and that was that bad people had been spending the money that ought to go to the sick children. Well, that was very wrong indeed. While he was speaking M. Aaron had been gesticulating with his hands, and his voice had taken on a very agreeable tone, and Trott thought that he looked exactly like a picture in his book of Sacred History which showed King David dancing before the Ark of the Covenant.

"You make out an admirable case," Mme. Ray remarked rather pointedly, "but don't you remember, M. Aaron, that even St. Martin himself gave only half of his cloak to the poor people?"

M. Aaron laughed—he always laughed at everything! He went on talking, telling anecdotes, and making epigrams, and at last he said:

"St. Martin was wrong. In a matter of charity I maintain that one ought to give either everything he has or else nothing. That's my notion of charity."

Well, that *was* a splendid idea, Trott thought. He could barely tolerate M. Aaron before, but now he was full of admiration for him. Teresa had been most terribly in the wrong when she had called M. Aaron an ugly, miserly Jew—but then, after all, he had said that he would give either everything or nothing, and, who knows? perhaps he gave nothing.

Suddenly the sound of a whining voice reached Trott's ears. It came from a poor old beggar crouching at the roadside, his clothes in rags and mud-stained. A bristly beard hung from his chin, thin hair trickled down beside his hollow cheeks, and his gnarled old hands held out to the passers-by an extraordinary object that bore some remote resemblance to a hat. He was so dirty, miserable, and pitiable, that any one would have preferred not to see him; but nobody could have helped taking pity on him, all the same.

Trott was full of excitement; what would M. Aaron do?

M. Aaron didn't seem to notice him. He went on laughing and telling stories to the ladies as if he had not seen the beggar. In another moment he would have passed on without knowing he was there.

But no! Suddenly he stopped. He thrust two fingers into the very waistcoat pocket from which a little while ago he had taken his little gold purse; he fumbled in it for a second, threw something into the old man's hat which made him call out loud blessings on him, and then continued to walk on and to talk jokingly, as if what he had done was the most natural thing in the world.

Trott's whole conception of M. Aaron was completely shattered, and in his eyes M. Aaron's face seemed suddenly to have become surrounded by a halo. Everything he had—everything! He had given it all to a poor old man, with a slight, quick gesture, just like that, without seeming to pay any attention to what he was doing. And surely in that purse he must have had a great number of copper and silver and gold coins. There were very few people who would do that; it was safe to say, *very* few people!

Then a hot blush swept over Trott's face. He opened his left hand, and in it lay his bright copper. He had never even thought of giving anything to the beggar. And he knew that he did not really need any cake or barley-sugar; he wanted to buy one or the other out of sheer greed. And perhaps the poor man had never tasted either cake or barley-sugar! A great bitterness engulfed Trott's soul. He looked back; but the old man had disappeared, and it was too late to turn back altogether. It was impossible, Trott knew, and he was heart-broken.

An abrupt halt of the party arrested Trott's melancholy, and then he found they were all going into the Winter Gardens. M. Aaron pointed out the refreshment room to mamma, and asked her if she would come with Mme. Ray and take tea with him. Mamma refused. But M. Aaron persisted, still smiling.

What a good man he was! He was much better than St. Martin even, for he had given away not only everything that he had, but he now wanted to give what he had not got! He had forgotten that he had no money left, and he was offering to pay for tea for these ladies. Trott was moved almost to tears. As for Trott himself—still, he would try to repair his fault. Ten centimes! Well, of course a little boy could buy much with that, but then perhaps a grown-up person might do something with a bright copper coin.

From somewhere about the height of his elbow M. Aaron heard a shrill little voice saying, "M. Aaron!"

M. Aaron looked down in bewilderment. He could see a little

fist held up above a little yellow head, and in the palm lay a shining copper coin.

" What is it, little man? " he asked.

" It's to pay for the tea, sir, because, you know, a few minutes ago you gave all your money to the poor old man."

Mme. Ray began to laugh heartily; mamma bit her lips. M. Aaron began to laugh as well, but he did not seem to do so very cordially. He stammered out a few words, such as " Good little chap! " " Well-deserved lesson," " Taken literally," and patted the astonished Trott on the shoulder.

They went into the refreshment room, sat down at a little table, and M. Aaron ordered tea and a big selection of cakes. A white-capped waitress brought them a number of good things to eat. Who was to pay for all this? Obviously it would have to be Mme. Ray or mamma, but M. Aaron didn't seem to be the least bit ashamed because of this, and to look at him any one would have said that it was he who was the host.

And, indeed, so he was. He put his hand into his waistcoat pocket and drew out the famous golden purse, where about a dozen gold pieces rolled about, and drew one out between his fingers.

Trott was dumb with astonishment, and his eyes nearly jumped out of his head. What was this? What could he say now, and what had he said a few minutes ago? What had he given to the beggar? Perhaps it was only ten centimes! Yet he had said that he would give everything or nothing! M. Aaron was merely a liar. Trott threw him a look full of hatred and anger.

M. Aaron held out the gold coin to the waitress. Trott suddenly jumped up on his chair.

" Please, I want to pay for my own cake," he said to her.

Proudly he put his bright copper into the girl's hand. At least M. Aaron should not have the satisfaction of paying for Trott's tea!

RUDOLF BRINGER
B. 1871

THE CAPTAIN'S LITTLE SECRET

WHEN it was learned by the town officials of Mondragon, a little place in the very heart of France, that Castagnol had just died at Tangier, and that he had bequeathed his immense fortune to his native place, so that it was absolutely necessary for some member of the Common Council to go at once to Morocco to take possession of this unexpected heritage—in this state of affairs there was no question as to Captain Lambounigue being the man who must go. Everything seemed to point to him as the proper man to make the journey.

In the first place, he had ample leisure, being a man enjoying a modest income, and wholly unoccupied. Then, he was a bachelor. Finally, he was an old sea-dog, who for more than thirty years had knocked about in all the countries of the world; and so this comparatively trifling journey could not alarm him.

It was only necessary to see Captain Lambounigue rolling about the streets of Mondragon to be thoroughly convinced that he was an old salt. In the first place, there was his costume, which he had never been able to abandon: his trousers with their legs flaring at the lower ends, his waistcoats of navy-blue adorned with gold buttons on which anchors were plainly to be seen. And the same emblem was embroidered in gold upon his cap. Even without this characteristic costume, his swaying gait and his continual tacking to and fro bore witness that the captain had far more often trod the deck of a ship than the quiet dwellings on shore. But if you heard him speak, doubt was no longer possible, for the captain never expressed himself but in nautical language, and his talk was richly embroidered with all the terms used by seafaring men.

Captain Lambounigue's story was a simple one, which he gladly told to everybody, and with which the youngest urchins of Mondragon were quite familiar. He had been born at a seaport, and was the son of a captain in the merchant service. As far back as he could remember he saw himself upon shipboard.

He had travelled to every country, sailed upon every ocean, visited all coasts, endured all tempests, escaped from untold shipwrecks, and he had always hoped to die on the sea, near which he had been born; but a diabolical illness had developed in him, a disease hitherto unknown, but terrible, which was called "salingitis." Yes, the captain had become salted, like an ordinary piece of fresh pork, by reason of having so long lived in the sea-air. The medical specialists whom he had consulted had all assured him that he would not live for three months unless he succeeded in unsalting himself considerably!

That was his reason for settling at Mondragon, far from the sea. And there he hoped that the warm sunshine and the fresh breezes and the wholesale fragrance of thyme and marjoram which came from the little hills would at last freshen him and so prolong his life.

He bought a little country house on the banks of the Lez, and he provisioned and rigged it like a ship. His delight was unbounded when, one happy day, he took into his service his faithful Figaou, who was a living caricature of himself.

Figaou was a native of Mondragon, whence he had gone away when about twelve years old, not having returned until he was forty, after a past which was entirely hidden in mystery. Upon reaching his native place, quite penniless, with all his kinsfolk dead, and incapable of working at any trade, he had presented himself to Captain Lambounigue seeking employment as a house-servant. Figaou was lazy as a sloth, mendacious as a juggler, drunken as a Pole, untrustworthy as a breeze. In a word, he had all the vices; but the captain received him joyfully, for Figaou, like himself, was an old sailor who had visited all quarters of the globe. He wore the pea-jacket and tarpaulin hat, he pitched to and fro as he walked, he chewed tobacco, he spoke the choicest nautical lingo, and he needed nothing more to make the captain consider him the pearl of servants.

So now it will be readily understood why the Common Council of Mondragon did not hesitate for an instant to commission Captain Lambounigue to undertake the delicate business of going to Tangier to take possession of the heritage bequeathed by Castagnol.

To tell the truth, Captain Lambounigue at first made a very wry face. This journey did not please him at all. He alleged the state of his health. His treatment had begun to operate. Day by day he could feel himself becoming less salt. Would not his malady become much worse if he suddenly went back to breathing the fatal air of the sea? But they told him that the voyage was so short that it was scarcely worth talking about, and, besides that, they would give him, upon his departure, an ample supply of thyme, the fragrance of which he could inhale during his entire journey!

Finally, they assured him that there was no one else who could go, for all of them were subject to sea-sickness, which would not trouble him in the least; and he knew Tangier and Morocco, and would be able to attend to the whole business. What could Captain Lambounigue say to all this? He accepted the commission, but without any enthusiasm, and when he went home in the evening he sank into an arm-chair and gave way to the blackest melancholy.

Ah, poor Captain Lambounigue was a prey to the darkest thoughts! Decidedly this journey was not at all to his taste. He sat brooding in his arm-chair for hours, and it became necessary for Figaou to inform him that his supper was ready. The faithful servant was at once impressed by his master's altered appearance, and, with his usual familiarity, asked him the cause of it.

"The cause, my poor Figaou," exclaimed the captain, "the cause is that we must weigh anchor and get under sail!"

"Get under sail?"

"Yes; for Tangier, and that at once."

"For Tangier!" Figaou repeated, his face growing noticeably longer. "But Tangier is far away, on the other side of the sea!"

"You are quite correct! It is two or three days' journey from here, and we shall sail upon the Mediterranean."

Figaou made no reply, but he turned pale. This voyage seemed to be no more pleasing to him than it was to the old sea-dog who had sailed over all the oceans.

"We were so quiet and comfortable here!" he said.

"Well, well! Do you suppose that this business pleases me? Still, we must go, all the same."

And three days afterwards they departed, very mournfully. At the railway station, indeed, in the presence of the Common Council, they bore themselves right gallantly, for the entire Common Council escorted them to the train. The good captain even squeezed the stationmaster's hand so vigorously that the officer could not help saying that the captain had a heart of oak and a hand like a vice!

But what a difference when they found themselves alone in their compartment! Leaning against the window, poor Figaou watched the disappearance of Mondragon, with its little hill, its ruined château and its dark tower, as though he never expected to see again his native place. The captain, buried in his corner, shut himself up in a mournful silence—he who generally could not keep quiet for more than half a minute.

When the tower disappeared at a turn of the railway, Figaou settled himself at the other side of the compartment and fixed his gaze upon his master.

"How calm and strong he is!" he murmured to himself with a deep sigh. "Ah, it is easy to see that he is an old sailor!"

They were silent, each absorbed in his own thoughts. Presently the train stopped and a guard called: " Tarascon! " Then the captain rose, as if moved by a spring, and handed his valise to Figaou.

" But we are not at Marseilles! " said Figaou.

" All the same, we get out of the train here."

" What? To go to Tangier? "

" Do not trouble yourself about that," said the captain with a confused air.

Figaou followed his master and with him installed himself in an express train which was just starting. Without trying to understand, he noted how they passed many railway stations. At last he understood, for, with all his faults, Figaou was by no means a fool. Instead of going to Tangier by water the captain meant to go there by land! No doubt because of the salingitis from which he suffered. And in proportion as they drew nearer to the frontier and, consequently, were farther removed from Marseilles, Figaou's heart recovered its wonted gaiety.

It was a long journey, a very long journey! All Spain to cross! But at last, one fine evening, they arrived at Algeçiras. To tell the truth, Figaou made a very ugly face when he saw the ocean in front of Algeçiras, raging and foaming. " We must cross! " he said to his master.

At the port the captain of a fishing-smack agreed to take them across the Straits of Gibraltar, a trifling distance, for a rather exorbitant price. Captain Lambounigue, however, made a very serious mistake: he paid the captain of the fishing-smack in advance and fully an hour before the time when they were to set sail.

An hour is a short time, but it was quite long enough for the fisherman and the sailors who formed his crew to find their way to a tavern and to get so outrageously drunk that, as soon as the vessel started, the three men rolled upon the deck and became insensible.

Captain Lambounigue, that hardy mariner, was already beginning to feel the approach of a frightful attack of sea-sickness; but the sight of the crew, quite incapable of the slightest effort, cured him as if by magic.

" Why, they are drunk, Figaou! " he said. " What are we to do? "

" There is nothing left for you, captain, but to take command! You understand that perfectly," answered Figaou, between two distressing hiccoughs. But Captain Lambounigue grew pale. At that moment the wind freshened, and the frail fishing-boat began to roll and to pitch in the most alarming way. Captain Lambounigue went close to his valet and said in a low, confused voice:

" Listen, Figaou! I have something terrible to tell you. I am no more a captain than the Great Turk is! All my life I have been only a simple Government functionary, the chief of an office in the

Department of Agriculture; and, by ill-luck, I employed my many hours of leisure in reading accounts of voyages. That is what induced me to play the part of an old sailor! You are not angry with me? Heaven knows that but for the dangerous situation in which we are placed I would never have made this confession!

"Now you understand why I did not embark at Marseilles. Listen, Figaou, and tremble! While I lived in Paris I was never able to travel on one of the little boats on the Seine, I am so subject to sea-sickness! So do not count upon me for anything about a ship. Take command! I will obey you!"

"Alas, captain! I, too, have lied!"

"What do you say?"

"All my life I have been nothing but a bottle-washer in a pharmacy on Rue Réaumur, and I am seeing the ocean for the first time to-day! In order to get you to hire me I made believe that I was a sailor; but I am really no more a sailor than a lead soldier!"

"Then we are lost!" cried Captain Lambounigue.

Luckily the wind drove the disabled craft on the coast for which it had started, and some fishermen rescued three men who were dead drunk, and two others in almost as deplorable a condition!

Lambounigue and Figaou, having recovered from their fright, were able to proceed to Tangier; but neither of them was ever willing to go back to Mondragon, on account of the voyage. The little house on the banks of the Lez was sold, and Captain Lambounigue settled for the rest of his life in Morocco, where he still lives, the happiest man imaginable, for he and Figaou continue to pose as stalwart old mariners who have dropped anchor in every port in the world.

PAUL RENAUDIN
B. 1873

ASHES

THE door of the night café swung back on its brass hinges and two showily-dressed women came out, followed by several men. The little group stood in the boulevard, which was already becoming deserted, and continued the merry conversation begun at supper.

A little woman with a thin black lace veil over her head had been standing waiting for some time outside the brightly lit bar, and as the party came out she walked stealthily past them, keeping well in the shade. At last she glanced at one of them—a very tall man with a pale face; and from that moment her eyes never left his face.

As the merrymakers parted, she hesitated, and then quickly went up to the man whom she had been watching.

"Excuse me," she said, "but are you not M. Francis Vernier?"

"What do you want me for?" he asked.

"It's for little Annette Blaise," she replied; "you know, the girl who used to be a friend of yours. She sent me to look for you because she is dying, poor little thing."

The young man started. As the woman uttered the girl's name, old memories revived and he was touched for a moment. But the cab he had called was waiting by the pavement and his companion was already inside it. He drew a sovereign from his pocket.

"Well," he said, "give her this."

The woman looked at the money which glittered in his hand under the light of the street lamp.

"That is not what she wants, sir," she answered. "She is not in need, even though she has nothing of her own. What she wants is to see you. She may die any moment. It is for a dying woman, sir, and surely a rich man like you could have a little pity."

Then, in a lower tone, she added: "You need not be afraid; it is not blackmail. It is only a fancy of the poor little thing, who still worships you."

A painted face and a large, flower-bedecked hat appeared at the cab door.

"What is keeping you, Francis?" the woman asked.

" It is a troublesome woman," the young man said in excuse.

" But you look worried, my duck! Is she telling you some unhappy story? "

" No, nothing of the sort."

" Then do hurry up."

He hesitated once more, but the woman came forward boldly.

" It is like this, Madame, and I know you will be pitiful," she said; " I am telling him about a poor, unfortunate woman who wants to talk to him before she dies. I swear that it is all out of friendship."

The scented lips, still moist with champagne and iced fruits, opened indulgently.

" Well, go on, dearie," she said. " It is lucky to do a good action, you know! Hurry up."

She pushed him away and left him standing alone with the poor woman on the pavement. A cab was passing, and he hailed it.

" Give the driver the address," he said angrily.

" Sixty, Rue Castagnary, Vaugirard," she answered rapidly, and got in beside him, looking tiny and bewildered, yet very happy.

The woman began to think how happy she was soon to make her friend, and sat still, not daring to break the silence. When she had promised a week ago to find Francis Vernier among the crowd of gay lads who haunt the boulevards, and to bring him to the dying girl, she had never thought that she would be able to keep her word. " He is very tall and pale, and has a curled moustache and pretty, closely-set teeth. He looks like a marquis." How often Annette had described him, always adding some new detail, even to the little scar on his chin which had come back to her memory! She had told her about his favourite haunts also. But Providence, which often gives a last chance to the unfortunate, had taken matters in hand.

" Has she been ill very long? " asked the young man without turning his head.

" Nearly a year, from what she says," was the reply. " I have only known her for about six months, since she came to live in the Rue Castagnary. Every one loves her, she is such a kind-hearted little thing; and then she saved my little boy's life, she took such good care of him. When that happened I vowed I would do anything in the world for her. Just think! For a whole week I have spent half my nights in looking for you, and people don't do that for everybody! And then when I go back I stay quite a long time with her. Oh, she hasn't got long to live now! Of course you will find she has altered a lot, sir. It is grief that has done that; and then, I am sorry to say, it is the life she has led as well. She has come down in the world since you knew her, sir. She came here with a hawker, a waster who used to beat her every night, and left her when she began to cough like this. She told me all about it, poor thing, though she is mighty proud."

All the time she was speaking the young man looked out of the window at the empty streets and avenues on the left bank of the river. This was a queer ending to an evening's amusement! He suddenly felt angry at the bad turn that fortune had played him; he resented being driven along with the poor woman by his side; he wanted to jump out of the cab or to bully the woman, and was haunted by a fear that he might be dragged into some awkward scrape and become ridiculous. All the same, he could not help listening to what his companion had to say. He had never forgotten Annette Blaise, with her great loving eyes, her vivid lips, her silken skin and warm heart, whom he had loved for a whole year, with the tenderness that one gives to a darling wife, in that little home of theirs where she lived between her sewing-machine and her crucifix. Since he had left her he knew that she had plunged into the vast maelstrom of Paris, following her star, for good or evil; he had been able to think of her without bitterness. But now that this wave had brought her, bruised and broken to his feet, how could he turn away his eyes and say that he knew her no longer?

" Is she really—dying? " he asked.

" Oh, I know enough about these things to know that she really is dying, sir. There are times when she would deceive you, when she is feverish and lively, but if you could hear her coughing all night long in the next room! And then, she is so thin; there is nothing of her! "

He tried to imagine her as he would shortly find her. But all the time it was the other Annette who came to his mind, the bright young girl who had come to him laughing and singing in all the joy of youth!

The cab stopped. Francis Vernier followed his companion into the passage of a humble house.

" It is Mme. Florent," she called out to the concièrge; " you need not trouble, M. Gaube."

They crossed a narrow and ill-paved courtyard, mounted a staircase without banisters and with steps so narrow that they struck against the toes, and then stopped at the second flat. Mme. Florent knocked gently twice and listened. Francis heard no reply. The woman glided into the room while he waited outside. He could hear some whispering going on, and then he was aware of a stifled exclamation that made his heart beat quickly. At last Mme. Florent returned.

" Come in," she said; " I will bring a light."

The room was full of the stale smell of poverty and ill-health.

He groped his way in, made out the bed from its whiteness in the gloom, and then spoke in quiet tones.

"It is you, Annette, isn't it? You asked for me, so I have come, you see."

She sat up. He went forward, took her two burning little hands in his, kept them from playing nervously on the coverlet, and pressed them gently. His breath and hers mingled in the darkness.

"Is it really true?" she murmured. "Oh, you are *too* good! I hope you will forgive me, Francis."

The lamp was burning behind him, on the mantelpiece. He could see her ravaged face, narrow temples, and the thin neck which showed from her half-opened night-gown. But in spite of this unhappy vision, her eyes shone, smiled and called to him as they used to do so long ago. It was Annette.

He smiled a little sadly.

"Then you have been ill for a long time?" he said. "And no one has been able to take care of you? I will send you a good medicine to-morrow, to make you well."

"Well? Oh, no; it is too late. And, besides, I don't want to go on any longer."

Exhausted by emotion, she fell back on the pillow and closed her eyes. Francis looked down at the Annette whom he had loved. The blood was coming back to her cheeks now, flushing her dying face. But every feature was marked with the stains of her miserable life.

"Annette," he murmured, "I have been a bad man to you. Why did you not send for me sooner?"

"Oh, I knew that you left me because you did not want me any more. I understood that at once. But it took me much longer to believe it. And then, later, I did not dare to send for you. If you only knew what I have gone through since then! When a woman is all alone with her—sin, she has to tread a long long path. But as for happiness and love, Francis dear, I have never had any one but you. I was really made to be an honest woman, you know."

A sob broke short her confession. With a sudden impulse the young man respectfully kissed the forehead of the unhappy woman.

"Annette," he said, "have you forgiven me?"

"Oh, I have always forgiven you, Francis," she answered, "because I have always loved you. Of course you have other girls; I have been only a tiny incident in your life; but you have been everything to me, you know, *everything*! When you first took me, you remember, in a room not much bigger than this, I gave you everything. I am not sorry that I did, because it is so good to be in love. Oh, Francis, how I have loved you! Only, when one gives everything, one doesn't give only one's own self; but much that belongs to other people as well. My mother and father, my sisters and brothers; I have given a little of their happiness and their honour. It is because of that that God has punished me."

"Haven't you seen them since then?"

"No, never. While I was with you, I wrote to them twice, without telling you, lest it should annoy you. I never had any reply. That didn't surprise me, you know, because my father is very proud; I was just as if I were dead to them, and I knew that perfectly. Then when you left me, I wouldn't go back to find them for anything in the world. I too have my pride. And besides, to show them what I had become; to give them still more trouble and shame,—oh no! I would rather they should believe me to be dead. A little sooner or later, what does it matter?"

A violent cough shook her from head to foot. Francis gently laid her head on the pillow and told her to rest. But she continued eagerly:

"I found that death was too long in coming. I had counted up my savings, and found that they went quicker than I. Then, a week ago, I opened the window wide, and sat by it, and stayed there for an hour. Death is very good, very sweet, when life is too hard. You must see me when I am dead, Francis. Yes, you must see me when I am dead."

She sat up, leaning on her elbows, her eyes wide open.

"Only, Death won't get a beautiful Annette! I am no spotless bride! Oh, why did I make you come here? Go away; go away; *don't* let me tell you these horrors! You hate me; I know you do! It is my own fault! Go away and let me die alone!"

Anguish marred her face as she thought of her lost youth; and she fell back sobbing.

"Oh, Francis, should I have been dead if I had stayed your little Annette?" she asked.

Deeply moved, he raised the head of the unfortunate girl and encircled it with his arm, as he had protected it in days gone by against the remorse of his love. And in this dim room where they sat alone, with those pictures on the walls which brought back to his memory the days of their happiness; in this room which still held the perfume of her presence, he could have believed himself to be back again in that little room where, four years earlier, she had given herself to him, had been folded in his arms as she was now, and was sheltered by his love against the terror of her sin and against the judgment of God and man. In those lovely days he had known how to reassure and console her; but to-day he could find nothing to say. He stammered—he knew not what.

"Darling, don't lose courage. We shall bring you back to life and health; there is no doubt of it. You only need a little care.

Now you shall have everything you want. And I will tell you what will make you better. Can you guess? I mean to find your father and mother, and tell them that you are in trouble and that they *must* forgive you."

The poor girl's face brightened immediately.

"Oh," she said, "you *are* kind! No, that would be too much; I shouldn't want to die any longer. But if only they could know that I was sorry, and that I had died better than I had lived; that is all I should want, Francis. I didn't dare to ask you to do this, but that is really why I wanted to see you so much, Francis. The other day Mme. Florent went to fetch me a priest. He was very kind and told me that God *would* forgive me. And I thought all the time about father and mother; perhaps they would forgive me too. Only, I don't know where they are now. But I will tell you exactly how bad a girl I have been. About a year ago I took my courage in both hands and said to myself: 'Mother must be very unhappy, and I must trample on my shame and go to see her.' Then I went to the Rue Foucault in Clichy, and blushed when I asked for Mme. Blaise. I had even put on a thick veil so that the concièrge should not recognise me. But she answered: 'They left here three months ago.' Then I went away, thinking that everything was all over, and I cried—oh, I cried, in the street. Afterwards I got the idea that perhaps they had had some misfortune, and that my father might have died. I ran to the factory where he used to work. When the workmen came out they told me I had better ask the foreman. I found out then that my father was working in Billancourt. I ought to have gone there, don't you think? But it was already very late. When I reached home again I would not say where I had been. I cried and got a thrashing, and the next day I hadn't the courage. Oh, it was terrible, terrible!"

Her breath was exhausted and her voice became strained. He made her stop talking. Then he promised that he would go away to make inquiries, that she should have their forgiveness, and that she should be happy.

"Thank you," she whispered; "you're very kind. I am quite happy now. Stay here for another minute, so that I can believe we are back in the old days. Francis, you were always kind, and you haven't changed a bit. Perhaps I am making you feel miserable; I ought to have died without your knowing anything about it. But I was so terribly lonely!"

She whispered the last words very low. He watched her close her eyes, and she lay still for a long time with one hand in his. The April dawn began to quicken outside the little window. He gently disengaged his hand; murmured, "I will soon come back again"; left two sovereigns on the mantelpiece; and went downstairs, groping along by walls, the steps and the doors until he was out again in the street.

The strange new sensation which he experienced in this deserted district, with its mean and unfamiliar houses and its narrow streets brightened by a misty dawn, seemed to prolong the dream from which he was now emerging. First he took the turning to the right and then the turning to the left, at once eager to make his escape and yet indifferent. It was only when he had at last reached his own house and the room that he had left after dressing for dinner, that he could feel he had returned to his normal life and individuality. Then in one swift moment he lived over again what he had undergone in the last few hours.

"Heavens," he exclaimed, "I never expected such an adventure!"

He had no wish to think over what had passed, but undressed quickly, so that he might sleep the sooner. Suddenly, changing his mind, he wrote a telegram to his doctor, and laid it on his dressing-table for his man in the morning; then went to bed and slept soundly.

The doctor's report did not come until late in the evening of the next day. It was quite formal, and gave no hope. It was useless to take the woman to the hospital; she had only two or three weeks at most to live.

Francis Vernier threw the letter into the fireplace where the embers were still burning, sank into a chair, and covered his face with his hands. All day long he had kept himself from thinking about her story; or, if he thought about it, he told himself that she was wrong and that she would recover if she were only well-cared for, and poverty and grief were removed; besides, he would take all on himself and would fully pay his debt. His mind had always been busy with other things; he had had but little inclination to take responsibilities in life; he had felt that everything would happen in the way best for himself. But the doctor's verdict now struck his optimism to the ground. "Poor little Annette!" he repeated several times aloud. Deepest pity gripped his heart; and suddenly, astonished to think that he could have made her suffer, and surprised at this new bond between herself and him, he murmured: "But I *did* love you. How ever could I have deserted you?"

In this warm, scented room, with all its pleasant invitations, playbills, memorials of bygone joys and loves, crowding the walls or laid upon his desk, the silence answered him.

"Whatever happens, she must have every possible comfort before she dies," he told himself. "I promised her that I would look for her parents, and I will set out to-morrow."

Immediately, so that his selfishness and natural indolence should not prevent him from carrying out the resolution he had made, he went over to his desk, sat down, took up a pen, and began to think how he could find the Blaise family.

But he went on dreaming about the task he had taken upon himself. Who were these Blaises whom he was about to track throughout Paris, urged on by this strange adventure? A household of ageing workpeople, with grown-up children, a daughter, and two sons who must now be men. Where did they live, and by what means? He tried to picture their looks and their home from the little that Annette had told him. But who would ever have believed that he would have to bother about people like that? Of course, on that evening when he had taken her to the room he had engaged for her, half as a surprise and half because he felt that he had made a conquest of her—this little work-girl whom he had met accidentally on the boulevards two months earlier—he knew very well that some one was waiting for her elsewhere; he had heard her whisper "Mother!" in the arm-chair where she had thrown herself weeping. But they had loved each other so deeply; no other souls had existed but just they two; and she had proved only more desirable because she had yielded so tremulously.

He cut short his dreaming and thought over the ways of redeeming his promise. Should he go to a private detective? No, that sort of thing was too ridiculous! The simplest way was to make inquiries at the dyeworks at Billancourt; perhaps to write to the managing director. He decided to do this, looked up the directory, and wrote two letters. If he were unsuccessful, at least he would have done all that he could.

Three days later a reply came, giving him all the information and the address he required: M. Blaise, employed by the Hallu factory for the last twelve months, 12, Rue des Peupliers, Billancourt.

So that was settled, and all he had to do was to carry out his mission. With the letter lying open before him, he began to think of what he should do, and for the first time the difficulty of the task came home to him. Yet it would make Annette happy. But, after all, the success of the whole affair depended on these people themselves! The father would not compromise his daughter's honour; she had told him so. Well, if they refused to acknowledge their own child, he would reason with them; he had no doubt of success.

He became quite exhilarated at the thought of their imagined resistance. Then he reflected that he ought to go that very evening and watch the workmen come from the factory, and came to the conclusion that he would have to start very soon if he were to be in time.

The next day was full of engagements. He thought he would let

Annette know what he had discovered; then thought it would be better to announce the reconciliation when it had been effected, so as not to raise false hopes in her.

But now he hesitated, wondering what would be the most propitious hour. Ought he perhaps to go in the morning to Billancourt, and find the mother there alone? Surely she would allow herself to be touched, for she was a woman and a mother. Yes, he would talk to her alone.

Or—should he simply write?

But as soon as this thought came to him, Francis unmasked it. This was the third day he had wasted since he had undertaken this commission. "What a slacker I am!" he said, took up his hat, and hailed a cab.

It was nearly six o'clock when Francis Vernier reached the corner of Rue du Vieux-Pont-du-Sevres. He got out of the cab and asked the man to wait for him until he should come back again. The sun was sinking into the gap made by the Seine, and shed its glow on the river, the high banks and the streets with detached houses; the air was full of the sweetness of early spring. Many children were playing under the trees or in the tiny gardens, bright with wall-flowers, which were before many of the houses. Women were gossiping at their gates, waiting for their men to come home. The evening meal was announced by the odour of cookery, wafted from the open windows and mingling with the perfume of the shrubs and trees.

Number 12, Rue des Peupliers, was one of these tiny houses, consisting of two storeys under a tiled roof, which could not hold more than two families at the most. A vine crept up the wall, and lilac-bushes showed green outside. Through the budding and still lace-like branches Francis noticed a young girl in one of the down-stairs rooms laying the table for supper. Instinctively he began to count the plates—three, four, five. Was this their home? He would have liked to loiter outside for a little to take stock of things, but fear of being noticed decided him, and he pushed open the gate. He walked down the garden path and knocked at the door. The girl came to open it.

"Does Madame Blaise live here, please?"

"Yes, sir."

He could have answered for her before she spoke. She was very much like her sister, not so pretty, and with coarser features, but like her in that curious indefinable way in which family resemblances come out. When she fixed her steady eyes upon him he dared not raise his own; it was with lowered eyes that he next spoke.

"Can I speak to her, please?"

" She will be back from the laundry in a minute or two, sir; I came out just before her."

" Then I will wait for her."

The girl took a chair from beside the wall and offered it to him. The polished sideboard, the folding-beds covered with chintz, and the cloth on the table, told of a certain comfort in this house; it was by no means the wretched hovel of the thriftless poor, but the scene of real home life. The girl had removed the plates and put them back on the sideboard.

" Please don't let me interrupt your work, Mademoiselle," said Francis, noticing this.

" Oh, that is all right, sir," she answered. With a grace and simplicity which doubled the value of her courtesy, she added, " I was really too early."

Several minutes went by. At last, in order to escape the silence as well as to avoid speech, Francis said, " I will take a little walk outside while I wait."

He came back, and his eyes fell on a photograph on the mantelpiece in which two little girls were pictured with their heads close together, their hair mingling. They had the same smile and the same way of saying, " See how united we are, and how fond of each other! "

He dared not stay in the room and went out again.

In the street men were coming home from their work, their bags on their shoulders. A boy of about sixteen or seventeen entered the Blaises' house with a round loaf of bread under his arm. And soon, in the distance, coming from the banks of the Seine, was a little woman, grey-haired, and loaded with a bundle of linen rolled up in a cloth. Francis followed her with his eyes until she reached the gate of Number 12. " She has no idea of the news I have to break to her," he thought. For a moment he let his mind wander over the day of a working-man, and his well-earned rest in the evening, with the father and the son coming in one after the other; and he thought of the girl who had not returned for four years and whose place was no longer laid for her at the table. Then he retraced his steps and knocked at the same door where he had been a short while ago.

" You are Madame Blaise, are you not? " he asked.

" Yes, sir," was the reply from the worn and worried-looking little woman.

Then suddenly he plunged into his story.

" I have been sent to you, Madame," he said, " by a lady who used to know your daughter Annette, and who is looking after her now. I am, unfortunately, the bearer of bad tidings. Your daughter is very ill indeed, and the doctor holds out no hope of being able to save her life."

Hardly had the name of Annette been pronounced than the wrinkled face of the little woman paled to her very lips, which began to tremble slightly, but she said nothing. Francis was more touched than he cared to be.

" She has not seen you for a long time, it seems," he went on.

Mme. Blaise lowered her head and shook it slowly. " No, not for a long time."

The young girl, who had put her arm protectingly round her mother, added: " My sister was just as if she were dead to us."

There was a silence in which only the old grief spoke: the true sorrow which this new blow had simply recalled and reawakened.

" It seems that she is most anxious to see you again before——" Francis stammered. " She knows she is dying. She has never dared to ask you to forgive her, has she? But I don't think you can refuse to give it to her any longer. I have been asked to tell you on her behalf that she is penitent and that she has asked to see a priest so that she may die a Christian."

A sob broke the silence of the lips which had for so long closed over their sorrow.

" We will go, mother, shan't we? " asked the girl, holding her mother close to her. " Don't you want to go now? "

The mother made an affirmative gesture, dried her eyes, and said, " Please forgive me, sir, but it's difficult to lose her twice over."

Francis Vernier waited to hear what questions they had to ask. But the two women were lost in thought. Sorrow did not rouse their curiosity, it was so familiar a guest.

Hastily he gave them her address, and was just about to go away when the door opened behind him and a man entered the house. He was tall, with hair and beard nearly white, and his eyes gleamed from his bronzed face. He bade the stranger good-evening, and looked at him slowly, steadily, and firmly. The same familiar look which had struck Francis a short time ago when he saw Annette's sister, now went to his heart as he looked at her father.

" Father," said the girl, speaking instead of Francis, " this gentleman has come here for some lady, to let us know that Annette is dying and that she wants to see us, to ask us to forgive her."

The man started suddenly; then, instead of answering his daughter, he said to the visitor, turning his head aside: " She was taken away from us long ago. We gave up thinking about her. We are only poor people, but we have our honour like every one else."

Then, slowly, having made this confession, he looked at Francis. The latter gave a sign of assent.

" Doubtless," went on the old man, " girls ought to take care of themselves when they earn their living, and we ought not to make excuses for them. But youth is inexperienced, and it is the others who are the real wrongdoers and criminals, because they know what they are doing. If I knew who had dishonoured her, sir, whether he were a plain man or a lord, I would crush him like that! We don't bring up our children in this house to live on their vices. There are plenty of girls on the boulevards, and there is no need to come and take ours."

Trembling, he shook his closed fist, and the stilted phrases he had used made his grief no whit less sincere nor his hatred less deep. He stopped himself suddenly as if to repress both these emotions. "You will excuse me, sir, won't you?" he said. "I know I ought not to speak like this before you, but I have suffered so much!"

He leaned on the sideboard and looked at the carpet without speaking. His daughter went over and stood beside him.

"You want us to go to see her, don't you, father?" she asked.

He made a gesture of assent.

"Will you come with us?"

He thought for a moment, then said, "No, go there by yourselves."

Then, turning to Francis, he said, "Monsieur knows where she is, I suppose?"

"Yes, at Rue Castagnary, Vaugirard."

The man seemed to be searching his memory.

"I lived there myself when I was young, near the railway. It is a poor part of the town! So she must be in great want, isn't she? These things always end like that!"

It was the old story over again, but it was his own. He went over it again to himself in silence, his forehead deeply lined, while the women made ready in the next room to go out. Behind him his two sons stood motionless. The setting sun shed its last glow in the room and lit up the walls with their customary brightness. But, though the men kept silent, they could hear the mother stifling her sobs in her haste to go away.

They were ready to set out. Francis suggested that he should take them to Paris in the cab which was waiting for him, so that they might see Annette the sooner. They accepted with some embarrassment.

"We have forgotten to thank you, sir," said M. Blaise, addressing him. "You must excuse us. It is even harder to show shame than grief."

The tears were falling from his bright eyes. Francis wished to show him his sympathy and held out his hand to him. The man took it and grasped it firmly. But their eyes did not meet; Francis had looked the other way.

Outside, he took the two women to the cab, gave the address, paid the man, and cut short their protestations by saying that he had some business to transact at Auteuil and would return on foot.

He saw the cab disappear in the distance, carrying the mother and daughter to the child who was awaiting them so anxiously. So now his work was over, and it had all come about so easily and happily. Now Annette would die forgiven and contented. He needn't think any more about it! But the part which he had just been obliged to play cut him to the heart. The man's handgrip burned his fingers. And they had understood nothing, suspected nothing. He thought of the stupid, easy solution, that any one of his own class would have proposed—a duel that would make no reparation at all, but might at least serve as a relief, and give one the sense of being a man of feeling. Before these poor people he had been able to look like an honest man; but he had done so only under a mask. . . .

He had come back now along the quay towards Passy. He was thinking about Annette and about their love for one another. Well, of course he had not deserved the hard lesson that Fate had thrown in his way any more than other men had done, but he had deserved it as much as they; and it went to his heart and his conscience. Then a furious longing came to him to shake off the lie which humiliated him, to see Annette again, to kiss her, and to ask for that forgiveness which he required much more than she. He found a cab and was carried away towards Vaugirard.

The darkened room was full of sobs. Annette, lying back on the bed, very pale, seemed to be waiting for death to come to her. Without taking any notice of the two women, Francis went to her and leaned over her bed.

"Annette," he whispered, "you are happy now, aren't you? Will you forgive me for the wrong I have done you?"

She opened her eyes, held out her arms, took the dear face between her two hands and pressed her lips to his.

Then, suddenly, he heard a cry behind him. The mother had seized his arm.

"Oh, it was you!" she cried. "It was you who wronged her! Out of my sight! Go!"

In his surprise he hesitated. But she placed herself between him and the bed, and repeated in a tremulous voice, "Go away at once! Go away and leave her to her mother!"

He drew back and went out without saying a word. He never saw Annette Blaise again, living or dead.

FREDERIC BOUTET
B. 1874

THE EXPERIMENT

MACPHERSON, the famous master of experimental physiology, tall, upright, his hands in his pockets, and his back to the fireplace in his study, leaned towards his listeners, Jeffries, the anatomist, and Moffat, the biologist, both men of world-wide fame; his face, powerfully moulded and clean-shaven under his short, white hair, was bent on them in fierce resolution.

" I took the liberty of calling you here this evening," he said, in a level voice that dwelt on each word, " to show you a dangerous and astonishing experiment which I am afraid to carry out alone. An ordinary man would not have the courage to undertake it. But the results may be so important for the whole human race that I cannot hesitate. Will you come into the laboratory? "

They followed him, silent and disquietened. They were friends of his—if he could be said to have any friends—and Macpherson had, that afternoon, mysteriously invited them to come at ten o'clock, and this in so abrupt and masterful a way that they had left everything in order to keep the appointment. His singular and daring genius always disconcerted them a little, and his lack of scruple in his experiments had already provoked some violent protestations and almost scandals. His preliminary speech now promised something very exceptional.

In the vast, closed laboratory, the high electric lamps poured down a harsh, white radiance. There, amid all the new, strange, scientific apparatus which was now familiar to them, the two men of science saw with astonishment an inexplicable bath. It had just been filled with hot water, for steam was rising from it. On one side, on a stool, sat a man clad only in a loose shirt and canvas trousers. He was livid, his shoulders trembled, and two pairs of handcuffs bound his wrists and ankles.

Towering above him, in a watchful attitude, was a young athletic negro, a servant of Macpherson's, who had been with him for years, and worshipped him with a dog's devotion.

" This man," said Macpherson to his visitors, " whom you see sitting here, tried yesterday in the street to murder me in order to rob me. Look at what he did."

He opened his waistcoat and shirt, revealing a long, deep wound over his left lung.

"But I caught him a blow under the chin, and knocked him out; sent him to sleep, as prize-fighters say. It happened just near my door, and I got my servant to bring the man indoors. I find he is Wilson, the notorious murderer. He has been practically condemned to death at two or three inquests, but the police have never been able to put their hands on him. Isn't it my plain duty to deliver him up and get him hanged?"

His words fell on a strange, heavy silence. The handcuffed man shuddered. Macpherson went on:

"But I have another idea. You know the applications I have made to the authorities for all condemned persons to be handed over to us for experiments in the cause of humanity. But there is so much silly prejudice that I have only discredited myself and my work by urging this most necessary reform. Well, now that chance has given me the power of life and death over Wilson, I have made a bargain with him. I won't give him up to the police, I will forgive the attack on me, and I will set him free and give him a thousand pounds, and arrange a free passage to any colony he may choose, if he will submit to a single experiment which, in all probability, will not end fatally."

"Whatever do you mean to do?" exclaimed Jeffries.

"I have discovered a serum," said Macpherson, "which I firmly believe can wholly take the place of human blood. It is, in fact, an artificial blood, possessing, I hope, vital qualities superior to those of natural blood. I say I hope, because I can't be sure until I have made a complete and definite experiment. This is where Wilson comes in. I shall open a vein in his arm in this bath. When his body is entirely bloodless, when, in fact, *he has been dead for several minutes,* I will inject my serum. It will, I feel certain, replace all the blood he has lost, and provoke the proper functioning of all his organs."

"What a revolution in medicine—if you are right!" said Moffat.

"Yes. If I am right," said Macpherson, "I may absolutely resuscitate Wilson. Of course, in every first experiment there are more chances against a successful result than there are chances for it. But there is a chance of success. I am positively sure of my discovery. So I have proposed to this man, already marked for the scaffold and the rope, that he should take this chance, and be born again, perhaps to a new life won through a pleasant, painless death. Wilson will tell you he accepts my conditions."

The chained man made an effort to swallow the saliva in his mouth.

"Yes," he said at last, in a thick voice, "I accept them."

"But it is impossible, Macpherson!" cried Moffat. "I will take no part in it. You are either going to murder this man, or else let loose again on society the most dangerous criminal of our time."

"If I come out of it all right"—the eyes of Wilson lighted up with wild energy. "If I come out of it all right, governor. . . . Ah, heavens! I'll go to Canada or Australia, and live as straight as a die!"

"I believe him," said Macpherson. "After what he is about to undergo, he'll fear death too much ever to risk his neck again. As for my responsibility . . . I don't suppose Scotland Yard will worry over the disappearance of John Wilson. So there remains only, my dear Moffat, a case of conscience. Will you see the thing through, or go?"

There was a few moments of silence. Moffat grew pale.

"I'll see it through," he said at last. "After all, he only risks a quiet, pleasant death instead of a horrible execution in prison."

"And you?" said Macpherson to the anatomist.

"Of course I'll stay," said Jeffries. "If you have discovered the serum. . . . What a gain for the whole human race! It ought to encourage you, Wilson."

"When you are where I am, you only think of yourself," said the man, in a dull voice. "But I've a chance. . . . And there's breakfast in prison, hangman, bandage, and the drop"—he shuddered. "No. Give me the bath!"

When the man, his hands untied, was lying in the bath, held down by the grip of the colossal negro, Macpherson came to him, raised his right arm, bent it, and rolled up the shirt-sleeve.

"You are still willing?" asked the physiologist. "You will not try to get away when the experiment is begun? You won't be able to then, I assure you."

"Go on with it," said the man. He closed his eyes, his teeth chattered. Macpherson leant over, a lancet in his fingers. The patient gave a slight jump, and a little red stream ran down his elbow; but Macpherson had already placed it in the warm water.

"You know what will happen, my friends?" he said to Moffat and Jeffries. "The pulse will grow quicker, the arterial tension will diminish, the patient will have fits of giddiness, a keen thirst, and then syncope will follow."

He stopped speaking. With his thumb on the right wrist of the man, who was now breathing heavily, he measured the pulse. Then by means of an instrument with a tube and dial he registered the arterial tension. A strange excitement came over the two assistants, in spite of their professional experience. The negro, upright and watchful, was like a machine of obedience. Macpherson remained calm. As for the patient, stretched out in the bath, he did not pant any more now. With pressed lips and eyes closed he seemed dead already. And the water grew redder and redder.

"The pulse is quickening, and the pressure diminishing," said Macpherson.

"I am thirsty!" cried Wilson suddenly, in a broken voice.

His lips were moistened, and a little while after he groaned twice. Slowly the minutes passed, slowly and terribly.

"I can't feel the pulse," said Macpherson. "The pressure is lowered. The end is near now."

"I feel . . . so . . . giddy," stammered a horrible voice.

The man opened his eyes—large, dilated—and they stared from his waxen face without seeing.

"Take me out!" he cried suddenly, making a feeble movement. "I won't . . . won't. . . ."

"Syncope," murmured Macpherson. "It's the end."

"No! No!" The man's throat rattled as he tried to speak. He gave a desperate effort as though to escape, but he could hardly lift himself up in a convulsive, shuddering leap. The negro held on his shoulders, with his great black hands. Wilson fell back in the red water, and his livid head tumbled on one side, lifeless.

"Syncope," said Macpherson. "He has bled to death."

Jeffries ran to the bath.

"It's all over," he exclaimed. "Now let us take him out of the water, wait five minutes, and inject the serum. The poor devil! He was plucky, all the same, and I should like to see him pull through. What a splendid thing it will be for you, Macpherson, if the experiment comes off!"

The physiologist smiled strangely.

"The experiment has come off," he said.

The two men of science stared at him.

"Yes," continued Macpherson. "I have not told you the truth. The experiment I have just made isn't what I promised to do. All we have carried out is a study in auto-suggestion. . . ."

"Auto-suggestion?" said Jeffries.

"Yes. Your meeting in this laboratory, this bath, my lancet, my talk were merely a fake to impress the patient. I wished to make an experiment in nervous impressionability, so to speak. This man has not been bled. He only thought he was, as you too thought."

The physiologist raised the reddened left arm of the subject, and wiped it, and held it up in the glare of the electric light.

"You see, there is no trace of bleeding. I only just scratched it with the tip of the lancet, and broke on the spot a pipette of warm red water. A simple apparatus fixed to the bath gradually tinged the water there. I dictated to the subject the feelings of being bled to death, and he reproduced these impressions, one by one, according to the indications given in my words, up to the profound swoon in which he now lies. It is a very curious experiment."

"It is more complete than you think!" cried Jeffries the anatomist, who had stooped and examined the subject. "The man is really dead."

"Well, it was only a condemned murderer," said Macpherson.

But, all the same, he grew somewhat pale.

PAUL CLESIO

THE MUSGRAVIUS MONOPOLY

MINERALOGY has come to be considered the freehold of the Musgravius family.

Georges Musgravius, founder of the dynasty, has occupied for the past thirty years the chair founded for him at the French Academy. His eldest son, Jean Musgravius, is professor of mineralogy at the Museum. His second son, Henri Musgravius, lectures on mineralogy at the Normal School. One son-in-law, Pierre Donon, is professor of mineralogy at the Sorbonne, while another son-in-law, Charles Bonniguet, like all the other members of the family, teaches mineralogy, but holds a less important position, being only a lecturer in the Faculty of Toulouse.

The fact that her second daughter was thus condemned to live in the provinces was Madame Musgravius' keenest sorrow. It was a great grief and privation imposed upon her that she was able to see this one of her children only three times a year—on New Year's Day, at Easter, and for a short time during the summer vacation. For this reason, when it became known that a new chair was to be founded at the Sorbonne for lectures on mineralogy, Madame Musgravius at once thought that this place should by right be given to Charles Bonniguet. With this idea in view she arrayed her husband in his best frock-coat, tied a smart white bow under his chin, and, giving him elaborate instructions for the interview, sent him to the minister to ask him to confer the position upon their son-in-law.

The minister had been expecting the visit for some days, and had prepared in advance the arguments by which he intended to refuse to grant the petition of the old scholar. He happened to have a candidate of his own of whom he thought very highly, a young man of great merits and promising future, and he resolved that he would force this young man upon the Musgravius monopoly.

The minister felt nervous, and prepared himself irritably for a scene when the door of his room opened and Musgravius entered. He addressed him in an abrupt tone which quite startled the professor:

" I am charmed to see you, my dear sir, and, as your visits are rare, I suppose you have something to ask of me."

" You have guessed correctly, Monsieur; I have been informed that you have decided to endow the Sorbonne with a new course of lectures on mineralogy."

" *I* have decided? *I* decided!—pardon me, but you seem to credit me with unlimited power. The Sorbonne demands a new course of lectures; the Superior Council is favourable; I simply agree."

" You are no doubt too modest, Monsieur, but the important fact remains that the course of lectures has been decided on."

" Have you a candidate to propose? "

" Precisely, Monsieur; Charles Bonniguet, a young man of great merit."

" Your son-in-law? "

" Yes, my son-in-law."

" Well, I will not deny that I have heard of the young man, but I do not wish to encourage false hopes, Monsieur Musgravius. This nomination is impossible, absolutely impossible! "

" What do you say, Monsieur? Has any one tried to injure Charles in your opinion? "

" No; no one has tried to injure him."

" He is a most distinguished candidate. His studies on cretaceous soils have even received notice from the Academy of Sciences."

" I do not dispute his merit."

" What, then? "

" You have the right to ask me to be candid with you, Monsieur Musgravius. If we do not appoint Monsieur Bonniguet to the Sorbonne, it is not because we consider him in any way incapable of filling the position. No, our motive is more serious than that."

" What is your motive, then? "

" Shall I tell you? It is because he is your son-in-law."

" Because he is my son-in-law? "

" Because you, your sons and your sons-in-law occupy every chair of mineralogy in Paris. You are creating a dynasty! "

" Well, there are other examples, Monsieur."

" I do not wish to know them. I am the sworn enemy of nepotism. I have promised to fight it whenever I encounter it."

" The sentiment does you honour, Monsieur, but at the same time you commit an act of injustice and, pretending to war against nepotism, appoint an undeserving candidate."

" An undeserving candidate! Is it true then, as people frequently say, that you imagine it is only in your family that mineralogists are to be found? "

" I make no such claim. Charles was my pupil before entering my family."

"Ah, on that subject you may set your mind at rest, for the young man whom I am going to appoint has also been your pupil. I may as well cut the matter short by telling you his name at once to avoid further arguments. It is Paul Granjean, who is at present a private tutor at the Normal School."

"Paul Granjean?"

"Yes. If I am not mistaken he has just written a brilliant thesis?"

"Yes, Monsieur."

"The report I have received concerning him is excellent."

"He is very young."

"So much the better; he will have so much more time before him in which to aid French education. Now, you must admit, Monsieur Musgravius, that in default of your son-in-law, my choice is a good one."

"Ah, it will be a blow to my wife!"

"No one regrets that more than I do, but at the same time I cannot make appointments just to please Madame Musgravius."

"But we counted on that course of lectures! Charles has a right to it. I submit, since you tell me it is impossible; but don't you think that you owe us some compensation?"

"Is he an officer of the Academy?"

"He has been at Toulouse for the last six years; he has the degree of doctor, is thirty-five years old and is still only a tutor. Couldn't you make him a professor? There is no chair of mineralogy at Toulouse. Found one! You do not want me to go back to my wife and tell her that I have obtained nothing, absolutely nothing. Really this much is due me!"

"I see that you are philosophical, Monsieur Musgravius, and I promise you I will do all I can."

"All you can! That is rather vague."

"I must consult with the Faculty, the Superior Council."

"Ah, if you really did wish it, Monsieur!"

"Of course I wish it. Well, you may count on me."

"The affair is settled, then. May I say so to my wife?"

"Yes, I promise that you may count on me, and Monsieur Bonniguet will be appointed professor."

The minister rose, as a sign that the interview was terminated. He congratulated himself on his victory, but was somewhat surprised at having met with so little opposition from Monsieur Musgravius. Holding out his hand to the old scholar, he said:

"You are not angry, Monsieur Musgravius?"

"No, I am not angry, Monsieur. Your choice is, after all, very suitable. My wife can console herself. Paul Granjean is affianced to our third daughter."

JACQUES CONSTANT

THE BETRAYAL

"At last, at last, Dmitri! Why do you frighten your Maroussia so? You leave directly after dinner without saying a word, and I have been awaiting your return, counting the hours, mad with anxiety. Where do you come from so late at night? What were you doing? Whom were you with?"

"No, I am not reproaching you, only I have been so afraid—I don't know why."

"No, don't joke. I know there are no wolves in Helsingfors, but there are men who are more ferocious than wolves. I know that the hospital of Saint-Vladimir is filled with wounded; that every night the soldiers fire upon people who walk through the streets after ten o'clock. It is dangerous to be out after that hour."

"Sleep when you are absent, exposed to danger? You know I could not do it."

"How did I pass my time? Crying, darling, and praying to God. Don't laugh, don't blaspheme, Heaven would punish us. As soon as I had put our little son, Sasha, to bed, I knelt before the image of the Virgin. My prayer was not in vain, for you have returned safely. You say you are thirsty? Have some of this vodka with water. Ah! I talk so much and I notice nothing! You are flushed, out of breath, covered with mud; you look gloomy and preoccupied, Dmitri, do you know that you have not even kissed me? And do you know that you went away without even kissing your son? Oh, bad papa! But—good God!—I hadn't seen it! You are wounded! Your right hand is covered with blood."

"Not your blood? What? You were attacked? You fought? You struck your adversary? Perhaps you killed him? Speak, tell me what has happened. You see that I had good reason for being anxious! "

" Some terrible mystery, and I must not know it! There are things you keep secret from me now. Still, think, I must know what you are doing in order not to compromise you. In these days a thoughtless phrase, an imprudent word, is enough to condemn a man to death or to Siberia."

" I understand now. I will say that you came home to dinner, and went to bed at ten o'clock as usual. If only no one saw you come in! I can guess that something very serious must have occurred. Why do you hesitate to confide in me, your wife? "

" I annoy you? You would not have said that to me two years ago. What has become of our loving intimacy, of those pleasant evenings we spent seated in front of the fire, while Sasha rolled at our feet on the bear rug, holding out his little hands and calling to us in his childish voice? You smoked your pipe, you know—the one that was carved in the likeness of Tolstoy."

"Dmitri, you are crying. Oh, why did you ever join this society of the Invisibles? "

" Don't deny it. I know it. A letter fell from your pocket one day with that horrible black seal. What were you preparing for? I don't know; but I do know that every one lowers his voice and looks about him in terror when the name of this mysterious association is pronounced. Besides, since you have been associating with these people you don't laugh any more, and you seem plunged in gloomy thoughts. You read books that speak of a better condition of society, liberty and justice, but counsel crime."

" Oh, it is possible that I do not understand. I have never studied as much as you have; only it seemed to me that Christ had already said the same things more humanely, more lovingly. Don't be angry, Dmitri; if all the world followed the precepts of the gospel there would be less suffering and less iniquity. Laws were not to be changed by violence, but by love. He who strikes with the sword shall perish by the sword."

" What do I care about the universe, Dmitri? You and Sasha are all the universe that I have, and that is why I am afraid when you leave me. My happiness may be selfish—so much the worse. Swear to me that you will not risk your life! There are plenty of men who have neither wives nor children; let them sacrifice themselves first."

———

"No, all rich men are not bad. Look at that little toy horse over there that Sasha received as a present to-day!"

———

"Who? I dare you to guess. Well it was a present from His Excellency, Prince Ourivan."

———

"Yes, the Governor of Helsingfors himself. But what is the matter with you? How curiously you are looking at me. Don't you remember that my cousin, Fedora, is governess at the palace? We met her this afternoon when we were out walking, and she insisted upon my seeing the apartments of the Prince. She thought he would be away all day, but he returned sooner than usual and entered the great ballroom where we were standing in ecstasy before the pictures and tapestries. But far from seeming to be annoyed, he showed us the greatest courtesy. Sasha conquered him at once; he took him on his knees, kissed him and complimented me on his looks. He thought he was very big for a boy five years of age."

———

"Why do you object to my accepting the toy which the Prince offered me so graciously? A refusal would have annoyed him."

———

"He certainly looks more like an honest man than a cruel butcher. I imagine that a good many evil deeds are attributed to him that he is in no way guilty of."

———

"Killed? How? By whom? Oh, this must be the act of some member of your terrible society. Sooner or later the assassin will be discovered and he will be punished as he deserves."

———

"You say he is prepared for death and martyrdom? Then you know him? He is one of your friends? I am sorry for him. But —how stupid I am! This inexplicable absence, this secret which you dare not reveal, the blood on your hands!

"This man might have been a thousand times worse than he was, yet he was one of God's creatures and you had no right to take his life. Oh, my darling, I feel sure that a terrible misfortune is about to happen to us. He who strikes with the sword shall perish by the sword."

. . . .

"Yes, your Excellency, I am the wife of Dmitri Propopov, lithographer; but, judge, I swear to you that I do not know for what reason they have brought me before you.

" This morning, when I awoke, the police brutally invaded our little house and compelled us to follow them. In spite of our protestations they took us to prison—my husband, me, and even this poor little innocent boy who is smiling at you now.

" There must be some mistake, judge. I know you are good and just, and I am confident that you will set us at liberty."

———

" The crime that was committed last night? "

———

" Prince Ourivan assassinated? It is horrible! I saw him only yesterday afternoon. He was such an amiable, good man."

———

" I met him because my cousin is governess at the palace. He gave my little boy a toy. Oh, this is a sad misfortune for Helsingfors! I suppose the assassins have already been arrested? "

———

" Dmitri suspected? But that is infamous, your Excellency. A man so quiet, so honest as he is would be incapable of such an action."

———

" You say that the information you have received about him is bad? Doubtless there are some people who hate him because he is proud and will not associate with them, because he earns his living honestly and fears no one. Besides, think for a moment, your Excellency: the crime, you say, was committed between midnight and one o'clock. At that hour Dmitri was asleep."

———

" Am I certain of that? Why, of course, I was lying beside him."

———

" You say my testimony is suspicious! Of course I have no one to corroborate it. My house is isolated, and we know few people. No one saw him go out that night, that is certain."

———

" Excellency, this is my son. He was asleep at the time, and besides, he is so little, he doesn't know. Sasha! Answer the gentleman! Do you love your papa? "

———

" Last night? Hush, Sasha, you're a bad boy. You do not know what you are saying."

———

" Judge, I will not allow him to annoy you any more with his babble! "

———

" It is false, your Excellency, it is false! The child has invented all that. You are crazy, Sasha! "

" I have no intention whatever of intimidating him, judge, but you can see yourself that he is lying. How could I have exclaimed: ' My God! It is midnight and Dmitri has not returned! ' when Dmitri was sleeping beside me? Oh, God! I tell you he was sleeping, sleeping soundly."

" No, you cannot, you must not believe what a child says. Your Excellency will certainly not credit his statement. He is subject to hallucinations, to nightmares—and yesterday, now I remember, he was very feverish. He dreamed all that he has just told you. Oh, my God, believe me, he has no notion of time. Yesterday or last week are all the same to him. Silence, Sasha! Yes, yes, yes, you know you are ill. But he is repeating it again and with an accent of sincerity! Oh! Children are terrible, your Excellency knows, and could cause a catastrophe without knowing what they are doing. But do not believe him, judge, do not believe him! "

" Oh, heaven, we are innocent! Be just, do not hold us under arrest! You have no proof! You could not be so cruel as to base your accusation upon the denunciation of a child who is only five years old, and does not know what he says. On my knees, Excellency, I beg of you; you have a wife, children. Sasha, poor child, get down on your knees and pray the judge to give you back your father."

" It is all useless. We are lost. My God! I do not believe in Your goodness and mercy any more, since You have permitted a child to betray its own father! "

GEORGES JAPY

THE MIRROR

It is really rather absurd to describe the Japanese as "the French of the East," as writers often do. For the fact is that these two peoples are in many ways utterly different.

In no respect does this inherent difference appear more clearly than in the innate vanity of the French baby-girl. It is said that these tiny coquettes will seize hold of a hand-mirror and gaze with insatiable delight upon the reflection of their own pretty faces; and that this ingrained passion for self-admiration grows stronger and more absorbing year by year. The French maiden of seventeen, we are told, likes nothing so well as the satisfaction of having mirrors all around her; and in the Palace of Versailles there is a room which for these young ladies contains all the bliss of Paradise. The walls of this great apartment are covered with mirrors reaching from the floor to the ceiling, and the floor itself is like a mirror, so highly polished is its surface. But such a room would be impossible in Japan, where feelings of this kind are unknown.

In the little village of Yowcuski, hidden away among the hills of Japan, such treasures as looking-glasses are unknown, and a girl cannot judge of her own appearance except by her lover's rapturous expressions. And a lover, as we all know, sometimes gives a rosier account of his beloved's charms than the mirror would afford.

In Yowcuski there lived a young man named Kiki-Tsum, who earned his living by pulling a rickshaw, for the convenience of any passenger who would hire his tiny vehicle and his swift, sturdy legs. One day this young rickshawman noticed a small pocket-mirror lying in the street, where it had been dropped by some foreigner travelling through the country.

Kiki-Tsum picked up this mysterious round object and scrutinised it with the profoundest interest. What could it be? He had never in his life seen anything at all like it. But as he looked, his interest changed to awe and reverence and wonder. A light-brown face, with deep earnest eyes and a mingled expression of fear and astonishment, looked out at him from the glittering jewel in his hand, and as he recognised the features he sank on to his knees in an ecstasy of devotion, exclaiming: "The image of my sainted father!

This is indeed a sign from the gods to me! How else should it have come here?"

He took out his handkerchief and wrapped it round the precious object, and placed it carefully at the bottom of his deep pocket. On reaching home he meditated long as to the safest place where he could hide it away, and finally chose the bottom of a deep vase which was unlikely to be disturbed. He said nothing about it to any one, having a sense that this miracle of his departed parent's image, revealed to him in such unwonted guise, was a thing too sacred to be mentioned. He said not a word even to his dear young wife, reflecting that "the curiosity of women is notorious, and they are not always innocent of talking about things."

The excitement of his recent discovery lasted for some time, and Kiki-Tsum could not bear to be long absent from his mystic treasure. He used to leave work and come home several times a day, in order to feast his eyes and heart with a sight of it. But such unusual conduct could hardly fail to arouse suspicion.

Japanese wives are much the same as all other wives, and are never satisfied until they get to the root of anything which seems incomprehensible or out of the ordinary. It was in vain that Kiki-Tsum protested to his fair companion that his sudden visits at all hours of the day were due to his desire to feast his eyes on her own pretty face. Lili-Tsee was at first satisfied with his explanations and his kisses; but when this had gone on for many days her woman's heart told her that something deeper lay behind these continual irruptions of her husband. And then, too, he always came in with such a strangely serious expression!

So Lili-Tsee, like many another woman all over the world, determined to get to the bottom of the mystery, and began to study the actions of Kiki-Tsum. She soon noticed that he invariably went all alone into a certain small room at the back of the house, before leaving again for his work. She therefore turned her attention to this room. There was no rest for her until she could discover the secret hidden there, but for many days she searched and searched in vain. At last, however, her diligence was rewarded.

One day Lili-Tsee opened the door of this little room suddenly, while her husband was there, and was just in time to see him replacing upon the shelf a tall blue vase which she used for drying rose-petals. She accepted with apparent composure his explanation that he was putting the vase straight, as it seemed unsteady; but she could hardly contain herself until he had gone, and then she ran back to the little room, climbed on a stool, and hastily lifted down the vase. Out came the secret treasure, and Lili-Tsee turned it curiously about in her hands. Whatever in the world could this strange thing be? Ah——! Now, when she looked into it, the dreadful mystery was revealed!

Could she really believe her eyes? There, before her, lay the portrait of a woman! And she had always been so sure that Kiki-Tsum was the very soul of honour, affection, and goodness!

The blow was too cruel! Lili-Tsee was utterly prostrated with misery. She sat on the floor, rocking her lithe body to and fro in anguish, the fatal portrait lying in her lap. So, then, it was to visit this woman's picture that her husband came home at all times of the day. This was the explanation of it all!

Then the bitterness of her sufferings flashed suddenly into anger, and she looked once more at the hateful woman. How could Kiki-Tsum admire a face like that, so dark and malignant as to be actually terrible? The eyes had a horrible look in them, which she had not noticed the first time she looked at the face, but which now made her shudder and forced her to put the abominable thing away.

But all the light had gone out of life for Lili-Tsee. The cruel picture fell into her lap, but she sat on, her anger rising to a great bitterness. When Kiki-Tsum reached home, there was no loving wife to greet him in the front room; no supper was prepared. He went through the house to seek her, and was greeted with a storm of reproaches which came as a cruel surprise.

"Is this the sort of love you have for me, then? Is it thus I am to be treated when we have hardly been married a year?"

"What are you talking about, Lili-Tsee?" cried the astonished husband, beginning to fear that his wife had gone off her head.

"What am I talking about? You should say, What are *you* talking about? To think of your hiding away portraits among my rose-petals! Here, take away your precious thing, and never let me see it again!" And Lili-Tsee burst into a miserable storm of weeping.

"I don't understand what it's all about," pleaded Kiki-Tsum, now utterly bewildered.

"You don't understand, don't you?" she cried, becoming hysterical. "Well, *I* understand quite well. You prefer an ugly, wicked woman like that to your own faithful wife. If she were only good-looking, it would not be so bad; but she is a vile, hideous creature, with a face full of every kind of wickedness. She might be a murderess, a cruel wretch, anything that is bad!"

"What are you talking about, Lili-Tsee?" asked the indignant husband, at last losing patience. "This is the picture of my sainted father, who is dead. I found it in the street some time ago, and I thought it would be safe in your vase."

At this shameless falsehood, as it seemed to her, Lili-Tsee's anger flamed up still higher. Her eyes blazed, and her words rose to a scream.

"Listen to that!" she cried. "Do you dare to tell me that I can't tell a woman's face from a man's?"

At this Kiki-Tsum lost his temper, and the altercation became a violent quarrel. The angry voices reached the street, for the door was ajar, and an old priest who was passing put in his head to see what was the matter.

" My dear children," he said benignantly, " what is the meaning of this wrangling, of such unseemly anger? "

" I am afraid, father, that my wife is out of her senses."

" My son, all women are more or less unreasonable," said the holy man. " When a man marries he is a fool to expect a paragon, and he must be content to abide by the bargain he has made. All wives are an affliction, and it is no good losing your temper with them."

" But she makes charges against me which are gross lies."

" They are no lies, holy father," cried Lili-Tsee. " My husband has a woman's picture hidden away in a vase of rose-petals."

" I swear to you," protested the poor Kiki-Tsum, " that I have no picture at all except the image of my father, of saintly memory."

" Come, come, my children," said the old priest magisterially, " let me see these pictures."

Lili-Tsee produced it. " There is only one," she said in a voice of cold sarcasm, " but it is one more than enough. Here it is."

The old priest took the mirror and gazed at it with rapt attention, finally saluting it reverently. " Dear children," he said, and his voice had an entirely different tone, " make up your quarrel, and let there be nothing but peace between you. Both of you are in error, and your delusion is quite incomprehensible. This picture is the sainted face of a holy and reverend priest, which I will take away with me. It shall be preserved among the most treasured relics of our church."

The holy man then gave them his blessing, and departed, taking with him the mirror which had been the innocent cause of so much trouble.

MARC LE GOUPILS

THE CROSS-ROADS

WHENCE she had come, and who she was, nobody knew at all.

The county police had never set eyes on her, and concluded that it would be a waste of time to make too deep enquiry into a matter which could lead to nothing. The entry in the register of deaths was simply:

"An unknown woman. Age supposed about sixty."

She was not even one of those ordinary beggars who have a certain round, and are known in the larger villages by some popular nickname, and whose social position the police can specify at once. She was a gipsy, an inveterate wanderer, living on the road rather by petty thefts than by charity, perhaps a derelict from some ragged tribe, prevented from following her companions by some illness, or it might be by drunkenness.

The only important point was that her death was due to natural causes, and permission for the burial had been granted at once. The Mayor of La Maladrerie gave orders that the tramp should be buried, in accordance with regulations, at the expense of the community, in the district in which her dead body had been found.

The death of this poor woman had, indeed, been the most natural in the world, and no fewer than fifteen witnesses were ready to testify to this. She had died at about eleven o'clock, near a gate leading into a meadow, at the side of the road, in the sight of the stars, one summer's night.

If she had been a drunkard, which was neither an impossible nor an unlikely supposition, she was certainly not drunk on that night. This had been stated authoritatively by those who had seen her and who had, they said, examined her thoroughly. Had she suffered from illness? Of course, since she had died. But it was unanimously agreed that her illness amounted to no more than exhaustion. About what age was she? Fifty or sixty years, who could say? Besides, they had been unable to get a word out of her about it, she was already so far gone when help had come to her. She had babbled a few incoherent syllables; that was all.

She had reached the hamlet of Carrefour-de-la-Forge at about half-past nine.

At the same moment the blacksmith's wife, nicknamed Mistress Nails, had come out to close the window-shutters. She had noticed this tall old beggar at once, standing in the middle of the cross-roads; she had kept quite still, but she seemed to be holding herself upright with all her strength by leaning on a long, knotted stick.

Seeing a carriage coming along at a good pace, Mistress Nails had called out to the beggar to keep out of its way, but she had made no attempt to move, and the carriage, in order to avoid knocking her down, had been obliged to swerve sharply.

Mistress Nails called out to her husband, who was inside the house, "Come out here, Philip. Perhaps you should ask that woman what is wrong with her."

Philip Nails came to the door-step. His wife and he looked first far along the road, for at this late hour both were naturally suspicious of the multitude of thieves and drunkards who wander about at night.

As the unknown woman, evidently frightened, but still standing stock-still, was mumbling unintelligible sounds, he went close up to her, and indeed walked right round her.

Mistress Nails suggested that she should wake her children, who were in bed and fast asleep, so that she could find out if this were the same woman whom they had seen a short time ago, when they had gone out to bring the sheep home, and whom they had spoken of as sitting with her feet in a ditch by the roadside, at a little distance from the village. But, on consideration, she remarked that their testimony could after all serve no important purpose.

At last the blacksmith went up to the poor creature, and spoke to her familiarly, in a voice which sounded kindly also: "Hullo, mother, you don't seem quite as well as you might be!"

There was no reply. Encouraged by this step, Mistress Nails in turn came forward, and both husband and wife examined the beggar. She was indeed a dreadful sight, but only because of her poverty and misfortune.

"She's a deader, I do believe!" the housewife pronounced at last.

They could not think what to do. They were good people and very neighbourly, as people often are in the country, but they were by no means well off, and could not afford much in the way of charity. Besides, they did not consider that they had any clear duty to fulfil to strangers and tramps, whose papers the police are always demanding, and against whom complaints are often made by workhouses, relief-committees, and parish councils. Vagrancy involves many dread mysteries.

Now this tall vagrant—for she certainly was one—standing there at the dark cross-roads, looked a very suspicious character. But, quite apart from the question of sheltering her it seemed only right to speak to her kindly, and perhaps to do a little more than that if her case were urgent.

" Are you ill, my good woman? " Mistress Nails asked.

There was no doubt about that. The poor soul nodded her head painfully, and, trying to find breath, made an effort to open her mouth.

" Good Heavens! " cried the countrywoman, horror-stricken; and, like the good soul that she was, stepped swiftly to the help of her failing fellow-creature. She put her hand under one of the arms that held the knotted stick so stiffly. " We can't leave her here! " she exclaimed.

" By Jove, that we can't! " the blacksmith agreed. But something stronger than he, some vague feeling which he could not have explained, came over him, so that his approval was only half-hearted.

" Come into the house for a little, and rest," Madame continued.

The vagrant made an attempt to walk, but her feet seemed glued to the ground, and her half-raised stick fell down heavily.

" Philip! " cried the blacksmith's wife. The man came at her call and took the other arm. Suddenly, while they were carrying rather than guiding her into the house, he suggested: " Suppose we let her sit outside on a chair? "

But his wife either did not hear or did not understand him: the poor woman was gradually led into the house, and seated in a comfortable arm-chair by the side of the fire.

" Can't you see that she's dying? " the blacksmith said sharply.

" Well, she looks like it, sure enough," his wife replied.

" Hurry up and see that she gets warm, so that she can go away soon," he said.

His words seemed reproachful, and his tone signified that it may not always be wise to play the good Samaritan.

" I don't want her to come to any harm," the wife replied.

" Neither do I; I want to cure her," he answered. " Didn't I speak to her first? But all the same, hurry up and get her warm."

With these words he knelt on the hearth, thrust in a handful of shavings, and made the embers underneath the ashes smoulder brightly, while the woman hurriedly brought brandy from the sideboard.

In the arm-chair, her thin hands clutching its arm, the beggar was gasping for breath, with her wan, bony, and corpse-like head thrown back. Her stick had fallen at her feet; and, slipping from her shoulder and hanging in mid-air, was an old and dirty canvas bag, full of holes; the string that held it had caught on the chair-back.

The fire burned briskly. A foot-warmer filled with ashes had been placed beneath the beggar's feet, and Mistress Nails, holding a glass to her lips, made her swallow three-quarters of a glass of strong spirit.

"My word, if I had that medicine," said the blacksmith, "I couldn't help getting better!"

For a few moments the woman seemed to have recovered. She could lift her head, utter a few sounds, and make a few gestures with her hands.

The hamlet of Carrefour consisted of four or five houses built at the roadside, and from these the neighbours came to see what unusual goings-on were taking place at the forge.

They looked at the dying woman, and felt an embarrassed and hesitating pity when confronted with the miserable rags of the vagrant and her besotted face, which had been ravaged by want and the vices attendant on a life which knows no hearth nor home. She was hideously ugly. Now that she had recovered her senses, she rolled her haggard eyes about in her foolish face. One wisp of grey hair strayed from beneath a dirty bonnet with cord-like ribbons.

Still, one must always help the dying, and all felt this duty so strongly that nobody uttered an inhospitable word. Each inwardly thanked his lucky stars that the lot had fallen to others rather than to himself, and every one praised highly the charity of the blacksmith and his wife.

"Wasn't I right, Philip?" the latter remarked, warmed by these compliments.

For some time they began to hope that she was less seriously ill than they had believed at first. La Fillotte, one of the neighbours, had gone home to look for a bottle made of thick and wonderful glass, the contents of which, an elixir, seemed to be a sovereign remedy. The beggar looked at every one in the room, and put several of her helpers out of countenance.

The hope that she would get up, take her stick and bag, and continue her journey under the stars, was strong in every one. They made fun of the matter, and then moralised: "These beggars are so hardy! They look as if they are dying; give them a glass of spirits and they're all right again. It's impossible to kill them! Curious life, all the same!"

Gaffer Durand, a gardener, and the most optimistic of the company, went out to observe the condition of the sky. It was a beautiful night: it would not become cool until nearly morning. This was very fortunate! For the unlucky woman, as well as for her hosts, who had plenty of troubles of their own, it had only been an alarming accident. In the house attached to the smithy voices rose in argument.

But optimism did not last long, and soon it became increasingly evident that the poor woman would die. Their uneasiness began to weigh on the observers. Making various excuses, several of the curious disappeared on tip-toe. A few remained, but looked as if they wished to follow suit.

"I wonder if I can put her out now?" the blacksmith said. He spoke interrogatively and not affirmatively, because he wanted public opinion to show him his duty, and he also wanted to give it a clue to the attitude he hoped it would adopt.

"I'm a Christian, by George!" replied Gaffer Durand.

Having said this, and Christian though he was, the gardener went away all the same. Yet, he added, in case he could help his neighbours, he would not go to bed just at once.

"My goodness, no, that woman's not going out," Mistress Nails declared in a firm voice. "We'll see what happens to-morrow."

The fire would have warmed any one but a dying person, for the evening was mild, and the room very hot. But there was nothing more to be done; on the pillow which had been slipped beneath her dishevelled and livid head the beggar was dying, and her breath came in rattling gasps.

About a quarter of an hour went by. The blacksmith suggested to his wife that he should fetch a doctor or the priest. Both lived a long distance away; but, since he was anxious to escape from the wretched scene, he did not mind that. His wife did not like to show him that she was afraid to wait there alone. But she made out that it would be a good errand on which to send one of their officious neighbours and counsellors. Her husband agreed, and went out to speak about the matter to the old gardener.

Durand had not yet gone to bed. He was talking to some one whose gig had pulled up at his door, on the opposite side of the road.

"Hullo, blacksmith!" the gardener called out. "Do you know what M. Vassort says? He tells me that if that woman dies in your house Blosseville will have to pay the funeral expenses."

"Yes, that's the law!" the gentleman in the gig added, turning to Nails. "And I imagine that the Mayor of Blosseville won't be too pleased about it!"

Then, only slightly interested in the story, M. Vassort whipped up his horse and was off at a canter.

Thunderstruck, the blacksmith forgot both doctor and priest. All he could think of was the terrible mayor of the district—the great, the old, and harsh Pierre Desfossés, whose anger nobody liked to rouse. And then what might not happen? The magistrate and the police would perhaps call on him. He swore he would have nothing more to do with the matter. A superior mind had rid him of the unpleasant task with which he had unwisely burdened himself, and he made up his mind immediately.

"In that case," he said, "I can't keep her. You surely see, Durand, the condition she's in. I can't keep her."

"I know, of course, what she's like," the gardener answered evasively.

But the blacksmith persisted. He wanted the other to realise that he was sending the wretched creature away only when she was dying, and he could do nothing more for her. But he saw something else, too; he wanted some assistant, or rather an associate, in a painful and delicate task. Gaffer Durand, greatly annoyed with himself for having suggested in any way the removal of the vagrant, followed him regretfully.

The blacksmith went back to his house with a firm step.

"I can't have her any longer," he declared.

Pushing open the swing-door, which at once began to close of its own accord, he put a stone against it to keep it open.

Briefly he stated the case to his wife; and she, without any false sentiment, approved of his resolution. The shrewd wife thanked Durand for giving her husband such good advice.

"One can't do these things all alone," she said to him ingenuously.

But they were obliged to set to work at once, for the poor woman could not last much longer.

"Fetch Gaffer Durand's wheelbarrow," she said; "it is better than ours. You can't carry that poor wretch: you'd choke her!"

Since it was all-important for their business that the beggar should be alive, they went off quickly. It was not from any religious scruple, nor from any superstitious fear, that these three peasants would not touch a corpse, but from a wholesome respect for the mysterious legislation which governs irregular deaths.

The wheelbarrow came at last, and both sides of the swing-door were fastened open.

The dying woman was carried out to her strange hearse by the three accomplices; her head lay on the pillow which the soft heart of the blacksmith's wife could not take from her, and her legs were made to rest on one of the handles of the barrow. Her eyes were already sightless and staring, and her breath came in slow gasps.

Once having cleared the door, the procession stopped short in the middle of the cross-roads. Where should they lay down this gloomy burden, which was certainly living, but was as certainly unable to give advice? It was a difficult problem.

Four districts meet exactly at the cross-roads: Bonnebosq, La Maladrerie, Blosseville, and Bretteville. The first two own none of the houses in the hamlet of Carrefour; old Durand had the only one in Bretteville, and all the other houses belong to Blosseville.

To which of these districts did the pauper belong? She had been standing on Bretteville soil, on the high road, when first discovered, and in the blacksmith's house she had become a denizen of Blosseville.

Gaffer Durand had no difficulty in finding that Blosseville had a right to rid itself of her, since she was not yet dead. He volunteered this information, but yet he would not permit that she should fall to the lot of his parish.

None of the neighbouring houses opened their doors, but the discussion was helped out by people at various windows.

"But, after all, it's quite an easy matter," Durand argued calmly. "Where did the woman come from? From Bretteville, of course. But where was she going? To La Maladrerie or to Bonnebosq? I am not finding fault with you, you know, but perhaps it would have been better to have let her find her own way."

The entire Blosseville portion of Carrefour warmly approved of these wise remarks. It was a man from Blosseville who had made the mistake, and the Brettevillian was showing himself a good neighbour, trying to redeem the false step his friends had taken.

"If you carry her only about fifty yards farther," said a voice from somewhere, "she'll be in Bonnebosq or La Maladrerie."

Her custodians hesitated between the two parishes, but the blacksmith's wife at last decided for the former, because it seemed to her that "the poor thing was looking more towards Bonnebosq" when she had first seen her. This argument seeming conclusive, they considered that she belonged to Bonnebosq.

Then they hurried off, the blacksmith pushing the barrow, his wife and Durand following. At fifty yards from the cross-roads they lifted the dying woman carefully, and laid her down as gently as possible beside a milestone; they then turned back, Mistress Nails carrying her pillow under her arm.

After they had walked a few steps in the peace and silence of the night, they heard a rattling sound.

"It's *her*!" said the woman.

"Very likely!" answered Durand.

"She has not long to live," the blacksmith remarked.

And they went on walking.

When they reached the cross-roads, the woman said, "Well, after all this, I'll bet it's past eleven."

At that moment a trap, coming swiftly out of the darkness, crossed Carrefour. The driver had to rein in his horse to keep him from running into the barrow, and he swore loudly. The pedestrians bade him good-night: he was Michael Leloup, the Mayor of Bonnebosq.

When he had gone by, the blacksmith laughed at the thought of the face Master Michael would wear next day when he found that a vagrant had died in his parish. But his laugh rang hollow: Master Michael Leloup, Mayor of Bonnebosq, was, like his colleague, Pierre Desfossés, one of those coarse peasants whom one is afraid to cross in any way.

A sound, the meaning of which was immediately clear to all, made them stop short: Michael's horse was shying violently in the road. What awful luck! The animal was afraid and refused to go past the milestone at the foot of which the poor woman was gasping her last breath.

Soon a storm of oaths broke out in the darkness, and a few minutes afterwards Master Michael, leading his horse by the bridle —for it had narrowly escaped throwing him into a ditch—came back to know why this dead, or dying, woman was lying at the roadside fifty yards from these curious specimens of Christianity who were wheeling a barrow at this unusual hour! This was indeed a pretty state of things.

They would have tried to lie, to say that they knew nothing about it, declare that they had left the vagrant where they had found her, had not the blacksmith been incriminated by the wheelbarrow, whose handles he still held. And, above all, the three were frightened by the authoritative voice of the doughty peasant who addressed them. They betrayed themselves at once in the confused and contradictory account that they gave of the incident.

Master Michael Leloup was neither more nor less sentimental than the inhabitants of Carrefour, and what angered him was the bad trick they had tried to play on him. He then asked if they were absolutely certain that she was dying. They replied that they were.

"Then you were going to make a fool of me! And you would have done if I had not passed!"

"You mustn't get in a temper like that, Master Michael!" the woman said. "There's no sense in that. We'll take her away again to please you. Come along with the barrow, Philip. Come on, Durand."

While this conversation had been going on with the Mayor of Bonnebosq, the other people of Carrefour had come to their windows. The smith now turned back with the barrow, and his wife and Durand went with him.

"She's not dead yet," said the smith, when they had nearly reached the milestone.

They could, indeed, hear her groans come out at long intervals.

This time, in their hurry, they dumped her on the barrow as if she had been a bundle, and Mistress Nails carried the pillow under her arm, without placing it under the poor creature's head again. The smith spat on his hands; then, lifting the barrow by the handles, trundled it along.

Master Michael, back in his trap again, waited until the procession had reached the centre of Carrefour.

"Now then," he said in a tone of relief, "good-night, every one!"

Without more ado, he urged on his horse with a click of his tongue, and disappeared.

The vagrant was once more at the spot where her strength had failed her, and our three burden-bearers were at their wits' end. But the whole of Carrefour was in an uproar about the dispute.

"Is she any better?" one of the neighbours asked hypocritically; he had been the first to slink out of the way.

"She's soon going to 'pass away,'" was the reply.

"Are you going to leave her there, in the middle of the road?" suggested one woman, who understood nothing of the whole squabble.

"That belongs to Bretteville," quickly replied Durand, the Brettevillian.

The vagrant, left alone in the wheelbarrow during this argument, continued gasping, a shapeless mass in the dim light of the starry night.

No one left his house: let the smith and his wife, who had taken the trouble to get mixed up with other people's concerns, and this old Durand, who had not got out of it in time, finish off the work they'd taken in hand! But from one window to another passed questions, replies, suggestions, denials.

"I can't hear her any longer."

"Yes, I can."

"It's a sad case of poverty."

"You should say a case of laziness."

"She was fuddled."

"They say she wasn't."

"Where are they going to put her?"

"Good! I thought I could hear the sound of horses' hoofs! What if it were the police? It's really a matter for the police."

And they made comments on the law about which they had heard a vague rumour. Some said it was iniquitous, others that it was very wise. But all agreed that it was the duty of the government to bury these folk, and, also, that the police should patrol the roads better.

But they also laughed at Master Michael's outburst of temper and at his way of taking care of his own parish. They approved of it and said he was a good mayor.

Doubtless the whole affair would merely have amused these country-people, wakened at such an unusual hour, if it had not been for the persistent gasping that came from the darkness of the cross-roads.

"Her bag! We left it in the house," said Mistress Nails, who had gone in for a moment. She threw the bag down upon the barrow on top of the poor woman.

"Well, good people," she continued, "it's time we decided what to do. For a quarter of an hour, Gaffer Durand, she was in Bretteville. She'll be dead in another five minutes, as sure as I'm standing here!"

Durand took off his cap and scratched his head for a moment.

"Do you know," he said finally, "what I think we ought to do? We ought to dump her down on La Maladrerie—it's a rich enough parish, surely! If you think this bad advice, say so; and, if they don't like it, they must get rid of her as best they can!"

La Maladrerie had no supporter in the hamlet to fight out the vexed question, and it therefore met with no objection.

The blacksmith entered at once into Durand's scheme, and he elaborated it.

"We'll put her at the gate of M. Petitjean's paddock," he said; "she'll be best there."

He did not explain why she would be better there than in any other spot, but nobody took the trouble to ask for the reason.

"Come on!" said Durand.

He now spat on his hands, in his turn, and wheeled the barrow along with a determined step. But he began to suspect that nobody was following, and so turned round.

"Well, really," he grumbled, "you must come with me."

"Oh, of course!" answered the smith half-heartedly.

It was only right: the treaty silently concluded between Bretteville and Blosseville demanded, in this act of mutual defence, that they should remain firmly welded to the end. The smith and his wife followed the barrow.

"Is she still alive?" some one asked.

"Oh, Lord, yes!" said Durand testily. "You may be sure she's still alive; very much so!"

In order that every one might judge of the truth of this assertion, he brought the barrow to a standstill. They could hear that persistent, heavy, choked breathing.

Then the barrow went on its way, and, turning towards Carrefour, it was swallowed up into the darkness along a road bordered by thick hawthorn hedges. It rattled along, going farther and farther away, for several minutes; and at last they heard it coming noisily back, rattling emptily along the stony road.

Durand and his fellow-conspirators went straight back into their houses. After he had cleared the door of his house with the barrow, old Durand could not restrain himself from saying, for the benefit of the inhabitants of Carrefour, who were waiting for it before going to bed:

"My goodness, no! I don't know whether she's dead or not. But, anyway, she doesn't make a sound now."

The windows closed immediately, and the Brettevillians and Blossevillians went to bed and slept soundly, while at the gate of M. Petitjean's paddock, on the La Maladrerie soil, leaning against a post, was the body of the poor woman who had come from nobody knew where; and her wide open eyes stared stupidly at the stars.

A. LE HÊTRE

TRAMP AND POET

"WHAT time is it, Bastide, my good clerk?"

"Five minutes to two, judge."

"Let us enjoy those five minutes, Bastide! It is so hot! Whose are those tomatoes upon the window-sill?"

"Those are some of the fruits of my garden, sir. This morning I pulled up one of my plants by mistake, the finest of them all, the one I had saved from the insects; and so I brought the poor tomatoes here, that they might ripen. It must be owned that monsieur the judge's room is so freely exposed to the sun——"

"That it seems made expressly to ripen your love-apples! You are right, Bastide. What the deuce are we going to have to-day? Some fine domestic drama?"

"Alas! sir, nothing but a simple tramp, but we must not be downhearted."

"I still hope, Bastide, I still hope! In the meantime let us examine Jean Clochepin, tramp by trade. A tramp! Good heavens, what a trade, and in such weather! Go and bring in this hero; it will be a charity to put him in the shade."

The judge let his arms drop along the sides of his chair. He had laid his cigarette close to his pen-rack; there rose from it a fine, silky smoke—a dainty keepsake from some invisible fairy's hand.

The judge saw in front of him, through the wide open window, the dazzling blue sky of a July afternoon, and the light tower of the college, which sprang up like a rosy stalk. A bee, that had rested upon a tomato that had burst open with a juicy laugh, bore away with his humming a faint echo of the snoring of the drowsy town.

At the same hour the sergeant and the substitute whom he had picked up dozed over their beer at the Café Tivoli. The professor of mathematics went back to his classes after having repeated to Mme. Graubjac, the proprietress, for the thousandth time, as he himself said, that her profile was growing more and more Grecian. The judge addressed verses to this lady, madrigals and sonnets, wherein he lamented her hard-heartedness. All this, however, was merely postprandial playfulness. The judge loved poetry, cultivated figures and rhythms, and in his court this was his only consolation and the secret of his even temper.

Weariness fell from the city walls with the grey dust of the plaster. The evening, with its quiet hours, was coming, when those good, motherly voices in the belfries would counsel folks to go to sleep. The judge longed to escape to some calm retreat—with a book of verses.

"Move on there! Quicker than that, you!"

The magistrate drew himself up. In front of him, under Buzenat the gendarme's black eye, and preceded by the clerk Bastide, the tramp entered; a tall, slouching body, bearded, and very hot. He had taken off his rusty felt hat, which looked like a mushroom. Two sea-green eyes shone under his bushy eyebrows, and his solidly planted nose projected over a red moustache. His beard foamed and flamed. He was dressed in an old suit of grey clothes, the colour of the roads.

The judge inspected his man with a glance. Then he let him approach without looking at him, affecting to be occupied with his papers and with the reports of the officers. This carelessness in regard to prisoners was the judge's favourite procedure.

He suddenly raised his head, looked at the man, and asked: "Your name?"

"Jean Clochepin, monsieur the judge, at your service."

"Thanks!" said the magistrate scornfully. "Jean Clochepin, you have already had dealings with the courts."

"That is true," said the tramp, bowing his head.

"You need not flatter yourself upon that account," said the judge. "For some days your movements have thrown the peaceful hamlet of Saint-Pierre-le-Fenille into a state of terror. You must have threatened the people or the crops, either by gesture or by words, or else the men would not have driven you away with pitchforks and pointed you out to the police."

The tramp replied in a calm voice: "Pointing out their field to them, I said to three peasants who refused me a piece of brown bread: 'Still, you have fine rye this year!' There was no anger in my gesture or my words. That field, monsieur the judge, was very beautiful. I love the dusty green of the rye. The ladies whom I saw last year all wore that shade of green."

Crac, cric, crac, went the clerk's impatient pen. One might have thought that it was a cricket learning to chirp. The judge bent down toward the worthy officer:

"You need not take anything down, Bastide. Do not fatigue yourself."

Then, turning to Jean Clochepin again:

"As to the ladies," he said, "you addressed unsuitable words to a young woman of Peyrilles, near the fountain. It was in the evening toward nine o'clock, fifteen or twenty minutes past nine—this type is not very clear. Nobody knows what might have happened if Grateloup, the postman, had not chanced to pass that way."

"It is possible, monsieur the judge, that I may have spoken some words of harmless gallantry to this woman, who I thought was very pretty, and who bore upon her head, with antique grace, an old copper pail adorned with flowers. But I can assure you that my words were in nowise disrespectful. Tramps, monsieur the judge, look at young women as at the blue sky of our land; they look with joy, but without hope."

"A queer, good fellow!" murmured the judge, who had been regarding Jean Clochepin with interest. "A queer, good fellow, indeed—but perhaps one ought to be distrustful. The happy warrior may be a rascal. Let us be wary!"

The tramp was getting talkative. The judge checked him with a gesture:

"Have you any papers?"

"Yes, monsieur the judge."

He placed a dogwood stick against the table and drew from his waistcoat a thick, fawn-coloured pocket-book, frayed, worn, full of folds and pockets, crammed with papers and plants, bulging like a poacher's game-bag.

"Give me that."

The judge took the pocket-book with a sudden movement, opened it upon the table, unfolded it, spread it out. There were ferns in it, pressed flowers, some blue or faded rose-colour on a pale yellow background.

"Why, this is a perfect herbarium!" said the magistrate. "Wait, here are some pages!"

The judge had come to a dead stop. He was reading. Sombre at first, his face began to brighten. The judge swayed his head back and forth, with half-open mouth.

"Is this your own?"

"Yes, monsieur the judge," the tramp confessed, embarrassed. "You know how it is! The length of the roads, the loneliness of the inns, the open air, the smell of the meadows, the adventures——"

The judge bent upon Jean Clochepin a face full of kindness.

"Will you leave me one of your poems?"

"If it pleases you, monsieur."

"Yes."

The judge glanced round the room: Buzenat, the gendarme, was stealthily drawing near the tomatoes; full, round-cheeked, swollen with rich juice, they temptingly diffused a warm and piquant fragrance in a wave of sunlight. Bastide, the clerk, his head upon his arms, was slumbering, a pleasant smile upon his lips.

The magistrate quickly drew from his pocket a five-franc piece and put it into the tramp's hand. The latter, having seen the movement, looked as if he would refuse the gift.

"It is the price of the verses," murmured the judge. "You are free."

And, rising, he himself opened the door for Jean Clochepin, tramp and poet.

GEORGES MAUREVERT

THE GOLD CHAIN

"*ESTÁ muerto!* He is dead!"

They believed him dead—impaled on the enclosure—killed instantly! From the entire amphitheatre a cry of horror rose to the dark-blue heavens.

The slender blade of Eusebio Moreno had bent into a circle and snapped like glass on the thick hide of the bull.

Miraculously spared, however, mute, haggard and ashy pale, the swordsman, his body caught between the sharp horns fast driven into the palisade, was trying desperately to extricate himself from his frightful position. The people grasped the situation and a stupefied silence at once fell upon the plaza.

The torero, Salvador Lopez, a wiry and nervous Castilian, nicknamed El Mico ("the Monkey") on account of his extraordinary agility and his small, dark and mobile face, leaped into the arena. He seized the bull by the tail, and the moment it succeeded in getting its horns out, with a supreme effort he pulled it back with so sudden and violent a jerk that the bull turned aside. Moreno cleared the palisade with a bound. He was saved!

"*Gracias!*"

He grasped Lopez by the hands and embraced him fervently, amid the acclamations of the multitude.

Already the bull was some distance off, attracted by the manœuvres of the chulos and banderilleros. Moreno, who had now selected another and well-tried blade, made signs to the men to drive the bull toward him. It was to be a battle to the death between the man and the monster.

The swordsman, an athletic Andalusian with a determined face, wished to try again the thrust that had so nearly cost him his life. Amid the breathless attention of the spectators he attracted the bull by calmly waving his muletilla, a cape attached to a rod. Right in front of the president's box he stood, with crossed arms, one foot placed upon the bench. The animal, a small Murcian bull, strong-necked, black and fiery, stopped in front of him, a sword's length off. His heaving breath agitated the blood-stained streamers hanging at his neck. From his muzzle ran thick slaver flecked with blood. With his round, red, fiery eyes he gazed at the swordsman as though hypnotised by the cold eye of his opponent. Fifteen thousand hearts beat high at the supreme and silent duel.

Suddenly the bull gave a long bellow, took one step forward and deliberately lowered his sharply-pointed horns. The arm of Moreno darted out like a flash, and a pale gleam of steel was visible. With lowered horns the animal staggered a moment, tumbled on his knees, then heavily sank to the ground at the feet of the torero, who stood impassive, his little sword still in his hand.

From the base to the summit of the amphitheatre a thunder of bravos went up. The vanquisher, splendid in his brilliant costume of red silk brocaded with gold, stood quietly wiping the bloody steel of his blade on the purple folds of his muletilla. Outwardly he was unmoved, but the delirious plaudits of the crowd filled his simple soul with the infinite pride of some barbaric king.

From every direction a frenzied tribute was poured on him. Hats, canes, fans, oranges, flowers and jewels flew toward him from all points of the circus.

A massive chain of gold struck him in the chest. The torero raised his eyes to the spot whence the gift had come and his face, up to this moment calm as a bronze statue, was irradiated by a flash of joy. Standing in a neighbouring box Lorenza Suarez, the beautiful interpreter of great tragedies, was wafting him showers of kisses with her clasped hands, her eyes aflame—Lorenza Suarez, the mistress of El Mico!

Moreno bent down and, amid the continuous rain of presents, picked up the chain and held it to his heart, bowing to the actress.

"*La oreja!* The ear!" shouted the crowd.

The president of the course, the Duke of Veragua, commanded that the ear of the bull be given to the victor. A chulo cut it off and, dropping on one knee, presented it to him.

"Don Eusebio!"

The swordsman turned toward the little chulo who had called him just as he came out of the plaza by a side door.

"What do you want of me, my boy?"

The boy carefully took a letter out of his pocket. "This is from a beautiful lady, Don Eusebio," said he timidly, his eyes cast down.

Moreno took the note and read:

"Follow the bearer. I am waiting for you and I love you.

"Lorenza."

Disguising his surprise and agitation, he asked: "And where are you to bring me, my boy?"

"To a villa near the gate of the city, on the cliff."

"Palacio de las Rosas?" queried Moreno, knowing that this was the name of the actress's villa.

"Yes, Don Eusebio. You know?"

"Very good. I shall not need you. I can go alone."

"All right, Don Eusebio. You are expected about eight o'clock."

"Thanks, my boy. Here, this is for you."

He put several pieces of money into his hand. The boy disappeared.

Moreno enveloped himself in his cloak, drew over his eyes his broad-brimmed felt hat, and, passing through the suburbs, made his way towards the sea.

He arrived at the beach as the sun was about to sink into the Atlantic. All along the horizon the sky was of a putrescent green; it almost seemed as if some cyclopean forge had overflowed and the fused metal, welling up, had circled the sky. Above the sun soared a long streamer of deep rose-coloured cloud, tingeing with its hue the white palaces standing near the sea. A profound peace brooded over the beach, broken only by the infrequent cries of gulls and the soft rhythmic breaking of the waves upon the sand.

In the west the sun was very near its goal. All at once it plunged below the horizon, drawing with it the long red streamer. In its disappearance the cloud grew vividly red, like a pool of blood betraying a murder.

A lurid light seemed to haunt the swordsman, but he did not know whether it was a reflection from the sun's last rays or the effect of the flaming eyes of the bull, which he had so fortunately poniarded, and to whose death he owed the happiness of being loved by one of the most beautiful women in Spain. But remorse haunted him on El Mico's account. Still, when one reflected what Lorenza's love was—! Six months ago Garcia was the favoured one; then it was Lopez, now it was he, Moreno. He would take his happiness, since it was offered to him.

He hastened on, leaving behind him the last villa. There was no longer anybody on the beach. At the extremity of the cliff, hidden by tall fir trees, stood the Palacio de las Rosas, which, by a whim of the actress, had been placed on the wild summit of the hill. He hurried on, longing now for the touch of Lorenza's scarlet lips, the intoxicating perfume of her hair.

"Bravo, Eusebio!" cried a mocking voice all at once. "Good! You are punctual at the trysting-place!"

A dark shadow flitted out of a niche in the rocks and advanced toward him. El Mico! He here, and at this hour? A terrible suspicion arose in Moreno's mind.

"Punctual at the trysting-place?" repeated he, in a tone which he endeavoured to make indifferent. "What do you mean?"

"You know very well, Moreno, you know very well. The note! Ha, ha!" El Mico burst into a bitter, sardonic laugh which reverberated weirdly along the cliff. "And the gold chain, Eusebio! Aha! Do you think I didn't see you when you picked it up? I know that chain well, for it was I who gave it to Lorenza."

"Mico, I assure you I did not know——"

"Ah! You didn't know, Eusebio? You didn't know? She sent you the chain—Lorenza—but it was I who sent you the note."

Moreno drew back a pace. "You, you?"

"I, myself, Eusebio! She loves you, the beautiful Lorenza—she told me so. And I—I hate you. Do you understand, Eusebio? I hate you like the devil."

He took a long knife out of his pocket. There was a sinister metallic click as he opened it.

Moreno drew still further back. "You want to kill me, Mico? And you saved my life a little while ago!"

"You saved mine a week ago. Now we are quits. And, besides, I didn't know then what I know now."

Moreno opened his cloak and bared his breast. "It is well, Salvador," said he gently. "Kill me, if you wish."

El Mico shrugged his shoulders. "I am not an assassin, Eusebio. I intend to kill you, but in fair fight, knife to knife."

"I have no weapon," said Moreno.

"That is nothing, Eusebio. Here is a weapon like mine."

He threw a knife at his rival's feet. Moreno crossed his arms upon his breast.

"I lied, Lopez. I am armed. But I will not fight with you. You may kill me if you wish."

El Mico came up to Moreno. "You say you won't fight, Eusebio? I say that you shall!"

He spat in his face.

With a cry of rage Moreno threw himself upon El Mico, knife in hand. "You devil! I'll kill you, Lopez."

El Mico stretched his arm out toward the cliff and said in a softened tone: "It is possible, Eusebio. But, first, come with me and let us pray to the Virgin."

He went toward a simple white statue concealed in one of the clefts of the rock. Trembling all over, Moreno followed him. The two men knelt in the fine sand, side by side, and prayed. El Mico rose first and withdrew a few paces. An instant later Moreno stood up.

They had thrown their cloaks upon the sand and were now face to face in their sumptuous apparel of the arena.

In silence the fight began, deadly and merciless. The first stars were piercing the faint blue of the sky; the silver crescent of the moon hung in the west. The pallid gleaming of the thrusting knives mingled in the fragrant twilight with the scintillations of the gold and silver spangles on the clothing of the combatants. Like a tiger El Mico circled rapidly around Moreno, with frequent feints, offering false openings, and ready to profit by any unguarded movement. Suddenly, with a loud cry, he leaped in the air—then rolled upon the sand, his throat pierced by the blade of his foeman.

Moreno dropped his poniard, closed his eyes with a groan, placed his hands on his breast and fell a few feet from his adversary. For a moment there was no sound, save that of faint moans suppressed by the pride of the dying men. A gentle breeze arose, wafting in a smell of seaweed.

"Eusebio," said Lopez in a broken voice, "it's all over. I am dying."

"And I, too, Salvador," said Moreno, trying to raise himself on one arm.

"Will you forgive me, Eusebio?" asked Lopez in a stifled voice.

There was a painful silence.

"I forgive you," said Moreno at last.

With an agonised effort Lopez dragged himself over to his foe, leaving a red trail behind him. "Eusebio, in ten minutes I shall be a dead man. Will you receive my confession? You can repeat it to the priest for me."

Something like a grin flickered on the face of the other man. "I need a priest myself, Lopez."

"Less than I do, Eusebio—less than I do! I know how I struck you. If you were destined to die you would be dead now. Listen, I beg of you."

His voice both implored and inspired hope in Moreno.

"I listen, my son," said he gravely.

"My father, bend toward me—I am very—weak——"

In a voice that could scarcely be heard, broken by moans, he whispered his solemn confession to the man who had given him his death wound. They were surrounded by a dark stain which spread from moment to moment over the rock.

"Bless me quickly, my father," pleaded El Mico.

"Die in peace, my son."

With his right hand Moreno made the sign of the cross over the dying man.

With a supreme effort Lopez raised himself on his arm.

"Now I can die!" he cried. His voice was stronger and clearer. "I lied, Eusebio Moreno! Do you hear? I lied! I know the thrust I gave you; in an hour you will follow me. No one will find you here on this lonely beach. And you—you cur—

you stealer of my love—you shall die burdened with my sins and your own—*unconfessed*—ah——!"

A crimson surge burst from his lips. He fell back dead.

SUICIDE

GEORGES MAUREVERT

SAN ROMANO! What a heavenly place! Here one fully understands the words of Flaubert, "There are some places in this world so beautiful that one has a desire to press them to his heart." What a pity that San Romano resembles an exquisite fruit whose taste is so bitter that we dare not eat it with impunity, since it causes death.

Unfortunately, the joyous peace that lies over the scene does not reign within the hearts of the people. On every side you meet sorrowful faces from whose lips these strange words seem to fall, "Oh, had I only placed it upon seven! The accursed *rouge*! Ten times in succession it won and I played *noir*!"

They pay little or no attention to the scenic beauty of San Romano. They are Œdipus in the struggle with the Sphinx Zero. The earth to them seems but as a gigantic *roulette* and the sky a slate of *trente et quarante*, for this is the Kingdom of Mammon, the Residence of the Demon Chance.

I, also, was a subject of his for a few months, lost a small fortune and became somewhat grey. One day, I wakened with only twelve francs in my pocket, and I owed the landlord fifteen. So I examined my pistol carefully and made sure that it was well loaded with six bullets, for these would certainly suffice to blow out a brain like mine.

I opened the window. "My last morning" was glorious—the heavens, azure blue; the waves, a shimmering green; and the air, heavy with the fragrance of the orange and the violet. I strolled down to the shore so as once more to breathe in the refreshing salt air; then I took a short walk and found that I was hungry. Before returning to the hotel, I bought a paper, the *Anti-San Romano,* a sensational weekly edged in black like a mourning letter.

During breakfast, I hastily turned the pages. The heading, "Suicides of the Week," drew my entire attention to it. "Here will also my death be reported within the next few days," I thought without much emotion. I even had a desire to thank the writer of my obituary in advance.

One notice, marked with a heavy black cross, attracted my attention and I read, "Yesterday, the body of Joshua Jacobson, an American, was found hanging from one of the palms that grow upon the terrace. The sum of three thousand francs was in his pockets—naturally!"

Joshua Jacobson, I had known him well—I might say that we had gambled away, side by side, one franc after the other. During the previous evening in the Casino, where he had lost his last penny, he had grasped my hand with much feeling, had looked sadly into my eyes and, smiling, said in a low voice, "I am ruined, utterly ruined! Farewell, my friend—" and went out, and—hanged himself.

Still, how was it possible that three thousand francs had been found on him, and what the devil did that "naturally" mean?

After a few moments, light began to dawn upon me. How stupid not to think of it at once! Of course the proprietors of the Casino had had the money put into his pockets so that we should not think his suicide due to his losses. That was self-evident. Then I began to wonder how much money would be placed in my pockets if I should carry out my intentions and take my life near the Casino. I think I had lost as much money as Jacobson. And then—suddenly an idea rushed into my head faster than the bullet I had intended for it. Excited, but with a light heart, I continued my breakfast. Then I went to the landlord, told him that I would pay him his fifteen francs that evening, "Provided," I added, with a sad smile, "that I am still alive."

"My dear sir, we trust you implicitly."

"Then," said I, "please lend me one hundred francs until this evening. I am expecting money from Paris."

"Certainly."

I spent the afternoon on the beach where, after careful deliberation, I planned the various steps of an advantageous suicide.

That evening at nine, I donned my best dress-suit, tied my most elegant cravat and went to the Casino. I made it quite evident I risked my last coin, and should have been greatly chagrined had I won. I lost, and assumed first a troubled, then an angry, then a meditative mien.

An attendant, who knew me, became interested in my fate. In low, sad tones, I told him of my ruin. He sympathised with me and sought to comfort me.

"You can still have your travelling expenses home, for the Casino makes it a point of honour to——"

" The way that I go needs no ticket," I interrupted with deep earnestness.

He looked at me, amazed. " You are not in earnest. You are not going to be a fool, I hope."

I remained silent and turned my back on him. Looking about carelessly after several minutes, I noticed the attendants of the Casino watching me. Towards eleven, the crowd of players arose. I went out among the last, hanging my head and looking thoroughly crushed.

The night was glorious. The moon bathed forest and sea in a flood of light. In the distance I heard violins. Deciding quickly, I directed my steps towards a great bush of rhododendron not far from the Casino, a place that seemed a fit setting for the joke I had planned. My hasty preparations were carried out in the presence of a marble nymph that seemed to smile, then—crack, crack, two shots rang out! I fell, not without care, upon a bench and waited. Voices in the distance came nearer and nearer, and shadows fell across my closed eyes.

" My God, it is he! "

" How awful, pierced with two bullets! "

Then the voice of the attendant whom I knew, " Hurry! hurry! before any one comes. Oh, the rascal, couldn't he have done this somewhere else? "

He bent over me and I felt that he slipped something into my pocket.

I almost choked. I groaned twice, slowly opened my eyes, raised myself with great care and looked in astonishment at the crowd. Unconcerned, I took my hat and my still smoking pistol and arose.

The crowd looked on with increasing astonishment. They stared at me as if I were some strange animal.

" This is unheard of! " I said angrily. " A man can't even kill himself without causing a sensation."

The attendant who knew me came toward me enraged. " My dear sir, I would—well, you—? " he stammered, confused. " What do you mean by this farce? I shall have you arrested for disturbing the peace."

" Disturbing the peace! " I repeated bitterly. " That is well said; that will become the watchword of the season. And I walked away, dignified but inwardly laughing at the crowd of people who had gathered out of curiosity.

I returned to my hotel and paid my debts out of the three thousand francs earned through my suicide.

The Bank made repeated efforts to collect the money from me, but it never entered my mind to return it, for I considered that it had been legally given to me. Furthermore, I believe that three thousand francs is not too large a fee for a suicide.

To vex them, I lived extravagantly for a few days upon the money and then went to Paris. Subsequently, I have heard that the sum bestowed by the Casino of San Romano has been considerably reduced.

A. ROGUENANT

A SILVER COIN

It was close upon midnight when Hector Merot left his office, after finishing the reading of his proof-sheets. During the previous week, when an article to which he had devoted an immense amount of trouble, and of which he had been justifiably proud, had been altogether ruined by a printer's error in its most important sentence, he had resolved never again to omit this precaution. He insisted on seeing a final proof each night, before allowing the next day's article to be printed.

It was a sharp night in early winter, and the wind blew chill against him as he walked along the Rue Montmartre toward the boulevards. The thought of his empty rooms was comfortless, and he turned aside as he came to a café, and sat down at an outside table, calling for a hot drink. He drank it quickly, for it was near closing-time, and the lights were already being turned out in the café; then he laid beside his glass a small silver coin for the waiter, rose from his seat, and turned to look for his stick.

At this moment, Hector saw a man glide swiftly up, seize the coin he had left, and make off hurriedly down the street and round the first corner. Pulling out another coin for the waiter and calling his attention to it, Hector ran after the thief.

It soon became plain that the man he was following was by no means a professional hand, and that he did not even know the district through which he fled. He ran forward blindly, dodging up and down one street after another, scared out of his wits by the pursuit, and was not long in coming back almost to the spot from which he had started. This odd behaviour gave Hector a keener interest in catching him, so that he might discover the reason of the man's eccentricity.

Himself familiar with all the alleys and byways of the district, Hector was able by superior tactics and by his swifter pace to meet suddenly, at a street corner, the wretched creature who was trying to escape from him. There was a lamp just above them as they stood together, while Hector sternly exclaimed, "Give me back my money!"

But then, as he caught sight of the other's face, his feeling changed utterly. The man stood silent and cowed, the picture of sheer hopeless misery. He was a young man, but thin and haggard, and his white face was made quite unearthly by the contrast of his dark hair and moustache. It was a desperately sad face, the most pitiable Hector had ever seen; and the man's clothes were equally worn and wretched.

Without a word the unhappy fellow held out the stolen coin to Hector, while the look of despair settled more deeply in his hungry eyes; and Hector suddenly felt that he himself was the criminal, standing before a silent accuser. Taking out his purse, he put the stolen coin into it, then, thrusting the purse hastily into the hands of the other, he turned away and passed quickly into the night.

Ten years passed. They were years of hard work and many struggles for Hector, but at the long last he had won for himself a recognised place in journalism and in the world of art. His critical pronouncements were undisputed. His articles on literature and the arts were read and quoted everywhere, and were eagerly awaited by his many readers. No other critic combined in such a high degree the qualities of sincerity, sheer ability and sound judgment.

Yet traces of those early years of trial still remained upon Hector, in spite of his present eminence, and were especially evident in that slight shade of sadness which had become so characteristic of him. This drama of humanity, which had been his life-long study, has so much tragedy in it, for those behind the scenes!

There was no mark of sadness about him, however, on a fair morning in May, the day of the opening of the Salon. Hector came briskly into the Restaurant Ledoyen, where many sculptors, painters, and journalists were gathered, and the more outstanding exhibits and their merits or demerits were being eagerly debated. There was quite a stir all round the room as he entered. In his usual careless yet cordial manner he shook hands with all who rose to greet him; then, moving to the little table where he always sat, he joined the two friends who awaited him—Paul Nielssery, the young landscape painter, and Charles Zirtius, the clever artist in water colour.

These three friends were always happy together; they shared the same tastes, the same love of art, and the same hatred and scorn of all that is base and unworthy.

"How happy you look to-day, Hector," Paul exclaimed. "Have you come into a fortune? Or where have you been?"

"I have been where all the world has been, of course," Hector replied. "I have been looking at the paintings and sculptures. There is one thing which is absolutely superb, a wonderful piece of work. It has given me an inspiration which will last with me for long!"

His two companions looked up with professional interest, and many at the nearest tables were silent, so that they might hear with their own ears the famous critic's verdict, which all the world would read in to-morrow's newspapers.

"There are some very good things in this year's Salon; but there is only one thing which in my opinion stands altogether above the ordinary. It is the kind of thing you only meet with once in ten years. I expect you know which I mean—Jean Meunier's 'Wreck.'"

The babble of satisfaction at the surrounding tables showed that Hector's admiration of the young sculptor's work was shared by all who heard him. The three friends went on with their meals, all of them in the highest spirits and enjoying themselves immensely; and general conversation was resumed throughout the room.

When they had reached their coffee, Charles Zirtius rose, and, crossing to the further end of the room, brought back with him a man of about thirty years of age, handsome, and well-dressed, obviously a gentleman. His dark brown eyes, full of intense passion, and not without a note of tragedy, were now gleaming with quiet joy, so that they transfigured the fine oval face. Fame at last had lent her laurels to his brow.

"Hector," said Charles, "let me introduce my friend Jean Meunier."

Hector sprang up and seized the sculptor's hand, exclaiming heartily, "I must thank you for a morning of the very greatest pleasure. Your 'Wreck' is a wonderful piece of work; no sculpture that I have ever seen has so delighted me."

The youthful artist glowed with pleasure at this praise from the famous critic, and gladly accepted their invitation to join them over their coffee.

The fine dark eyes with their unearthly earnestness seemed strangely familiar to Hector, and he studied Jean Meunier's wonderful face as they sat and talked, but without being able to remember when or where they could have met. He ransacked his mind for all the possible meeting-places—cafés, clubs, the studios of many friends—but all in vain.

Convinced at last that he must have been deceived by a chance likeness to another person, Hector gave up the problem, and was soon far too deeply interested in the conversation of his artist friends to think any more about it. The room was now almost empty. Summoning the waiter, he paid for their dinner, laying the money on the table. One silver coin, destined for the waiter himself, was hidden by the rim of a plate, so that the man failed to notice it, until Hector called after him, "Here, take this!"

Jean Meunier looked up swiftly at these words, and glanced from the coin to Hector, shivering as if deadly cold, while his face became ghastly white and his eyes gleamed with sudden terror. Immediately, Hector saw in a flash that face of hopeless misery which he had seen years ago under the street lamp, on that night in November. He turned to the young man with a gaze of friendship and understanding; and as the little party rose from the table, held out his hand in friendship. Jean Meunier seized it, and the fervent pressure of his clasp held all the grateful devotion of a lifetime.

The intimacy thus begun grew closer day by day; and at last the day came when Hector heard the story of the terrible straits from which he had saved the young sculptor when on the verge of despair, and when his little sister was at the point of death. This sister was now twenty years of age, and was the darling of her brother's life. She was a joyous, radiant, lovely girl, and filled Jean's home with sunshine.

Hector's steps turned ever more frequently to that happy place, and by degrees all melancholy vanished from his expression. Not many months had passed before a notice appeared in the papers: "A marriage will shortly take place between Hector Merot, the well-known art-critic, and Mlle. Hélène Meunier, sister of Jean Meunier, sculptor of that celebrated work, 'The Wreck.'"

MAURICE SAINT-AGUET

THE CROISSEY YEW

I

I AM going to tell you, monsieur, why I come every evening to smoke my pipe under the Croissey Yew.

My story goes back to the end of the year 1812. Brought up by an old uncle, the curé of a neighbouring village, and having already a footing in the Pope's army, I had escaped the requisitions of the Emperor; as an ecclesiastic the conscription had spared me. But almost at the same time my old uncle died, and the worthy man, from having given all he possessed to the poor, even to the shirt off his back, had nothing to leave to his nephew but the poverty from which he had drawn others. There was I, then, at twenty, free, alone in the world, without means, and full of disgust at my calling, but undecided as to all others; in short, in that state in which one is at the mercy of mere chance.

I have told you that I loved to dream, while waiting for the means of living; and I often came to this spot to rebuild the "Château en Espagne" I had reared the night before, and which had crumbled in the interval. But I had wearied of standing at the foot of this colossal yew tree which covers in and freezes us with its shade, and which stands on the edge of the precipice expressly to shelter the spectator, and I had established a sort of dwelling-place in its branches, where I succeeded in making myself believe that I was isolated like an eagle on the watch, and secure from discovery as the most confirmed misanthrope or dullest philosopher could desire to be.

One evening I was at my post. The moon was rising. Suddenly I heard something below me: it was the voice, or rather the sob, of a woman, saying:

"The last time!"

Then I heard something which sounded to me extremely like a kiss, followed by the voice of a man, replying:

"Come, come, Louise; a little courage!"

Another voice, that of a young girl, soft but decided, then said:

"No, no—not the last time—I will not have it so, I tell you!"

Considerably mystified by this stray fragment of conversation, I peered through the branches, and perceived in the moonlight a young man in the dress of a workman, having in his hat the bow of ribbons and the fatal number. He was supporting with his right arm a young girl, who was weeping on his bosom, and giving his left hand to another and smaller girl, who was not weeping. It was she, doubtless, who had said, " I will not have it so." I quickly understood that it was the conscript's parting that was taking place.

" Poor Christine," replied the young man, smiling sadly; " your will goes for nothing in this matter, sister—I am not the master."

" But, brother, it is you who have reared me, you are the father of the family! You must not go away—besides, you are married, for you are betrothed to Louise—who does nothing but weep, as if *that* would do anything! "

And the pretty rebel, who in the moonlight appeared to be charming, fell to crying too. Louise replied in a voice broken by sobs:

" Christine—is unreasonable—isn't she, Eugène—unreasonable? "

" My poor dears! " replied Eugène tenderly pressing them to his bosom.

" Well, then, Louise," cried Christine suddenly, " prove to me the strength of your courage! Since he will not listen to either of us—since he believes that we can do nothing for him—you see the quarry before us; it is deep and goes straight down from the brink—come with me! "

And, completely losing her head, she took the hands of Louise and drew her from the arms of Eugène.

" Are you both mad? " cried Eugène. " Can't you see that I must go with the others to fight for France?—for you?—for the cross? Louise, Christine, I shall return in eight years, and if I do not find my sister and my beloved one then, what will there be left for me? Do you wish me also to kill myself?—that I should not have the memory of you in my heart, to make me fight like a lion, to bring you back a pair of epaulettes? Let me go; one only has to serve one's time, and all is said."

" Oh, his time! " replied Christine. " There was Stephane, the mechanic, who went away with the others to Russia: *he* served his time—he died at Moscow—and his mother is in mourning for him. The others, will they ever come back. His time! with their dog of an Emper——"

" Will you hold your tongue? " interrupted Eugène, clapping his hand over her mouth.

" No, I will not hold my tongue! Haven't you a colonel—he who enrolled you? Well, go to him, throw yourself on your knees before him and say, ' Monseigneur, I don't want to go with you—I don't want to be killed. I have a sister and a wife who cannot live without me, and who will throw themselves into the river if I am taken from them. Beat me, Colonel—put me in prison, but don't take me away for a soldier. Long live the Emperor!—he's a worthy man; let him leave me in peace and go wherever he likes. Look you, Colonel, I am a man, I am free, and I have no right to leave my sister Christine against her will—and she'll detest you, Colonel, if you compel me to go.' "

"That would be pretty conduct on the part of a soldier!" replied Eugène, who could not help laughing.

"Unfeeling, cruel brother!" she cried, in tears, throwing herself into the arms of Louise.

II

A moment of silence followed. I was deeply touched—so absorbed in the situation, that I forgot my own. Presently Christine raised herself, and was apparently a little more calm.

"Heavens!" she said, "is there not a man—a comrade— who will replace you? Others have means. Oh, how I would love him!"

"It could all be done as you say," assented Eugène, "only to do it we need money—and that by to-morrow."

"Well," cried Christine, "I'll give all I have—my gold cross, my earrings, my neck-handkerchiefs, my lace collars, all my jewellery—to whoever will go in your place."

"All that would not make the price of a man," replied Eugène.

Christine reflected for a while, and then, seizing her brother's arm, said:

"But I—I am worth a man—more than a man; I am sure I am! I'll give myself; I'll say to some one: 'Go instead of my brother, and I'll be your wife! See! I'm good-looking—a little overpetted, but that's no harm. I'll love you so dearly, if you save my brother!'—I swear it on the gold cross in which there is a lock of my mother's white hair! I'll cheerfully marry whoever will devote himself for you."

"Good sister, I know you would do all you say, but you are overexcited to-night, and do not see how utterly impracticable are all your dear follies. Let us get away from here," he added, laughingly, "for if you go on, I shall really become afraid of the precipice before us."

I could not catch what Christine said in reply, and presently I lost sight of all three in the shadow of the trees; but both my head and my heart remained filled with the charming girl, and I became lost in thought.

That evening, as they were seated at their supper without being able to eat a morsel, and gazing at each other through their tears, somebody knocked loudly at the door.

" Come in! " cried the young man, hastily drying his eyes.

An old sergeant appeared before them and said:

" Good evening! Does the conscript Eugène Livou live here? "

" Yes, sergeant."

" That's for you, then," said the trooper, throwing a letter on the table.

Eugène read, at first slowly, then devouring the contents. It was a release in form!

He looked up at the old soldier in bewilderment.

" It says that you have been replaced, conscript—that's all. But I can't congratulate you—because a little gunpowder would have made your moustache sprout. Different people, different tastes—if you are satisfied, all's said. Good evening to you."

He had turned to go, but stopped suddenly and cried:

" Thousand bullets! I was forgetting half my errand. You have a sister—Mam'zelle Christine—where is she? "

" Here, sergeant," said Eugène, indicating Christine, pale with happiness and surprise.

" This is for you, mam'zelle "; and he threw a second letter on the table.

" You'll drink a glass of wine, soldier? " asked Eugène.

" With all my heart, conscript."

While Eugène was preparing to ask the old soldier a number of questions, Louise, out of her senses with joy, kissed her betrothed again and again, half crying, half laughing, while placing fresh bottles on the table and filling the glasses.

Agitated, trembling, Christine sat, holding the letter and looking fixedly at the table.

" What is the matter? " asked Eugène anxiously. " It is that letter distresses you? Who has written to you? Let me see it, dear."

He hastily read the letter, which he had taken from her unresisting hands.

" Read it aloud," she said: " it is all the same to me—all the same! "

Eugène read out the letter:

" Mademoiselle, I demand nothing, I go without making any condition, I replace your brother; you have need of him, no one has any need of me. But I love you—have loved you ever since I saw your tears. I send you a ring which belonged to my mother. If you feel pity for me, you will take the cross containing a lock of your mother's white hair, which shone on your neck this evening in the light of the moon, and place it in a crack in the side of the great yew tree, high up, near the branches. To-morrow morning I will go for it. You will wait for me two years, and, if I am not dead, I will bring it back to you. Will you remember that you have made an oath on that cross? Adieu! "

"What does this mean? How could anybody know?" said Eugène slowly. "Do you understand this, sergeant?"

"Oh! a vedette near you? Bah! I have it! it comes from a novice—a youth who knows how to write, but, for want of practice, doesn't know how to tell a woman just what he means," replied the sergeant, laughing.

Eugène shook his head.

"Your hand, soldier," he said; "I'll not accept this substitute—my sister shall not be sacrificed; I'll go with you."

And taking up his release he was about to tear it up, when Christine stayed his hand.

"But if I wish it!" she said. "He has acted nobly. He is going away unconditionally; he is unhappy. I have no other means of keeping him—and—and I want to love him! For the rest, he has done well not to show himself—perhaps I might have regretted it too much. I will take my cross, as he directs; but I should like to know—Sergeant, have you seen him?"

"Yes, I've set eyes on him."

"Well, he's not hunchbacked or bandy-legged, is he?"

"Thousand thunders! Hunchbacks and bandy-legs in the French army!" cried the sergeant, scandalised.

"Is he a good fellow?" asked Eugène.

"That I can answer for," replied the old soldier heartily.

"Well, then," said Christine, detaching her cross with its black ribbon from her pretty neck, "tell him that what he has done was well done; and, yourself, put this cross in the side of the great yew tree. Do not tell him anything about it: but do not lose sight of him, and try and return with him; he is worthy of you—he has begun as a brave man, and he will continue as a brave Frenchman."

Eugène and Louise gazed at her without being able to speak. The grenadier rose, and received the cross, while tears sparkled in his eyes.

Christine then turned towards her brother and future sister. She was no longer the same: her character had suddenly become serious. She said to Louise:

"I, too, am betrothed; my pledge is in the hands of a soldier of the guard."

Next morning, on setting off, my knapsack on my back, I found the cross hidden in the side of the yew tree—and I fancied I saw amid the close-grown branches the uniform and red epaulettes of a sergeant of the guard who was watching me.

III

A year later, the campaign of Saxony was finished: the campaign of France was going to begin. Eugène was married to Louise.

The terrible requisition reached him as well as others, but this time he was not kept back. It was foreseen that the anxiety would not be of long duration; and then it was so clearly evident that the defence of France was necessary; lads ran away from their colleges to get to the frontier, and it would have been shameful in any man who, in default of a sword, had not seized up his ploughshare, shameful in the woman who still hung upon the arm of that man.

Eugène went this time, and joined the army in Champagne. At the bridge of Montereau, after having fought long at the outposts, he found himself without cartridges, and was defending himself as well as he could with his short infantry sabre against five Austrian grenadiers, when a lieutenant of carabineers sprang before him, crying:

"Conscript, go and find your sister and your wife; leave those to die who have nothing to live for!"

And the lieutenant cut down two whitecoats with his long sabre. But his horse received a bayonet stab and fell under him. He received two others and fell also. A French fusillade laid low the three men of the enemy; and Eugène, who had sprung to the body of his rescuer, carried him to a neighbouring house and brought him back to life.

The soldier and the officer became friends and brothers in arms; but the soldier could not understand the devotion of the officer, nor the sense of the words that had accompanied it. He was but the more proud, the more fascinated; and then, the officer was so fond of him and spoke to him so kindly, that he was wholly at a loss how to repay so much goodness. When, at the end of the drama, the armies were disbanded, he said to him:

"Lieutenant, if you have neither father, children, nor family—if you are alone in the world—come to my home. I am only a workman, but my people will be very fond of you. I have a good wife and a pretty sister—you hear what I am saying, Monsieur Charles? You will not disdain my family, even if you do not consent to make part of it? At least you will not deny me the pleasure of showing them my preserver."

The lieutenant could only throw himself on Eugène's neck and thank him warmly. A week afterwards, Eugène, stifled in the embraces of Louise and Christine, tore himself free from their arms and, pointing to the friend he had brought home with him, cried:

"Here is a brave man who saved my life without knowing me, and exposed his own because he had no family to weep for his death; but now he has one! He is my brother; he has said that he will not disdain my home—let it be his! We will work together, and some day, perhaps, we shall be rich and my house more worthy of a lieutenant."

"A lieutenant!" cried Christine involuntarily.

"Sister," whispered Eugène, "this one is worth more than the other."

Christine cast down her eyes and looked furtively at the officer. He was not ill-looking; his epaulettes, his wounds received for a dear brother, and, above all, his determined efforts to please Christine and prove to Eugène that he did not despise his family, resulted, at the end of two months, in causing her to appear thoughtful, while blushes suffused her cheeks in answer to the expressive looks of Charles; at which signs Eugène smiled.

One day he took his friend and his sister apart.

"I am very happy," he said. "You love my sister, Charles?"

"I love her," replied the lieutenant, gazing on Christine, pleadingly.

"Do you love him, sister?"

"Yes."

"More than you love me?"

"In a different way," she answered simply.

Imagine my delight, monsieur! for I was the lieutenant. I who had repented of having engaged the young girl's promise, and had wished to die, so as to release her from it. I who longed to win her free and voluntary love! I fell on my knees before her.

"Will you be his wife, Christine?" asked Eugène.

"No," she replied, sadly, but firmly; "no, I have given my promise to another. I am betrothed."

"Folly!" cried Eugène. "Betrothed!—to a man you have never even seen—who asks nothing of you—who is ugly, perhaps, and as old as I am?—a man, in short, who has never cared to show himself, and who by this time is dead, no doubt!"

"Dead! If so, he died for you, Eugène. Have you forgotten the year of happiness you owe to him, of which I am the price? The bargain is sacred. If he is dead, the pledge returns to me, and I will wear mourning for him as for a husband. If he is not dead, I will wait."

"But have not the two years passed?"

"Though that may be, I will still wait for him who, poor and friendless, trusted in my promise. Oh no, let him come; let him return me my gold cross—and, if he pleases, set me free!"

Eugène was losing patience, but I restrained him by a gesture. I was still kneeling at Christine's feet.

"Christine, Eugène," I said, "it is time that you should know all. It was I, my friend, who replaced you; I who, hidden in the great yew tree, overheard your tearful parting; I who accepted Christine's pledge; I who love her and who ask her, on my knees, to restore to me my mother's ring."

"You! you!" they both cried at once. Christine had already

drawn from her bosom the ring and the letter enclosing it; but suddenly she paused.

"Do not deceive me," she cried. "Can it be possible? Ah, you have agreed together, you and my brother! He has told you the secret! Where is my gold cross?"

"What!" I exclaimed, "do you refuse to believe me? Is not my voice that of truth?—my soldier's word?"

"The cross! the cross!" she repeated.

"I have it not," I replied sadly. "I have it no more! It was the old sergeant——"

"Where is he?" asked Christine.

"He is dead—he died at Leipsic," I replied hopelessly.

"No—thousand thunders!—I'm not dead," cried a voice behind us; "and I've arrived just in the nick of time, or I'm a Prussian! Lieutenant, don't you recognise me?"

"What! are you still living?" I cried, throwing my arms about him.

"As you can see for yourself! I've come from the hospitals at Leipsic; but while I've been grunting there—thousand bombshells!—changes have been going on, it seems. The Little Corporal—but enough of that for the present; we'll talk about it some other time. What we've got to deal with is Monsieur Charles's affair. Look at him, mam'zelle—though he had not courage to speak to you under his Jesuit's cassock, he knew how to fight under his tonsure. I saw him slip your cross out of the old yew tree. kiss it, and put it under his uniform—where I have mine now; but that's not the same thing. I followed him everywhere. He went under fire—thousand cartridges!—as if he were entering a ballroom! At Dresden, owing to his education and his dare-devilry, he was made a sub-lieutenant. At Leipsic, in a tussle on the bridge, I saw him dash right upon the crowd of whitecoats, and I said to myself: 'What is he about? Does he want to get himself wiped off the roll?' Then I took the liberty of laying hold of the tail of his coat, and saying to him: 'Lieutenant, are you forgetting that you have a pledge to return to somebody—down yonder?'

"That told him that I knew all about the business, and he said to me: 'I've seen you somewhere—yes, I remember. Here is the pledge you speak of. Take it to Croissey; it weighs on my conscience. I have no friends, and I would not tempt fate by buying a wife—I leave that to the Turks. To give her back her liberty I am going to get myself killed. Fly! Save yourself! Let the old moustaches return to France—they have need of one another!' I wished to take an oath; but, bah! he was gone. As for myself, I got jammed between a gun-carriage and the parapet of the bridge; and that laid me up in bed for eleven months, with a dozen poultices to keep me company. But here I am, at last, and—no disrespect to my lieutenant—I find him still a bit of a conscript where women are in the case."

"How could I win her trust in me?" I said, looking beseechingly at Christine.

"Forgive me," she cried, throwing herself into my arms; "forgive me for having been too faithful to you! I will love you twice as much."

"The cross! the cross!" cried Eugène, mimicking her voice.

"Here it is!" replied the old sergeant delightedly.

Christine took it with transport, and, holding it, between our kisses said to me:

"May it render them sacred!"

We are now old married people. The sergeant died at Waterloo. Eugène and I have prospered by labour: we conduct the manufactures of M. de V——; we live in the little white and rose-coloured house you see in the midst of the foliage of the island yonder, and every evening I come to smoke my pipe under the Croissey Yew.

SAINT-JUIRS

NICETTE

"You are a dead man!" said the doctor, looking intently at Anatole.

Anatole staggered.

He had come gaily to pass the evening with his old friend, Dr. Bardais, the illustrious *savant* whose works on venomous substances are known all over the world, whose nobility of heart and almost paternal goodness Anatole had learned to know better than any other living soul; and now, without the least hesitation or preparation, he heard this terrible prognostication issue from those authoritative lips!

"Unhappy boy, what have you done?" continued the doctor.

"Nothing that I know of," stammered Anatole, greatly agitated.

"Tax your memory, tell me what you have eaten or drunk—what you have inhaled?"

The last word was a ray of light to Anatole. That very morning he had received a letter from one of his friends who was travelling in India; in the letter was a flower plucked on a bank of the Ganges by the traveller—a strangely formed red flower, the perfume of which—he now recalled the fact vividly—had appeared to him to be singularly penetrating. He hastily drew forth his pocket-book and produced the letter with its contents and handed them to the *savant*.

"No doubt is possible!" cried the doctor; "it is the *Pyramenensis Indica*! the deadly flower, the flower of blood!"

"Then,—you—really think——?"

"Alas! I am sure of it."

"But—it is impossible!—I am only five-and-twenty years of age, and feel full of life and health!——"

"At what hour did you open that fatal letter?"

"This morning, at nine o'clock."

"Well—to-morrow morning, at the same hour, at the same minute, in full health, as you say, you will feel a pain in your heart—and all will be over."

"And you know of no remedy—no means of——"

" None! " said the doctor.

And, covering his face with his hands, he sank into a chair overcome by grief.

In face of the profound emotion of his old friend, Anatole understood that he was really condemned.

He hurried from the doctor's house like a madman. His forehead bathed in cold perspiration, his ideas all confused; going he knew not whither, he sped on and on amid the darkness of the night, taking no heed of the loneliness of the streets he was traversing. For a long time he pursued this blind course, until at length, finding a bench, he sank down upon it.

How many hours had he still to live?

The persistent and distressing sound of a racking cough brought him back to consciousness; he looked in the direction whence it came, and saw, seated upon the same bench, a pale and weak little flowergirl—a child not more than eight years old, who, as François Coppée says,

> Dies of the winter while offering us the spring.

That verse of the poet's recurred to the mind of Anatole; he felt in his waistcoat-pocket and found there two sous and two louis. He was going to give the poor child the two sous; but recollecting that he had only a few hours longer to live, he gave her the two louis.

This incident did him good.

He had been like a man stunned by a blow on the head; his bewilderment was overcome now, and he began to reassemble his dislocated ideas.

" My situation," he said to himself, " is that of a man condemned to death. A man in that position may still, however, hope for pardon—many of that sort are pardoned in our days. In past times even, some have been saved from the axe or the cord, to devote themselves to some difficult or dangerous piece of work—the launching of a ship for example, or, as in the time of Louis XI, to marry an old woman. If I were consulted in the matter, I should prefer to launch a ship. Unfortunately, I shall not be consulted during the short interval of time that remains to me. But, by the way, how long *have* I got to live? " He looked at his watch.

" Three o'clock in the morning!—it is time to go to bed. To bed!—waste in sleep my last six hours! Not if I know it. I have certainly something better than that to do. But what? Of course—to make my will."

A restaurant—one of those which keep open all night—was not far off. Anatole entered it.

" Garçon, a bottle of champagne—and ink and paper."

He drank a glass of Cliquot and looked thoughtfully at the sheet of paper before him.

"To whom shall I bequeath my six thousand francs a year? I have neither father nor mother—happily for them! Amongst the persons who interest me, I see only one—Nicette."

Nicette was a charming girl of eighteen, with blonde tresses and large black eyes; an orphan like himself—a community in misfortune which had long established between them a secret and complete sympathy.

His last will and testament was speedily drawn up: universal legatee, Nicette.

That done, he drank a second glass of champagne.

"Poor Nicette," he mused; "she was very sad when I last saw her. Her guardian, who knows nothing of the world outside his class of wind instruments at the Conservatoire de Musique, had taken upon himself to promise her hand to a brute of an amateur of fencing whom she detests—the more because she has given her heart to somebody else—who is that happy mortal?—I haven't the least idea; but he is certainly worthy of her, or she would never have chosen him. Good, gentle, beautiful, loving Nicette deserves the ideal husband. Ah! she is the very wife that would have suited me, if—if—— By Jove, it's an infamy, to compel her to destroy her life—by confiding such a treasure to such a brute! I have never before so well understood the generous ardour which fired the breasts of the wandering knights, and spurred them on to the deliverance of oppressed beauty!—And now I come to think of it, what hinders me from becoming the knight-errant of Nicette? My fate is settled—at nine o'clock—after that it will be too late; now, therefore, is the time for action! The hour is a little unusual for visiting people; but, when I reflect that, five hours hence, I shall be no more, I conclude that I have not time for standing on etiquette. Forward!—my life for Nicette!"

Anatole rose—and then, perceiving that he had no money, he gave his gold watch to the waiter in payment for the champagne—a watch worth five hundred francs.

The garçon took the chronometer, and examined it closely—weighed it in his hand, opened it,—and finally put it in his pocket doubtfully and without thanking Anatole.

It was four o'clock in the morning when he rang at the door of Monsieur Bouvard, the guardian of Nicette. He rang once, twice, and, at the third tug, broke the bell-wire. At length Monsieur Bouvard himself, in his night-dress and in great alarm, came and opened the door.

"What is the matter—is the house on fire?"

"No, my dear Monsieur Bouvard," said Anatole; "I am only paying you a little visit."

"At this hour!"

"It is pleasant to see you at any hour, my dear Monsieur Bouvard! But you are so lightly dressed—pray get into bed again."

"I am going to do so. But, I suppose, Monsieur, that it was not simply to trouble me in this way that you have come at such an hour? You have something of importance to say to me?"

"Very important, Monsieur Bouvard! It is to tell you that you must renounce the idea of marrying my cousin Nicette to Monsieur Capdenac."

"What do you say?"

"You must renounce that project."

"Never, Monsieur!—never!"

"Don't fly in the face of Providence by using such language!"

"My resolution is fixed, Monsieur; this marriage will take place."

"It will not, Monsieur!"

"We will see about that. And, now that you have had my answer, Monsieur, I'll not detain you."

"A speech none too polite, Monsieur Bouvard; but, as I am as good-natured as I am tenacious, I will pass over it, and—remain."

"Stay if it pleases you to do so; but I shall consider you gone, and hold no further conversation with you."

Saying which, Monsieur Bouvard turned his face to the wall, grumbling to himself:

"Was ever such a thing seen!—rousing a man at such an hour!—breaking his sleep, only to pour into his ears such a pack of nonsense!——"

Suddenly Monsieur Bouvard sprang to a sitting posture in his bed.

Anatole had possessed himself of the professor's trombone, into which he was blowing like a deaf man, and sending from the tortured instrument sounds of indescribable detestableness.

"My presentation trombone!—given me by my pupils! Let that instrument alone, Monsieur!"

"Monsieur, you consider me gone; I shall consider you—absent, and shall amuse myself until you return. Couac! couac!—fromn! brout! Eh?—that was a fine note!"

"You will get me turned out of the house; my landlord will not allow a trombone to be played here after midnight."

"A man who evidently hath not music in his soul! Frrout! frrout, prrr!"

"You will split my ears!—you'll spoil my instrument!—a trombone badly played on is a trombone destroyed, Monsieur!"

"Couac! prounn, pra—pra—prrrr——"

"For mercy's sake give over!"

"Will you consent?"

" To what? "

" To renounce the idea of that marriage? "

" Monsieur, I cannot! "

" Then—couac!——"

" Monsieur Capdenac——"

" Prrrroum!——"

" Is a terrible man to deal with! "

" Frrroutt!——"

" If I were to offer him such an affront, he would kill me."

" Is that the only reason which stops you? "

" That—and several others."

" In that case leave the matter to me; only swear to me that if I obtain Monsieur Capdenac's renunciation, my cousin shall be free to choose a husband for herself."

" Really, Monsieur, you abuse——"

" Couas, frrroutt, ffuit, brrrout!——"

" Monsieur, Monsieur,—she shall be free."

" Bravo! I have your word. Will you now allow me to retire? By the way, where does your Capdenac live? "

" Number 100 Rue des Deux-Epées."

" I fly thither!—Until we meet again! "

" You are going to throw yourself into the lion's mouth, and he will teach you a lesson you deserve," said Monsieur Bouvard, as Anatole hurried from the bedchamber and shut the door after him.

Without a moment's hesitation Anatole betook himself to the address of the fire-eating fencer; it was just six o'clock when he arrived there. He rang the door-bell.

" Who is there? " demanded a rough voice behind the door.

" Open!—very important communication from Monsieur Bouvard."

The sounds of a night-chain and the turning of a key in a heavy lock were heard.

" Here is a man who does not forget to protect himself against unwelcome visitors! " remarked Anatole to himself.

The door opened at length. Anatole found himself in the presence of a gentleman with a moustache fiercely upturned, whose night-dress appeared to be the complete costume of the fencing school.

" You see, always ready; it's my motto."

The walls of the swordsman's antechamber were completely covered with panoplies of arms of all descriptions; yatagans, poisoned arrows, sabres, rapiers, one- and two-handed swords, pistols—a regular arsenal—enough to terrify any timid-minded observer.

" Bah! " thought Anatole, " what do I now risk!—at most two hours and a half! "

" Monsieur," said Capdenac, " may I be allowed to know——"

" Monsieur," replied Anatole, " you want to marry Mademoiselle Nicette? "

" Yes, Monsieur."

" Monsieur, you will not marry her! "

" Ah! thunder!—blood! who will prevent me? "

" I shall, Monsieur! "

Capdenac stared at Anatole, who was not very big, but appeared to be very decided.

" Ah!—young man, you are very lucky to have found me in one of my placable moments. Take advantage of it—save yourself while you have time; otherwise I will not answer for your life! "

" Nor I for yours."

" A challenge!—to me!—Capdenac!—Do you know that I have been a master of the art of fencing for ten years! "

" There's nothing of-fencive about me, Monsieur! "

" I have fought twenty duels—and had the misfortune to kill five of my adversaries, besides wounding the fifteen others! Come, I have taken pity on your youth!—once more, go away."

" I see, by your preparations, that you are an adversary worthy of me and my long growing desire to confront a man so redoubtable. Let's see! what shall we fight with? Those two double-handed swords standing by the fireplace? Or those two boarding-axes? With cavalry sabres, or would you prefer a pair of curved yatagans? You hesitate: can't you make up your mind? "

" I am thinking of your mother and her coming distress."

" I haven't a mother to be distressed. Would you rather fight with a carbine?—pistol? or revolver? "

"Young man—don't play with fire-arms."

" Are you afraid? You are trembling! "

" Trembling! I? It's with cold."

" Then fight, or at once renounce the hand of Nicette."

" Renounce the hand of Mademoiselle Nicette! By Jove, I admire your bravery! and brave men are made to understand one another. Shall I make a confession to you? "

" Speak! "

" For some time past I have myself had thoughts of breaking off this marriage, but I did not know how to do it. I consent, therefore, with pleasure to do what you wish; but, at the same time, you must see that I cannot appear to give way to threats, and you have threatened me."

" I retract them."

" In that case, all is understood."

" You will give me, in writing, your renunciation? "

" Young man, you have so completely won my sympathy that I can refuse you nothing."

Furnished with the precious document, Anatole flew back to the dwelling-place of Monsieur Bouvard: he had a considerable distance to walk, and by the time he reached the professor's door it was nearly eight o'clock in the morning.

" Who is there? "

" Anatole."

" Go home, and go to bed! " cried the professor savagely.

" I have got Capdenac's renunciation of Nicette's hand! Open the door, or I will break it down."

Monsieur Bouvard admitted him, and Anatole placed in his hand the momentous paper. That done, he rushed to the door of Nicette's room and cried:

" Cousin, get up—dress yourself quickly and come here! "

" It appears, Monsieur, that I am no longer master in my own home! " exclaimed Monsieur Bouvard; " you go and come, and order as you please! To make you understand that I will have nothing more to say to you, I—I will go back to my morning newspaper, in the reading of which you have interrupted me! "

A few minutes later, Nicette, looking fresh as dawn, arrived in the drawing-room.

" What is the matter? "

" The matter," said Monsieur Bouvard, " is that your cousin is mad! "

" Mad? So be it! " replied Anatole. " Last night, my dear little cousin, I obtained two things: the renunciation of your hand by Monsieur Capdenac, and the promise of your worthy guardian to bestow it on the man of your choice—the man you love."

" Do you really wish me to marry Anatole, guardian? "

" Eh? " cried Anatole, his breath nearly taken away.

" Since I love you, cousin! "

At that moment Anatole felt his heart beat violently. Was it from pleasure at the unexpected avowal made by Nicette, or was it the agony, the death symptom predicted by the doctor?

" Unfortunate that I am! " he cried. " She loves me—I am within reach of happiness, and am to die without attaining it! "

Then, taking the hands of Nicette feverishly within his own, he told her all about the letter, the venomous flower he had scented, the prognostication of his old friend, the will he had written, and the steps he had successfully taken to release her from the claim of Capdenac.

" And now," he said, in conclusion, " I have only to go home and die! "

" But it is impossible! " cried Nicette. " This doctor must have been mistaken; who is he? "

" A man who is never in error, Nicette—Dr. Bardais."

" Bardais! Bardais! " cried Bouvard, bursting into laughter.

"Listen to what my newspaper here says: 'The learned Dr. Bardais has been suddenly seized with mental alienation. The madness with which he has been stricken is of a scientific character. It is well known that he was absorbingly engaged in an inquiry into the nature of venomous substances, and latterly he had fallen into the delusion that everybody he met was under the influence of poison, and endeavoured to persuade them that such was their condition. He was last night transported to the Maison de Santé of Dr. Blank.'"

"Nicette!"

"Anatole!"

The two young persons fell into each other's arms.

RAYMOND SCHWAB

THE PRINCESS "JUST BECAUSE"

When the little Princess lowered her head, any older persons who were looking down on her from above and had seen the shadow of her heavy hair on her forehead and of her eyelashes on her cheeks, the lines round her mouth, and the curve of her neck and her rounded shoulders, would at once have forgotten how slight her figure was and would have taken her to be grown up. Any one who had seen her sitting down would have come to her side to talk about all manner of things, for she had the look of one who understands everything. Looking at her in full face, she had the features of a woman of thirty whom suffering has not embittered but has somewhat broken. Yet, when she turned her head and showed her profile, it was easy to judge how very young she was from the concave line of her retroussé nose and the pout of her tightly closed lips. And those whom she deigned to allow to kiss her hand had noticed the groove which forms a natural bracelet on a baby's wrist. The creases in her fingers, arms, and neck were not set lines, but were rather dimples.

The Infanta's favourite attitude was one in which she stood up straight in her immense stiff skirt, her hands crossed at the back, and her arms hanging straight down. Sometimes, although not a hair would be out of place, she would raise her right hand with a tired gesture and would smooth her forehead with her palm, closing her eyes at the same time as though she were making an effort. And just as her profile seemed a contradiction to her grown-up face, so was her hand, which seemed full of vitality and independence, so that every gesture was complete and perfect.

The soul of this young girl was always very near to the very heart of things, and far from her fellow-creatures. Just as one recognises a friend by his voice, so with closed eyes she knew every month of the year by its particular odour.

When she came out of her room, she ran her fingers caressingly down the richly chased blades of the halberds which the guards lowered before her. The lady-in-waiting warned her to be careful of the sharp edges of the blades, and asked her what pleasure she could find in such an action. And when the Princess's uncle, Don Fabian—who was nicknamed "The Bully"—replied in his rude way, "She finds pleasure in it, Madame, because she is touching the weapons that destroy our enemies," the little girl let his remark pass without deigning to contradict it; she merely shrugged her shoulders disdainfully. But the old lady-in-waiting hurried angrily after her, grumbling out; "But why do you do it? Why?" And the little girl, answering as a little girl must do when surprised in some wrong action, yet certain of herself, said in a humble though obstinate tone: "I do it—just because!"

When it was noticed that she took an extraordinary pleasure in touching or looking at brilliantly coloured or highly polished objects, she was taken to the royal portrait gallery. The lady-in-waiting showed her the portraits of her ancestors in their gorgeous robes, and introduced them in passing; once she stopped in front of the picture of a child with a sallow skin and faded features, awkwardly represented in a costume whose colours had faded so that they mingled with those of the wooded countryside that served as a background. "You must love this child, Madame," she said, "because he was your brother." The little Infanta, following her lead, made the sign of the Cross, because, just as she had never sinned against etiquette, she did not wish to lose any opportunity of showing her reverence to God, the most powerful of all princes, Who rules the kings of the earth.

But suddenly she resumed her childish vivacity and ran toward another picture in which, from above garments of bright colours, there rose a very beautiful little face, which seemed to be continually changing, and always full of life. She stood there thoughtfully for some time and then, as if in an ecstasy, she said: "It is *here,* Madame, that it would more befit us to praise God and pray to Him."

The lady-in-waiting showed by a look of astonishment and a swift interrogation that she was paying unwarrantable honour to a mere court dwarf, a plaything dead and now forgotten even in name. But the little girl kept on looking from a distance in her dreamy way at the picture where the greens and the blues were so bright, and she murmured: "Because—because——"

No one understood her. They smiled when with evident joy she caressed French silks, soft and fluid as water; Moorish leather whose roughness had been obliterated by art and the hand of time; when she stood still in amazement to kiss rare gems and necklaces; and when she opened her eyes wide, careless of the amusement of her companions, on a wonderful piece of tapestry. Sometimes her maids of honour would hint at hereditary weaknesses which had afflicted her father's line, and at the manifold follies which in olden times had been committed by representatives of the dynasty. They dressed up her dolls in rich stuffs, captured from pirates and long ago sold by Venetian merchants to the Great Turk; every yard of material had cost several human lives and in their dull designs were flat-looking stains which were, perhaps, splashes of blood. And every time the Infanta undressed or dressed her dolls she wept.

She won much reputation in the court for her affectionate soul, because for six months she had carefully treasured the hair of a little dead peasant-girl who had been brought up at her own expense, because they had been born on the same day. Often she would spread it out on her hands like a skein, and would caress it with her fingers or curl and uncurl it; but she never kissed the hair. Once when the dead child's father threw himself on his knees before her to beg for some favour, she had him sent away spurned, and all day long she shrank from the thought of his eyes, where colour had been all dissolved in tears. She would allow no one to serve who did not excel in beauty and in dress. And they said that not all the beauty of the world would satisfy her longing.

No one ever asked her now why she liked such and such a thing; it had become a household jest among her footmen when courting her maids to say, "I love you for our little Infanta's reason."

"What's that?"

"Oh, just because——!"

And they called her "The Princess Just Because——!"

The favourite resort of the princess was a little old ante-room which smelled so musty that no one would go past it alone. Even the palace guards were no longer ordered to inspect it, because the dreadful odour of mortality so unnerved them that more than once its horror had led to suicide. Many ugly stories were current about corpses in the walls, and about an unnatural gloom which was said to haunt this desolate chamber. Yet this queer child had some strange predilection for the ancient smell of the leather which lined its walls.

On her tenth birthday the little Infanta, robed in blue brocade, appeared for the first time at a royal ball and danced the minuet, She had been a dancer ever since she had learned to walk, and her appearance at the ball was one continuous triumph. When she sat out she was in an ecstasy far beyond thought, and no one could evoke a reply to even the most fervid compliment. She would only bow her head slightly, and no one could tell whether her fatigue was due to the dance, or to the emotion aroused by the applause, or to the unaccustomed delight of hearing music; for she had never before attended a royal concert. The conductor of the orchestra, touching the strings of his violin with an affected gesture, glanced boldly towards the Princess. Noticing this, the aged duenna remarked: "How music uplifts and carries away the soul!" The little girl rose in a temper, and without a word went back to her own apartment.

From that day forward she forsook the leather-lined ante-room, and no longer took delights in scents; she no longer caressed swords nor the richest stuffs of the East. Instead, the delicate tips of her fingers began to pucker, as if they had been kept too long soaked in water. The most brilliant colours no longer evoked any response from her expressive eyes. And when from time to time she looked out below drooping eyelids, it was noticed that those wonderful eyes were now growing pale, and it was soon whispered that her sight was failing. This went from bad to worse, yet still the court-physicians dared not tell the King that the little princess had difficulty in breathing, that her hands were only too like those of a paralytic, and that she would probably become blind.

And now "Princess Just Because——," altering her style of hair-dressing, no longer let her hair fall in heavy masses over her ears; but at the same time her voice became more powerful, and so sweet that it seemed to be raised in one long song. Until now she had ever been silent, but now her chattering never ceased, as if she were greedy of hearing her own voice and generous of it to others.

All that extraordinary delight which she had taken in the senses of sight and smell and touch, had now become transferred to the sense of hearing. She, who had always been so greatly admired for her elegance and courtly manners, her wonderful knowledge of the etiquette of the royal Court and of the proprieties before the Sanctuary, had now fallen exclusively in love with Sound. Music, as it seemed to her, welcomed and uplifted its hearers, and made a majestic and reverent accompaniment to all their thoughts. Above all, she loved the strains which had the honour of guiding her own steps, the music of her own minuet. She was insatiable in her desire for it, and ever moved unconsciously to its stately rhythm.

But now, when rather more tired than usual, she no longer moved at all, nor even opened her eyes; and even breathing seemed too great an effort. And one day, lying inert upon a regal couch, still robed in the blue brocade, but now without eyes for the treasures of art, she summoned the musicians to play her minuet. But even as the merry instruments were tuning up, the sweet child suddenly drew her last breath, and by virtue of her immaculate innocence, and her utter love of all beauty, went straight in the blue brocade to heaven.

Yet the music still pursued her through celestial space; she was still aware of the symphony now resounding through the palace far below. Angels bore her in their arms and guided her unaccustomed way, but though their voices joined in sweeter chorus than any ever heard on earth, she begged them haughtily to be silent, and bent forward from their arms to hear the music of her minuet.

When at last she arrived before the throne of God, the music no longer resounded in her ears. She found the Court far less gorgeous than she had expected from the churches in Spain, and became sulky and fractious as a peevish and ill-tempered child. All that they could do was to place her in a cloud as blue as her brocade, and there St. Cecilia played her the most touching melodies.

But the little Infanta had no desire for moving strains. She neither loved nor understood the saint. St. Cecilia, in an ecstasy, listened to her own music; she played only for her own pleasure, without caring about the unhappy maiden. "Princess Just Because——" did not understand these melodies, which came from the heart and hoped to reach the heart, these simple and yet subtle airs, so insinuating, which might make even princesses submissive to their sweetness; she wanted something less caressing, less direct, less heartfelt, but with more majesty and more reserve. She wanted the music of procession and of precedence, slow marches in time with the pacing of heralds and courtiers, or, better still, the dance music of royal courts where one may hear the swish of silken trains, while the wailing strings evoke the dignity and grace of people of high degree. Above all, she wished to hear her own minuet; but, whenever she lilted a few of the bars which capriciously crossed her memory, St. Cecilia caught them up and wove them into a hymn inflamed by a devotion of which the little Infanta had no knowledge. Thus eternity stole from the blind and paralysed princess her last joy. The insatiable little creature did not indeed become deaf; but, stiff and solitary in her blue brocade, she heard the majestic symphonies of Heaven pass over her, as she lay there insensitive.

. . . .

HENRY KISTEMAEKERS[1]
B. 1851

IN EXILE

I HAD made up my mind to go down into my cabin when a rather elegant but melancholy-looking passenger—I had noticed him during dinner—approached me on the upper deck.

" A beautiful night, isn't it? " he remarked.

" Extraordinarily beautiful! "

" Do you land in Alexandria? "

" Yes, to-morrow morning."

" We touch there about daybreak. As you will see for yourself, the picture of Alexandria as it takes shape in the golden and rosy glow of an Egyptian daybreak is a sight like some enchanting fairy scene. I know nothing so beautiful, so graceful as this city of Aphrodite, poised like a jewel casket on the edge of the desert. Truly Alexandria is beautiful; it is like some hymn of light. There is only one spot in the world that is more bewitching, and that is Paris! Do you know Paris? "

" It is my native city," I returned.

" Just as I thought—I felt it. Even blindfold I can single out a Parisian in any crowd." He leaned over the ship's railing, watching the phosphorescent arabesques that formed in the wake of the boat. Then he murmured: " What a happy man you are! "

He turned suddenly on me, his eyes flashing wildly, and fixed his gaze steadily on me. " You are an extremely fortunate mortal —you do not realise your good fortune. You have before you a man who adores Paris; one who has Paris in his blood, in his veins—and will never see Paris again. Can you imagine anything more ghastly? "

" Are you exiled? " I queried. In a tone that was most matter-of-fact he answered: " Far worse than that. I am dead! "

[1] Henry Kistemaekers and the brothers Boëx (J. H. Rosny) though Belgian by birth are so essentially French by residence, training, and sympathy, that they are seldom classed with the authors of their native country, and here they are included with the French, the Belgian section being devoted entirely to the authors of Belgian origin whose literary work has remained native in inspiration.—ED.

My features must have betrayed my sensations at such a confidence, for he added rapidly: " Don't be frightened; you are not confronted by a maniac. Don't look up at the rigging so anxiously; you are in absolutely no danger, for I am the sanest and most peaceable man in the world. My story will prove it—of course, you must guess that there is a story to tell, inasmuch as I claim to be dead and you see me here alive in the stern of this boat. Have you five minutes' time to give to me? " I thought it best to humour him and nodded assent, seating myself on one of the deck benches. He lit a cigar, placed himself opposite me, and began: " Have you ever heard the name Saint Mai? "

" I know not only the name but also the works of that great master," I answered. " Are you going to tell me something about him? "

" Exactly—about the famous Saint Mai, author of ' Heracles,' the thousandth performance of which took place last night; about the creator of ' Marie,' and ' The Woman of the Sabots '—in short, of all those works that have had such tremendous success in the last ten years. I want to tell you about Saint Mai, who died without having tasted of fame——"

" Well, what about him? "

" Only that it is all a mistake and that Saint Mai is alive. Don't look so surprised, for it is just as true that he is alive as that I am here before you. In fact, Saint Mai and I are one and the same person."

" Oh! " I cried, and my voice sounded my alarm.

" True! It was just about ten years ago that I began to vegetate. A concert of my compositions had been noticed with the most prominent indifference; my opera, ' Marie,' had flattened its nose against the portals of the Opéra Comique, and bore the honour of having been the greatest failure since that of ' Carmen ' was recorded in the annals of modern French music. My portfolio was bulging with unpublished works, and I withdrew to a small corner of Brittany to ruminate over my fate and to economise in my expenditures. It was during this retirement that one fine morning I got hold of a Paris newspaper and discovered in it the announcement that I was dead! A laconic despatch from some news agency brought the information that I had been ship-wrecked in a bark. I have never been able to discover the motive of the news correspondent who reported me dead; but as a matter of fact this incident decided my career."

" How is that possible? "

" Let me proceed: When I read this news item the first impulse that arose in me was to run to some telegraph station and contradict the report. The nearest telegraph office was four miles from my place of seclusion. On the road there I pondered the matter and realised that it would cost me one sou per word to contradict the report, and that a telegram would have to be sent to each one of the ten prominent Paris newspapers. The total cost of all this telegraphing would have made a fearful hole in my meagre purse. As I considered these things I gazed out upon the ocean from the high cliff, and the thought flashed across my mind: It might be a very interesting thing to discover just how much of an event my death would be, and what would be said about me after my death. So I decided to wait until the following day before recalling the news.

"Without boring you with many details, let me assure you that I had a magnificent press. Some of my intimate friends tried to besmirch me with mud by spreading evil reports about my private life; but they only succeeded in raising me in the estimation of those people who had not known me personally, and the latter praised me to the skies. Within comparatively few hours I was made the object of most tender consideration. I became the subject of laudatory magazine articles—they are not very difficult to write, for the formula is ready at hand and there exist numberless phrases that were coined at the time of Bizet's death and are still available as models. In short, it was unhesitatingly asserted that I had been a genius. My opera, 'Marie,' which had been a failure, was hurriedly put on the boards again and had a tremendous success. At the Paris Grand Opera, in the archives of which the score of 'Heracles' had been slumbering, every effort was made to produce that work—and at its première it was frantically applauded.

"Meanwhile I was still in Brittany. I had come to realise my position and did not dare risk endangering my successes by breaking the silence. I was mightily convinced of the fact that the position of a dead composer was much easier than that of a living one—the dead composer finding a ready publisher for his works and eager managers to produce them; and thus he achieves a success that living composers cannot dream of tasting until after their death. I am in a position to assert this!

"And now let me tell you the rest of my story. I had a nephew who was absolutely without morals, and I determined to press him into service. Carefully disguised and with precautions of secrecy of which you can have no idea, I hunted him up, this conscienceless young man, and made him a proposition. After much deliberation we arrived at an agreement that my death was to be declared a suicide; the evidences were to be found in the letter that I had ostensibly written to my nephew on the evening before my death. In this letter I named him my sole heir. Other documents that gradually came to life confirmed this disposal of my property. At the point on the coast where I was supposed to have been wrecked my nephew found some of my belongings that the sea had thrown back, and among them was my portfolio containing valuable manuscripts.

"As my sole heir he was entitled to all the royalties of my works, and we agreed that he was to pay over to me three-fourths of the sums thus collected. Furthermore, I had named him as the heir to all my unpublished manuscripts and had stated that he was to publish them at his discretion. In this way it has become possible for me since my death to have written six operas, and I hope to write more. I wish to make the whole world gasp in amazement. I wish to make the universe marvel at the tremendous number of operas I had written before the breath of life departed from me! To this end I work with a fiery energy—I am a corpse of most remarkable zeal.

"Since I have died I have allowed myself extravagances that were denied me during life. I own plantations in India, a palace in Rio, and a harem in Damascus. All these fancies cost money, and I have to work hard; yet I am convinced that never before has a corpse enjoyed life so vividly.

"But alas, that all this happiness should be marred by a speck of discontent! Each of us carries his own unhappiness in himself, and my misfortune is that I love Paris so dearly; that I adore the city which I cannot see again without risking resurrection. And that is my continued nostalgia. Oh, Paris! One cannot find you in Rio, nor in India, nor in Damascus; not even in Paradise! Apropos, do you happen to know little Evelinette, of the Theatre of Varieties?"

"I should rather think I do!"

"How strange! And you see her occasionally?"

"Very frequently; she is quite my most intimate friend."

"Really?"

"Most assuredly!"

"What a coincidence! Has she ever spoken to you about me?"

"Never!"

He suddenly grew thoughtful; then, after a short silence, he remarked: "You see, there are some disadvantages in being dead. That little minx Evelinette was my last love, my only one. And yet she has succeeded in forgetting me entirely!"

J. H. ROSNY

(HENRY AND JUSTIN BOËX)

B. 1856 and 1859

THE GARDEN

I WAS born for love, and more especially for that sacrificial kind of love wherein a man gives himself entirely into a woman's hands " for better, for worse," so that he is ready to live or to die for her. Fate has twice struck me down: the first time when my fiancée died from some sudden illness during our engagement; the second when my beloved, after having seemed to love me very dearly, ran away with a mandolinist from Chile.

These disillusionments had been so cruel that I despaired altogether of my future happiness. They left me listless, without dreams or desires. I went into solitary retirement in a deserted cloister near Lyons, and spent every day in a huge garden where none of the trees had been touched for a hundred years. It was a perfect wilderness of birds and tiny creatures, and a thousand chances had enriched it with flowers and grass, strange newts and long, glittering, timid snakes. A stag wandered about with his graceful herd of hinds and fawns; I cannot think how he came into that hermitage. He soon became a great friend of mine; and one day when I was unable to go out, he walked up the steps leading to the ancient convent and moaned most mournfully; he threw back his great antlers and gazed at me uneasily.

I roamed about this garden early in the morning, and at night when the sun seemed to set the trees on fire, and later while the clouds played their comedies in countless wonderful scenes. But I never found any pleasure in it. My heart was as withered as dead autumnal leaves. The sorrowful words of Ecclesiastes were ever in my mind. I was always nursing my grief amid the amazing scenery of this wilderness, where oaks, elms, and beeches made a virgin forest.

One morning, when I had gone to the far end of the garden, and stood beside the crumbling wall, I saw a door open and admit the startling figure of a girl. Her dress was scarlet, embroidered with gold, and hung in heavy folds about her; she wore a dazzling emerald necklace; her hair, fastened by tiny pearl combs, fell in waves of light over her shoulders, and was as silky as a spider's web. Her eyes were of a delicate river-green, her complexion pink and white, her cheeks finely rounded, her lips were sensitive and her form was supple; and all this beauty made her look like a fairy, a nymph, a sylvan queen of story in the lovely old garden.

She seemed to be frightened and threw me a timid glance. I was too much overcome to be able to move, but I still knew how to show proper respect to this fair divinity.

"Please take no notice of me," I said sadly. "This garden is altogether at your service, if you will only let me stay here!"

She smiled, and I saw that I had quite reassured her.

"I thought it was quite deserted," she said, speaking in a voice that made me think of running, crystal water; "I have often spent hours here without meeting anybody."

"It used to be deserted," I answered, "and we may still call it so."

We then fell a-talking of the old trees, the stag, and the newts, and to me there was a great charm in our conversation. This young fairy was so fresh and sweet; she loved books and living nature equally; she was as much at home in fields and woods as when deep in the romances of George Sand, Lamartine, Bulwer-Lytton, and Alfred de Vigny. She chose her words carefully and well, and there seemed to be something whimsical even in her silence. Every now and then she had a far-away look in her eyes, and at last I noticed that she seemed to be gazing right beyond the old wall.

"What are you looking at?" I asked.

"Well," she answered, "it is just this: *I have left my body in my bedroom*. I am a little bit worried about it, because I am always afraid it might want to go out *alone*!"

I saw, of course, that her mind was disordered, but this only aroused my deeper interest.

She came back again; at first after fairly long intervals, then nearly every day. I was sure there was nothing wrong in this, and as for the future, how could I foresee anything when I didn't care a hang about my life? First spring, then summer, passed by, and a pleasant autumn began to dry up the flowers and verdure. Then, one September morning, I discovered that the unhappy exile had awakened the love that slumbered in the poor mad girl's heart. It was the first vivid emotion that I had experienced since I went into retreat, and it roused my pity and my fear. I wanted to wean my kindly friend from her love, but I saw that she was growing paler and thinner every day; and thinking over our many conversations, I knew that she had a loyal heart, and that, like mine, it was made for lasting love and unswerving devotion. Then my heart was torn, and I bitterly repented my rash conduct.

"Why should I not make reparation to her?" I asked inwardly. "Why should I not give the rest of my gloomy life into her keeping, poor soul?"

I had hardly conceived this idea before my veins ran molten fire. I could see the resurrection of the love I had believed was dead, and I felt once more the breath of hope. And why not? Lucienne's trifling delusion was a secret known only to herself and to me. She lived with a doting aunt and several faithful old servants; there was no legal hindrance to our marriage; my destiny was all that was at stake, and that was a dull one with no promise of living joy.

It was nearly twilight. The huge stag had ceased to bell in the gathering shadows, and clouds like celestial flowers strewed the sky. We could see amber, ruby, and sapphire lights breaking through the mists, scattering them and filling them with fairy dreams.

Lucienne drew closer to me, and together we looked upward beyond the branches. My heart was full of a great tenderness. My lovely companion, with her hair as beautiful as the twilight and her soft white face lit up by the seductive evening glow, brought back to me the days of my joy and youth.

She seemed sad and uneasy, and very much on the alert. With all gentleness I took her little hand in mine.

"Lucienne, my little Lucienne," I murmured, "why should we not watch the twilight together until the end of our days?"

She became paler still and began to tremble, then her hand closed in mine and she spoke as if in a dream.

"Don't you know," she said, "that I care for nothing in this world unless I can share it with you?"

She leaned close to me, shyly and nearly fainting. I pressed her to my heart, and as my lips met hers I felt that I had found the happiness I had lost before.

I am now married to Lucienne. We did not give up the old garden, and it has become the garden of Eden. My charming wife has healed my wounds and repaid me a hundredfold for my lost joys. Even her queer delusion endears her to me. Often, after we have been walking together under the oaks or beeches on a fine night, while the owls fly past and the young rabbits run away in the moonlight, Lucienne begins to talk about "her body left in the house." And then I feel that I am wandering in the spirit-world, with the loveliest of spirits, until I hear a silvery voice murmur:

"Are you not growing anxious? *It* has been left alone so long!"

And really for a moment I feel deliciously uneasy. We go back home, and when we are safely back in our nuptial nest and I clasp my sweet wife in a close embrace, I really feel that I have met her body again after having walked with her soul.

And the hallucination of this gentle being has become a kind of symbol, a misty, pleasant, and smiling allegory.

A LOST SOUL

J. H. Rosny

"No," he replied, "I have got nothing to grumble about; Fortune has always been kind to me and lavish of her gifts. My misery is simply the product of my own imagination, and all that keeps me from being radiantly happy is an absurd fiction which seems more terrible to me than anything real could be.

"I suppose you remember how enthusiastic I was that evening when we first met little Léa Dambère? Everything about her made her so lovely that I have never been able to think of any other woman afterwards. Her movements were so winning, her lips so sweet and beautiful, her dark eyes were so wonderfully gentle and full of womanly kindness; and then she had countless different ways of smiling that wholly transfigured her, and a little trick of bending her sweet head under the weight of that glorious hair which made me mad with love.

"Now, as you know, I have always detested myself, and with good reason. I know that I look very gloomy and dull; I am awkward, coarse of feature, and of ashen complexion; I find conversation difficult, and succeed only in uttering the most dismal phrases; and, what is worse, I am incapable of paying those trifling attentions which compensate for many graver errors. With all this in my mind, I could not, of course, hope to make this incomparable girl my wife. I had to be content with admiring her from a distance and with seeing her whenever I could; but it was in the same way as we wait for a gleam of sunshine, or seek a welcome shade, or the murmur of a hillside rivulet. And there is no doubt whatever that my relation with her would have remained at this stage, if chance had not given me an adventurous opening.

"Her father had challenged a cheat at the gaming-table. There was a fearful scene, and they went for one another tooth and nail. I was privileged to intervene. I took Dambère's side, which happened to be the side of justice, and had the satisfaction of routing the card-sharper, who was an alien Spaniard from the Balearic Isles.

"This little affair determined the rest of my life. Good old Dambère was so pleased with what I had done that he became monstrously friendly with me and thrust invitations upon me. It was thus that I came to meet Léa and soon knew her intimately, with the result that my love was altogether engaged. I thought of nothing but Léa all through those terrible nights when insomnia hovered over me like a bird of darkness.

"But it was a lonely love, for I never dared to show it to the mistress of my heart. The most that I could do was to speak to her very gently, and for the most part to be silent in her presence. I never hoped to be able to win her love; but, by slow degrees, as I saw that she was indifferent to other men who courted her, I began to dream of marriage. For a long time I revolved this idea in my mind, and my ardour was unequalled except by my unfathomable humility. It is quite possible that I might have remained all my life in this state of indecision, if I had not accidentally betrayed myself while talking to Dambère. As soon as I had done so he became greatly excited and ran away to ask his daughter what she thought about the matter. An hour later he came back to me. You know how effusive he can be!

"'She's in love with you, my dear old chap,' he told me; 'and she is wonderfully happy!'

"I put these words down to the blindness of friendship. Nevertheless, they implied that Léa was quite ready to consent, and so made me as happy as if they had been really true.

"Our engagement was short and delightful. Léa was always ready to welcome me and to keep close to me, to the exclusion of every one else. She showed evident delight in listening to me, and my adoration of her was unbounded. Her whole manner showed wonderful kindness. I never dreamed that it was a proof of her attachment to me; and, indeed, I rarely spoke of love at all, for fear of evoking conventional avowals of affection.

"I trembled whenever I thought of that formidable wedding-day, and when it had passed and we were alone together, the evening began for me in a kind of fear. But contrary to every expectation, I found a joyfully-yielding wife; her lips were brimming over with tenderness as I held her in a close embrace. And when the summer dawn showed silvery through the window, I looked down on her smiling rosy face, and asked: 'So you don't detest me altogether, Léa?'

"'Are you blind, dear husband of mine?' she said. 'Do you mean to say that you have never noticed that you are the only man in the world at whom I ever look? Don't you know that my soul is filled with joy at your mere presence?'

"I was overwhelmed by this avowal of love, and for the first few days of our married life I replied to it by an intensity of passion. Then a strange sense formed itself within me, and at last became my dominant impression. It was, that I ought not to be loved by such a perfect being as Léa, and that the whole situation was absurd and wrong. In proportion as this impression grew, my tenderness for my wife diminished. When she drew me to her gentle breast I experienced not so much joy, as a curious shame, and a feeling of moral uneasiness. It seemed to me to be abnormal for her to kiss me; I felt as if, by doing this, she was committing some perverse crime against nature. And then, sometimes, I felt that vague kind of hatred that strikes us when we see a very pretty girl become the wife of a repulsively ugly man. Yes, it is no more than the truth, that in the end I hated her for being fond of me; I had to keep myself from reproaching her for her bad taste.

"What more is there to tell you? This morbid state of mind has become chronic with me. She has changed me into an absolutely miserable creature; for I have a burning desire for love, a fanatical need of adoration, yet it would be impossible for me to transfer my love to any one but Léa. She seems to me to be the only beautiful and interesting woman alive; she sums up for me all grace, sweetness, and pleasure. I cannot love her because she is in love with me; and yet I should be carried away by passion if only she could feel nothing but friendship and affection for me. But she goes on loving me more and more as the years go by, and it looks as if I should never find a cure for my disease."

on her smiling rosy face, and asked: "So you don't detest me altogether, Lea?"

"Are you blind, dear husband of mine?" she said. "Do you mean to say that you have never noticed that you are the only man in the world at whom I ever look? Don't you know that my soul is filled with joy at your mere presence?"

I was overwhelmed by this avowal of love, and for the first few days of our married life I replied to it by an intensity of passion. Then a strange sense formed itself within me, and at last became my dominant impression. It was that I ought not to be loved by such a perfect being as Lea, and that the whole situation was absurd and wrong. In proportion as this impression grew my tenderness for my wife diminished. When she drew me to her gentle breast I experienced not so much joy as a curious shame, and a feeling of moral uneasiness. It seemed to me to be abnormal for her to kiss me; I felt as if, by doing that, she was committing some perverse crime against nature. And then, sometimes, I felt that vague kind of hatred that strikes us when we see a very pretty girl become the wife of a repulsively ugly man. Yes, it is no more than the truth that in the end I hated her for being fond of me; I had to keep myself from reproaching her for her bad taste.

"What more is there to tell you? This morbid state of mind has become chronic with me. She has changed me into an absolutely miserable creature, for I have a burning desire for love, a ravenous need of admiration, yet it would be impossible for me to transfer my love to any one but Lea. She seems to me to be the only beautiful and interesting woman alive; she sums up for me all grace, sweetness, and pleasure. I cannot love her because she is in love with me; and yet I should be carried away by passion if only she could feel nothing but friendship and affection for me. But she goes on loving me more and more as the years go by, and it looks as if I should never find a cure for my disease."

THE BELGIAN STORY-TELLERS

THE art of the short story as it has been developed in Belgium is fairly illustrated by the examples brought together in the following pages. It will be noticed that, though all these stories were written during the last sixty-five years, they present remarkable contrasts. There are in fact few periods in the history of European literature so rich in originality and diversity of style. After dwindling into insignificance during the seventeenth and eighteenth centuries, when the Belgian provinces were placed under foreign domination, national literature burst out in every direction, and asserted itself with a vigour and authority which, in ordinary circumstances, could never have shown themselves among a young people. This alone should be a sufficient proof that, if politically the kingdom was new, its spirit was as old as that of any great European nation.

When, in 1850, Decoster for the French-speaking part of the community, and Gezelle for the Flemings, succeeded in freeing Belgian literature from French and Dutch influences, they took up the thread where Commines, Froissart, Van Maerlant, and Ruysbroeck had left it. They expressed a spirit which had never ceased to exist since the early Middle Ages, but which had had no opportunity during the last centuries of manifesting itself. They tapped old sources of knowledge and inspiration which had for a long time remained hidden to the world ;

they were helped in their work by the accumulated energy of centuries of silence.

This long interval, during which the Belgian soul remained unexpressed, accounts for most of the characteristics of Belgian contemporary literature, for its richness, for its contrasts. Elsewhere, in France for instance, we could not find such glaring opposition as exists between realists like Eekhoud and Hubert Krains and symbolist writers such as Rodenbach and Blanche Rousseau. Still less could we discover authors like Lemonnier or Franz Hellens who pass constantly from one mood to another. This strange mixture of sensuality and mysticism is foreign to the French modern spirit and taste. French originality is held within bounds by a strong classic education. Mediaeval dreams have been regulated by a rationalist religion, mediaeval violence has been tamed by criticism and irony.

The French as a rule wonder at these wild outbursts of physical and spiritual energy through which the Belgians endeavour to express their aspirations. They look upon Lemonnier's novels or Verhaeren's poems as upon strange elementary forces, which it is impossible to master or classify. They generously recognise the power of Belgian writers, but they feel in their works a want of measure and of balance, and some Englishmen of French education will share this feeling.

Others will, no doubt, derive some pleasure from the extreme diversity of subjects and talents which may be found in Belgian contemporary literature, and appreciate the popular spirit and the deep sincerity which characterise its production. There is a striking analogy between the Belgian modern movement and some writers of the Elizabethan period. The subjects differ, of course, but the temperaments are to a great extent akin to each other. Pre-Shakespearian writers indulge in the same excesses of language, the same outburst of congenial vitality and, at the same time, display a delicacy of feeling, a sense of mystery, which has never been equalled abroad since the Renaissance, but which manifests itself over and over again in the works of Belgian modern writers.

CHARLES DECOSTER

Charles Decoster (1827–1879) is at present considered as the founder of Belgian modern literature. Before his time, Belgian letters were entirely in the hands of uninspired writers, imitators of the French, especially of Victor Hugo. It is typical of the conditions prevailing in the middle of the nineteenth century in Belgium that, outside a small group of friends, Decoster remained practically unknown. He led an obscure life, making his living by journalistic work in the Brussels papers, and by occupying a small post as a State employee. It was only twenty years after his death that, thanks to the efforts of Camille Lemonnier, justice was rendered to Decoster, and that a monument was erected to commemorate his national epic, "The Legend of Thyl Uylenspiegel" (1867), which Mr. Geoffrey Whitworth translated into English in 1918. The story of "The Three Princesses" is taken from an early work of Decoster, "Flemish Legends" (1858). We have tried as far as possible to preserve in the translation the archaic form of the original.

CAMILLE LEMONNIER

Considered from a purely critical point of view, the works of Camille Lemonnier (1845–1913) do not reveal the same originality and are sometimes unequal. Out of the forty novels which he published from 1869 to 1910, a certain number will not survive him. But from the point of view of the development of Belgian literature, the action of Lemonnier has been considerable. He was the first Belgian writer to make a living by his writings and to reap some Parisian success. Though strongly influenced by Zola and his school, he succeeded in preserving his national temperament, and fought obstinately for the recognition of a purely Belgian literature. His headquarters remained in Brussels, and the best of his works, such as "Le Vent dans les Moulins," "Le Petit Homme de Dieu," "La Vie Belge," have been devoted to the exaltation of his country's spirit and beauty. Lemonnier was also an art-critic, and it has been said of him that "he wrote with a brush." His power for description and his sense of colour are characteristically Flemish. Lemonnier was the forerunner of an important group of Belgian poets and story-tellers who gathered round Max Waller (Maurice Warlomont), the editor of *La Jeune Belgique*. This group included all the most prominent Belgian modern writers, not excepting Maeterlinck and Verhaeren. Though deeply divided as regards ideals and methods of expression, the contributors of *La Jeune Belgique* agreed on one point: the right of Belgium to a national literature, distinct from France, finding in the country and the people its main source of inspiration.

EEKHOUD—RODENBACH

Georges Eekhoud (1854–1927), faithful to this programme, described the people of Antwerp, his native city, and of the surrounding countryside, as in " The Little Servant," in " Mes Communions," " Le Cycle Patibulaire," etc. ; he studied types of outlaws and vagabonds. He published also several excellent translations from Marlowe and Beaumont and Fletcher, and essays on the Elizabethan dramatists. Georges Rodenbach (1855–1898) is better known for his works of verse, such as " Les Tristesses " and " Vies encloses," than for his prose works. Though born in Tournai, he was brought up in Bruges and felt the charm of the " dead city " so keenly that he devoted all his talent to it. He went to Paris early in his life, and became there the recognised poet of Bruges. " Lace of Bruges " is his best effort in the short-story form, and essentially characteristic of his genius.

EUGÈNE DEMOLDER

Eugène Demolder (1862–1919) was also one of the first promoters of *La Jeune Belgique*. Together with Lemonnier and with a great number of Flemish writers, he was strongly influenced by his admiration for the artists of his country. His " Contes d'Yperdamme," " Récits de Nazareth," and other works are merely literary transpositions of the art of old Flemish masters, such as Peter Breughel, and of their method of interpreting the Gospel. Those acquainted with these works will remember that the events which they describe—such as the Nativity, the Massacre of the Innocents, the Adoration of the Magi, etc.—are not represented as happening in the past, in a far-away country, amidst Eastern surroundings, but as if they had taken place in seventeenth-century Flanders, in a landscape of ice and snow, among Flemish peasants and landsknechten in armour. Whether such interpretation was due to sheer ignorance or to the popular belief—so often expressed in folksongs—that the Gospel story is eternally true, ever present, and intimately mingled in the people's everyday life, Demolder adopted it with delight, emphasising the humorous effects of anachronism while preserving the reverent treatment of the old masters.

MAETERLINCK

The dramas and essays of Maurice Maeterlinck (b. 1862) have gained for him universal celebrity. His first contributions to *La Jeune Belgique* were, however, in verse, and it is interesting to recall here that it was through the short story, "The Massacre of the Innocents," that he drew upon himself for the first time the attention of the Belgian public. This story at once stamps its author as a Fleming, not only on account of the influence of Peter Breughel, which is as evident here as in Demolder's works, but also the painter's methods are substituted for the writer's, the story being told through a series of pictures, not through a connected and logical narrative.

HUBERT KRAINS

While most of the Belgian poets are of Flemish origin, the story-tellers are generally Walloons. But the latter, far from being absorbed by France, as might be expected, deal almost exclusively with their local surroundings. Hubert Krains (b. 1862) describes in a realistic and somewhat sombre vein the life of the peasants and small "bourgeois" of the country near Liège.

A GROUP OF WALLOONS

Prominent representatives of the group of Walloon story-tellers are Georges Garnier (b. 1868), Maurice des Ombriaux (b. 1868), and Louis Delattre (b. 1870). All three were born in Hainault and, like most Belgian prose writers, prefer to deal with the life of the country-side. They express the lighter side of the Belgian spirit, but, in spite of their dry humour, never lose an intense feeling for the landscape in which their pictures are framed. A Walloon can laugh at the human comedy better than a Fleming, but he shares his northern brother's delight in nature, and grows poetical when placed before some beautiful scenery.

Perhaps the most delicate prose-writer now in Belgium is Blanche Rousseau (Mme. Maurice Belval) (b. 1875), author of the delicate little fairy story, "The Little House in the Midst of the Woods." She has only published four or five books, but every one of them is full of poetry and of the most refined sense of the pathetic and humorous side of life. Her tales are symbolic without being forced, and she has succeeded in renewing the art of legend-writing. The symbol with her is never cumbrous, and, though entirely original in their subjects, her stories seem as natural and genuine as any familiar fairy tale.

In concluding these notes, it is scarcely necessary to add that the editors of this " library " have not attempted to do more than illustrate the national genius of Belgium in the field of the short story, and it may be claimed for this brief section that it is at least representative of the style and character of the Belgian story-tellers, though by no means representative of the general body of Belgian literature, in which the short story holds a less conspicuous place than in the literature of most other European nations. E. C.

*** All the Belgian stories, with the exception of those by Maeterlinck and Rodenbach, have been expressly translated for this volume by Mrs. Tita Brand Cammaerts.

CHARLES DECOSTER
1827–1879

THE THREE PRINCESSES

I

Of the three noble virgins and of their great beauty

In the year of our Lord Jesus Christ 690, lived three lovely maidens, issue in the male line of the noble family of the great Emperor Octavian.

Their names were Blanche, Clara, and Candida.

If they had consecrated to God the flower of their virginity, it must not be thought that 'twas for lack of lovers.

For each day a large gathering of people assembled to see them pass to church, and each one said to the other, "Behold their fair eyes, behold their white hands."

And many a one, too, gazing upon them with longing, added lamenting, "Must these sweet virgins make a vow to God when there are eleven thousand, yea, more, already in His Paradise?" "But not so dainty as these," replied one aged and asthmatic man behind them, as he drew in the perfume of their robes. And walking thus, this aged one, espying some youth spitting in the water or stretched upon his belly on the grass warming his back in the sun, would deliver him a kick, saying, "Up—wilt thou not see the most beauteous flowers in the world?"

II

How a young Prince of Arabia doted upon the youngest, and what came of it

Many would have persuaded them to wed, but failing of their purpose, pined and faded visibly.

Among these was a Prince of Arabia, who with great ceremony was baptized, and 'twas expressly for the love of the youngest maid. Moreover, not obtaining what he would, either by prayer or force, one morning on the threshold of the door he pierced his heart with his dagger.

The maiden, hearing this noble lord cry out, descended in great haste, and caused him to be laid upon her couch, whereat he who was not yet quite dead, greatly rejoiced.

But when she stooped above him to bind and dress his wound, he found a little strength, kissed her lovely mouth, sighed as one relieved, and gave up his soul in great joy.

But the virgin was ill pleased with this kiss, for she thought it taken from the rights of Jesus her Divine Spouse. Nevertheless she let fall a tear or so for the sake of the noble knight.

III

In which is seen how Satan pursues those maidens who desire to fly the world

Oft were there many lovers before the virgins' house, some singing plaintive songs, others seated proudly upon the backs of brave prancing chargers, others in silence sad gazing the livelong day up at the windows. And ofttimes would they fight among themselves and kill each other for jealousy. At which the maidens were right troubled. "Ah," said the eldest to the youngest, "pray for us, Blanche, thou well-named one, white of soul and white of body, pray for us, dear one, Jesus hearkens willingly to the prayers of such maids as thee."

"My sisters," replied the youngest, "I am more unworthy than you, but I will pray if you desire it."

"Yes," said they.

Then these three virgins cast themselves upon their knees and thus the youngest prayed:

"Sweet Jesus, we have surely sinned against Thee, else wouldst Thou allow the Evil One to stir these miserable men to love by our beauty? Yea, we have sinned, but wretched that we are, 'twas all against our will, Lord. Ah, pardon us, for we are sorely grieved. Thou wishedst us to be Thine, and all that is ours for Thee we have kept, our youth and beauty, melancholy and mirth, wishes and prayers, body and soul, thought and deed, all. In the morning, at midday, and at night—at every hour and moment—do we not think of Thee? When Thy bright sun arises, O Beloved, and also when in Thy heaven gleam the bright stars, they can see us praying and offering to Thee, not gold, incense, nor myrrh, but our humble love and our poor heart. 'Tis not enough, we know it well. Alas, teach us to do more." And pausing here all three began to utter piteous lament.

"Sweet Jesus," said the youngest yet again, "we know right well the will of these men. They think that they are proud and fair to look upon, and that thus they should win our love, but they are neither fair, nor good, nor proud as Thou art, Jesus. Therefore Thine are we, Thine will ever be, and never theirs. Wilt Thou love us just a little still, for Thou alone art all our comfort, all our joy, in this sad world, Jesus. Thou wilt not forsake us. The earthly husband leaves not the spouse in danger, nor eke the bridegroom the bride. Art Thou not better than they all, and wilt Thou not protect us from the enemy's snares? If Thou dost not wish it, do it not, but then might they rob us of our virginity, which is Thine. Ah, rather, Dear Beloved, make us to pass all our lives withered and hideous, then into Hell descend in midst of devils, flames, and sulphur, and there abide till Thou shalt judge us pure enough at last to receive us into Thy Paradise, where we may look upon Thee and love Thee eternally. Have pity upon us. AMEN."

And having thus spoken, the poor maiden fell a-weeping and her sisters likewise, saying, "Pity, Jesus, pity."

IV

Of the voice of the Divine Bridegroom and of the fair knight in silver armour

On a sudden heard they a sweet voice saying, "Take courage." "Hearken," said they, "the Bridegroom deigneth speak to His brides."

Then was the chamber filled with a perfume sweeter than that which rises from finest incense burning in a censer.

Then the voice spoke again. "To-morrow morn," it said, "at sunrise leave the town, mount on your palfreys, and still riding go your way straight forward, not caring for the road. I will protect you."

"We will obey Thee," said they, "Oh, Thou who makest us the happiest among all the daughters of men." And rising, they embraced each other joyfully.

Meanwhile, as they were listening to the voice, there came to the place a fair knight in silver armour. Upon his head was a golden helmet, on which fluttered like a bird, a plume brighter than flame. His steed was white as snow.

None had perceived his coming, he seemed to rise from out the ground among the crowd of wooers, who, seized with fear, ventured not to look upon him.

"Ye evil men," said he, "Avaunt, remove your steeds. Know ye not that the sound of their hoofs disturbs these ladies' orisons?" Thus having said, he departed riding towards the East.

"Ah," said the wooers one to another, "Saw ye that silver armour and that plume of fire? Surely 'twas the angel of God, come down from Paradise to seek these ladies." And the most wanton muttered, "He did not forbid us to stand here on foot before the door, therefore can we do it modestly."

V

How, according to Divine command, the three virgins adventured on their journey

Upon the morrow, before the dawn of day, came many, but having left their chargers in their stalls. The sun having risen, they beheld the three virgins, according to the command of God, each mounted on her palfrey, thus issuing from their home. Thinking that they were going into the neighbouring meadows to inhale the fresh morning air they followed, singing joyous carols in their honour. While still within the town, the steeds moved with a stately tread, but leaving it, they quickened their pace.

Then did the lovers try to follow on foot, but finally one by one they fell upon the road, exhausted. Having gone for several leagues, the palfreys stopped. And the three virgins, seeing that they were now delivered from their troubles, resolved to proclaim the wondrous aid of God and to build in His honour a fair church.

Where? they knew not. But the matter was already plain in Paradise, as you shall see anon.

For no sooner were they seated on their palfreys again than, led by the Spirit of God, these beasts galloped away. And they leapt across rivers, went through deep forests, passed through towns whose gates opened before them and closed again behind them, sprang over walls. And fear struck the heart of every one as those three white horses and those three fair ladies passed by him, swift as the wind.

And thus sped they on a thousand leagues and more.

VI

Of the diamond hammer and of the foundations which were uptorn out of the earth

At Haeckendover in the Duchy of Brabant the steeds stayed their course and neighed, and would take no further step neither forwards nor yet backwards. For 'twas that spot which God had chosen for His church. But the Virgins, gathering that the palfreys were a-weary, went on foot as far as Hoy Bout and there judged that 'twould be well to build the church.

Therefore they assembled the most sturdy workmen, masons, and artists in so great number that in one day the foundations were raised two handbreadths at the least.

At seeing which the maidens rejoiced much, believing that their work was pleasing unto God.

But on the morrow morn, behold all the foundations torn from out the earth.

Thinking that some traitorous heretic fortuitously there lay buried, who at night had shaken the sacred stones of the church with his accursed bones, went they to Steenen Berg with all these masons and there accomplished like work as at Hoy Bout.

But the morrow saw again the foundations torn from earth.

'Twas because the Lord desired to be adored at Haeckendover only. And He had sent His angels in the night, with diamond hammers from the storehouse of Paradise, and had made them to destroy the work of the three virgins, who, grievously troubled and full of woe, fell upon their knees, imploring and praying God to tell them where He would be adored.

VII

Of the youngest maiden and the beauteous angel

On a sudden beheld they a youth of celestial beauty, clothed with a robe of the colour of the setting sun. Benignly he looked upon them. Knowing him to be the angel of God the three maids prostrated themselves with faces to the earth. But the youngest, most full of hardihood, as are children, ventured to raise her eyes to that fair messenger and seeing him so well looking, gained courage and smiled.

The angel took her hand, saying to her and to her sisters, "Rise and follow me," which the virgins straightway did.

Thus came they to the spot where standeth now the church, and said the angel then, "Here is the place."

"We thank thee, sir," replied the youngest maiden gleefully.

VIII

How the three virgins beheld a green isle, and of the fair flowers and birds which were there

'Twas the thirteenth day after Epiphany. Much snow had fallen, and 'twas freezing hard on account of the bitter wind which blew. And the virgins beheld before them amidst the snow, as 'twere a green isle. And this isle had a girdle of silk thread of purple hue. And all within the isle was springtide, blossoming roses, violets, and jessamine, whose perfume is as balm. Without was winter blast and fearsome cold.

Towards the centre, where to-day standeth the high altar, was seen an evergreen oak, all in flower, as if 'twere truly Persian jessamine. Amidst the branches, redwings, nightingales, and finches emulated one another in singing the sweet song of Paradise. For they were the angels, who decking themselves in feathers warbled thus in praise of God. A sweet nightingale, the lovelier singer of all, bore in its right claw a parchment strip whereon was writ in letters of finest gold: " Here is the place, chosen of God, divinely shown unto the three virgins, wherein that they might build a church unto the glory of our Lord and Saviour, Jesus Christ."

Great was the joy of the virgins, and the youngest said unto the angel, " Herein we see that God a little loveth us. What behoveth it us to do, Sir Angel? "

" It behoveth you, fair maid," replied the gentle messenger, " here to build a church, and choose unto that end twelve of the finest workmen, neither more nor less; God Himself will be the thirteenth."

Having thus spoken, up to high heaven mounted he again.

IX

Of the church of Haeckendover and of the wondrous mason who worked thereat

Thus the three, in greatest haste, chose out from among all the twelve fine masons, who straightway laid the foundations of the church where had been the purple-hued silken thread.

The work advanced now so well that in truth it was a joy to see how fast the stones rose one upon another. But lo, the miracle was that at the hours of work there were ever thirteen masons, but at the hours of dinner and of payment, only twelve.

For the Lord deigned to work with them, but not to eat nor to drink—He who hath such fine broth in His Paradise, such sweet fruits and wine from the fountain of Saphir, the which is a fountain wherefrom floweth ever wine yellower than would be molten gold. Neither suffereth He lack of money, which is a pain reserved for us, needy, wretched, and necessitous of nature.

Thus it befell that soon the bell was placed as is ever done whenas a church is perfectly completed. Then entered the three virgins, and falling on her knees the youngest said:

" By whom, O Spouse Divine and Well-Beloved Jesus, must this Thy church raised in Thy honour be dedicated? "

Whereto the Lord replied, " Myself will dedicate and consecrate this church unto Myself. Let none come to consecrate it after Me."

X

Of the two Bishops, and of their withered hands

Ne'ertheless two venerable Bishops then in Haeckendover, seeing the new church, desired to bless it—naught knowing of the words of Jesus to the three virgins, else had they never done a deed so bold.

But terrible was their punishment. For while the one was busy blessing the water, on a sudden he became blind. The other held the holy water brush with arms aloft to bless the church, and these were withered and all power to move bereft them. But lo, the Bishops who had sinned were full of contrition, and prayed the Lord that He would deign to pardon them.

And they were pardoned for that they had sinned in ignorance.

And thereafter came they ofttimes in devout pilgrimage to Haeckendover.

CAMILLE LEMONNIER
1845–1913

THE FEAST OF SAINT CATHERINE

Two little children came and went in the corridor with an air of mystery, watching the clocks, for it was customary not to celebrate the grandmother's saint's-day until a few minutes before dinner.

Outside in the streets, the snow was spreading a white cloak, and the flakes bounded in the air like shuttlecocks from invisible battle-dores. None of the poor folks who ventured out in such weather along the side walks could have suspected that something was being plotted that day within the house; it wore its accustomed appearance, there was not a tile more on the roof, nor a curtain more at the windows; but inside it was not the same thing. Everyone wanted to laugh, and yet appeared as if nothing were the matter; there were whisperings behind doors, and sudden silences. Some one went upstairs quickly, then came down again on tiptoe; and quite quietly, as if by enchantment, in the most secret corner of the house bouquets and cakes arrived.

" Tick-tack " went the kitchen clock, but one could have heard more easily still the tick-tack of the two little children's hearts. How long these hours were! Up to mid-day it was nothing: one waited, one was patient, and then sometimes the confectioner was late, but the afternoon seemed as if it would never end. Then there was rage against the wretched clock!

The two children were very small; even if they climbed upon a chair they could not reach its face, otherwise they would certainly have pushed on the hands with their little pink fingers. At last, however, it seemed to have made up its mind to move a little quicker. The tick-tack became more frequent, and finally when night fell one could not have told which beat more irregularly, the pendulum of the clock or the hearts of the two children. For my part, I think it was the hearts of the children.

Without any one knowing how it happened, the fire was found alight in the big room, as it was on Sunday afternoons, and the grandmother had just settled herself by it in her red plush armchair, worn out at the place where her arms rest. Then evening fell, the servant closed the shutters, and the light of the lamps made stars in the shadows inside the room.

The front-door bell had tinkled many times that day, and people had come in carrying *things* in big paper wrappings and baskets. What things? The children knew all about it, but it was a secret which they would not have disclosed for anything in the world. Lids of hampers were raised, paper stripped off, and four little hands beat together, while eyes gleamed; and the grandmother, shut in her room, coughed as hard as she could, pretending she had not heard.

Tap! tap! tap! It was her walnut cane. Then every one scampered off so as not to be found in her way, and the grandmother, who heard doors slam in every direction, passed on murmuring, "All right . . . all right," in a voice which said, "Go on. I have seen nothing. I know nothing." She even tapped her stick on the ground a little harder than usual to warn every one of her coming. Thus the day passed until the moment when the hand pointed to six o'clock.

Then one might have seen every one in the house going to that mysterious corner where the presents were hidden; and long before getting there a smell of violets and vanilla gave notice of the presence of extraordinary things. Voices buzzed confusedly, plates clattered against one another, people came and went on tiptoe. The two little children looked like fat red peonies then, their cheeks were so flushed, and their eyes blinked hard in the effort to remember the verses which had been taught them.

The father, an old servant, and several neighbours were there too —only the mother was absent, having gone before them to the grave; but it is not at all sure that her soul was not fluttering at that moment around the lips of her children.

Then they set off, the children first, the father following, and behind the father came the old servant in her turn, carrying in her hands a pot of mignonette or a little rose tree in bloom. They wound through the hall, crossed the dining-room, and the sound of their feet stopped suddenly before the drawing-room door—only for a moment it is true—for the father turned the handle and the children rushed into the room, holding out their little arms and mixing up their verses.

How four candles had lighted themselves upon the mantelpiece was no more known than how the fire was made. On the table the special Sunday lamp was burning, yellow and bright beneath its glass shade; and in the cupboard the glasses faintly rang, as if to remind one that they would also like to take part in the merrymaking.

Although the door has creaked as it opens, the grandmother has not turned her head, but the two little children raise their voices so high that she pretends to awake, and passes her hand over her face. Then a slight trembling passes over her whole body. She wants to speak, but cannot, but two happy tears run slowly down her cheeks, and in her turn she holds out her arms to them. No doubt it happens that her dress makes acquaintance with the cream from the tarts, but who would think of a little spot on one's dress at such a moment? Bouquets and cakes are placed upon her knees and each one, as he offers his gift, kisses her on her dear cheeks, which quiver like jelly.

When every one has finished, it is the old servant's turn; she offers her flowers, then wipes her mouth on her sleeve, and asks to be allowed to kiss the grandmother like the others. While she presses her fat, honest face against each cheek, you can see her laughing and crying at the same time, and the two little children show their white teeth and shout, "Long live Saint Catherine!"

Is it the light from the hearth, the reflection of the curtains, or the brightness of the candles which suddenly sends, as it were, a pink fire over the face of the grandmother? No; it is the joy of her heart, and a new youth seems to have begun for her with this hour which brings her good wishes and kisses. The lips of little children make old grandmothers young again. And she admires the cakes and bouquets, and claps her hands.

"Really, is to-day Saint Catherine?" says she. "I had not thought of it!"

She does not notice that her best cap with ribbons and lace betrays her. "Why, then, have you made yourself so fine, grandmother?" And everything in the room seems to be in admiration of her flowered silk dress.

Then the table is laid, courses are left out so as to come more quickly to the cakes. Letters in sugar run all over the almond icing and the cream, and all together make up the wish, "Long live Saint Catherine!" From the cellars now come old bottles covered with spiders' webs, and the glasses fill with a golden wine which seems to reflect the happiness in every one's eyes.

The grandmother raises her glass up high, and thanks big and small for this happy day. No one present but is touched, and while all look at her, the light of the lamp makes around her, as it were, an aureole which fades softly into the shadows.

Thus it is with her memory, for all this is but a vision of long ago; but each year brings back the feast of Saint Catherine, and sometimes it snows again as it did in the old days. Then I hear through the room the echo of her tap, tap, and I feel that I shall see her leaning on her stick, and coughing under the lace frill of her cap. Alas, it is only a thick branch which the wind strikes against my window-pane; but the little grandchild of former years has a grandchild now in her turn, and they go together through the quiet country to the cemetery where the beloved grandmother sleeps, and a voice seems to rise from the earth and to speak to them through the silence of things, saying:

" Really, is it already the feast of Saint Catherine? I had not thought of it, my children."

GEORGES EEKHOUD
B. 1854

THE LITTLE SERVANT

LITTLE servant from over there, unused to service, bearing in your countenance, in your hair, on your lips, and, above all, in the depths of your great eyes, the quivering atmosphere and dreamy sky of the dear country. . . .

Recommended and introduced by Master Martens, a thoroughly good fellow, the little servant crossed our threshold one morning. A man from Brabantsputte, one of those pedlars who carry the products of the slender village industries to Brussels every Monday, and relieved of their roll of goods return to their own clock-tower towards the end of the week, had piloted his little fellow-villager to our door.

In a somewhat choked voice, which she tried to steady, the little girl asked her escort to say a last farewell to her mother, her elder brother, and her little sister.

"All right."

The pedlar took off his cap, adjusted his pack on his shoulders, and went off, emitting his nasal and guttural cry.

After putting down her modest belongings, tied up in a red cotton handkerchief, she glanced round the kitchen with her large brown autumn-coloured eyes, and said simply, "I think I shall like being here."

In the tone in which this tribute was spoken I distinguished a touching expression.

I read in it an appeal to our indulgence, the wish to settle down, the courage of a fifteen-year-old heart which doubts its own strength. It seemed to say, "You look kind people, and if I am clumsy and slow at first, you will not be hard on me, will you? You will be patient and remember that I am only a child, and that I have never been away from my own village before?"

She added aloud, "Mr. Martens told me to do him credit and to be very good and polite."

Surely she was a credit to the girls of the Campine and to Mr.

Martens' confidence. From the early morning she was at work, but, in spite of her activity, at dinner-time she could not eat.

Next day found her with red eyes and a drawn face.

"She is homesick, but this trouble, which shows a good heart, will not last," we said to ourselves.

On the following days she showed the same energy over her work, but she had no appetite, and her colour, fresh as a peony, faded.

On Saturday, his round finished, the pedlar Franske came to ask news of her. As he went off, she called out after him, "Be sure to tell them that I am very, very happy, and that I don't want to go back to Brabantsputte." And, as if proud of her strength of soul, she said to me eagerly, "You heard, sir, he will tell my mother how happy I am with you."

Good little thing! I felt suspicious, however, of this.

I guessed that she had cut short the interview with the pedlar of Putte to prevent herself from being tempted to go off with him to her native paths through the pine trees, for when I went down to the kitchen again, she did not turn away quickly enough to hide the tears trickling over her long dark lashes, and drowning in a November gloom the September richness of her great eyes.

In the afternoon she scrubbed the hall. From my room I heard her giving energetic blows with the broom handle. She continued to make the pump groan and to swish pailfuls of water over the tiles.

"That's a good thing, I thought. She is throwing off her depression. I should not be surprised if she began to sing to cheer herself up at her work. The song did not come, though; instead, the prelude became tempestuous. At last the hubbub prevented me from working. I went down to entreat the over-zealous worker to use her implements—brushes and pails—more discreetly.

I paused on the landing. The poor thing was indeed lifting up her voice in the noise.

But what a sad song! What a heart-breaking lament!

It was to stifle the sound of her sobs that the little servant had made such a to-do. Thanks to the noise I was able to go up to her without her having heard me coming.

"Well," said I, touching her shoulder, "is this the way you are settling down?"

She dropped her things, covered her face with her hands, and through a fresh outburst of tears, she confessed to me her weakness —her sacred weakness.

"Forgive me, sir . . . when I think of home it is stronger than my will and power. I must cry out or I would choke. . . . It is as if they had tied a string to my heart and were pulling over there as hard as they could. . . . They are pulling, and they'll end by getting me over to them . . . otherwise they'll drag out my soul. . . . It's stupid, I know. And how they will laugh at me in the village! I can't help it. . . . And it isn't your fault either. Surely I am well-treated! Yes, indeed, only too well-treated here . . . . But, you see, if you were better still, Madame and you, if you were the Blessed Lord and the Holy Virgin themselves, I would pack up my things all the same. . . . So let me go back on Saturday with Franske, the pedlar. . . ."

There was no way of keeping her; in vain during the week did she strive—touched by our words, our sympathy, and care—to fight against her obsession. Several times she declared her resolution to remain, and to be sensible. But even at the moment of this elation, the tone and look and pitiful smile denied her words. On the very eve of the visit of her fellow-villager, irresolute, not knowing whether she should obey her head or her heart, she packed and unpacked her humble luggage.

"My mother promised to come and see me; very well, I'll wait till she comes and go back with her if it isn't any better."

"That's settled, then?"

"That's settled."

A minute after this decision the demented girl ran mechanically to consult the clock, and found the hours already too long which separated her from the appearance of Franske, the deliverer. No; it would never be any better! It was unnecessary to confess to us her lack of courage. We released her from her promise.

The last night passed, and she got up long before day. The pedlar never came very early, but this did not prevent the little country girl from trembling at the milkman's ring. All ready, with her bundle in her hand, she awaited Franske in the hall. Suppose he should forget to pass to-day! Suppose he had not sold his wares! Suppose he should be afraid of troubling us! Any amount of cruel suppositions tortured the poor little thing, too inexperienced to set out on her journey alone, and find the way to her beloved clock-tower.

There was another ring, and it was at last he to whom she opened. . . .

The fellow was not a little amazed at this sudden change of decision. He laughed at his protégée, and undertook to make her listen to reason.

The big fair fellow, with his deliberate way, knew the town better. For five years he had walked through Brussels every week, calling his wares in the most distant streets, and if the capital had not succeeded in seducing and corrupting him, it had at least ceased to frighten him.

The wise exhortations of the pedlar did not persuade the little one in the least. Rather than stay she would have clung on to him as one would on to a life-buoy. The fellow was quite embarrassed, and apologised for her. If he had not kept her in the half-open doorway, she would have gone without saying good-bye to us.

I laughed condescendingly. "Did you ever see such a silly little thing? She ran away as if the house were falling down."

Pose, affectation, a mask, all that, my good friend! In my heart I was thinking—I don't blame you for this desertion, my poor child. And your people will be wrong if they make fun of you. You are not the only one who pines far from your lair. I, too, control myself and set my face. Noisily I dig and delve to dull my senses. And if I stir and bustle about, it is in order that they may not hear the beating of my heart. Like you, little one, it is when I seem most active and gay that I am on the point of breaking down and admitting myself beaten. . . . Dear little girl, my sister in the holy religion of patriotism, do you remember the day when the boy from Brabantsputte brought you news of your village and of what was happening on the Dutch frontier? I went by with an indifferent air to catch some scraps of your conversation, and inquired in a casual tone of those good people who had forgotten me, or who had never known me, but who are "from yonder," bear names like ours, speak the dear dialect, haunt the heather or the meadows where I spent my best, my only life.

As foolish as you, in my crazy affection, I am inclined to believe that the sun, and especially the stars of the Campine, are different from those here, unless, like myself, the exiled stars put on an enigmatical face and hide their unquenchable suffering under a mask of coldness and scepticism.

Franske said, "And the son of Widow Hendrikx of the 'Cosy Corner' is going to marry Bella, the cobbler's girl. . . . The Marinckx killed their pig on Saturday. . . . And Bastyns is going away. And Machiels is coming back. . . . And Nand is. . . . And the band plays on Saturdays now at Laveldoms."

At this spoken village journal, interrupted by your simple exclamations, "Zou het? Hoor je!" (Really? Just listen!)—at this monotonous rosary told by the pedlar—such intimate, touching recollections surged up in my heart. . . .

Oh! I could have listened to this melancholy song for hours—for long, long hours—as I listened to the wind in the leaves, the lowing of the cattle, and the sound of the church bells. . . .

After the departure of this fellow my books seemed more dull, my friends more affected, my business more unbearable, and the town more stuffy.

Between ourselves, dear little one, I am as weak as you. The carnival of town life wearies me more and more; my mask and city disguise begin to weigh terribly upon me. May the time soon come for me also to go back at all costs to my own countryside, if it be only to sleep close to the church, you know where, at the foot of its slate tower, with its crooked roof which calls over its curtain of trees on Sundays to the laggards who are about to miss the Elevation of the Host; you know—the place where the youths confess their love, and talk in low tones so as not to tempt the dead.

GEORGES RODENBACH
1855-1898

LACE OF BRUGES

SPRING had thrown its green mantle over the fields beyond the city where, standing by itself, is the Sisterhood of Bruges. From a window of the little convent, Sister Ursula was watching the twigs and branches of the elms, clothed with young foliage, slowly swaying in the light breeze, with movements recalling those of infancy. The lawn was brightly green, and green as grass were the little doors in line along the cloister; but elsewhere white was the only colour, as if green, the colour of hope, lived here together with the white of innocence. All around were walls of snowy whitewash, white as the linen-covered altar-rails; at the windows were curtains of spotless muslin—everything was lily-white. Here and there went quiet sisters under their quaint head-dress, moving like the swans of the Bruges canals, and scarcely disturbing the silence more than the swans disturb the water.

Sister Ursula was a study in white, her ivory complexion reflecting the white of her linen cap. She had early lost her parents, and had spent the years of childhood in an Ursuline convent before coming to the Sisterhood at Bruges. Young as she was, she had no memory of hearth and home, nor echo of the voice of other days. And having thus lived always among strangers, she was full of thoughts to which she had never given utterance. Yet sadness had no place in her heart. She was habitually silent with the silence which came to her from this peaceful cloister, where footsteps fell soundlessly upon the pavement, as if the whole place were part of the church, or the church had thrown over the garden its mystic atmosphere, heavy with old chants, and dim with incense mounting upwards. This mystical silence was all the vaster and more profound for the incessant falling through it of the chiming of the bells from city steeples, like flakes of music falling one by one.

Sister Ursula was very happy. She lived in the spirit of the hour and the place, more and more absorbing the character of the Sisterhood, her little soul echoing the chiming of the bells, and becoming herself a cloister surrounded by white curtains, festooned with the pale blue ribbons of floating incense.

Ursula and five of her sisters inhabited a tiny gabled cottage, one of many which together constituted this religious house. Their days were taken up with various duties; there was the Divine Office to say, and prayers, and all the housework to do, and a little manual work. In their case this was needlework, well suited to the delicate white hands of these innocent creatures. Most of them, indeed, were engaged in lace-making, which is the chief and oldest industry of their order. It is a gentle craft, and not unworthy of hands weary of the rosary. In every one of these convents you may see from an early hour the sisters in their workroom, sitting in line against the wall, and holding on their knees the cushions over which their cunning fingers chase the bobbins.

Sister Ursula was known as one of the cleverest lacemakers, and her marvellous work well supported the fame of that precious lace of Bruges, which has ever adorned the robes of queens. She loved this work with all an artist's love. For her it was indeed an art, and her fingers played among the threads of her cushion as those of a musician on his harp. Often she would improvise, suddenly inventing a new design, perhaps a cluster of rose-traceries, great white ornate flowers, such as she had seen one winter's night in frosted pattern on her window-pane and all at once now came back to mind. Sometimes you might have thought from her expression that she was working with threads lent by the Blessed Virgin. What snowy wonders she made as if in play! Sometimes an invisible spider's web like a net in which stars had been entangled; sometimes an intricate scheme which seemed mere confusion, but finally became an ornament of finest filigree. Is not lace, after all, the jewellery of flaxen tissue?

When working at her best, Ursula was carried quite out of herself. She scarcely looked at the pattern, and even delighted in making variations on it, and in boldly creating some new effect to change the everlasting spring of these virginal roses. She would add some swift movement of her soul to those immemorial patterns which were the pride of the Order and had been copied for centuries; no one knows how they originated! perhaps it was at the time of the folk-songs and by the same unrecorded impulse. These laces are no more than flowers treated decoratively, as the songs of the people are redolent of natural life. Indeed, so close is the analogy between lace and music that even at Divine Office in the church, as Ursula listened to the chant, she instinctively followed the movement of an anthem as if it had been a lacework of sounds in the making.

But a deeper and more spiritual joy also pervaded Sister Ursula's humble heart whenever she remembered, many times a day, that her work was destined for use of worship and that her hands were actually serving God. Her work was given only to the adornment of churches and altars and to vestments for the celebration of the mass. Surely these hours of hers were spent in a form of prayer. Her bobbins passed through her fingers like the beads of a swift rosary, where the fingers rather than the lips are engaged in prayer; and her fabrics were a kind of story or litany recited in praise of God. For this reason she refused to take orders for lace except from religious communities and from priests, for the convents and parishes of the city, or for the sacristies of the countryside. She knew well enough that the wonderful lace of Bruges, renowned throughout the world, was bought and sold and carried far away, often to be employed to far less saintly ends. It might become the servant of coquetry and luxury, adorn garments of vanity, and even frame the sinful picture of bare necks and shoulders. It was in vain that any one applied to her for lace to be used for such profane purposes as these; she had never hesitated to refuse every application of the kind, wishing to see in her dearly-loved craft nothing but ornaments kept for God alone, and having no other purpose than His honour.

In spite of her modesty and against her will, her reputation as an artist had spread all around. She was known throughout Bruges and all the province as the most expert and cleverest exponent of the art. Her work was asked for by name, and was recognised by connoisseurs as if she had signed it. It was the very last word in lace, fantastic, intriguing.

The dealers were soon upon her track, and knocked often at the convent doors. Some came from far, and were from other countries, to secure specimens of her astonishing work. But Sister Ursula rejected every offer and reward. She had entered religion. Her renunciation of the world involved the entire devotion of her labour to God; and the restriction of her lace to the adornment of divine worship and of those engaged in it was altogether in the spirit of her intention. She refused to be moved from this resolution, as if it had been one of the vows of her vocation.

But one day, when the sister-portress had called her to the parlour and she had come obediently, though annoyed and unwilling, expecting to see only one more of these incessant commercial buyers, she was surprised to find three visitors of a different kind. One was an elderly lady; with her was a girl, plainly her daughter, for she was like a youthful portrait of her mother; and the third was a tall and handsome youth with some strange charm about him, especially a certain candour and directness of gaze. He spoke for the others. He was about to be married, and was engaged to the sweet girl beside him. He wished to make her a present of some of the most beautiful lace procurable, to adorn the bridal gown. He knew that Sister Ursula's gift was unique.

The gentle nun was much troubled by this request. She meant at first to refuse, saying as was her custom, that she only worked for churches and for religious communities. But somehow, she did not dare this time refuse abruptly. The young man had spoken with such confidence that his request would be granted, such touching certainty that love cannot but obtain all that it asks, and there was something so resolute in all his manner, that Sister Ursula sought in vain for her accustomed formula of refusal. She caught sight, as it were, of the word, and could even touch it, but for some reason she was unable to seize that uncompromising negative, which might have given her instant freedom, but seemed to escape each of her attempts and to hide or vanish with diabolical sport.

Without giving her any opportunity of refusing his request, the young man had asked Ursula to show them a few specimens of her work. She brought them several pieces arranged like a long scarf. The two women went into ecstasies, the girl examining the lace while the young man gazed upon her. He happened at one moment himself to take up the end of the fabric to study in detail, and the two young figures seemed to be linked together by this bond more insubstantial than a dream.

The two of them were so touching that Ursula could not watch them without emotion. The girl was of that pink and white complexion, a peculiarly Flemish attractiveness, which would soon fade under the shadow of the belfries and massive towers. With what loving confidence her great eyes turned toward her lover as she spoke, and how tender were his tones when he replied! He called her "Dorothy" in every phrase, loving to repeat her name in the language of love, which was still somewhat strange to him. He spoke her name with a sense of something precious in it, as though every syllable were a caress. And Ursula, too, felt herself carried away by the music of this voice, which seemed to her as though she could not but follow it, though it should be to the end of the world. She felt herself no longer able, nor even at liberty, to refuse the request which these good people had made. Indeed, even while he was speaking, she had found plausible reasons for giving way; this was no dealer, she said to herself, and God would surely not be jealous. Surely the good God would be very pleased, inasmuch as the nuptial lace, which just for once she meant to give them, would still take some small part in worship, united as it would be to a great sacrament of the holy faith.

Eagerly the little nun set to work. She had set her heart on doing a supreme piece of work, on surpassing herself indeed, and began at once to design a pattern which should express a new and symbolic idea: two flowers springing from a single thread; two birds cooing upon the edge of a nest. The bobbins flew hither and thither through the forest of pins. She seemed to be improvising. Rapt in spirit, she worked on her lace as a player upon his instrument, while her fingers now swift and now slow, moved over the lace beneath them as if over a keyboard or zither.

Nevertheless, deep in her soul she was dimly doubtful of her part in providing the garments of a bride. Sometimes her fingers lagged and the threads became entangled, especially when she remembered how they looked in the parlour—the gaze which taught her what love is, nay, the gaze of love itself. And how they must have loved!

But what, after all, is love? Until now, she had known nothing of it but its name. She had never really thought of it, but now she knew that it made you happy. This charming, mysterious, and tragic influence, from which she recoiled as from a sin, had at last taken human form in the traits of the commanding young man whom she could not forget. Ah, how lovely it must be to be looked on so, by such a face as that!

Sister Ursula knew very well that she would never know this superhuman joy. She was vowed to God, and was even wedded to God, but it was in the black robes of mourning, instead of the shining white garments which this happy Dorothy would wear, garments which she herself was helping to adorn. Do not imagine that Ursula envied her. The homesickness of love was with her, yet not clearly recognised. She never dreamed of loving any one, for she had taken a vow of chastity, fortified by every ascetic practice. Yet love no longer frightened her; the word haunted her mind, and her lips pronounced it. She began to love —Love itself.

And now, as she worked among her sisters, bending over the lace pillow, the bridal pair were often in her mind. She saw them as she had seen so many others like them, on the days when she went down to the town to make some trifling purchase, or to go to confession at Holy Saviour's, or to make the "Way of the Cross," in the chapel of Jerusalem. Hitherto she had never noticed them, but now they were obvious to her at a glance. She knew the devotees of love by their slower and closer movement, by their clear and happy expression, even by a light which seemed to surround them like the halo she had noticed round the moon. And springtime now came into the conspiracy, the season of love. A tender sweetness invaded the breeze. The poplars reflected in the canals swayed to the light airs, their reflections seeking and flying one another, and uniting in the trembling water. Even the leaves met as in a kiss.

And now Ursula saw the sparrows twittering on the branchlets of the trees and on the gables, courting and fighting in playful encounters. She could not fail to understand. She remembered the two lovers in the convent parlour, and other lovers whom she had seen at eventide along the quays. A thousand trifles which she had never before observed now became significant. For instance, this Minnewater, the great sleepy lake which surrounded the outer walls of the convent, on which the windows of her room had always opened, had often struck her by its silence, its reflections of the moving clouds, and the water-lilies as white as the soul of infancy. Yet she had never realised the meaning of its charming name, Minnewater, "the lake of love," or more exactly, "the lake of lovers." It was well named indeed; for now Ursula, less innocent, was incessantly conscious of the happy pairs of lovers who wandered round the shores of the lake, happy as the lovers whom she had seen in the parlour. Even their reflections as they walked by the lake united in the water under the pale moonlight.

Leaning out through her window Ursula watched the night, enervated and shaken with a storm of feeling. Sleep was impossible, but she tried to pray. In order to quiet her anxious thoughts by the repetition of words, she opened her prayer-book and read: "Lord, give us grace that we may be so filled with Divine love that we may give You all our heart." Hurriedly and eagerly she recited prayers which always brought back to her the word which she wished to escape; and the name of "love" seemed sometimes lawful, transfigured, burning like Isaiah's coal from the altar, but quite as often profane and sweet and earthly, touching her lips with the warmth of human kisses.

So the hours passed away in feverish vigil, marked at intervals by the slow striking of the clocks from the towers of Bruges. At every hour there was a disordered concert of sounds, the great deep old bells of the parish churches mingling with the high silvery tones of the convent bells. Sister Ursula knelt at these moments and muttered the canonical prayer: "The angel of the Lord declared unto Mary——"

And now she trembled with a great emotion and shook from head to foot. She had never hitherto gone very deeply into the significance of her prayers. But now, all of a sudden, she was plunged into this intimate and mysterious meaning, in which the Divine mystery emerged from the accustomed words. Her love had at last attained to more than the idea of love; and she was immediately convinced that she had lost in purity what she had gained in womanhood. She was ashamed of herself, and was struck with dreadful remorse. She knew now that all these thoughts, which were no longer venial, could be traced back to her acceptance of the order for the bridal robe. Surely she could not work at that any longer! She feared this beautiful lace which she had begun, just as she would have feared any other sin. She threw it aside as if it had been some bad book which she could no longer read. She knew that the Evil One, seeking her destruction, had devised this so innocent-seeming stratagem. All the pains of hell were hidden in these folds of lace. Strange medium for so deadly a poison!

Penitently Sister Ursula called to her patron saint for help, and started a novena to her. Every day she visited St. Ursula's shrine in Bruges, and lit a candle to burn many hours before it, a tiny quiet flame symbolising her own obedient heart. Peace soon came to the poor little sister. There was a heavenly calm in this shrine, where Memling's genius had painted St. Ursula, with her eleven thousand virgin companions, accepting death rather than the choice of sin. What a lesson of chastity they taught, standing fearlessly before the brutal soldiery and offering their breasts to the arrows of martyrdom!

And soon these holy observances, the novena and many rosaries and burning candles, and chiefly the intercession of St. Ursula herself, brought back our nun to the quietness of virtue. Temptation ceased to annoy her, and a resolution which came to her was carried at once into effect. She would immediately complete and deliver the order which too long had led her into doubtful ways. Inward peace was hers again. The pure laces of the sanctuary and altar now occupied her hours, instead of that dreadful marriage-lace which she had quite forgotten. Happy, heavenly thoughts now made their home in her soul, instead of the risky guesses and dreams of days gone by. She never thought of all that now, except as a danger of the past, which she had happily escaped. Yet sometimes a skiff, entering harbour, sees in one lightning flash all the raging sea behind; and this was Sister Ursula's experience one day when she was called to the parlour, and there found Dorothy, who had once been so charming and pretty. But what a difference there was now! The girl was thin, wan, greatly changed, and all alone. The nun recognised her voice rather than her features. For a moment Dorothy was silent, while Ursula trembled, wondering whether her own temptations had returned.

At last her young visitor was able to speak, with broken accents, while her poor little fragile body shook with sobs. She had not been married after all. No, there would never be a marriage. And so—this beautiful lace would not be needed; she had brought it back, and hoped that it would be accepted for a veil for Our Lady. And was it not, in fact, for Our Lady that Sister Ursula always made her lace?

The nun listened eagerly, and began to understand; the mystery seemed to clear up.

Yes, poor little Dorothy's fatal mistake had been that of wishing to take to herself Our Lady's lace. Dorothy had tried to believe just for once these votive laces might be appropriated to her own pleasure and her own wedding-gown. But all her delusive dream, that she had really been loved, had only been a devil's snare. She herself had not believed in it. She had never believed in it, but had only pretended to believe. The child confessed that she had known it was all a pretence, yet that she had been unable to resist it; and that in all the miserable comedy she had only enjoyed one moment, that moment when they had come to tempt Sister Ursula, to teach her what love meant, and to show her their faces glowing with love. Dorothy confessed that she had been no more than the puppet of fate. She knew now that it was all over, and had come quite simply to return the pieces of lace, like a theatrical costume which has played its part. It all seemed very natural and logical. Ursula did not even ask her why she had brought them back herself, and had not rather returned his gift to the young man. Doubtless, she supposed, he was no longer available; he had disappeared, invisibly, through the air. It must have been no other than the Tempter, Satan himself, who had taken that attractive form, and had enlisted this pretty accomplice only to gain access with her to this holy retreat, all in order to seduce one poor little nun, and by tantalising her with the vision of a kiss to infect her with desires which must lead to her destruction.

Poor little Dorothy had only been the hapless instrument in the hands of the power of hell. Even now she was completing her task by coming to show the picture of love's to-morrow, with its melancholy face, the culminating disillusion of this clutch at happiness, all the perils indeed which the nun had escaped by entering religion. Dorothy showed her all that she might have been and mercifully had not been, all those dire effects of the hurricane which lays the soul in ruins from which it can never recover. Ursula gazed on her, deeply affected. The child was so wan and frail; she held out the lace with the broken-hearted mien of a beggar who has only her hair to sell. With tears streaming from her eyes, Ursula seized her hands. "Poor Dorothy! poor little Dorothy!" she cried, and even then remembered how the lover had uttered this name. Sister Ursula gave Dorothy's lace to the sister-sacristan, after arranging it as a long veil to drape the statue of Our Lady on Sundays and the principal feasts.

Soon afterward came round the Feast of the Assumption, which is celebrated by a great procession, following on Benediction, through the streets of Bruges. In order to get a good view of the ceremony, Sister Ursula had taken her place on one of the quays near an Altar of Repose. Here for some moments the white procession was halted, a picture of snowy surplices, lilies, and candles, while the white swans assembled on the dark canal. The silvery jingling of censers was heard, and the sounds of a holy chant arose. Down from the high steeples the bells flung their huge clamour, to be lost among the fragrant herbs and flowers which had been scattered along the streets.

Sister Ursula, kneeling, watched the solemn rite. Immediately before her, surrounded by banners and statues, stood high the image of Our Lady, smiling under her long lace veil, Dorothy's veil, the veil of temptation, which, like Ursula's soul itself, after having fallen into evil hands, had come home at last to adorn the service of God.

EUGÈNE DEMOLDER
B. 1862

THE DAUGHTER OF JAIRUS

A WHITE monk came out of Jairus's mansion with Joe, the servant, and said: " I will go to the Prémontrés Monastery and see that the bells are rung."

" God receive her within the Paradise of Virgins," replied Joe.

" Amen," said the monk.

And pulling up his hood he moved away, gliding along the walls like a shadow, with arms crossed on his breast.

Joe was left alone and thought: " The bells toll for the dead to-day! . . . It is like fasting on Easter Day."

Do they pour wine in the organ pipes on All Souls' Day when they blow for the Dies Irae? But it is all the same to me after all, for I must stop to look after the house.

But what a fair! The bells will make the very heavens sad. To go and dance to the sound of the bells tolling for your dead! And indeed the festival was being prepared on the market-place of Yper-damme. From the balcony of the Town Hall, where presently the aldermen were going to appear, hung rich rugs from Smyrna. On every house front were fastened flags and banners. Tables were being laid before the doors of the inns, and heavy brewers' drays deposited full barrels.

At one end of the market-place were planted poles, decorated with garlands of flowers and shields, a platform was being erected, and the guild carpenters made the beams and planks ring beneath the blows of their hammers.

Further on, there was a merry-go-round with wooden horses, which was already practising to the sound of a clarionette and a horn. And along the principal street stretched a line of booths, with awnings and open stalls newly set up in anticipation of the buyers at the fair.

Amongst these preparations, which the people and the sunshine made for a brotherly festivity, the mansion of Jairus alone remained sullen, with its closed shutters, its rich portico ungarlanded on this joyous morning, and the melancholy lights faintly glimmering behind the windows of Ephraima's room. Oh, the gleam of those candles! like a star of ill omen rising on a peaceful horizon, or some will-o'-the-wisp, with thoughts of death, lighted suddenly above the flower-beds of a spring garden. The townspeople of Yperdamme cast pitying glances at the mournful house, and cursed Death who had that day mown down the most lovely flower of their city.

At that moment the noble lord Zacharius arrived. He wore a large felt hat with a yellow feather, a grey doublet frogged with silver, and one hand upon the rich guard of his sword, with the other he twirled his moustache proudly. He tapped Joe on the shoulder.

"Your master?"

"My master, my lord Zacharius! He has gone to look for Jesus. My master's daughter is dead."

"Ephraima?"

"Yes, my lord—this morning. Market was just over. She still heard the finches and warblers which the peasants brought into the market-place."

"A week ago she was dancing the minuet at my castle! . . . So your master has gone to Jesus?"

"Yes, sir."

"Waste of time! How old was she?"

"Sixteen."

"She was very pretty. So sweet and dainty! graceful and with eyes like forget-me-nots. What a divine Magdalen she would have made in one of our performances!"

"Yes, sir."

"For she had hair like an angel. And all that mown down. Oh, the mournful harvest, the cruel harvest. I will write some verses on her death."

"Yes, sir."

"Unhappy Jairus! What is the use of all his wealth? His ramparts of sapphire and emeralds have not prevented Death from entering his house and stealing his most precious jewel! And now he has gone to look for Jesus?"

"Yes, sir; may he succeed in his undertaking."

"Ha! ha! I should like to see that. Poor Ephraima! Poor little girl! But I must go and meet my rhetoricians, who are coming here to act the story of Joseph sold by his brethren. I advise you, Joe, to see the performance which we are going to give presently, over there. Do you see? They are putting up the stage. There will be an orchestra, and two dromedaries which a travelling Asiatic merchant has lent us. You will see the King of Egypt in a velvet gown, surrounded by guards, then Joseph and his brethren, the story of the dreams. Madame Potiphar will recite some verses which I have written."

"Yes, sir."

But Zacharius, catching sight of a procession arriving on the market-place, cried out, "There they are! there they are! there they are! I must join them."

"Good-bye, sir."

The rhetoricians arrived on the market-place in carts decorated with laurel wreaths. They were very boisterous, and the opening of the stone bottles of Louvain beer resounded. Sturdy horses with beribboned manes drew them, making a great show beneath the windows, which were thrown open. The actors wore odd costumes, large swaggering hats, and light cloaks. Their faces were animated, and they showed, in between the festoons of foliage hung around their conveyances, merry, comic, hilarious countenances, greedy mouths, sunburnt cheeks generously flushed. Gross pleasure oozed from every pore of these vehicles, like the scum from cider moistening the joins of a fermenting barrel. And what strange things to swing about on the wheels of the carts!—drums, lances, beards, armour which gleamed in the distance, a gilded sceptre, a tin crown, and Roman draperies. All these things were scattered around the stage under the direction of my lord Zacharius. Curtains were hung over the laths and wooden bars, and all around was a crowd of curious children.

A nun appeared at Jairus's balcony.

"She is tired of saying paternosters," said Joe to himself. "Other years it was Ephraima who came out on to the balcony. Well, well! a fortnight's mourning and then she will be forgotten, for the earth swallows up more than the bodies of the dead!"

And he went sadly along a path close to the houses between the spread tables. Mine host, polishing a pewter mug at the door of his inn, stopped him, saying: "You look very miserable, Joe."

"Ephraima is dead!"

"I saw the Holy Sacrament carried into Jairus's house this morning. But the candle-light makes a wretched illumination at the fair! Especially as my inn is so close to the house of death! It makes you think about too unhappy things, Joe! . . . And then Jairus cannot let his fine purple flag, embroidered with golden lions, flap over the front of his house this year."

"Jairus has gone to look for Jesus."

"I saw Jesus curing a paralytic one day. What magic, Joe! I couldn't believe my poor eyes! But here comes the crowd. I must tap my barrels. There are the vendors of gingerbread and fritters. The market-place will smell good of frizzling butter and caramels and fat. Ha! ha! They will have to gulp down a lot of beer to float all those pancakes and waffles into their stomachs! Here is the Guild of St. George coming to the cross-bow competition with the banner on which you see St. George with lance in hand! They are passing under the belfry. What lovely weather! The sun is pouring on to the cross-bows! The weather-cock on the Town Hall gleams like a coin in the sky! A good omen for our purses, Joe!"

Mine host and Joe were chatting thus in the midst of the animation on the market-place when a great noise arose at the side of the stage.

It was a crowd of beggars quarrelling with the rhetoricians! A little while before they had been at the gates of the town, attracted by the profits of the fair. They moved, descending the banks with strange contortions like hunted toads, hopping and struggling along with their deformed limbs. Some leaning on crutches, one poor fellow with a guitar on his back, others, out of breath, crawling like snails, dragging their swollen limbs wrapped in muddy rags; then the blind, with red eyelids, knocking themselves against the passers-by; one wretch had only one foot, but to make up for it, bagpipes slung on his shoulder. Poor things, mangy musicians of the fair, dirty street-singers, they bore their deformities as a means of livelihood. Some of them were real monsters out of the Revelations: horrible were their contortions, for they were twisted like the trunks of oaks in their repulsive rags. All this scurvy regiment, propped up on their stumps, hunchbacked and with sores, like a group of monstrous snails or chipped gargoyles, sent out pitiful glances from under their weak eyelids.

"It was over there," began one of them, "on the high road near the Post Horn Inn. We were on the bank, poor wretched toads, with the dust of the road on our rags. One was turning the handle of his hurdy-gurdy; one offering to tell fortunes. Jesus appeared. It seemed to me that the birds were singing in the orchards of Hoogeland Farm as I had never heard them sing before. People were passing on the road going to the fair. I had been blind for many years. But at the approach of Jesus my eyelids became transparent, with a soft silver-white light, and as soon as He had touched these miserable red-bordered lids with His hands which smelled of incense—ah, my brothers! I saw again, beyond His linen robe, over the crowd, and in the joy of the light pouring on my eyes through the flags of the fair, yes, I saw the windmills turning in the sky, and the meadows through which winds the Lys! I was intoxicated as if I had drunk all the sky. And the treasures which God has collected for the poor in the magnificent casket of the firmament once again enriched my eyes. I danced with joy! The crowd had stopped, and I saw others who had thrown down their crutches and their sticks and their ulcerous bandages, and who leapt in the full light of midday. Butterflies, my brothers, who had cast off the larva of misery. Oh, the holy blessedness!"

The rhetoricians burst out laughing and exclaiming:

"Ha! ha! ha!"

"This Jesus is a magician!"

"He will be burnt as was the witch of Maldeghem."

"No, He will be crucified!"

"Like a slave, on the shameful gibbet!"

"This feigned Son of God! He! he! he! Who is no more the Son of God than you were blind or paralytic, crowd of mountebanks! A few blows with a cudgel would have made the most lame among you run like hares—and the most dumb, scream like peacocks!"

But under this hail of derision which beat upon the newly opened flowers of his faith, the beggar continued:

"Jesus will come here and will raise up the daughter of Jairus."

"Ha! ha! ha!"

"Jesus will raise her up! He has just cured Saint Peter's mother-in-law."

"Saint Peter's mother-in-law! Ha! ha! ha!"

"When Jesus had sown health and light around Him near Hoogeland Farm, He went away with Saint Peter and Jairus, who had come to meet Him. He went to the house of Peter's mother-in-law, who was suffering from a fever, and the crowd followed them. The poor woman was lying in a recess protected by red check curtains. Oh, the quiet cottage. Fishing-nets drying at the door, a silent spinning-wheel by the fireplace, a few loose faggots on the hearth crackled beneath a saucepan in which some marshmallows were boiling.

"Jesus only touched the sick woman: she rose up with great gestures of gratitude, and having put on a white bonnet and a red skirt, such as the shrimp-fishers wear, she served the visitors with fresh cheese, radishes, and a jug of beer. They sat down on little wooden stools and ate, while the old woman drew down a yellow muslin curtain over the window, which bathed them in a warm, golden light."

But the angry rhetoricians would not let these poetic accounts be finished. They cried out:

"Cunning rogues! You are sly politicians."

Some waved lances out of their unharnessed carts, others made faces. One among them, dressed as a fool, imitated the gestures of the beggar. Then they shouted out: "Come and see our plays and mysteries. They are sincere and honest, entertaining, with beautiful costumes and attractive women. We shall represent to you the Seven Deadly Sins. You shall see Pride and Deceit.

But we play our plays without pretending that we are descended from David."

"Or calling ourselves the sons of God."

"These intriguers always come to a bad end."

"The rope is ready for them."

"Go to Calvary and count the skulls of which the vultures have emptied the sockets."

In the meantime the distant sound of trumpets of the guilds entering the town could be heard. A light breeze made the banners wave, and the crowd was like the sea which breaks its sun-bathed waves between the breakwaters.

Beneath the flags everything was in movement.

A Jew came out of the crowd with a face like a goat, and laying his crooked finger under the nose of the beggar who had just been so happily singing the glory of Christ, he said: "He shall be killed, your Jesus. The soldiers shall cast their lots upon His garments, the people will spit upon His face, the red executioners will make His flesh bleed, and your eyes shall be torn out with pincers."

The people cried: "The Jew! the Jew! the Jew!"

"The juggler who spirits away our money."

"He has the beak and claws of a magpie."

A workman struck the Semite, who fled towards the rhetoricians, "Protect me, noble lords, against this mob."

Some of the actors drew their swords. The workmen caught up tools.

Mine host cried out: "Will you quarrel like this at a fair? Be careful of my windows. Be careful of my windows!" And the nun at the balcony of Jairus entered quickly, crossing herself, without closing the windows.

But at the Monastery of Prémontrés the bells tolled slowly for the dead. When bells proclaim the death of a young girl, they are particularly heartrending. All the sadness of faded springtime veils their hearts. For they are also feminine and virgin, and understand the sorrow of the poor Ophelias plucked by destiny in the harvest of the world. They weep for the unfinished flower garlands, for the lace neglected by pale hands, for the unopened loves. . . .

Then Jesus came while the actors and beggars and people were disputing among themselves. He was dressed in a long robe like the pilgrims, and a cape with shells; and He leant upon a big staff from the end of which hung a flask. A felt hat thrown back from His head remained hanging on His back. A supernatural light hovered over His white face, with its fair beard, which was gentle and glowing as a fountain of light.

Jairus, in gorgeous Eastern costume, opened a path through

the crowd. The rich jeweller wore a silken turban with a diamond aigrette, a pink jacket with gold embroidered satin belt; his soft leather boots were tapped by a curved, ivory-handled sabre.

Jesus raised His hand to those who were disputing.

"Why make ye such ado? The maid is not dead, but sleepeth."

A great silence spread suddenly over the market-place of Yperdamme.

When Jesus reached Jairus's mansion, He mounted the steps, followed by Saint Peter, whose old sunburnt face and worn-out brown toga contrasted with the brilliant dress of the jeweller. It was a mansion, the corridor of which, decorated with splendid pictures by famous artists and paved with marble, seemed, like the resonant avenue with its chiming clock, leading to some oasis of happiness.

He mounted a staircase covered with gorgeous tapestries and reached Ephraima's room.

Jairus was in despair. He was shedding tears and kneeling upon every step to kiss Jesus's hands. He cried aloud:

"O Thou, Jesus, Who made the leprous woman fresh as a rose, Who with a spark of Thy power lighted again the dead lanterns of the blind, Thou Who madest the lame to dance in a ring, and gavest strength and suppleness to the cripple, Jesus, on this festive day on which Thy Father lighted the most splendid luminary which He ever made to glow above forest and sea, Jesus, give back to the cold fruit of my holy and lawful love, that warmth which clothed it with fair youth!

"My daughter is dead, but come and lay Thy hand upon her, and she shall live. O Son of David, to Thee I sacrifice my wrought shrines by the finest jewellers of Bruges, my tapestries wherein are woven in gold the lives of the Holy Martyrs, and my ceremonial collars. Take from their frames my most magnificent canvasses, carry away my Utrecht velvets and my Malines lace."

But Jesus entering the room replied: "Man, be it unto thee according to thy faith. But keep thy wealth, or divide it among the poor. It will not help to gain the Kingdom of Heaven."

The beggars and the rhetoricians had collected around the door of the mansion. In the distance, through the streets, crackers went off, and through the open window, with the clear blue air, came the music of the merry-go-rounds, turning yonder, their tinsel glittering like rounds of fireflies above the heads of the crowd in its Sunday best.

And all these sounds rose up towards Ephraima, whose hair, still moist with the pale sweat of the agony, fell on the pillow like an unbound distaff-full of faded gold around her waxen face and closed eyes. She lay with folded hands, like a figure on a tomb, and on the white silk which covered her slender body had been placed branches of box and a diamond crucifix. She lay immovable among the flowers of her satin curtains, and one might have said that at the sound of the tolling bells and the orchestras of the fair, this sumptuous bed amidst birds, she floated down the dream-river which leads to Paradise.

But already her delicate hands were cold, her eyes like closed caskets, and one felt upon the brow, but yesterday bathed with the light of dawn, the hideous trace of the finger which condemned the flesh of this child to the branding of worms and the shame of death.

Candles were burning and a psalter with silver clasps lay on the table among the phials. The nun had put her hands into her black sleeves and dropped her eyelids beneath the white wings of her cap. Jesus approached the dead. He laid His hand upon Ephraima's brow, and in the alcove it was as if all the larks awakened. One had said that the spirit of the springtime, summoned by the mystic gesture of the Prophet, had come to hover over the daughter of Jairus. The dried-up streams when they take up their course flow softly from their sources, murmuring hymns of flowers and sky. Little by little, daisies once more freshly gem their borders. Goldfinches again come to quench their thirst in the water which mirrors the periwinkles. It is festival for all the dwellers on the rivers, and through the meadows once more the stream makes the radiant cords of its reflection vibrate in the light. Thus in her bed, which seemed enchanted, Ephraima awoke. The red blood took up its course through her veins and bathed her cheeks again with living colour. Her stiff hands slowly relaxed and stretched out towards Jesus as if she offered Him a lily of prayer gathered in Heaven. Her breast rose again. Then her eyes opened. And they seemed surprised. They were radiant and strange. Ah, when Jesus gave back to the blind the treasures veiled by their dark lids, He raised them up but to the light. They had retained a warm heart in their breast. But Ephraima's body had become cold, her flesh insensible to the caress of the air. From what sights had she been snatched away? She had looked upon that which our ancestors see who sleep beneath the brass plates in the cathedral, the mystery of the tomb had been unfolded for her. She bore on her looks and gesture a gleam from beyond the sky. And about her as she woke there hung a soft white air such as surrounds the saints and martyrs when they appear on earth. The bells for the dead had ceased their sobbing, and from all the church towers of Yperdamme, with one accord, burst forth a wild and joyous peal. The crosses gleamed brighter upon the spires. The procession poured on to the market-place—banners fluttered above the white dresses of girls, and seemed like great butterflies over blooming flower-beds.

The richly dressed aldermen were seated on the balcony of the Town Hall. Trumpets scattered around on every side through the blue air the red flourish of their brass. Already the crowd knew that Ephraima had been raised up to life. The beggars sang hymns. The rhetoricians, converted, waved their hats and feathers, and carried baskets of flowers to the door of the house where the miracle had been performed. Yes, there arose throughout all Yperdamme a mighty hymn of praise—a hymn of praise to life rising up to the sublime ball of fire which pours joy through space. It was he, the symbol of life; and Jesus, standing before the young girl slowly called back to the joys of life, seemed to have descended from the sun. Jairus, with eyes red with weeping, kissed the Prophet's robe. The nun upon her knees murmured a litany. Beneath the brotherly look of Christ, Ephraima, having regained the splendour of her youth, spread out her arms amazed.

MAURICE MAETERLINCK
B. 1862

THE MASSACRE OF THE INNOCENTS

TOWARDS the hour of supper on Friday, the twenty-sixth day of the month of December, a little shepherd lad came into Nazareth, crying bitterly.

Some peasants who were drinking ale in the Blue Lion opened the shutters to look into the village orchard, and saw the child running over the snow. They recognised him as the son of Korneliz, and called from the window: "What is the matter? It's time you were abed!"

But sobbing still, and shaking with terror, the boy cried that the Spaniards had come, that they had set fire to the farm, had hanged his mother among the nut trees, and bound his nine little sisters to the trunk of a big tree. At this the peasants rushed out of the inn. Surrounding the child they stunned him with their questionings and outcries. Between his sobs he added that the soldiers were on horseback and wore armour, that they had taken away the cattle of his uncle, Petrus Krayer, and would soon be in the forest with the sheep and cows. All now ran to the Golden Sun, where, as they knew, Korneliz and his brother-in-law were also drinking their mug of ale. The moment the innkeeper heard these terrifying tidings, he hurried into the village, crying that the Spaniards were at hand.

What a stir, what an uproar there was then in Nazareth! Women opened windows, and peasants hurriedly left their houses, carrying lights which were put out when they reached the orchard, where, because of the snow and the full moon, one could see as well as at midday.

Later, they gathered round Korneliz and Krayer, in the open space which faced the inns. Several of them had brought pitchforks and rakes, and consulted together, terror-stricken, under the trees.

But, as they did not know what to do, one of them ran to fetch the curé, who owned Korneliz's farm. He came out of the house with the sacristan carrying the keys of the church. All followed him into the churchyard, whither his cry came to them from the top of the tower, that he beheld nothing either in the fields, or by the forest, but that around the farm he saw ominous red clouds, for all that the sky was of a deep blue and agleam with stars over the rest of the plain.

After taking counsel for a long time in the churchyard, they decided to hide in the wood through which the Spaniards must pass, and, if these were not too numerous, to attack them and recover Peter Krayer's cattle and the plunder which they had taken from the farm.

Having armed themselves with pitchforks and spades, while the women remained outside the church with the curé, they sought a suitable ambuscade. Approaching a mill on a rising ground adjacent to the verge of the forest, they saw the light of the burning farm flaming against the stars. There they waited under enormous oaks, before a frozen mere.

A shepherd known as Red Dwarf climbed the hill to warn the miller, who had stopped his mill when he saw the flames on the horizon. He bade the peasant enter, and both men went to a window to stare out into the night.

Before them the moon shone over the burning farmstead, and in its light they saw a long procession winding athwart the snow. Having carefully scrutinised it, the Dwarf descended where his comrades waited under the trees, and now, they too gradually distinguished four men on horseback behind a flock which moved grazing on the plain.

While the peasants in their blue breeches and red cloaks continued to search about the margins of the mere and under the snowlit trees, the sacristan pointed out to them a box hedge, behind which they hid.

The Spaniards, driving before them the sheep and the cattle, advanced upon the ice. When the sheep reached the hedge they began to nibble at the green stuff, and now Korneliz broke from the shadows of the bushes, followed by the others with their pitchforks. Then in the midst of the huddled-up sheep and of the cows who stared affrighted, the savage strife was fought out beneath the moon, and ended in a massacre.

When they had slain not only the Spaniards, but also their horses, Korneliz rushed thence across the meadow in the direction of the flames, while the others plundered and stripped the dead. Thereafter all returned to the village with their flocks. The women, who were observing the dark forest from behind the churchyard walls, saw them coming through the trees and ran with the curé to meet them, and all returned dancing joyously, amid the laughter of the children and the barking of the dogs.

But while they made merry under the pear trees of the orchard, where the Red Dwarf had hung lanterns in honour of the kermesse, they anxiously demanded of the curé what was to be done.

The outcome of this was the harnessing of a horse to a cart in order to fetch the bodies of the woman and the nine little girls to the village. The sisters and other relations of the dead woman got into the cart along with the curé, who, being old and very fat, could not walk so far.

In silence they entered the forest and emerged upon the moonlit plain. There, in the white light, they descried the dead men, rigid and naked, among the slain horses. Then they moved onward toward the farm, which still burned in the midst of the plain.

When they came to the orchard of the flaming house, they stopped at the gate of the garden, dumb before the overwhelming misfortune of the peasant. For there his wife hung, quite naked, on the branches of an enormous nut tree among which he himself was now mounting on a ladder, and beneath which, on the frozen grass, lay his nine little daughters. Korneliz had already climbed along the vast boughs, when suddenly, by the light of the snow, he saw the crowd, who, horror-struck, watched his every movement. With tears in his eyes, he made a sign to them to help him, whereat the innkeepers of the Blue Lion and the Golden Sun, the curé, with a lantern, and many others, climbed up in the moonshine amid the snow-laden branches to unfasten the dead. The women of the village received the corpse in their arms at the foot of the tree—even as our Lord Jesus Christ was received by the women at the foot of the Cross.

On the morrow they buried her, and for the week thereafter nothing unusual happened in Nazareth.

But the following Sunday, hungry wolves ran through the village after High Mass, and it snowed until midday. Then, suddenly, the sun shone brilliantly, and the peasants went to dine as was their wont, and dressed for Benediction.

There was no one to be seen on the Place, for it froze bitterly. Only the dogs and chickens roamed about under the trees, or the sheep nibbled at a three-cornered bit of grass, while the curé's servant swept away the snow from his garden.

At that moment a troop of armed men crossed the stone bridge at the end of the village, and halted in the orchard. Peasants hurried from their houses, but, recognising the new-comers as Spaniards, they retreated terrified, and went to the windows to see what would happen.

About thirty soldiers, in full armour, surrounded an old man with a white beard. Behind them, on pillions, rode red and yellow lancers, who jumped down and ran over the snow to shake off their stiffness, while several of the soldiers in armour dismounted likewise, and fastened their horses to the trees.

Then they moved in the direction of the Golden Sun and knocked at the door. It was opened reluctantly; the soldiers went in, warmed themselves near the fire, and called for ale.

Presently they came out of the inn, carrying pots, jugs, and rye bread for their companions, who surrounded the man with the white beard, where he waited behind the hedge of lances.

As the street remained deserted, the commander sent some horsemen to the back of the houses, to guard the village on the country side. He then ordered the lancers to bring him all the children of two years old and under to be massacred, as is written in the Gospel of Saint Matthew.

The soldiers first went to the little inn of the Green Cabbage, and to the barber's cottage, which stood side by side midway in the street.

One of them opened a sty and a litter of pigs wandered into the village. The innkeeper and the barber came out and humbly asked the men what they wanted; but they did not understand Flemish, and went into the houses to look for the children.

The innkeeper had one child, who, in its little shift, was screaming on the table where they had just dined. A soldier took it in his arms and carried it away under the apple trees, while the father and mother followed, crying.

Thereafter the lancers opened other stable doors—those of the cooper, the blacksmith, the cobbler—and calves, cows, asses, pigs, goats, and sheep roamed about the square. When they broke the carpenter's windows, several of the oldest and richest habitants of the village assembled in the street, and went to meet the Spaniards. Respectfully they took off their caps and hats to the leader in the velvet mantle, and asked him what he was going to do. He did not, however, understand their language; so some one ran to fetch the curé.

The priest was putting on a gold chasuble in the vestry, in readiness for Benediction. The peasant cried: "The Spaniards are in the orchard!" Horrified, the curé ran to the door of the church, and the choir-boys followed, carrying wax-tapers and censer.

As he stood there, he saw the animals from the pens and stables wandering on the snow and on the grass, the horsemen in the village, the soldiers before the doors, horses tied to trees all along the street, men and women entreating the man who held the child in its little shift.

The curé hastened into the churchyard, and the peasants turned anxiously towards him as he came through the pear trees, like the Divine Presence itself in white and gold. They crowded about him where he confronted the man with the white beard.

He spoke in Flemish and in Latin, but the commander merely shrugged his shoulders to show that he did not understand.

The villagers asked their priest in a low voice: "What does he say? What is he going to do?" Others, when they saw the curé in the orchard, came cautiously from their cottages, women hurried up and whispered in groups, while the soldiers, till that moment besieging an inn, ran back at sight of the crowd in the square.

Then the man who held the innkeeper's child by the leg cut off its head with his sword.

The people saw the head fall, and thereafter the body lie bleeding upon the grass. The mother picked it up and carried it away, but forgot the head. She ran towards her home, but stumbling against a tree, fell prone on the snow, where she lay in a swoon, while the father struggled between two soldiers.

Some young peasants cast stones and blocks of wood at the Spaniards, but the horsemen all lowered their lances; the women fled and the curé with his parishioners began to shriek with horror, amid the bleating of the sheep, the cackling of the geese, and the barking of the dogs.

But as the soldiers moved away again into the street, the crowd stood silent to see what would happen.

A troop entered the shop kept by the sacristan's sisters, but came out quietly, without harming the seven women, who knelt on the threshold praying.

From there they went to the inn of St. Nicholas, which belonged to the Hunchback. Here, too, so as to appease them, the door was opened at once; but, when the soldiers reappeared amid a great uproar, they carried three children in their arms. The marauders were surrounded by the Hunchback, his wife, and daughters, all with clasped hands, imploring for mercy.

When the soldiers came to their white-bearded leader, they placed the children at the foot of an elm, where the little ones remained seated on the snow in their Sunday clothes. But one of them in a yellow frock got up and toddled unsteadily towards the sheep. A soldier followed with bare sword; and the child died with his face in the grass, while the others were killed around the tree.

The peasants' and the innkeepers' daughters all fled screaming, and shut themselves up in their houses. The curé, who was left alone in the orchard, threw himself on his knees, first before one horseman then another, and with crossed arms, supplicated the Spaniards piteously, while the fathers and mothers seated on the snow beyond wept bitterly for the dead children whom they held upon their knees.

As the lancers passed along the street, they noticed a big blue farmstead. When they had tried in vain to force open the oaken door studdied with nails, they clambered atop of some tubs which were frozen over near the threshold, and by this means gained the house through the upper windows.

There had been a kermesse in this farm. At sound of the broken window-panes, the families who had assembled there to eat gaufres, custards, and hams, crowded together behind the table on which still stood some empty jugs and dishes. The soldiers entered the kitchen, and after a savage struggle in which many were wounded, they seized all the little boys and girls; then, with these, and the servant who had bitten a lancer's thumb, they left the house and fastened the door behind them in such a way that the parents could not get out.

The villagers who had no children slowly left their houses, and followed the soldiers at a distance. They saw them throw down their victims on the grass before the old man, and callously kill them with lance and sword. During this, men and women leaned out of all the windows of the blue house, and out of the barn, blaspheming and flinging their hands to heaven, when they saw the red, pink, and white frocks of their motionless little ones on the grass between the trees. The soldiers next hanged the farm servant at the sign of the Half Moon on the other side of the street, and there was a long silence in the village.

The massacre now became general. Mothers fled from their houses, and attempted to escape through the flower and vegetable gardens, and so into the country beyond, but the horsemen pursued them and drove them back into the street. Peasants with caps in their clasped hands knelt before the men who dragged away their children, while amid the confusion the dogs barked joyously. The curé, with hands upraised to heaven, rushed up and down in front of the houses and under the trees, praying desperately; here and there, soldiers, trembling with cold, blew on their fingers as they moved about the road, or waited with hands in their breeches pockets, and swords under their arms, before the windows of the houses which were being scaled.

Everywhere, as in small bands of twos and threes they moved along the streets, where these scenes were being enacted, and entered the houses, they beheld the piteous grief of the peasants The wife of a market-gardener, who occupied a red brick cottage near the church, pursued with a wooden stool the two men who carried off her children in a wheelbarrow. When she saw them die, a horrible sickness came upon her, and they thrust her down on the stool, under a tree by the roadside.

Other soldiers swarmed up the lime trees in front of a farmstead with its blank walls tinted mauve, and entered the house by removing the tiles. When they came back on to the roof, the father and mother, with outstretched arms, tried to follow them through the opening, but the soldiers repeatedly pushed them back, and had at last to strike them on the head with their swords before they could disengage themselves and regain the street.

One family, shut up in the cellar of a large cottage, lamented near the grating, through which the father wildly brandished a pitchfork. Outside on a heap of manure, a bald old man sobbed all alone; in the square, a woman in a yellow dress had swooned, and her weeping husband now supported her under the arms, against a pear tree; another woman in red fondled her little girl, bereft of her hands, and lifted now one tiny arm, now the other, to see if the child would not move. Yet another woman fled towards the country; but the soldiers pursued her among the hayricks, which stood out in black relief against the fields of snow.

Beneath the inn of the Four Sons of Aymon a surging tumult reigned. The inhabitants had formed a barricade, and the soldiers went round and round the house without being able to enter. Then they were attempting to climb up to the signboard by the creepers, when they noticed a ladder behind the garden door. This they raised against the wall, and went up it in file. But the innkeeper and all his family hurled tables, stools, plates, and cradles down upon them from the windows; the ladder was overturned, and the soldiers fell.

In a wooden hut at the end of the village, another band found a peasant woman washing her children in a tub near the fire. Being old and very deaf, she did not hear them enter. Two men took the tub and carried it away, and the stupefied woman followed with the clothes in which she was about to dress the children. But when she saw traces of blood everywhere in the village, swords in the orchards, cradles overturned in the street, women on their knees, others who wrung their hands over the dead, she began to scream and beat the soldiers, who put down the tub to defend themselves. The curé hastened up also, and, with hands clasped over his chasuble, entreated the Spaniards before the naked little ones howling in the water. Some soldiers came up, tied the mad peasant to a tree, and carried off the children.

The butcher, who had hidden his little girl, leaned against his shop and looked on callously. A lancer and one of the men in armour entered the house and found the child in a copper boiler. Then the butcher in despair took one of his knives and rushed after them into the street, but soldiers who were passing disarmed him, and hanged him by the hands to the hooks in the wall—there, among the flayed animals, he kicked and struggled, blaspheming, until the evening.

Near the churchyard, there was a great gathering before a long, low house, painted green. The owner, standing on his threshold, shed bitter tears; as he was very fat and jovial-looking, he excited the pity of some soldiers who were seated in the sun against the wall, patting a dog. The one, too, who dragged away his child by the hand, gesticulated as if to say: " What can I do? It's not my fault! "

A peasant who was pursued jumped into a boat, moored near the stone bridge, and with his wife and children moved away across the unfrozen part of the narrow lagoon. Not daring to follow, the soldiers strode furiously through the reeds. They climbed up into the willows on the banks to try to reach the fugitives with their lances—as they did not succeed, they continued for a long time to threaten the terrified family adrift upon the black water.

The orchard was still full of people, for it was there, in front of the white-bearded man who directed the massacre, that most of the children were killed. Little dots who could just walk alone stood side by side munching their slices of bread and jam, and stared curiously at the slaying of their helpless playmates, or collected round the village fool who played his flute on the grass.

Then suddenly there was a uniform movement in the village. The peasants ran towards the castle, which stood on the brown rising ground at the end of the street. They had seen their seigneur leaning on the battlements of his tower and watching the massacre. Men, women, old people, with hands outstretched, supplicated to him, in his velvet mantle and his gold cap, as to a king in heaven. But he raised his arms and shrugged his shoulders to show his helplessness, and when they implored him more and more persistently, kneeling in the snow, with bared heads, and uttering piteous cries, he turned slowly into the tower, and the peasants' last hope was gone.

When all the children were slain, the tired soldiers wiped their swords on the grass and supped under the pear trees. Then they mounted one behind the other, and rode out of Nazareth across the stone bridge, by which they had come.

The setting of the sun behind the forest made the woods aflame and dyed the village blood-red. Exhausted with running and entreating, the curé had thrown himself upon the snow, in front of the church, and his servant stood near him. They stared upon the street and the orchard, both thronged with the peasants in their best clothes. Before many thresholds, parents with dead children on their knees bewailed with ever fresh amaze their bitter grief. Others still lamented over the children where they had died, near a barrel, under a barrow, or at the edge of a pool. Others carried away the dead in silence. There were some who began to wash the benches, the stools, the tables, the blood-stained shifts, and to pick up the cradles which had been thrown into the street. Mother by mother moaned under the trees over the dead bodies which lay upon the grass, little mutilated bodies which they recognised by their woollen frocks. Those who were childless moved aimlessly through the square, stopping at times in front of the bereaved, who wailed and sobbed in their sorrow. The men, who no longer wept, sullenly pursued their strayed animals, around which the barking dogs coursed; or, in silence, repaired so far their broken windows and rifled roofs. As the moon solemnly rose through the quietudes of the sky, deep silence as of sleep descended upon the village, where now not the shadow of a living thing stirred.

HUBERT KRAINS
B. 1862

CHRISTMAS EVE

I HAD gone, that night with my parents, to a farm at the end of the village where they were keeping Christmas Eve. The guests arrived in little groups. They could be heard far off, for it was freezing, and their sabots and hobnailed boots made a great commotion in the silent streets. When they opened the door, a blast of cold air entered the house. The women took off their broad-brimmed hats and shawls, the men unwound their mufflers, and all drew reddened hands out of their woollen mittens. Then they sat down around a big roaring stove above which the smoke of the pipes hung in a cloud.

They had put us, Marie and me, at a little table in a corner. We had before us a Liège almanac and a gorgeously illustrated Bible. After having gazed for a long time at the astronomer with his pointed hat who looks at the stars through a big telescope, we admired one after another the ingenuous prints representing the Seasons. Marie asked me explanations every moment, and, in order to understand better, bent her roguish head on my shoulder. I felt her soft fair hair tickling my cheek, her red lips smiled at me, and her blue eyes looked deep into mine with affection. We were about to pass on to the Bible when the conversation among those grouped around the stove suddenly stopped. " Sh! " said Marie, putting her finger to her lips, " they are going to tell a story."

We folded our hands on the table, turning towards an old man at whom every one was looking eagerly, and who seemed to be considering, with his head propped in his hand.

At last he raised his slender body, and after glancing round with a mischievous look he began:

" Once upon a time. . . ."

At that moment the door opened, a head appeared at the opening, and a frightened voice cried:

" They have just found a dead man out in the country. . . ."

Every one was struck with terror, and we all rushed out of the house with the exception of a few women. The street was full of people running fast. The moon had just risen; its thin crescent, with slightly iridescent edges, gleamed like a crystal in the depth of the sky, thousands of stars twinkled, and two rows of poplars raising their thin skeletons along the fields, cast weird mysterious shadows. Before us, the heads of the crowd moved up and down through a dull sound; this monotonous murmur was sometimes interrupted by a strident call, answered by a frightened childish voice. In a quarter of an hour we were out in the open fields, and soon we saw a group of people in the middle of a roadway. They formed a circle, bending over the body of a man lying on his side. One who was kneeeling by, from time to time, took a match from his pocket, struck it on his trousers, and passed it in front of the dead man's face. Then the pale still face could be seen, the eyes white between half-closed lids, the pinched lips, wrinkles on cheeks and brow; his hair was grey, and so was his long beard, which flowed down over his breast; his left arm was folded under him, while his right hand lay on the ground palm upwards; with his big body, which obstructed the whole pathway, he looked like a warrior of olden times.

" Does any one of you know this dead man? " asked the one who had been kneeling by the body, as he got up.

" No! " answered every one present in a chorus.

" He is a beggar," said some one. " Look, his clothes are all torn, there is his stick in the rut, and here is his wallet," he added, picking up something from the ground, which looked like an empty bag.

A strange silence followed these words, everything was still around us; you only heard the irregular breathing of the people. The more timid remained at the back, immovable, quiet, and oppressed, from time to time craning their necks over their neighbours' shoulders to cast a rapid glance at the corpse. On all sides the country, bare and flat, stretched out like a desert.

Suddenly a man asked me:

" You have never seen a dead man, little chap? "

" No," said I, " I have never seen one."

" Then you must touch him; otherwise he will appear to you every night in your dreams."

For one instant I wanted to run away, but the fear of finding myself alone in the lonely fields held me back. I went up, trembling in every limb. If it had been in daylight very likely I should not have been so frightened, but to touch this huge immovable body in the dark, under the eyes of all those vague faces moving in the stillness around me, seemed to me something appallingly dangerous. I made up my mind, however. I put out my hand—but drew it back at once. Finally, with a resolute effort,

I laid it on the forehead of the dead. God! how cold it was! I shivered from head to foot. A crowd of thoughts buzzed in my head, and for several minutes I saw nothing but a black mass melting into the earth. Meanwhile, steps sounded in the distance; we saw a little light swinging to and fro as it drew near, and soon a man with a lantern pushed his way through us up to the corpse, near which two workmen placed a stretcher.

The three of them together casually turned over the body, laid it on its back, and then put the lantern close to the face, which suddenly appeared brightly lighted as if illuminated by a fire. After having examined it carefully they announced that they had never seen this man in the country. They spoke low and very slowly; in the oppressive silence, among the terrified people, their words acquired an extraordinary solemnity; it seemed to me at times as if I heard supernatural voices coming from the depths of the earth. Then they took up the body by the shoulders and feet. The cold having stiffened it, the men groaned as if they were lifting the trunk of a tree. When it was on the stretcher they crossed his hands upon his breast, and after raising his head, which was bending backwards, they set off. A man walked in front, with the lantern in his hand; we followed in silence. Presently some one said that we ought to pray. An old woman, thin and bent, began to tell her beads. Our voices made a melancholy murmur, the sound of our irregular steps became rhythmic with the steps of the bearers, the light of the lantern reflected by the ice in the ruts threw occasional gleams upon us, and when the unevenness of the road forced us to separate a little, I saw the corpse tremble on the litter. When we arrived at the village hedges, some one cried out suddenly: "Wait!"

Every one stopped. Where was the body to be taken? The question had not yet arisen, and although every one was full of pity for the unfortunate man, and felt obliged by natural feelings of humanity to pay him funeral rites as decently as possible, no one felt inclined to receive into his house the dead body of an unknown man. So no one answered, and the bearers stood ranged to the right and left of the litter waiting in vain for the order to go on. Finally, the farmer with whom he had gone to spend the evening went up and said:

"There is an empty stable at my place; you could put him there for the time."

The procession went on. We had arrived by this time under the poplars whose branches showed up against the sky where the moon continued her slow and calm ascent.

When we got to the farm, three dogs rushed out barking. The house door opened and women appeared on the threshold. Then there was a great coming and going. Lanterns ran here and there, for the stable had to be cleared of harness and farm implements which had been put there. During this time the body remained upon the litter, near the dung-heap. At last it was carried into the stable and placed upon a heap of straw which had been arranged into a sort of slanting couch.

A woman removed the spiders' webs which hung in a corner, another brought a crucifix and laid it upon the dead man's breast, while a third wound a rosary round his hands. Then we said three Pater Nosters and three Aves. Before leaving we all gazed at him: in spite of the slight bruise on the cheek, caused by his fall, the face was calm and noble, and his great height as well as his long beard made him as majestic as a bishop.

When we were once more assembled in the house we felt first of all an unutterable sensation of well-being. Enjoying the soft warmth of the fire we looked with delight upon our neighbours' faces, which now appeared glowing with life and devoid of all mystery, and very one secretly congratulated himself that neither he nor any of those belonging to him had fallen victim to an accident which might just as well have happened to us as to this stranger who had just been found, lifeless, in the open fields. Our thoughts soon clouded. The dead man obsessed us, we felt unable to speak of anything else; but as we did not want to enter into melancholy conversation, every one was quiet, and a painful silence reigned in the house. We heard voices in the street; people, no doubt, who had collected together in front of the farm to discuss the event. Suddenly our host turned to a servant:

"Call the dogs in," said he, "for they will howl if they are left out in the yard."

The three dogs came in one after the other with their heads hanging: they slipped in between the chairs and stretched down quietly before the stove.

But who was this man whom no one had ever seen in the country? Where did he come from? What had he thought of before he died?

"He must have suffered terribly," said some one. "Did you notice how he had scratched the soil around him?"

"Yes," said another, "the tips of his fingers were worn to the bone."

Meanwhile the voices outside had died away; a great stillness spread over the farm, but soon the sounds of a violin and an accordion were heard in the distance; other people, who had gathered like us to make merry on this Christmas Eve, were making music; they were singing too, and fragments of verses rose here and there through the silence. This cheerfulness, which at other times would certainly have added to our merriment, now only plunged us deeper into our gloomy thoughts; besides it did not sound genuine, a kind of vague sorrow was mingled with it, it had something funereal which suited well with our melancholy reflections on the fragility of human life. . . .

" You touched the body," said Marie suddenly.

" Yes," said I.

" With that hand? "

She took it in hers, examined it curiously, then pushed it away with disgust.

" Come," cried the farmer in a cheerful voice, " we are not here to make ourselves miserable. The man is dead; we may think of him as much as we like, we cannot bring him to life again. Besides, people die every day. The cemeteries are full of them. . . . Somebody had just begun a story," he added, " now is the time to finish it. While we are in good health let us enjoy life, for we too shall have to die one day or another."

Again the thin old man glanced round with a mischievous look, and said, after clearing his throat:

" Once upon a time. . . ."

But the farmer's words had impressed a little old woman, the one who had led the prayers following the dead body, and she murmured in a weak and trembling voice, ignoring the narrator:

" God grant that it be in a bed, without too much suffering, in the midst of our family, and after having received the Holy Sacrament."

GEORGES GARNIER

B. 1868

JACCLARD

WHEN Monsieur Bonchamps, the notary, left his house on the opening day of the shooting season, with his legs in new gaiters, his starched smock magnifying the ampleness of his form, his brightly polished gun under his arm, the villagers ran to their doors and followed him with their eyes until he disappeared at the end of the high road. Jangette, the lad who carried the game-bag round which hung a smell of game, due to the congealed blood which had remained in it from the previous season, walked behind him, like a choir boy following the priest in a procession, respectful and proud. The dog, Bok, ran on in front, with nose in air: a strapping little spaniel, with muscular chest, and the intelligent, keen, and gentle eyes peculiar to the race, thick glossy coat, with strong mouth and a straight, well-carried tail.

The spaniel was making his first appearance in public. Monsieur Bonchamps had bought him the week before from a breeder at Bessons. After having tried him in the woods and in the open, he had paid, not without much hesitation, 500 francs for him—so high a price that he had not ventured to admit it to Madame Bonchamps.

As he passed the last house on the high road, a peasant leaning on a fence, by a hedge surrounding a vegetable garden, greeted him cunningly, taking off his cap.

"Good day, sir, there's plenty o' game. You'll have good sport, sir."

The notary seemed disagreeably surprised; he looked at him askance and answered coolly, "Good day." Evidently this man, whose name was Pierre Jacclard, had leant out there to address him as he went by, and the whole of a recent incident passed through Monsieur Bonchamps' mind.

Six months previously, he had surprised Jacclard in Halines Wood, swinging a brace of hare in his left hand and holding his loaded gun under his right arm. It was catching him redhanded, and Jacclard threw himself at the notary's feet, swearing that it should be the very last time he would ever poach. But a sportsman never forgives any one who robs him of his game. The poacher was prosecuted. Jaccard was condemned. On account of former offences he was given three months' imprisonment. This sentence had enraged him.

" I understand that the keepers nab us," he said. " They earn their living by watching the preserves, it is their business to spy on poachers; but if the sportsmen themselves interfere, it's not fair-play."

To him, poaching was a fight, a battle of wits, of cunning and care, played frankly between the keeper who watches and the thief who hides; a contest just like the one between the sportsman and the game, the keeper being armed with the law, as the sportsman is with his gun. As he left the court, he flung at Bonchamps, who watched him being led away:

" I'll be even with yer yet, Mister Notary! "

It was said in so clear, calm, and decided a voice, with the expression of a man so sure of himself, that the threat remained a long time in Monsieur Bonchamps' ears. He was on his guard for several weeks, then, as time passed, he forgot the matter. And now this morning the man as he greeted him had the same bold, quietly mocking look which the notary had seen on the day of the sentence. The poacher was known as a rogue capable on occasion of playing a nasty trick. He lived, no one knew quite how, with his father and mother, both over seventy years of age. Old Jacclard was paralysed, unable to bend his hips to sit down. He slept on a mattress on the floor, and in the morning his wife hoisted him up by planting his feet against the wall, as one raises a heavy ladder. As stiff as a board, he went off supported by two sticks as inflexible as his old legs; he mounted the steep village street as if on stilts, with bent back. It took him an hour, in fine weather, to get over the four hundred yards which separated his house from the place he was going to. Half way he stopped to take breath, and the hostess of the Black Lion, according to a charitable tradition inaugurated the day on which he became crippled, brought him out a " Jack," a big glass of gin, which he swallowed, leaning against the wall of the inn. Arriving at last at his rock, he propped himself up against the smooth vertical side: upright, unable to sit or stoop, by dint of using a hammer with a very long handle he broke stones for mending the road. He was paid by the cubic foot, and in the best days he earned as much as 1*s*. 6*d*. He did not beg, but accepted the gifts which pitying passers-by put into his hand. During this time his son, Pierre Jacclard, poached in the river. Quick as none other, he caught barbels and pike with his hands, drew up the lines he had laid over-night, threw dynamite cartridges in the richest pools, and limed the trout in the streams; when evening came he set traps for hares and rabbits; he had even caught deer.

The best hotels in Liège were secretly supplied by him, on occasion he knew how to secure the peasants' discretion by a brace of partridges or a thick-backed hare. As for the boys who surprised him, he gave them spankings, halfpence, or cigarettes according to their age. But, unlike his fellow plunderers, if by chance the keepers turned up, he never resisted. When he hoped he had not been seen, he flattened himself upon the ground, tried to slip into the underwood with the swift suppleness of an adder, with the tricks of a Red Indian disappearing into the prairie grass. Otherwise he allowed himself to be taken with a good grace, giving himself up quietly.

Well on guard against any foolish movement of anger, he never once made as if to shoot, nor attempted to intimidate "authority." He took off his cap politely; he was nabbed, so much the worse! These are the disadvantages of the trade; and he submitted to them like a sensible fellow, preferring a fine and prison to the court of assizes and penal servitude. He went in for still another kind of business: on Sundays in summer he walked as many as twenty or thirty miles to play at skittles in the village fairs; and he always came back with money, forks and spoons, and hams. He carried off all the prizes with such ease and calm that the players began to know him, and shouted out when he arrived. You should have seen him then, cordial and pleasant, joking with them, playing tricks, making faces, confusing them, entertaining the society with chatter. And all the time so merry, with such a genial and cheery manner, with his cap over one ear, shoulders and arms like a young Hercules, red lips laughing through an auburn beard, that he ended by cajoling them: he entered the game after all, and was the last to leave at nightfall, grinning, rich with spoils, and jingling his money. Strong as an ox and agile as a squirrel, he never shirked a scuffle; he fought for pleasure, delighting in it, without anger or ill-will. One day, having been on a spree with a poacher from Houdémont, and being tipsy, he said to him, "As we are such good friends, we'll fight to see who's strongest."

The other agreed, and immediately, in the inn itself, they stripped off their coats and set to. The man from Houdémont, who was looked upon as the strongest in the country, got a sound drubbing, and it took him three weeks to get over it. From that day Jacclard's reputation was made, and as he also owned a cock and two chaffinches unrivalled in the "singing competitions," this well-built and uncomfortably sly rascal began to be regarded with deference. And so this morning his former anxieties came back to the notary; his cheerful, round, clean-shaven face, with red hanging cheeks, clouded as he climbed the hill. He seemed to hear the poacher coming out of court, "I'll be even with yer yet, Mister Notary," and he felt a discomfort which quite spoilt the "opening" day. However, it was a splendid morning, real weather for sport, a bright sun in the pink sky of dawn promising victory to the shrewd sportsman. The heat would increase presently, but a good breeze was blowing from the east, passing in long waves and sweeping over the country with a healthy freshness. When he arrived at last on the upland with his dog and game-carrier, he spied a large field of beetroot and wanted to go in at once, certain of raising some partridges.

But while he slipped a couple of cartridges into his rifle he saw his dog suddenly sniff and seize in his mouth something grey-looking, which he could not quite see. He was certain, at once, that it was a poisoned bait, and in a voice trembling with fear he called out, "Here!" The dog was afraid of having this unlooked-for titbit torn from him, and swallowed it at one gulp. The result was instantaneous: he beat the air with his paws and rolled over on his back. Monsieur Bonchamps threw down his gun, ran up bravely and plunged his hand into the dog's mouth, trying to reach the piece of meat, which had perhaps stuck in the throat; he risked being badly bitten, for the dog's jaws were working in convulsions. For three minutes he struggled, the notary kneeling by him, still holding the jaws open. But Bok bit him deeply in the thumb and he was obliged to let go. While the notary stood distracted at the sight of the dying dog, the game-carrier picked something from the ground, and, stammering with fear, said:

"Look, here's another of 'em. Its strychnine."

The bait he held out was made of two pieces of ham stuck together and dusted over on the inner sides with poison. Monsieur Bonchamps looked at the piece of meat, and then when he had seen it, when the truth appeared evident and palpable, he was shaken with the fury of a wild beast; he stammered, choked with a rush of blood to his head, only grasping one thing, that his 500 franc dog had been poisoned, that this dog was dying before his eyes, would be dead in ten minutes, and that the rogue guilty of this was. . . . Suddenly Jacclard's big body appeared fifty yards off on the upland. The poacher advanced cautiously, sly and defiant; his eyes full of mischief, merry and mocking. He behaved as if he had not seen the dog, and, as if he guessed nothing of the scene, said in his taunting voice:

"Well, haven't yer got any game, sir, to . . ."

Before he could end, the notary had seized his rifle, and without replying or making a sound, mad with rage, he aimed. Jangette, the game-carrier, screamed and flung himself flat upon the ground so as not to see. But the poacher awaited the blow, turned rapidly, made a great spring in the air, and received the shot full in the back. Suddenly there was a great silence, the silence of death; the game-carrier had stopped yelling and was hiding his face in a beetroot, not daring to look. Jacclard, fallen on his face, remained immovable; the dog had done struggling; and it seemed to Monsieur Bonchamps that all of a sudden the wind had ceased to blow, the blades of grass to tremble, and the sun to shine.

He was stunned, stupefied, like a drunken man, with his rifle smoking in his hand. Only then did he realise; the revelation was appalling; he had shot at a man, bang! the blow had brought him to the earth, it had been done in a flash of lightning! and now it was irrevocable, no human power could make this thing undone. He saw himself placed between the dead dog and this man lying on his face, whose trousers were becoming covered with red spots. The frightful horror that clutched his heart developed into a mad idea of a precipitate flight, a wild rush across the fields; but seeing the man move, he went towards him, overwhelmed with horror, shaking on his legs. He said, as needing to justify this shot which made a murderer of him:

" It was you who killed my dog."

The other chuckled on the ground without even dreaming of denying it:

" Me? Your dog? Yer'll have ter prove that; when yer do, I'll kiss yer dirty——" The notary asked again, looking at the red spots growing on the seat of the trousers:

" Are you—are you——"

" I dunno. I don't care. We shall see. All I know is, I'm hurt bad enough to have yer up for trial in court "; and gleefully, fiercely, jeering:

" Well, I said I should be even with yer yet."

MAURICE DES OMBRIAUX
B. 1868

ZIRÉ BUZETTE

FOR many years Ziré Buzette had coughed his soul out, one of those hard dry coughs which seem to shake and tear the chest, and make those who hear it say: " He has not long to live."

It was true, for a long time already Ziré Buzette had not had long to live.

Plasterer during the summer, he was seen going out early in the morning with his bucket, chalk, blue, brushes and sleeves, coughing all the time.

" Poor Ziré Buzette," said every one, " to do that sort of work with his health. It is the lime eating away his lungs. No, indeed, he has not long to live."

" That miserable Ziré Buzette, how brave he is; nothing will induce him to go into the infirmary; he persists in working, and all the while the ' blue ' is poisoning his blood. He won't last long, that's certain."

And Ziré went off to make the house spick-and-span with white-wash, cough-coughing on his ladder, with a face as white as his apron. He used to whitewash kitchens and rooms too, and he was well looked after out of sympathy. For pity, and because his prices were moderate, he was ordered everywhere, and his services were bespoken long beforehand. Even in the humblest cottages a piece of meat was put in the oven for him.

" That poor Ziré Buzette," said they, " he needs strengthening. He is worn to a thread. He won't last long."

In the farms he was made to drink a mouthful of good wine every day; he needed it too, not having long to live!

Yet Ziré Buzette still went on. So much so, that on Sundays, at the fairs, on the platforms made of four casks covered with boards, near the dung-heaps, he played the fiddle for the young people to dance. Still coughing, he scratched his Stradivarius between the clarionet and the trombone.

" Poor Ziré Buzette, he must be hard up to chill himself like that, sitting out during a whole evening with such an illness. He has no strength in his blood. It makes your heart ache to see him shivering and coughing. Ah no, indeed, he won't last long!"

And so at every pause he was offered either beer or gin, or even champagne, as well as large slices of cake. It was the least one could do for this miserable wreck, who had not long to live. And he was liked as a musician; it was he who led the little orchestra, and nobody could make one dance as he could. He played with such a swing and rhythm that the clumsiest legs, and even the beginners, went of themselves. The leaders of the parties arranged with him from the beginning of the year to be quite sure that he would not fail them. How he was spoiled! How he was 'treated'! For his sake a cask of beer was placed on the musicians' platform. Good old Ziré Buzette must be well looked after, for he would not play much longer, and who would make them dance then?

Ziré Buzette never refused anything, drank everything, ate everything, slowly, without ever hurrying himself. To see him thus one would not have said that he had not long to live. A regular gulf was Ziré Buzette.

"It's his disease," they thought. "Ah, he needs all that to keep him up, poor fellow! Yes, one may well say so, and in spite of that he has not long to live."

He had the mild, gentle, resigned expression of the violinist.

Ziré Buzette also went to the big houses of the neighbourhood to make the young folks waltz at christenings, weddings, or engagements. And everywhere he was treated above a workman or servant. There was always something extra for him; an interest was taken in him. He was regarded almost as a friend. I know not what else to say, except that, in fact, he was the one who had not long to live.

In winter no whitewashing was done, and there were no fairs. To earn his living, then, and occupy his leisure hours, Ziré Buzette, still coughing, plied the trade of bootmaker. He was not, truth to tell, remarkably capable at this profession, I had almost said this art, but work never failed him. People ordered slippers from him. He mounted those which had been embroidered or woven by housewives or girls for petted husbands or to fascinate lovers. He also made the children's boots.

"Poor Ziré Buzette! Goodness, he must live. It is a charity, a duty. He will not last long."

Weakly, sickly, perpetually coughing, Ziré Buzette, who had not long to live, had nevertheless already buried two wives. His first had married him out of pity, it was said.

"Let us risk it, one might as well," she had thought; "it does not bind one to much. He will not last long."

She died of a chill.

The second had married him for his modest hoard.

" It is a good business," she speculated. " I have nothing, and as he will not last long, I shall inherit from him, and can find whom I like after him."

She died.

And now the rumour spread through the village that he was going to be married again, for the third time, to a girl who was only twenty years of age.

" Did you ever hear of such a thing? " said the gossips. " He will do for himself, poor Ziré Buzette, and he has not long to live in any case."

" There is another who has an eye on his house and orchard," said others. " What a shamefaced thing! She knows well enough that he won't last long."

" After all, why shouldn't he, if he likes? We should do the same thing in his place. He has no time to lose, for he won't last long."

Ziré Buzette had his little house and piece of ground surrounded by the property of the Brothers Blairaux, the richest people in the village. One was mayor, another farmer, the third treasurer of the Charity Organisation, and all three were bachelors. Big robust fellows, with powerful limbs, strong and wiry as a whip handle, they looked as if they were made to live a hundred years. They owned over a hundred acres of land, and bought more every year. It was said that half the village belonged to them. The farm, field, garden and orchard made a splendid place. It was the finest property in the village. It had cost them a great deal of money and trouble. They had had to buy a bit of land from one, a ruined cottage from another, a hut here, a bakehouse there, pulling down, filling up, levelling; in order that the estate should be complete and the whole perfect, they only needed Ziré Buzette's cottage.

" He won't last long," they said to themselves. " We shall have it for nothing at his death."

But their wish finally became stronger than their reason. They wanted to have the estate at once, as soon as possible, for who knows if, after Ziré's death, his heirs will not make difficulties and, in the circumstances, exorbitant demands?

After all sorts of advances, manœuvres, with numerous peasants' tricks, they entered into negotiations with the plasterer. But their cunning plans were of no use, Ziré Buzette would not hear of it. He shook his head with its pale face, and, coughing, said:

" Ask me anything, sirs; but not to leave the house of my grandfathers. You know I have not long to live. Be patient. I won't go anywhere else for the short time that is left me. I will die in the house where I was born and where all my people have died."

He met the pressing entreaties of his neighbours with a gentle and polite obstinacy. There was nothing to be done. He remained resolute. They tried frightening him with threats. In vain. They withdrew their custom, and the Mayor engaged another musician for the village fair. Ziré Buzette felt wounded by this blow; he coughed more than ever. All the peasants took his part; all the village youth deserted the official dance and paid for Ziré Buzette's orchestra themselves. The first county magistrate was roundly abused.

"Treat a poor fellow, who has not long to live, in that way! You must be heartless!"

There was quite a hubbub. The incident was used against the Burgomaster at the elections, and it was suggested that Ziré Buzette should be among the candidates. He was sure to be elected, and as he had not long to live he would not give any trouble. But he had the good sense to refuse.

The Blairaux, to avoid danger, made peace with him. They increased their offers. But in spite of these being tempting, Ziré answered, still coughing:

"No, sirs, a house like mine is worth 8 per cent. At the price you offer I should lose . . . and, besides, I want to die in my father's house."

"Sell it to us and you shall keep the use of it during your lifetime," said the collector of the Charity Organisation, who thought that Ziré Buzette would not last long. The idea pleased the plasterer. They discussed the matter and finally agreed. Ziré Buzette was to retain the use of his cottage until his death, and the Blairaux would pay the rent once or twice at most, for Ziré Buzette would not last long.

And the whole village said:

"Those Blairaux are fine foxes. You don't catch them napping. They've bought Ziré Buzette's place for an old song, for he won't last long."

Every year Ziré Buzette got his rent. Each time the Blairaux rubbed their hands together, saying to themselves that they had paid the last annuity.

The Mayor died without having seen the orchard joined to his land. The two brothers looked glum when Ziré Buzette called for his due.

The farmer died, also without annexing the fiddler's little domain, and Ziré, who had not long to live, continued, still coughing, to draw his rent. The collector of the Charity Organisation threatened ruin to Ziré, who, everlasting in his state of dilapidation, went on coughing, and getting the money. He had already pocketed two or three times the value of his field. But in the village they continued to say:

"This Blairaux is a lucky fellow. He has got Ziré Buzette's house for nothing, for the poor fellow will not last long."

A mad desire to strangle the plasterer made his fingers itch every time he had to hand over the precious gold pieces. Unable to control himself he could not help saying:

" Ah, there you are. Are you never going to die? "

" Monsieur Blairaux, how can you say such a thing to a poor man like me, who has not long to live? " answered Ziré, pitiful and coughing.

He buried the third Blairaux and died, over a hundred years old. For over three-quarters of a century he had not had long to live.

LOUIS DELATTRE
B. 1870

THE NEWS

At the beginning of April the weather changed, and in one night spring opened like a primrose in the wood.

Monsieur Quât, in his little house on the town walls, was very glad of it. He told his servant to go to the end of the garden, climb on to the big stone at the foot of the wall, and peep over to see if the fine weather had really come back.

It had. The servant vowed, in a voice as clear as her blue eyes and blonde hair, that the wind would remain in the fair quarter of the sky. And she moistened her lips.

Monsieur Quât was delighted to hear it, and he believed her. He had only to make the sign which she expected, and with her large, red, affectionate hands she brought him the clothes suitable for such a day. The trousers of the colour of café-au-lait—goat's milk which makes the coffee yellower—the black cutaway coat, with its perfectly darned moth-eaten places, the Indian silk comforter with a pattern of gherkins, the hat, brightened by a drop of oil, and the good solid stick, a sapling oak with ivory knob.

Monsieur Quât thus tinkered up, the servant took his arm to help him down the front steps, and led him to the middle of the road. He felt his feet while she, steadying him with one hand in the back, pushed a pebble out of his way with her sabot. "There we are!" she said. "I'm off," he answered, and bending forward, he started.

He walked with short steps, tapping the ground with his heels. His outstretched neck kept his head high, which nodded "Yes" all the time. For a long time already if Monsieur Quât wished to say "No" he has had to do so with great energy, for his neck trembles, and even so, he sometimes signs "No" awry.

To-day his head's "Yes, yes" quickened. His eyes twinkled in their nest of wrinkles and grey hair. The keen air moistened them with cold tears which made them look like some beautiful old jewels. "Yes, yes, yes . . ." and he gazed at the freshly cleaned blue of the sky, as if he drew from it something subtle which others could not see; especially over there, between the rounded hills of Blanche Maison and Rond Chêne, where the silky air shimmers with such bright gaiety. His stick tapped the ground and Monsieur Quât went on and on.

A big drop trembled at the end of his nose. On the Place du Trieu where he arrived, the old man suddenly acquired the aspect of a child delighting in the things which belong to the whole world —without reserve or shame.

" Hullo, Father Quât," cries the wheelwright working on the road in front of his shop. He holds his pipe in one hand and in the other the adze with which he was just chipping pieces off some post. He is flushed with pleasure and with working in the wind.

" So there you are, the fine weather has come again! "

" April air, my boy; it is the April air," cries Monsieur Quât at the top of his voice without pausing, smiling, sniffing, tapping the ground with his stick.

" Good morning! Good morning! "

And on he goes. Now he is opposite the blacksmith's forge. The bellows roar; the hammer strikes the red-hot iron rod with a hurried sound. The blacksmith cannot stop. Still, he laughs as he sees Monsieur Quât, only in little jerks, because he is hitting hard.

" Good day, Father Quât! Winter is over. Ha! ha! I know where the fine weather is leading you. Hey! the good for nothing! "

" Ha! ha! ha! " and the old pink hoary head goes on. " Yes, yes, yes. . . ."

At the end of the square, in the little inn with a bunch of holly hanging over the door as a sign, Monsieur Quât is in the house of his sweetheart! He is eighty years old, but she is not yet twenty. From the window of her house where she was sewing, she had seen him coming. She opens the door to him as he climbs the step. Held between her teeth some bits of cotton flutter in the wind, like spiders' threads caught on a hedge. Her face is serious and beautiful. The pleasure of seeing Monsieur Quât, absent during the whole winter, illuminated it frankly. She leads him to the low chair close to the dogs, settles him against the iron stove, and pours him out in a thick crystal glass, which could be filled by a finger's length, a drop of gin. Then she goes on with her sewing.

Gently, without haste, she tells him the village news which had not travelled as far as Monsieur Quât's house; she tells him of those who have died and of those who have been born.

" Dear, dear! . . . The things that happen . . . in my time . . ."

But Monsieur Quât lets his sentence drop halfway, tired with stringing so many words together. And then, he is so happy!

The time passes, and inside the house, as the pale gold of the sun rises along the walls, the smell of the simmering soup at the point of perfection is spread abroad. Monsieur Quât rises.

" You are going? " asks the innkeeper.

She goes to the mantelpiece and from between the crucifix and the copper pot of sulphur matches she takes a folded newspaper, yellow, dirty, and worn at the edges.

" Take the news with you. You can read it at your leisure."

" Thank you," says Monsieur Quât. " Yes, yes. I will bring it back next week when I have finished."

He has started off again. By dint of little steps with his heels and taps with his stick on the ground, and of doing " Yes, yes," he has arrived home. He has eaten his soup out of his little plate decorated with faded flowers, with his tin spoon, worn on one side. Seated in his cane armchair, armed with his magnifying glass whose lens is so scratched that it seems to be covered with spiders' webs, he spells out the news. There is a great deal. What things! . . . But soon the light is no longer bright enough. Monsieur Quât folds up the newspaper exactly in the old creases. He will read on, to-morrow.

" The things that happen! " say his lips. While his gentle little, cheerful, faded soul murmurs like a suppressed song, " And what is the use of it all? "

And yet he will go on reading the gazette to the end. And when he has finished, he will carry the paper carefully back to the inn on the market-place. So that after him, this summer, or next winter, in the village which sleeps like a lilac spread open in the sun, another inquisitive person may still learn the news of the world—the great world, yonder, far away.

He who has nuts, cracks them;
He who has none, lacks them.

BLANCHE ROUSSEAU (MADAME BELVAL) B. 1875

THE LITTLE HOUSE IN THE MIDST OF THE WOODS

GOTTE and Nanette lived in a little house in the woods. Gotte was young; Nanette was old.

"Alas! alas!" said Nanette, "what will become of Gotte when I die?"

"I will look after her," said Pierre. And that was why, on the day on which they carried Nanette to the grave, he went to look for Gotte and said to her, "Will you be my wife?"

"Wait a little," said Gotte, "until I have made my dresses. First the black dress and then the white dress. We will see about it next spring." And she worked away busily at the black dress.

In Gotte's little house everything was neat, quiet, and poor. Nanette's stool in the corner by the hearth, the bread bin, the bed, and the little cupboard with its starched curtains. As for ornaments, there was a bunch of anemones or buttercups in a glass of water, and in winter the pot of ivy in the corner of the window-sill. We must not forget that there was also, on the chimney-piece, a sacred picture, and on the walls, a cuckoo clock and two everlasting flowers dried, in the form of a cross, on grey cardboard neatly framed. Then there was the work-basket, with the thimble, scissors, and cotton, and the little rattling case full of needles, for Gotte earned her living by sewing.

She had two friends, Pierre, who gave her love, and her cat Jude, who gave her friendship. Pierre was young and strong: his stroke felled the oaks, and he lifted Gotte in one arm, as easily as a child can rob a nest.

Jude, old and bald, could only miaow and rub himself against Gotte's skirts, or sit on his tail beside her while his big sea-green eyes, full of little floating seaweeds, watched her thoughtfully. But at night he slept on Gotte's feet. And every one knew him to be a real devil, all teeth and claws, if one wished to touch his mistress.

One day, as Gotte was sewing at the window, a knight passed, magnificently attired, and followed by a great pack of hounds. He looked at Gotte, and seeing her so charming, asked her name.

"I am called Gotte," she answered, blushing.

"Gotte," said the knight, "do you know that you are lovely?"

"I have no mirror," said Gotte.

"Take mine," said the splendid knight, and he gave her his silver mirror, and Gotte saw that she was fair.

Next day he came again.

"Gotte," said he to her, "would you not like to be a princess?"

"You are mocking me," said Gotte, laughing.

But at night she asked herself seriously:

"Would I not like to be a princess?"

"It rests with you to become one," said the knight on the following day. And he bore Gotte off upon his steed. When Pierre came back to the little house he found it deserted, the fire dead, and Jude tied to the bread bin by a piece of string. And thus did Gotte become a princess.

She lived in a magnificent palace and had people to wait upon her, and costly dresses and jewels. But she did not sleep at night, for a voice cried in the park from nightfall until dawn. "I know that voice," thought Gotte. And she drew the sheets over her face, but she did not sleep. Tired with sleeplessness she rose, hid her lamp behind her hand, and went and looked through the curtains. And she saw Pierre wandering in the park, lamenting. The next day she called her husband and said to him:

"A man disturbs me, crying in the park at night. Give orders, I entreat you, to have him driven from the country."

And Pierre was driven from the country.

But next night other cries sounded in the park. And it was Jude who wandered, lamenting. Therefore the princess said to her husband:

"A cat wanders at night in the park and disturbs me. Give orders, I entreat you, to have it drowned."

And Jude was drowned in the pond.

But next night the princess, slumbering, heard a voice calling in her dreams. And the voice said, "I am the thimble; I am the thimble." And another voice cried out at the same time, "I am the needle; I am the needle." And other voices cried out all together, "I am Nanette's stool. . . ." "I am the window. . . ." and "I am the bin!" "Gotte! Gotte! do you hear us?"

Then Gotte rose up without a sound. She went out in the dark night and set light to a bundle of wood before the door of the little house in the woods. But at the same time she burnt a swallow's nest which hung under the eaves, and this brings ill luck, as every one knows.

And that was why Gotte could not sleep the following night because of a swallow which fled around her windows crying for its young ones.

They tried to kill it too, but no arrow could reach it.

" My fortune to any one who will kill the swallow," cried Gotte. But it was no use promising fortunes, no one could kill it. And thus Gotte lost her sleep and withered miserably at the side of a prince in a splendid castle.

SWISS SOLOMON GESSNER[1]

1730–1788

JEALOUSY

THE most odious of all passions is jealousy; it is the most poisonous reptile that can inhabit our bosom. This Alexis found to his cost. He was in love with Daphne and she loved him. Both were handsome: he manly and brown, she wise and innocent as the lily opening its petals to the first rosy kiss of the dawn. They had plighted their troth of eternal love, and Venus and the gods of love seemed to have filled their cup of happiness to the brim. Alexis' father had just recovered from a long and painful illness, and calling his son to his side said:

" Dear son, I have taken a vow to sacrifice six sheep to the goddess of health. Go and take them to her temple! "

It was two long days' journey to the temple of the goddess; but Alexis took leave of his sweetheart with tears in his eyes, as if he was going on a long sea-voyage, and sorrowfully he drove the sheep along before him. Thus going on his long way sighing, sighing like the breeze in the willow trees that line the brook, he passed the rich fields and meadows without seeing them. The finest views lay stretched before him and remained unnoticed. He only felt his love, he only saw his sweetheart; saw her in her cottage, saw her sitting by the spring in the shadow of the great rock, heard her call his name—and still he sighed. Thus he walked on behind his sheep, vexed because they were not as fleet as the deer, and finally arrived at the temple.

The sheep were slaughtered, the sacrifice made; on the wings

[1] The most noteworthy imaginative literature of Switzerland has been written in the German tongue, and indeed three of the following four stories are the work of authors usually classed among German writers, though they were of Swiss origin. In the German-speaking part of Switzerland a certain amount of vernacular literature has been produced in the German dialect known as "Swiss," but it is peculiarly local in its interest. Just as Gessner, Keller, and Meyer are usually classed with German authors, so is Edouard Rod included among the French, but it has seemed desirable to group them here in accordance with our territorial plan as the representatives of Switzerland in the art of the Short Story.—ED.

of his love he hastened back towards his home. In a wooded glade, however, a thorn entered the sole of his foot, and his pain was so great that he was hardly able to reach a hut that was lying close by. A kind old couple received him and soon treated his wound with healing herbs. "How unhappy I am," he kept on saying, sighing the while and counting every hour; each minute seemed to him like a long winter's night, and to add to his misery some unkind goddess planted in his heart the seeds of jealousy. "Ye gods! What a thought!" he murmured to himself, looking around anxiously. "Daphne might be unfaithful! Ugly thought! But girls will be girls, and Daphne is beautiful. Who can look upon her without desiring her? And Daphis her neighbour has long desired her! And he is a fine fellow; who could hear him sing and remain unmoved? Who can play the flute as he plays it? His cottage stands close to Daphne's, and the space that divides them is but small. Oh leave me, leave me, wicked thoughts!"

But deeper and deeper this jealousy sank its root in his mind—torturing him by day and night. Often at night in his dreams and by day in his imagination he saw his sweetheart making her way to the spring in the shade of the trees to meet Daphis, who sang to her of his great love. He saw her gazing languishingly into his eyes and her bosom rising and falling in happy agitation. Or he saw his beloved resting in the soft shadows of the lofty trees asleep, saw Daphis stealthily approaching, gliding gently nearer and fixing his scorching gaze upon her every beauty. He bends over her, kisses her hand, and she doesn't wake. He kisses her cheeks, he kisses her lips—"And she doesn't wake!" he cries out at the top of his voice. "Oh miserable fellow that I am! What fearful pictures my brain creates! Why must I keep on thinking these dreadful thoughts, why torture myself with these fancies that are an offence against her innocence?"

Already he had lain there six days and his wound was still not quite healed. In vain the old couple begged him to delay. He could wait no longer, and embracing his benefactors and thanking them fervently he resumed his journey, travelling as fast as his wound would let him. Darkness began to fall when at last he came in sight of his loved one's cottage, and the full moon rose behind the wooded upland. "Ha, away with you, you ugly, torturing dreams! There my love awaits me, and to-night I shall weep with joy and hold her in my arms!" And saying this he hurried on. From under the rose-covered walk that led up to her gate he saw her slowly emerging. "Yes, it is she! Yes, it is Daphne, her slender lovely figure, her graceful walk, her snow-white dress! It is she, ye gods! But where is she going so late in the evening? It is dangerous for young girls to go out into the open fields so late at night. But perhaps she is coming out in the hope of meeting me?" he told himself. But there—a figure darts out from the covered walk behind her, runs to her side, and laughingly she takes his hands into hers. He hands her a basket of flowers, which with a graceful bow she hangs on her arm; and now they walk away from the cottage in the pale light of the full moon.

Terror-stricken, Alexis stands motionless, trembling from head to toe. "What do I see! It was only too true then, too true all that I feared; a compassionate goddess prepared me for this shock. Ah! poor wretch that I am, where, oh where is the goddess who warned me of this misfortune! Come to my aid now and avenge me; yes, avenge this infidelity, strike down these miserable beings and then let me die!"

Arm in arm the while that girlish figure and the youth went on their way in the moonlight towards the myrtle-grove where the little shrine of Venus stood, talking happily as they sauntered along.

"They are going into those myrtle-groves!" Alexis said to himself wrathfully, "into those shadows where she has so often pledged me her love! Now they are entering the wood. Ah! I have lost sight of them, and they, they will be sitting under yonder trees. But no, here they are again, I can see her white dress in the moonlight gleaming through the shrubs and the trunks. They have stopped; here is a fine open space and soft beautiful grass. Faithless ones! Yes, sit down there, opposite the watching moon, and there protest to one another your dishonourable and degrading passion. May all the devils persecute you! But what is this? The song of the nightingale and the cooing of the doves! How is it possible, when these low creatures sit there in their midst? They are moving on; yes, they are going to the temple of Venus; I shall go after them and listen, and spy on them."

With these words he made his way towards the grove, keeping carefully in the shadows. Nearer and nearer the couple in front of him drew to the temple whose white marble pillars, gleaming in the moonlight, reached high into the dark sky. "What, they dare to enter! Will the goddess of love bless this black outrage against her holiest vows?" Thus he spoke to himself as the girl, the basket of flowers still on her arm, ascended the steps and slowly made her way in between the stately pillars, while the youth, leaning against one of them, appeared to gaze after her lovingly. In the shadow of the temple Alexis approached closer and pulled himself up on to the pillared verandah. Mad with rage and despair he crept along in the shadow of one of the great pillars, and hugging it closely saw Daphne walking up to the statue of Venus, who, standing there in the rays of the moon in marble of milky whiteness, seems to shrink back in her holiness from the astonished gaze of the mortals who come to sacrifice at her shrine. Daphne sank on her knees before the goddess, deposited the wreaths and flowers at the foot of the pedestal, and sobbing loudly began in great misery to pray: "Listen to my prayers and accept the wreaths and flowers which I sacrifice at your shrine. The evening dew on them is mingled with my tears! Ah! Already six days have passed since Alexis left me! Oh, good and sweet goddess! Guide him back to my arms unhurt! Guard and watch over him on his way, and send him back to me as devoted and loving a sweetheart as he left me!"

In wonder Alexis listened to her prayers, then his eyes travelled to where the youth was standing, on whose face just then the rays of the full moon fell. Now he sees—it is Daphne's brother; he had accompanied her on her nightly pilgrimage to the temple, thinking it not wise to let so young a girl go there alone.

Alexis came out from behind the pillar. Daphne was overwhelmed with joy at seeing him, and he was full of gladness and shame. They embraced one another and then sank down in thankfulness before the goddess and prayed.

SWISS GOTTFRIED KELLER

1819-1890

A PRINCE IN DISGUISE

On a dismal November day a poor devil of a tailor was walking along the country road to Goldach, a little wealthy town but a few miles from Seldwyla. The tailor carried nothing in his pocket but his thimble, which in lieu of coin he was incessantly twirling between his fingers; it was so cold that he was obliged to keep his hands in the pockets of his trousers, and his fingers began to ache smartly, what with this eternal twirling and twisting. He had lost his pay and his work at the same time, because some head tailor at Seldwyla had failed, and there was nothing for it but to take to the road. A couple of snowflakes that had blown into his mouth were the only breakfast he had had, and there was as little prospect of any dinner. Begging was made difficult, ay, seemed quite out of the question; because over his black Sunday suit, which was the only one he had, he wore an ample dark grey mantle faced with black velvet, which gave its wearer a noble and romantic exterior, the more so as his long black hair and little moustache were well cared for, and he was the happy possessor of pale, regular features.

Attire of the sort described had become a necessity to him, and he indulged in it with no evil or deceitful purpose; he was quite contented when he was not interfered with and left in peace to do his work, but he would sooner have starved than give up his mantle and Polish fur-cap, which he managed to wear with an inimitable grace.

For this reason he could work only in good-sized towns, where he did not become too conspicuous; when on the road and without savings he was in a sorry enough plight. Did he approach a house, he was looked at with surprise and curiosity, and there was nothing farther from the thoughts of the inhabitants than that he would beg; so the words died on his lips, the more so as he was not a possessor of many words, and he became in truth a martyr of his mantle, and suffered hunger as dark and dismal as the latter's velvet lining.

As he was wearily ascending a rise of ground he came upon a new and comfortable carriage, which a gentleman's coachman had fetched from Basle for his master, a foreign count who was awaiting it somewhere in Switzerland on an old estate he had bought or leased. The carriage was designed for travelling, and had all sorts of arrangements to hold luggage, so that it seemed to be heavily loaded, although it was empty. The coachman was walking by his horses on account of the steepness of the road. When he reached the top of the hill he got up on the box again, and asked the tailor if he would not have a ride; for it was beginning to rain, and he saw at a glance that the poor fellow was faintly and sorrowfully trudging along.

He gratefully and humbly accepted the offer, whereupon the carriage took him at a rapid pace over the rest of the road, so that in one short hour they passed, with a hollow, thundering sound, through the town gate of Goldach. Before the best hotel, called Zur Woge, the elegant turn-out stopped, and at once the groom pulled the bell violently, so that the wire nearly broke. Down came the host and his people and pulled open the carriage door; the children and neighbours came crowding about the splendid carriage, full of curiosity to see what kernel could be contained in this marvellous shell, and when the dumbfounded tailor came forth in his mantle, pale and handsome, gazing pensively upon the ground, he seemed to them to be a mysterious prince or count at the very least. The space between the carriage and the door of the hotel was narrow, and the rest of the pavement pretty well blocked by the curious crowd. It may have been due to a certain lack of presence of mind, or possibly of courage, that he did not break through the rabble and simply go on his way; he did not, but weakly allowed himself to be escorted into the house and upstairs, and did not become fully conscious of his new and remarkable position until he found himself in a comfortable dining-room, and his portentous mantle was being officiously removed.

"The gentlemen wishes to dine?" said a voice. "Dinner will be served at once; it is nearly ready."

Without waiting for a reply the host rushed for the kitchen, and cried: "In the name of three devils! now we have nothing but beef and a mutton joint! I dare not cut the partridge-pie, because that was ordered for the gentlemen coming this evening. *Isn't* this a shame? The only day when we don't expect any such person, and when there is nothing in the house, so fine a gentleman must turn up! And the coachman has a coat-of-arms on his buttons, and the carriage is good enough for a duke! And the young man is so grand that he doesn't so much as open his mouth!" And the phlegmatic cook said: "Well there is nothing to grumble about, sir. Of course he shall have the partridge-pie;

he won't eat it up! We'll serve it on small plates for the gentlemen this evening. We can get out six platefuls!"

"Six platefuls? You must forget that the gentlemen are accustomed to eat their fill at *my* hotel!" answered the host; but the cook looked unmoved, and continued: "And so they shall! We must send for half-a-dozen of cutlets; we need them for the stranger as it is; and what he leaves I'll cut up into little squares and mix it in the pie. Just leave all that to me!"

But the honest host said, with a serious mien, "Cook, I have told you before that such things cannot be in this town and in this house! I wish to be respectable and honourable, and can afford to be so."

"Ye saints!" cried the cook, "one must do the best one can! Here are two snipes that I bought from the hunter this minute; I'll put them in the pie. A partridge-pie adulterated with snipe will be good enough for your gluttons! And then there are some trout; the biggest I threw into the water as that remarkable carriage came to the door; and there is some soup in that little pan. So then we have fish, beef, cutlets with vegetables, the joint, and the pie. Just give me the keys now, so that I can get out the sweetmeats and the dessert! And, by the way, you might do me the honour, sir, to entrust the key to me once for all, so that I wouldn't have to run after you for it and get into awful straits."

"Good woman, you must not bear me a grudge for that. I promised my wife on her deathbed never to give the key out of my hands, so it's a matter of principle, not of mistrust. Here are the cucumbers, and here are the cherries; here are the pears, and here the apricots; but this old, stale pastry cannot be used. Quick! send Lise to the pastry-cook's to get fresh cakes, three dishes full, and if he has a good tart he may send it also."

"Dear me, sir! you can't put all that on one gentleman's bill. It will cost you more than it is worth!"

"Never mind that. It's all for the honour! It won't kill me, and when a grand swell like that passes through our town he shall be able to say he dined well, though he was not expected, and it was in winter! I won't have it said of me as they say of the hosts of Seldwyla, that they eat everything good themselves and leave the bones for their customers. Go ahead, then, all of you, and do your best!"

. . . .

Without further delay he was asked to table, a chair was placed for him, and as the fragrant odour of the savoury soup, the like of which he had not smelled for many a day, robbed him completely of his will, he sat down in God's name and at once dipped his heavy spoon into the golden brown liquid. In deep silence did he refresh his wearied spirits, and he was waited upon in respectfully hushed awe.

When he had emptied his plate, and the host saw how he had relished it, he encouraged him politely to have another spoonful; it would do him good, the weather being so inclement. Now the trout was served adorned with greens, and the host helped him to a generous piece. But the tailor, tormented by anxiety, did not venture in his shyness boldly to use his knife, but coyly and shamefacedly dabbed at it with his fork. The cook, who was watching behind the door to see the grand gentleman, noticed it, and she said to her subordinates, "Praised be our Lord Jesus Christ! There is one who knows how to eat a fine fish, as he should; he does not saw the delicate thing with his knife as if he were butchering a calf. That is a person of quality. I'd swear to that if it were not wicked! And how handsome and sad he is! There isn't a doubt of it, he is in love with some grand lady whom they won't let him have. Ah yes, grand people have their troubles as well as others!" Meanwhile the host, seeing that his guest left his glass untouched, said deferentially, "My table wine is not to your honour's taste. Permit me to bring you a glass of good Bordeaux, which I can greatly recommend."

And then and there did the tailor commit his first spontaneous fault by obediently saying yes instead of no; and thereupon did the landlord of the Woge betake himself in person to his cellar to pick out a choice bottle; for he was greatly concerned to have it said that there was something first-class to be had in the place. When his guest, suffering under the torments of an evil conscience, ventured only to sip faint-heartedly of the contents of his glass, the host ran exulting into the kitchen, smacked his tongue, and cried: "The devil take me, there's one to the manner born; there's a judge of good wine for you. He takes it on his tongue as one would lay a ducat on the gold scales!" So dinner took its course, very slowly indeed, for the poor tailor ate and drank very coyly and undecidedly; and the host, to give him time, left everything on the table for longer than ordinary. For all that, what the guest had eaten up to this time was not worth speaking of; but now his hunger, which was constantly being tempted in so dangerous a manner, began to conquer his terror, and when the partridge-pie appeared the mood of the tailor suddenly changed, and one fixed thought began to master him. "Things are as they are," he said to himself, warmed and incited by a new glass of wine. "I were a fool now if I should bear the brunt of the coming shame and persecution without having eaten my fill for it! So look to it while it is time. This is likely to be the last dish; I will devote myself to this, come what may! What I once have in my stomach no king can rob me of!"

No sooner said than done. With the boldness of despair he attacked the savoury pie, with no thought of stopping, so that in less than five minutes it was half gone, and the cause of the gentlemen who had ordered it was sadly in want of support. Meat, mushrooms, balls, crust, and top he swallowed without distinction, only anxious to bag it all before a cruel destiny should overtake him. He drank his wine in a hearty draught, and put enormous bits of bread into his mouth; in short, it was a lively innings, as when before a storm the hay from the near meadow is cast into the barn with a pitch-fork. Again the host ran to the kitchen and cried: "Look, he is eating up the pie, while he scarcely touched the roast! And the Bordeaux he drinks by glassfuls!"

"Let him," said the cook. "He knows a partridge when he sees it! If he were a common fellow, he would have gorged on the roast!"

Meanwhile the coachman had had his horses fed, had eaten a substantial meal himself in the servants' room, and as he was in haste, he had ordered his horses to be harnessed again. The menials could not resist asking him, before it was too late, who his master was and what was his name. The coachman, a jolly and sly fellow, said, "Has he not told you himself?" "No," they said; and he replied, "It is no wonder. He doesn't have much to say from morning till night. Well, he is Count Strapinsky! He is going to stay here all day, perhaps longer, for he told me to take the carriage home."

He perpetrated this vicious joke to take revenge on the tailor, who had, as he thought, without giving him a word of thanks for his kindness, gone into the hotel to play the false *rôle* of a gentleman. Carrying his waggishness still further, he got up on his box without so much as asking what there was to pay for himself and his horses, cracked his whip, and drove out of town, no one interfering, for it was all put down on the bill of our friend the tailor.

KONRAD FERDINAND MEYER
1825-1898 SWISS

PLAUTUS IN A NUNNERY

At the end of a hot summer's day a group of cultured Florentines had gathered round Cosmos Medici, the "father of the fatherland," in front of a casino in the Medician Gardens to enjoy the cool evening air. Above them, in wondrously changing hues, was the clearest of evening skies.

Amongst the company, quietly drinking and chatting, the finely-chiselled features of a white-haired head stood out; on his eloquent lips seemed to hang the attention of all the company, yet the expression of the intelligent, mobile face was singularly mixed; over the gay forehead and the laughing mouth lay the shadow of a great sorrow.

"My dear Poggio," began Cosmos Medici, the intellect of the man showing in the well-set eyes in his ugly face, "the other day I looked again through your *Liber Facetiarum,* and though I know it all by heart, I enjoyed at least once more the admirable turning of your clever and happy phrases; it has since occurred to me that surely there must be still some story that your critical mind had excluded from this volume as being either too salacious or not salacious enough for its pages. Think, friend, and give us, who understand the slightest allusions and would forgive the coarsest joke, a 'Facetia inedita'; and then, talking and sipping your wine, you will forget your troubles!"

The new sorrow to which Cosmos referred, as something known to all, had fallen on the aged Poggio Bracciolini—now Secretary to the Florentine Republic, and formerly Secretary in turn to five Popes—at the hands of one of his clever and good-for-nothing sons. This unhappy youth had committed an offence akin to robbery and theft, and had brought not only misery, but also heavy monetary loss on his already deeply suffering old father.

"Those stories that would amuse you, Cosmos," replied Poggio, "I hardly now like to recall. Innocent of wrong as they were in my youth, they yet seem to me to testify to my then lack of balance and seriousness, and they may have some bearing on the results now showing so disastrously in my sons! "

" Don't moralise, Poggio! " interrupted one of the younger ones, " you who gave back to the world the Comedies of Plautus! "

" Thank you for your reminder, Romolo! Yes, thank you, for let the finding of Plautus be the Facetia with which I will amuse you to-night! "

" My Facetia," said Poggio, aping the style of the inevitable introduction to the Italian novel of the time, " concerns two crosses, a light one and a heavy one, and two barbarian nuns, a novice and an abbess."

" Great! Poggio," interrupted a neighbour, " the same style of Germanic vestals, I hope, as you mention in your *Letters of Travel*, the finest thing you ever wrote! "

" Oh, then I exaggerated, friends, knowing your tastes; however, here goes, and I venture you'll enjoy my barbarian females! Those days, dear Cosmos, when we struck the surplus heads off our holy Church, then distorted to a Lernæan Serpent, found me attending the Council of Constance. My spare time I divided between pondering the wretched composition of the Council—piety, cleverness, science, cunning, buffoonery—with all its attendant unchaste company mixed up together—and my search for old manuscripts in the surrounding convents. Various scents and clues led me to believe that in a neighbouring nunnery a Plautus lay hidden —think of it, friends—a Plautus, at a time when only a few scraps of that great Roman comic writer were known to the world! For nights I lay awake thinking of a way to secure this jewel. If only I had left everything and there and then had gone after this treasure instead of attending to the election of Pope Otto Colonna!

" Thus it happened that one of my followers—a blundering ass, and unfortunately one of our countrymen—to whom in my excitement I had given an inkling of the great find, had got there before me, and worse still, without getting the classic, *per fas et nefas*, had only succeeded in arousing the suspicion of the abbess. At last, in spite of the election of his Holiness, I got away, and hiring a sturdy mule and drover—one Anselino de Spiuga—I set out. Anselino, who, to my great surprise, had accepted my first small offer for his services, showed as we proceeded on our way a gradually increasing fit of depression, which in my happiness I laid myself out to dispel. I only partially succeeded, but I culled from him the following strange love-story.

" Coming to Constance some time back in the train of his Bishop he had later found work as a carpenter, and was employed in the building of an additional wing to a neighbouring convent. Here he got to know a maid named Gertrude who lived in the vicinity, and as the two spent much time in each other's company they mutually fell in love—' in all honour and chastity,' he added, ' for she is a good girl.' Suddenly she had given him up without apparent reason, and without telling him why, and to-morrow she was to take the veil—and now I knew why he had hired himself to me as drover for such a small sum; he was going to attend the ceremony, to see the girl for the last time, and to make sure with his own eyes how this maiden who had loved him, and who, strange to say, had expressed a deep abhorrence of the nunnery, a fear almost, was going to become a nun.

" He relapsed again into his brooding silence and asked to be left behind as soon as the convent came into view amongst the vineyards in the distance. On my inquiring about the abbess he told me that she was a nasty little woman, but a wonderful administrator, who had rehabilitated the convent, and whom the people called ' Brigittchen von Trogen.'

" I continued on my way, and arriving at the convent witnessed a queer performance. Some large unwieldy object, which I afterwards saw was a gruesome black cross of ancient make, was being raised now and again by one or the other of the large company assembled there. It was a motley crowd; not one man seemed able to lift the heavy cross, and every time it had been raised it would have come crashing down had not other helping hands supported it. Yells of vulgar laughter resounded when these attempts failed, and the crowd of peasants, townsfolk, pedlars, gipsies and wandering players who had been attracted here from Constance to witness the ceremony, grew bolder and rowdier as the huge wooden mugs filled with convent wine were handed round, passing from mouth to mouth. A queer figure the barbarian abbess made on the newly-cut grass; she skipped in and out of the throng full of glee—and as it seemed to me also full of her convent wine—shrieking and gesticulating wildly. ' Not one of you can lift this cross of our sainted Duchess Amalaswinta, yet to-morrow,' she said with a grin, ' Sister Gertrude will lift it up like a feather. Good people, this wonder has been performed for a thousand years and still it goes on! ' I was sure now that this good abbess had imbibed her wine too freely on that bright summer's day.

" While I was lost in thought, trying to put two and two together, Anselino's story and the queer performance I was witnessing running through my brain, the barbarian abbess, with a roseate colour on her vulgar face, and with a bestial mouth, espied me.

" ' Hi, there, Roman scribbler,' she called out. ' Come a little nearer, and try to lift this cross of our sainted Amalaswinta! '

" Every eye was on me, and then jeeringly and with rough Germanic pushes I was sent into the middle of the crowd. I excused myself, saying, ' Friends, look at my poor, short, weakly arms! '

" ' Ho! ho! ' cried the abbess, ' the longer fingered are you, my fine fellow.' And really my fingers were rather long, having grown so through my occupation in continuous writing.

"Uproarious yells greeted this sally, and though I missed the exact point of it I mentally chalked it up against the abbess to be paid for presently. Annoyed I turned away and made my way to the chapel, the main entrance of which I found open, and entering there I sought peace and quietness in its fine and sombre interior. I stopped before a picture, which from its position in the nave I gathered to be something special, and on closer examination was not disappointed to find it so. The stone frame held a huge cross, an exact replica of the one I had seen upon the meadow, and beside it two figures; one, a big powerful woman, a crown of thorns on her head, held up the cross on her broad shoulders, and yet was borne down by its weight, for her knees bent beneath her: the other the small figure of a lovely child, with a halo around its head, also supported the cross, helping to lighten the tremendous burden. The figures were crude, but the painter had put into the faces all the life and soul that he was capable of, and he had succeeded in portraying in one profound despair and a deep compassion in the other.

"Stepping back to get a better view, I suddenly noticed, kneeling at the other side of the picture, the figure of a girl, apparently a native of the place—almost as well built as the Duchess of the picture—with the hood of her white cassock thrown back from a head crowned with a wealth of fair hair and a strong, well-shaped neck. She rose and, brushing away her tears, made as if to go. A novice, I thought, and, addressing her gently, begged her to explain to me the meaning of the painting.

"In simple language she told me that it represented a Duchess, the founder of this convent, who, having poisoned her husband, came here crowned with thorns and carrying that heavy cross to atone for her sins. Doubting her salvation she was supposed to have asked God for a sign of His forgiveness, and having had this cross made which no man could lift unaided, she would have broken down under it had not the Holy Virgin helped her to carry it in answer to her prayers.

"Seeing my doubting look, the girl brusquely insisted that the legend was perfectly true. I asked her name, and, as I had already guessed, it was Gertrude—the Gertrude of whom Anselino had spoken. Gaining her confidence, she confessed to me that she was taking the veil in fulfilment of a vow she had made after the death of her father when quite young; her mother had then fallen seriously ill, and she had, in her desperation at the thought of being left quite alone in the world, prayed to the Holy Virgin to spare her the mother until she should reach her twentieth year at least. A few weeks ago, near the end of the term set in all her prayers, her mother had died, and now the time had run out and she would gladly take the veil and give up her life to God. At the same time, she owned, that often, since she had learned to love Anselino, she had wavered in her resolution, but she would faithfully persist in it, provided the Holy Virgin also came to her aid, and helped her to carry that heavy cross on the morrow, as she had helped every novice since the time when the old Duchess entered the convent.

"I suggested that a clever girl might easily extricate herself by stumbling, but immediately her eyes flamed up and she said, 'Would you have me act a lie, sir? As surely as I want God, Father, Son, and Holy Ghost to help me in my last hour, so surely will I endeavour to carry that cross!' And with these words she raised her arms as if already holding it up. Her sleeves fell back and disclosed her well-moulded young arms, on which, as a true Florentine, I could not help but feast my eyes in artistic pleasure. She noticed this and puckering her forehead, turned away offended.

"I sat down in one of the confessionals, rested my head in my hands, and pondering deeply, saw my way to gain that Plautus! I thought I saw at last through the incredible and through the fraud. This was my reasoning. The heavy cross being undoubtedly real, a barbarian woman a thousand years ago might have lifted it with the giant's strength of desperation and devotion; however, this deed could not have repeated itself, and for hundreds of years must have been accomplished by fraud. Who, and what, originated this fraud? Probably misplaced zeal to fill the convent, and calculated greed. Yet even Gertrude had assured me that she witnessed the feeble and ailing Lisbeth of Weinfelden carry that same cross just nine years ago.

"There must be two crosses, I told myself, a light one to be cleverly substituted for the heavy one at the right moment, and of the existence of that light fraudulent cross I was by then convinced. In this knowledge and in the fact that I had been one of the members of the Congress for the reformation and purification of the nunneries, I held two good weapons wherewith to fight my fine abbess. The net was closing upon her.

"Slowly I ascended the steps of the choir, and turning to the right, into a lofty and finely domed vestry, I found the place—adorned with many grand inscriptions—where the heavy black cross was usually stationed against the high wall. Two doors led off from here. One was locked, and opening the other I found myself in an ill-lit lumber-room, where, on rough shelves round the walls, the poor library of the convent reposed. I trembled with excitement at this discovery, and had I found here, covered in dust and cobwebs, those Comedies of Plautus, I would have kissed the dirt off the priceless pages. Alas, all I found were merely religious Rituals and Liturgies that left me cold. No Codex of Plautus! It was quite true, that stupid fellow had been before me, and the Plautus evidently had now been hidden by the crafty abbess. I found—and it was my only plunder—*The Confessions of St. Augustine,* and put it in my pocket to read at night before seeking rest. All at once, like lightning the abbess appeared, and rushing at me and feeling my gown, triumphantly produced the *St. Augustine,* which was nestling in my bosom.

" 'Fellow, fellow!' she shrieked, 'I knew from your long nose that you were one of those southern book thieves who are the curse of our convents. But mark me, there is a difference between a befuddled monk of St. Gallus and a sturdy maid of Appenzell who keeps her brain clear. I know what you are after! We had another of your Lombardine robbers here the other day; and I found that, when he had finished admiring our holy relics, he tried to depart with a parchment of comic writings under his habit. We never knew we had this valuable pigskin of comic writings here, but I soon consulted the vicar at Dietenhofen, who likes a good mug of convent wine, and is a most learned man. "Goodness gracious!" he called out as soon as he had set his eyes on it, "Mother Abbess, this is worth something! This will build you another out-house and wine-press! Take it and hold it well, sleep on it and wait until you find an honest buyer!" And this I have done ever since, though I have found it pretty hard to rest on.'

" I had to hide a smile when I thought of the poor Plautus lying beneath the pillow of this virago's bed; but putting on my most solemn mien, I said:

" 'Abbess, you mistake me. I am one of the fathers now assembled at Constance, one of the reverend persons charged with the reformation of the nunneries.' With these words I held before her a finely engrossed parchment which I had by me from my last sojourn in Rome. 'In the name,' I read out, 'and with the authority of the seventeenth solemn Council. The hands of none of our holy Vestals must be soiled by any unclean writings, whether in Latin or other language. The practice of trickery and imposture, whether traditional or otherwise, is prohibited, and must be punished without delay—even in the case of an abbess—with death at the stake.'

She paled visibly, but immediately recovered herself, and with wonderful presence of mind said, 'God be thanked, that at last He is setting about the ordering of His holy Church!' and with these words produced from a cupboard in the corner a little volume, adding, 'This, a Lombardian cardinal left behind after his visit here, and the vicar of Dietenhofen pronounced it the profanest book he had ever seen, and the work of a cleric! So pray relieve us of this plague! ' And she handed me—my *Faceticæ*.

" I knew this was pure accident, yet I was much chagrined, and began to hate this abbess thoroughly, especially so as I knew my writings to be destitute of any offensive remarks against holy Church.

" ' It is well,' I said, ' and do you wish also to be proved innocent of the second, and more important, matter? I have witnessed your promise of a miracle on yonder meadow; beware, then, lest your miracle be examined.'

" Her knees began to give way and her eyes seemed to roll. ' Follow me,' I continued severely, ' and let us inquire into the working of that miracle! '

" We made our way to the vestry, where the heavy cross had been replaced, and I tried in vain to lift it. Resolutely I turned to the locked door at the side where I thought the second cross would be kept, and sternly commanded her to produce the key. With eyes protruding and terror-struck she cried, ' Lost, your holiness! Lost, these past ten years! '

" ' Woman! ' I cried in my hardest, most terrible tones, ' your life is in danger! If I find here a lighter cross which is a copy of yonder heavy one, you will burn at the stake, burn as sure as that heretic Huss and as guilty as he! '

" With chattering teeth and tottering knees she produced an old key and opened the door. And there stood against the wall the same black sister cross, but light as cork. So perfectly was it fashioned after the other, that involuntarily I said aloud, ' A masterpiece! Perfect! ' not in admiration of the fraud, but of the skill, the art that had fashioned this copy.

" ' Jester, jester,' leered the brazen woman, who had been watching me closely, ' you have outwitted me, and I know your price, take your buffooning sheets of pigskin, which I will fetch you at once, keep your mouth shut and leave us in peace! ' Quickly I decided what to do. I forced her to tell me how she had been initiated in this thousand-year-old fraud, how her predecessor on her death-bed had impressed her with the glory of keeping it up for the good of the convent and of holy Church, how she had been made to realise its deep significance and secret power, and finally she even insisted to me that in perpetrating the fraud she had done nothing unworthy.

" ' I pardon you, so that holy Church may not be disgraced by any revelations,' I told her; but I also commanded her to burn the fraudulent cross immediately after the ceremony on the morrow had taken place—to prohibit the latter I thought unwise—and to produce the Plautus immediately.

" The abbess, grumbling and reluctant, obeyed, and I am sure my commands were quite in conformity with the wishes of the Council of Constance, though they were without the knowledge of the Council.

"I had taken the key from the lock of the all-important door and left it on the latch, while the abbess was fetching my Plautus, and had gone to my quarters at the inn across the way. Presently heavy knocks resounded on the oaken door of my room and the abbess furiously demanded the key. However, I told her calmly that it was not in my possession, which was quite true, for I had dropped it into a crevice between two pews in the chapel—where probably it still rests—and by and by the holy mother departed, moaning and lamenting pitifully. I was happy in the possession of my classic, and after beguiling my brain with the glorious treasure deep into the night I finally retired to rest.

"Startled out of my sleep I jumped up. It was morning. One half of the little window stood open and I heard from the chapel near by alternate wailing and groaning, and then again a stifled cry. Hastily I threw on some garments and hurried to the chapel. At the door of the vestry I halted, for there before the heavy cross I saw Gertrude on her knees beating the stone-flagged floor and wringing her hands, which were bleeding. She had been lying here all night in prayer and subjection; her voice was hoarse and her words came with difficulty from between her parched lips.

"'Mary, Mother of God, pity me! Let me be buried under the heavy cross, for I cannot carry it! I hate the cell! I cannot live in it, I shall knock my head against the low ceiling, against the walls! But if you do help me to carry the cross, then lighten my heart also; for see, if you do not I shall dash out my brains on the flagstones!' Exhausted, she sank down.

After a while I approached her gently, for I had made up my mind to save this girl, and though I had given the abbess my word —she had required this of me—not to speak to Gertrude, I saw my way to enlighten her.

"She saw me confusedly at first, but soon watched my actions more alertly, and later with perfect clearness. I walked up to the heavy cross and deliberately taking out my knife cut into it, near the crosspiece, a good sized notch. Then taking the requisite steps towards the unlocked door, where the other cross was hidden, I laughed loudly and called out, 'The truth on the wall, the lie in the hall!' Then slapping my hands and crying, 'He presto!' I called out, 'The lie on the wall, the truth in the hall!'

"Looking sideways at the novice I scrutinised her face and saw that her curiosity had been aroused, and knew that she would find out the rest for herself. I now quietly made my way back to my room, and throwing myself on my bed found a few hours more rest, until I was wakened again, this time by the ringing of bells and the singing of the crowds on their way to the convent.

"Just as I entered the vestry once more I saw Gertrude, pale as death returning from a pilgrimage—a necessary part of the ceremonial to facilitate the changing of the crosses no doubt—to a neighbouring chapel. The preparation of the novice then began. In a circle of chanting nuns she first tied round her hips the thrice knotted cord, then slowly cast her shoes off her strong but well-formed feet, and having the crown of thorns handed to her pressed it viciously upon her hair, partly lacerating her forehead in doing so. The nuns drew back affrighted before her wild looks. Six of them—no doubt fully initiated into the sham—then placed the spurious cross upon her shoulders, imitating but poorly the carrying of a heavy load.

"But now events moved quickly. Gertrude, casting an eye rapidly on the part where I had heavily notched the real cross, found this one unmarked, and with a yell of rage slipping it off her shoulder, caught hold of it with both her hands and dashed it to pieces on the flagstones with a fearful cry. Then, with insane laughter, like one possessed, she ran to the vestry, and there in the unlocked closet found the real cross. With unearthly yells she hoisted it on her shoulders and staggered under it slowly and haltingly into full view of the congregation, in spite of the efforts of the abbess and her six co-conspirators to hold her back.

"'Now Mary, Mother of God, I pray you decide my fate honestly!' she screamed, and breathing heavily she tottered a few more steps, only to break down under the fearful load; again she raised herself with superhuman strength upon one knee and arm, only to collapse suddenly and completely and be crushed down under the heavy cross. This was the blood-stained truth and not the lying sham. A deep sigh escaped every breast in all that throng—which had witnessed this tragedy as if transfixed. The nuns were busily engaged trying to restore the bleeding girl to consciousness, and presently she opened her eyes, then stood up, passed her hand over her brow, and smiling slightly spoke in an almost clear voice full of happiness, 'You do not want me, Blessed Virgin, so I will give myself to another!' and ascending the steps of the choir she called, 'Anselino!' A deep manly voice answering her, she continued, 'Will you have me still?' 'Yes, with all my heart,' came the reply, and so descending again she went with swaying steps to the arms of her lover, her thorny crown still on her bleeding forehead.

"As I followed her down the choir steps my messenger from Constance touched my sleeve and brought me the news that at last the election of the Pope had been completed. When I looked up again Gertrude had disappeared. The crowd, however, was now seething with uproar and confusion, cries of 'Sham! Fraud! Shame!' against the abbess, mingled with shouts of 'Sinner! Traitress! Shameless hussy!' against Gertrude. The uproar was frightful. Whether either party knew the whole significance of the proceedings I know not, yet in any case the wonder-working cross was completely discredited, the power of the miracle gone for ever. To put an end to the raving of the people and the haranguing of the abbess, who in her fury yelled to me to get out of her sight, I ascended the chancel, and gaining some sort of silence for myself, proclaimed to the assembled Christians in sonorous tones, 'Habemus Pontificem Dominum Othonem de Colonna!' and started a rousing Te Deum; at first only the nuns joined in this, but soon all the multitude took part.

"*Plaudit amici!* I have finished. When, too, the Council at Constance, which lasted longer than this story, had finished, I returned with my Plautus and my superior, his Holiness, Martin V., over the mountains to Lombardy. But on our way we stayed at the inn at Spiuga, just north of the dangerous pass of the same name, where Anselino and Gertrude had made their home, and where she now carried the cross of matrimony.

"This, friend Cosmos, is my 'Facetia inedita.'"

With many acclamations Poggio was laughingly thanked by all his assembled friends, and the discussion went on to other things—parchments of the old world—the greatness of the present century.

EDOUARD ROD — SWISS

1857–1910

THE GOLDEN WEDDING

At the end of the Rue Lafontaine, in Auteuil, leading to goodness knows where, a certain married couple had lived for the last five or six years. Their name was Walter, a cosmopolitan name which gives one no clue to their birth or station in life; and their strange personalities caused as much talk in this quiet part of the world, where we fraternise somewhat, as if they were in the provinces.

Twice a day, at eleven o'clock and again at four, Monsieur Walter took a constitutional walk. He held himself very erect, and in spite of his seventy-five years his step was quite brisk. His complexion had that artificial look of freshness that is peculiar to well-preserved apples; his frock-coat was very well-fitting, and he had the ribbon of some foreign order in his buttonhole. On wet days he curtailed his walks, went into a café, read the papers, and exchanged a few words with its frequenters. He spoke with affected brevity and with an accent which told as little as his name; it was slightly guttural and therefore might be German, but the dipthongs were quite English, and the aspirates might have been those of a Russian. No sooner had he left a group of people than someone would ask, "Where the deuce does that fellow come from?" At once conjectures would be offered. One man was sure that he was a German, trying to hide his nationality; another thought he was an Englishman, with the saturnine temperament of that race; a third would declare he was a Russian, whose delight was to make a mystery of himself.

As for Madame Walter, she never left home except on shopping expeditions, and spoke to no one but tradespeople. She was several years younger than her husband, but looked older: her hair was quite white, and her complexion mottled; she stooped and was short-sighted; and her whole mien was that of some poor soul who has seen much trouble. She did all her household duties with the aid of a charwoman, whose name was Marianne. This was the wife of a journeyman upholsterer; she came in the early morning and left at mid-day, just when M. Walter came back to lunch after his daily walk. Marianne's work was to clean out the rooms and do the heavier jobs, for Mme. Walter did all the cooking herself. Her cooking was perhaps plain, but was certainly excellent, and she was skilled in all kinds of foreign dishes, so that her cookery indicated her origin as little as her name.

Of the private life of the couple Marianne knew nothing at all. Once, when she had returned to the house to look for something she had accidentally left behind, she heard M. Walter's voice raised angrily in the dining-room. Two or three days later she made some excuse for repeating her action, and again she heard the man's irritable tones. But after this she was warned by Mme. Walter that if she were ever to come back to the flat except during "her proper hours" she would be instantly dismissed; so Marianne restrained her curiosity. From the glimpse she had had of the household, however, Marianne gathered that M. Walter was a glutton and a tyrant, and that his wife shut herself up from the world so that no one should know of their quarrels. With this idea running in her mind, you can imagine her astonishment when Mme. Walter said to her one day: "Can you stay here the whole of to-morrow, Marianne? I am having a dinner-party and I shall need you to help me."

Marianne knew that such a question was purely rhetorical and required no answer, but her curiosity got the better of her.

"Are you expecting visitors, madame?" she asked.

Instead of withering her with a glance, the lady condescended to explain.

"No, I am not having visitors; but to-morrow is the anniversary of our golden wedding, and we mean to have a rather special little dinner. I want to enjoy a meal without leaving the table after each course. You understand, I am sure."

Marianne understood perfectly, and with the subtle instinct of her class, which can grasp and unravel the complicated problems in the life of a neighbour, she knew at once that something mysterious was about to take place, and that the golden wedding would be something quite out of the ordinary.

. . . .

The golden wedding had, very naturally, not been forgotten by M. Walter. One day, after certain unpleasant remarks on a curry which was not hot enough for his taste, he had said: "By the way, do you know that the fourteenth of October will soon be here?"

It was so long since any anniversary had made any difference in their lives, for even Easter, Christmas Day and New Year were passed over very quietly in this household, that Mme. Walter saw no significance in this date.

" Well? " she asked.

" What! is that all you have to say? " her husband replied. " Does the date convey nothing to your mind? But that's exactly like you: you have about as much heart as brains. . . . Why, the fourteenth of October is the anniversary of our wedding—the fiftieth, my dear—our golden wedding day! We ought to celebrate it somehow, don't you think? . . . What do you say to a jolly little dinner, the kind you used to make when you were at your best, with a bottle of champagne to drink with the dessert? That would revive our youth, wouldn't it? "

A jolly little dinner with wine and dessert! Yes, that was all M. Walter thought of when the date had suddenly occurred to him. Since he never on any occasion troubled himself about his wife, he did not perceive that she had suddenly grown very white and had refused to eat any more. In calm expectation he awaited the " great day."

As for Mme. Walter, she was completely overwhelmed. Fifty years! was it really so long as all that? For fifty years, then, she had dragged on in this slow sacrifice of her life; for fifty years she had been growing old, and the whole time she had been waiting for the day when a ray of happiness or affection should come to her; for fifty years she had felt those rebellious thoughts rising within her, and every time she had crushed them down.

Fifty years ago, when she was a young girl, fair-haired, pretty, intelligent, and warm-hearted, she had given her small hand trustingly into this man's keeping. But that happened far away, it doesn't matter where, in a southern land, on a warm, sunny day, amid the smiles of nature, amid songs, laughter, gaiety and dances. He was young and she had loved him. She believed in him utterly, and dreamed that a golden future awaited them under blue skies. Yet her disappointment began on the very day after the wedding, when she found that the heart of this man, whom she had endowed with every grace of soul, was ruled by a colossal egoism. The disillusionment had grown from day to day, from year to year, wrought by his absurd self-sufficiency, realised more fully as they journeyed together from one end of the world to the other, and perfected when he refused to share in griefs which should have been common to them but which he brushed aside from his vision as hurtful to his well-being. And yet, in spite of the tears she so often unwilling shed, time had passed so quickly that now life held but little for her in the short years she had still to spend on earth, and there was little hope for her now save in the mysterious Beyond.

And yet even this last hope had been somewhat damaged by the withering egoism of her man. Had he not tarnished her pure faith with just such jests as he had thrown upon her girlish dreams of happiness? And now, careless of the ruins in which he still contrived to stand upright, scorning the notion of treasuring any pleasant memory of bygone years, turning aside from those which still were possible, indifferent to past regrets as to the future menace, all he thought of now was a good dinner, with champagne at dessert! Oh, wretched dinner! If she could only make it into a means of revenge! If the poor wretch could only have instilled into it all the bitterness, all the poisons she had absorbed drop by drop! If it could only be the last dinner of their common life! If she could only find courage to carry out, even at this latest hour, the plans she had so often played with, to break loose from her bondage and leave him to his own devices, while she would live out her remaining days far away from him!

. . . .

On the night of their golden wedding day M. Walter was in high good-humour, waiting for the " little dinner " such as his wife knew so well how to prepare and he to enjoy. To speak candidly, his good-humour was hardly less disagreeable than his bad temper: it showed itself in many little pleasantries in a bitter and malicious vein, and he underlined his thin jests with a grating laugh which was an outward expression of the creature's soul. Three or four times in the course of that day he spoke to his wife in this way, thinking himself a great wit. He had never loved her, he said brightly; she was of no use except to prepare his meals; and other clever little things he said which hurt as not the grossest insult could have done. To these his wife made no reply except by an occasional appealing look, but he never realised their grief-stricken significance. The hours went by.

At long last the gaudy clock which had followed them everywhere on their travels and divided their hours with its mellow chimes, struck six, and at the last stroke M. Walter, who returned from his constitutional with the most precise regularity, opened the dining-room door. The table was not even laid!

There is nothing in the world so heartrending as to find that some long-expected pleasure is to be deferred; and the sight of that empty room, with its threat of delay in accomplishment of M. Walter's desires, put him in a state of actual fury. Hardly able to control himself, his face purple with rage, his lips brimming over with insults, he rushed into the kitchen. On the threshold he stood still in amazement, for there he found—Marianne! And Marianne was there alone!

" Where is my wife? " he asked.

" She has gone out," the woman replied.

" What, gone out? Where? What message did she leave? "

" She said that you were not going to dine until seven o'clock to-day."

"Seven o'clock! Another hour to wait! And she has gone out! Why did she go out?"

That hour seemed a century of waiting. M. Walter had never before been so thwarted in his life. He paced up and down the room, trying to solve the puzzle which engrossed his whole attention. Why had his wife gone out, on this day of all days, and why had she altered the dinner-hour? The riddle grew in his mind until it assumed gigantic proportions, and at last M. Walter, who was the least imaginative man on earth, came to entertain all kinds of mad notions; it struck him that possibly his wife had suddenly lost her senses, and he could well imagine how annoying such a misfortune would be to him. When the clock had struck seven and the hands continued to creep round slowly, the dining-room became too small for him, and he began to pace about in all the other rooms of the flat, opening and shutting the doors, and counting his own steps for the sake of distraction; and he ended up his walk with another visit to the kitchen. He felt sure that Marianne could enlighten him a little, but she held aloof. She watched him closely, a queer smile on her face, but luckily he was too much wrapped up in himself to be observant and he never noticed her looks. At last he broke the silence.

"Well," he queried, "she has not returned yet?"

"Oh, I forgot to tell you, sir; Mme. Walter told me to say that you were not to be anxious if she came back a little late."

"A little late!" Why, it was a whole hour after the time fixed on for to-day! And the dinner, the festal dinner, the golden wedding dinner—she had handed it over to a charwoman who knew nothing in the world about cookery!

"What is there for dinner?" he asked Marianne roughly.

"Madame told me not to say anything about it to you, sir," the woman answered slyly, "because it was to be a surprise dinner."

A surprise dinner! This word cleared the air at once. Why, of course, his wife had gone out to purchase some rare and unheard-of delicacy; perhaps it had come from a long way off and had not arrived until the afternoon train, and she could not bring it home any sooner? So she was a dutiful wife after all! His anger suddenly melted away into a feeling of vague and misty affection, and this helped to whet his appetite still more.

. . . .

There was the sound of a footstep on the stair, then the door opened, and Mme. Walter came in. She was looking rather pale, and was out of breath after her climb up four flights of stairs. Her hands were empty; she had brought no surprise parcels with her!

"Oh, so you are here at last! Why, it is nearly eight o'clock. What do you mean by such conduct?"

"I don't mean anything by it. I preferred to have dinner later to-day, that's all. Marianne, you may serve the dinner now."

M. Walter had assumed the attitude of a wrathful despot, and the calm reply had disconcerted him. The couple sat down silently at the table, and Marianne brought in a tureen of steaming soup.

" Pumpkin soup! Pumpkin soup! Why, you know I simply detest it! "

" Yes, but I am very fond of it," Mme. Walter replied calmly, in a tone that admitted of no reply; " and it is more than thirty years since I have tasted it."

M. Walter was dumbfounded. With his mouth wide open in astonishment, he looked at his wife, speechless. In the meantime Mme. Walter swallowed a few spoonfuls with difficulty, trying to look at her ease.

" Oh, here's the fish! "

" Look here, are you making fun of me? Why did you order a pike? And you have dressed it with sauce hollandaise, too! You know perfectly well that I only like sea fish! "

" Yes, but I like fresh-water fish and dislike the others."

In spite of this preference, Mme. Walter scarcely touched the portion on her plate. With dreaming eyes she gazed into the void, into the wasted past she had left behind her, in which her youth, beauty, high spirits, her love and her strength had been swallowed up; and she lived over again the fifty years of bondage that had been all her life. Her heart was black with hatred, and when her glance rested on her husband, sitting in bewilderment opposite her, feeling humiliated and vaguely nervous, she was full of triumph at the thought of the childish trick which had been her only sign of rebellion and revenge.

" This *is* a cheerful golden wedding and no mistake! " Marianne murmured to herself, as she brought in the jugged hare.

" Look here, is this a wager? " M. Walter broke out at last. " You have provided everything that I hate."

" But everything that I particularly like."

" Any one would say that you had done this on purpose."

" Oh, so you have seen through it at last, have you? Well, I may as well admit that I did arrange this dinner on purpose."

M. Walter rose, his face purple with rage, and he raised his fist.

" I arranged it on purpose," Mme. Walter repeated in her colourless voice.

Her calmness and rebellion seemed to him such enormities that M. Walter sat down again, silenced and somewhat alarmed.

" But look here," he said, " I don't understand all this. Explain yourself. Have you gone mad? Do you realise what you are saying? Isn't this my golden wedding? "

" Yes, but it is mine too, alas! " Mme. Walter answered. " And you need not think I have gone mad. And if you want me to explain what I have been thinking, I'll tell you. For fifty whole long years you have made me submit to your whims and give in to all your wishes without even once considering that I could have an idea of my own or a feeling that you would be capable of wounding. For fifty years I have been nothing but your slave. Well, I thought I should like you to be my slave for one hour, just one hour, to the very smallest details of our life. Afterwards you will resume your liberty, and I shall have to take up my yoke again. I should really have liked to shake you off altogether and then to have gone away and left you to yourself. But I simply can't do it: I am too old, and I'm afraid. Now, do you understand? "

The poor woman was trembling in every limb and her eyes were already dumbly pleading for pardon. While she was speaking M. Walter's face lit up. So that was all it was! It was a crisis that would soon be tided over; indeed, instinctively he felt that it had already passed and that he could now worry her, scold her and run her down, and that she would merely beg his pardon in return; and for the first time in his life, doubtless because his nerves had been on the rack and were now released, he was generous. His smile, then, was almost pleasant, and with a shrug of his shoulders he murmured: " After all, I suppose that women will be women until the end of time! "

Several tears had rolled down Mme. Walter's withered cheek into her empty plate. She dried her eyes, and then said very timidly: " We had better have the rest of the dinner brought in. I have cooked something for you that you like. It is a duck pie."

M. Walter's eyes brightened.

" From Amiens? " he asked.

She made a gesture of assent.

" Well, you have spoilt my appetite, but I think it will come back again later on. And the champagne—did you purposely omit that too? "

" No, it is there, in ice."

The old man's face grew bright at once.

" In ice! " he echoed in high glee. " Now you're yourself again! And you needn't leave me; I forgive you for everything! "

ACKNOWLEDGMENTS

Most of the translations in the Masterpiece Library of Short Stories have been made expressly for this work, but in several instances previously published translations have been reprinted, and among these the following acknowledgments have to be made:

To Messrs. George Newnes, Ltd., Southampton Street, Strand, London, W.C.

For their courteous permission to reprint from *The Strand Magazine* the excellent translations of these stories: "The Helmet," by Fernand Beissier; "The Treasure," by Georges Beaume; "Jacques Brulefert's Death," by Georges Renard; "The Croissey Yew," by Maurice Saint-Aguet, and "Nicette," by Saint-Juirs.

To the Editor of "Everyman," London.

For the use of the translation of "Mlle. Heudier's Husband," by Marcel Prévost, which originally appeared in *Everyman*.

The Editor's thanks are also due to the notable living authors of France and Belgium represented in this volume for the courtesy which has made its compilation possible.

Made and Printed in Great Britain by
Hazell, Watson & Viney Ltd. London and Aylesbury